BELLA WALLIS

By the same author

Memoir

Keeping Mum: A Wartime Childhood
Clever Girl: Growing up in the 1950s
A Corner of Paradise: a Love Story
(with the usual reservations)

BELLA WALLIS

A Victorian Mystery Quartet

BRIAN THOMPSON

Chatto & Windus
LONDON

Published by Chatto & Windus 2013

2 4 6 8 10 9 7 5 3 1

Copyright © Brian Thompson 2013

First published in Great Britain in 2013 by
Chatto & Windus
Random House, 20 Vauxhall Bridge Road,
London SW1V 2SA

www.vintage-books.co.uk

Addresses for companies within The Random House Group Limited can
be found at: www.randomhouse.co.uk/offices.htm

The Random House Group Limited Reg. No. 954009

A CIP catalogue record for this book
is available from the British Library

ISBN 9780701185596

The Random House Group Limited supports the
Forest Stewardship Council® (FSC®), the leading international
forest-certification organisation. Our books carrying the FSC label are
printed on FSC®-certified paper. FSC is the only forest-certification
scheme supported by the leading environmental organisations,
including Greenpeace. Our paper procurement policy can be found at
www.randomhouse.co.uk/environment

MIX
Paper from
responsible sources
FSC® C016897

Typeset by Palimpsest Book Production Ltd, Falkirk, Stirlingshire
Printed and bound in Great Britain by Clays Ltd, St Ives plc

To Jake

Contents

THE
WIDOW'S SECRET

ONE

Early-morning mists promised a fine day. There was talk at breakfast of a barge journey along the canal, culminating in a picnic at Stone Saxton where the druids had once danced. But to Arthur Gration's great disappointment these mists refused to rise like a theatre curtain and reveal the estate in all its splendour. Instead, they thickened. In the space of an hour, cows in the low meadow that had seemed to float like ducks disappeared from view altogether. Long before the last guest came down to breakfast, the mist had become emboldened enough to lick at the long windows, nudging aside trees and shrubs as it advanced.

Gration consulted Billings, his butler.

'I doubt we shall see much change, my lord. Tidyman walked up from the village with the day staff and says there it is as thick as porridge, his words for it.'

'What can be done?'

'I should not like to answer for conditions along the canal. But if a picnic is still called for –'

'– it has been promised –'

'– yes, indeed. Then may I suggest we open the ballroom and bring along the paper lanterns and such that went with Lady Celia's birthday last year? They might make a pleasant enough show. And it occurs to me just now, my lord, I could send to Compton for the village band, or the steadier parts of it.'

Gration looked at his butler with the kind of admiration another man might reserve for a Fellow of the Royal Society.

'Billings, you are wasted in service here. You should be an admiral or something of the sort. By land, a major-general.'

'Your lordship is too kind,' Billings said calmly. He was thinking of how to coerce the housekeeper into clearing the ballroom, last used the previous November and generally considered a handy depot for things broken, things unwanted, and any amount of suitcases, steamer trunks and empty tea chests.

Only two people from the breakfast table braved the weather. One of these was Mrs Bella Wallis, a widow, but a very assured one, not at all dismayed by circumstance. She was a striking-looking woman in her late thirties, tall, maybe a little on the buxom side, her undoubted appeal amplified by a humorous mouth and wonderfully grey eyes. The previous evening she had been much admired by the entire house party for her genial common sense and – this from her own sex – a comfortably elegant way with clothes. Men found her entrancing.

Now, when she proposed a walk, the first to jump up was Philip Westland, as agreeable a companion as she could have wished for. She waited for him in the hall, a half-smile on her face, as he banged about looking for his hat, trying it on and then deciding against it.

'You will go bareheaded, Mr Westland?'

'I shall risk being wetted, I think.'

When a servant opened the door for them, the fog rolled in.

'But don't you see, if you only had a hat in your hand you could waft away the weather,' she chided, laughing.

'In the past, I have suceeded in that line with wasps. And have heard it sometimes works with cows.'

He ushered her on to the gravel path that led away from the house and they set off together, boots crunching in unison. They were by no means complete strangers. But they only met on occasions such as this – weekend house parties, dinners for twenty or more, the crush bars of theatres and so forth. It was not in Bella's nature to be flirtatious but she was free with Philip Westland in a way she found difficult with others. Part of the pleasure she found in his company today came from knowing that he sailed for India on Tuesday.

Westland was tall, dark and unhandsome. He walked like a sailor with his arms held apart from his body. His hair was unbrushed, his figure on the portly side already. He had no small talk – or not of the kind that is obligatory for weekends in the country.

'Look!' Bella teased. 'A young girl from the village is waiting to ambush you.'

They paused before a statue depicting a goddess with perfectly round breasts and plump arms, beckoning seductively. A marble skirt clung to the chub of her hips.

'I recognize her,' Westland said. 'She is the stationmaster's daughter. I have warned her of going about naked. But she's headstrong.'

'Shall you miss England?'

'On days like this, yes, I suppose I shall. I know nothing at all about India. It is hot there, I believe.'

Bella laughed.

'You make such determined efforts to be offhand. You'll go, you'll fall in love with some very serious young woman and be happy ever after.'

'It is no use my saying I would rather stand about in the fog with you?' he asked. 'Maybe not here. Maybe in some other place in the world where there is nothing but fog.'

Bella flushed. His meaning was unmistakable. She covered the statue's ears with her palms, feeling her gloves drench. Philip smiled and took her hands away.

'You were born to draw love like a magnet, Bella, but I like you best for hardly being aware of it. Think of me henceforth as Westland, the man who went to India and married the colonel's daughter.'

'Shall we go on?' Bella asked in a shaky voice.

'Good Lord, yes. There are any amount of ditches we can fall into. I shall make you walk until your very unsuitable London boots are filled to the brim with dew.'

She drew his head down and kissed him on the lips.

'I am very nearly forty, my dearest Philip, and about as much use to you as a tea-strainer. Or watering can.'

'Watering can is good,' he said. 'A fellow asked me at billiards last night who the devil you were. Meaning where does she come from, has she any money, et cetera. I said that among women you were the finished article.'

'That was gallant of you.'

'He seemed perplexed. He mentioned the name Broxtowe to me.'

At once, Bella's eyes flashed.

'Did he indeed? I like you less for telling me that. Lord Broxtowe is a friend in the way I should like you to be a friend to me. Who was this billiards player?'

'Bella, please,' Westland murmured.

'You won't tell me? Well, damn country-house weekends. And damn you too for not knocking him to the carpet there and then. Broxtowe has been my particular friend since my husband died. He is old enough to be both my grandfather and yours. Never was a more honourable man.'

'Would I have mentioned a single word of this if I knew it was going to cause you so much anguish?'

'I am not anguished. I am disappointed.'

'In me?'

'In men.'

'I am very sorry to hear it. People do say some very stupid things when playing at billiards. Often it is the brandy that talks.'

'No,' she warned sharply. 'I will not be humoured.'

'Does it really matter who it was who made these remarks?'

'It matters to me.'

Still with the warmth of her lips on his, he capitulated. 'The fellow's name is Freddie –'

Before he could say another word, she clapped her hands together in annoyance.

'That mincing idiot? I have been overhearing his interminable prattle all weekend but I'm surprised to find *you* hobnobbing. How disgusting.'

There was enough of the cynic in Westland to think she was protesting too much, but she turned and set off into the blank fog without another glance. There was a faint cry a few moments later and he found her flat on her back at the bottom of a mown bank. She was either laughing or crying.

She was crying with laughter. Arthur Gration loomed out of the fog.

'My God, Mrs Wallis,' he exclaimed. 'You might have broken your neck! And then where should we be? This is worse than when Mrs Profitt fell into the lake.'

'Hardly worse, surely?'

'Much worse. Who gave a fig for Frances Profitt and her ridiculous verses? Westland, be a good fellow and steer this lady back to the house. Damnation take the English weather. Did you see a boy sent to Compton for the village band?'

'We have seen no one,' Westland said.

'No, and how could you? We might as well be in Patagonia. It is foggy there all the time. Most of the hurricane lamps in the world are bought by the natives to lighten their gloom.'

Bella and Westland exchanged glances.

'I was just saying to Mrs Wallis that I should like to live there, under certain conditions.'

'And is that so? Then you're a bigger fool than I took you for.'

But as he made his dramatic exit, melting back into the gloom like Hamlet's ghost, he smiled warmly at Bella, his lips finishing in a knowing purse, halfway to a kiss.

The ballroom picnic was judged a great success. Giant paper parasols had been set up and cushions fetched from all over the house. The Compton band played country tunes and a village child sang unaccompanied airs of such sweetness that one or two of the house-guests felt their eyelids prickle. Gration was delighted with the whole effect.

'This was a very good idea of mine, Billings,' he said to his butler.

'I must congratulate you, sir,' Billings said with his habitual gravity. 'I could never have thought of it for myself, I am sure.'

'What's the matter with that shit, Freddie Bolsover?' Gration asked, pointing. Billings gently drew down his master's arm, as though smoothing out the line of a coat, or giving a last touch to a tablecloth.

'I believe his lordship is talking to Mrs Wallis,' he murmured.

'I can see that. Why is her face bright red? That's my point, Billings.'

Bright red was an exaggeration but certainly Bella's cheeks had begun to flush. In matters touching her own honour, she believed in coming straight to the point; and so it was now.

'I understand that at billiards last night you were anxious to know where I came from, Lord Bolsover. And expressed some curiousity about a very valued friend of mine.'

'Did I appear anxious?' he bantered. 'As for being curious, in the sense you intend, I am seldom guilty of that. Who you know is of not the slightest interest to me, madam. Gossip is very dull.'

'I am pleased to hear you say so. Nevertheless. Neither subject is any of your business, as I'm sure you will acknowledge.'

He seemed surprised by the quiet vehemence with which she spoke.

'Well, well, Mrs Whatever-your-name-is,' he drawled. 'I see I am being given a lesson in etiquette.'

'I think you must mean manners, my lord.'

His eyes widened and a muscle in his cheek twitched. Belle felt a stab of fear at the momentary transformation in his face, which bespoke, not irritation, but pure hatred. And not of her particularly, but women generally. All women.

Bolsover was tall and heavy-jowled. Some earls liked to be addressed as examples of God's benign intentions towards the social order: this one clearly thought of himself in more rakish terms. His clothes were perfectly cut but of a faintly theatrical nature, as for example the turned-back cuffs to his sleeves, finished with a thin silver brocade. The weight that he wore round his shoulders and gut was a sign of dissolute living, as was the crooked smile he gave her, revealing crooked teeth.

'You have said nothing, sir.'

'I am trying to eat a bun, madam,' he retorted, holding his plate up for inspection. Someone nearby giggled.

Bella was rescued by Philip Westland.

'I have found the book we were talking about.' He smiled, holding up a calf-bound volume from Gration's library. 'If you will excuse us,' he added, taking Bella by the elbow.

But the odious man had already turned and sauntered away, handing his plate of crumbs to an astonished young curate from Milfield.

'I believe I can fight my own battles,' Bella said, red in the face.

'Of course you can.'

She opened the book he proffered and burst out laughing. It was *Scenes descriptive of the Manners & Customs of the Inhabitants of Tierra del Fuego, together with a Scheme for the Abatement of Vice in that Country.*

There was a sudden delighted cry from Arthur Gration: the fog was lifting and now nothing would do but a contest of archery for those who were in no hurry to get away. The long-suffering Billings could be seen through the long windows, supervising the erection of the targets on the South Lawn.

'We could stay another evening,' Westland suggested. 'I have already spoken to Gration.'

'Between bows and arrows and the London train there can be no contest,' Bella said, feeling her heart lurch at the gratitude that shone in his face.

And the decision to remain when carriages took others to the station turned out beautifully. A slant sun poured over Gration's elms and his neighbours stayed on in enough numbers to make the archery into a genuine contest. Westland and the curate from Milfield shot it out for the grand prize, a dozen of claret recklessly donated by their host.

'By God, Westland!' Lord Gration cried. 'Cupid himself could not do better. Although, yes, now that I recall –'

Bella's rich laugh floated out across the lawn.

Next day, travelling back to London, Philip Westland plucked up the courage to ask Bella an obvious question.

'Did you know we were to meet at Arthur Gration's?'

'I knew you were invited.'

'And as a consequence you invited yourself?'

Bella had been looking out of the window in an abstracted sort of way. She turned her head and studied Westland with her fine grey eyes.

'Well, I don't think it works exactly like that, does it?'

'You can be cruel, Bella.'

'I wanted to say goodbye,' she explained gently. 'I shall miss you terribly.'

'I know that isn't true.'

'Why do you say that? Any man that can win a dozen of claret with such a negligent display of prowess –'

But she stopped when she saw how much more serious the moment was for him. Westland was smiling but his eyes were troubled.

'I wanted to say goodbye to a dear friend in the nicest way I knew how,' she insisted. 'And as to that, when we come into St Pancras, better we part at once, as though India was, I don't know, no further than Margate.'

'As you wish. There are so many things I don't know about you, Bella.'

'Now whatever can they be, I wonder?' she chided. He easily detected the tiny tremor of warning in her remark.

'I don't mean whether you have ever eaten whelks, or snore when you sleep on trains. Darker things.'

'Do I have dark things about me?'

'You are wrapped in mysteries.'

'Ah that! Very well. I am a Home Office spy,' she suggested lightly.

'I can almost believe you.'

'Such nonsense! I am an old London gossip, my dear. Look, I will show you my place of work.' She smiled, drawing him to the carriage window.

They were running through suburbs of harsh new brick. But on the horizon, mixed in with church steeples, were a hundred tall chimneys poking up into the sky. Westland stared. In the pleasant afternoon haze, they did a little resemble gossip factories. He took her hand and kissed it.

'Then I have wasted my last weekend in England paying court to an awful old gossip without a heart of her own.'

'That is how it is,' she agreed, pulling down his head and kissing him full on the lips.

At St Pancras, they did as she wished. Westland had style. After putting her into a cab, he turned and did not look back.

At eleven that evening, Bella Wallis could be found in her house in Orange Street, writing in quirkily irregular script, a brandy at her elbow, a cheroot smouldering in its saucer. Neither Westland, nor Arthur Gration, nor anyone else was on mind. Instead, her pen chased the previous day's fog, trying to describe the delicacy of its colour and the strange texture it had, like water rearranged and stretched fine for inspection. The hurdy-gurdy man was playing in Leicester Square, the notes carried by a trick of the wind. A mouse scratched disobligingly behind the wainscot. Bella wrote on, patient and unhurried.

TWO

Westland was gone, save for a faint echo received by postcard from Gibraltar. In its entirety, the news from the Rock was this: *Sad want of fog*. There was no signature. After a little hesitation, Bella did not add the card to the morning-room fire but tucked it under a cushion, feeling uncomfortably schoolgirlish about it, too. Then she marched upstairs to the bathroom, banging and entering in one bad-tempered sweep of her hips.

Lying in the bath was a pale young woman wearing a white linen mobcap to guard her hair. Her skin was the colour of pearl, as though at any moment it would become completely translucent, which only served to emphasize how delicately formed she was, how angelically perfect. There was not a single blemish on her nakedness save one – a mole that kept coy company with her navel. But Bella was in no mood for aesthetic ecstasies.

'Do you think it is fair to Mrs Venn to have her fetch you hot water all damn morning when she has better and more important things to do?'

The girl in the bath stared up at Bella.

'You are going out,' she said, making an accusation of it.

'Yes, I am going out and you, *ma petite*, are leaving this bathroom in the next thirty seconds.'

'With whom do you go?'

'Is that really any concern of yours?'

'You are in a foul mood.'

'Your grasp of idiom is improving. I am going down-stairs to calm myself with a pot of coffee, then I am being fetched by a ridiculous man and taken to one of London's most romantic locations. And now,' she bellowed, 'if you don't get out of that bath I shall drown you in it.'

And so, by mid-morning cab to the Royal Agricultural Hall in Upper Street. The horse was mettlesome and the cabbie young and eager, his plum-coloured coat and brass buttons as good as livery. Bella was used to surly men who smoked or spat, exchanged ribaldries or the time of day with their friends in the trade; in short, hard-bitten Londoners. This one still had the blush of the novice about him. Bella guessed that driving up the Pentonville Road at such a good lick was for him a metaphor for setting out in life.

As to the occasion, she had given some thought as to what to wear, settling on a sprigged dress and a hat that might be seen by some to have associations with the countryside. The wing feather of a pheasant (she supposed) perked up at a jaunty angle and she wore the brim low over her eyes. Of her two parasols, she chose the sage green.

'I say, you look most awfully pretty,' Henry Pattison said, as they rattled along. 'Quite the thing, in fact.'

'Thank you. And shall we see some of your own beasts today?'

His face fell and he gripped his cane with something like anguish.

'Oh Bella,' he cried. 'I see I have not made myself clear. It is the Royal Agricultural to be sure but there will be no cattle. We are on our way to an exhibition of farm machinery. The new and improved drain cutter – I thought I had mentioned it – of Dutch manufacture –'

Bella laid her gloved hand on his.

'Dear Henry, please be easy about it. It is all new to me. And I imagine as unlike Gloucestershire as anywhere in London.'

'That much is true,' Pattison agreed gloomily.

In the Great Hall, she walked about with her arm tucked inside his, a tall and buxom figure, with a decidedly full jaw he had never noticed previously. What had entranced him when they first met was her eyes – intelligent, searching eyes – and the air of mystery that hung about her. She was a widow who never spoke of her late husband. But she had such an alluring presence that Henry was torn between wishing to throw himself into the principal exhibit (a steam threshing machine) and blurting out the contents of his heart.

'It's all rather like a railway station,' Bella observed, pointing to the glass canopy, where pigeons squabbled with sparrows. She was secretly impressed by the number of bluff men with reddened cheeks and veiny noses who wished to raise their hats to Pattison.

'You are being most incredibly game about it all, I know,' he groaned. 'And I accept, there are more romantic locations.'

But Bella had a directness that had unsettled better men than him.

'I don't think we came here for romance,' she snapped, just a fraction too tart. Then relented and patted his arm.

'I have never been to Islington before, if that's where we are. And everything is interesting to an open mind, is it not? For example, that steam engine, such a potent symbol of progress, as you have described, is making a devil of a lot of old-fashioned smuts and cinders. Look.'

She held out the sleeve of her dress for his inspection and laughed. And in that instant Henry knew he had lost her.

They had met a week since at a musical soirée in Bedford Square and people had warned Henry she was a tricky fish to land. There was some fellow called Westland she had toyed with and then packed off to India with a broken heart. There were rumours that she smoked, a thing Henry associated with men: if with women at all, then Irish biddies sitting with clay pipes on the steps of caravans when the travelling people came to pester the margins of his property. Otherwise, smoking went with billiards; or brandy.

Though he was staggeringly rich, Pattison knew little of London, or widows, or courtship. He was not young any longer but neither was he particularly wise. He took a London musical soirée to be much the same as a vicarage tea or a weekend shooting party at home – that is, along with everything else a display case of eligible young women. Not for the first time in his life he had gravely misread the manners of the capital city. That night he would go back down to Bromhead Gate, the ancestral seat, wishing himself dead.

'Who is the gentleman tending the new and improved thresher? He is remarkably well dressed for an engineer.'

'That is Lord Yelverton,' Henry said through gritted teeth. 'He has four thousand acres in Somerset. The machine is of his design.'

Bella merely nodded.

They inspected everything: they took a not very good lunch: Bella saw by how much she had unintentionally hurt him.

'My dear,' she murmured, 'I would not have missed this, truly I wouldn't. But I do not go about much and it was the purest accident that we met at Lady Cornford's. That is how it is. And that is all it is.'

'I had hoped we might be friends.'

'Were I ever to live in Gloucestershire, perhaps we might. Neighbours are generally friends in the countryside, I understand.'

'And that is it?'

'That is it.'

'I shall never understand London,' Pattison cried spitefully.

'Nor I,' agreed Bella, who was born there.

On the journey back from Islington, he several times apologized for the scenery. He meant in addition the people in the landscape, dressed in black, stunted, stuttering in their way of moving, their heads swinging this way and that, the faces louring and suspicious. Their dogs raced to greet the cab.

'Mongrels,' Pattison exclaimed in disgust.

Bella raised her eyebrows and let them fall. The truth was, she was already forgetting her companion, his innocence and waif-like insecurity. Her mind was on work, but such work as Mr Henry Pattison could never have imagined.

'You may set me down in the Strand, if you will,' she murmured.

'I shall take you to your door,' he insisted.

The house in Orange Street astonished him. He had some sense of what constituted a good address in London and this was not it. The roadway was none too clean and he was astonished to find a legless beggar right outside Bella's front door, his rump protected from the pavement by a flattened carton. He was smoking and reading.

'Do come in for a moment,' Bella said without too much enthusiasm.

'I am quite comfy here, ma'am,' the beggar replied wittily.

Pattison was irritated by this. Legless beggars should not read. Apples should not be left to roll about the gutter, nor newspapers cling to the railings. As for the house itself, an unpromising façade should not conceal an interior of such casual elegance. Nor was he used to being offered wine at four in the afternoon.

'You have no servants,' he observed.

'Well, I hardly think I would call one to pour two small glasses of Madeira.'

'Did I happen to see your daughter peering over the top of the stairs when we came in?'

'I have no children,' Bella replied offhandedly.

And that was it! Pattison thought with sudden exhilaration: she is a demirep and the girl is her maid. I am in a house of harlotry. He was planning how to go forward with this discovery when he caught Bella's withering and mind-reading gaze and blushed from his waistcoat to his hairline.

'Such a pretty little sitting room,' he mumbled, feeling his legs tremble under him. If the truth were known, he was seeing it as one looks at the sun from the bottom of a lagoon, shortly after falling out of the native canoe. He sat down far too heavily.

'I think you were about to say something else, Mr Pattison,' Bella suggested icily.

'I assure you,' he protested.

'Say what was in your heart.'

Pattison looked at her imploringly.

'Perhaps – you will understand I mean no offence in saying this – it was in my mind that you are a woman of mystery, Bella.'

Poor fellow. He realized at once that he had said exactly the wrong thing. She set down her glass and rose. Her face was like stone.

'How very perceptive of you,' she murmured, handing him his gloves and hat.

Only much later, on his way home to Bromhead Gate, did it occur to him that he may have said something very significant touching Mrs Bella Wallis. But being Henry Pattison, he could not pinpoint what it was.

THREE

A hundred yards or so away, in Haymarket, the sort of whores Pattison had in mind were assembling for their evening parade – well-dressed and grave young women who kept up the kind of manners likely to seduce impressionable subalterns, country squires and the more unworldly lawyers and judges. They sauntered up and down in twos and threes, chatting and giggling behind their gloved hands. Sex came in a package that included supper at Thenevon's in Glasshouse Street or Air Street; or, if the mark looked promising enough, the Café Royal. Girls who a year or so ago had been milking cows or cutting hay were now engaged on more lucrative forms of farming. Their selling point was a quite staggering self-assurance.

Mallet's, halfway along this daily promenade, had once been a small hotel. The man whose name it bore borrowed from future clients to turn it into a club, suitable for gentlemen who never for a moment supposed the strolling Araminta to be a bishop's daughter or Lou a refugee from Hungary, but who could recognize them at once as Molly from the Fens of Cambridgeshire, or Jane from Liverpool.

Lord Bolsover liked Mallet's for its male-only ambience and quite colossal snobbery. It was famously said that when Sir Charles Dilke tried to dine there he was turned away by a uniformed doorman with the memorable remark, 'Your name is not known to me, chum.' The club rooms were small and uncomfortable and Bolsover liked that about the place, too. The food was schoolroom fare. Only the cellar was in any way exceptional. Mallet knew wine far better than he knew himself.

Lord Bolsover was happy to make this crusty and over-mannered man his crony. That afternoon they sat drinking Krug in Mallet's tiny first-floor sitting room, boasting a window that overlooked the street.

'The girl in black striped silk really is what she says she is,' he observed. 'Her father is the most crashing bore but was indeed at one time Consul to some godforsaken Balkan outpost. She was raised on the banks of the Danube. Pa thought to save her from sin and mosquitoes by sending her home, a kindness she has repaid most ungenerously.'

'Name?' Bolsover enquired indolently.

'His name? Pelligrew. The sister married that Irish oaf, Mont Styal. Big house out in the peat bogs somewhere. Very good horses. The girl is called Pauletta, a piece of nonsense wished on her by the mother.'

'You surprise me by knowing as much about this young pox-box as you do.'

'Pox-box?'

'She is a slut, George dearest.'

Mallet smiled. 'I know an amazing amount about a great many people.'

For example, he thought secretly, how you came home early last night with your shirt-front black with blood. But Bolsover waved away the remark.

'Women are sewers. I have yet to meet one who wasn't. I dine my German here tonight, by the way.'

'The gallant Colonel. You might tell me: how did he come by his extraordinary wounds?'

'By standing too close to the flames.' Bolsover laughed, lumbering to his feet. 'That is his unhappy story. One must be nimble, George. Fearless, of course. But nimble!'

Vircow-Ucquart was indeed an awful sight, even when disguised in evening dress. It took courage to look him in his remaining eye and to ignore the ancient ruination of the rest of his face. He sat at table with a ramrod back, breaking a bread roll with blunt fingers.

'Never again a thing such as last night, Freddie,' he warned in a booming whisper, even before he picked up his soup spoon. Bolsover laughed.

'Don't be so foolish. Life is appetite, or it is nothing.'

'But I must tell you –'

'Must? *Must?* You are overreaching yourself, my dear. We are not on the parade ground now; and while I find some of your orders thrilling, you will confine them to the bedroom. Or some dark Teutonic wood. A shooting lodge, perhaps, tended by a pretty boy of both our choosing.'

Vircow-Ucquart realized tardily that his host was already too drunk to eat.

'You have caused our Oxford friend a great deal of anxiety,' he grumbled.

'Do you know what?' Bolsover said suddenly. 'This is a very boring topic. I do not tolerate being spoken of behind my back and I will not be told what I must and must not do. The waiter's name is Charles. He will see to your meal. Good evening to you.'

And with that he pushed back his chair with the greatest possible show of petulance and stalked from the room. Vircow-Ucquart was left with a spoonful of soup halfway to his lips. He laid it back into his plate and wiped his mouth. Mallet appeared as if from nowhere.

'Dear, dear,' he sniggered. 'Whatever can have upset him?'

Bella was also engaged for supper that night but made a small detour into the Strand, having the cab drop her off at Fleur de Lys Court. There was still plenty of light left in the sky and the evening was balmy. The cabbie watched her walk into the narrow entrance of the court, interested enough to produce a low whistle. It was not the most obvious destination for a well-set-up judy in a sweeping lilac dress. But no sooner had she disappeared than a bully-boy of a man came out and hauled himself into the cab.

'Bit of a to-do in there, is there, guvnor?'

'Parrot,' the man said obscurely. 'Take me up to Holborn.'

'A parrot, you say?'

'Listen,' the new fare said with dangerous reasonableness, 'just drive the bloody horse.'

Fleur de Lys Court was small and dark, the walls plastered with advertising. Nobody lived there. What had once been artisan hovels were now lock-up premises. Two were empty, their windows so filthy that little of anything could be seen inside. Three more were offices, of a kind.

Pushing past a gaggle of ragged onlookers, all of them gazing upwards, Bella came across Captain Quigley, who nodded to her, his brown teeth clamped on a reeking cigar.

'There is your problem,' he explained, pointing. 'The bird has been chained at the leg and when it flitted, took the chain with it. Which we now see tangled in the bars of old Solomon's top window.'

Quigley: troubled, uncertain, a blustering man with an actor's painful facetiousness. In his own way of describing it (but only as it applied to others) a classic fourpenny-bit. Twenty or more years ago he had been thrown from a troop transport on his way to the Crimea, pitched over the rail by his disgusted comrades. So ended a private soldier's service that had lasted just nineteen weeks, from the time he turned up drunk at Dover Barracks to flying arse over tip into the inky dark of the Mediterranean. That was Quigley's principal absurdity. He was as much a Captain of Dragoons as Bella was a Chinese washerwoman.

Forty feet above the ground, yet more securely fastened than ever it had been in the public of the Duke of Connaught, the parrot alternately flapped upwards with frantic wingbeats and swung exhausted and upside down like a green clock pendulum. Little feathers drifted down and were caught by street Arabs with outstretched hands.

'O' course, it could have been a cow,' the Captain chuckled, who was not supposed to know where Bella had been that day. But then that was his value to her – his unsleeping interference in other people's business.

'What can be done for the creature?' Bella asked with as much haughtiness as she could muster.

'They have sent for Hampsy, the egg collector. Nimble youth, cleft palate, ginger hair, lives across the river by the Shot Tower. Can climb cliffs of all sizes. Collects eggs for the gentry, who take him to Scotland and other parts.'

'He's going to climb Solomon's warehouse?' Bella asked.

'He's fearless but he's not the human fly. Nah. Boost him up on to the tiles and have him shinny down a rope of some kind.'

He waved his arm at the crowd, indicating that it was this they had come to see. Standing to one side was old Solomon himself, swamped by an ankle-length overcoat that had once been a fashionable dove grey. Though it was his property on which the parrot was entangled, it never occurred to anyone to ask him to walk up to the top floor of his premises and open or smash the window.

'Which he never would, no-how,' Captain Quigley explained. 'Useless to ask him, point firmly established. Not a Christian. Understood.'

The previous night, a young prostitute called Welsh Alice had been found with her throat cut behind some scaffolding in Maiden Lane, only a hundred yards away. Her murder had not created half the excitement generated by the parrot – in fact, even now one of the prime suspects was among the crowd shouting advice and encouragement to the bird.

Bella might have watched longer but when a small girl crouched and extruded a pale, glistening turd almost at her feet, one that curled as it fell, she grimaced, struck the man in front of her with her green parasol and pushed her way deeper into the Court, where lay the door to an office.

'Or Temple of Vanities,' Quigley smirked cheerfully, opening the sticking door for her by throwing his shoulder against the woodwork. His supper lay on the topmost page of a heap of manuscript in the centre of a good, once excellent rosewood table.

'You and I must come to a reckoning,' Bella cried, vexed.

'Who is this talking now – Mrs Bella Wallis? Or that mighty wordsmith, Henry Ellis Margam?'

Bella winced. Though he liked to fancy himself as arch, Quigley had all the finesse of a coal hammer.

'Why not take a megaphone and shout that name up and down the Strand?'

For that was the secret she had withheld from Philip Westland, the one that Henry Pattison could not have guessed at in a hundred years. She was indeed Henry Ellis Margam, writer of sensational novels.

It happened that both men had read a Margam novel. Westland had skimmed a few chapters and thrown his copy into the sea with an indulgent laugh. Pattison read his in a first-class railway carriage, feeling uncomfortable stirrings in the trouser department. Asking cautiously around at his club, he discovered this was by no means unusual.

'Piffle, of course,' the aged and decrepit General Chalmers observed, 'but then you have to hand it to the fellow. He knows women.'

Margam was one of those lucky authors whose reputation grows by stealth. Only a very few people in London knew of his real identity and Bella had never heard his name mentioned by readers otherwise only too anxious to discuss, for example, Wilkie Collins. Bella had once heard Collins described with reverence as a troubled aspen: Henry Ellis Margam was, by comparison, hardly more troubled than a trench of asparagus. He wrote fluently and expressively about sex and betrayal, money and lust as it affected the kind of men – and the readers were nearly always men – who came from Bella's own class. In that one narrow sense, the stories were high-flying adventures; and they had their own eerie style. But they made no pretensions to literature and this was the greatest part of their appeal. They were guilty pleasures for gentlemen who associated pleasure with guilt.

'Quigley, I employ you with more or less cheerfulness,' Bella said now. 'But sometimes your impudence can go too far.'

'My dear madam,' Quigley blustered, clearing his plate by the simple expedient of tossing the ruined contents through the front door. 'Your secret is safe with me. And I ask myself sometimes – in fact, I'll ask myself now – who sought out who? Did I come round your gaff in Orange Street begging for help? I think not. So don't go topping it the society lady, oh no, no thank you. I am here to oblige Henry Ellis Margam. I flatter myself I have done that great weaver of dreams some service.'

'This is his office,' Bella countered. 'His – my – place of work.'

'I understand.'

'I wonder sometimes if you do,' she said, fanning the door to remove the frowst of the Captain's overnight occupancy. Quigley, the great baby of the world, did her the honour of blushing. A thought occurred to her, producing a smile. Pattison, coming across Captain Quigley any-where at all on his rolling acres, would have despatched him, left and right barrels, without a second thought.

'You have found some humour in our situation,' the Captain suggested.

'This is the smile of quiet desperation.'

'Poetry!' Captain Quigley exclaimed gallantly.

There was a sudden joyous shout from outside. The simpleton boy Hampsy had arrived on Solomon's roof and was hanging upside down from the gutters, his ratty face cracked open by a grin.

'A guinea says he breaks his neck,' a sporting parson up from Wiltshire cried. But then his foot slipped on some-thing soft and upon examining his boot he found he had stepped a fraction too far into the exciting life of the Lon-don poor. He retreated into the Strand, wiping his feet on the flagstones, the sweat of humiliation wetting his back and belly.

Henry Ellis Margam derived his plots from weak men like Henry Pattison, whom he turned into monsters of depravity. His work attracted no serious reviews and the books sold by word of mouth – sold in their thousands. His readers shared a common itch. As a genre, sensation-alist fiction depended upon weary devices like heirs hid-den away at birth, octoroon Misses who dabbled in voodoo, wills that cast down the villain and raised in his place the remittance man roaming the veldt. The women in these stories were termagant foreigners who were discov-ered to be dead shots with a pistol; titled society whores; girls hardly out of their childhood tied to trees by ropes that bit into their firm young flesh.

What Margam could do was realize these fantasies and locate them. He could scratch the itch. That Mexican beauty with the cruel mouth and pearl-handled pistol, for example. Was she not unlike the sulky Italian woman glimpsed at Harrogate, strolling in the grounds of the Old Swan Hotel? The fictional Lady Witney was surely the actual Lady Eynsham, the hateful snob who once cut the reader's wife stone dead at a charity dinner? As for the damsel in distress with her hands tied behind her, every man with a daughter felt a shameful prod at her predicament. It was Celia semi-naked, watched through the bathroom keyhole by a daddy with sweating palms.

Very, very few of Margam's readers imagined that the book they held in their hand was written by a woman. Nor that the story began its life in a dusty and largely sunless courtyard off the Strand. Margam was a bookseller in Tetbury. He was an attaché at the Paris Embassy. He was a hopeless alcoholic hanging on by his fingertips in Constantinople. He was almost anybody but Mrs Bella Wallis.

FOUR

'Well, and did the boy fall?' the ancient and papery Lord Broxtowe wanted to know. His lordship was entertaining Bella that same night at dining rooms in a far kinder part of London. The surroundings fitted the old man perfectly, for it was the kind of place that lay off the beaten track and persisted in a decidedly old-fashioned way of going on. Among the diners there was hardly anyone younger than sixty and they ate their chops and fresh peas in an almost sepulchral gloom. The oak wainscotting smelled agreeably of many coatings of beeswax, the first laid down in the days when that monster Napoleon mastered Europe.

'The boy survived,' Bella smiled. 'The parrot died of shock, however.'

'Poor creature,' his lordship whispered, flicking his thumb out from his closed fist a few times. And then shrugged humorously, his faded blue eyes fixed fast on Bella's face.

'What great adventures you have,' the old man said. 'What life there is in *your* life.'

'Fie, my lord,' she reproached him.

Bella sometimes wondered whether Lord Broxtowe, whose estates were in Yorkshire, was not above a little slumming when he came to town, and whether she was not a part of those pleasures. On the other hand, he treated her with the effortless manners of an earlier age and would have been horrified to hear her voice what she occasionally thought.

'And tell me,' he asked. 'How does it stand with the agricultural fellow? Mr Pattison?'

'He has gone home to his rolling acres.'

'Which are not inconsiderable, together with a pretty little house and deer park. But I cannot say you have missed a trick there. His conversation is all cogs and drive-shafts. We met at Bowood once.'

'I had no idea you knew of our connection, however slight.'

'My dear child, a musical soirée is nothing if it is not a rumour mill. Lady Cornford was quite sure you were made for one another.'

'That was forward of her. I hardly know the gentleman.'

'Then it is a story about Cissie Cornford,' Lord Broxtowe said with a smile. 'I do seriously mistrust a woman of her advanced years who keeps up with pale mauve mittens.'

They regarded each other very fondly across the table and on an impulse she reached out and sought his papery hand.

'What a friend you are,' she murmured.

'And you a most beautiful woman, Bella,' he returned.

Broxtowe was much nearer eighty than seventy. He had inherited from his uncle at the age of fourteen, when George IV was on the throne. Broxtowe Hall, where, as he put it, he rattled around, was set in a dale painted by

Turner. In one particular work by the artist, if one peered through what seemed like a gale of sleet lit by a sudden explosion of red in the sky – 'rather like the reflection of the accursed Bradford getting its comeuppance' – if one stared intently enough, the Hall could be seen in the low foreground as a liquid slash of grey.

'The fellow came to stay with us while he was daubing, you know,' he mused aloud. 'I have seen blind beggars with stronger eyesight.'

'Turner?' Bella guessed, well used to her friend's habit of continuing in speech what a second before had been a private reverie. Broxtowe smiled.

'How clever you are, how good for me. Tell me what is troubling you.'

'Margam is troubling me.'

He looked up sharply.

'You haven't told this Pattison fellow –?'

'No, of course not.' Bella smiled. 'You and perhaps half a dozen others know the identity of Henry Ellis Margam. Some through necessity. And some –' she inclined her head towards him – 'for other and better reasons.'

'I saw a parson on the train yesterday. He was reading *Lady Nugent's Letter* with the greatest enthusiasm. A mere boy in appearance, though I thought he blushed prettily.'

He summoned the waiter by a lift of his eyebrow.

'Your lordship?'

'A second bottle of the hock if you will, Joe. And perhaps, in a little while, a plate of glazed pears.'

Broxtowe studied his companion amiably.

'This is Margam's seventh novel, I believe.'

'Curse him.'

'Some say he is a well-placed member of the government, some a bitter old stick like me. I have never met anyone that supposes he is the invention of the remarkable woman I see before me now.'

'He is just another novelist.'

'But what a fellow, all the same. In his latest, Lady Nugent is perfectly recognizable but who else could have invented Henshawe, the implacable Henshawe? What a grudge the man has! And what a place to nurture it, working half naked in the opal mines, coming out only to have his eyes ruined by the cruel Australian sunlight. Those blue spectacles! Spinning in the mill-race below Nugent Hall!'

Bella laughed.

'I like what you write,' Broxtowe protested equably. 'Fellow tried to sell me some French pornography once. It's very poor stuff, you know. I always think about pornography that it only works in certain situations. For example, discovering a single copy of some lubricious convent doings hidden away in the Dean of Windsor's library would be wonderful. One such work is always profoundly erotic, wherever you come across it. Yet two or more are, as I say, dull.'

'I would not know.'

'Stuff!' Broxtowe retorted. 'The thing about Mr Margam's work is that the stories are strictly – how shall we say – improper but they uncover and identify the evil in society. You are a moralist, Bella.'

She considered, her hand still in his. If London society were to be believed, her friend had not been completely untouched by sin in the days of his youth, sin redder than any pillar box. Only his great wealth had protected him then. Now extreme old age placed him beyond reproach.

'I write these books in the first instance for pleasure,' she murmured. 'You are kind to say they have a moral dimension. Yet were my husband still to be alive . . .'

'Oh yes,' Broxtowe said with a kindly smile. 'Things would be very different for you, I am sure. I am sorry never to have met him.'

There was a delicate pause. Just once had he asked her a direct question about who Garnett Wallis was and how he had died. But even to him she refused to divulge even the slightest information. The two friends sat back as Joe the waiter brought them their bottle.

Bella defused the slight embarrassment caused by the direction the conversation had taken. 'Were you really able to guess at the true identity of Lady Nugent?' she asked.

'I met the original at a ball in York quite recently. She is of course furious with the infamous Margam, enough to have engaged private detectives to hunt him down. I directed her attention to a rather squalid set of rooms in Paris. And a man who had been turned out as a butler in Eaton Square some five years since.'

Bella laughed.

'It is you who should be the fictionalist.'

'No, but such a man *was* shown the door by the Countess of Thame and *does* now live in Paris. La Nugent thanked me profusely and rushed home to set her myrmidons on his trail. I should imagine he is having the cravat applied liberally to his back at this very moment.'

'What is his name?'

'Burrell. Born for the horsewhip.'

His keen blue eyes studied hers.

'There is more. A poor fellow called Hearnshaw but not Henshawe has resigned his commission in the Kent Militia and fled the country into Germany. Unluckily for him, he bragged to his fellow officers once too often about owning shares in an opal mine in Cooperpedie. They took him to be the remorseless devil who drove Lady Nugent's daughter into the madhouse.'

'Oh fie!' Bella exclaimed. 'By appearing to the girl as half-man, half-lizard? Are people so very credulous?'

'When it touches their own dark desires, yes. Who would not secretly wish to be the Henshawe of the tale, gazing down on the virginal Lydia Nugent, her breast rising and falling with such palpable innocence?'

'Palpable was good,' Bella admitted, blushing.

'All London has heard of Mr Philip Hearnshaw and his daemonic lust, so thinly disguised in name by that sensational novelist, Mr Henry Margam.'

'Poor devil.'

'A member of the Garrick,' Broxtowe sniffed.

Bella said nothing to this because if the truth were told she was already acquainted with Hearnshaw's fate. When she told the very few people who knew of her second life that she wrote for pleasure, she did not add that part of that pleasure was to do down her enemies. In this instance there was enough of Hearnshaw in Henshawe to seal his fate: his tattooed arm, his laundress mother, his touchiness when it came to matters of social slight. A dozen tiny details confirmed him as the model for a fictional character who came halfway round the world to seduce a mother and her daughter in a frenzy of lust.

'You have not yet said why you are out of love with the estimable novelist,' Broxtowe prompted gently.

'Making parsons blush is all too easy,' Bella said.

The Fifth Earl seldom laughed out loud, but when he did it sounded like a musical peal.

'The real Lady Nugent, as we might term her, prostituted an ugly and not very intelligent daughter for the chance to acquire a coal pit in Derbyshire. I would say a handsome cloak of fiction was thrown over these poor details. Is that so very easy?'

'Easier than you think.'

'Maybe so,' Broxtowe said. He laid his spoon gently on the rim of the plate in the old-fashioned manner. When he sat back, his face was disturbingly out of the light, so that she could not read his expression.

'You are disgusted by Margam, Bella. And you think it demeaning in some way to stamp your foot on such cockroaches as Hearnshaw. I think not. Mr Margam is an important man. What does he look like, by the by?'

'Small,' Bella said, who had given the matter some thought. 'Small and plump, like Napoleon. Earnest. Pontificating. With hands like a mole. You would not wish to touch the dampness of his skin, nor to breathe the roaring stink that comes out of his clothes. Not the gentleman, Broxtowe.'

'Does he have to be a gentleman at all?' his lordship objected, but in such a reflective way that the remark followed her home.

* * *

The house in Orange Street welcomed her and calmed her nerves. Its principal room was papered blue-grey, a colour that reminded Bella of France, interrupted by gilt-framed oils, none of them contemporary and all rescued from the sort of dealers known to Captain Quigley – that is to say, stolen, or in the Captain's more neutral way of putting it, recently acquired.

At the end of the drawing room were windows that framed a huge and sprawling fig, suggesting secret gardens beyond. But in truth, this foliage concealed a blank wall only a few feet from the end of the property and the fig's stem rose from an ancient pavement of broken York stone. The screen of green she looked out on now was, Bella acknowledged with a sigh, yet another deception. She flung herself into a chair and kicked off her shoes.

And so she slept, until roused by the click of the door latch. Standing on the threshold was her companion and perhaps the consolation of her life, Marie Claude d'Anville. Nearly twenty years younger than Bella, hardly more than five feet tall, Marie Claude was in her night-gown, her hair braided into a single plait.

'Where have you been?' the girl asked with her habitual downturned lips.

'Don't be angry,' Bella chided.

'This is not the way to be happy,' Marie Claude said.

And Bella laughed, jumping up to embrace her in the doorway.

'This way of life? The habit of sleeping in chairs? Before I left him tonight, Lord Broxtowe sent you his love. And that made me very happy. Come, Marie Claude. Look into my face. Do you not see a happy woman?'

'You are hard to love.'

'Ah well,' Bella said. 'That is a completely different matter.'

Captain Quigley had made some efforts to tidy the office – in fact, his employer caught him sweeping it out with a borrowed broom, billows of dust at his feet. Moreover, he was wearing the better of his two tunic jackets and a pair of canvas trousers that concertina-ed slightly less than usual. Bella peered. The gallant Captain had shaved, or been shaved, the razor skirting his mutton-chop whiskers and greying moustache. His skin glistened red.

'There is work,' he explained briefly. 'The cove they took up last night for Welsh Alice's murder has been released. Boiler-plate alibi. Was in Poplar the night of the crime, having been run over by a dray. Eight witnesses, one of them a justice of the peace.'

'What was he doing in Poplar?'

'Drinking,' Quigley said.

'And how is this become work for us?'

The Captain fiddled in his tunic pocket and produced a leather cigar case. He passed it to her with an elaborate flourish. It was empty, save for half a dozen green breast feathers.

'And how did the police miss this?'

'On account it was nicked by the first to arrive at the scene.'

'Who was?'

Quigley whistled, as if for a dog. After a moment or two, the same little girl who had defecated at her feet the previous day appeared. She was clutching in both arms a ruined applewood crate. Bella peered. Inside were a handful of crushed and mangled potatoes and a single carrot.

'What is your name?'

'Can't speak,' Quigley advised. 'Has spoken, used to speak. But not now. A good girl, however. Name of Betsy.'

'You've been shopping, Betsy.'

'Scratting. Up at the market. Gutter work,' the Captain explained.

'And this little case you found. It's for your treasures, is it? Like the parrot feathers?'

Betsy nodded.

'And where did you find it?'

To point, she had to set down her gleanings from the Covent Garden gutters. Her stick-like arm indicated the general direction of Maiden Lane, where the body had been discovered. Quigley caught Bella's eye.

'Story stands up. Found the body, found the case, ran into the Strand, found a bluebottle. Subsequent hue and cry. Betsy bunked off. Smart girl,' he added approvingly.

Bella tipped the feathers into the palm of her hand. A small gilt crest became apparent, embossed in the bottom of the case.

'Just so,' Captain Quigley observed quietly.

'Do you recognize it?'

The Captain shrugged. 'I thought you might. Now this here Betsy was wondering if you would like to buy her cigar case for a consideration. And o' course, somewhere new to keep her feathers.'

'Well now, would this sweetie tin be a good place to keep them safe?'

Betsy held out her hand. Depicted on the lid of the tin a child no older than herself stood by a sundial, surrounded by lupins. A little way off an indulgent grandfather stood with a hoe in his hand. We were in Mummersetshire, where things are ordered differently.

'What do you say, Betsy?'

'That, and a florin. Made up of little silver joeys,' Quigley proposed, ruffling the urchin's hair.

'And how long would she hang on to that?' Bella wondered.

For answer, Betsy spat in both palms and held her dukes up, chin bristling.

'I am not a police reporter,' Bella said, an hour or so later. She was feeling sour: something in the way Quigley cosseted her was proving repellent. But the Captain knew her moods and lounged against the doorpost, picking his teeth with a bristle from the broom.

'Have you told the French Missie about Lieutenant Hearnshaw?' he asked, opening a new line of conversation.

'Not yet.' Something in his expression alerted her. 'Why? Is there further news?'

'Tried to blow his brains out in Germany. Missed, took off an ear and most of his jaw. In quarters now at Brussels. Very low.'

Bella's eyes glittered.

'How many times has Quigley offered to fight your fights for you?' the Captain asked gently. 'I would have cut the young gentleman so that he never walked again, leave alone presented arms down a dark alley to a respectable young Frenchwoman. Your way better. The living death of literature. Excellent. But it's taking something out of you, dear lady.'

'Will he live?' Bella asked.

'After a fashion.'

She rose and paced the room for a moment or two, her hands trembling.

'Are you my conscience now, Quigley?'

'We must hope not.'

'But this is about Welsh Alice, all the same?'

'I draw your attention to it, is all.'

'I knew nothing about her in life,' she muttered. 'Was she an honest, kindly girl?'

'She was a shilling whore. But who followed her out of the market and slit her throat, just because he thought he could?'

Bella considered and then held out her hand for the cigar case with the armorial crest. Quigley was right: it was work, of a kind. Her books always began with a modest discovery, like walking into a dark and trackless forest and finding a single pearl earring hanging from a twig. That was the opening scene of *Belinda Hetherington*, which, for the purposes of the plot, took place in Ceylon, an island Bella had never visited. The earring was her own, however, and the villain whose vanity and sexual cruelty was unmasked by its discovery was equally real.

FIVE

France: Boulogne. The tide has filled and the Gare Maritime is afflicted with the smoke that announces the arrival of the packet from England. The best hotels have sent carriages to the landing stage; humbler citizens who have rooms to let are jostling each other at the foot of the gangway.

It is midday. By standing order of the garrison commander, Lieutenant Mercier has marched a file of soldiers out from the post guarding the Bassin Loubet. It is exercise for them and a mild demonstration of the might of the Third Republic to the flustered and ill-tempered rosbifs who are alighting from Folkestone.

From Mercier's point of view it is also an utter waste of time, as well as an insult to his rank. He has written the adjutant three letters on the subject. To show the might of the Republic it would surely be better to have a mounted officer at the head of the column? The adjutant is his cousin and generously overlooks the tone of these letters, in one of which Mercier complains of being made to walk about like a postman.

Colonel Duprat, the garrison commander, takes a different view: he dislikes his junior officers almost as much as he detests his posting. While Mercier trudges back to his post on foot, Duprat sips an anis and leafs through a book on the antiquities of Asia Minor. Examining himself at the shaving mirror that morning, he has concluded he is still a devilish handsome man, even if one without immediate prospects of promotion. He lays aside his book and lights a Turkish cigarette.

The novels of Henry Ellis Margam were published by the firm of Naismith & Frean in a list that included the ramblings of Indian Army veterinary surgeons; grim old men who understood the workings of the Lunacy Laws; and pederastical schoolmasters. Composite title: *Diseases of the Young Mind in Tropical Climates, by an Army Surgeon.* The fiction in the catalogue, until the partners discovered Bella, was likewise on the whimsical side. For sixteen years past, a Mrs Toaze-Bonnett had supplied an annual story of the American Plains, peopled by such characters as Old Seth, Sheriff Jinks, and the mysterious and shape-changing Redstick Indian, Dancing Feet.

It was always broodingly hot in Mrs Toaze-Bonnett's world and the rattlesnakes exhibited more impudence in her pages than ever they do in life. In *Tall Tales from Tolliver Creek*, Jim Dalloway astonishes the company at a church social by shooting the knitting bag out from under Lilian Fairbrother's chair. The despicable fortune hunter Colonel Mortimer is all for having Jim horsewhipped there and then but when the tapestry bag is opened, a rattler is revealed coiled in Lilian's skeins of wool. Romance ensues. 'I'm a rough diamond,' Jim explains, 'but many a second son has turned out likewise.'

The cheerful and undemanding Naismith, who oversaw the outpourings of Mrs Toaze-Bonnett's pen, dropped dead under the Euston Arch one frosty morning on his way to see the lady, who lived at Pinner. The surviving partner, the much more various Elias Frean, retreated, as he had always planned, to a house a little way from Boulogne. There he lived alone, save for a young male companion of lissom good looks. And to that place, before the commencement of any new Henry Ellis Margam novel, he liked to summon Bella Wallis.

Though in the fullness of his years, Frean was no taller than a child. His bald head and beaked nose gave him an unwanted resemblance to the handle of a lady's umbrella – was he ever likely to forgive General Sir George Milman's supposition that he slept for the most part in the hall, with walking sticks for companions? Bella liked him for his incurable avarice. Even among publishers, he was stinginess personified.

'You stay at the Boule d'Or, I believe?'

'As always, Mr Frean.'

His chuckle was that of a glass being emptied of stale water.

'Decidedly expensive. Ruinously so. But then, ah yes, the artistic temperament . . .'

They were smoking Dutch cheroots either side of an octagonal rattan table on which lay the firm's most recent publications, all too obviously unread. Frean had an uncertain taste when it came to interior design: the little table was of a piece with several huge fretted vessels in brass and a low-relief panel depicting native boys swimming. The floor was scattered with Baluchistan rugs. There were three sofas, so low to the ground that only the most romantic of minds would consider abandoning themselves to them.

Though he would have died to admit it, Frean was a little in awe of his top-selling author. Bustiman's *A Young Boy's Make-up* had sold well year on year – to a largely disappointed readership – but its sales figures were as nothing to the novels of Henry Ellis Margam. Frean had accidentally struck gold – and if he tiptoed around the problem of keeping Bella sweet, it was not just that he was, on the whole, a woman hater. After all, he knew next to nothing about the sex and had never, in a long life, seen one naked. What made Frean nervous was that he was dealing with intellect, something a decent publishing house avoided like the plague.

'You have an idea for your next book?' he suggested, after the usual civilities. Bella passed him the cigar case from Maiden Lane.

'Ha!' he cried, inspecting the crest within. 'What people won't do for armorial bearings. In my day the government was right to raise tax on them. Have you taken this to the College of Arms, at all?'

'I have not. The case was found on a gentleman murdered in Maiden Lane a fortnight since. His assassin was a young woman called Alice Protheroe.'

Bella watched him closely. It was her habit to take actual events and twist them to her purpose. The poor drab known as Welsh Alice had thus become a governess newly returned from India and the man who killed her was reinvented as the victim. It seemed unlikely that Frean, preoccupied with his life in Boulogne, would know of the real events witnessed by the mute girl, Betsy. And so it proved.

'And this is your plot?'

'It is the opening to my story,' Bella corrected.

'What is the name of this gentleman?'

'I propose to call him Colonel Abbs.'

'Oh, a very bad name for a soldier. Oh dear, no.'

'You may have a better suggestion.'

'He should be called Luckhurst,' Frean said at once. 'Or possibly Luckless. Luckless is good. He too is from India? I do hope he isn't from India.'

'From Bad Gastein. Where he has a small set of rooms in the Hotel d'Angleterre.'

She watched Frean's lips move, as though he were chewing on the idea and had discovered a morsel of gristle. He shrugged.

'And how did the lady do for him?'

'With a hatpin to the carotid artery. Only an expert could have been sure of her mark.'

Frean touched his own neck with fluttering fingers.

'Well,' he muttered.

'That is how the story begins,' Bella concluded briskly. 'I am looking for my usual terms, Mr Frean. You may have the manuscript six months from today's date.'

'Yes, but a governess,' he objected. 'I'm not sure –'

'Miss Protheroe is merely the instrument of someone else's vengeance. Someone of an even darker hue.'

'And who might that be?'

But Bella understood the workings of a publisher's mind only too well. Captain Quigley had once summed up the ideal strategy for meetings like this: go in, make your pitch and leave. It was a lesson learned from his own dealings with the police and other authorities.

'Relevant papers lodged at Chatham. Their business to trace. Material witness now in lodgings at Portsmouth. Statements must be sought. Always remember, dear lady, the more you explain, the more you have to explain.'

With these wise words from an expert echoing in her ears, Bella held out her hand for the cigar case. Frean hung on to it, peering closely at the crest.

'If you will send your standard contract to the hotel for signature,' she pressed gently, 'I shall be in Boulogne one more afternoon. I leave for England tomorrow morning.'

'Yes, but – this vexing little detail here –'

'It is my experience, as it is yours, that the world is filling up with false coats of arms. We can say, if you like, this particular one is the invention of Colonel Abbs. Or Luckless.'

But Frean was by no means as stupid as he sometimes appeared.

'Colonel Luckless, as I understand it, is a figment of your fecund imagination. However, this cigar case exists in the real world. And, according to you, was found at the scene of an actual murder. Or have I misunderstood you?'

'No,' Bella said slowly. 'All that is true.'

'Then, would it not be helpful to know whose crest it is?'

He picked up a copper cowbell and shook it. After a minute or so, his companion Pardew glided into the room. Bella gawped. The Oriental décor had got to Billy Pardew in a big way: he was wearing a clinging muslin gown and had dyed his hair a marmalade orange. His fingernails were painted silver.

'Mrs Wallis,' he lisped. 'How lovely. I see you come up the path from my bedroom.'

The last time she had seen the light of Frean's life, he was a faintly podgy youth in white flannels and a rowing vest. Clearly, he was now striking out on his own. When he reached for Bella's hand it was to bow low, kiss it lightly and then lay the back of it against his forehead.

'How nice to see you again, Mr Pardew,' she murmured.

'Should you like some iced sherbet?' he asked solicitously.

'I think not. Is that henna on your feet?'

He plucked up the hem of his gown.

'These are my henna socks,' he giggled. 'Mr Frean disapproves. Don't you, Mr Frean?'

'Billy, tell us what you can about this,' his master muttered, passing him the cigar case. 'The crest therein.'

Pardew opened the case and peered, a half-smile on his luscious lips.

'Well, blow me,' he exclaimed. 'Ancient heraldry. Or perhaps not so ancient. I don't think we'd see *this* on a knight's shield. Dear me, no.'

'You recognize it?'

'Well, I'm not exactly Garter King of Arms, am I!' he shrilled. 'It rings a bell, Mrs Wallis, I'll say no more than that. It stirs a memory. But now you're making me blush.'

'You *should* blush,' Frean said. 'I have seen this crest before. To be bold about it, on a pair of cufflinks you have in your room, from a time before you took to henna socks.'

'Oh!' Billy cried petulantly. 'My room is my room, I thought we agreed. Have you taken to snooping again, Mr Frean? Have you no trust at all left in you? Fie and for shame!'

Bella wondered why Frean had never taken this impudent telegram boy, as he was in former life, and chained him to the wall with his feet in a bucket of scorpions.

'Either you do recognize it or you don't,' she said tersely.

For a second, all the play actor in Pardew disappeared and he looked at her with a flash of his old aboriginal self. He turned away and minced out of the room.

'*He* is not the man we're looking for,' Frean laughed uncertainly.

'I imagine not,' Bella snapped.

'These cufflinks –'

'You need not explain how he came by them.'

It was a remark she immediately wished she could take back: Frean's face crumpled. When she took a step towards him, he flapped his hand and turned his back on her.

She caught up with Billy on the terrace, where his muslin gown was flattened against his body by the wind. He stood under a trellis, his henna-ed feet plunged into white and pink rose petals. He pouted sulkily.

'I don't have to tell you nothing, I believe, Mrs Wallis.'

'You have already told me something, you little fool. Whose crest is it?'

He chewed on his lower lip, trying to think his way past the yawning pit that lay in his path.

'I seen something similar on the arch over a door in Oxford once.'

'A college?'

'Big house. Just happened to notice it. In passing.'

'Of course.'

'You're wondering if I'm telling you the truth.'

'I am wondering whether to box your ears.'

'A very cool remark, I must say.'

'An arch over a doorway?'

'I just told you.'

'And the cufflinks?'

'You don't own me, neither of you,' Pardew screeched. 'It is the same crest that I seen over the door. While I was waiting for a gentleman.'

'The crest wasn't his?'

'Him!' he hooted. 'I should say so, I don't think! And now I've said all I'm going to say.'

Bella raked him with one last glance and then walked back indoors to say goodbye to Frean. His head barely came as high as her chest and his hand, when it was offered, had the touch of forest mushrooms. Bella resisted a mischievous impulse to further ruin his morning by hugging him.

'My best regards to Mademoiselle d'Anville,' Frean whispered, peering up past her bust at her grave and composed face. Unconsciously, but still horrible for all that, he licked his lips. 'Such a pretty little thing.'

'I shall be sure to tell her so,' Bella replied.

'And as for Billy, I shall speak sharply to him, you may bank on it.'

'You would do better to kick his backside.'

She walked away down his gravel path, her parasol on her shoulder. There was a view of a sea no more troubled than a silk bedsheet. The French flag wagged over the roof of the *mairie* and somewhere a band was playing airs from Suppé. In that instant, she resolved to cashier Colonel Abbs, or Luckless. By the time the manuscript was delivered,

Frean would have forgotten all about him. The very idea of soldiers disgusted her more than she could say.

The walk back into Boulogne lay along a modest enough esplanade with the sea on one side and houses like Mr Frean's on the other. In places, the way was paved and in others last year's high tides had dumped drifts of sand that were churned to a powdery grey. Holidaymakers walked out here for the very French thrill of being at least ten minutes from a decent restaurant: there were a few telescopes flourished at the fishing boats coming on the tide. A rich papa with a mahogany and brass plate camera was trying to arrange a photograph of his wife and daughter and pleading with mama to look less like a fisherwoman with a grudge against life. Out of courtesy, Bella stopped for a moment to allow him to expose his plate.

Standing in her path, his hat hanging loose in his hand, was a pale man she could see at a glance was English. There was something about the abject modesty with which he acknowledged her, his silver hair unkempt and ruffled by the breeze, his eyes soft and downcast, that tugged at Bella's memory. When he saw that she did not immediately recognize him, he smiled ruefully.

'Charles Urmiston, Mrs Wallis,' he murmured. 'I knew your husband a little.'

Bella let out a sharp and genuine little cry and extended her hand.

'What must you think of me, Mr Urmiston?' she exclaimed. 'My mind was quite elsewhere.'

Look at the boots if you want to find a gentleman's balance at the bank, was one of Captain Quigley's rules of thumb. Urmiston was wearing ridiculously yellow boots, their toes scuffed. His suit was in a too loud, far too ancient check and the collar to his shirt rumpled and none too clean. Bella guessed that each item, even down to the shirt, had come from the Caledonian Market.

'And Mrs Urmiston? How is she?' she asked, remembering a tall thin woman with a long nose, on whom her husband doted.

'She had such fond memories of Boulogne. And asked to be brought here in her final illness. I buried her yesterday,' he added, his voice trembling. He looked into Bella's face with such sweet simplicity that now she had him. This ruined man had once been a land agent to the Great Western Railway, with a pretty house on Campden Hill and a carriage of his own. There was some story of a calamitous court case, the details of which she could not bring to the front of her mind.

'Mr Urmiston, my husband had such high opinions of you both. I am deeply grieved to hear of your loss. Where do you stay in London?'

'Just at the moment, I am across the river in Lambeth,' he replied uneasily.

'And whereabouts, particularly?'

'Does it matter?' he asked with a feeble spark of testiness. But then repented, blushing.

'Do you know the Black Prince Road?'

Enough to realize you're a man on his uppers, she thought, feeling a hot rush of sympathy. From Campden Hill to Black Prince Road was a journey as painful as falling out of a balloon on to spiked railings.

'I stay at the Boule d'Or here in Boulogne. Will you not walk that way with me? I shall very much like it if we can take lunch together.'

Urmiston plucked at the fabric to his jacket, his eyes filling with tears. Bella immediately understood.

'Come now,' she said, perhaps a little too sharply. 'Friendship does not stand upon the tailoring of a suit. You shall be my guest and we will talk of better times, happier times.'

To her complete dismay, Urmiston turned and ran, an ungainly and clumsy Englishman scattering children in his path. An irate French papa raised his cane and cracked it across the poor man's shoulders. The sob he gave was hideous to hear. He leapt a low wall and landed on hands and knees in dirty sand. People on the beach stopped their promenades to stare at him in amazement.

The rest of the day should have been filled with reflections on the absurd Billy Pardew and his transformation from a frog into an Eastern princess. But instead she could not rid her mind of Charles Urmiston and his flight. Using hotel stationery, she tried to capture the essence of their meeting.

In her fiction, it was generally women who fell from grace. Lucy Akehurst defended Captain Williamson from charges of fraud and embezzlement, only to discover that the plausible captain, with his rolling sea gait and piercing blue eyes, was a pirate when it came to women. She was undone by girlish innocence and the refusal to face facts until it was too late. Hedley Martineau, who might have saved her, drew back at the last moment. Lucy was left high and dry in Alexandria, lodging with Margarita Busoni, her cats and parakeets. Her bedroom window looked out over the souk and when she woke in the morning, her floor was peppered with flowers and little screws of coloured paper. The reader was left in no doubt. If there was a fate worse than death for the guileless Lucy, La Busoni was planning it.

Charles Urmiston was the first man Bella had come across to be so comprehensively unhorsed in the same way. You could not live in London and not meet ruined gentlemen who had gambled away their inheritance or married the wrong woman. Yet by and large their disgrace was softened by the circumstance of their birth. The best houses might refuse them but they had enough cousinage to see them through. Urmiston, by contrast, had no one. Another man, offered a free lunch by an unattached woman, might have leapt at the offer. Urmiston, the gangling fool, had bolted.

Next day, she looked for him on the boat, but he was not to be found.

'Not a college?'

'Billy says not.'

Quigley shrugged. 'That is good for us. That narrows the field.'

'I thought so too,' Bella said.

'Cigar case not a souvenir of happy days spent construing the Greek. Some mutton-chopped old goat at the head of the class. Stained-glass windows and college port. Rowing. Possibly a bit of hunting to hounds. Nothing of that.'

'You know your Oxford,' Bella exclaimed, with as much sarcasm as would sink the average Thames steamer.

'I do,' the Captain acknowledged, blithe.

'Can you find the place that Billy was talking about, however?'

'I should say so,' he replied judiciously. 'It would seem likely. They are slow down there but if a thing is put simply enough, they can be made to understand.'

'There is one other thing before you set off. In Boulogne, I met a man called Urmiston.'

'Yes?' Quigley leered.

'A Mr Charles Urmiston, late of Campden Hill. A gentleman I would like to help.'

To her surprise, the Captain flinched slightly at the name.

'You know him?' she asked, startled.

'This address in Campden Hill: magnolia in the front? Householder some sort of gent with connections to the railway?'

'I believe so.'

'There is a problem.'

'I'd like to know what that is.'

'You have a picture in your house, of a foreign-looking dinah, a bit on the plump side. Not a stitch on her and looking out the window at some palm trees adjacent. With altogether somewhat of a pensive air, you might say.'

Bella passed this painting on the staircase every morning. She stared into Quigley's face, her eyes narrowing with dreadful suspicion.

'And?'

'It belongs to this Urmiston cove.'

'You sold me a stolen painting?'

'Did I say I stole it? I come by it in the normal way.'

'Which is to say theft. Do I have anything else of his acquired in the same way?'

'I was offered the work at a knock-down price –'

'You received stolen goods.'

'This can go on all day,' the Captain blustered. 'I'll hook it out of your gaff before I set off for the dreaming spires.'

'You will have it removed this afternoon. Mr Urmiston was a friend of my late husband. To say I am angry is to understate the case: I am furious.'

'If I was to meet the gentleman and explain an honest mistake –'

'You will have first to find him. He lives somewhere along the Black Prince Road –'

'A neighbourhood known to me,' Quigley supplied hastily. 'I could nip across the river –'

'What is the name of your associate, the cross-eyed man with a horse and cart?'

'Murch.'

'You will find Mr Murch, go to my house and remove that painting. Right now. Indeed, at once.'

'And Black Prince Road?'

'I will attend to that myself.'

It was a little on Quigley's mind to issue a general weather warning about the Borough of Lambeth, as though there it rained soot and disaster; but the pale fury in Bella's face deterred him. Instead of saying anything, he smoothed down his moustaches with one hand, and jingled the change in his pocket with the other. Murch the carter a reliable sort of cove. No art lover, but then again that did not come into it.

SIX

This, included in a small parcel franked with French stamps to an address in Oxford, the paper reeking of patchouli, one edge decorated with a henna thumbprint:

Hoping that I find you well and that you remember a cheeky boy you once knew and I hope you have not forgot. Enclosed please find something that I confess might have been nicked from you once though it was done out of desperation. But now I find my circumstances much changed and for the better, the sea air agrees with me, haha! A lady I won't name was round at my domicile asking questions and you can be sure I sent her off with a flea in her ear. Nothing serious but I thought you ought to know. Please don't try to trace me though I know you never would anyway. The moving finger writes and having writ moves on. This green ink is tres joli, n'est pas? From yours A Friend.

Vircow-Ucquart was something of a crack shot. He and Bolsover lay out on the roof of the earl's Berkshire seat, picnicking on chicken and cold lamb cutlets. From time to time, the German applied his one good eye to the back sight of a long-barrelled game rifle, aimed down the lawn and blew another unfortunate rook into eternity.

Bolsover was delighted: the birds did not simply expire but became a sudden puff of feathers and guts. They disintegrated.

There were estate workers clustered at one side of the carriage drive, elderly men with veiny arms who were cleaning out the brook that ran alongside.

'Oh how I wish that fucking breech would blow back in his face,' Claude Atkins muttered.

'Why, m' oldun, time hangs heavy when you'm waiting for nightfall.'

'And what happens at nightfall?'

'They turn into them chaps with the sharp teeth.'

'Vampires,' someone supplied.

'Those are the boys. Vampires, hot and strong.'

There was laughter: but it was uneasy. Another shot, another black snowball of feathers and guts.

'If you were to shoot one of those men down there,' Bolsover wondered idly, 'would they make as pretty a mess, do you think?'

'About this, you should not joke,' the German said.

'Would they blow to pieces?'

'Freddie, listen to me. You are wise to come down here to the country. I will find things to amuse you, provided it is done discreetly. But no more London adventures for a while. We live quiet, we eat well, we stay calm.'

'I am always calm,' Bolsover said. 'I leave panic to others. You have been talking to a certain clerical gentleman in Oxford, I detect.'

Vircow-Ucquart frowned.

'He is concerned for you. You would expect as much from an old friend. He has only your well-being at heart.'

'Well, God damn him for his solicitude,' Bolsover shouted.

He snatched up the rifle and levelled it at the German and closed his finger round the trigger. But the weapon was not loaded and all that resulted was a dry click. Lord Bolsover's manic laugh floated out over the lawns and was caught by the estate workers below.

'Now what?' Claude Atkins demanded.

'The Prussian has said something comical, doubtless.'

Bella was in Lambeth. Persuading a cab to cross the river had involved a conference in the cab shelter by the gardens in Leicester Square.

'Money is money,' she protested.

'Lord love you,' an excitable cabbie exclaimed. 'The way we see it, time is money. That is our trade. I say nothing against the people over there – my old woman was one of them, in her day. But you want me to take you there, have me hang about while you make some enquiries and then bring you back. That's going on for two hours. I could be up and down Regent Street a dozen times for that – *and* run a body to Victoria or Euston. Or into Knightsbridge, say.'

'I will take you,' a frail old man interrupted. There was a roar of laughter.

'That horse of your'n 'll get as far as Lambeth Bridge and then give hisself up to the nearest copper. He ain't got the strength left in his body enough to blow a decent fart, begging your presence, madam.'

And the horse, who was called Perce, did seem in the autumn of his years. But Mossman, whose horse he was, whispered a few encouraging words, and they set off at a leisurely pace. Indeed, so slowly did they progress, the terrors of the Black Prince Road seemed lessened as they drew towards them.

'Do you have a house number?' Mossman called in encouragement as they crossed the crown of Lambeth Bridge.

'Are we close by?'

'Not exactly as such,' the cabbie conceded. They drew up just beyond the Doulton factory for a conference.

'The fact is, I am here to search for a man. I do not have his exact address, nor can I be sure it is in Black Prince Road, even. But the man I am looking for is mild-mannered enough and a gentleman. Albeit one down on his luck.'

Mossman had intelligent eyes and listened in silence.

'You do not have a servant who could do this work on foot?'

'I do not. Is there a problem?'

'There might be. If your gentleman is a black gentleman or a Chinee, that might make things easier. But a great many clerkly-looking chaps live along that road. Which is nothing much to write home about, to be sure. But is not the poorest place in Lambeth. He's not black, the cove?'

'He is tall and thin, with a refined air about him.'

Mossman's smile was tiny but carried enough reproof about it to make Bella blush.

'We can do no more than try,' he said. 'Does he have a name?'

'His name is Charles Urmiston.'

'Better than Smith, then,' the cabbie said, speaking to Perce as much as to his fare.

The search began badly. Though Black Prince Road was cheerless, it was recognizable enough to Bella as a poor but proud street of houses, not all of them subdivided into lodgings. It was true that what had been a pleasant zephyr on the far side of the river was here a sharp and gritty wind, blowing dust and papers up into the air; and though Mossman had the place set down as a bolt-hole for clerks and the better sort of warehousemen, almost the first thing Bella saw was a woman her own age stretched out in the roadway, either unconscious or dead. Her black straw bonnet was rolling gently towards them.

'Stop the cab,' she cried and leapt down to help. On the pavement, five men were fighting each other. While Bella knelt by the woman, dozens of people appeared as if from nowhere and a general milling ensued.

'Take me to Tait's,' the woman mumbled through bloody teeth.

'Tait's?'

'The dairy.'

Mr Tait, if he was the man who gave his name to the premises, was outside, feverishly putting up chocolate-brown shutters. As if in a fairy tale, the five who had been fighting had multiplied to more than fifty: when Bella glanced back, she saw Mossman on foot, dragging Perce round by the head and leading him away.

'Get her in the shop,' Tait shouted.

Once inside, the woman collapsed on to the sanded floor.

'I'm done for,' she sighed.

'No, you're not,' Bella said in the gloom. 'But you've been stabbed, I think. I am going to undo your blouse and stays.'

When Tait came in, locking the door behind him, she glanced up and asked him to fetch his wife.

'This is my wife,' he said, bleak.

'Then fetch me some clean linen and a bowl of hot water.'

'Are you a doctor?'

'Just do as I say.'

The wound, when it was discovered, was superficial. Mrs Tait was cut across the breast and in the fleshy part of her arm. Her husband watched uneasily as Bella swabbed the paper-white flesh and dressed the cut with a bandage torn from a sheet that was by comparison a dirty grey.

'Who are you?' the victim whispered.

'I came down here to find a man called Urmiston.'

'Him as lost his wife recent?'

'You know him?' Bella exclaimed.

'On a better day, I sell him his milk,' Mrs Tait replied.

There was a knock on the door. Mossman's face peered in.

Back in Orange Street Bella reviled herself for not staying in Lambeth a moment longer than it took to jump into Mossman's cab and shrink back against the horsehair upholstery. She had no idea what all the fighting had been about nor who had stabbed Mrs Tait. Much more to the point, she had done nothing to track down Urmiston to his lair. Only when the cab was wheeling her up Whitehall – a wonderfully comforting and orderly Whitehall – did she regret bolting.

The answer was to write to him. There was a terse and faintly aggressive side to all Bella's correspondence. In the end, she sent him no more than a note, inviting him to call on Fleur de Lys at his convenience. For an hour or more this single sheet of paper and its dozen or so words lay on her desk. In this time, Urmiston's future hung in the balance. Bella grimaced, she smoked, she read. On an impulse, she went upstairs and changed her clothes. She wished she had sent Quigley to Lambeth and gone in his place to Oxford. She resolved to take Marie Claude to supper at Fracatelli's and changed her mind.

Only then did she bundle the note into an envelope and find a stamp. There was a postbox fifty yards from the house and she walked there with complete indifference to Charles Urmiston's fate in her heart. He could do as he wished. She could hardly care less. However, even thinking that vexed her. She felt like kicking someone.

SEVEN

Captain Quigley knew some parts of Oxford better than others. For a time, before he took up with Mrs Bella Wallis (as he liked to phrase it), he had lived in a hut by the canal, indulged in his every whim by a stout woman from Norfolk, who left his bed each morning to unload barges. Big Barbara had once won a substantial wager by tossing a hundredweight sack of coal over a five-foot fence from a mark drawn in the mud of the towpath. Her challenger had been the stroke of the Merton boat, who stripped to his white waistcoat to attempt the feat, employing the press-and-lift method, which took the sack above his head, showering dust on to his blond curls. He failed, injuring his groin into the bargain. Barbs won the day by snuggling the coal to her waist and then tossing it clean across the fence, with the same sort of economy lesser women would have employed in emptying their aprons of peapods.

Which story the Captain was now retelling in the snug of the Eagle and Child, every detail closely followed by Mr Blossom, a sweating tub of lard, porter to the missionary gentlemen along the Banbury Road. Blossom, as he had already confessed, was an eight-pint man of an evening, every one of which was needed to look after his flock without himself going mad or running amok.

'A rum lot of coves, are they?'

'Not in the sense you might intend. Not so to say rum as you and I might understand. For a start there's on'y sixteen of them.'

'Brutes, though?' Quigley suggested, who knew very well what their character was, having observed their comings and goings for two days.

'Brutes? A bunch of mollies if you ask me.'

'You don't say!'

'Gentlemen who want to missionarize the heathen,' Blossom explained. 'Who have received in their undergraduate years a call for that sort of thing and now nothing will satisfy them but that they go to some poor benighted country and pester the life out of the savages there.'

'Know the type,' Quigley confirmed. 'Forever close to tears. Handshake wetter than lettuce.'

'You have them off to a T,' Blossom said, admiringly.

'Is there a guvnor to this place at all?'

'Mr Hagley,' the porter responded. 'The Reverend Mr Anthony Hagley.'

'Himself a missionary once, I wager.'

'Him!' Blossom cried. 'I doubt he's been further east than Paddington Station. Or,' he added, tapping his nose significantly, 'maybe certain parts of Moorfields, eh?'

The porter had a laugh that could shake plaster loose. Quigley feared for his new friend's life as what was intended as genial punctuation turned to paroxysm. Drink called for. A small gold watch accepted, which Blossom swallowed off, chasing it with a pint of the ditchwater passing as Best Bitter. The porter had raised a considerable wad of phlegm that he disposed of by opening the window and hawking vigorously into the night. There followed a more orderly conversation about the qualities required in a missionary, chief of which was that a Christian soldier should know how to biff.

'A good clout first and let the word of God follow after. I don't say it is always called for, but often enough. Now these gentlemen of mine could not crack a walnut without wincing.'

Quigley began to like Mr Blossom.

'You were handy once,' he guessed.

'I call to mind an occasion in Malta. Hot there, and it makes the locals bad-tempered. As it happens, a very religious island, you understand, but all of them left-footers. However. One night I had the necessity to square up to an Arab sort of cove trying to sell me pomegranates. Which is no kind of a fruit at all. He was an evil bugger with a blue scar down across his eye, like this. So I said to him, I said –'

'Not to interrupt, old son, but aren't those some of your gentlemen in the saloon? Just walked in?'

Three young men were standing awkwardly at the bar, trying to decide how to order a pint without announcing themselves to the world as the tares among the wheat.

'Them three poor buggers are off to the Zambezi,' Blossom said, with grim satisfaction. 'They sail at midnight on Friday to certain death. Goners, each and every one.'

'Then I must buy them a pint,' Quigley declared exuberantly.

'And the more fool you,' the porter retorted.

But the Captain's move into the parlour bar was a shrewd one, for in this way he found the answer to a question that had exercised his mind for two days and two nights. What was a bunch of religious nellies, sincere though they might be, doing with crested knick-knacks like cigar cases? For the house with the decorated keystone over the porch was where these poor devils lived.

'For me, gentlemen, the Cross was my blazon. Fashioned from twigs, tied with seagrass, held high aloft. Accompanied by psalms, hymns, the whole bang shoot.'

It was the concluding trope of an inspirational account of how he had walked the desert beaches of North Africa in search of another Christian soul, a yarn all the more persuasive for happening to be true. He omitted to say how he came to be in such a quarter of the world and how far he had swum to get there.

Two of his listeners had the abstracted air of men who could already foresee death coming at them like the train from Didcot, but the slightly more garrulous Tobias Ross-Whymper offered what the Captain was seeking.

'Our Hall, you must understand, is no part of the University,' he volunteered, as if giving the Captain his due as a man of the world.

'Well it wouldn't be, would it?' Quigley agreed cheerfully.

Ross-Whymper stared him down. 'I myself am a former Christ Church scholar, however.'

Quigley adjusted sights hastily.

'I could see that at a glance. But to be clear, the old crest over the door. That's your badge of honour, so to speak?'

'You could say so.'

'I mention this because a curious thing happened in London recently. Fellow punts me a cigar case with those same arms emblazoned.'

'He punts you it?' Ross-Whymper asked, bemused.

'Beggar type. Offers the case for sale.'

'A cigar case?'

'The same. My curiosity was sorely piqued,' Quigley added, borrowing a line from *Lady Nugent's Letter*.

'Some of the fellows smoke. But hardly cigars. Do you have the case with you?'

'My dear sir,' the Captain protested gently, 'it was my clear and bounden duty to run the scoundrel and his swag to the nearest constable.'

But Ross-Whymper wasn't listening. He turned to his neighbour.

'I say, Ralph. Who do we know in B.H. who smokes cigars?'

'Only Principal Hagley,' Ralph replied, obliging Quigley greatly. He wished the gentlemen well of their voyage, made his excuses, and left.

It was natural in him to walk a hundred yards up the Banbury Road and study the crest one last time. The book-lined room he had noticed on a previous reconnaissance, the one to the right of the entrance, had also given up its secrets. The man lighting a reading lamp was clearly the guvnor, the Reverend Mr Hagley. If he looked spooky, it was because Quigley wished this character upon him.

'You didn't meet him?' Bella asked.

'No, but easily done. The gentleman's not going nowhere. Lives at the Hall, skates about the town all day in clerical dress. However, your obedient ess, finding himself strapped for cash, forced to retire. Has returned to aitch-coo for further orders.'

'You seriously believe a minister of religion, such as you describe, capable of murder? Of slitting a girl's throat?'

'I'm only telling you what I found out. This cove Blossom –'

'Yes, Blossom. An utterly reliable witness I am quite sure –'

Quigley gave her the old level stare, the one that turneth away wrath.

'This Blossom says the Reverend has mislaid his case and searched for it high and low. Thinks he may have left it on the train.'

'We can say he was in London that night?' Bella asked swiftly.

'Not much of a story if he wasn't. Yes, he was out and about that night. Why not say it? He was in Maiden Lane when Welsh Alice was done.'

'And it was he who killed her?'

'Never in a million years,' Quigley said blithely. 'Unless of course,' he added, 'you want to make it so.'

Bella slapped her palm down on the rosewood table that served as her writing desk. To say that she was exasperated with the Captain was to understate the case. It was no use admitting that part of his usefulness to her was just this habit of cheery insolence. It stung: but it made her think. He was the wasp at her picnic.

'He was there,' Quigley repeated. 'But I don't reckon him for a killer. I made it my business to come alongside and give him the hard glance when he was walking down St Giles, they call it. That's –'

'I know where St Giles is in Oxford.'

'So like I say I give him the once-over. Head to toe. And what do I conclude? Not capable of the dastardly deed. Twittish.'

'Then what?'

'Why,' Quigley crowed, 'just afore I left, I'm having a swiftie with Blossom before setting out for the station, when he ups and says that Mr Hagley has found his cigar case after all. My eye.'

All this while, the Captain was practising at the Indian clubs, the wooden billets occasionally crashing into the wall. He had the idea that he would, within a day or so, exercise a few pounds of fat from his bones. His face was an alarming purple. Bella watched him from behind her writing desk.

'Telling Blossom he had found the case was a lie?'

'You can bet your Christmas goose on it. He was there all right but there was others with him. The plot thickens, Mr Margam, sir.'

One of the clubs came loose from the Captain's grip and sailed out of the open door, carooming off the building opposite. Vexed, he threw the other after it.

'What self-respecting Indian ever jigged about with this nonsense?' he muttered. 'Hadn't the time. Served the mem her cucumber sandwiches. Painted the flagpole. Dug the occasional useful ditch.'

'This weight thing is bothering you, I take it?'

'I was called a fat bastard in the Bag o' Nails last evening. Remonstrations. Quarrel taken outside at the request of the landlord. Opponent: Stoker Miller of Gosport. Honours even but it led to a period of quiet reflection.'

'Are you forever going to be quoting from me, Captain Quigley?'

'I am one with an infinite capacity for easeful contemplation,' he countered adroitly, lifting a line she wished she had not written in the otherwise heated pages of *Deveril's Disgrace*. 'I should add, by the way, Stoker Miller very anxious to tender his services to the firm.'

'I thought he was in the Navy?'

'If they ever catch up with him again, yes, that would be so.'

'I think we have enough military genius to cope with, without Stoker Miller.'

'You are in the right of it, as always,' the Captain agreed comfortably.

Charles Urmiston turned up at Fleur de Lys Court two days later. Though he had made a great effort with the clothes brush and a pail of soapy water from the landlady in which to wash his shirt, he still looked decidedly frowsty. He had walked to the Strand in a light shower of rain. Poverty came off him like the smell of a dog's wet fur. When he asked after Mrs Wallis, he was told she had yet to come in. He looked around him with some anxiety.

'I do have the right address, I hope.'

'This is the place all right. And, knowing that you were coming, I have stirred my stumps, Mr Urmiston. I believe this here picture is yours.'

Urmiston stared in amazement as the harem scene was unveiled.

'How on earth –?'

'Quigley has means,' the Captain asserted grandly. 'Has contacts with the fraternity, you might say. The lady was warehoused in a hooky kind of gaff behind Paddington Lock. I took the liberty of making some enquiries. Among art-lovers, the picture valued at twenty sovs.'

These art-lovers were in fact the people who had stolen the painting in the first place. It was one of the Captain's better wheezes. He and Murch had removed the work from Bella's staircase, driven it round to Paddington, offered it for resale (a tenner, topsides) but lingered long enough to identify a portrait by G. F. Watts, lifted only a fortnight earlier from a house in Belgravia. That changed matters to a cove with his wits about him. That is to say, someone like the Captain. Negotiations took a sudden new turn.

'How about this, then?' Quigley suggested jovially. 'A straight swap. The fat china showing all she's got for the lady in the red hat.'

'Pull the other one, Captain,' Frenchie Thomas said. 'This here likeness is a work of genius by one of our greatest living portraitists.'

'And what a crying shame if the law sniffed out where it was and asked how it come to be lodged in your garden shed.'

Thomas narrowed his eyes.

'Dangerous talk.'

'We are men of the world, Frenchie. We both play the long game.'

'How much?' the fence demanded. And then, a moment later, incredulous, '*How* much?'

'Think of it as the price of silence. And of course, an expression of unbroken goodwill between friends.'

Urmiston stared at the painting leaning against the back wall of Bella's office with something like a child's amazement. Quigley smiled.

'Your picture was stolen, do you see? I have extracted twenty sovereigns from the thieves, money that I have in this here handkerchief.'

'Captain Quigley,' Urmiston said, embracing him, 'you are a man of business, sir. I put myself under your command.'

'A rough-and-ready soldier is all,' the Captain smirked.

'Then count me as a very willing recruit. May I offer you a finder's fee from my unexpected windfall?'

'Do you drink at all?' his new friend asked hopefully.

'A glass of something with you by all means! And perhaps a pie. The excitement has whetted my appetite.'

'The Coal Hole the very place, sir. Or maybe, nearer still, the Cyder Cellars.'

'Whatever will please you best.'

Which was how Bella came to find them later in the day, at their ease in her office, feet on the desk, smoking shilling cigars. Captain Quigley waved her into their presence.

'Mr Urmiston has already earned his corn, dear lady. Tell her, Charlie.'

'Anthony Hagley is the living incarnation of the devil who helped lose me my place with the Great Western. The biggest humbug in Christendom, I would style him. Such a cad as is seldom produced in England, even among the aristocracy.'

'And is he such a one?'

'Such a one what?'

'You are drunk, Mr Urmiston,' Bella said wonderingly.

'I probably am. Now there's a less than honest answer – I *am* drunk. But if it's Hagley you're after – that wicked man hiding beneath clerical dress, that Ananias –'

Quigley patted him comfortingly on the sleeve. He rose from his seat – not without difficulty – and walked to the door, where he let fly a huge and stentorian 'Oi!' After a moment or two a boy of ten or so appeared, wiping his nose on his sleeve and in the same flourish saluting the Captain.

'Nip to Tonio's and ask him for a can of fresh coffee. Fresh, you understand. And a couple of biscuits for yourself. Chop chop, double quick.'

EIGHT

Urmiston's story began with a curiously drab view of Berkshire, like a snatched glimpse of nothing in particular seen through a railway-carriage window. The image was not of that dereliction and emptiness that seems to crowd the trackside of mainline routes, as if the homeless have come to watch the rich ride by: all that could be seen were densely packed trees, their trunks glistening. Trees and fallen boughs, emerald moss and a darker carpet of brambles. All set in the sort of unromantic gloom that carries with it a faint air of menace.

In 1869, a little to the west of Wallingford Road Station on the Great Western line from London to Bristol, the company sought a minor alteration to the permanent way. In a fold of woodland, engineers making a routine inspection discovered early indicators of ground subsidence, caused by a particularly wet summer and boisterous autumn.

Their report began to creep its way through the GWR management, accumulating additional papers and memoranda as it went. At a directors' meeting in Swindon, it was agreed that the problem was serious enough to recommend the building of stone revetments along forty yards of track and – most importantly – the provision of a three-hundred-foot run-off channel, to be built in brick, ending in a twenty-foot sump. They sent Urmiston to negotiate terms for the work.

'This is not uncommon?' Bella interrupted. 'I mean from time to time there will be unavoidable repair works to the permanent way?'

'The company has a statutory duty to inspect for just those contingencies when they arise, yes.'

'Then where was the problem?'

Urmiston sipped at his coffee. Bella and Quigley waited while he gathered his thoughts. Though his hands shook, the shabby clothes he was wearing seemed to have fallen from him and in their place he was dressed as the man he had once been. He was back in the moment, speaking the language he had once used. But it gave him no joy.

'Sometimes the repairs are limited to the ground on which the rails actually run – that's to say, the property of the operating company, in this case Great Western. But to build our run-off, we had to seek permission from the man who owned the woods.'

'Makes good sense,' encouraged the impatient Quigley, nodding vigorously all the while. He knew – or thought he knew – how the story came out. Urmiston studied him for a long moment.

'Just so. In this case, the landowner refused point-blank to let us set foot on his property. Not one foot.'

The Captain tugged on his moustaches.

'An awkward cove,' he prompted.

'For the sake of clarity,' Bella intervened, 'I wonder if Mr Urmiston can be allowed to tell this story in his own way, without your contributions.'

'I will come to the point,' Urmiston said. 'Because of this prohibition – which was of course highly unusual – the regional engineering superintendent and I were obliged to walk out along the permanent way to the point where the work was to be done.'

'And how far was that?'

'Just under three miles. In heavy rain and a blustery gale. The site was in a valley, almost a tunnel of trees –'

He spread his hands helplessly.

'You were able to see at once what was at fault,' Bella suggested.

'Oh, there was time and enough for that. We were kept waiting nearly an hour for the arrival of the landowner's representative.'

'Now we're getting to it,' the incorrigible Quigley chortled. 'Now we're nearly there. Tell her what happened next.'

'Normally, such a person would be a lawyer, perhaps a local solicitor –'

'No, but tell her!' Quigley insisted happily.

'In time, a party came down through the woods, led by a man in clerical dress. Who introduced himself to us as the Reverend Anthony James Hagley, vicar of Brailston.'

Bella stared.

'Hagley was the agent for this business?'

'He had a letter with him granting him full powers of negotiation.'

'A *vicar*?'

'Exactly. From that first moment, there was not the slightest chance of a reconciliation between the two parties. The Regional Superintendent and I were forced to walk a little way off and confer. The situation was unprecedented.'

Bella was picturing the scene – the sluicing rain, the discomforted GWR party, the gale rattling the trees all around. And Hagley, the vicar of Brailston, under his umbrella. A thought occurred to her.

'You say there were others in Hagley's party?'

'There were two gamekeepers with shotguns. I don't know them to have been gamekeepers for a fact – but anyway, men with sacks over their shoulders to keep off the rain and with guns under their arms.'

'Breeches broken, though,' Quigley prompted. 'Safety observed, I don't doubt.'

'No, it was not. The first thing this Hagley said was that if we attempted to step one inch off the company's property, he would order his men to prevent us. Tufton – the engineering superintendent – was a country man. He saw the guns were loaded.'

'This is an incredible story, Mr Urmiston.'

'I can't tell you how offensive Hagley was, how arrogant and aggressive.'

'Now why was that?'

'Why? He was spokesman for an equally vicious and arrogant master.'

'And this man? Who was he?' Bella asked gently.

'The woods and all about belonged to a Lord Bolsover,' Urmiston replied in all innocence.

It was as if he had thrown a grenade. Even Quigley was startled by Bella's reaction. She jumped up and rummaged in the drawers of a battered military chest, a piece of furniture the Captain liked to assure his more gullible cronies was his own. At last she found what she was looking for.

'Is this his crest?'

Urmiston took the cigar case from her and examined its interior.

'Yes,' he said wonderingly. 'But how did you come by it?'

'You are quite sure the crest is part of Lord Bolsover's arms?'

'I am certain.'

Bella glanced at Quigley, who had the decency to look as consternated as she felt. Out in the Strand, the evening traffic grumbled.

'What have I said?' Urmiston asked, confused.

'I want you to go for a walk for a few minutes, Mr Urmiston, the better to gather your thoughts. Perhaps you might walk as far as Temple Bar and back.'

'I am in full charge of myself, Mrs Wallis.'

'I am sure you are. But I am not. I shall be grateful for time to think. Captain Quigley will send out for a bite of supper. Let us meet again in ten minutes.'

They resumed over a plate of mutton and a can of beer each. There was still some light in the sky but hardly any of it percolated to Fleur de Lys Court. They ate by candle-light. The only people to enter the court were men, passers-by who came to relieve themselves against walls scabbed with theatre posters and advertisements for patent medicines.

'What else happened at that meeting?' Bella asked at last.

'I tried to talk Hagley into walking back to Wallingford with us, where we could discuss things in a more businesslike manner. I even offered him dinner that night at the Woolpack. He just laughed in my face.'

'You explained your difficulty in dealing with him as Bolsover's agent?'

'In the most offhand manner, he said that the company should not bother to send another clerk after him. He had served his notice on us and that was the end of the matter. Then he and his bullies turned their backs on us and walked off.'

'And then what?'

Urmiston's smile was bleak as midnight.

'You must remember that I was at the time something more distinguished than how you find me tonight. I was a senior man from the London office, acting on behalf of a very great public enterprise. In the normal course of things I travelled first class, was put up at the best hotels. I went back to town later that afternoon and wrote a short report, the intention of which was to pass the matter up to the most senior levels.'

He thought for a moment and Bella was astonished to see tears in his eyes.

'I had gone straight from Paddington to my house and I wrote this note at my own desk in Campden Hill. What was needed was advice from counsel, obviously. That was my recommendation. I have wished a thousand times the story ended there.'

'But something else happened?'

'Yes,' Urmiston said heavily. 'Marguerite – my wife – said that I should fight them. That I should not be so –' he glanced round – 'I am not ashamed to use her words for it – that I should not be so passive.'

'You do not have to tell us this,' Bella said in her gentlest voice.

'No, but I do. She was ill, to be sure, but her infirmity forced the truth from her. That night, I reviewed the whole calamity – Hagley's contempt, the engineering superintendent's barely disguised disgust, my own sense of bewilderment – and resolved to fight them.'

'You mean to fight Bolsover. He was surely the principal.'

'I never met Lord Bolsover. The management sent me to see him both in London and at his house in Berkshire but he would not admit me. The fight was between me and Hagley. The thing became something of an office joke; here's old Urmiston run off the rails by a country vicar. You should go down to Berkshire and kick his arse from here to Christmas Eve, Charles. Or send your wife, perhaps.'

'And so, in the end?'

'Yes,' Urmiston said, grim. 'In the end, they broke me. They knew they would have to concede eventually but it gave them pleasure meanwhile to stretch me on the rack. After a year of quite indescribable agitation and confusion, I was summoned to a meeting of the directors and dismissed. Very foolishly, I attempted to sue the company. Within another year, I was as good as destitute.'

'But these alterations were essential to public safety, surely? Weren't they covered by Acts of Parliament?'

'Oh, his lordship had no choice in the matter, as he knew from the start.'

'Then what was his game?' Quigley asked, indignant.

'His game?'

'You never met him, he never met you. What stroke was he trying to pull, for all love?'

Urmiston made a face. 'Maybe he found it amusing.'

This was not at all an answer to Captain Quigley's taste. He cleared the greasy plates by banging them together and throwing knives and forks into the tin dish covers. The tray on which the meal had been delivered went out of the door like a sled.

'I do not like these buggers,' he said. 'This Bolsover bird I know nothing about, but you know that the Reverend Hagley is poncing round Oxford this very night in all his clerical glory as Principal of some tuppenny-ha'penny mission to the heathen?'

'You told me this earlier.'

'Well, I don't like it. By God I don't.'

Bella stood and held out both hands to Urmiston.

'I understand you have some money from Captain Quigley for the recovery of your painting. In place of walking back to Lambeth tonight, let him find you a room nearby. Merton's Hotel is small but clean. It will do until something else is found. I will bother you with one last question before the Captain takes you there.'

'I am at your service,' Urmiston muttered.

'Why do you think Bolsover appointed Hagley to look after his interests? No, I will sharpen the question. Did you form any idea of the kind of relationship there was between these two men?'

'They were intimates,' he replied, blushing. 'The Captain asked me what their game was. That was it: to take a mild-mannered man such as me and humiliate him. I was not as they were.'

That night, Bella lay in bed with Marie Claude, stroking her lover's hair and, after a while, patting her back gently, as one would pacify a fractious child. The Frenchwoman had been out earlier in the evening, to the Aquarium, and endured her usual chapter of insults. A waiter had been rude in his address; at a neighbouring table someone had said something unkind about her hat. Certain young men had looked at her in a leering sort of way and one – a bold blond in a mint-green suit – had the temerity to speak to her in French. It was useless to protest that none of these things mattered; Marie Claude was as sensitive as a snail.

'I should have been with you,' Bella said. 'Your friend Miss Titcombe was no defence at all, I see.'

'She is an idiot,' Marie Claude confirmed gloomily. 'Tonight she was dressed in clothes I would not wear for a ballooning trip.'

In spite of herself, Bella laughed out loud. The manly side of Miss Titcombe led her into many a mistake. One of these was a penchant for tweed, which when draped across her ample bosom gave her a decidedly aldermanic look. On her only visit to the house in Orange Street she had astonished Bella by smoking a pipe; not a comely sort of a pipe at all but one with a long stem and tiny bowl, like a caricature or child's drawing of the object.

Bella kissed her companion on the neck.

'Shall we go ballooning one day, you and I? Over the Alps, perhaps, or along some Norwegian fiord?'

Marie Claude raised her head from Bella's breast.

'Yes, now you make fun of me. I am so very unhappy.'

'I would not have you any other way.'

'You should write my story.'

'Easily done! A beautiful but sad girl lives in a cottage under the walls of a castle. People come from all around to hear her cry, which is a sound like the north wind sighing. Her tears are collected in little glass phials, made in Venice. Many men fall in love with her and wish to dance and flirt with her under the castle's chandeliers. But every evening, as the sun sets, she walks into the wood and becomes a silver birch. Only the moon knows where she is.'

Marie Claude considered.

'It is a story for children,' she said.

'Can there be anything more truthful than that?'

'So then, these other things you write, stories about only stupid people, why do you waste your time on them?'

'They are important to me.' Bella pushed her away. 'Go to your own room now. The next time you visit the Aquarium, I shall come with you.'

'And Lydia Titcombe?'

'Can stay at home and cobble her boots, or wax her moustache.'

Marie Claude smiled, a rare event. After she left, Bella lay on her back, gazing at the ceiling. She was picturing four or five men standing in a dank wood, their capes heavy with rain, while the express to Paddington thundered past on the up-line. That one of them was Urmiston was almost, but not quite, beside the point. What attracted her to the image was its sombre monochrome, relieved only by the glint of light on the rails and – she added a further touch – the rags of steam left hanging in the branches of the trees.

On the ground, her naked neck and breast as white as paper, her disordered hair mingling with the mud, lay Welsh Alice. Her eyes were open and her body unmarked. It bore a disturbing resemblance to Marie Claude's. Bella felt a shudder run through her, enough to make her sit up abruptly, her fingers plucking the hem of the sheet. The true beginning to her next novel had presented itself, implacable and as stern as headstones in a graveyard.

As to where these horrors might lead, she had no idea. That was the particular reason she rented the place in Fleur de Lys Court. Otherwise, the images she had just conjured would dissipate like the spring snow. She sat up abruptly and lit a cigarette, something she had promised Marie Claude never to do in the upstairs rooms. With a little twinge of guilt she opened a window. It helped. Cool air slipped into the room and dried her moist hair.

What else was a well-appointed house for, if not to keep such nightmares at bay? Why else choose this curtain fabric over that, or place such-and-such an ornament there and nowhere else? The house in Orange Street was her home, to be sure, but it was also an elaborated spell. Quite recently Bella had bought a massive sponge for the bathroom, quite as big as a small cat. It was a toy for Marie Claude to play with but also in some obscure way a means of fending off disaster. It went along with Bella's collection of glass paperweights, the eighteenth-century rummers, the naval chest that stood in the hall and all the rest of it.

There was a simpler reason still for the office in Fleur de Lys Court. It was where Henry Ellis Margam lived and worked. Even its crabby accommodations were too grand for the monster she had created. He was being punished for his ugliness. Ideally, Bella would like Margam to live in a hollow log out in the woods and drink from puddles. He would run on all fours like a dog.

She rose early enough to walk to Merton's and find Charles Urmiston at breakfast. He looked up guiltily from a steak with a poached egg balanced on it.

'Money has made me reckless,' he said.

He smelled of soap and his face was close shaved. His dreadful old suit had been taken away during the night and sponged and pressed. Merton, who had a keen eye, had sent his daughter round to Jaworski's in Henrietta Street, and that amiable bear of a man had opened early to furnish some fresh linen and a yellow cravat. Urmiston was still the unfinished sketch but a night's sleep and twenty sovereigns in his pocket had made a dramatic change in him.

'You are on your way somewhere, perhaps?' he asked, proffering Bella a bit of toast and the marmalade dish.

'To Fleur de Lys Court.'

'I must ask you: what exactly is it that goes on there?'

'Mischief,' she teased. But Urmiston brushed the remark away.

'You have some complaint of your own against Mr Hagley, perhaps?'

There was no one else in the breakfast room, the windows of which were wide open to the street. Londoners passed by, most of them with the peculiar air of abstraction that people have in the early morning, as if listening to interior voices, or ghostly music. Bella hesitated and then told him what she knew of Hagley and Bolsover and the suspicion she had that they were both implicated in some way in the murder of a drab called Welsh Alice. Urmiston looked out of the window, nodding, watching the world go by, asking no questions.

'I will never be your bravest ally, Mrs Wallis, but if you are about seeing these two villains done down, I would like to be of your party.'

There was more agreeable business to conduct first. Driven by Quigley's friend, the laconic Murch, Charles Urmiston took his newly recovered painting to an address in Shepherd's Bush. Penny, Murch's elderly mare, drew their cart along through early-morning sunshine that had, from the amount of dust hanging in the air, the texture of gauze. Murch pointed out one or two landmarks with his ribboned whip, a thing never to be used on Penny and carried only as a badge of office and as punctuation in disputes with other road-users.

'You are not a London man then, sir?'

'As it happens, I am, Mr Murch.'

'Well, down this here road, afore we go much farther, we shall see sheep and thatch. Is all my meaning.'

'This is hardly beyond Bayswater, Mr Murch. The natives are rich and friendly. As you see, many of them wear trousers in the Christian way and their womenfolk are as chaste as rounds of cheese.'

'I ain't lost,' Murch replied, niggled.

Their destination was a picture dealer called Cussins, someone known to Urmiston slightly, a calm and comforting presence wearing a frogged velvet jacket and smoking a carved meerschaum. He had the pleasant habit of bouncing lightly on the balls of his feet when talking.

'This is a Venneke,' he said of the painting. 'And quite a good one. But of course you know that, Mr Urmiston, for it was I that sold it to you some years past – yes, that's it, the pretty little house on Campden Hill, I remember it well – and now here it is again. Venneke of course has fled – you didn't know that? – fled the country, yes, and is living in Rome, the reprobate, on the Spanish Steps if you please. With a *very* young creature not at all in the likeness of our Turkish lady here. The model for her was a splendid woman, not at all some guttersnipe child, no, but a landlady to a public house in Ladbroke Grove – what was her name now? – ah, yes, Mrs Hill.'

'I had no idea,' Urmiston said faintly.

'Well, I would not have told you such homely details when you were the prospective purchaser, oh dear no. But now, of course, you wish to sell. I suggest a hundred and twenty guineas.'

The deal was struck over a glass of Marsala and little cakes. Cussins looked thoughtfully at his former client.

'I should mention, by the by, how saddened I was to hear of your dismissal at the hands of the Great Western. A shabby affair and you have my sympathies. May Lord Bolsover repent of his sins at leisure.'

But for all his earlier protestations to Bella, Urmiston barely registered the name. He was moonstruck. In the space of twenty-four hours he was richer by a hundred and forty sovereigns, a wonderful sum, a gift as it might be from heaven itself. He forced himself to meet Cussins' curious gaze.

'Lord Bolsover will get his comeuppance, you may be sure of it,' he said with what he hoped was not too foolish a grin. 'I am with new people nowadays.'

They looked up at the sound of an altercation just outside the window. At the back of Murch's cart was a rolled tarpaulin and some unwary chancer had taken it into his head to steal it. While Penny munched placidly on her mid-morning oats, Murch had seized this thief in a head-lock and run him full tilt into Mr Cussins' gatepost. The man staggered to his feet and groped about like the victim in a game of blind man's bluff. He found a pillar box in his path and embraced it feebly before sinking to the pavement.

'My best wishes to you, Mr Urmiston,' Cussins said reverently.

'And mine to you, sir.'

NINE

Lord Broxtowe was giving Bella lunch at Lord's, comprising chicken and game pie served from a wicker hamper and an excellent Niersteiner. A match was taking place but his lordship could not say who the visitors were, nor did he attend overmuch to the score. He was there in his capacity as a committee member of the Marylebone Cricket Club, a faintly dizzying honour he had held off and on his entire adult life.

'In 1844,' he said, pointing with a wavery gesture, 'we had some Red Indians out in the middle, dancing and stamping, and giving displays of archery. A rum business. Good shots, but surly buggers, I thought them. Feathers and so forth. You may believe this or not, but some of their trousers had no backside to them.'

He smiled. 'Could you not work that story into one of your tales?'

'Where had they come from?'

'You mean who brought them here? I have no idea. Perhaps they came in canoes, of their own accord.'

There were other ladies present, some of them suspiciously young, though none so radiant as Bella. The picnic they were having began to attract glances.

'These other gentlemen nearby, they are also committee members?' she asked in a quiet aside.

'Some of them are from the Middlesex Club, who would like to make this their permanent ground. A piece of damned impertinence if you ask me.'

'What I wished to ask you, Broxtowe, was whether you knew a family called Bolsover.'

'Knew the Second Earl – he played here in the Eton–Harrow match I can't remember how many years ago. Before the Red Indians, probably. He married my cousin Lydgate, who had but one leg. The other she left in a public garden in Mentone, which gives you a good idea of the morals of that unhappy branch of the family.'

'But losing her leg was surely an accident? Some beast attacked her, I imagine. A savage dog, perhaps.'

'A dancing bear. What a disgusting thing for a young girl to wish to witness in the first place.'

He proffered her his serviette with which to wipe her chin.

'You want to know about the Third Earl, of course. An out-and-out snake, my dear. There is a small house of some kind in the Thames Valley. I dined there in his father's time. A gentleman would not keep his dogs in the south wing, which is where I was put to bed. Elizabethan, they claimed.'

He hesitated.

'You are a sanguine enough creature, Bella, and so I will tell you. The boy – Freddie, his doting mother called him – played wife to a hulking great servant they had, a footman of some sort. You understand me sufficiently, I think.'

There was a shout and a ball clattered on the steps to the newly erected pavilion. Lord Broxtowe was the only man present not to applaud, merely adjusting his top hat to a more comfortable tilt.

'The man's altogether a subject worthy of your pen, I'd say. Reckless, notoriously so. Vulgar. The very devil when it comes to an argument. Lacking altogether in gentlemanly conduct. Some say he is deranged.'

'Have you heard his name in connection with a man called Anthony Hagley?'

'The parson fellow? Didn't he set him up in Oxford a year or so back? Some nonsense about missionarizing the heathen. My neighbour Fullerton sent his son there. The boy wanted to Christianize China. Was given Tahiti, I think it was.'

'What happened?'

'I imagine they ate him. Are there cannibals on Tahiti?' Bella had no idea.

'Quite the most stupid boy in Yorkshire, anyway. Resigned his commission, went to Tahiti – if it was Tahiti – never been heard of since. And I must say,' Broxtowe added, warming to his theme, 'the world is littered with the graves of these poor devils. As soon as the quinine and the tinned sausages run out, pfft. Harry Fullerton commissioned a fellow to go out there and photograph his son's grave. A very foolish act of piety.'

'Did the man come home with anything?'

'He has never been heard of since. Also eaten, I dare say. But we were talking about Bolsover. A goddamn monster, Bella. Fifty anvils would not weigh that fellow down. Want me to ask around about him?'

'If you would.'

'Care to say why?'

'Monsters make good reading,' she said evasively.

He patted her hand.

'If we had only met when I was younger,' he declared gallantly, and loud enough to disconcert a gaitered bishop sitting nearby. 'That bodice. How many little buttons does it have, now?'

The bishop inclined his head eagerly.

'Forty, my lord,' Bella said smiling. 'But not all of them are functional. Otherwise, where would we be in the mornings?'

Lord Broxtowe's shouted laugh floated out across the ground just at the moment the receiving batsman was playing forward to a fast delivery. He edged the ball to slip and then stood disbelievingly as it was gathered in.

'Mr Copley has been dismissed, my lord,' the servant provided by Broxtowe's hotel explained. 'On a score of ninety-eight at that.'

'Two buttons short,' Broxtowe murmured, causing the bishop to convulse in silent laughter.

Meanwhile, Quigley was playing the part of adjutant, a role he greatly enjoyed. He was taking a pot of tea with Mrs Bardsoe in Shelton Street, a little below Seven Dials. That is to say, she had offered and he had graciously accepted. His feet were planted square on what had once been a very good Indian carpet, his arm laid along the lace tablecloth. The Laughing Cavalier, no less. Moustaches tweaked from time to time, eyes (he hoped) twinkling.

''E's not an actor, is he?' Hannah Bardsoe asked suddenly.

'He is a gentleman, ma. I already told you.'

'Well, if he's a gentleman, what's he doing wanting to come round here?'

The house was tall and narrow, the ground floor given over to a little shop selling herbal remedies and the more explosive kinds of proprietary medicines. There was a steady trade in Hensher's Bile Pills and Dr Eagleton's Linctus for the Throat and Chest; but the front window also advertised open jars of quinine bark, liquorice sticks, the dried flowers of feverfew, cinnamon, cloves and – some people swore by it – nettle tea.

'He is a gentleman who has recently buried his wife. Poor woman planted on foreign soil, leading to a grief too deep for words.'

'Are you still messing with that Mrs Wallis?' Mrs Bardsoe wanted to know suspiciously.

'Don't change the subject. Urmiston's the name. Doesn't hardly smoke, drinks no more'n a hummingbird, the very figure of a saint.'

'And a bit on the shy side I'd say,' she added. 'And for why? Because he ain't here is for why!'

'I left a note for Billy Murch to fetch him round.'

'Billy Murch!' Mrs Bardsoe exclaimed fondly. 'Is he still with us?'

'He's not fifty yet,' Quigley retorted.

'He and my Harry had some times together, so they did. Well, if he's Billy's mate, that puts a different complexion on the thing. That's putting a bow on the dog all right. I thought you was trying to palm off some friend of your'n, Captain. Which is to say, trouble in trousers.'

Urmiston arrived shortly after and was shown three rooms on the top floor. The presence of Mrs Bardsoe gave a useful scale: she was almost as broad as a door.

'A sunny aspect,' Urmiston observed politely, indicating a bar of sunshine not much wider than a tea tray.

'There's a good half an hour of that,' she observed. 'But I make no claims, sir – it *is* a gloomy sort of house. Bardsoe was from Sussex, originally. He found it terrible going here in winter-time. Though we took our Christmas regular with his people and the wind from the sea down there would take your leg off.'

'Your late husband was a herbalist by profession, I think?'

'Profession is ripe, very ripe. No, he was a bit on the slow side, to speak frankly. The little business you see downstairs was my idea.'

'And are you at heart a countrywoman, Mrs Bardsoe?'

'However did you guess?' she asked, pleased. 'From Uxbridge.'

She left him alone to explore the accommodation and he felt a sharp pang of yearning to hear a woman's tread on the stairs, even one so formidably clunky as Mrs Bardsoe's. As for the house and its location, Urmiston could not say that this was as low as he had ever fallen, for measured by the single room he rented in Lambeth, he was on the way up. Though the floorboards sank as he moved over them and the walls were none too straight, the place was scrupulously clean and smelled faintly of apples.

When he went back downstairs, Murch and the Captain had gone. Urmiston had the strong impression that something had been cooked up during his absence. Mrs Bardsoe passed him what he took to be a cordial but which turned out to be best Martinique rum.

'Now you listen here, sir,' she said. 'You won't find a shrewder judge of character than me, you can go to Timbuktu to search for one. And I say this: you will do. I am a respectable widow woman and while there are some in this street that are no better than they ought to be, you will find me straight.'

'An impression I have already formed, Mrs Bardsoe.'

'As may be,' she said. 'As to terms, I would take it well if you was to have some breakfast with me of a morning, but I do not intend to cook for you, nor do your wash. You can come and go as you please and for the rest, kiss my arse – I beg pardon – if I won't look after you a treat.'

'What would you like to know about me, Mrs Bardsoe?'

'Bless you, sir, I already said, I read you like an open book. Your are friends with Mrs Wallis?'

'I knew her late husband well.'

'Then we shall have no trouble, Mr Urmiston.'

'I shall need to buy a few sticks of furniture.'

She laughed, a wonderful round bell-like sound.

'The Captain is your man for that. Good Lord, yes. None better, the thieving old rogue.'

'He has been very kind to me, Mrs B.'

'They do say Dick Turpin was kind,' Mrs Bardsoe pointed out, though blushing for pleasure at the way her name had been shortened to almost an endearment. To Urmiston's amazement, when he extended his hand she brushed it aside and kissed him lightly on the cheek.

'You'll do for me,' she said briskly. 'We ain't going to stand on no ceremony here, I do hope.'

Urmiston was saved by the single clack of the shop bell. A young woman in a shawl stood there, and when he walked out with Mrs Bardsoe from her parlour, waited for him to leave before she consulted with the widowed herbalist on a topic unfit for a man's ears.

'She seems to know you,' Urmiston said of his new landlady, an hour or so later. Bella was smoking a cheroot, with her feet up on a second chair.

'Tell me,' she asked. 'Do you think the Middlesex Club should play at Lord's on a permanent basis?'

'Of course.'

'Do you have reasons to say so?'

Urmiston considered.

'Progress,' he said. 'Or inevitability, if you like.'

'I like the word progress better,' Bella decided. 'As to Mrs Bardsoe, yes, I know her a little through Quigley. I seem to know half London by that conduit. But here's a thing, Charles. The other London, the one that you and I were born to, knows nothing of it. I could sit outside Mrs Bardsoe's little shop, smoking a pipe and spitting into the gutter, and not one friend from that other place would be any the wiser.'

'Yet it seems a world filled with kindness.'

'Oh, what nonsense. Everyone you have met since we came across each other in Boulogne is standing at the edge of a black swamp of cruelty and despair. About which we can never speak.'

'Not even Quigley?'

'Not even he.'

'And me, Bella? Where does that leave me?'

'You must find your own place. But a little moral instruction from a friend never goes amiss and I should welcome that. Without ever having met the Reverend Mr Hagley and exchanging few words with Lord Bolsover, I find I hate them with a passion. You must stop me from poisoning myself.'

Though she spoke lightly, her eyes were dark. Impulsively, he took her hand and so they sat until the return of Captain Quigley. He was carrying a plush chair on his head. Murch followed with a rolled carpet.

'Before we takes this round to Shelton Street,' the Captain asked, 'will you be needing a desk of any kind?'

'A desk? I don't believe I shall be writing anything.'

'You'll leave that to the experts, will you?'

It was the ghastly knowing wink that did it. Urmiston turned to Bella enquiringly.

'There is something I have to tell you about myself,' she said with a sigh.

But it made no difference to Urmiston. He had never heard of Henry Ellis Margam and though he made all the polite expressions of wonder and congratulation, such as authors pretend to disdain but love to hear, she saw that the day had been altogether too joyful for him to care. When she had finished explaining her purely literary interest in Lord Frederick Augustus Bolsover and the Reverend Mr Hagley, she waited for a response. He fiddled with a pencil he picked up from the rosewood table, his lower lip thrust out in thought.

'Mrs Bardsoe seems a very pleasant woman,' he said dreamily.

Bella laughed.

'Urmiston, I have just confided to you my most precious secret.'

'That you write books? Excellent. Should I read one, do you think? Well, I should: it would be a kindness.'

'What do you read normally?'

'Ah,' he said, awkward. 'I have a fitful interest in travel books. There's a fellow called Oliphant who's done some daring things – he rode into Sevastapol disguised as a merchant just before we went to war in the Crimea and –' his voice trailed off to be replaced by a shy smile. 'As you can see, your secret's very safe with me.'

'What did you want to ask me about Mrs Bardsoe?' Bella murmured.

'Oh,' he said, flustered. 'There is one thing, perhaps. I was going to ask you whether I was not compromising her good name by being her sole lodger. You know, a strange man about the house.'

'What exquisite manners you have,' Bella complimented him, keeping her face straight by a superhuman effort. 'I would say she is very pleased to have the company.'

'Yes,' Urmiston said gratefully. 'Yes, of course. That is the way to look at it.'

Bella's hooted laughter followed him out into the Strand. Ears burning, he turned up into Southampton Street and, passing along the edge of the Market, bought his landlady a sheaf of roses. When he got them home, the look of astonishment on Mrs Bardsoe's face sent him scampering upstairs as red as a beetroot. And there he stayed, his hands between his knees, staring at the pattern on his new carpet.

TEN

Captain Quigley went back to Oxford. For three days he dogged the Reverend Hagley through the streets, meeting many interesting and entirely irrelevant people along the way. In his own mind he moved about as unnoticed as the shadow of leaves upon the pavement; or perhaps something in the Chinese way of things, silent, pattering, inscrutable and remorseless.

Luckily for these fantasies, Hagley was an easy man to follow. In the early mornings he went for a constitutional in Christ Church Meadows. Clergymen were as plentiful there as rooks in a cornfield, but none of them with Hagley's haughty swoop. On the way home he undertook what Quigley thought of as a town patrol, raising his mortarboard to as many dons and scholars as he met. Some he acknowledged in a curt way, some with greater elaboration. Very few were seized with a desire to engage him in conversation. Nothing abashed, he made his way home for lunch and in the afternoon walked one or other of his young gentlemen up the Banbury Road and down again. Their conversation was entirely theological.

In the evenings, Hagley dined as a guest in this or that college, allowing the Captain ample drinking time in the King's Arms, the pub he made his headquarters.

A conversation with a porter from New College established how long the gentlemen's snouts would be in the trough. It seemed to depend on how generous Fellows were with their wine. Wadham scored highly.

'I have seen McIlvanie of Worcester brought away by wheelbarrow from there,' the porter said. 'Hertford is a more abstemious place these last few years. Dr Pike the exception to the rule. That is Pike there in the back bar.'

Quigley saw a man apparently with two beards, one overlaying the other, fashioning the idea of a cider press or perhaps a bilge pump with his hands. These gestures accompanied a harsh and grating monologue, from which occasional key words flew like rocketing pheasants. A semi-comatose cleric listened, a wineglass balanced on his stomach. Quigley edged within hearing. The subject of Dr Pike's address was not mechanical engineering but certain field stones in Littondale and their misinterpretation by the thrice-cursed Summerscale, Prebendary Dean of Ripon Cathedral.

'What are field stones?' Quigley asked the New College porter.

'They are stones, matey. That is the in and the out of it.'

On the last evening of his surveillance, Quigley drank off his pint and sauntered out past the Radcliffe and across the High to wait for Hagley in Oriel Square. The dusk had that appealing mauve colour: he watched appreciatively as a young man walked towards him down Merton Street in white flannels and a rowing blazer, transformed from an oaf to a wavering will-o'-the-wisp.

Quigley himself had little poetry in him, but the light and the location provided the magic. His cigar was drawing well and for a moment or two he seriously contemplated joining the University in some capacity or other. One of his chance acquaintances of the last two nights' drinking had been a servant of the Bodleian Library, a job he described as light work in a largely unsupervised environment. It was true that this particular man had been given the old heave-ho for accidentally locking Stebbings of Keble in the Divinity Schools the previous Christmas Day but the point held. There was an actor asleep inside Quigley and here was a city full of them, with a stage large enough for all their ill-assorted vanities.

The boy in the rowing blazer came abreast of the Captain, who was startled to see blood spattered on his sleeve and shirt.

'There's a fellow down there that needs your help,' he said in a stiff voice. Quigley peered.

In the gloom, a gentleman in black was sitting on the cobbles outside Merton, his head on his chest. Dignity prevented him from howling – that and a broken nose. As Quigley drew closer, he saw that it was none other than the Reverend Anthony Hagley himself. Frisked up by a final glass of the Oriel port, he had come out into the alluring dusk and said the wrong thing to the wrong man.

'I have stumbled and fallen,' Hagley said.

'Generously put, sir, but the scoundrel that struck you passed me not two minutes ago.'

Hagley considered for a moment and then nodded, spraying the cobbles with gobs of bloody snot.

'An unprovoked attack. I was asking directions.'

'Why, Mr Hagley sir, you know this city like the back of your hand,' Quigley chided. 'Ah! I see you have broke your nose. If you'll permit an old soldier?'

He grasped the flesh of Hagley's nose between his thumb and forefinger and tweaked vigorously.

'How do you know my name?' the injured man said, tears of pain starting in his eyes.

'What Christian has not heard of it? In St Cuthbert's-by-the-Wall, we speak of little else. Percy Quigley, sir, sexton. Up you get now and let us navigate our way home.'

'Is there blood on my face?'

'Somewhat.'

He passed Hagley a snuff handkerchief which the cleric had the speed of thought to refuse.

'You are a sexton?'

'That is my honour.'

'You said you were a soldier.'

'A veteran of Balaclava. And now sexton to Mr Pons.'

'What name is that?'

'The Reverend George Pons. Him of the silver hair and wooden leg.'

And this, Quigley thought, is as good as any Margam novel. Hagley threw off his helping hand.

'I can find my own way,' he said.

'Quigley begs to differ. The young fellow that gave you one up the hooter had indignation writ all over his countenance. I left him looking for a constable.'

'What?' Hagley cried.

'Our passage home should be by indirection, I fancy. What's more, I believe we should leg it.'

Seizing his man just under the elbow, he ran him down Merton Street into the High. Just as they were about to cross the road into Longwall, he had a bright idea, or perhaps a rush of blood to the brain, and threw his free hand up in a dramatic gesture.

'Why, if that is not Lord Bolsover!'

'Where?' Hagley yelped.

'I could swear. Shall I run after him, Mr Hagley?'

'I have no idea what you're talking about.'

'Yes, you do,' the Captain leered.

He cupped both hands to his mouth and bellowed Bolsover's name. Hagley took his chance and bolted.

'In short, he knows we're on to him,' Quigley smirked at the end of his report. 'Called at the Hall the following morning, Principal unable to receive me. Was penning an urgent note which he sent out by my old pal Blossom. Contents of which you have in front of you now.'

'Pons?' Bella wanted to know first. 'Mr Pons of St Cuthbert's-by-the-Wall?'

'A mere flourish.'

'And the gentleman's wooden leg?'

'The same.'

'I thought it rather a good touch,' Urmiston said loyally.

There was time to discuss these details because Hagley's letter was brief. *There is mischief in Oxford*, it said. *Meet Thurs.* The note was written on Bolsover Hall paper but unsigned. The addressee was Colonel Walter von Vircow-Ucquart. Bella examined the envelope.

'Who is this?'

'My dear lady,' Quigley smiled indulgently. 'Is that a real name? I think not. What you got there is an alias. Such as to disguise this Lord Bolsover as keeps cropping up. All plain as a pikestaff to me. Mr Hagley wishes to confer with his old pal.'

'If this *is* Bolsover in disguise, he has the cheek of the devil to put up at Claridge's,' Urmiston observed.

'Black eyepatch,' Quigley suggested. 'Empty sleeve.'

'I don't believe that for all his boldness he is walking around London as Lord Nelson,' Bella snapped.

'I have seen wonders done with an empty sleeve.'

'You say you have never met Bolsover, Charles?' she asked, ignoring the Captain.

'That is so.'

'Then we shall go to tea at Claridge's.'

Urmiston brushed the lapels to his new suit with something like real pleasure. His linen was crisp and only that morning Mrs Bardsoe had tied his stock just so, saying in addition that he looked a fine, well-set-up gentleman, though perhaps in need of a haircut.

'Who do you go as?' Quigley asked of Bella.

'Albert Edward Pons, brother to the one-legged George,' she replied with a flashing look. 'Is anyone watching the hotel?'

'Murch,' the Captain said, deflated.

Vircow-Ucquart walked with the aid of a stick. His huge lump of a head was shaven and blue glasses were looped over his ears. Bella and Urmiston alighted from a cab just as he entered Claridge's. Murch, who was lounging nearby, indicated his identity by laying a hand across his chest, his index finger extended. For good measure, he semaphored with his eyebrows.

'It is not Bolsover, of course,' Bella said in an undertone.

'I am very relieved to hear it. An ugly-looking brute.'

'The question is, who is he?'

'Here, my good fellow,' Urmiston said, palming Murch the letter from Hagley. 'Put this to good use. You'll know what to do.'

He took Bella's arm and they smiled their way past the doorman. Vircow-Ucquart was on his way in to tea. When seen closer to, the greatest surprise was the left side to the man's face. Fire had pulled down one cheek and emptied the eye to the socket. What had once been jowly flesh was replaced by a glistening white scar, wrinkled like boiling milk. Bella exchanged glances with Urmiston.

They took a table facing the Colonel and watched him order tea and sandwiches. His English, though murmured, was curt and guttural in tone. The waiter nodded and left at once to do his bidding. Bella bit her lip.

'Let us see how he reacts to the letter,' Urmiston whispered.

This had been hand-delivered by Murch to the doorman, who gave it to a page, who gave it to the reception desk. In time it was brought in on a small silver tray by a frail old messenger with snow-white hair. Vircow-Ucquart merely glanced at the envelope and laid it down by his napkin. Then he resumed his expressionless inspection of the room. His head turned in Bella's direction, paused a moment, and then swung back. His tea arrived and he waited patiently for the waiter to arrange everything to a nicety.

'Do you speak any German?' Bella asked with sudden inspiration. Urmiston patted her sleeve. He rose and walked over to Vircow-Ucquart's table.

'You will forgive me for disturbing you, Excellencz,' he said in schoolboy German. 'But do I have the honour of addressing one of the Crown Prince's most able lieutenants?'

'And who are you?'

'Medley, of *The Times*.'

'I have never heard of you,' Vircow-Ucquart replied with the greatest possible nonchalance.

'Then it was not you that I spoke with at Metz; and later outside the walls of Paris in 1870?'

'I do not speak to the press, in France or anywhere else.'

'Then I must apologize for the intrusion. Would you pass my kindest regards to the Reverend Mr Hagley when next you see him?'

This got Vircow-Ucquart's attention. He removed his glasses and gave Urmiston a dreadful Cyclops stare. A little tear ran from the corner of the empty eyesocket.

'Tell me again your name?'

'Henry Medley, Oslo correspondent of *The Times*.'

'Oslo!' the German boomed. He had very few facial expressions left, one of which was intended to indicate mirth. It involved a baring of his teeth, such as might be needed to eat a still-living fish or tear flesh from a particularly acidic orange. Urmiston bowed and retreated.

'Well done,' Bella said when he returned to their table. 'Where did you learn your German?'

'Charlotte Street,' he replied obscurely. 'What do we do now?'

To his great surprise, Bella laughed a deep-throated laugh, enough to turn heads at the adjoining tables.

'Do you know, that's a question I can't answer. Hagley and this fellow know each other, obviously. The mischief referred to in the letter would seem to make him complicit in the general scheme of things. I liked it when you mentioned Hagley's name: he seemed to react positively. But where they are to meet on Thursday is still unknown.'

'In Oxford, perhaps?'

'That would suit Captain Quigley very well. But I think not. Perhaps here.'

Urmiston touched her wrist. Vircow-Ucquart was at last opening the letter. He read it through at a glance and then threw it down. In place of a guilty start or smothered oath, he piled gâteau on to his fork and masticated it with awful thoroughness. Bella studied him.

'He is a mere go-between,' she concluded. 'Rather a forbidding one at that. You mentioned Charlotte Street earlier.'

'I was a waiter at Sieghardt's for two years when my financial situation was at its most pressing,' Urmiston said, blushing.

'Did you wear one of their long white aprons? I should like to have seen you.'

'You probably did. Waiters are indistinguishable one from another to most diners.'

Bella rapped the table with her teaspoon.

'What nonsense you do talk from time to time. You are a very handsome man, Charles. Look! Our gallant Colonel has become bored with cake.'

Vircow-Ucquart was indeed scraping back his chair. At the last moment he remembered the letter and stuffed it anyhow into his trouser pocket.

'Note how he does not look at you as he leaves,' Bella whispered. 'This must mean that he has no intention of killing you in the immediate future.'

'You relieve me greatly.'

'Unless,' she teased, 'he has gone upstairs to fetch his pistol.'

'As to that,' Urmiston said thoughtfully, 'does it not strike you that we have somewhat overplayed our hand? All three of us are now known to Hagley and the German. And thus to Bolsover, too.'

'Yes, but we are not investigating a crime, though one has certainly been committed. We must not be distracted by Quigley, who sees it all in his own too lurid light. We are not policemen, or avenging angels. We are simply students of human nature, which is mystery enough. We are looking for the one unburned stick in the bonfire's ashes.'

'And is this how books are written?'

'It is my method,' Bella retorted cheerfully. 'This German – and even Hagley – are minor characters. Lord Bolsover is our villain. I am increasingly sure that he is.'

'But why would he so lightly kill a girl in Covent Garden? And how, if at all, is he connected to this German?'

'We say in novels: the plot thickens.'

'In novels! Then I have it,' Urmiston mocked. 'We are actually following Bolsover's half-brother here, the one that was locked in the east tower since birth, to be fed and raised by a blind mulatto woman. The real Bolsover, discovering the existence of a twin, blinded by rage at the realization that the half-brother has a greater claim on the estate and having in his possession some loose sticks of gelignite –'

'I do hope you are not about to descend into mere facetiousness,' Bella snapped. A red flush was creeping up her neck. Urmiston was alarmed to find her very angry indeed.

When they came out of Claridge's and he found her a cab, she went straight home to Orange Street with barely more than a nod. Murch was waiting and watching from across the road and the two men walked out of the West End together, wrapped in companionable silence.

Vircow-Ucquart followed them at a convenient distance, clearing the Oxford Street pavements of mere Englishmen who strayed across his path with slashing strokes of his cane.

In Orange Street, Bella was still smarting from Urmiston's mockery. She attempted to calm herself with a third glass of Pouilly, through it was hardly yet six o'clock. Useless to acknowledge that Urmiston was as baffled as she with the addition of Vircow-Ucquart to the plot, and that he might have spoken out of exasperation. She had shown him anger and that was an emotion Bella prided herself on keeping in check. The true culprit, she thought with a fine irrationality, was Henry Ellis Margam. Even the six syllables of his ridiculous name annoyed her.

Vircow-Ucquart was the stuff of sensationalist fiction all right, belonging to that ruined world of death by fire, death by water, the innocent dragged down with the guilty, the stench of sulphur rising through otherwise unexceptional city pavements. But Bella's purpose in writing novels was, she hoped, more sophisticated. If she created monsters, she preferred them to be home-grown, although (and it shamed her to remember this) the plot of *Deveril's Disgrace* hinged on a babblingly mad octoroon girl with blue eyes.

For something to do to vent her ill-temper, she kicked her shoes up and down the drawing room. Had Urmiston been there, she would have kicked him, too. As for Hagley, who was beginning to elbow aside Bolsover in her anxious thoughts, had he been present she would have torn his ears off, the way epaulettes are stripped from a dishonoured soldier.

At this unfortunate moment, Marie Claude came in from a visit with Miss Titcombe to the National Gallery. She hesitated in the doorway, recognized Bella's mood, thought about saying something but settled instead for rolling her eyes.

'*What?*' Bella shouted.

'Nothing.'

'Are you coming into the room or are you going to hover there like a moth? Or a fruit bat or something?'

Marie Claude fled. Bella pursued her as far as the foot of the staircase.

'I am *not* merely some foolish woman with a talent for scribbling!' she bellowed. 'And if you dare to utter one word more to suggest that I am, I will lock you in your room until you starve to death, you ungrateful child.'

'I have said nothing!' Marie Claude yelped.

'No, you haven't. But don't you *ever* roll your eyes at me again!'

'Will you please stop shouting?'

Bella found she had a shoe in her hand. She threw it at the landing and watched it bounce off the banisters and fall back at her feet. Marie Claude ran screaming to her room. Bella retrieved the shoe and went back to look for its partner. Under the sofa.

As always happened when in this frantic mood, she thought of her husband, Garnett. The memory of him only came to her when she was truly angry. It was a realization that made her blush. She sat down, defeated.

Garnett Wallis had gone out early one morning from their home in Hertfordshire, riding across the fields to join the local hunt. It was three days before Christmas and the mantelpiece was littered with invitation cards sent from five or even ten miles away.

The ground was frozen, a perfectly unremarkable circumstance, given the season. Garnett's horse slipped on an ice pond at the bottom of a neighbour's meadow, breaking its leg and pinning the rider down with a broken pelvis. And even then Garnett might have survived the accident but for the pure ordinariness of a sudden but prolonged snowfall. He was found a little after two in the afternoon and carried home on a hurdle. Doctors were summoned, telegrams sent. It was all to no purpose. Pneumonia, that unfailing friend to old people, took the ebullient and adored Garnett Wallis off in his thirty-sixth year.

In his pocket, intended for the postbox outside the inn where the hunt was to meet, was a letter to a mistress Bella had not known existed. Six days after the funeral, she found the woman's letters to him. She thought the whole morning about reading them and then burned them one by one in the drawing-room grate. Watching them curl and blacken was a greater horror than closing Garnett's eyes with the stroke of her thumb.

She looked up from this reverie as Marie Claude entered the room.

'The Captain Quigley has sent a message by a child. You are to go at once to Shelton Street.'

It took Bella a moment or two to clear her mind and remember that was where Charles Urmiston lodged. Then she jumped up, her face white.

'A cab, Marie Claude. As fast as ever you like. Run into Leicester Square if you must. But find me a man who will drive like the devil. Say it is life or death.'

The cabbie was young and superlatively cocky. When he heard where he was to take his fare he pointed out that a one-legged chicken could walk there in five minutes. Bella flung two florins full into his chest and that, along with the terrible expression on her face, closed his mouth. The crack of his whip rang like a pistol shot down Orange Street.

She was met at the little shop by Mrs Bardsoe, a mixture of blunt common sense and quivering outrage.

'The foreign brute followed Mr Charles into the parlour here, swept me right out the road and straightways began belabouring the gentleman with his stick, his cane. Not a word said, no sign of a prologue, that poor brave man defending himself as best he could. Bottles smashed, that picture there knocked clean off the wall.'

'He truly said nothing?'

'Not a word. I took him to be a robber of some sort, was slow to get a picture of it in my mind. But then I ups and hits him to the side of the head with that stone mortar of mine on the table there. He went down like a sack of taters. So now I'm out in the street shouting blue murder. I find Ma Rawnsley's boy, a bright enough spark, and has him run to Captain Quigley's double-quick smart.'

'You knocked the German unconscious?'

'German, was he? I laid him out like a corpse, ma'am. So anyway, there I am wringing me hands when who should pitch up but Billy Murch? As soon as he sees the state I'm in, he breaks into a run and we go in to see to Mr Urmiston. Billy gives him the fireman's lift up to his rooms and I'm to wait behind locked doors until the Captain shows.'

Simply by reciting the story, Mrs Bardsoe's composure was beginning to crack. Bella opened her arms and the plump little body melted against her.

'Not a strong man, Mrs Wallis,' she wailed, 'never a one for the rough-and-tumble of life. But game as you like.'

'Where is the German now?'

'Why, the Captain and Billy are seeing to him. Murch fetches his cart round, the animal is rolled into my parlour carpet, and off they go.'

'Do you know where, Mrs Bardsoe?'

'Well, not to no hospital, I'll swear to that.'

'And Mr Urmiston? Has a doctor been called?'

'Bless you, Hannah Bardsoe can set him to rights faster than any doctor you'll find round here. Come.'

Urmiston lay on his bed, naked to the belly. When he saw the women he made a shamefaced attempt to cover his paper-white ribs and chest, crisscrossed with ugly red weals. Bella ran to him and knelt by his head.

'Never mind that for a moment, Charles,' she whispered, her breath fanning his cheek. 'It is a ridiculous question, but are you all right?'

'Nothing is broken. I have that from Mrs B,' he smiled. 'Though I feel like a spring-cleaned carpet. This is what they mean by being given a dusting, I believe.'

'We'll have you up on your feet in no time at all, sir,' Mrs Bardsoe said from the shadows. 'Think of it as nothing more serious than falling out this here window.'

Urmiston tried to laugh, but a huge wince pinched the sound in his chest. Bella turned to the landlady.

'There is truly nothing broken?'

'I'll wager my life on it. Two dislocated fingers what I have pulled straight. A powerful bruised left hip. The rest is what you see.'

'Where is Vircow-Ucquart?' Urmiston whispered.

'Quigley and Mr Murch have him.'

'Poor devil,' he replied. 'I would like you to know, Bella, it was Mrs B that saved me from being thrashed to death. She is a very brave woman.'

'Stone me, Mr Charles,' she cried. 'It was my furniture he was knocking about. But you're right – I fetched him one the side of the head he won't forget in a hurry.'

Bella smoothed the hair from Urmiston's brow.

'Listen, my dear. Mrs Bardsoe and I are going downstairs to make all well in her parlour and I hope take a little restorative together. Shall you manage here for a while? Is there anything you need?'

Blushing, Charles Urmiston beckoned her closer. But Mrs Bardsoe easily guessed what he was saying.

'Now do you find your way down those awful old stairs, Mrs Wallis, and I shall just tidy him up, the same as I have done enough times before. I mean with other invalids,' she added hastily.

'Perhaps, though –' the patient mewed.

'Now, now, Mr Urmiston. Don't come it the green girl with Hannah Bardsoe. We'll attend to what's needed and then I will knock you up a salve that would inspire a dead horse. I have it all in mind what's needed. And then, when you're plumped up on more pillows than what you have now, you shall have a poached egg or a bit of herring roe, whichever you choose.'

Down in the parlour, Bella was sweeping up broken glass with a battered brush and pan. The man she most wanted to meet on earth was the Reverend Anthony Hagley. From a shard of glass picked up from under the table, she recognized one of Mrs Bardsoe's treasures, a memorial mug issued for the funeral of the Iron Duke. Completely unbidden, she burst into tears.

'Why!' Hannah Bardsoe cried, bustling in on her. 'This won't do, my dear. This won't do at all. What's a few knick-knacks, compared to the saving of that good man upstairs? Though a glass of rum with you, Mrs Wallis, by all means.'

'Now then, Fritzi,' Captain Quigley whispered, patting Vircow-Ucquart on his good cheek. 'Can you smell the river? Because that's where you are. This gentleman here is for gutting you with a rusty bale hook, ain't that right, Billy?'

'That, or reach down his throat and pull his liver out with my bare hands,' Murch suggested by way of alternative.

The German licked his lips. He sat tied to a chair in his shirt and trousers, a lump above his ear the size of a teacup.

'This is kidnap,' he muttered. 'My government shall be informed.'

'You're talking through the cheeks of your arse now, Fritz. Moored up outside, waiting on the tide, is a brick wherry going round the Naze to Ipswich. The boys have promised to give you a lift halfway home. The Goodwin Sands is where they'll drop you off. Wasn't that it, Billy?'

'The same.'

Vircow-Ucquart squinted furiously.

'This you cannot do. I am a German officer. I am a *gentleman.*'

'You are a murdering bastard.'

The captive laughed, in spite of the peril he was in.

'That weakling? I give him only a good thrashing, that is all. For his impertinence.'

'I am talking about Welsh Alice,' Murch said, his cross eyes terrible to behold.

Vircow-Ucquart looked genuinely at a loss.

'What person is this?'

'Slashed to death in Maiden Lane.'

'Where is such a place?'

'At the bottom of Covent Garden.'

Quigley was watching carefully: he saw a very slight compression of the German's lips.

'I know only Hyde Park. I have not been in this garden.'

'Welsh Alice. Young girl, china-doll face. Police looking for you. This here boat trip I'm talking about is to save you from the gallows. You and the chair both, over the side, kaboosh. Like a Viking funeral sort of thing.'

Murch suddenly pushed the Captain out of the way and put his face within an inch of the German's.

'You killed her, you wicked basket. And I shall have you for it. Before you drown, you'll suffer, so help me.'

'I did not kill this girl!'

'No?'

'That is not my way,' he yelped.

'Captain,' Murch growled, 'let me at him with the tin-snips.'

'Shears,' Quigley explained. Turning back to Murch he asked, 'And for why do we need those tin-snips, Billy boy?'

'I'm going to trim off his murdering fingers for starters. And then –'

'Not his todger, Bill, for all love! Leave him his todger.'

'It was not me!' Vircow-Ucquart roared. 'I was not even there any longer. It was Freddie!'

'Freddie,' Quigley scoffed.

'Lord Bolsover!'

'Oh, very rich. A made-up name if ever I heard one.'

'Ask your friend Medley. Medley of *The Times.*'

The Captain sighed. 'Do you know what he's talking about?'

'That's where you found me! In Medley's lodgings! You are all of the same gang in some way. But I have money. Whatever it is you need, you say. Say now! And then all is forgotten.'

'I'll look them shears out, Bill. The old tin-snips.'

He wandered away in the gloom at the back of the go-down, his boots crunching on little drifts of grain.

'Listen to me,' the German said urgently to Murch. 'You must believe me. I was not there. I don't play games with women. You have got the wrong man. Lord Bolsover –'

'Not one word more,' Murch commanded. 'Take your punishment like a man. Toes and fingers first and then a trip down the Thames. But better you go with empty pockets.'

He reached into the German's trousers and found the letter from Oxford.

'What's this?'

'It's not important.'

'*Meet Thursday?* And where is that to be? Captain!' he called. 'This here gentleman is to meet someone on Thursday.'

'What's that to us, Bill?' Quigley responded from the back of the empty warehouse. His position now was betrayed by the clash and clank of metal and some vile curses.

'Can I lay my hands on those old snips?' he shouted. 'I cannot. And there's rats here as big as armadillios. I seen nothing like it since Dick's day.'

A claw-hammer skittered out of the gloom. Vircow-Ucquart flinched.

'My friend,' he whispered to Murch. 'The money, we were talking about some money. Gold sovereigns –'

'Hold your horses,' Quigley cried in triumph. 'Here we are.'

'Very well!' their victim cried hastily. 'We meet on Thursday and I take you to him.'

'What's he saying now, Bill?' Quigley called.

'He's on about this Bolsover again, I don't doubt.'

'Pay him no mind, Bill. Never was such a person.'

'I take you to him,' the German bellowed at parade-ground volume. 'In Paris! He is in Paris! The Hotel Louvois maybe.'

'Which they are rusty,' Quigley said quietly, standing directly behind Vircow-Ucquart's chair.

'Pass them here.'

There really was a pair of tin shears. Without the least hesitation, Murch opened the blades wide under the screaming man's nostrils and cut off the tip of his nose. Then they opened the door at the end of the shed and ran the chair and its occupant across the plank flooring and, taking a side each, pitched it out into the Thames.

There was no brick barge; and far from filling, the tide had yet to reach its ebb. Vircow-Ucquart fell into three feet of grey-black ooze. They watched for a few moments while the German thrashed about, trying to avoid being buried alive. His roaring attracted three naked urchins a hundred yards off, panning the river bed for treasure. One by one they shaded their eyes with their forearms.

A thought occurred to Captain Quigley.

'How did you know about them tin shears, Bill?'

'I never expected you to find none,' Murch protested mildly. 'Once found, it would have been a crime not to use 'em. Give me a hand to sweep up some of this here corn for my old horse.'

ELEVEN

Murch went back to Rotherhithe next day to spy out the lay of the land from his acquaintance the thoroughly evil M'Gurk but refused his offer of a drink, pleading an engagement later that morning. Accordingly the two men leaned on a cranky wooden fence overlooking the Thames, a short way from where Vircow-Ucquart had been flung from the grain loft. The river was busy. They watched a grimy paddle steamer running downstream. M'Gurk pointed.

'You want to keep your eye on that. There's boilers there that'll blow any day soon.'

'You don't say?'

'The wife's brother has the care of them,' M'Gurk explained.

'You paint a picture. What does she carry, the old tub?'

'Enough,' the Wapping man said shortly.

There was a properly businesslike pause before Murch broached the next topic.

'You haven't come across a Fritzi by any chance? Fell out the sky, seemingly, along with his chair?'

'I knew it had to be you,' M'Gurk rumbled.

'How is he today?'

'He has mentioned money.'

'Listen, Ollie,' Murch said suddenly, 'is it right that your Liza should wade about with the boys in her birthday suit? And her no more than a maid?'

'Been having a gander, have you? She ain't got nothing they don't already know about. So mind your own bleedin' business,' her father added. He leaned over the fence and spat into the lap of the tide. Then, for good measure, he eased himself with a foghorn fart.

'He done you some wrong, the foreign bloke,' he suggested.

'Got on my wick,' Murch confirmed.

'How much d'you want for your part in it?'

'He's all yours,' Murch said. 'God help him.'

'Slow to rile, that Billy, but once he gets his dander up there is no stopping him. My late husband was the same.'

Mrs Bardsoe was helping Charles Urmiston to his first faltering steps since the beating, his arm round her neck and shoulders, hers encircling his waist. The salve she had prepared for his wounds smelled very agreeably of wet summer meadows. Urmiston tottered about in his nightshirt, unable to prevent himself easing his ribs against his landlady's pillowy bosom. The sensation was disturbing.

'You don't think cutting the man's nose off was a step too far, Mrs B?' he asked, to cover the first faint prod of arousal.

'I do not. Whatever was he thinking of, coming over here and interfering with the rights of true-born Englishmen? And him with only one eye in his head.'

'He survived, though?'

'Bless you, sir, the M'Gurks have him safe. Though I wouldn't like to say when he'll see the West End again.

And as for blowing his nose, well, he won't need no wipes no more!'

Her laughter jiggled her breasts and set Urmiston's pulse racing all over again. He reached out with his hands and balanced himself against the bedroom wall.

'Do I detect a healthsome little show of sweat?' Mrs Bardsoe asked, not without a secret smile. 'Shall I fetch up the tin bath and a pail of hot water?'

'I believe I shall manage without,' Urmiston said. 'Let your healing balm have its full effect. But I tell you what it is, Mrs B, I must get down to Fleur de Lys Court today.'

'Ho!' Mrs Bardsoe cried. 'Never think of it! There's a bruise on your hip as big as a cowpat. No, no, the others must come to you. Go to Fleur de Lys Court, forsooth! If that don't beat all.'

'Well then,' Urmiston said uncertainly, 'at the very least I must send them a letter.'

He managed to shoo her out long enough to find his trousers, which he put on as if for the first time in his life, his fingers extremely slow in the matter of buttons. Socks and boots defeated him utterly.

'Now,' his landlady said, coming in with a kettle of hot water. 'What a sorry sight we have here. No ducking nor schoolgirl blushing, I'm going give you a general once-over and spruce-up before your friends arrive – I have sent an intelligent boy to fetch them. A shave and a clean shirt will set you to rights. And after that a nettle tea.'

'Could I not have coffee?' Urmiston remonstrated weakly. Mrs Bardsoe smiled.

'Go on then,' she relented. 'And I suppose a cigar would be to your taste as well? Men! Now hold your head very still while I have this here razor in my hand. And for why, Mr Urmiston, dear? In case I cuts your blessed nose off, that's for why!'

This witty sally sent her into peals of laughter. There was something irrepressible about her that gladdened Urmiston's creaking gate of a heart. When she had finished shaving him, he reached impulsively for her warm, moist hand. Her eyes widened.

'Whatever next?' she wondered in the least chiding way possible. They were both blushing. But Urmiston had a ready change of subject, bringing forward something that had been on his mind all night.

'I have to ask you, Mrs B. This cutting-off of noses. Is that really the way things are settled in the real world?'

'Ho! What does a quiet body like me know of the real world? If by those words you mean *your* world? All I know is that we are forced to look after our own in this station of life. I know the policeman Higgins, the local bobby, for he comes in here for salve to his piles, which he has something crucial. But I would no more ask him his opinion on how to go on in life than I would one of them china dogs you see downstairs in my parlour.'

'He is unreliable?' Urmiston suggested stupidly. Mrs Bardsoe smiled.

'He is a copper,' she explained gently, as if talking to a visiting Trobriand Islander. 'He joined for the boots and his brains are right there in his feet. A nice enough cove and his wife is a pleasant body. But oh dear me, if we had to depend on the coppers for our justice, the world would come to a stop by next Friday teatime.'

'I hadn't realized.'

'That's because you're made of better stuff than us.'

'If there is better stuff than you, Mrs B, I hope to meet it before I die.'

'Go on out of it,' she squealed, delighted.

But there was a problem with these hints and glances, as there almost always is. Urmiston had loved his wife after his own fashion, making loyalty and a great deal of patience his way of showing it. Towards the end Marguerite – more and more so after his dismissal by the Great Western – had grown fractious and weepy. Tears he could cope with, for he very often felt like crying himself, trudging home to Lambeth from his waiting job at Sieghardt's and realizing he would never again buy new shoes or own decent linen. But then came silence between them, a long and bitter silence that lasted until her death.

Lodging with Mrs Bardsoe had already shown him some of what he had missed in his own life – earthiness, a careless physicality, delight in the small pleasures of the day and (like the conversation he had just had about the policeman) a brutal realism. The widower in Urmiston liked Hannah Bardsoe far too much. Aroused, as he was now, he felt guilty. And she, intelligent soul, sensed it.

Captain Quigley was the first to arrive, his fist filled, preposterously, with a nosegay of violets. They were made of cloth.

'Care of patient exemplary,' he noted. 'Lady of the house preparing coffee. And at my suggestion, a thimbleful of rum.'

'I am in your debt once again, Captain. The villain found more than his match in you, I believe.'

'What is that smell?' Quigley asked.

'Mrs Bardsoe's balm. Er, goose fat and other ingredients.'

'Is it red, the mixture?'

'Green.'

'A red ointment the only thing. Chilli pepper. Camphor. Maybe a pinch or so of gunpowder. Strong salts various.'

'Mrs B tells me Vircow-Ucquart is captured by the mudlarks.'

'The M'Gurk family. Which is terrible for him.'

'Has he talked?'

'Before he lost his bugle, he did say this Bolsover character was jaunting off to Paris.'

'You think Mr Hagley plans to meet him there? It seems unlikely.'

'Ah, now, as to that –'

He was about to review the whole campaign when Bella appeared, bearing a tray of coffee. She kissed Urmiston lightly on the cheek.

'You are looking more human this morning, Charles.'

'I expect to be fighting fit by tomorrow.'

'We shall see. Captain Quigley has told you about Paris, I don't doubt.'

'The Hotel Louvois,' Quigley supplied helpfully.

'I'm assured by the Captain that in his extensive military experience, time spent on reconnaissance is seldom wasted. All the same, we stay where we are. And *that*,' she added, turning to Quigley, 'is my final word on the matter.'

Urmiston thought for a moment or two and then nodded his agreement.

'We have perhaps been fishing in too deep waters,' he said.

'Vircow-Ucquart would have killed you if he could. Or would not have shown a moment's remorse had you died under his hands. It has made me think. What is it that they don't want us to find out about them?'

Captain Quigley blew out his cheeks and absentmindedly drank the medicinal rum he had prescribed for the patient.

'What else, if not blue bloody murder?'

Urmiston shifted uncomfortably inside his shirt. The broken skin on his ribs and back was itching and his head throbbed.

'We don't know,' he said. The words came out far too bluntly.

'Steady the front rank,' Quigley muttered.

'I realize I am a tyro when it comes to situations like this. My opinion counts for very little. But nothing sharpens the mind better than a good drubbing. With your permission, I would like to put forward a theory.'

'Please,' Bella encouraged.

'I start by making a very large assumption, that it was Bolsover who killed the girl in Maiden Lane.'

'You can be sure of it,' Quigley cried.

'No, Captain,' Urmiston said quietly. 'We can't, not entirely.'

'What is your theory?' Bella asked.

'It came to me last night that we could divide the story –' he nodded to her politely at the use of the term – 'into two quite separate moments. The first is when his lordship, for whatever reason, uses a part of his capital to endow a missionary enterprise in Oxford and install his particular friend as Warden, or Principal. At the very least, Bolsover bought a house for Hagley. A very large and commodious house.'

'Go on.'

'We don't know and it hardly matters how it benefits them both – I'm sorry if I am coming it the lawyer somewhat.'

Bella studied him calmly, her grey eyes searching his face for the last scrap of meaning.

'Is it your point that he was perfectly free to do whatever he liked with his own money?' she asked.

'There is no crime in being philanthropic.'

The three of them sat digesting this for a moment or two. Captain Quigley clog-danced briefly on the bare boards, coughed, smoothed his moustache.

'But a rum do, all the same.'

'Yes. Given Bolsover's moral character, as far I have understood it, very strange.'

Quigley leered hideously.

'Perhaps it was done for love.'

'Would that be so wrong either? Then again perhaps he was tricked into it, blackmailed even. Anything's possible. But the outcome was a good one and I think what the Captain has discovered in Oxford stands apart from all the rest of it.'

'You say so,' Quigley protested. 'But there's a lot we don't yet know about what goes on there.'

'The second part of your theory?' Bella prompted with the same attempted calm.

'Concerns the murder of Welsh Alice. We can say three, possibly more, people were present but almost certainly

Bolsover, Hagley, and now, according to the most recent evidence, this German fellow. They make a most ill-assorted trio on the face of it.'

'And?'

I think we must assume they know each other well, perhaps very well, but I do not think it feasible that three friends, after a supper somewhere, decide to go out – in *harness* – to find and murder a young girl. And certainly not behind some scaffolding in a residential street within cry of two popular pubs.

'And if one of them – or all of them – hated women enough,' Urmiston blushed, 'Well, I know little of the subject but I believe there are houses to accommodate that particular kind of lust.'

Bella turned to the Captain, who shrugged. 'The point is that we must believe one of these men – and we really can't say which one – killed Welsh Alice.'

Urmiston gave way to impulse and scratched the wounds on his chest. Little flowers of blood appeared on his linen almost at once. 'The poor creature died of a sudden, irrational, ungovernable impulse on the part of one of these men. The three of them were walking together somewhere, we can't say where, with nothing more on their minds than commonplaces. They are interrupted – let's say they are propositioned – and within seconds a woman has fallen to the pavement with her throat slashed. And then they walk on.'

Captain Quigley marched to the window and opened it a crack. Urmiston was at a loss for a moment to know why, until he realized that what had begun as the scent of summer meadows in the room was changing now to a more foetid stink. It was the smell that comes from river weeds stirred by a stick, or oar.

'Mrs Bardsoe swears by this concoction,' he apologized faintly. 'It did wonders for Penny. Mr Murch's horse.'

'Linseed the only remedy for a horse,' Quigley corrected. 'I suggest we fumigate quarters with a cheroot each.'

'That would be agreeable,' Bella said. 'But not one word to Mrs Bardsoe about linseed, horses, or any other medical topic, understood?'

For a while they smoked in silence. Urmiston concentrated all his attention on not setting fire to the sheets. Quigley sat with one leg cocked up on the other, gazing judiciously at the ceiling and giving the company his impersonation of a man in deep thought. Bella mused.

'Very well,' she said at last. 'Among those three men, the one most capable of a sudden irrational act is Bolsover. Is that what you're saying?'

'That is my theory,' Urmiston murmured. 'We know what Vircow-Ucquart is capable of with a cane, in a Prussian sort of way; but it is hard to suppose that Hagley carries a knife or razor with him when he goes to supper. That only leaves his lordship.'

'Does your theory support any further conclusions?'

'Only that we don't know half enough about Lord Bolsover.'

'Suppose,' Quigley proposed quietly, 'suppose he has done this sort of thing before?'

'We don't know and we can't say,' Urmiston said.

'Because, my dears, if he has,' the Captain continued, unabashed, 'wouldn't that explain a bit why Mr Hagley and the Fritz were with him? To keep him on the leash, as it were.'

'Too fanciful,' Bella objected.

'You don't slash a girl the way he did in Maiden Lane just because she says the wrong thing to you,' the Captain persisted. 'If you're a belted earl, you don't go out to dinner with a razor in your pocket.'

'Was it a razor?'

'That's what the police doctor thinks.'

Bella jumped up and walked to the window. She pushed the sash up as far as it would go and perched uncomfortably on the sill. Three floors below, the citizens of Shelton Street bickered and called to each other, or rummaged in the vegetable and old-clothes stalls. There were patterns in the way people moved and interacted, much clearer to the eye than ever they would be at street level. Because, she thought ruefully, in the gutter the observer was part of the story.

Urmiston and Quigley watched and waited.

'If all this is so,' she asked almost absently, her eyes still on the scene below, 'why does Hagley wish to meet him now?'

'You are forgetting,' Urmiston reminded her gently. 'As it turned out, he wished only to meet Vircow-Ucquart.'

'All right, but why?'

'Because,' Quigley suggested with telling simplicity, 'they are his lordship's minders. Bolsover a gentleman who likes the smell of blood. Same as he likes bully lads and fine wines.'

'If I had a friend as combustible as Lord Bolsover,' Urmiston agreed gloomily, 'I would not let him out of my sight. They have no idea whether the police have discovered witnesses, nor whether there is some other trail of evidence that might lead to them. They know we know something. Hagley in particular realizes he left his cigar case at the scene.'

'That ties him nicely to Bolsover in any court of law,' the Captain added.

'What do the police say about Alice's murder?' Bella asked.

'Nothing so fanciful,' Quigley grunted. 'A tart with no drawers has her throat cut behind some scaffolding. Not much of a story there.'

Bella turned away from the window with a set expression, picked up her gloves and quitted the sickroom without another word. Her cheroot was left smouldering in a saucer, the smoke drawn to the open window in an undulating blue-grey wave.

Steyne, Bolsover's house in Berkshire, looked well enough in sunshine but on an overcast day, such as this was, its yellowy stones darkened and – the thought flew into Hagley's mind by association – sulked. That morning, to the consternation of his servants, his lordship had ordered fires lit in every room. No sooner done than he further commanded all the windows to be opened. Hagley was received in a gale of woodsmoke, attended by rushing maids and footmen.

'There is some reason for all this, is there?' he enquired too jovially.

Bolsover stared at him. 'It is what I want,' he said.

'Yes, but the reason –'

'I have given you the reason. You have come from Oxford?'

'From London. We are in trouble, Freddie.'

'I am not in the least trouble, unless it is that the house will shortly burn down. And if it does, what's that to you?'

Hagley walked to each mullion window in turn and drew it close. Bolsover had flung himself on to a huge couch and resumed his glass of claret. He looked tired and drawn.

'You are beginning to creep about, Anthony, my dear,' he scoffed. 'Too much holy Moses, or whatever it is you do. Too much snuffling round your young gentlemen. Do you kiss them all goodnight? Is that what has induced the bent back and the tiptoe steps?'

'Vircow-Ucquart has disappeared.'

'How I wish that were true. I favoured him at first because of his appalling ugliness – you can have no idea of the horror that face inspires in others. It was thrilling for a while. But I am tired of it now. He is the bad penny that one throws into the gutter, only to see it back in your pocket the next day.'

Hagley poured himself a brandy, pleased to find his hands were shaking only very gently.

'This room was once precious to us both,' he observed.

'That was in the days when you were more impressionable. And far more reckless. I have largely forgotten those times.'

The sheer impudence of the remark made Hagley want to go over and slap his face. Instead, he controlled his voice.

'Vircow-Ucquart is a loyal friend. As am I, still. I tell you now, there is trouble for all three of us. A rogue of some kind has been asking questions in Oxford. Two other people, unknown to me, were spying on Vircow-Ucquart at Claridge's, one of them claiming to be a *Times* reporter. The other was a woman. The Prussian scribbled me a note and set off after them. He has not been seen since.'

'And what did they want to know, these people?'

'There are things about a recent event in Covent Garden that would be better kept secret.'

Bolsover yawned.

'A shilling whore who joined the choir invisible a few years earlier than she expected? How many times does that happen a week? Ring for Maudsley.'

When he came, the butler was ordered to find someone called Jean and bring her to the drawing room. Maudsley was not the usual image of a senior servant. He was broad and clumsy, with thick wrists and huge square hands. He hesitated for a mere fraction of a second and then nodded.

'You don't bow, Maudsley?'

'I have trouble remembering that,' the man said with equal insolence.

Jean, when she came, was a girl of about twenty. Hagley's presence startled her for a moment, but she made him a bob and then stood with her hands folded in front of her.

'This is Jean,' Bolsover drawled. 'Tell Mr Hagley your duties, Jean.'

'Well,' she said uncertainly, 'I am your lordship's maid.'

'As you might be to the lady of the house in a different circumstance?'

'I have never worked nowhere else,' she said cautiously.

'Mr Hagley and I have been discussing aspects of the Bible just now and in particular the role of the handmaiden. It is Mr Hagley's contention that I do not like women enough to grasp the concept.'

'Sir?'

'This is quite enough,' Hagley said, feeling the blood run to his cheeks.

'Have I ever frightened you, Jean?'

'No, sir.'

'Threatened you?'

'No, sir.'

'Do you like being my handmaiden?'

'As far as I understand it, yes.'

Her eyes flicked to Hagley, who stood. He reached and took both her hands in his. They were moist with sweat and, close to, he could see her burning face.

'This has been most useful testimony, my child,' he said with all the clerical unction he could muster. 'We need not detain you further.'

'Have I ever seen you naked, Jean?' Bolsover interrupted. She bit her lip.

'I believe you have, sir,' she said in a tiny voice.

'And were you afraid then?'

'Never in life,' she whispered.

After she had gone, Hagley wiped his hands on a handkerchief before rounding on his host and former lover.

'Are you quite mad? Do you think this extenuates in any way what I came here to talk about? I am trying to tell you, Freddie, we are in very great trouble.'

'You know,' Bolsover said dreamily, 'you can get people to do anything you want with money. Last night I

- 134 -

entertained your successor at Brailston, a very different sort of parson. A hearty innocent. He plays village cricket and botanizes. I told him I wished to make him a generous donation to the fabric of the church.'

'That was decent of you,' Hagley said carefully.

'It was. He turned up on the dot of eight, and we dined *à deux*. I thought it would be amusing to have the food served him by naked servants. He managed not to blink an eye. I can do that sort of thing. I can do anything.'

'Your servants agreed to all this?'

'For a consideration. I chose only the ugliest, the grossest among them. We were given our soup by a venerable kitchenmaid almost too old to see. Other dishes were brought in by my groom and a simpleton boy from the gardener's staff.'

'Freddie,' Hagley whispered helplessly, 'I am only here to save you.'

'You are here because if I go down, you will go with me.'

And that, Hagley thought, was the beginning, middle and end of it. The death of the Covent Garden drab brought their whole relationship into sharper focus. More than that, it opened a box of similar nightmares better left untouched.

'You are thinking of crossing into the Continent, I believe?'

Bolsover laughed. 'You walk like a parson and damn me if you don't begin to talk like one. I am going to Paris for a few days or a week. I buy my shirts there. Are you going to advise against it?'

'I was hoping to accompany you,' Hagley protested gently.

'Well, well, this is a romantic gesture indeed. I stay at the Louvois.'

He said this with some considerable spin and laughed at Hagley's reaction.

'A good-class family hotel, as the manager has insisted more than once in the past. That is, when attempting to explain certain house rules that appeared to have been broken by the distinguished English milord and his clerical friend.'

'Do you not think,' Hagley asked with as much innocence as he could muster for the question, 'we might go to Rheims instead?'

'Generally speaking, I detest champagne. And I certainly detest provincial cities. No, Paris suits very well.'

'But not the Louvois.'

'We shall see,' Bolsover said, laughing.

And how I hope you fall overboard and drown before you get anywhere near France, was the Reverend Mr Hagley's most unchristian thought. His smile was as flimsy as tissue paper.

'Then Paris it is,' he said.

Marie Claude had taken Bella at her word. That evening the two women went to the Aquarium, a place of such moral squalor, as it seemed to Bella, that she was alarmed for her companion. Perhaps Marie Claude liked the place for its faint echo of café life, the buzzing of waiters and the sauntering crowds that passed, seemingly at ease but as nervously alert as any fish. Bella was not so entranced.

'Hello, ma,' a pimply young clerk addressed her cheekily. 'Out for a spin with your daughter, is it?'

'Will you be a good little boy and go away?'

But he took this as an invitation to banter further.

'May I?' he asked, scraping back a chair. 'How about a nice ice or another cup of coffee?'

'Go away,' Marie Claude said.

'Ah, a French miss! Albert Judd. Firm of Minshall and Greaves. Man about town, bong viveur. I know France. I had a day trip to Zeebrugge just this last May.'

'Albert,' Bella began. But at that moment an altogether different kind of man stood over them.

'Is this little bag of wind troubling you, madam?'

Judd jumped up at once.

'Never argue with the navy, that's always been my motto.'

'Good lad. Now hop off.'

The sailor was a far more respectable proposition. His face was seriously whiskered and his hands blunt. His eyes were a startling blue. On an impulse, Bella asked him to join them.

'Well,' he said uncertainly.

'We are perfectly respectable,' she said, laughing.

His name was Bolt and he was in London on the last day of shore leave. He joined his ship next morning in Portsmouth.

'And where do you go?' Marie Claude asked.

'Channel Squadron,' he said, smiling. 'No palm trees, miss, nor no other exotic climes neither.'

'But you have been to such places?'

'I have seen Japan in '63, serving in the *Havoc*, a little wooden tub you would not cross the Channel in. Though we had our say, when the time came. Brisk work at Kagosima Harbour.'

'Was there a war there at that time, Mr Bolt?'

'There was shot and shell to be sure.'

'What are they like, the Japanese?'

'I would say bloody-minded little chaps.'

Bella warmed to him.

'Would you take a glass of brandy with us?'

'No to the brandy, with grateful thanks. But I will smoke a pipe if you permit.'

'Are you married?' Marie Claude wanted to know.

'Bless you, miss – yes, and with a daughter I hope turns out half as pretty as you.'

'Oh how I have always longed to be a sailor!' she cried. Bolt was amused.

'And many a jack would be happy to serve with you, I can swear to that! But it is not all glory, miss, not by a long shot. Some of it is a very dirty business.'

'Were you born within sight of the sea, Mr Bolt?' Marie Claude wanted to know. 'Is that what drew you to faraway places?'

He laughed indulgently, forgetting himself so far as to pat her hand.

'I am from Berkshire, my dear. My old father had the Feathers on the road to Wallingford. I knew nothing of the sea until I was fourteen.'

'You said Wallingford?' Bella asked.

'Do you know that lovely old place?'

In novels – like the one she was carrying around in her head – such a coincidence would lead to a revelation and the plot would bound forward; and it did occur to Bella that she had only to ask the right question to have Bolsover rise as if from the pages of a pop-up book. Bolt studied her attentively, waiting for her reply. It was a dramatic moment: the noise, the crush, the question left hanging in the air, Bolt as the innocent messenger of some crucial piece of intelligence. Bella smiled.

'I had an aunt who lived there once,' she improvised.

Bolt nodded. He tucked his pipe away inside his breast and reached for his uniform cap.

'That's how it is – one thing leads to another. We are all connected in some small way. 'Tis but all one story, however big the book may be. Every life touches every other. And if that is not the good Lord's purpose, then I'd like to know what is.'

He stood, and in his frank seaman-like way, touched his cap to them.

'You will not take coffee or a plate of cakes?'

'I will not. I bid you goodnight, ladies.'

That night Bella and Marie Claude slept together in the same bed, something that did not happen often. Marie Claude's neediness was hardly ever carnal. She liked to be admired for her almost cat-like beauty, that concealed a hidden truculence none but another woman could under-stand or tolerate. And Bella did so admire her, marvelling at her narrow hips, the extraordinary delicacy of her wrists and ankles. It was a body born for white shell beaches or the greenest tropical forests and not London's reckless vulgarities. For her, Marie Claude was like a picture in an exhibition, beckoning but at the same time unknowable. The burden of her pillow talk was how happy she had been in Paris and how miserable she was in London. Neither statement was true. Naked and sleeping, as she was now, one arm flung across her face, the other folded on her gently fluttering stomach, she was, Bella considered, a creature from some other dimension altogether. I am, she thought, merely her curator.

And a bulky one at that. She nudged the sheets away with her feet and let the night air flow over her body, suddenly as glum as Marie Claude was silent. She thought of her fellow novelist, Mrs Toaze-Bonnett, tucked up in Pinner under far more chaste arrangements, her hair doubtless under a little linen cap and not clinging to shoulders slick with sweat. Mrs Toaze-Bonnett (like Bella, a widow) wrote five hundred words a day, pruned roses, sang in the parish church choir and forgave the rest of the world its sins. By any standards, she was the most thumping bore in Christendom. But, Bella reflected bitterly, she had grasped one essential truth about life: that happiness was the greatest fiction of them all.

It was said that the sage old fool Sheriff Jinks, the hero of her novels, was based on her late husband, a shipping agent for Pierotti & Clunes. Nobody could remember a thing about this unhappy man, unless it was his eccentric habit of walking each year from Pinner to Ramsgate, the town of his birth. 'I use the pistol but sparingly,' Sheriff Jinks confided in *Handiman's Revenge*, 'but trust rather in the word of God and a rough-hewn wit. I believe in tall trees and plain speaking.'

Bella slipped out of bed, found her nightgown and patted down her body with it. Moving with excessive caution she opened the door to the bedroom and crept downstairs, where the scent of beeswax mingled with tobacco and that faintly sulphurous smell that even a summer's day delivered from the streets outside.

She walked about the drawing room, thinking over the novel that might come from all these recent alarms and revelations. Bolsover was the villain of the piece; but who was the hero? Urmiston it could not be. He was too gentle and compliant, too self-effacing. Murch (she smiled to herself) was the physical type, crossed eyes and all – there was something glamorous in his bony self-containment and want of a smile. Suppose, for example, that Murch was not just another ruined Londoner but the greatest fencing master in all Europe? She found him a place to live – the royal mews in Stuttgart – and changed his unfortunate eyes to – yes! a vow of silence he had undertaken the day he accidentally killed his brother in a duel with sabres.

But then again, why do stories need heroes? It seemed to Bella that what the world wanted was innocence – to read of young men and women polished like wineglasses, reflecting back not the world as it was, but mere sunlight. Murch would not do, after all. She liked him for the very things wineglasses were designed not to be – an awful matter-of-factness, the absence in him of promise and celebration.

She fell into her spoonback chair and thought of Mr Bolt and his beefy sailor's figure, sitting with the mail-bags, waiting for the first train down to Portsmouth. A little of the desolation in that imagined scene crept into her heart.

When she went back to bed, she folded Marie Claude into her arms without waking her and lay waiting for the first light of the day to march bit by bit across the ceiling. If there was a satisfaction in being Mr Henry Ellis Margam that morning, she was as far from it as Kagosima Harbour lay from Leicester Square.

TWELVE

The next day turned out to be sultry and overcast. The hazy cloud that obscured London raised the temperature and thickened the air. In the mid-morning, feeling tetchy and ill-tempered, Bella had a sudden recuperative idea. She asked Charles Urmiston to dinner that night, promising a cab at the door of Shelton Street for seven. He was on no account to accept the invitation out of duty. If he felt too battered to attend, then he must refuse. But she knew he would not. Nor did he – the boy that took round her note returned it with 'At Seven' scrawled across the bottom. Those additional stains were not from tears of gratitude – the invitation had caught Urmiston in the tin bath, wearing a helmet of suds.

Bella spent a happy half-hour in the principal cellar of the house in Orange Street, choosing wine. In the afternoon she walked out into Leicester Square to buy flowers. These exceptional preparations astonished Marie Claude.

'Does the Prince of Wales come tonight?'

'Don't be impertinent.'

'If it is Lord Broxtowe I am going out.'

'When has Lord Broxtowe ever dined with us? And if he ever did, don't you suppose I would pack you off with the blessed Lydia Titcombe for the evening?'

For answer, Marie Claude burst into tears. It seemed that two nights ago Miss Titcombe had been shown the door. She had lately inherited a cottage on the Kent coast from her aged grandmother and there she planned to set up house with her beloved, keeping chickens and growing vegetables. There were other romantic inducements. The property had a well from which to draw water and from her early childhood visits Lydia remembered bacon hanging on hooks. Rare orchids hid in the fields roundabout and any amount of wading birds decorated the mud flats. Bella was stunned.

'She has no idea who you are,' she observed incautiously.

'Oh yes!' Marie Claude shouted. 'Do find it funny, why not!'

'I find it sad. Poor Miss Titcombe. Who will she ever find as beautiful as you?'

'I hate you both! I wish I were dead!'

'No you don't. Or not more than usual.' She embraced the sobbing girl. 'You will live a very long time and see miracles,' Bella promised.

'I don't want to see miracles.'

'Twentieth-century miracles.'

Marie Claude howled. By the time Urmiston arrived, Bella was emotionally exhausted.

'This is kind of you,' he said shyly.

'It is something I have wanted to do. I entertain very seldom.'

Marie Claude came to table in a surly and jealous mood but found their guest to have impeccable manners, which was to say French manners. He knew Paris; and of course, Boulogne. Without revealing the reason for his journey, he gave a pleasant and witty account of travelling by train to Mentone and the people he had met along the way.

'This *comtesse*, the mystery woman, offered you a job?' she asked incredulously.

'As tutor to her daughter.'

'Was she beautiful, the girl?'

'I was shown a daguerrotype.'

'The picture bewitched you?'

'I am slow to bewitch,' Urmiston smiled.

'But about that you can't say. No one can say.'

'Well, let's say it has happened to me very seldom in a long, long life. And it did not happen that afternoon.'

'Tcchh!' Marie Claude scolded.

After taking coffee and cognac with them in the sitting room, she excused herself and Bella was at last free to lay out what she wished to say. During the day something had happened, the way things do happen – tiny vexations, unbidden thoughts. When she finally came to the point, it was this: she did not wish to continue any further along the path that led to Bolsover.

Urmiston listened with grave attention.

'I take it you mean that you have uncovered enough about this monster to write your next book,' he murmured. 'And that anything else – any further twist or turn – would not further your interest.'

'Could you make the writing of a book sound a little less effete? A novel is an exercise in imagination, Charles. How it all comes out in the end, I mean in real life, is none of my business. You look shocked.'

He steepled his fingers, gazing at the carpet. When he looked up again, his smile was tentative.

'I must ask you: have you come all this way simply out of literary curiosity? You don't care at all for the outcome?'

'I am struggling to find the outcome.'

'I mean in what you term real life, Bella.'

'I already see one obvious possibility. We give the cigar case to the police. Quigley deposes a statement saying how he came by it and the thing is out of our hands. The three villains we have identified are brought to justice.'

'Or not.'

'Yes!' Bella exclaimed, niggled. 'Brought to justice or not. But can't we rely on the police to do their duty?'

'I have no idea. I have never spoken to one, other than to ask directions.'

She found herself losing her temper. Pouring another cognac for them both, a little of it splashed over her wrist. She sucked at her skin, not without failing to notice his tiny wince of dismay.

'You are disappointed in me.'

'I am surprised.'

'You think we should go to Paris, as Quigley wants?'

'I shall go,' he said simply.

'Oh, Charles,' she cried. 'Are you going to be my hero?'

Charles Urmiston was in no way Philip Westland when it came to pleasantries. Instead of batting the shuttlecock back over the net, he fell to examining the carpet again. She waited. At last he rose and carefully set down his glass.

'I understand what you have said but find I cannot leave things at that. Bolsover wronged me. Without his essential viciousness my dear wife might have lived a little longer – or at the very least ended her days in comfort and not squalor. Moreover, the evidence has convinced me that he murdered that poor Welsh drab and for that too I shall hunt him down. To the ends of the earth, if necessary.'

'As a form of adventure?'

'As a means of exacting justice,' Urmiston corrected, perhaps a little too sharply. 'I thought we had just agreed that romance was your department.'

'This is very cool, Charles.'

'Perhaps. I must thank you for an excellent meal.'

'We are to part on such stiff terms?'

Urmiston hesitated.

'I am much more the coward than I should like to have people believe,' he said. 'You can see that in me, I am sure. But somehow, with all this, I have crossed over into a different country.'

'Then beware,' Bella cried. 'Percy Quigley can be no guide at all to you in this new place.'

His smile was very faint.

'The Captain? I have met his kind before, though in a very adulterated form. He is the dog who runs after a thrown stick and cannot always find it. Who peers pitifully from the bushes. No, the man who has stiffened my backbone is Billy Murch.'

'*This* is your new friend?'

'I have hardly exchanged a dozen words with him. But there is something implacable in him that I have never met with before.'

He tried to continue the thought and then shrugged.

'My wife used to ask when we would go back to Campden Hill, to things as they had been. She thought – well, it doesn't matter what she thought. I promised her that we would. And even half-believed it myself. I know now I can never go back to who I once was. I will help kill Bolsover for that one realization alone.'

'But your fortunes might change,' she cried.

'It is not about money, Bella. It never was about money. Billy Murch has somehow shown me that, without asking a single question of me.'

Quigley knew a man who lived close by Victoria Station in Gillingham Mews. Mr Cumberledge's hobby was to file and cross-reference newspapers, a work he had started with his daughter, and after her death, his granddaughter. William Cumberledge would have done this work for love, for he was in character a saintly fool with something of the common squirrel about him. The newspapers he had hoarded over fifty years filled the basement from floor to ceiling, the earliest editions several inches deep in water. The all-important abstracts were cut and pasted into folios that were shelved in his living quarters, where he received from time to time lawyers' clerks, amateur will hunters, incurably inquisitive local historians and members of the criminal classes.

'You have,' he explained to Quigley, 'deaths by fire, by shipwreck, avalanche, by balloon, railway – this last subdivided into collision, explosion, runaway trains, stationary trains, bridge disaster, signal failure –'

'Has there ever been death by disappearance on the railways?' Quigley asked with his usual whimsy.

'Of the entire train, do you mean?' Cumberledge responded. 'In 1861, yes. The Bombay Express left Poona at seven in the evening and was never seen again.'

'What happened to it?' Quigley asked, squelched.

'History offers nothing but wild conjecture. But it carried 127 officers and men of the Warwickshire Regiment and any number of Hindus. Plus, of course, Lady Bantling, her children and their paternal uncle, Colonel Horace Bantling of the 15th Hussars.'

'Never seen again?'

'I thought everybody knew the story,' old Cumberledge murmured peaceably. Behind his chair, his granddaughter Amy put her thumbs to her temple and wiggled her fingers. She was a child of extraordinary beauty, even seen in the half-light of what would have been the sitting room in any other circumstances. Quigley admired her firm young bosom, surely not got from mixing flour-and-water paste for her grandfather? He dragged his mind to the matter in hand.

'For a consideration, my clients are interested in murders, unsolved, involving young women, perhaps in a country setting.'

'By gunshot, stabbing, strangulation or poison?' Cumberledge asked at once. 'If poison, by rare agents or household products? Presenting symptoms of wasting illness or sudden and convulsive disorder?'

'Probably not poison. Strangulation the most likely.'

'Ah yes. By cord or rope, scarf, stocking or other underclothes; or manually? By day, at night, in public or domestically –?'

'In the Wallingford area.'

Cumberledge sat back with disappointment written all over his face.

'My dear Captain Quigley. You have made it too easy for me. Amy, would you reach down Murders, Unsolved, Berkshire?'

Quigley gazed appreciatively as the little minx fetched a library step and strained to reach the topmost shelf, on which were ranged the most recent files. He saw by what means her girlish bust had been developed. Cumberledge sat with his head in his hands, genuinely dashed.

'From memory, in recent years there have been eleven recorded cases of unsolved murders in Berkshire and adjoining parishes of Oxfordshire, of which seven were probably instances of domestic violence.'

'Wifey bashed over the head with the garden spade,' Quigley suggested. 'Husband does a bunk, never seen again. Lodging with relatives in Norfolk.'

Cumberledge stirred slightly in his chair, taken by these imaginary details.

'Norfolk?' he mused.

Amy dropped a folio into her grandfather's lap and announced that she must go out and buy a bit of fish for their supper that night. Quigley was sorry to see her leave, enough to give her the old lascivious wink, getting in return the tip of her tongue pushed between cherry red lips. Oblivious, Cumberledge searched the ledger.

'Ah! A person that might interest you is a Miss Jane Dorriman of Laburnum Lodge, Newbury. Not Wallingford, of course, but not entirely unadjacent. Daughter to the locomotive engineer and designer Negley Dorriman.'

'There are people in the world called Negley?' Quigley wondered.

'Now – it says here – residing at Portland Place. Can that be right? It must be a very lucrative business designing steam engines. Is the family armigerous at all?'

He stood, looking distracted.

'I have here somewhere a file of prominent persons from the world of industry presently resident in London, cross-indexed by length of residence.'

'Do not trouble yourself, old cock.'

'But I think I must.'

While he squirrelled, Captain Quigley read an inch or so of yellowing newsprint. Jane Dorriman was nineteen years old at the time of her death. Her character was described as unblemished. She lived a quiet childhood in Newbury until brought to London by her widower father for a medical consultation about her asthma. She was found in Hyde Park with her clothing disarranged and her throat cut. Quigley came upon what he was looking for in the last two sentences of the Reuters report, touching on the bereaved father's anguish. Negley Dorriman was a director of the Great Western Railway.

Urmiston went to Portland Place later that day. He was shown by a butler into a high-ceilinged room where a plumply nondescript kind of man sat with a shawl round his knees, hands clenched in his lap. The furniture and decorations were in impeccable taste but it was plain to see that Mr Dorriman took no pleasure in them. At the side of his chair was an occasional table crammed with medicines.

Even after Urmiston had completed his introduction, the engineer sat as if mute, his eyes blank.

'I know who you are, Mr Urmiston,' he said after a long pause.

'We met socially once, sir, at the time I was employed by the company.'

'I remember that. And the case that provoked your dismissal.'

'Mr Dorriman –'

'I have not left this house for nearly three years. I think you know the cause. At first I thought I could control my grief. I toured the world – can you picture that to yourself, Mr Urmiston? I taught myself to hunt and shoot. For a while I had with me a girl I represented to the greater world as my daughter. I took her to places Jane had always wanted to see.' He glanced. 'I was of course quite deranged. I don't suppose I exchanged more than half an hour's conversation with the poor creature in all that time.'

'What happened to her?'

'We parted in Calcutta. More specifically, she ran away.'

They sat in silence for a while. A servant came in, bearing a bottle of wine and one glass. Dorriman indicated by a wave of his hand that Urmiston alone should drink.

'Jane was my only child. You must not think of her as a simpering miss. Sparks flew from her. She was the flint. Bolsover was the powder.'

The shock of hearing this name so casually introduced brought Urmiston bolt upright. He so far forgot himself as to jump up and walk the room. Dorriman watched, dabbing at his mouth with a cambric handkerchief.

'If I had not recognized your name, I would not have had you admitted, Mr Urmiston. You can say if you like that I have been waiting for you. We are two ruined men, destroyed by the same villain. There may be others like us. Are you going to patrol the carpet or will you sit down again?'

'I beg your pardon.'

He sat, his emotions churning. Again, Dorriman waited.

'You met Lord Bolsover?' Urmiston asked at length.

'He was her murderer, there can be no doubt. Yes, we met at dinner in the Café Royal. He said something insulting to Jane and she replied, with more than a little force.'

'Is it possible to ask what was the nature of the insult?'

'It was a remark of such indecency that I took him to be drunk. There was a scene such as happens when one meets boorish people and we left the restaurant without completing our meal. Twenty-four hours later, my daughter was dead.'

'You say there can be no doubt as to Lord Bolsover's guilt.'

'I have none in my own mind. It happened that the Prince of Wales was dining at a nearby table that night. He sent a note to our hotel reprehending Bolsover's words and actions and saying he had made known his displeasure to the author of them. The next morning, when walking in Burlington Arcade, Bolsover accosted us and called us upstart swine. A better man than I would have struck him. I should have knocked him to the ground. Or at the very least slashed my cane across his face.'

'Your daughter was found in Hyde Park?'

'Not very far in. It was thought she had been dragged from the pavement in the Bayswater Road.'

'And had she a reason for being in that vicinity?'

'She was walking back to our hotel.'

Dorriman broke his composure long enough to touch his cheek. There were tears running into the lined and weary face. Urmiston bit his lip.

'Forgive me, sir. These are shocking stories yet they do not constitute proof of who killed your daughter.'

'What has made me rich, Mr Urmiston, has been the twenty-seven patents held on engines designed by me. I have seen the product of my inventions at work in nine different countries. I am in every other respect an unimaginative man. I cannot prove but I *know* Bolsover is guilty of that crime.'

'When Jane was discovered, you of course at once alerted the authorities. You made known to them the story you have just told me?'

'I went to the police, yes. You have to imagine willing but not very intelligent men. I urged them at the very least to take a statement from Lord Bolsover. This they were very loath to do. In the end it did not matter. Bolsover had fled to France that very morning.'

Dorriman smiled wanly.

'The verb is mine. It was explained to me with great patience that he had gone to Paris to attend a reception at the British Embassy. He travelled over with the Foreign Secretary. This made a great impression on the investigating officers. That, and the singular fact that a month later, he used some of his wealth to endow a missionary charity in Oxford.'

He wet his lips with the tip of his tongue.

'I received a letter about this great example of Christian philanthropy from William Ewart Gladstone. It seemed to him inconceivable that the man I was pursuing so relentlessly could be what I said he was. Mr Gladstone had prayed hard and long for guidance on the matter. He could not rid his mind of the idea that I was very close to a charge of criminal slander made against a true-blue Englishman.'

'How could he make such a reckless assertion?'

'He and the Second Earl were at Christ Church together. Bolsover's father, you understand.'

'But how does that alter cases?'

'According to Gladstone, never was a more pious man. There was in time a coroner's inquest at which a verdict of murder by a person or persons unknown was returned.'

'Forgive me, but you never thought to take the law into your own hands?'

'It happens in novels,' Dorriman admitted, brushing feebly at the rug over his knees. He turned his head away towards the window and, after a few moments, Urmiston realized that the interview was at an end.

Walking back down Oxford Street, he thought of going to see Bella and laying before her this latest crumb of the story but the noise and the crowds worked on him like an opium dream. Here were hundreds of men who were not Hagley or Bolsover; and as many women who were not Jane Dorriman. They streamed towards him, their minds on hats and shoes, toffee apples, schooners of sherry, wedding veils and feather beds. They were the innocents.

Literature could not make heroes or heroines of them, any more than Urmiston could stop one in his tracks and tell him about a man with a rug over his knees whose daughter was so casually murdered in the Bayswater Road by a peer of the realm.

THIRTEEN

For a third morning running, the sky was overcast. An intolerable night of damp sweats gave way to daylight streaked with brown. The house stank and opening all the windows made things, if anything, worse.

Bella lay in the bath, reading and smoking her first cheroot of the day. The water was unheated but she had forced herself to make this her summer practice. For Marie Claude (who appeared briefly to snatch a kimono from the chair) cold baths were an infallible sign of Anglo-Saxon stupidity. As for reading in the bath, that was, in her opinion, simply trying to appear clever.

'You would not read in the sea.'

'But I did. Last year, in Etretat.'

'You must always have the last word,' she shouted, before flouncing out. Bella threw her book at the door and clambered out after it. Her skin was reddened, her heels an alarming blue. She wrapped herself in a towel and padded back to her bedroom goose-pimpled and contrite.

In all the earlier Margam novels she had found a plot that borrowed from the world she knew best, of garden parties and musical evenings, gossip and intrigue. The books were popular because the violence was largely sexual.

Pistols were brandished to intimidate weepingly indecisive women and girls too young to realize the effect they were having on out-and-out villains invited the kind of frenzy that had them locked in steamer trunks or tied hand and foot in railway carriages careering down the track to Carlisle.

Naked, she studied herself in the pier glass, seeing a healthy woman with much more of the peasant about her than she would care to admit. Her hips were broadening and there was a roundness to her belly she deplored but could do nothing about. Without shoes to pitch her forward a little, she appeared a very solid figure indeed. Moreover, she reflected gloomily, one more than usually anxious, a new thing for her.

Still naked, she marched to Marie Claude's room. Dressed in the silk kimono, the Frenchwoman had returned to bed, her arm dramatically flung over her brow.

'It is disgusting, what you do,' she complained. 'To walk about without a robe.'

'I wanted to ask you about Mr Urmiston.'

Marie Claude's shrug sent the kimono up round her ears.

'I have no opinion.'

'He has an enemy, a bad man. He wants to kill him.'

'Men always want to kill each other. It's very childish. To kill, you need big hands and that big jaw, like an ape. Not little hands and a long nose.'

'Do you still love me?' Bella demanded suddenly. The question astonished her more than Marie Claude.

'Mrs Venn is bringing me some coffee,' the young girl warned in a small voice.

'Could the question be any simpler?'

Like a mouse diving behind the curtains, Marie Claude burrowed into the bedsheets, shrieking.

'I cannot bear to live like this another hour!' Bella said.

She turned and fled, meeting the housekeeper at the top of the stairs.

'If not with her, then without her,' Captain Quigley repeated.

He and Urmiston were sitting in the snug of the Six Bells, where the Captain liked to sup and meditate his next moves. His manner was unusually quiet, not because of any special burden of thought, but rather that he had in the past waged a campaign to empty the pub of its rowdier and more jocular elements, either by sarcasms or fisticuffs. He liked the present arrangements better. Where market porters had once drunk themselves into a stupor there now sat meek little tally clerks and the better sort of cabmen. In this new calm, Quigley had installed himself as the equivalent of President of the Mess. The booth they sat in was reserved exclusively for him. It was known as Quigley's Corner.

The two men were of course talking about Bella. As if to signal that the leadership of the group must change, Quigley was wearing the kind of braided cap favoured by park-keepers and missionary explorers. It was also a day for medals. The Captain had four, all got from a junk dealer in Old Compton Street. One was English, one French and two Turkish. The ribbons to all of them had been refurbished from the same bit of scarlet silk found in the gutter outside this very pub.

'I think she has gone as far as she wishes to go,' Urmiston agreed.

'I don't say as how I'm surprised. What's left of this is men's work.'

'As to that, it may be too early to praise God,' his companion warned, speaking as much to himself as to anyone else.

In front of them was a page torn from a child's atlas, depicting a political map of Western Europe. Britain was coloured pink, France an unusually pale green. Prussia spread like an emerging purple bruise. The Captain smoothed the sheet with a none-too-clean hand and blew a little smoke across the Channel.

'France,' he observed. 'Paris. The Hotel Louvois.'

Urmiston felt dismay sweeping over him. He did not like to dampen Quigley's enthusiasm, nor to throw obstacles in his path, but the thought of the two of them wandering the Left Bank together left him horribly underwhelmed.

'Lucky for us you speak the lingo,' Quigley continued, very blithe. 'Though we might consider taking old Solomon with us as a sort of local guide. Comes from Trier. Father a distinguished rabbi in those parts. Dead now, at a guess. Pushing up the German daisies.'

He peered at the map.

'Paris a different kettle of fish,' he admitted. 'Can you think up some wheeze to fetch his lordship back to London – some guise or pretext, as they say?'

'I cannot.'

Though it was hardly past ten in the morning the Captain was on his third brandy and water. It was abundantly clear to everyone except himself that he did not have a huge appetite for the descent on Paris. He drummed absent-mindedly with a box of matches.

'Bring Billy Murch in, possibly,' he said. 'Maybe this sailor I was telling you about – Stoker Miller. Good man in a tight corner. Four of us. Travel light, live off the land if necessary. Weapons? Pistols, I think.'

Urmiston cut him off before he could go any further.

'I am going back to Shelton Street, Captain. I suggest we both give this more thought before we involve anyone else.'

'Ha! Cold feet, is it?'

'As you yourself have observed on more than one occasion,' Urmiston snapped testily, 'time spent on reconnaissance is seldom wasted. Or, as my grandfather was fond of saying, measure twice, cut once.'

'You had a grandfather, did you?'

Urmiston rose and walked out on stiff legs. By a huge effort of will he managed to control his irritation and crossed Covent Garden looking much less like a stalking pigeon. By the time he got to Mrs Bardsoe's, he was in a cheerful, even a skittish frame of mind.

Waiting for him in Mrs Bardsoe's downstairs parlour was the man Urmiston least expected to see.

The Reverend Anthony Hagley did not trouble himself by rising but sat very much at his ease in a red plush chair, reading his Bible. When he raised his eyes from the page, they were the colour of flint. The two men examined each other, much in the manner of a *Punch* cartoon for which the caption had yet to be written.

'Vircow-Ucquart told you where to find me,' Urmiston guessed.

'He is in hospital. The German Embassy has been informed and is considering its position. There may be diplomatic consequences.'

'I can quite believe he is in hospital. The rest I do not credit.'

Hannah Bardsoe came in with coffee, her lips set in a straight line. The clerical visitor had left her distinctly unimpressed and some of her black mood seemed to be directed at Urmiston also. In the middle of her ministrations the shop bell went.

'Leave that tray to me, Mrs B,' Urmiston said, springing up.

'Which there is very little milk and none at all of cake or biscuit,' she said sourly. 'On account of we are not a hotel.'

Hagley ignored the rebuke, save for a faint lifting of the eyebrows and the smallest of smiles. Urmiston trembled. The hand that poured the coffee shook.

'Such is domestic bliss,' Hagley suggested with a smirk.

'I wonder why you are here to witness it.'

'I can hardly claim I was in the neighbourhood. I am in London to attend a meeting at Exeter Hall. Your situation has changed a little since we last met, Mr Urmiston.'

'And yours too, I understand. You are now at Oxford, I believe?'

Hagley brushed away the remark.

'Let us come to cases. You and your confederates – one of them a ruffian calling himself Quigley – will cease this foolishness forthwith. If you don't, I shall take steps to see that you do.'

'Very little of threat in that. Were you present at the murder of a poor Welsh girl, not half a mile from here?

– 161 –

Did you help in getting the killer away? Or was that Vircow-Ucquart's job?'

'A Welsh girl?'

'Don't play with me, Mr Hagley. You are aiding and abetting a murderer.'

Hagley seemed startled, not so much at the accusation as the tone of voice Urmiston employed.

'These allegations are all very heated. I wonder at you, Mr Urmiston.'

'Nevertheless –'

'Ah, there is more to be said, is there?'

'This one last question, yes. Were you also present in London the night Miss Jane Dorriman had her throat slit?'

Hagley brushed the front of his coat with two or three passes of his hand, a sign to those who knew him well that he was very angry indeed.

'I don't know how you came to fall in with the man Quigley but you would be well advised to break off the connection.'

The two men sat staring at each other while Mrs Bardsoe's clock ticked on the mantelpiece and the boards of the shop creaked as she moved about on the other side of the door. Hagley had learned the knack of dominating an awkward moment – he sat as still as a china cat. It was Urmiston's heart that was going like a trip-hammer. More extraneous sounds: a handcart passing in the street outside, its iron rims ching-chinging on the cobbles. A child's voice screeching. A dog yelping. Still Hagley did not move a muscle. Urmiston wetted his lips.

'Miss Dorriman's father is neither a thug nor a bully. I have found him a most responsible witness.'

'What airs you give yourself, Mr Urmiston.'

'His daughter was murdered in the most foul way imaginable, some would say by the hand of a madman.'

For a moment it seemed as though Hagley was going to let that go by. But then he reached for his coffee cup with the greatest possible display of negligence and managed a mild laugh.

'You have conjured a deal of moral indignation since your dismissal from the Great Western, Mr Urmiston. You are harbouring a grudge the size of Gibraltar, my dear fellow. Lord Bolsover is no more capable of murder than I am. And, just to be clear about it, no madman either.'

'I have yet to mention that gentleman's name,' Urmiston pointed out in a quiet and trembling voice. 'I am grateful to you, therefore, for confirming it to me in such a frank and open way.'

In the deathly silence that followed, Hagley's cheeks flushed and he seemed to find difficulty in controlling his hands. Urmiston watched, his chest pounding. But the Reverend Hagley had been this way before. The fight for his self-possession finally subsided. He pulled out a silver hunter from his fob and managed a theatrically elaborate sigh.

'Ask the person who works in the shop to send out for a cab, will you? I am a little pushed for time.'

'You may find your way to Cambridge Circus and search for one there. I should tell you, Mr Hagley, your friend will be hunted down and destroyed, like a mad dog. He will end up in a ditch with holes in his waistcoat, whether here or in France, it makes no matter.'

A muscle jumped in Hagley's cheek.

'You ridiculous little understrapper,' he exclaimed. 'You think you can speak to me in this way? You think you can utter any threat you like against a gentleman of irreproachable character? I shall have you taken up in charge for it.'

'There is a police station in St Martin's Lane. Let us walk down there together. I shall welcome the chance to make a statement.'

'And what will that amount to? The testimony of a man who was dismissed his post, presently living in a slum hovel? Against the word of a gentleman? You are forgetting yourself.'

'The night before Lord Bolsover killed Miss Dorriman, he excited the indignation of the Prince of Wales who was dining at the same restaurant and overheard some of what was being said. According to today's Court Circular, the Prince returns from Aldershot this morning. Tomorrow I intend to lay the facts as I know them before him and ask his advice about what to do next.'

Hagley's contempt was bottomless.

'And where will that interview take place? At his club?'

'Wherever His Royal Highness is gracious enough to receive me.'

'You poor devil. I really fear for your mental condition.'

'But I don't think it is *my* mental condition that has brought you to London this morning.'

Hagley flushed and slapped the table with his Bible, enough to make the cups rattle.

'Damn your impertinence, Urmiston.'

He looked up as Mrs Bardsoe entered.

'The Reverend had best be off, oaths and all,' she said. 'For I have took the trouble to send for Billy Murch who I know would like to debate him on several points.'

'Murch?' Hagley asked, bewildered.

'Concerning the German gentleman who lost his nose recent.'

Hagley turned back to Urmiston.

'You are swimming in very deep and treacherous waters. I will not be threatened.'

'If you walk to the top of the street and turn left, you will come eventually into Cambridge Circus,' Urmiston murmured. 'Good day to you, Mr Hagley.'

'You are a fool, Urmiston. You always were a weakling but I had not realized the extent of your naïveté. Someone is behind this – not you, not your ugly friends, Quigley and this other fellow just mentioned –'

'I wouldn't call Murch ugly, sir, not to his face, oh no, not for a thousand pounds,' Mrs Bardsoe warned, her face brick red.

Hagley flapped his hand as if batting away a housefly.

'This has nothing to do with you, madam. You will oblige me by holding your tongue.'

'And in my own parlour!' Mrs Bardsoe exclaimed wonderingly.

'I came here to warn you,' Hagley said to Urmiston. 'There will be no more criminal interference in my affairs. Whoever is pulling the strings in this sorry Punch and Judy show had better beware. They are out of their depth.'

After he had left, hardly before the shop bell had ceased vibrating, Mrs Bardsoe turned to her lodger. She took his hands and bounced them against her chest, her eyes dark with apprehension.

'I don't know what all that was about but you saw him off. My word, you gave him what for.'

'I am terrified,' Urmiston muttered.

'Of him? Some jumped-up parson?'

'I am fearful of what I have brought to this house.'

'Well,' Mrs Bardsoe allowed, 'there's never been a dull moment since you first hung your hat on the peg, that much I grant you.'

Impulsively, Urmiston took hold of her soft and doughy upper arms and kissed her. He was aiming for her cheek but she turned her head expertly and their lips touched, hers fragranced by liquorice, from a twig of the same she used to clean her teeth in the mornings. The kiss became an embrace.

'Now!' she said, pretending to be shocked. 'Here's a nice thing to come out of a few harmless remarks, I must say.'

'How lucky I am to have met you, Hannah,' Urmiston whispered.

'That's still to find out,' she said, her voice muffled by his shoulder. 'But I should take it kindly if you was not to get your head blowed off before we go any further down this particular road. I aren't altogether stupid, my dear. You are up to something.'

'There are vile people in this world, Hannah.'

'And don't I know it. The less we have to do with them, the better I shall like it.'

He smiled and kissed her again, more lingeringly.

'Is Mr Murch truly coming here?'

'If I am not mistook, that is him coming through the shop at this very instant,' she said, disengaging herself with a final peck on Urmiston's chin.

It was not Murch, but Bella. One glance was enough for her to realize what she had interrupted. Hannah Bardsoe's distracted laugh and Urmiston's burning face told the story.

'Which I shall just run round to the Welshman for a can of milk and a bag of buns,' Mrs Bardsoe cried, sweeping her forearm over her hair.

'I have come to apologize for how I spoke to you recently,' Bella began. 'I know Quigley is representing it as desertion. But I am a writer, Charles, not a warrior. And neither are you. I beg you to let it go.'

'Which is the greater enormity? To kill him or to let him go scot-free? It's a moot point, don't you think? Hagley –'

'Yes, what of him?'

'He was here. You missed him by two minutes.'

'He was *here*?'

'He came to warn me off.'

Bella searched his face with her fine grey eyes.

'This is bringing things very close to home.'

'I think I realize that.'

'All right,' she said. 'I admit it: I am happy not to have met him. What is he like?'

And at once snapped one hand into the palm of the other, annoyed with herself for providing Urmiston with proof that she was living this crisis at second hand.

'Not one word spoken of Marguerite, not one recognition of my widowerhood. But cheap jibes directed at Mrs Bardsoe and this house, that he is pleased to call a slum.'

'And how did you answer him on that?'

Urmiston flushed. His silence touched Bella to her heart.

'It is not in your nature to play the avenging angel,' she said. 'You are too kind, too gentle. We – all of us – would do better to draw a line and let it all go hang. I am appalled at what you are planning.'

'I take it you have been speaking to the Captain.'

'Not half an hour since. He is for setting out today or tomorrow, crossing by the Folkestone boat. I came straight round to warn you.'

'It is my day for warnings,' Urmiston said in too light a tone. 'I am scarcely enthusiastic about the idea, Bella, as I think you realize. And it has occurred to me more than once that your novel will do for Bolsover what I may fail to do in life. I mean, destroy him. But I cannot leave it as it is. I cannot.'

'You mean three decent and generally harmless men will go to kill a fourth, upon the mere suspicion of murder? I could not write such a plot, not even I. Are you really such a man of action?'

'You are right, I am not, not in the least. But I shudder to admit that I am a man capable of this one isolated action. Yes.'

'Then I must come with you,' Bella declared.

'The Captain has described our expedition as man's work,' Urmiston pointed out.

'I am not coming to load your pistols for you. It is to save you from the consequences of knowing Captain Quigley. And to bring you home safe to those who love you.'

At which, though it was a most general remark, Charles Urmiston blushed. Pat upon her cue, the shop bell rang and Mrs Bardsoe bustled in, talking, as was her habit, the moment she crossed the threshold. Before Urmiston became her lodger her remarks were addressed to the empty air. But now, as Bella had divined only too well, she had an audience only dreamed of since the death of her husband.

'And I suppose you have been gassing about the reverend gentleman's visit,' she said, dumping her bag of buns on the table.

'We have been talking about sandcastles,' Urmiston said. 'And how it is wise never to build them too close to the tide.'

'I have seen many a child's heart broke for that reason. What a fund of common sense you have.'

Bella laughed delightedly and kissed her on the cheek.

'We do not needs buns, we need a good bit of halibut. If Syrett's is still in business round the corner, let us sit down together at one of his little tables and do justice to his fish.'

'And if you don't have a memory like an elephant!' Hannah Bardsoe cried admiringly. 'Syrett's! I haven't been there in many a moon.'

They crossed to France the following morning in flat calm. Though there was fog in the Channel, Bella and Urmiston sat in deckchairs abaft the saloon. Quigley and Murch were inside. It was the Captain's fond belief that the smoky and fussy little steamer carried what he called Ship's Bitter, an almost fabled restorative, best drunk with a mutton chop and a plate of mashed potatoes.

'And if that's not available, a glass or two of the India Pale Ale, Billy. And for ballast, a Melton Mowbray and some pickled red cabbage. Maybe a plate of ham on the side.'

'That purser,' Murch observed idly, 'is none other than Walter Neary, that used to have the Rose in Coleman Street.'

Quigley peered.

'Buggered if you're not right. It's a small world and no mistake.'

The thought cheered him through half a dozen bottles of Ind Coope.

Mr Neary's duties took him to pass the time of day with the deck passengers and in this way he happened on Bella and Charles Urmiston. They agreed it was a disappointing morning for telescope work, more was the pity, for the purser had it of the first mate, who had it of the captain, that Admiral Sir Geoffrey Thomas Phillips Hornby was in passage that morning with the battleship *Alexandra*.

'A rare sight, madam. A passing rare sight.'

'You are a long-serving sea-officer yourself, Mr Neary?' Bella enquired.

'Bless you, madam, I should say so,' Mr Neary lied amiably, who came from Hoxton and until this present service had never been nearer the sea than Margate, where his sister-in-law kept a brothel. He saluted and paced slowly away, his hands clasped behind his back.

'What a staunch-looking fellow,' Urmiston murmured, causing Bella quite visibly to wince. By a slight diminution of the thrumming noise made by the deck plates, she divined that Calais was in the offing. There was a piercing shriek from the ship's siren as the vessel cut like a blunt knife through the becalmed French herring fleet. Quigley appeared at the saloon door, wiping froth from his whiskers. His face could not conceal a certain unease, not to say outright anxiety.

'It is like watching a child hesitating to jump into a river,' Bella sighed. 'I wonder I have put with him all these years.'

'Mr Murch looks the part, however.'

And this was true. The lanky Murch had the knack of posing, one shin crossed over the other, his battered top hat tipped at a jaunty angle. People excused themselves to him as they streamed from the saloon to catch their first whiff of France. The Captain they simply pushed aside by the small of his back, cigar or no cigar. Quigley had left behind his peaked cap and was sporting a wide-brimmed straw. He resembled the French painter Courbet, had Courbet legs no longer than a Shetland pony.

Bella asserted her authority on the train to Paris by taking this ludicrous headgear and skimming it out of the window, where it sailed into a glassy river covered in harvest dust.

'Sunstroke to follow,' Quigley lamented.

'We are not travelling in the deserts of Mexico,' she retorted. 'Nor is it necessary to shout when addressing the natives. Nor to examine the contents of a sandwich before eating it. What Mr Murch calls meat paste the French call *rillette*, which is delicious.'

'Handsome,' Murch admitted. 'If a trifle salted.'

The sandwich had been offered by an elderly woman whose piglet was peering morosely out of a jute sack. She was, she explained to Urmiston, on her way to see her daughter in Ménilmontant, she who had so recklessly married the first man she met. This had taken place on market day in Rouen, not bad weather, raining a little but what can you expect of March? Who could have foreseen it? No sooner had the old lady turned her back to buy a yard or two of embroidered tape – for the chairs, you understand, that her own dear mother had bequeathed and were now most cruelly in want of repair (for which she blamed the cat – not a bad cat, in fact a furious mouser, though like all cats of an independent turn of mind – and blind in one eye), anyway, no sooner had she turned her back but what Suzette was snaffled by a discharged soldier with one arm. Worse than that, a Parisian.

'*Et maintenant,*' the old countrywoman added triumphantly, making a pun of how she had been snaffled, '*elle est fauchée comme les blés.*'

'Stony broke,' Bella supplied.

They took a cab to the Hotel Louvois on the Left Bank. It was not, as Urmiston had guessed, of the first rank, but neither could it be said that it was modest. Its keynote was a seedy flamboyance. The five-step marble staircase was attended by two doormen in ankle-length green overcoats, their top hats buffed to a shiny gleam and finished off by broad white satin bands from which the ends hung loose. What looked like an elegant clientele could be seen taking lunch in a yellow-and-gilt salon and the sound of a string ensemble floated out across the pavements.

At the Captain's suggestion, the English party made a pretence of peering into the Seine for a few minutes, the better to inspect comings and goings on the opposite side of the road.

'So, can you picture our man staying at a gaff like this?' Captain Quigley asked Urmiston.

'Very easily. The three girls going in now do not have entirely the appearance of innocence, for example.'

'Professionals, you'd say. And the old cove with them in the top hat –'

Bella started forward.

The man entering the hotel was Lord Broxtowe.

FOURTEEN

'I am here for a funeral,' Lord Broxtowe explained with sly good humour. 'My cousin Ferrensby. Nice man. Lived here for more than forty years. Married a dancer in his youth, exquisite chit of a girl. She died in '62. They were very much in love, you understand. Ferrensby the most enormously fat man with as much wit as a cabbage. But kind.'

He smiled at Bella.

'Did you perhaps harbour some other, darker explanation for my presence?'

'I was amazed to see you, was all.'

'I used to come to Paris for venial pleasures quite often as a younger man. But in the end – have I mentioned this before? – everything palls. I am in the hotel here with Dr Duddington, the fellow you met at Goodwood once. The good Bishop Duddington. A person of irreproachable morals, Bella.'

She remembered a man half Broxtowe's age, as plump as his friend was gaunt and blessed with a truly beautiful shy smile.

'Has the funeral taken place?'

'Yesterday,' Lord Broxtowe confirmed. 'Duddington did the honours. Damn good turn-out and in addition a very decent class of people. The Ambassador's wife came to the service and I gather the Mayor of Paris was there too. It seems that Ferrensby endowed not one but two ballet schools and a dogs' hospital. The French like that sort of thing in an Englishman.'

Lord Broxtowe's suite overlooked the river and he asked Bella to drag a small couch to where they might sit side by side and watch the barges fuss past. In one, perhaps a hundred cattle were standing patient and unmoving, their heads held low, as if listening to the river chuckling under their hooves.

'Little do they know what awaits them,' Broxtowe said. 'Though I'm told that when they smell the blood of the abattoir they can get fractious. As I think I shall, when the time comes.'

As was his way, he held Bella's hand lightly in his and for a long time he seemed to be dreaming, his pale lips moving in the unconscious manner of a very old man. When he spoke again, she was startled.

'I am very disappointed to find you here.'

'Why should you say that?' she asked uneasily.

'I am guessing at your reasons. You will end as a corpse in one of your own stories before you have finished.'

'I am in Paris very unwillingly,' she allowed. 'In one sense, to protect a friend.'

'Not that ghastly fellow Quigley, I hope.'

'Hardly, though he is of our party.'

Lord Broxtowe nodded. For a while his eyes returned to the river, where the water was broken up into silver streamers by the passage of another barge, this one with washing strung from the wheelhouse to the forward hatch.

A bold woman stood at the prow, arms akimbo. Bella was taken unawares when he gently disengaged his hand from hers.

'Mark me, Bella: you will do better with a pen than a dagger when it comes to someone like Bolsover. I take it that's your purpose in being here?'

'Yes.'

'You should go home. I only wish I had the power to make you.'

There was a knock at the door and the silver-haired Duddington drifted in. Over his clerical vest he wore a linen jacket of the kind worn by some gardeners. Pickwickian glasses hung from the sagging top pocket.

'My dear Mrs Wallis,' he said at once. 'What a pleasant surprise.'

'I'm astonished you remember me, my lord,' Bella exclaimed.

'We met at Goodwood. You wore the most wonderful hat that day. I will not attempt to describe it but it – and the wearer –' he added gallantly – 'have long stuck in my mind.'

'Duddington's good at this sort of thing,' Lord Broxtowe muttered.

The bishop smiled his angelic smile.

'I think I was offered champagne half an hour since.'

'Then be a good fellow and give a tug to the sash thing over there. Our friend Marcel will oblige us.'

Henry Treloar Duddington was as well connected a bishop as any who sat in the House of Lords. His wife was a lady-in-waiting to the Queen when she was at Windsor and a rich woman in her own right. The two were devoted to each other.

'We were discussing earlier,' he explained to Bella, 'whether there is ever a wrong hour for champagne. My wife, for example, takes half a pint at breakfast in a silver mug. That is a very appealing sight. Your friend Broxtowe here is of a more sentimental nature. Or perhaps the better word for it is traditional. For him champagne goes with red plush and candlelight, face powder and pier glasses. Garters, even.'

'That is true,' Lord Broxtowe grumbled. 'But since you are exhibiting your worldly side, Duddington, I will tell you straight that Mrs Wallis is here to meet that infernal swine Bolsover. Not to meet – meet is quite the wrong word. To confront.'

Duddington made her a polite but noncommittal nod.

'Well,' his friend complained tetchily, 'you might say more.'

'I take it you already know the nature of the man. I have met him twice, once as it happens here in Paris. Indeed, in this very hotel. A dissolute, Mrs Wallis. I would say a woeful desperado. You would do well to steer clear.'

'Thank you for that,' Lord Broxtowe muttered.

'Have you heard he is in Paris?'

'I cannot be sure,' Bella said.

'Then –?'

Duddington's glance was quizzical, in the warm manner of a clever fellow with all the answers. Bella bridled.

'I have reason to believe he has killed at least two young women,' she said. 'In the most hideous way.'

Duddington blinked. He was saved from replying by the knock and entry of a hotel servant, bearing a silver ice-bucket of champagne. Marcel was one of those grave and unsmiling servants who manage to convey the manners of the better sort of undertaker. He bowed courteously but briefly to Bella.

'Marcel, would you be so kind as to fetch another glass for our guest? And perhaps a plate of those little cakes, tiny little cakes, that look like rosebuds?'

'*Avec plaisir*, milord.'

Duddington waited until the door closed.

'Let us come to cases, Mrs Wallis. Do you have proof of these accusations?'

Bella hesitated. She saw that Duddington was capable of more expressions than a winning smile. His face was now composed into an attentive seriousness and his whole demeanour was no longer that of a chubby and gently-mannered angel. While he waited for her answer he took the spectacles from his breast pocket and polished them slowly on the hem of his jacket. His eyes never left hers.

'A street girl was murdered in London a fortnight ago,' Bella said. 'Her throat was slashed with a razor. I will not trouble you with the details but I am at least certain that Bolsover was in London that night and at the scene of the crime. I have no direct proof that he was the killer.'

'Then – forgive me – are you wise to take him on?'

'Bella would like to settle his hash,' Lord Broxtowe observed testily. 'At the very least, push him down a long flight of stairs or something of the kind.'

'I must tell you both, I have friends who have come here prepared to kill him.'

'Well,' Duddington responded, 'I hope they will attempt nothing of the kind. There is a Christian text to hand –'

'– Vengeance is mine and so forth –' his friend supplied.

'Exactly. You would expect me to say as much, I am sure.' His tone was very sombre. Bella gave him a polite nod, realizing what a faintly ridiculous figure she must cut. She could see that the bishop enjoyed the company of women quite as much as his friend Broxtowe but never perhaps as an unwilling accomplice to murder. She cast about for a change of direction.

'May I ask how and where else you came to meet Lord Bolsover?' she asked Duddington.

'At Windsor. He recently gave over a part of his fortune to found a missionary enterprise in Oxford – but I see that you know about this. The Queen was interested in him – there are many bees in that poor sad woman's bonnet – and he was to have been presented to Her Majesty. However, her secretary Ponsonby is far too nimble a fellow to encourage any such thing and he was shown the door. The man who took his place was an insufferable little squit called Hagley. Or as he styles himself, Principal Hagley.'

'Duddington won't at all mind if you do for him,' Lord Broxtowe chuckled.

'It *is* jolly, I suppose,' the bishop chided, 'in the way that all evil is if you stand far enough back. But of course I have a professional duty to go down to the ringside, as it were. There it is not so pretty. I will tell you what you may already know, Mrs Wallis. Hagley is here in Paris. He had the vile impudence to attend the service for poor Ferrensby yesterday morning and to my utter amazement actually tried to engage in conversation with me.'

'Did he know Lord Ferrensby in life?' Bella asked.

'So he claimed. I doubt it very much.'

She was agitated enough to rise from the couch and walk about the room. Through the window she could see Billy Murch lounging against a parapet, hands plunged into his pockets. Even in such an indolent posture, there was enough about Murch to make those who strolled past give him a wide berth. There was danger in him and the idea of that gave Bella strength.

'I am hoping Mr Hagley will lead me to his friend.'

'You must forgive me: but is that really your concern?'

'He kills women, my lord. He has not yet killed a bishop.'

'Withdraw that remark,' Broxtowe snapped, red spots in his cheeks. Bella blushed.

'I apologize.'

Duddington smiled. 'My intention was never to patronise you. But I was once told – by no less an authority than Darwin – that you can never outrun an enraged bear.'

He glanced at his friend and Broxtowe nodded.

'I cannot tell you where Mr Hagley is today but I know how he can be found. When Marcel comes back in, we shall put the problem to him. I do not like what you are attempting – indeed I heartily deprecate it. But I see you cannot be altered in your course.'

'Far better you were put over someone's knee, given six on your bottom and sent home,' Lord Broxtowe exclaimed absent-mindedly.

Duddington's blush was a wonder to behold, rising from his neck into his cheeks in a single instant. Bella anchored her lower lip between her teeth to prevent making matters worse.

'No, but seriously, Bella, you are standing in the anteroom to hell,' her old friend ruminated. 'Leave it be, while you still have chance.'

She was to remember this remark a very long time.

It was not Marcel that they met later in a café in Rue de la Huchette but his nephew Jojo. He was a grave and courteous boy with a shortened right leg and a convict's haircut. His linen was clean and though his suit was threadbare, it was well-brushed.

'I will make enquiries,' he said to Bella in a voice that was barely more than a whisper.

'I must tell you, M'sieu Jojo, this is a gentleman – how shall I put it? – of a certain disposition. We may say having unusual interests and desires.'

Jojo smiled faintly. Bella was about to say more when Urmiston laid his hand on her wrist. The boy made an almost imperceptible nod of gratitude.

'We are who we are, madame,' he murmured, causing Bella to blush in furious shame. 'Do you have a hotel in this quarter?'

'The Dacia. Quite close by.'

The Frenchman nodded.

'Give me four hours,' he said, rising and shaking hands with all of them in turn.

'Well,' Captain Quigley blustered, when Jojo had limped out, 'he don't exactly get my vote.'

'A civil enough cove, though,' Murch objected.

'We should eat,' Urmiston said. 'Here is as good as any place and our friend will come back before midnight.'

'Run after him, Charles. Run after him now and give him my apology,' Bella said, flushed.

'And what apology's that?' Quigley wanted to know.

But Urmiston was gone.

He caught up with Jojo quite easily, crossing the Seine by the Petit Pont. Urmiston proposed a further glass of red and they walked into the Ile de la Cité to a small corner bar, kept by a man who nodded amiably to them both.

'Is Marcel truly your uncle?' Urmiston asked in the most conversational tone he could find. The question still sounded horribly obvious. Jojo smiled.

'He is my mother's brother. We come originally from Boissy-Saint-Léger. His kind – our kind – are not easily tolerated there. You realize of course that he recognized at once the man you are searching for. But he has to be discreet. It is also in his nature,' he added.

'Has your uncle ever mentioned another Englishman, a milord? Who has also stayed at the Hotel Louvois in past times?'

A faint wince of irritation crossed Jojo's face.

'I am not a police spy, m'sieu. I do you this small service tonight as a mark of respect for Marcel. Whom I admire. Tremendously. And that is all I will say.'

'Forgive me, but I must ask –'

'You want to know how I will recognize M'sieu Hagley. We are not engaged in a wild goose chase, I promise you,' the boy whispered drily. 'I do not promise what I cannot deliver. But now I must ask you a question. Has the gentleman met you? Will he recognize you?'

'We are old enemies.'

'Then you must surely return to your companions. Tell me what you want to know about him.'

'Where he stays, at what hotel. And most importantly, what he is doing here in Paris. And where he plans to go next.'

The boy opened his hands briefly and then with a sigh let them fall back to the table.

'What you really want to know is whether Freddie is in Paris with him.'

It took Urmiston a moment to recognize the name but then he nodded.

'At this moment, I cannot say. And now, I think, you should rejoin your friends. Where I go next you would not wish to follow. And in any case –'

Jojo pointed with his chin through the window of the café. The man perched on a stone hitching post, smoking peaceably, was Murch.

'Just keeping an eye on things,' he explained when Urmiston joined him. 'This here church behind us. Would that be the Notre-Dame at all?'

'Does Mrs Wallis not trust me one jot? Am I to be forever followed about like a child in need of a nanny?' Urmiston cried.

'She loves you better'n a brother,' Murch said gently. 'Come away and watch Quigley eat his pigeon, which he has ordered. It will be a sight for sore eyes.'

He took Urmiston by the crook of his elbow and so they retraced their steps. Halfway across the Petit Pont, Murch laughed.

'I forgot to tell you. Hannah Bardsoe reminds you to lay off the garlic, which she considers the devil's work.'

Urmiston experienced a sudden flood of yearning for his landlady. At this hour, when dusk was falling over London like purple soot, she would be grappling with the written word. She was a devoted fan of Mrs Ioaze-Bonnett's works and was halfway through *Jake Masterman, River Pilot*, a story she followed with moving lips, her hand inside her blouse, spectacles balanced on the pudge of her nose.

'Are we wasting our time, Billy?' he found himself asking, slowing to a halt and staring into his companion's face.

'Don't you know how very matter-of-fact these things are, Mr Urmiston? As we might say, simple to grasp and understand? I have not come here to look at churches. When the time comes it will be better that you are off to one side, so to speak. Stay a step or two behind the game. The same goes for the lady and Captain Quigley. But I have the stomach for it.'

Shockingly, he held his bony hands in front of him, unmistakably miming a stranglehold. His crossed eyes held Urmiston's.

'Little Alice Tarrant – Welsh Alice as we called her – was never close, as you might say. But I knew her since a babby. Among our class of people, we know what to do. It's not pretty, always, but we look after our own. You will see.'

Quigley managed his pigeon, Bella and Urmiston ate veal, and Murch investigated an omelette Savoyarde, a dish that so utterly delighted him that he rose and shook the patron's hand, mumbling cockney thanks.

'*Un vrai type,*' the burly M. Texier commented, though secretly pleased, enough to present a *digestif* to the whole table.

'Now this is more like it,' Captain Quigley opined. 'For want of a pack of cards, I say we wait the evening out with a round of ghost stories. Mrs Wallis to be handicapped by the stewards as follows: that she does not speak for more than two minutes by this old watch.'

This was agreed. The most interesting of the four tales that resulted was Murch's. In his days as a fencing master, he was walking home one night when he chanced upon a man with a naked sabre tucked under his arm.

'Make that a dark and stormy night, Billy,' Quigley suggested.

'It happened to be as calm and starlit as you like. There never was a quieter sky. I first came across him in Lamb's Conduit Street –'

'Now why on earth was you up there? You said you was on your way home –'

'Will you *please* shut up!' Bella exclaimed. 'Go on, Mr Murch.'

The fencing master was intrigued enough by the man with the sabre to follow him across Theobald's Road and into Holborn, so to the top of Drury Lane. He took him to be an actor in costume and was on the point of catching up and explaining that to carry a sabre about without its sheath was asking for trouble, the police being what they were. But before he can say a kindly word, the gentleman turns in at the White Hart. Murch paused for effect.

'The Captain can confirm that is a very ancient pub indeed.'

'I can, I do. So, to make no bones, when you gets inside, he is not there, the cove.'

Murch stared at Quigley for a full half-minute.

'He was not there. But on the floor was a woman, hacked to pieces most dreadful. I know the sabre, do you see, and these were sabre cuts. Her blood was running out of her in rivers and her eyes already glassy.'

Murch looked at them each in turn.

'The only problem was nobody but me took a blind bit of notice. It was busy enough, I'd say very busy. I said to myself, never having been to this particular house before, I said, what kind of people are these?'

Urmiston stirred uneasily.

'You were transfixed, I imagine, Mr Murch.'

'I would say more outraged. More – I have heard the word used – incensed. I take one pace inside the place and –'

The door to the café opened and Jojo staggered in, his shirt red with blood. He fell to the floor, taking a chair and table with him.

The café's patron, Texier, was quicker than any of them, rushing from behind the bar and kneeling beside the boy, Jojo's lolling head cradled on his knee. He bent his head to the dying youth's lips and listened as the blood bubbled. At last he looked up.

'Hotel Malines, Rue des Pommiers,' he said.

'Is he dead?' Bella whispered, distraught. 'This wasn't Hagley. It can't have been Hagley.'

'One of you must find Marcel,' Texier ordered. 'Bring him here.'

'Did he say the word Hagley to you?'

'Madame, pay me the courtesy of doing as I ask. Run and fetch Marcel. I have something else to do.'

'I'm coming with you,' Murch said.

'I will come too,' Urmiston said, rising.

Murch pushed him back down into his seat. Texier walked behind his counter and produced a short axe. Though he spoke no English, he could read ice-cold anger when he saw it in another's face and passed Murch a wooden billet, painted black.

'Have a care, Billy,' Quigley muttered.

'Mrs Wallis to find Marcel and bring him here. You and Mr Urmiston to tidy up. Take the boy into the back and have him laid out proper. Then go back to our hotel. You understand? Go back and wait. Let there be no ifs and buts about any of this.'

Texier said something that Bella translated.

'He says that it is not strictly our quarrel.'

'Tell him Murch begs to differ.'

He nodded to Texier and they left.

The Malines was a homosexual brothel from its front step to its fifth floor. Texier announced his intentions in the lobby by swinging the axe and decapitating a plaster statue of a naked shepherd boy. Two youths sitting on a red velvet couch fled, one directly into the street, his peignoir flying.

'Armand,' the manager remonstrated in an agitated voice, his hands fluttering. 'Did any of us know this was going to happen?'

'The boy bled to death on the floor of my café.'

'Mon Dieu!'

'We shall speak later, Albert. Where is he?'

When he got no answer he swung the axe again and buried it deep into the *comptoir*. Murch, who spoke no French at all, could understand well enough the burden of what was being said. He reached across and plucked the man clean out of his cubbyhole, sending him sprawling on to the marble floor. Before Armand could stop him, he brought his billet down on to both exposed shins. There was a spurt of blood: the manager had half bitten off his own tongue.

'I will ask you again,' Armand murmured.

They ran up the stairs, pushing aside tiny shoals of boys who screamed at their approach. On the third floor there was a suite. Texier spat on the palm that was to hold the axe. Murch pushed him gently aside. He raised his boot and kicked in the door.

Inside was not Principal Hagley, but Vircow-Ucquart. He sat at a table, drinking with his companion, who jumped up as soon as he recognized Armand, his hands folded over his bare chest.

'It has nothing to do with me,' he screamed. 'I only came in ten minutes ago! Armand, you must believe me!'

Vircow-Ucquart sat stock-still, a gauze veil over the lower half of his face, his one good eye unblinkingly calm.

'What he says is true,' he grunted. 'You have come for me. Make it quick.' He spoke in English.

'Where is Hagley?'

'Would I tell you?'

Later that night, when the story of the Englishman and the German was told in the café, Armand supposed Murch to have been a butcher by trade. Using only the black truncheon, Murch reduced Vircow-Ucquart's body to a set of broken bones, first the major skeleton and then the fingers, wrists, ankles, knees.

'You and I would have slashed in fury,' the patron said in an incredulous whisper, '*mais, mon Dieu*, with him I saw something completely different. The German bore the first two or three blows in silence – oh, a brave enough man, yes – but then he seemed to realize what was befalling him. Crack! Another bone shattered. He began to cry.'

'He sobbed for mercy,' someone suggested.

'No,' Armand corrected. 'He cried, like a child. He gave up his soul, like a child.'

'The Englishman killed him.'

Armand shook his head and poured another Armagnac with meticulous attention. The company watched him uneasily. A passer-by entered the café, caught the mood at once and retreated. The silence was unbearable.

'He died,' he said at last. 'When we left, he was still breathing. But there was nothing left in him that was human. Please God I never see such a thing again.'

The dining room of the Hotel Dacia was unlit and had already been set for breakfast but the proprietor, a woman, cleared away a table and provided what she thought of as appropriate to the occasion: a piercingly dry Muscadet and some thirty-year-old cognac, almost as thick and smooth as honey. Marcel sat and sipped, his hand shaking only very slightly, his expression inalterably grave.

'He was an excellent boy. His mother had him late, you understand, and died of the fever in bringing him into the world. He was raised by my second sister as her own, a little runabout child with a fistful of flowers in his hand as often as not. There are a few good souls in Boissy who remember him with affection and that's where he'll be laid to rest.'

Bella gently placed her hand over his and after a moment or so, he sighed out a smile.

'I am perfectly calm, I think. Mr Hagley and the German were, as you suspected, guardians to the mad one, Lord Bolsover. I do not think he is here in Paris. The German, we know about. His body is being taken by barge to a certain location beyond the limits of the Prefecture; it travels in a sack of cobbles and one supposes will resurface in the fullness of time. Months, maybe.'

'And Mr Hagley?' Urmiston asked in a low voice.

'Has fled. I imagine back to London. I can find out if you wish. It was probably the German who killed Jojo. But Monsieur Hagley was there, we can be certain.'

Urmiston shook his head.

'I think Bolsover was also there. I think he killed the boy.'

'If he did, he is a dead man.'

'Marcel, we all of us feel a great guilt for the grief we have visited on you,' Bella said, tears in her eyes. Marcel smiled.

'About grief, madame, we can say that it is like love, a cake that cannot be cut more than two ways.'

Quigley, who had said nothing for a quarter of an hour, scraped back his chair and offered Marcel his hand. The eloquent simplicity of the gesture caught the Frenchman off guard for a moment but then, as his nephew had done only a few hours earlier, he shook hands with each of them in turn.

The person missing from this midnight meeting was Billy Murch. He stood in the shadows of the Gare du Nord, arms folded, his back against a grimy brick column, seemingly half-asleep. Once or twice whores accosted him. He pushed them away gently with the flat of his hand. A drunken soldier came to harangue him. After a few moments of trying to waken a response in coal-dark eyes, the man saw the danger he was in and weaved away. Not until three in the morning did Murch give up his vigil – and then only because he was moved on by a caped gendarme with the same flinty expression as his own.

'Why the Gare du Nord?' Quigley whispered when he finally arrived back at the Hotel Dacia.

'I had the idea they would try to flit.'

'What, at this hour of the morning?'

'I would, if I were them.'

'Marcel says the bloke that runs the brothel knows nothing about no Lord Bolsover.'

'That's what he said to me,' Murch said calmly. 'To begin with.'

Quigley was not a Catholic and barely a churchgoer in any sense of the word at all, but when he heard this last remark of Billy Murch's, he did as he had seen done from time to time, and crossed himself vigorously.

FIFTEEN

Immediately after Jojo's stabbing, Hagley had the presence of mind to dress Bolsover and himself and run downstairs. As in a fairy story, their way was signposted by little rivers of blood. They picked up a cab up in the Boulevard Raspail, two drunken and dishevelled figures who might just conceivably have been to dinner with friends. Bolsover, quite horribly, was laughing. Hooligans in opera capes.

'*Eh bien?*' the cabbie asked.

Hagley's thoughts were wild as unbroken horses.

'A St Denis,' he commanded.

'Rue St Denis?'

'*Non. La ville mê me.*'

It was ten kilometres distant. To make his meaning clear, Hagley opened his pocketbook and thrust a handful of banknotes at the man.

They travelled with the blinds down and Hagley absolutely forbade his companion to speak a word during the journey, which seemed to last for ever. From time to time on the road out of Paris he peeked into the dark that was the real France, as contrasted with the naphtha flares and electric light strings they had so recently left behind. Bolsover lounged in a corner of the carriage, drinking brandy from the neck of the bottle.

The cabman was frail and grandfatherly but not stupid. He could recognize disaster when he saw it. To the huge fare was added as much again to stop the man's mouth and more yet to have him find them a crabby hotel behind a brickworks. The windows were shuttered and not a light showed anywhere. As Hagley banged on the door for attention, the cabbie slapped the reins over his horse's rump and neck and disappeared into the dark. Bolsover, released from the injunction to remain silent, bellowed after him like an enraged ox.

The unshaven brute who finally admitted them was in his nightshirt and reeked of alcohol. There was a ridiculous scuffling as the three men negotiated a short passage side by side and tumbled into a bleak reception area. Bolsover at once ordered champagne. The man leaned past him to spit on the floor.

'Wine,' he corrected. 'Or nothing at all.'

'We require rooms,' Hagley said in a shaky voice.

'I am sure you do. You will of course be gone by seven in the morning.'

'What kind of a hotel is this?' Bolsover asked.

'One known to the police,' the man said meaningfully. He tossed a key on to the desk. 'I have one room vacant. There is a bed and a couch of sorts. You will find nails on which to hang your fine clothes. Sleep well.'

'The wine,' Bolsover reminded him.

'But of course. The finest our cellars can provide.'

The room stank of cheap perfume and the bed was unmade, the bottom sheet rucked up and stained. Hagley opened the window and unhinged the shutters. There was a view of a hundred yards or so of ruined meadow, beyond which the brick ovens roared. Bolsover threw himself on to the bed and began to laugh.

'Is this really so funny?' Hagley scowled.

'Why stop here? Why not press on to the Marne? Or further still? There must be a deserted mineshaft somewhere where we can eat mice and grow our beards for a year or two.'

'Would you prefer prison?'

'I have heard such very dull reports of it. They say the room service is abominable. How lovely you are when indignant, incidentally.'

Hagley sat on the filthy couch and stood up again immediately. The pain of being sober was as terrible as toothache.

'You killed that boy,' he yelled.

'He was annoying me. And who is to say he is dead?'

'Of course he is dead. How much spilt blood does there have to be?'

'Do I need a sermon at this hour of the night? I think not. Where is this place?'

'We are in St Denis.'

'Really? The Duchess of Berthon-Gaultier has a villa here, did you know? We went in a party to lay flowers at the statue of Marie Antoinette. Another cheap whore.'

'You have just murdered someone,' Hagley shouted.

'And what if I have? Vircow-Ucquart will sort things out. He loves playing nanny.'

There was a knock and the patron entered with a bottle and two water glasses pinched between his fingers.

'You can be heard downstairs,' he growled. 'Drink your wine, sleep it off and then sling your hook. There is a train back to Paris at five past the hour, every hour. I will wake you at six.'

'Do you offer weekly rates?' Bolsover enquired. 'This is such a fine hotel, I can't imagine why people would ever wish to stay at the Ritz.'

The man hitched his nightshirt and scratched his groin. He addressed himself to Hagley.

'Make it clear to your nancy friend that I was a guest at Vincennes before I took this place. If he says anything amusing I promise to laugh. Right now I am debating whether to throw him through the window there.'

'He is tired and the medicine he is prescribed has mixed badly with an evening's drinking.'

'Is that so? I don't really give a shit but if you value your freedom, keep your voices down.'

'Spoken like a gentleman,' Bolsover said. 'Stay and have a drink with us. And do carry on scratching your balls. It's charming.'

'You don't listen,' the patron decided. He took an easy step forward and punched the Third Earl of Bolsover to the carpet. Blood spurted from his nose and he began a choking fit. 'Both of you can clear off right now.'

'There will be no more trouble,' Hagley promised in an agonized whisper.

The hotelier held out his hand for money, and yet more money.

'Everything's fine,' Hagley said. 'You haven't seen us, we were never here.'

'My lips are sealed,' the man said sarcastically.

After he had gone, Hagley helped Bolsover to the bed and washed his face with water from the jug and ewer.

Loosened his tie and waistband, removed his shoes. Opened the shutters wide and peered out into the night. Lit by the red glow from the brickworks, an emaciated pony cantered around, sometimes silhouetted, sometimes moving like smoke.

'What a strange evening,' Bolsover said absently, a handkerchief to his swollen nose.

'This is the last time I try to save you from yourself,' Hagley replied bitterly.

'I think that's wise. You have no great aptitude for the task.'

'Has he broken your nose?'

'I don't think so. I found it arousing.'

'You don't know what you're saying any longer, Freddie.'

For the rest of the night, Hagley sat over his friend like an anxious nanny, listening to the caa-caa of his snore. His eyes ached and thoughts darted like bullets through the fog of what had happened to them. It grew light shortly after four and when he saw what desolation they were in, he put his head in his hands and prayed. And, like a man suddenly flung furthest from God, wept.

True to his word, the patron of the hotel woke them at six. It amused him to see them in evening clothes, drinking a bowl each of foul coffee, their bread rolls untouched on the pine refectory table at which his guests took all their meals. An army of flies swarmed.

'The station?'

The patron pointed laconically. 'That way the brickworks. That way the station.'

The train they took back to Paris was filled with commuting workers, some of them with sacks of tools between their boots but some quite clearly waiters and bar staff. From these they attracted very sharp glances, all the more because Bolsover, in the ruins of his evening dress, cadged cigarettes and kept up an inane monologue about Marie Antoinette.

They dived into a Turkish bath next door to the terminus station. Were shaved by an attentive Algerian, had their clothes sent out to be sponged and cleaned. Lay in the steam room, surrounded by walrus-like figures. Hagley, but not Bolsover, staggered to a tiled alcove where he was hosed down by a naked attendant. He asked the time. It was barely nine o'clock. While he cowered under the hose, he heard a loud and imperious voice ordering champagne.

A contrite Bolsover was far worse than the same man drunk. He cried, he flung his arms round Hagley. His naked flesh wobbled and the sweat that ran from it was an ugly grey.

Because they had once been lovers, Hagley submitted to the tears and the distracted gestures. He knew he should send to the brothel and find out what had happened after they left. Then he must track down Vircow-Ucquart and make him get Bolsover away, maybe into Germany for a while. He should *act*. Instead, Bolsover clung and blubbered, not letting him move an inch. Their naked skin slid and skidded.

'Nobody has loved me as you do, not since the day I was born.'

'That isn't true, is it?' Hagley said, bitter. 'Tomorrow you will feel quite differently. You will forget the pain you are feeling now.'

Bolsover looked at him, his eyes very dark. Hagley knew what he had just said was the truth. Tomorrow, in clean linen and with his hair re-curled, his former lover would revert to playing the fallen angel. The clock would run backwards to the time when his theatrical beauty was at its most irresistible. He would be a different kind of child altogether. It was a shock to realize that he hated Bolsover, loathed him to the roots of his being.

'I have to return to England,' he heard himself saying.

'A feeling that has swept over you very suddenly, I take it?'

'Perhaps I am trying to distinguish between work and leisure.'

'Work?'

'I am the Principal of a missionary college.'

'How you have learned to prate since your elevation. We shall have you writing pamphlets soon. A bishopric beckons. In New Zealand, possibly. Would that be far enough away?'

'Be sensible, Freddie. I am only thinking of our safety.'

'You are thinking of your own skin.'

'Yes,' Hagley said.

'Then go.' Bolsover sulked, searching for his towel.

'You should do the same.'

Bolsover stood, flecks of spit in the corners of his mouth.

'I will not be betrayed, d'you understand?'

Hagley felt a terror rise in him.

'This is not the time to speak so wildly.'

'It is a solemn warning. You and I will come to a reckoning one day,' Bolsover promised.

It was not the threat contained in these words but the utter impossibility of dealing rationally with him that sent Hagley away to dress. Locked inside a mahogany cubicle, his hands trembling, he said his goodbyes to the man who had seduced him from being a licentious parson to an accessory to murder. In other circumstances he would have tried one last reconciliation. But this was a day for finalities. It was, he reflected ruefully, a day for betrayal.

He made no attempt to search for Bolsover in the bowels of the premises but stepped out into classic Parisian sunshine. For some reason he thought it better to find his way to the Rue des Pommiers on foot and so it was that he went, about as conspicuous in the streets as a sailor wading ashore from a shipwreck. His whole body trembled and only with great effort could he prevent his teeth from chattering.

When he came to the brothel, he found that during the night the place had burned down. All the pretty boys had escaped unharmed, a vicious old concierge from across the street reported; but M. Albert, who came originally from Marseilles and whose house it was, was taken away by ambulance minus his front teeth and with both arms broken.

'And as I explained to M. le Commissaire Garnier, that doesn't happen just by falling downstairs,' the woman concluded comfortably, at the same time eyeing Hagley with the sort of close attention that policemen love. He raised his hat to her and walked back out into the Boulevard Raspail, his linen wet with sweat. His whole being had the effect of floating. He had read somewhere there were spiders that travelled hundreds of miles across the Pacific

Ocean, borne along by their own gossamer. Whether they ever found dry land again was a matter of chance. That was exactly his case.

It occurred to him too late that he had gone to the Rue des Pommiers to ask after Vircow-Ucquart. It caused him to falter in his step only for a second. Wherever he was, the German was on his own. As for the once-bewitching Freddie, for all Anthony Hagley cared, he could stay in the Turkish bath until he died. The thing now was to get away. To flee. There was common sense in that useful word. Whatever the future risk, he should run, and keep running. He should teach himself to believe that what had happened was a specially hideous nightmare.

SIXTEEN

Urmiston had barely slept, tossing and turning on a mattress that sagged with the imprint of a hundred other bodies, the oval mirror by the washstand thickened by flitting ghosts of men and women he would never meet. Twice in the night he got up to push open the shutters and lean on the sill of the open window, staring out at the dark, his body trembling.

On the second occasion – or had he dreamed this? – there was the faintest knock at the door. When he opened it, Bella stood there in a crushed and damp nightgown, straight from bed. Her expression was blank enough to suggest sleepwalking but then she lifted her arm and brushed her hair away from her brow and her eyes came into focus. He found he could not speak to her. The two figures stood either side of the threshold for a full minute before Bella turned and floated away down the hotel corridor. Her bare feet made not the smallest sound.

When he came down to breakfast he was revolted by the faintly caramel stink of the unaired rooms. It was as though yesterday, like a recalcitrant guest, had refused to leave. Bella sat with him, mute and grey-faced. They passed toast and coffee to each other without making a single eye contact. Murch and Captain Quigley sat apart, at a table on the far side of the room. It filled Urmiston with a thick rage that they seemed to be acting and talking normally, as though the previous night they had done nothing more dangerous than smoke one cigar too many.

'Murch has to go,' he heard himself saying.

Bella looked up.

'You have changed your tune, I think.'

'I thought I had the guts for this but I see now that I don't. There's nothing wrong with Billy – he's a brave and resourceful man. But I want no more of it. If you like, a little late common sense has surfaced.'

'Perhaps you are saying it is you who must go.'

'I think that must be it,' he said stiffly. When she stared him down, he added, 'We have killed someone, Bella.'

'I have killed nobody.'

'Because we came to Paris two people are dead. You don't see that? Are we merely characters in some book by Margam? Two people who were alive yesterday are dead today.'

'You might wish to keep your voice down.'

'None of this is worth one line of literature.'

She half rose in her seat and slapped him hard against his cheek, her eyes blazing. A dozen heads turned.

'I think three days ago in London you were lecturing me on the moral obligations you felt that I, apparently, did not. How dare you speak to me in this way?'

She pushed back her chair and left the breakfast room, walking fast and soon enough breaking into a run. Bewildered waiters stepped aside to let her pass.

Murch – brisk, close shaven, his wiry hair flattened with water – quitted his conversation with Quigley to join

Urmiston. He had left the hotel earlier and bought a single rose from an old lady humping a wicker basket of them down the Boulevard St-Michel. It was intended for Bella. He laid it on the table in front of her empty place.

'Want to say what that was about?' Murch enquired in his calm and steady way.

'You might make a guess.'

'Won't say? We came to do a job, I suppose?'

'I can go no further,' Urmiston heard himself saying. 'In any case, I think we have all come too far. The question is, whether we lay what we know before the police.'

Murch rapped his nails sharply on the lid of the coffee pot.

'There will be no talk of the police. Where has she gone?'

Urmiston shrugged. When he finally left the table, he forgot to bring the rose with him.

Half an hour later, the four of them found each other again in the foyer of the hotel. Fellow guests were assembling, studying maps and flyers from restaurants and bars, sharing information with their neighbours about museums, churches or simply the best way to Montmartre. In this timid but noisy gathering was a pale man with blond hair, carrying an easel and a case of tubes and brushes. Seeing a quartet apparently undecided how to spend their day, and very much wanting to advertise his own reason for being in Paris, he hovered nearby, smiling shyly. When he finally plucked up the courage to speak, his greeting was in German.

'Just what we need,' Quigley muttered.

Only Urmiston could face talking to him.

Dressed in corduroys, his neck decorated by a faded square of red silk, the slender Herr Mueller wore a leather harness, on the back of which was a beech frame supporting several canvases.

'You see at once my purpose in being here,' he explained happily, turning so that his work could be inspected. 'I have never before painted this way, never with such blue in the palette. Can you see? It is almost a spiritual quest. At home –'

'Yes, where is home?'

'In Münster. We are farmers there, shopkeepers. Churchgoers. Here it is a little like looking into heaven.'

'I do not paint,' Urmiston muttered lamely.

'No, but come with me! I show you where I set my easel! It is not far. I beg of you, sir.'

Urmiston would gladly have followed him all the way home to Münster. He felt as light as thistledown. But immediately he stepped outside the frowst of the hotel, he felt better. The staff were hosing down the pavements in front of the building with silvery ropes of water and a stirring breeze pointed to a cloudless sky. Mueller waited with his ridiculous wooden harness, like a milkman who has lost his churn.

When they reached the Seine, he indicated some steps leading down to the river, as if welcoming Urmiston to his studio. The painting he was making of Notre-Dame, when reverentially unwrapped from its cloths and set up on its easel, was – to Urmiston's untutored eye – very good indeed.

'You have some genuine ability, I would say.'

'You are kind. But oh, if only I had words to describe what is in my heart!'

'You have the painting.'

'Yes,' the artist replied after a moment, deeply gratified. 'You are in Paris long? May we meet later and talk?'

'Alas, I go home today.'

'Such a pity. You are a man who understands life. I can see that. I myself must return home soon. And then the dream will fade.'

'Is that all this is? A dream?'

The German's face fell. 'Maybe I don't express myself so good. At home, yes, I have all that a man might wish – wife, children, pupils, patrons. In my garden find an apple tree, under which I may sit –'

Out of the corner of his eye Urmiston noticed Captain Quigley and Billy Murch, waiting for him on the opposite pavement. He excused himself and crossed the road.

'The Captain and me are staying on for a few days,' Murch said in a low voice. 'We will see the boy buried in his home village.'

'You don't think it wiser to make yourself scarce?'

'We'll come to no harm. We'll be back in London the end of the week, beginning of the next.'

'Billy –'

The Captain squared himself up, looking up and down the street with what he hoped might seem a keen eye.

'All discussed with the lady of the party, deployment of forces agreed.'

'Maybe I should come with you to Boissy. Indeed, I think it my duty.'

Murch shook his head.

'Mrs Wallis is very low. She will need someone to see her home. I don't say this to cause offence, but you too are in no state to hang on here a moment longer than is necessary. With the Captain and me, things is different.'

'How, different?'

'Look here, Charlie,' Quigley interrupted them in a kindly voice. 'The boy is dead. We can't put that right but me and Billy have been this way before. We know what has to be done.'

'I can't discuss this on the street,' Urmiston said, far more shakily than he intended. 'Come back to the hotel.'

'It's all decided,' Murch contradicted gently. 'You should go home and forget the whole thing.'

'Forget! Do you think I shall ever forget last night?'

'I don't lose my temper with you, Mr Urmiston, but put it this way. Just do as you're told.'

'Let us at least go to where that poor boy was murdered and see what else we can find out.'

'Nothing much left to look at.'

His expression was completely neutral but Quigley understood at once. He knew what smoke smelt like when it penetrated wool and serge. The bedroom he had shared with Murch stank like Paddington Station, a simile he had employed when they rose to shave. Only now did it make sense.

'Wake up to it, Charlie,' he said. 'These are marching orders he's giving you.'

With that, the two friends set off for Armand's café, Quigley stepping straight off the pavement and walking across the Boulevard St-Michel in an unwavering straight line, as though the morning traffic did not exist.

Down by the Seine the painter had removed his jacket and jammed a straw hat on his sparse blond hair. Watched with envy by Urmiston, he lit the first pipe of the day and gazed in rapture at a Paris innocent of all nightmares. Under the wide brim of his hat, he further shaded his eyes with his hand, like a child looking into a sun-filled bay.

Urmiston walked slowly back into the hotel.

Halfway home across the Channel, the ferry gave a single blast on the ship's whistle, slowed and hove to. Those in the saloon, seeing the sailors' dark blue guernseys running past the windows, joined the deck passengers crowding the starboard rail. There was a faint edge of panic flooding over the ship, not made any the less by the stentorian boom of a bosun telling everyone to keep calm. A foolish woman screamed: the mob of people swayed as if struck. Against her will, Bella set down her coffee cup and followed outside.

In the lee of the ferry, two men were clinging to a greasy yellow spar. A third body bobbed in the chop of the waves. It was the corpse of a shoeless child, his shirt inverted over his head, his arms outstretched.

Once the ferry passengers realized they were not themselves in any danger, there was a ghoulish interest in watching the rescue of the survivors. A deckhand jumped over the forepeak to secure a line to the dead boy. Horribly, he was cheered. Even more horribly, he waved his appreciation.

Bella forced herself to watch, though with only half her mind on the scene. She had gone to France to protect Charles Urmiston and in that she had failed catastrophically. At this moment, he sat on a slatted bench, his back to all the commotion. Although things between them could not be made any clearer, there was enough of the slighted woman in Bella to be huffed. Not for the first time since she began writing the Margam novels, someone had taken her to be far stronger than she actually was.

'A mere child,' a woman passenger observed, indicating the tarpaulin under which the dead boy lay. 'Were they all drunk, do you think, to be smashed into like that by some other vessel?'

'Is that how it pleases you to think?' Bella asked.

'Well, I don't know!' the woman exclaimed wonderingly. 'I was only asking a civil question, I'm sure. I beg your pardon for speaking at all.'

Bella pushed her gently aside and walked to where Urmiston sat.

'Are we to carry on like this indefinitely?'

He looked up at her with empty eyes.

'What has happened?' he asked.

'A fishing smack was run down in the night. But I asked you a question, Charles.'

'I cannot answer. I cannot think.'

'That is sentimental nonsense.'

'I am not the person I thought I was,' he whispered.

'And if I say I need you?'

He looked up, shaking his head.

'And that others may need you even more?'

When he did not reply, she walked back into the saloon. There, a florid man was passing around his billycock hat, soliciting donations to the welfare of the fishing-smack survivors. A little silver and a single banknote lay in the bottom.

'They're from Ramsgate, the lads. Never stood a chance. Two others, one of them the boy's father, gone to the bottom.'

And, she thought bitterly, how well you shape the story, how complete the dotting of the i's. How simple it all is.

'Do you know the name of the sailor who jumped into the sea to save them?'

The florid man stared at her.

'Devil I do. It ain't hardly about him. He was doing his duty, brave lad that he is. This is about widows, missus.'

The deck plates began to thrum and the ferry came round by its head. Bella opened her purse.

'Your husband out there has took it bad,' the man said, nodding to the figure of Urmiston. She glanced. He sat with his head in his hands, cloaked in misery.

'What is it?' Hannah Bardsoe wanted to know.

'I think we can call it Street Scene with Tabac,' Urmiston said, his voice trembling. 'Those blue tables are where the local people sit to gossip.'

'And did you sit there in your turn?' she asked carefully. 'And are those tables really blue, I mean in life?'

She propped the little canvas against the teapot and stood back, lips pursed.

'You took a fancy to it,' she decided.

'I bought it for you, Hannah, if you will accept it.'

'For me!' she cried.

'I thought we might go there one day. Sit down at an empty table – see, there is one, next to the red door –'

'You bought me a painting?' she asked, unsteady.

Urmiston sat down in her spoonback chair and, putting his head into his hands, burst into tears. He did more: he began howling like a dog. Nothing would comfort him, not a word, not her warm arm around his shoulders.

'My dear, my dear,' Hannah cried, terrified out of her wits. He disengaged her arm and flung himself out of the room, running upstairs, his howling turned to urgent barks of despair.

'Whatever have you done?' she screamed after him.

In the picture, a kind of soporific calm prevailed. Herr Mueller, the innocent from Münster, had painted the little bar in the Rue de la Huchette as though it were a way station on the road to paradise. A figure – maybe Jojo, maybe a girl, but anyway represented by a single stroke of red – walked away into the rapturous blue fog Mueller had discovered while smoking his pipe and trembling for joy at the glorious abundance of the material world.

SEVENTEEN

At Orange Street, there was a note from Marie Claude. She had accepted an invitation from Fern Jellicott to go painting and sketching in Cromer. If Bella could remove herself to Paris at only a few hours' notice, then why couldn't she, Marie Claude, do as she wished? They were hardly married, she added spitefully, and it was her own money she was spending. Mrs Venn confirmed: the mam'selle had set off with four pieces of luggage – dear Lord, enough for a visit to the ends of the earth. She was wearing the steel-grey dress Mrs Wallis had bought her in the spring, and had sent to the Burlington Arcade for a box of watercolours. It arrived soon after she left.

Bella was too tired to be angry. She went to Marie Claude's room. In the pages of fiction it would have been in wild disarray, with discarded scarves and scattered shoes everywhere. But the Frenchwoman had habits of tidiness that would not have disgraced royalty. The bed slept soundly under its silk cover, the little green chair dozed by the empty hearth, the studio photograph of Bella (from Mr Debenham in Regent Street) was centred exactly on the mantelpiece. It was as though Marie Claude had not left the previous day, but some months ago.

While she was still poking about – the sponge as big as a cat had gone from the bathroom, along with the blue-and-white kimono – there was a distant knock at the front door and Mrs Venn dragged herself upstairs to announce that she had shown a gentleman into the drawing room.

'A Mr Philip Westland, who has called on the off-chance of seeing you and so forth.'

Bella ran downstairs at the risk of killing herself.

'I got as far as Cairo,' Westland explained. 'Hated the people on the boat, set up at Shepheard's, fed the gazelle they have wandering about in the gardens there and just could not bring myself to rejoin the party. They sailed without me.'

'Oh fie,' Bella said. To Westland's amazement she burst into tears.

'I half hoped you might be pleased,' he muttered, greatly embarrassed. She flung herself into his arms.

'Have you ever read a work of fiction?' she howled.

'*Pickwick Papers*. Does that count?'

'Philip, you are come like a knight in shining armour, just when I need you most. I can't tell you how unhappy I am.'

'How happy I am to hear it,' he said drolly, kissing her first on the forehead and then on her lips. 'Should we sit down, or should we go out somewhere? Would the Café de Paris suit?'

'No, it would not. Would you consider taking me away out of London altogether? I mean for a day or two? I can't think where, but far, far away. And not Cromer.'

Westland studied her. His gaze was so intense that she could not meet it and dropped her chin to her chest.

'For a day or two, I think you said.'

'I cannot deceive you with the promise of anything else.'

'Has it occurred to you that I might have jumped ship at Cairo for a reason?'

'It has,' she admitted, blushing. He smiled.

'You are too honest, Bella. But I will tell you this. My cousin has a cottage he keeps for me at his place in Shropshire.'

'You would take me there on such meagre terms? A chance to run away for a few days in the company of a bad-tempered woman?'

'I should of course say no. And thrice no.'

At last she looked up.

'And what do you say?'

'First, we will sit down and you will tell me why you are so unhappy. Omitting nothing, Bella. I have not come home to be beguiled by mysteries. You must speak frankly, the way they do in bad plays.'

'I cannot tell you everything.'

'Then tell me nothing at all and I will be on my way.'

She pulled him to her side and told him everything. He listened; in places he laughed. When she came to what had happened in Paris his eyes darkened and he took her hand in his.

'This fellow Urmiston. You say you went there to look after him? Is he some kind of special ninny, then?'

'You and he would get on well, the way men do. But I am not his nurse, no. And acting jealous doesn't suit you, Westland.'

'I suppose I am jealous, a little. I feel the need to invent some rival personalities, like the flame-haired Mrs McCorquadale, or Aaisa, the Berber temptress. But what it is truthfully, Bella, I care even less for this fellow Margam, who has led you into such reckless danger.'

'I said I was unhappy earlier. I should have said I was miserable. I am trying to get you to see me as I am. Margam is part of it but nothing like as dangerous a companion as you wish to make out. He puts the bread on my table.'

She put up her face to be kissed.

'Nothing and no one stands between us,' she whispered.

'Except Miss d'Anville perhaps.'

The unexpectedness of this remark and the flatness in his tone jolted her upright. She had described her relationship with Marie Claude in completely honest terms, something she had never before attempted to do before another living soul.

'Think about it, Philip. She is very young. One day – it might be tomorrow – she will take wing and fly.'

'In the present circumstances, doesn't that come a little too pat?'

'Have you been listening at all? I returned from Paris in turmoil I could never have imagined. Until you came, I was at my wits' end. And then this, something wonderful. Could I care less what happens with Marie Claude?'

'I don't know,' he said with dreadful heaviness.

She rose and walked the room, very shaken by the turn the conversation had taken. Westland's eyes followed her.

'I held you to be the person most likely to understand who I am, who I really am. As you demanded of me, I have told you everything. If everything is not enough, then let us part now.'

For a moment she thought she had lost him but then he sighed hugely and asked if she had a Bradshaw's in the house.

'If ever I were to give myself over to another man for the rest of my life, it would be you, Westland,' she said, standing with her naked feet in the dew, watching the early-morning sun diffuse light down the valley. He stood behind her, his arms round her waist.

'That must be my fate, then. To wait for you.'

'No,' she said. 'I mustn't be selfish. But you are the kindest and gentlest man in the world.'

He kissed the nape of her neck.

'Did I tell you I had my fortune told in Cairo? An ancient crone dashed the coffee from my cup and read the grounds. She saw me living on an island – but not, she warned, these islands. After the exchange of some geographical possibilities, I took her to mean Cuba.'

'That was romantic.'

'Well, it was more kindly than romantic. After all, if you looked into the bottom of a cup and saw a poor naked wretch eating shellfish with nothing but a goatskin umbrella to keep the sun off him, you would want to improve his fortunes a little, I should think.'

'Did she mention me?'

'No, she did not.'

She turned and kissed him lingeringly. For a single beat in history she considered how happy she might be with him. But telling him about Marie Claude had been a mistake. In all other respects so quick and generous, he failed to understand. Quite accidentally, she had provided the excuse he needed not to pursue her any further. He felt he was betraying an existing relationship.

'If Garnett were still alive and thus you found yourself in love with a married woman, would it make a difference?'

'Listen, Bella. I am a rather nondescript sort of fellow who has taken great pains never to be hurt by life. You have not hurt me now. I am perplexed, is all. I shall go away at the end of what is for you a holiday and find somewhere I can wait things out. I think Cuba is a bit extreme. The Scillies, possibly.'

'You have a very exalted idea of honour.'

'Of love,' he said.

They walked, because that is what one does on holidays of this kind. Seeing a church tower a country mile or so distant, they walked there, making their way along the edges of fields, jumping ditches. Westland, just as she had imagined, was a clumsy explorer. His shoes found mud, the elbows to his linen suit were greened. He had nothing to say about the church when they found it but sat on a bank outside the lych-gate, fanning himself with the straw hat he had plucked from its peg in the cottage. There was a public house nearby: they drank lemonade served to them by a young girl in a faded dress and bare feet.

'You are townspeople,' she suggested.

'From London,' Bella confirmed.

'I heard tell of it often,' the girl said, not to be outfaced.

'You think you might go there one day?'

'And for what reason? There's nothing there for me, I shouldn't think.'

'You are right,' Westland said. 'You can do better.'

'I never said that,' the girl muttered, aggrieved. She felt she was being patronized. The gentle Westland saw it at once.

'I was meaning to say that here is better,' he explained softly. 'Else, why would we be here?'

'Ho!' the girl said knowingly.

They followed the river down to a bridge, exchanged pleasantries with the parson who was fishing there, crossed over to the other bank and waded through chest-high mallows to find their bearings.

'There is never a policeman about when one wants them,' Westland said, peering doubtfully at the landscape.

'Touching what I told you about Paris, you have not said a single word, I notice.'

'No. I don't say I understand half of it either. To be completely frank, if it *is* this fellow Margam who is leading you about by the nose, then you should brain him with one of his own books. Put his eyes out with a steel nib. He isn't you, Bella.'

'I have made him me.'

'What rot. In life you would kick him downstairs without a second thought. Is he here now, for example?'

'Of course not.'

'He won't jump out of that blackthorn with a thrilling piece of plot?'

'It seems unlikely.'

'Thank God for that. Needlework or petit point is the only consolation a lady needs.'

They lay down at the edge of a cornfield and he submitted to being kissed on the eyes and lips, the weight of Bella's body across his. Larks floated far above their heads. For ten sublime minutes Bella lay listening to his heart.

'Of course,' Westland said, almost to himself, 'it is Margam that is my real rival and not some ethereal French beauty.'

The remark lasted out the whole of their stay.

'Where will you go next?' Bella asked on their last night together.

'Not far,' he answered. 'A man at my club has offered a berth on his yacht. Norway and so forth. The salmon there are as big as women and twice as willing. This is the promise he has made anyway.'

'Won't you fall in and drown?'

'No,' Westland said. 'I shall save myself for other battles. Considering the mortal sin into which you have plunged me, I think it permissible to say that I love you, Bella. I shall fight. In my own way, I shall persevere.'

'I can promise you nothing,' she warned.

It was dusk and they had been in bed since late afternoon. He got up and, stark naked, began lighting the fire inside a cranky and rusting stove.

'I don't know whether you like stew,' he said. 'But that is what you're getting.'

'Where did you learn to cook at all?'

'In a tent, at the bottom of the garden. Quite a long time ago.'

She jumped up and – also naked – hugged him.

'What if I say I love you?'

'It is what I came home to hear.'

'And will you truly wait for me?'

'Oh, I should think so,' Westland said.

EIGHTEEN

The rest of that summer passed with its usual calendar of triumphs and reversals. A Scotsman called Coffey drove a thousand geese from Norfolk to London without losing a single one. As widely reported, they followed the sound of his bagpipes. In Ireland, Lady Keniry was discovered in bed with a foot servant by her husband: the aggrieved party shot her and eight of the nine house servants, including a fourteen-year-old girl, before turning the gun on himself. A two-headed lamb was born in Dorset; in Ayr a man fell a hundred feet from a church tower and survived without a scratch on him. A horse called Moncur won a two-mile handicap at Doncaster by the biggest margin ever recorded.

There was a letter from Oslo. The writer had not fallen overboard once but had contrived to be left behind on a tiny island in Norway's greenest fiord. This had not been planned but was a consequence of his friend's absent-mindedness. (And a ridiculous dalliance with an Italian lady they had picked up along the way.) The island showed some promise but was smaller than the one illustrated at the bottom of a Cairene coffee cup. The Italian lady resembled a wardrobe to be found in the Army & Navy Stores, Victoria. The letter was signed by a single initial.

In September, Bella's publisher, Mr Frean, wrote her a note expressing the hope that the new work was progressing well, that the London autumn was not too melancholy (though he had heard from sources that the first of the fogs had created three days of havoc by water and on land) and that she continued in good health, as ever. Never one to interrupt an author in mid-stream, he hoped nevertheless he was free to mention a curious case reported in *The Times:* the mysterious disappearance of a noted Oxford divine, the Reverend Mr Hagley. How strange the world wagged, he concluded cheerfully, when a clergyman should vanish completely in a city filled with such notorious gossips. Finally, he himself was well, indeed blooming, having been introduced to sea-bathing by a charming boy with one blue eye and one brown.

Three months had passed since Paris and Frean's news of Hagley was itself a fortnight old. He had not been seen since the afternoon of 3 September, when he left Bolsover Hall to call on the Dean of Balliol.

'Which my old pal Blossom says was to have been tea and toast, along with remarks pertinent to the Gospel, et cetera.'

Quigley had returned to Oxford on his own initiative. He and Blossom were reunited in the Eagle and Child and spent two happy evenings on the ale, returning to a deserted Bolsover Hall for generous measures of the Principal's whisky. Only a fallout over the monarchy had brought this idyll to its close.

'Who was it, I wonder, who offered the fateful insult?' Bella asked lazily.

The finished pages to her work lay lodged in a small leather suitcase at her feet. In the late summer, she had taken Marie Claude away to Devon for a week, so that the office could be re-whitewashed and given what Quigley called a general tarting-up. This was the prelude to making the final copy of the new novel, as yet untitled.

For once the Captain had made no mistakes over his commission and the place looked cheerful and in its own small way, homely. The only false note struck was the presence of a clothes mangle, promised to a neighbour, acquired in the Quigley way of things, but never collected. Bella actually enjoyed its presence. Often, she paused to search for a word and found herself studying the mangle as if the answer was to be found within its bleached rollers and the heavy seriousness of the cast-iron frame.

'I may have said something untoward about the Royals,' Quigley admitted. 'But Blossom will hear no ill about any of them. A man who has shaken hands with the Prince of Wales, d'you see?'

'And where was this?'

'On the up platform of Oxford Station. Both of them half-cut, of course.'

Bella grimaced, enough for Quigley to change tack. He pointed to the suitcase.

'I see you have finally managed to cobble together something.'

'We call the process literature,' Bella responded, tart.

'You got a story out of old Bolsover in the end.'

'Yes,' she said. 'I got a story out of him.'

'And who,' the Captain wondered, 'was the damsel in distress?'

'I beg your pardon?'

'Doesn't there always have to be a damsel in distress?'

He waggled his eyebrows, driving Bella to snatch up her bonnet and depart for lunch.

The thing that was missing was not the identity of the lady in distress, for such women hung on racks like clothes in a wardrobe. Walking down the Strand, Bella could see any of half a dozen likely candidates, pale girls with their tippets drawn up around their necks, their gloved hands joined, their little narrow feet as delicate as foxes'. Hadn't Marie Claude fallen in love with one such, the vapid Jellicott? Miss Jellicott lived in Barnes and barely had the strength to lift her arms to unpin her hair.

'She is a lost soul,' Marie Claude explained. 'She goes for help to séances in Camberwell.'

'Never the ideal place to find yourself.'

Fern Jellicott, with her milk-white body and childlike breasts, her elaborated habits of indecision, the trembling lower lip that began the moment she was asked even the simplest question, was now immortalized in the pages of fiction. She was – although the thought made Bella uncomfortable – Bolsover's last victim, to be snatched from death at the very last moment by Billy Murch, or the version of Murch that appeared in the story. It was the Murch-like Willem Meinherzen's shadow that flitted over the tumbling fury of a hundred-foot waterfall in Bohemia, marking his prodigious leap to pluck the girl to safety. Bolsover – Bella had not yet decided on his fictional name – stumbled, slipped on a wet rock and plunged to his ghastly death in the pool the locals called the Cauldron.

Such is literature. In life, Bella would cheerfully have pitched Fern Jellicott over a gloomy Bohemian cliff, along with her cloaks and capes, her watercolour boxes and diary written in purple ink. It annoyed her that Murch, now transfigured as Meinherzen, international fencing master, should have to dart through the air like a swallow to save such a puling ninny.

For two days past, she had been trying to think up a more spectacular end for Bolsover. It did not make much of a story that he brought about his own death by the accident of wearing the wrong shoes in a rural setting. Bella had killed him several different ways, most dramatically by having him pierced by a lifeboat rocket in a catastrophic explosion of magenta and white smoke. But in the end art imitated life, with the usual unsatisfactory consequences. Bolsover departed the novel with a sneer on his lips, a monster never brought to justice. In one version of his demise, he had not fallen into the Cauldron, but seeing the end was at hand, evaded his pursuers by executing the perfect swallow dive.

'Sometimes it is better this way,' Murch-Meinherzen declared, his slim bare arms around the hideous Jellicott, as the rescue party, led by a man very like Urmiston, announced itself with hunting horns. The rain lashed down on a Bohemia that had some striking resemblances to Dartmoor.

Murch had become Meinherzen so comfortably because little had been seen of him since what Quigley persisted in calling the Paris jaunt. When they came back from seeing Jojo properly buried, Murch, as if sensing that the mood was against him, drifted away from the group. Mrs Bardsoe had heard that he had sold his cart and sent Penny into retirement in Kent. Quigley believed him to be still in London, though untraceable. He had gone to ground, some said on the south bank of the river, some as far north as Edmonton.

That suited Bella very well. What he had to offer her in the pages of a novel was a character that she found both repellent and attractive. His calm and unblinking ruthlessness fascinated her: tricked out with a new accent and a more acceptable social background, he was a hero such as she had never before attempted. Meinherzen spoke seldom, moved with stunning economy, fenced, shot, tracked a human trace with the cunning of a stag-hunter. He spoke five languages but only those closest to him knew that he was born an Englishman. (This was another inspired inversion of reality. That year's Derby-winner was called Galopin: his owner was Prince Gustavus Batthyany, a Hungarian who but for his name many would have supposed an English aristocrat of the first water. Bella was introduced to him at the Goodwood meeting and the germ of a better idea was born.)

Meinherzen had the aristocratic trick of never explaining himself. In the drawing rooms of the rich, no one could remember him entering the room or leaving it: he was talking to his hostess one moment and then, when she looked round, he was gone. His evening clothes were of impeccable cut, his linen whiter than snow. Where he lodged in London, how he came to know Prague so well, or Nice, who gave him the scar that ran from his brow to his jaw – none of these things were known.

He travelled alone. Lady Troughton quizzed him extensively at a ball in the Paris Embassy about his taste in women, by which she meant their absence in his life. Meinherzen was saved from replying by the intervention of the

Foreign Secretary, who drew him away into the library to discuss highly secret matters of state. When her ladyship next asked after Meinherzen, he had gone. Two days later, a peasant girl of the Jura, attracted by a riderless horse cropping the lush grass in some out-of-the-way valley, had caught him bathing naked, his body backlit by the sun. From the dusty clothes scattered about, she took him to be the servant of a rich master. Thinking to steal from his saddlebag, her hands had closed on a pistol. When she turned round, Meinherzen was levelling its twin at her breast.

Bella could not have written so effectively about this mystery man without creating someone who in turn was hunting him. The foil to Meinherzen's cruel implacability was a bumbling and soft-edged Englishman with weak eyes. He too was a driven man, tempered by a conscience that had him wake up sweating. Meinherzen flew like an arrow, his pursuer with the erratic zigzag of a butterfly.

For a time during the summer, the Reverend Anthony Hagley acted like the man who believes that by not mentioning a problem it will go away of its own accord – dwindle to a point somehow and disappear.

There were other things to occupy him. True to Blossom's prediction, the three missionaries sent to the Zambezi did indeed perish. One – perhaps the luckiest of them in the circumstances – was drowned trying to land in an open boat at the mouth of the river. The huge surf that ran across the sandbars plucked him into the life eternal before he had set foot in Africa. His patented oilskin valise (to which was bound an enormous white sun umbrella) was discovered a week or so later; but the body of Mr Wilson Priddie, late of Magdalen College, Oxford, was never found.

The anxious and unimaginative Hainsworth died of the bloody flux a month after landing. The missionary Hagley thought about most was the man with whom Captain Quigley had enjoyed a brief conversation in the Eagle and Child. Immune to the portfolio of killing diseases that seemed spilt so carelessly along the river, Tobias Ross-Whymper swiftly became the admiration of all who met him. He was calm, he was energetic, above all ceaselessly devoted to the service of God. And then, one afternoon, he walked out from a camp among some native grass huts with nothing in his hand but a canvas bucket – and was never seen again.

Hagley could not rid his mind of this mystery.

'We cannot believe he is dead,' the father explained over dinner in the Randolph Hotel. 'The boy was intended for the diplomatic service, as you know. Then God chose him for this other purpose and it seems inconceivable that He should not have guided his steps accordingly.'

Hagley inclined his head. The grim old stick in unfashionable evening clothes pushed away his plate.

'I know it is none of your business directly how these ventures are organized –'

'In this particular case you will recall that Bishop Colenso –'

'Yes, yes,' Ross-Whymper's father said testily. He seemed to want to say more but instead pulled a letter from his jacket.

'You had better read this,' he said.

Hagley recognized the handwriting at once. He scanned the contents with mounting dismay and then laid it by his plate, his face crimson.

'Do you have the honour of knowing Lord Bolsover?' he asked.

'You stand accused by him of incompetence and gross dereliction of your duty as moral guardian to my boy.'

'During his time at the Hall, your son had nothing but kind words for me,' Hagley objected, his voice wobbling.

'This fellow Bolsover endowed your charitable enterprise?'

'That is widely known. He himself is esteemed as a Christian patriot. Mr Gladstone –'

'Goddammit, sir, do not talk to me of Gladstone. Is any of this true? That you have acted carelessly and – Bolsover's word for it – viciously in the execution of your duties?'

'I cannot imagine what his lordship means by that passage in his letter,' Hagley said, his head swimming.

'You have a servant, Blossom?' Ross-Whymper asked.

'I recently turned him off, for drunkenness. An utterly unreliable witness.'

'I have met Blossom,' the old man said with glittering eyes. 'I do not like you, Mr Hagley. Do not like you and cannot trust you. I have laid a complaint against you with the Charity Commissioners.'

'And will that bring back your son?'

Ross-Whymper stared at him, his eyes popping.

'You are, as others have said of you, a cad. And don't talk to me of the dignity of your cloth. You are not fit to wear it.'

* * *

And then the worst news of all, all the more painful for being so predictable. On a blustery day in late September, Bella turned in at Fracatelli's, where the tablecloths glowed like snow and the chandeliers chattered. It was Signor Fracatelli's whim to have his waiters reach on tiptoe and flick them as they passed, giving a pleasant impression of secret tinkling conversations going on above the diners' heads.

She was ushered towards a particular table by Fracatelli himself. The man who rose to greet her was Bishop Duddington.

'Mrs Wallis, how delighted I am to see you.'

Fracatelli beamed, saw to it that Bella was seated just so, and fawning over the bishop, snapped his fingers for his most amiable waiter. Duddington smiled.

'Everybody likes a uniform,' he murmured, indicating his purple vest, his britches and clerical gaiters. 'I go to the House this afternoon. We are debating amendments to a bill on a subject of such high importance that I cannot disclose its contents, even if I could remember them. This lunch is my reward.'

'You have dined here before?'

'Oh, as to that, we are here because Broxtowe told me it would please you.'

'Was his death peaceful?' Bella asked in far too casual a tone. Duddington at once tempered his expression. His smile became more grave

'I saw him ten days since. He was frail. No less genial, I should add, but quieter. Have you ever been to his house in Yorkshire?'

She shook her head. When he saw the tiny tears clinging to her eyelashes, Duddington nodded sympathetically.

'It is sad,' he agreed, 'but what he faced was something we all must come to. And I believe with all my heart that God was waiting to welcome him.'

'You were speaking about his house,' Bella said in a choked voice. Duddington searched her eyes with his.

'There never was a more devoted staff. The draughts from the doors and windows could dry a prodigious amount of corn, it is true, but nobody except me seemed to notice. Broxtowe has always engaged his servants together with their families, so that the place is more akin to a village green than a private home. The children played at cricket in the long gallery. There were of course any number of exceeding pretty girls about.'

Bella smiled dutifully, though the tears were still there.

'I must thank you for the tact you have employed.'

He reached for a bottle cooling in its bucket.

'We agreed this particular conversation was a job calling for champagne. He even specified the year.'

Bella could hold herself in no longer. Her sob could be heard the length of the restaurant. It had been on Duddington's mind to invite Urmiston to this same lunch; and now he wished he had. Luckily for him he stayed silent. Had he mentioned the name, Bella would almost certainly have fled back out into the Strand. He fished for the handkerchief in the sleeve of his coat and passed it across.

'My dear Mrs Wallis, I am most awfully sorry. I had no wish to upset you.'

He raised his glass. After a moment or so, Bella joined him.

'To a dear friend,' Duddington proposed.

'And to friendship,' she replied, pleasing him greatly, even though she spoke in such a tiny voice.

'Will you go to the funeral?' he asked. 'I shall be happy to accompany you.'

'I cannot,' she said. 'I hope it is not unchristian of me, but I cannot.'

Duddington nodded and with his trademark elegance changed the subject, launching out into more anecdotes of Broxtowe's servants, including an account of his hermit, a draper from Leeds who lived in a limestone cave on a remote part of the estate.

Above their heads, the chandeliers tinkled prettily.

NINETEEN

'Nothing?' Captain Quigley asked, accepting a plate of ham and some cold pease. 'Not a word,' Hannah Bardsoe confirmed in a beaten-down tone of voice. The Captain poured her a pale ale. When, on an impulse, he reached and held her clenched hand in his, she smiled weakly.

'Oh, I have no call on him, I know that. But a line or two to say he's safe would be gratifying to a body.'

'How long has it been now, ma?'

'Nine weeks and two days,' Hannah Bardsoe said instantly. 'He walks out that door, six in the morning, wearing his suit with the little check, a nice grey stock I bought him and that silly old hat he sometimes wears and pfffft! Neither hide nor hair has been seen of him since.'

'Don't you worry.'

'Easy for you to say, Quigley. I *do* worry. I know you and Billy done your best to find him but –' she hesitated a moment – 'well, it's not in his nature to hurt a person, not a man to give heedless offence. The gentlest of gentle souls. And it seems to me,' she added, her eyes filling with tears, 'what as how I am the only one now who give a brass farthing as to his well-being and present whereabouts. It seems to me his other friends have forgot him.'

'Blimey, ma,' Quigley protested with a full mouth.

'Eat your ham, you fat-arsed chancer,' Mrs Bardsoe said, wiping the tears from her cheeks.

In Cornwall, it was a day of scudding clouds and brief intervals of watery sunshine. Urmiston had taken to regular walks along the cliff path after lunch, more often than not, even in the sunniest weather, plucked at by the steady and uproarious westerlies that seemed to blow over the Lizard peninsula. The sea – which he feared with a townsman's dread – crashed on to brown and black rocks and though his way took him more than a hundred feet above the turmoil of it, at night he tasted salt on his lips and smelled it on his clothes.

Seldom a day passed without him witnessing what he took to be maritime disasters, some of them an ignorant misreading of the price of fish but every so often a genuine calamity. In the late August gales a waterlogged and dismasted barque ran aground on the Manacles. Five of the crew survived. They were Frenchmen, short, ugly men with something of the character of pencil stubs, blunt and well-used. Offered brandy, they sat in the gorse with their heads between their knees, as though disgraced in love.

Lucette Landrieux was also French, a tall woman, taller than Urmiston himself. Her cottage was in a sunken lane, gable end to the sea, about a mile from the cliffs. A painter, her studio was a cow byre. Unlike Urmiston, she seldom walked further than the lane end, where a Mrs Howard furnished milk and home-made bread.

'My poor Charles,' she smiled, softening his name to the French pronunciation. 'I think you go out along the cliffs to feed the terror inside you. And in those boots it is only a matter of time before something terrible will happen.'

She had the pleasing habit of drinking tea in the Cornish manner, from handle-less mugs as big as flower vases. And, scandalously, she smoked cigarettes one after another, sometimes lighting the next before the first was out. Her wiry grey hair flew from her head like a tangled bush and she had solved the problem of keeping warm by wearing a fisherman's smock and black serge trousers.

'Mrs Howard wants to know if you are suffering from a wasting disease.'

'What did you tell her?'

'That you had lost the knack of being alive.'

He shrugged. He knew this was a lie: Mrs Howard dealt in commonplaces. She would not have understood the remark. Her husband Jem was a lobster fisherman: they both walked four miles to chapel every Sunday, singing heartily on the way home. To lose the knack of being alive was to be dead already in Mrs Howard's way of looking at things.

'Today, while you were out, a man called on the chance of enjoying a cream tea. He saw these very practical trousers, searched with his eyes for the breasts within my smock, blushed bright pink and beat a hasty retreat.'

'What kind of a man?'

'An Englishman.'

'I cannot stay here, Lucette,' Urmiston said suddenly. 'It solves nothing. It buys me nothing. I have treated

Mrs Bardsoe most unkindly. I was caught up in something that I could not control – I mean the other business I have told you about, the Paris business. I was too weak to bear it.'

'She will understand. Or rather, she will if you tell her everything. I have been waiting for you to leave, *mon cher*.'

'Have I made trouble for you, being here?'

Lucette laughed.

'You are my lodger,' she said. 'I have enjoyed your company. I like silence in a man. And you eat very little.'

'Don't tease, Lucette.'

'Was I teasing you? I am a solitary by nature. You are not. I shall miss you for a few weeks and then I shall forget you. Not entirely, but enough. I came here to forget, dearest Charles, and that is what I have done. You, I think, could stay here another ten years and still worry after London.'

'Is that what it is?' Urmiston wondered.

'After other people, then. People you know, people you have yet to meet. In Béziers I have a complete house with almost a hectare of grounds. I have not seen it for fifteen years. Perhaps I never will again. That is the difference between us. Having you here has been in effect a holiday. I had forgotten how important history is for some people, how much it explains.'

All this while she had been rolling them both cigarettes. She proffered his with a reddened hand, dabs of paint on her wrist.

'Come and see the studio for a last time.'

Her paintings were large. Though she lived by the sea, none of the canvases illustrated it or the local landscape. They were flower studies, intensely detailed, almost obsessively so. Nor was the light that fell on them that cruel, heartless clarity that seemed to Urmiston to belong specifically to Cornwall. These flowers seemed to stand bathed in gold. There was another inexplicable detail. All of them, in all of the paintings, had been cut. In the moment of their representation, they were already dying.

'You don't like them, do you?'

'They make me uneasy,' Urmiston admitted.

'But of course,' Lucette murmured. 'That is the right way to look at them.'

'Why do you paint this way?'

'I have no idea. One day Mrs Howard will come down to find out how I am and find me dead behind my easel. And then perhaps her husband will turn the canvases and use them to patch his boat. Or his roof, where it leaks.'

'I wish you would not talk that way.'

She laughed.

'Shall I tell you something, Charles? Remorse is a very indigestible meal. You have done nothing with which to reproach yourself. While it is still warm, you should take the bath out on to the lawn and scrub yourself free of Cornwall. And, if I may suggest, shave off your beard. I don't say this because you are in the least unclean, dearest Charles – you are in fact one of the most particular men I have ever met. No, you must think of it as a ritual of some kind. Preparations towards a journey.'

'You have been such a good friend, Lucette.'

'Oh, friends!' she laughed. 'What a store men set by friendship. I am not your jolly good egg, M'sieu Urmiston. I like you – and if it won't set you running off down the lane in terror – I even love you. But what is more, I know you. Friendship is for clubs, or public houses.'

He kissed her, standing on tiptoe to reach her lips. It was their first and last kiss: the singing in his ears was as real to him as the nap of her sleeve or the hands with which she framed his face.

'This is knowing someone,' she explained gently, as if to a child. Even his beard failed to conceal the blood that had rushed into his face. His ears burned like lamps.

'Someone is thinking of you,' she laughed, kissing him again on his forehead.

The next day he set off by cart to Helston, in company with four ladies and what seemed to be an itinerant village idiot. At one o'clock, he took the coach to Penzance, where the road to London lay along glistening iron rails. While he was waiting on the up platform, shivering a little from nervous anticipation, a day-old newspaper caught his eye.

Hagley had been discovered with his throat slit in a Bath hotel. The razor lay in his lax hand and there were no other signs of disorder. He was naked but that could be put down to circumstance. Inspector Todmarton deduced that the gentleman had risen from his bath and was about to shave when despair had overwhelmed him.

Todmarton was a giant of a man with a lantern jaw and very little imagination. There were four or five suicides a year in the city's hotel rooms and in his time on the force he had seen three other clerical gentlemen who topped themselves, two of them expressing doubts about the Trinity in notes propped against the mantelpiece. He was a chapel man himself.

There were one or two little anomalies. A guest towel was missing from the bathroom and on the carpet of the sitting room was the imprint of a shoe heel, outlined in blood. These were pointed out to Todmarton by the hotel manager, a Mr Bellamy. But then Bellamy was just the sort of supercilious sod that the Inspector disliked most in life. Everybody thought they could do a policeman's job better than the man in charge.

'I see a man with his throat cut, holding an open razor in his hand,' he boomed. 'That tells me all I need to know. My poor weak brain has, I believe, managed to grasp the essence of the matter. We are not in some Henry Ellis Margam novel here, Mr Bellamy,' he added spitefully.

Bellamy winced. It was in this very hotel that Guy Liddell had leapt from a first-floor window in *The Devil's Knapsack*, landing foursquare on Sir John Repington as he made his escape, the smoking gun still in his hand. It was an early Margam but he was inclined to make too much of it, especially when talking to persons of a literary bent.

'You don't think that at some point there were two people in this suite?' the manager persisted.

'Very grateful to you for your help, sir,' Todmarton said with maddening complacency. For emphasis, he pulled out a pipe from his jacket and lit it, sending clouds of smoke billowing. Looking for somewhere to dispose of the match, he returned it absent-mindedly to his pocket.

'I have arranged for the body to be removed to the morgue. My Sergeant Perkins will tidy up the details. But please, I beg of you, set your mind at rest. The Reverend did himself in. You get a feel for these things, you know.'

Bellamy went downstairs in a fury and snatched a sheet of hotel stationery towards him. His letter to Henry Ellis Margam was addressed care of his publisher. When it arrived in London, a young clerk found a second envelope and sent it along unopened to a poste restante address in the Strand. There Quigley picked it up as part of his daily duties. He was ambling back to Fleur de Lys Court when he was clapped tentatively on the shoulder by a familiar presence.

'Well I never!' he exclaimed, pumping Urmiston's hand with genuine pleasure. 'Loveaduck, if I didn't think you was gone for good.'

'I was ill, you understand, Captain, but I am better now.'

'And I all the better for seeing you, dear old lad.'

'I read that Mr Hagley has committed suicide in Wiltshire.'

'And good riddance to bad rubbish, as the saying goes. Look here, do you turn in at this old pub on the corner and wait five minutes while I fetch the memsahib. Which she will be as pleased as punch to see your ugly mug, no doubt about that.'

He peered at Urmiston and laid his hand on his shoulder.

'I see a touch of grey about the old temples. And a man sorely in need of something to blow out his kite, I would say. The lamb shank and a plate of cabbage for you before we go another half-hour!'

It was clear from the way he plucked at his moustache that he was preparing to say more. When he found the words, they came out shyly, with more delicacy than was usual with the Captain.

'Will you be going round to see Hannah Bardsoe later, at all?'

'If she will see *me*.'

Quigley chuckled. 'Oh, that's a good one! That's very rich. Which she has waited for you like a lovesick girl. Hands clasped, eyes to heaven.'

Mrs Bardsoe listened to the story of Urmiston's time on the Lizard with tears pouring from her eyes. They sat knee to knee, holding hands, pushed by love into an horizonless fog. She asked no questions, made no comment, but her eyes seldom left his.

'You see, dearest Hannah, how little I know about the human heart, how clumsy my actions have been. They are a very earnest and particular people down there and it was this that gradually acted on me. I have come back to ask your forgiveness.'

'As if it were needed,' she cried. 'You have nothing to reproach yourself with. I was sorely feared I would never see your kind face again but that was all.'

'I came back to tell you that I loved you,' Urmiston concluded, trembling.

She leaned back, astonished.

'Well, if there are happier words to be spoke this afternoon, I should like to hear them. I will tell you straight, Mr Charles, I love you back. Indeed I do. Body and soul, my dear.'

He looked around the parlour, savouring its supreme ordinariness. The china spaniels stood either side of the clock. Hannah's sewing basket sat in the corner and her table was littered with what seemed the very same muddle of drying herbs, the teapot, and a cheese dish big enough to house a cat.

'The picture,' he remembered with a sudden start. 'The picture from Paris.'

'And did you think I had chucked it out?' she asked fondly. 'You will find it over my bed and 'tis the last thing I see before I blows out the light.'

'I hope it is hung at the best height to show it off.'

'That is for me to know and you to find out,' she said, arch.

They were interrupted, as they knew they would be, by the arrival of Bella, bearing a huge cream cake. She was followed soon after by the Captain.

'Well,' Hannah Bardsoe said in a high state of playfulness, 'I hope I can call for a bit of a knees-up. And whyever not, on such a happy day?'

The shop bell clattered and announced a third guest, as unexpected as might have been Gladstone or the Prussian Bismarck. Murch stood in the doorway, dressed in a black tail coat, his neck decorated with a red snuff handkerchief worn as a cravat. By way of greeting, he merely nodded to the company, though giving Urmiston a brief and wry smile.

'Sit down, Mr Murch,' Bella said, absolutely astonished. 'However did you know to find us here?'

'Word gets around,' he said calmly.

'Another prodigal returns,' Mrs Bardsoe cried. Murch smiled again and walked to the least comfortable chair in the room.

'And where have you been then, Billy?' the Captain asked.

'Round and about.'

All this passed over Urmiston's head. He busied himself with the corkscrew, his face brick red with pleasure. He knew that when he was in this mood all the mirrors in the world began to lie. In them, he was transformed from a middle-aged man to the voluble, overheated boy he once had been at Christmas parties. He served cake, he tripped over Mrs Bardsoe's carpet and found even the slightest thing amazingly funny.

Only half an hour later, after a single glass of wine, Murch had gone.

TWENTY

Hannah Bardsoe read the headstone with unselfconscious deliberation and then knelt and placed her posy of flowers at its base. Urmiston watched, feeling that he too was being watched. A cloudless but pale sky stretched back across the Channel, where the white horses pranced. Several close-hauled fishing smacks buffeted the waves. It was a cold day, with a biting onshore wind.

Coming back to Boulogne was entirely Hannah's idea – indeed, she insisted on it. She was a much better traveller than someone like Quigley and while she could be nothing but an Englishwoman, as described by her dress, there was a seriousness, an alert awareness that endeared her to the French. They had spent the morning walking round the fish market and taking an aperitif in a café that, while it was not exactly like the one Mueller had painted in Paris, was sufficiently romantic in her eyes.

Urmiston was used to people, even the best sort of people, treating France as some kind of zoo. But there was a calm and common sense about Hannah that he loved. At least in the district round about the fish market, she was as if at home.

'Well, if he isn't eating mussels!' she observed of their neighbour in the café.

'Would you like some?'

'Would I ever! And though I know you will take a glass of wine with yours, what I should like most is a glass of beer. For the shape of the glass as much as anything.'

When *la patronne* fetched the drinks and put the wine in front of her and the beer in front of Urmiston, Hannah switched them about with such a warm smile that he felt his heart would burst.

'Now it's at times like this that a body can say she's content with the little things,' she observed. 'Same as on the boat, were we not happy with that wicked old soup that would hardly stay in the plate?'

'You are easy to please, Hannah.'

'Maybe that's why you took up with me,' she suggested.

But their true business in being there was to visit Marguerite's grave in the Protestant cemetery. Borrowing from the quiet desolation and moreover as the only people present, their mood was chastened.

'Would she have liked me?' Hannah asked doubtfully.

'She was a parson's daughter from Wivenhoe,' Urmiston explained. 'Very shy, not at all the jolly person you are. And in her last years, too ill to take much note of other people. A good woman, Hannah, but in the end an unhappy one.'

'Well,' she said, 'I am glad we come. I truly am. Do you want a few moments alone with your thoughts, my dear?'

'No,' Urmiston said gently, pressing her gloved hand to his lips.

They turned and walked slowly away, her arm in his.

'And was it ever your thought to live here, out of England, Charlie?'

'Never once. Else, how could we have met?'

She reached on tiptoe to kiss him, her warm lips against his icy cheek.

'Now don't you go saying it was all in the stars,' she warned. 'That wouldn't be the right thing to say. No, not at all. Not today of all days.'

'It was chance, then. But a lucky chance, such as comes to very few men.'

'And you ain't ashamed of me for my common ways?'

'I have asked you to marry me,' Urmiston protested.

'Yes,' she said, chewing her bottom lip. 'That.'

She had given herself to him the previous night in a little commercial hotel, more anxious than she could remember since being a foolish young maid in Uxbridge. She had nothing to fear from his love-making, which was of such a dreamy nature that she took it to be an excessive form of politeness. But afterwards, cradling his head on her pillowy breasts and watching the moon through unshuttered windows, she began to cry.

'My dear,' Urmiston said with alarm. 'Whatever is the matter?'

She could not tell him that in the silent and modest minutes they had just spent she had seen, as clearly as the passing of the Lord Mayor's Show, the whole of his first marriage.

'My dearest boy,' she whispered, stroking his naked shoulder. ' Nothing at all is the matter and whyever should it be?'

'I have disappointed you.'

'What a wicked, wicked thing to say,' she howled, bursting into bad-tempered sobs. For good measure, she punched him on the breast-bone and snatched the duvet back to her side of the bed. She thought at first he too was crying but it became apparent that he was shaking with suppressed laughter.

'Right!' she said. 'We'll see who's disappointed.'

Pulling off her nightgown and kicking off the duvet, she straddled his narrow hips, the tips of her breasts dipping into his eyes. Her kiss, when it came, was like the brisk bang of a post-office date stamp on a letter. So much so, in fact, he feared for his front teeth.

Quite by chance, the Captain came across Murch in Cecil Court when he was going about a little piece of business (fifty or so fine bindings that had come into his possession in the usual way). He declared himself as astonished as the jack tar who married a mermaid.

'I don't see you for weeks on end and now bless me if we don't meet twice in ten days.'

Billy Murch was cagey, claiming to have been in Gravesend, visiting a former colleague in the West Kents, now down on his luck.

'And do I know this cove?'

'I shouldn't think so. I thought your mob was the 18th Hussars,' Murch said pointedly.

On the spur of the moment, the Captain invited him to a meal at the Coal Hole, suggesting they might stroll up west later on the old *qui vive*, the only two accurately pronounced words of French he possessed.

'Well, I am busy,' Billy declared. 'As I see you are.'

'Are we chums or are we not chums?' the Captain demanded.

'Let us say that we are,' Murch allowed, after a too-lengthy pause. 'Tomorrow night, then.'

When he set his mind to it, Murch could come it the toff with the best of them and appeared next evening in a frogged velvet jacket and fashionably narrow trousers, sporting a pair of boots that were almost brand new. The reason for this pride in his appearance was very evident, for on his arm he escorted Molly Clunn, known to both of them as a glamorous figure from a different world. And so much for a pal in Gravesend, the Captain thought bitterly.

Molly's glory days were past, as happens to music-hall artistes, though perhaps they were never as glorious as she allowed people to believe. Nevertheless, for someone born in Brewer Street above a pork butcher's shop, she had done well. In her day she had played to audiences at the Mogul in Drury Lane, at Gatti's, and across the river at the Canterbury, where she was famously retained for six consecutive weeks. Molly was taller than Captain Quigley and almost as tall as Billy Murch. Her hips were square and her shoulders broad. This physical presence dictated the kind of act she was known for. She was a comic singer and actor, one with enough fame for her catchword to follow her round. 'Well, this ain't like no saveloy I ever saw' – a line from a dire sketch – was still shouted at her in the street.

'Molly, if you don't look as lovely as ever,' the Captain exclaimed, dragging back a chair for her and trying to conceal his astonishment.

'And yourself, Captain?' she asked with just that touch of negligence that had made her a star.

'Bully, my dear, bully.'

Close to, he could see the lines etched either side of her mouth and the faint scrawniness of her neck. Her bosom was whitened with rice powder.

'And which hall are you working at the moment?' he asked gallantly.

'I buried my poor mother in January last and that has set me back, my word it has. I remember dear old Marie Collis telling me, right when I started, a fortnight out of this game and you are as good as forgot, as good as though you never had been. I mean in London, you understand me.'

'Molly's been starring in the circus,' Murch said.

'Yes, dear,' she muttered. 'Topping the bill with the Peking Kings and Walter the Talking Horse.'

'But only at the best venues, I wager,' Captain Quigley suggested.

'If you count Kidderminster and Stourbridge and the like. The truth is, boys, Molly's not as young as she was. I've known you chumps more than twenty years and I was on the halls even then.'

'Has it really been twenty years?'

'I knew *you*,' she flashed, pointing at the Captain, 'when you was merely Percy Quigley, market porter. Before you won your medals,' she added with a raucous laugh.

Wine for Molly, stout for the men. The conversation ranged over people they had known and music halls they had visited or played. While they talked, they ate. Patting her chest to aid her digestion, a cloud of white powder rose from Molly's busom, the marks of her fingers remaining in orange outline. A strand of her hair came down.

'I'll tell you the real truth,' she said as the waiter uncorked the second bottle. 'Old Molly's on her beam ends. If I had a gun tonight and the Peking Kings were to come in here to the dear old Coal Hole, I would shoot the little bastards stone dead, so help me God. They say people run away to join the life of the circus and it's true, we have one in the company now. But for the most part we are a sorry lot. Flotsam and jetsam, Captain.'

'Can we not come and see you?'

'Bicester's the closest I've been to London for six months. I'm only in town now because MacGilligan, the cove that owns the business, is down the docks taking delivery of an elephant. That they aim to run up to Paddington somehow and shove in a goods van to Oxford.'

'An elephant, eh?'

'Me and the beast to open the show. If he's got anything about him at all, the animal, I don't doubt he'll get top billing and I'll be on my way.'

'And this MacGilligan?'

'Like no saveloy I ever saw. Irish. The breath on him could pickle eggs.'

'Well, this is a sorry tale and no mistake. If I wasn't took up with business, I would make it my pleasure and bounden duty to bring you back into the halls under your old flag. Flying your old flag, if you follow my drift.'

All this while, Murch had been ruminating in his cross-eyed way.

'This new bloke you mentioned. The one run away to join you. Can't you make a pal of him?'

'Him! A toff who speaks with a mouthful of marbles? Who can't be taught even the simplest thing, no, not even to pull the right rope when the ring is being rigged? I don't think so.'

'He's a toff?'

'A true-blue toff. Spikka da German but he's about as much a fritzi as my old ma's chamber pot, God rest her soul.'

Quigley was about to say something but Murch laid his hand on the Captain's wrist. And not in the most friendly way either.

'What it is,' he grunted, 'me and Molly have it in mind to go up west for an hour or so. So shall take it kindly if you was to hop off.'

'Well, where are you staying, Molly my beloved?' Quigley asked.

'Only me and Billy know that,' she laughed. When she stood, she staggered.

'A breath of fresh air will set me right,' she said doubtfully. 'I aren't used to the bright city lights no longer. And me, who played the Canterbury for six solid weeks.'

'Would I be such a gooseberry if I was to come along with you?' Quigley asked hopefully.

'Yes, you would,' Billy Murch said, rising. Without knowing a blind thing about his transfiguration as Meinherzen, the way he handed Molly to the door was gentlemanly perfection.

The Captain supped off and for want of something to do, decided to go up to Paddington in hopes of seeing the elephant board the train to Oxford. It was a long shot but he had never seen an elephant. No call for it. However, someone had once told him that they took offence easily and ran amok at the smallest insult to their dignity. It would be worth the price of an omnibus fare to see that.

After a quick patrol round the darker parts of the station – smelling more of fish than elephant – and being told to garn off out of it by indignant porters, he gave up on the idea and strolled to a pub on the Wharf Road near Paddington Basin. There he stayed until chucking-out time, musing on Molly Clunn and the historic favours bestowed on him when he was a likely lad and she an altogether more reckless sort.

'You say she took a shine to you?'

'To me and no other.'

'And what's her name again?'

'Molly Clunn.'

'I never heard of her, mate.'

'And that's because you're an ignorant no-nothing get.'

The bloke was bigger than him but a bit slow on his feet. Quigley was wearing his best boots, however, and what they lacked in style they made up for in thickness of leather. A flying kick on the shins and a thumb in the eye worked their magic.

'I'll wait for you outside,' the Captain promised but legged it as soon as he got through the door.

Walking back towards Praed Street along the blackened walls of the station (one last gander, time spent on reconnaissance, et cetera) he was rewarded by seeing a grey and shambling giant being coaxed through some handy gates, attended by MacGilligan's men and a crowd of drunks and whores. A child walked past with some souvenir dung under his arm.

'Has the animal run amok yet?' Quigley asked.

'Drunk two buckets of ale, scoffed up half a dozen cabbages, give us his trumpet noise an' everythink,' the child said. 'Woman fainted, was carried down to St Mary's. Circus coves pissed as newts.'

The Captain pushed his way to the gates, where the elephant was of a mind to turn round and walk back to the pub for more beer. There was great shouting and jostling and cheers as MacGilligan was dragged this way and that by a chain hanging from the elephant's neck.

'This is prime,' Quigley said to a neighbour.

Since he had never met Bolsover, he did not recognize him, putting him down merely as a fat cove with fleshy lips, wearing a seal-hunter's cap, the earpieces tied under his chin. The man was so drunk – or perhaps elated – he clung on to the Captain's shoulders for a few seconds before moving away to aim a kick at the animal's wrinkly backside.

'That's the way,' a whore shouted. 'Show him who's master.'

Bolsover turned and flashed her a hideous grin.

'Absolutely,' he drawled.

TWENTY-ONE

As if signalling the change of seasons, it rained for a week in London, turning the streets to rivers of mud and filth. Damp plaster and ruined carpets. Coal and more coal fetched up from the cellars. The air grew yellow and sulphurous and out of doors breathing became something only to be done through a scarf or handkerchief. The whores and horsemen were driven from Hyde Park and miseries that had remained invisible in the summer – because dispersed like dust and pollen – now became starkly obvious. Beggars and vagrants formed villages under the railway arches at Charing Cross, where they roared and fought in front of huge fires fed by park benches, beer crates, stolen barrows, even young trees.

Some stories of the incessant rain acquired an almost biblical significance. In Tooley Street, opposite the Tower of London, rats rose out of the cellars, at first in their dozens, then as a moving carpet of hundreds. Very few people actually saw this happen but the news of it spread like wildfire across the river. By nightfall, everyone knew someone who had seen this army, its battalions led by a grinning king variously estimated as the size of a rabbit, cat, or dog. The rats swam the Thames in a single compact mass and were last seen at dusk on Tower Hill, terrorizing pedestrians. Or in Leadenhall Street, or St Paul's Churchyard, according to the powers of invention in this or that pub.

Then, with the abruptness of an electrical switch, the weather changed. Cold air rushed in from the north, bringing with it dry, crisp conditions and morning frosts. Bella rose with the pale sun and walked each day as far west as Kensington Gardens. It was a pleasure to walk across grass stiffened with rime and among bare trees brought to a juddering halt by the cold, their arms outstretched. In the hotels along the Bayswater Road, wan lights burned with an almost Japanese delicacy.

On the second of these dawn walks, the only other human being Bella met was someone she recognized. The Foreign Secretary was picking his way by horseback across an empty Hyde Park. His face pinched red by the frost – and perhaps by the early hour – he touched the brim of his top hat to her with a laconic salute that had come down from Wellington's day.

It was an impressive moment. It occurred to her that perhaps this was how Meinherzen might receive the thanks of a grateful country, not with medals and speeches but by a single nonchalant gesture. It was not too late to interpolate such a scene. But then she shrugged her coat closer to her and went on.

At the beginning of the week, she had moved the manuscript of her novel back to Orange Street, where it was kept under the bed, the place anxious old ladies hid their best spoons and silver picture frames. The story's value to her was not that it was good but that it was finished. Meinherzen would have to make do with what he had been given, a final sight of Miss Fern Jellicott at the window of her train to Paris, before he turned and slipped away into the shadows of the Vienna Bahnhof.

The moment a Margam story was finished (which happened at more or less the same time every year) it was Bella's habit to move out of Fleur de Lys Court, leaving the office for Quigley to furnish as his winter quarters. It was an emphatic seasonal punctuation that suited both parties. For three months she barely picked up a pen. For his part, the Captain fetched in his bed and coaxed a draught from the chimney, cooked himself chaotic bachelor meals and entertained his cronies.

Winter was when Quigley made his real living. This year, within a day or so of Bella moving out, the office was stacked with two hundred orange and marmalade tiles from a garden path and the front door towards which it had led. Tucked in a corner under wraps was the sword drawn by Sir Henry Havelock in his conquest of Sind – or if not that sword, one very like it. Half a dozen naval cutlasses, stolen from the same house in Belgravia, were waiting similiar authentication. Easier to dispose of: a hundred brass stair-rods and their fixings.

The MacGilligan elephant made the letters pages of *The Times*. It fell out that MacGilligan's was the smallest travelling circus ever to acquire such an attraction and the owner was roundly castigated for his impudence. In a correspondence begun by an anxious vicar, very indignant men from the shires who had seen India wrote in to assure the Editor that the beast would die of pneumonia, run berserk and kill innocent bystanders, or simply pine away. A professor of zoology was more brutal yet: the elephant would starve to death for want of his native foodstuffs. Though he had come no further than a barn outside Maastricht and was as domesticated as the average cat, it appeared that Quigley had witnessed an historic moment in the long history of cruelty to animals in England.

'Seemed sprightly enough to me,' he commented. 'And according to Molly Clunn, nothing wrong with his stools or motions, neither. Not a merry beast, not jovial in his dealings with others, but then they never fetched him over for his sense of humour.'

Bella endured these reflections from the Captain on her last visit to the office, already horribly disordered by its translation to winter quarters. (She noticed with a pang that the mangle had gone, though it pleased her to see that the rosewood table that served her as a desk was struck out of harm's way.) Quigley was of course trying to throw a smokescreen over the embarrassment of having spoken to Bolsover without knowing who he was.

'Could any of you have done better on the night, I wonder? I think not.'

There was injury in this as well as bombast. It had been Murch who tumbled at once to the possibility that the toff who pretended to be German was Bolsover. And thanks to the romantic streak in Molly that responded to Billy's soldierly way of courting, there was an energetic spy in the camp. The only problem was that none of the information she gathered came back to Fleur de Lys Court. Murch had not been seen in London for more than a fortnight.

'Executing a long-range patrol, I don't doubt,' the Captain explained.

'It is all the same to me if he has emigrated to Canada.'

Bella meant this. Murch (and Bolsover) could go to hell. There were plenty of other things to occupy her. She was planning to take her manuscript to Frean in Boulogne and then rescue Marie Claude from Fern Jellicott's struggle to find her lost soul. The medium in Camberwell had suggested to Fern that it might be found in America, advice that was channelled through a two-day-old girl who had died in an Indian attack in 1832.

There was also the matter of Urmiston's marriage to Hannah Bardsoe. The two women met for tea at Gunter's.

'Well, these are nice prices, I must say,' Hannah whispered, secretly very impressed.

'Where do you and Charles intend to live when you are wed?' Bella asked.

'Right where we are now. He is teaching himself herbal remedies from books he has scratted together – books, mind you! – and says he wants no better life. We can call this the honeymoon period,' Mrs Bardsoe added with her usual realism, 'for if he sticks at it, it will surprise me no end. The good Lord knows it is a low trade. And if the clientele ever found out we was dosing them from *books*, the balloon would go up and no mistake.'

'But you are happy all the same?'

'Oh yes,' she replied with a shy glance. 'All that side of it's going very well.'

'Do you think you might ever leave London at all, Hannah?'

'Bless me, no. No more than you should ever let it cross your mind. You love Miss Anvil with a passion but leaving this dear old place for her sake would never do.'

She had been momentarily perplexed by Marie Claude when they met at dinner in Orange Street but rallied when the French girl complimented her on her laugh, which it was true would raise the dead from their sleep. About the relationship between the two women, Mrs Bardsoe had nothing to speak but praise.

'If she is not the most beautiful little creature ever to wear bangles,' she exclaimed admiringly. 'And what a fortunate child she is in knowing you.'

'You should remind her of that from time to time,' Bella laughed.

Hannah Bardsoe seized her moment.

'Charles is very anxious that we should not lose touch,' she said carefully. 'None more relieved than him to be done with this Bolsover business, for he often says he made a fool of himself over it. But would be highly mortified not to keep your acquaintance.'

'In these winter months I seldom stray out of doors. This is not to evade the question, dearest Hannah, for I hold you both in total esteem. But from now until Easter I shall grow fat and lazy at home.'

She saw at once she had said the wrong thing.

'Of course, I hope to dance at your wedding,' she added, flustered.

'Ho! As to that, I am talking the dear man out of a church wedding. It would not do, would not do at all. I am already as married to him as ever a woman could be and no form of words can make it otherwise.'

Bella went to see Urmiston a day or so later. She found him in the shop, wearing a baize apron and pounding a dark red mixture in a stone mortar.

'Cough medicine,' he explained.

'It smells delightful.'

'That is the peppermint oil. I don't understand how exactly, but we have also released something called menthol. The colour is a mere additive. People won't buy pills or lozenges unless they look dangerously red. May I present you with a box? They are perfectly safe.'

'You do look the complete article,' Bella said admiringly.

'The neighbourhood have taken to me. I am sublimely happy.'

'May I fetch a chair and watch you work?'

'No, come into the parlour and we shall have coffee and chocolate cake. Hannah is out. She will be sorry to have missed you.'

The big surprise was the change in character of Hannah Bardsoe's parlour. All the usual fixtures were in place but along the length of the only blank wall Urmiston had installed shelves, on which were housed his library of treatises and texts on herbal medicine.

He took his visitor out to inspect improvements to the scullery. He had been busy with saw and plane, scratch-building cupboards and hanging a new back door. There was a yard that housed the privy but was too sunless for even the most good-natured plants. Bella was amused to discover the mangle that had decorated her office in the summer housed in a new lean-to shed; but the pride of the entire street was surely the bird pavilion Urmiston had built Hannah, an intricate structure of dowels and fretwork mounted on a ten-foot pole.

'Did you know there was such a bird as a coal tit? We watch them from the bedroom window,' he explained shyly.

'But it is beautiful!' Bella declared. 'You have talents I knew nothing of.'

'My grandfather was a master craftsman, a wheelwright. He taught me a small fraction of what he knew.'

'There cannot be another thing like this in all London.'

Urmiston laughed. 'Hannah is at pains to point that out to neighbours.'

'How I envy you both.'

In the house behind them, the kettle began to sing.

'I believe I know why you are here,' Urmiston murmured. 'It is from something Hannah may have said at Gunter's. I do not wish to lose you, Bella.'

On an impulse, she kissed him.

'Never dream of it. You – both of you – are very important to me. This late business has changed me more than I realized. Let us go inside. There is so much I wish to say.'

But of course, once inside, she found herself tongue-tied. Her heart was too full to bring out what she wanted to say most: that she was jealous of the happiness she found in that crabby parlour and the dusty little shop, as if it had stolen her friends away from her. Urmiston understood, as clearly as if she had spoken aloud.

'There will be other occasions when you may need to call on one or both of us for help and support. I can't imagine what these might be, or how they will come about. But wherever and whenever you are in jeopardy, you may count on us. I think you know this.'

'In jeopardy?'

Urmiston smiled. 'Whenever Henry Ellis Margam next takes up his pen.'

* * *

'And how is Mrs Vickery?' Bella asked dutifully, mentioning Fern Jellicott's Camberwell medium. Marie Claude glowered.

'I have told you a thousand times it is not Mrs Vickery who speaks but Charity Caudwell, the spirit voice from Conestoga Springs.'

'And how is she? I mean, I know she is dead – obviously – and only two days old at that but how is she getting along generally?'

Marie Claude burst into floods of tears.

'I hate her.'

'Charity?'

'Fern!'

'Good!' Bella said cheerfully.

The summer trip to Cromer had been a disaster: something had happened that was never to be mentioned in Orange Street, no, not for a million pounds. But Fern was needy in a way that shocked even Bella. Almost every day a letter arrived for Marie Claude in a pale green envelope, many containing poems – or at any rate verses. These were opened, read on the spot and then flung into the breakfast-room fire, the recipient in floods of tears.

Bella's brief adventure with Philip Westland was likewise a secret – one much easier to keep. Since they parted at the end of the trip to Shropshire she had heard nothing from him. Lady Cornford, who made everyone in London her business, was quite certain he had gone back to Cairo, where he had taken a houseboat on the unfashionable bank of the Nile. Her sister Alice had it of a Captain Dunscombe, an unimpeachable source. But a gentleman overhearing this told Bella a few minutes later that Westland had been spotted in Mentone. Or perhaps it might have been Florence.

'At all events he is married,' he concluded, not without a pitying glance.

There are some things a woman knows for a fact. Westland married was as unlikely as the Queen in labour. Bella wrote to him twice care of his club, light, bantering notes that mentioned lemonade and skylarks. The composition of these tiny letters with their measured archness cost her more than a chapter of the book she had just finished. Well, Mrs Venn observed, when Bella wondered a bit too nakedly how Mr Westland was going on these days, he knows where you live, my dear.

'Look at me, child,' Bella said to Marie Claude. 'Don't grind your teeth but look at me. Miss Jellicott is an idiot. You can do better. Next Wednesday you and I will go by train to Marseilles and thence by steamer to Cyprus. For two months.'

'To Cyprus?'

'For two months.'

'But why?'

'Because I love you.'

Marie Claude shook her head gloomily.

'I know you don't love me.'

'Well then, because I am devoted to you. If you don't believe that either, because I would like to make you happy. It is the island of Aphrodite, Marie Claude. Peasants with huge moustaches will kneel in the road to worship you. I shall have you carried about on a golden throne.'

'We have never been away at this time of the year before.'

'More's the pity.'

Marie Claude considered some other objections to the plan and then rose and embraced Bella. That is to say she leaned against her, her lax arms round Bella's waist.

'And if I don't like it?' she asked with her usual petulance.

'I shall chuck you into the sea. And then I shall smoke a cigar and talk to the village elders about wine. And olives.'

'Is it because you are writing another story? Is that why we are going?'

'How suspicious you are! I do not care if I never pick up a pen again.'

Marie Claude smiled through her tears. She lifted her face to be kissed.

'Poor Mr Frean. You will break his heart. He will cry his eyes out until he is dead.'

Bella stroked the girl's hair.

'Perhaps he won't die. Perhaps he will buy a bath chair and be wheeled about Boulogne by some handsome young man in white trousers, remembering me as the lady who went to Cyprus for two months but stayed there for ever.'

For the briefest flicker of time, that actually seemed a possible outcome. But then Bella's realism came flooding back in. She was going to Cyprus to forget. Two months would be ample. After all, there was only so much to be said about olives.

'Will we stay in a hotel?'

'Would I waste you on a hotel full of old colonels and Egyptian widows? We shall stay in a villa I have rented, surrounded by cypresses, with a fine view of the sea. Now go upstairs and begin packing a few sensible clothes; and a great many more that are ridiculous. You will know exactly how to choose.'

The manuscript of the book lay parcelled on the table, neatly tied up by Mrs Venn with blobs of sealing wax on every knot. Tomorrow it would set off for France. And, she thought vengefully, if a certain section of her readership did not recognize Lord Bellsilver for who he was in life, then she was not the writer Mr Frean so often assured her she was.

Murch had the patience that went with living from time to time like a predator from the animal kingdom. His natural habitat was London. Cellar steps that gave a worm's-eye view of snowy pavements; mossy front rooms where the plaster clung to the walls with the last of its strength and the fires of strangers had been conjured over months and even years from floorboards and banisters; the stone huts of railway workers or nightwatchmen's ramshackle sheds. Yet unlike many Londoners, he had no fear of the countryside either. More resourceful than Quigley, less fastidious than Urmiston, he could adapt his mind to anything. It was not the journey but the destination that mattered. Murch believed in outcome.

Accordingly, for three days he laid up in woodland beside the road into Tetbury, waiting for MacGilligan's wagons to roll into view. A huge Gloucestershire sky grizzled overhead – not a heavy rain, more like a widow's inconsolable snuffling and sneezing. Murch's Snider-Enfield rifle, stolen from the same house in Belgravia that had furnished Quigley with a cavalry sword and half a dozen naval cutlasses, was a souvenir from the 1870 siege of Paris. Wrapped in sacking, it was the one reasonably dry thing in the entire wood, save for the three cartridges Murch carried in a pouch next to his heart.

True to the way Bella had imagined Meinherzen, Murch's self-possession was complete, or almost so. Never the man to reveal too much, inside him there was an indigestible crust of disappointment at the cards life had dealt him. Molly Clunn was merry, she was courageous even, but the romantic in Murch found itself thwarted by her raucous laughter and incurable habit of self-advertisement. They had spent some riotous evenings in High Street inns in godforsaken towns where Molly used these stolen moments to perform, as though upon a stage.

'Who's the miserable sod you're with tonight?' randy farmers would ask, pointing to Murch sitting a little apart, the one still thing in a whirl of music-hall song and what he saw as bumpkin revels. Later, in bed, she would collapse into sobs and promises.

'I'm no good, Billy. I can't hardly remember how a woman – I mean a real woman – behaves.'

In the dark, he silently agreed.

'If you was to get me out of it, say we started up a little business together in one of these towns, I could be so good for you. We would make a right team. Partners.'

She was used to his habits and did not scold when he failed to reply.

She ran on until she was too exhausted to speak any more and then slept, her mouth ajar, her fists opening and closing.

For his part, he lay on his back, wide awake. Without him knowing it, Bella had sent him this way before – with

Constanza, Duchess of Vrac, another chatterbox a little too fond of the wine. In the novel, the accommodations had been far superior to those of the Fox Inn, Norton Parva: a marble-floored bedroom that boasted a sunken bath. But the mood had been the same. Constanza was a spoiled creature, the consequence of having inherited too much money far too soon. Meinherzen let her down gently, slipping out of the Duchess's bed and shinning down a trellis to be sure, but leaving behind on the pillow a single rose.

The originals for characters in fiction never recognize themselves. *The Widow's Secret*, when it came to be published, would be one of the few books Murch read from cover to cover, though more as an examination of technique and craftsmanship than any interest in the story. Murch in the act of reading was much like Urmiston running his hand down the grain of a choice piece of walnut or admiring a particularly well-seated mortice and tenon. It was an exercise for the eye. Here in the woods, he bivouacked against a dry-stone wall during the hours of darkness and felt the same satisfaction in a well-made thing.

Now, at last, Molly Clunn came striding along the road into Tetbury. She was singing loud enough for the sound to carry to the wood in which Murch lay: the song was a favourite of hers – 'I'm always the one that's last out the door.' Behind her the rest of the circus rumbled in five gypsy caravans, each of them with smoke rising from the chimney. The elephant ambled in the shafts of the first. A man – MacGilligan – sat on its back blowing a trumpet. One by one figures jumped down from the other caravans. But no sign of Bolsover. Or not yet. Murch studied the little convoy carefully and began undoing the sacking that covered the Snider-Enfield. It released a sudden and very agreeable tang of machine oil, as exciting to him as the smell of cooking.

A few children came out from the town to greet the circus which obligingly paused on the high-arched viaduct that led into the town over some ancient watermeadows. The elephant came to an obedient halt, drums and fifes were added to MacGilligan's trumpet: the zanies in the company began to leap and caper. More of the curious came down past the church and on to the bridge. The music resolved itself into a jig.

Bolsover came out of the third caravan, dragging on an embroidered felt overcoat. He joked with the children, whirling several round by the wrists. Although Murch had never seen him before, constant questioning of Molly had furnished a description that was unmistakable. He opened the breech of the rifle and inserted a cartridge warmed by the heat of his skin. He estimated the range at two hundred and fifty yards. The bolt closed.

You could say that Bolsover was being given his chance. Two hundred and fifty yards was hardly a distance but Murch knew he would be extremely lucky to get off two clear shots. In the Crimea, he had downed a man at nine hundred paces, bringing him the approbation of Lord Raglan himself (a vague wave of the hand from behind an olive press, the Commander-in-Chief's horse cropping unconcernedly as clods of frozen turf flew round his head as his master nibbled on a ship's biscuit). But the Crimea was an old story and the Russian battery commander Murch had sent into eternity was dust. Two hundred and fifty yards, some would say, constituted a sporting shot.

Bolsover was a clumsy circus hand. He was the butt of the troupe, their grinning but hapless dancing bear. A clown darted up and jammed a cap with antlers on his head. The townsfolk laughed as he jumped on to the parapet and skipped his way along it. Murch lowered his rifle. His target was dancing out of range. His breathing remained perfectly steady. Perhaps the only sign of his heightened tension was that the sound of music and laughter coming from the viaduct seemed to reach him from under the sea, distorted and very, very faint. He swallowed.

Bolsover turned and began dancing back again, clapping his hands over his head like a child on a lawn. His antlers bobbed, his coat flew out into wings behind him. And then, abruptly, he was blown off the coping as if by a sudden and savage gust of wind.

The report of the rifle boomed down the valley a fraction of a second later. Panicked, the elephant ran on into town, scattering the crowd. Screams, shouts; even hysterical laughter from those who wanted it all to be a showman's trick. There was a fifty-foot fall to the water-meadow and some credulous people were hanging over the parapet to see whether and when the stupid fat man would rise up again.

Up in the woods, towards which the shrewder of the locals were looking, Murch stood, rubbed his thighs and shins to restore some warmth to them, and sauntered away. Never the man to waste a single unnecessary gesture, he walked casually to the pit he had dug for the rifle, dropped it in and scuffed the soil and leaves over it. There was a gate at the end of the copse and he climbed it easily and calmly. A pheasant rocketed up from a hedge. He loped along the field's edge, jumping puddles, disappearing over the brow of the hill. Rooks who were stalking in the furrows rose in a lazy whirl and settled again. The sky pressed down.

THE
SAILOR'S RANSOM

ONE

London, one late August afternoon in 1876. Hyde Park is busy with people, the better sort strolling on the dusty paths, herding their children gently in front of them. From time to time these family groups are overtaken by men in frock coats who have given up their carriages and are taking the air at a brisk pace. In this way one might encounter someone like Lord Hartington of the War Office, moving at a suitably military clip and trailing two or three secretaries behind him. At the sound of the great man's approach – and Hartington does not stint but comes on like a cheery yet urgent tornado – gentlemen raise their hats, the parasols part and boys in sailor suits stand to attention. The better sort (or maybe only the more impudent) salute.

So it is also along the sanded carriage drive that runs around the edge of the park. On a mild and windless day such as this is, men of affairs, peers of the realm, half-pay admirals, dowager duchesses and distinguished foreigners roll gently past under the trees. The public likes to congregate in knots to watch them. There is a sudden flurry of hat-raising – the Queen's youngest son, Prince Leopold, is seen to be taking the air, looking well, according to some bystanders, looking drawn and hunted to others. The ladies with him in the royal landau are identified as Lady

Breadalbane and Sir Henry Ponsonby's good-natured wife, Mary.

Prince Leopold's mama, if she ever got wind of such innocent pleasures, would at once put a stop to them: she has it in her head that her boy is an incurable invalid, quite as likely to fall out of his carriage as to enjoy its easy motion. As everyone knows, there is something wrong with his blood and even the slightest accident with scissors might threaten his life. He has the anguished sympathy of those who watch. There is a scattering of applause and one or two muted huzzas. A recent story tells how, when in Oxford for the funeral of Dean Liddell's dearest daughter, Leopold took a white rose from his buttonhole and laid it on the coffin. There was gallantry in this gesture but also some real emotion. None of Victoria's other sons could have done such a thing – or not with such unassuming grace.

The Prince, who has impeccable manners, raises his hat a little, just a very little, at the warm reception given to his carriage. His smile is soft and diffident. Lady Ponsonby, who sees everything and knows everyone, dips her head in grateful acknowledgement of the crowd's kindness. Tonight, a hundred or so gentle souls will speak about their encounter with Prince Leopold as though he had stepped from the carriage and shaken each of them by the hand. This pale haemophiliac, with a student's beard and uncertain blue eyes, is somehow their connection to what makes England great.

But by far the larger number in the park today are men and women from another world altogether. They sprawl, they drink, they fornicate. Hundreds of empty bottles reflect the sun and the dusty grass is stiff with broken glass. From time to time the police sprint after thieves or form in knots to prevent a breach of public order, as, for example, when a ragged file of former soldiers pass, playing battered instruments. They are almost too drunk to stand, these men, and their behaviour insults the few scraps of uniform they wear. Their intention is to reach the mamas and their children, the better to wring their hearts. The police have drawn truncheons to prevent them.

There are people here who have been turned off from distant factories, agricultural labourers who have not seen work for months, dismissed servants, French and German exiles, beggars, whores and bully boys. The hubbub that is carried on the sultry breeze comes in part from hundreds of them bathing in the Serpentine, as near naked as makes no difference, roaring like seals, copulating, occasionally fighting, just like seals.

Foreign visitors are amazed by these sights, but to Londoners it is just another day in the park. In Berlin, in the Tiergarten, such a spectacle as these nameless and face-less beasts that roam and bicker on the tawny grass would be unimaginable. In Paris, the Jardin du Luxembourg is cleansed of the unwelcome and the unwaged by that same French sense of propriety that also ensures the pollarded trees are as near identical as possible and the iron benches aligned like parade soldiers.

Here in London, the rich pass among the poor with something like equanimity. Mortice locks and insurance policies are one form of defence; that nebulous idea, the Law (meaning the courts of justice, the treadmill, bread and water) another. Most of all, a Londoner of the better class will tell you that it is only very occasionally one has to meet the lower classes face to face. Even a hundred yards makes a difference.

The afternoon wears on, the parasols twink and slowly disappear. In an hour or two the roads around the park will be filled with traffic on its way to very different addresses. In some of the more popular streets and squares, there will be a queue of vehicles waiting to discharge elegant and perfumed guests, not at a little distance from their destinations, but immediately outside the front door. The human animals with whom they shared the afternoon are forgotten. This is a different – and most would say – a better world.

On this particular autumn day, Mrs Bella Wallis was saying goodbye to her godson, Jack. Earlier they had been to Shepherd's studio in Long Acre, where the boy was photographed in his spanking new ensign's uniform, doing his best to look worldly and as far as was possible, languid, one arm cocked against a white glaze jardinière. His right boot was planted on the head that decorated a tiger rug and an occasional table bore books and a rolled map. Young though he looked, he carried off this make-believe well, with one sorry exception. The moustache he had been ordered to grow by his adjutant was too sparse and pale for the camera: with the greatest tact Mr Shepherd suggested some judicious darkening. There were blushes and indignation at this but Bella held his chin firm and applied a very little rouge, so that Ensign Starling was captured for posterity in his blues, a thirty-guinea sword at just the right angle, his boot on a tiger's head – and a red streak across his upper lip.

'You look very well, sir,' Shepherd smiled. 'If I may say so, a credit to your regiment.'

'He sails for Capetown tonight,' Bella said, busying herself with a handkerchief at Jack's upper lip. Though she had been a widow for more than ten years, and had not seen her godson for five, she could all the same feel the heat of childish lust coming off him. His excited breath fanned her cheeks. Bella sighed. The new subaltern, like most of his kind, was a danger to shipping.

She offered him early dinner at Fracatelli's but he asked instead to go back with her to the house in Orange Street. As they walked, he gave her his arm.

'You really are most incredibly beautiful,' the boy blurted as they crossed the road into St Martin's Lane. Bella laughed.

'Why, Jack, that isn't often said of me.'

'I should so like to kiss you.'

'May we not take the thought for the deed?'

He followed her glance and saw a dishevelled figure saluting them both. The man wore a faded red tunic of ancient cut and concertina canvas trousers. Dundreary whiskers decorated a face heated by drink. To amuse passers-by (at any rate to his own satisfaction) he was marching with one foot in the gutter and one on the pavement.

'Who is that?' Jack asked, alarmed.

'I have no idea,' his godmother said in a very guarded tone.

'But he seems to know you. If not, if he is merely being importunate, allow me to deal with him.'

'You'll do no such thing.'

The old soldier, if that is what he was, laid his finger along his nose, straightened his back and executed an extravagant right-wheel into New Row. Jack stared after him in amazement.

'That fellow has the impudence of the devil.'

'Yes,' Bella agreed grimly.

'But does he know you?'

'His name is Quigley, these are his streets and he has quite as much right to walk in them as anyone else. And you, my dear, are nineteen years old, take ship for Africa later on tonight and must try to learn not to be such a confounded owl.'

'I beg your pardon,' Jack said, perking up his chin and blushing to the roots of his hair.

Though he knew London hardly at all, Orange Street was not very much his idea of a good address. Starling had been warned by his mother that dear, dear Bella was quite the woman of mystery, which to Mrs Starling was the same as saying she had a wooden leg. The faintly raucous street Bella lived in was mystery enough to Jack, as was the house itself, shabby on the outside but wonderfully calm and elegant within. Bella's drawing room was small but – to his young eyes – perfect. The blue-grey walls were set off by some very good paintings. Once seated (or sprawled, remembering to cross his legs at the ankle as did all the fellows in the mess) he was calmed by a glass of very good claret and the present she made him of a leather writing wallet.

'I wish to apologise for my earlier behaviour,' he said with stiff formality.

Bella jumped up and kissed him on his forehead. 'You are such a chump, dearest Jack. We are friends, as much as more or less complete strangers can be. By midnight tonight you will quite forget me. That is entirely as it should be. In three weeks' time you will be at the Cape, cutting a dash with your fellow officers and letting the adjutant win at billiards.'

He laughed. What he saw in front of him was a woman in her early forties, with wonderfully grey eyes and a humorous mouth. There was a magic about her, not least because she lived alone with the sort of self-possession his own mother lacked completely. The dusty old fool they had stumbled across in St Martin's Lane was a poser, to be sure: what on earth was his godmother doing by being able to name such a dreg? But there was a bud of common-sense in Ensign Jack Starling that would grow and blossom in time – far, far beyond this present moment – to adorn a general's rank. He saw that he was dealing with a real person and not some cypher.

He toasted her across the rim of his glass. 'Well,' he said gallantly, 'I apologise for wanting to kiss you but insist upon describing you as the most beautiful woman I have ever met.'

'Spoken like a gentleman.'

And then he was gone, in a flurry of cabs and trunks. It would not have broken his heart but might have piqued him to know that within an hour the beautiful Bella Wallis had more or less forgotten his existence. She read, she yawned, she ate a plate of cold cuts; and as the night drew in, lit lamps. In order not to shock her godson she had abstained from smoking in his presence but now she lay back in her favourite chair with her shoes kicked off and a cheroot smouldering in a saucer.

The boy Jack was her sister-in-law's child, from happier days. Then Bella had lived in some style in Hertfordshire with her husband Garnett. When he died, she moved back to London and set about reinventing herself, not as a society lady and certainly not as a grieving widow. There were no children of the marriage and not much money left to her in Garnett's will. She lived quietly. Though for a giddy year or so she was embroiled – and that was the very word for it – with the beautiful and childlike Marie Claude D'Anville, represented to the wider world as her companion, Bella Wallis was one of those lucky people who have an exact idea of who they are.

She was someone who could live alone and not shrivel like an apple. Marie Claude was gone, more or less amicably; and while there were plenty of men only too willing to take her place, Bella enjoyed her own company. There was a pleasure to be got from listening, as now, to the sighing of the house as it settled for the night: the bumps and creaks and faint gurgle of water in the pipes that was as familiar to her as conversation.

'Ah, but where are her wellsprings?' an intelligent woman had once asked. 'What is the source of this perpetual refreshment?'

No one knew. At eleven by the clock, Bella flung her arms back over her head to ease her spine and walked upstairs, unbuttoning as she went. She unpinned her hair, scooped water into her face and eyes, completed her undressing and slipped naked into bed.

If there was one being who could bring down the walls she had built around herself, whose genial good nature could beguile her more than any other man she had ever known (and that included her late husband), he was not in London tonight, and probably not in England either. Philip Westland shared her own knack of seeming to walk alone. They were lovers in the strictly technical sense – an exuberantly romantic weekend in Shropshire – but had circled each other since like sun and moon.

Bella fell asleep with his name upon her lips. And then woke at two, cursed roundly, padded downstairs and found – by feeling gently along the mantelpiece – a pasteboard invitation. She took it upstairs in the dark and laid it on the second pillow to remind herself in the morning, before diving once more into dreamless sleep.

As for Jack Starling, he lay on his back in a cabin hardly bigger than a wardrobe, his mouth filled with bile and about as far from sleep as was the English Channel from the Cape of Good Hope. A choppy head sea, though it barely troubled the massive three-decker he was sailing in, had uncorked smells that did nothing for the stomach. For three hours he had taken his farewell of dear old England with his head in a tin basin.

Bella was both right and wrong about Philip Westland's whereabouts. He was out of England but on his way home. He was in fact in Calais, talking none too willingly with a man called Alcock from the British Embassy in Paris.

Alcock was a former naval commander with some of the brusquerie of that profession.

'You saw our friend in Cognac, I believe,' he suggested.

'I saw the man you sent me to meet, yes.'

Westland's attraction to both men and women was a shambolic sort of charm. He was tall but maybe a stone or so overweight. His expression was frank and unflinching but could be misunderstood as slow-wittedness. Alcock, for example, who suffered under the delusion that he could tell a man's worth by the way he picked up a wineglass, or a spoon, considered Westland a bit of an ox.

'How was he?' he persisted. 'How was our friend?'

'I wonder why you keep calling him our friend,' Westland mused. 'The feeling is not reciprocated. But, to answer your question, he is very well aware of the interest taken in him and responded accordingly.'

'Ha! He was on the qui vive, shall we say?'

'I think weary resignation is a better description.'

'There is a young wife, I believe?'

'There is indeed. Her name is Laetitia.'

Alcock chewed his lip for a moment or two.

'You gave him the Ambassador's letter?'

'I gave him the letter you gave me. I might as well have given him a handful of gravel scooped from the hotel grounds. I must tell you, Commander Alcock, I am about as fitted for this sort of business as a one-legged bosun.'

'Bosun? Why do you say bosun?' Alcock cried sharply.

'Don't the best bosuns have two legs?'

Alcock lit a cigarette. This fellow Westland was either some sort of simpleton or had just said something very deep. 'You have managed a very small but quite significant piece of intrigue for your country,' he explained. 'And I think you should be proud. I will not trouble you further tonight, Mr Westland. I believe you catch the early boat?'

'That is so.'

'I hope we may call on your services again.'

'Oh, I shouldn't bother,' Philip Westland murmured. 'The French postal services can do as well, or better. And, of course, with them you get to keep the stamp.'

The man's an idiot, Commander Alcock decided. This impression was reinforced when they stood to shake hands. Westland overtopped him by more than a foot. He would not do, the Commander noted to himself. Would not do at all.

TWO

'I go to Lady Cornford's tonight, Mrs Venn,' Bella said, tracking her housekeeper to the cellars, where that good woman had strung washing lines, as if sheets needed dark to dry them. She was mangling by the light that came through a dusty grille and singing hymns to keep her spirits up. There was a very pleasant smell of damp linen and palm oil soap, as well as coal dust and lime.

'I have a piece of stewing steak that needs cooking,' Mrs Venn warned. 'Shall you have that when you come home? In a small pie, with mushrooms?'

'Well, I think not. Tomorrow, perhaps.'

'You don't eat enough to gratify a bee.'

'So I have heard you say, often. But the mushrooms sound appealing.'

'From some old country boy selling door to door. Speaking in such a Hertfordshire accent, you could cut it with a knife. Though I don't say as how the shrooms come from those parts.'

'Not too likely,' Bella agreed, edging towards the cellar steps.

'But a decent enough old country character. Leather gaiters and all, you know. And only trying to earn a crust, like the rest of us.'

Bella paused with one foot on the stone stairs. 'Was there something else you wanted to say, Mrs Venn?'

'It is not my part to say anything,' the housekeeper confessed shyly. 'I know that – and may the Lord guide my words now. I will say what is in my heart. I cannot bear to see you lonely, Mrs Wallis.'

Bella walked back into the gloom and embraced her right there by the mangle and – for good measure – kissed her on her burning cheek. Then, being sensible women both of them, they burst out laughing.

What to wear, however? Cissie Cornford liked her men to appear in white tie, which more or less forced the ladies into full evening gowns. Since many of her female acquaintance were elderly, like herself, it was almost an imposition upon younger guests to show rather more bosom than they might wish. Snowy bosoms and bare arms, a little jewellery from the family inheritance – these made anyone under fifty a ready topic of conversation. Beady-eyed old dames studied the figures, dress and deportment of certain guests – particularly the unwary, or the impudent – with mumbling relish. Wrong necklace, I think! My dear, quite the wrong colour gloves! And so on.

Bella left the house in one of her favourite outfits, a pale blue dress with a short train and the least concession possible to the line created by the obligatory bustle. Her jewellery was antique, to be sure, but did not come down from her mother. The necklace of exquisitely cut turquoise had first been seen at the opening night of Rossini's *William Tell* in another country altogether and recovered fifty years later from a boutique in Paris by the most adorable man in Britain. More's the pity he was not there to admire it, nor to fix the tricky clasp.

Lady Cecily Cornford's house was located in Bedford Square. To the virtues of a tall and chaste Georgian design were added gates that protected the square itself; and in the centre a locked garden, seldom entered. Many a tradesman cursed when having to deliver goods to Bedford Square, because under the terms of the leasehold, drays and vans were not admitted. Everything, from a bouquet of flowers to a ton of coals had to be carried in by hand. Sofas, like pianos, followed the same pavement route.

Cissie Cornford, if she thought about it at all, considered these arrangements perfectly normal. To her mind, all London was shaped by iron railings and marble doorsteps. How else would people choose to live? She seldom ventured beyond Bloomsbury, and since the death of her husband cultivated an eccentricity she was sure was nobody's business but her own. It had one pleasing consequence, however. Every month she gave a chaotic at-home that her more loyal friends talked of as Cissie Cornford's salon. This was a description she disliked.

'It's buns and bounce,' she explained with a vague wave of her hand. 'And of course, the servants adore it.'

If they did, they moved from guest to guest without too much bounce of their own. The youngest was sixty. Their task, as explained by the butler, was to stop her ladyship from setting fire to the place, for a feature of these evenings was the colossal number of lamps and candelabra scattered about the principal rooms. Already that night, Lady Yeadon had cause to be extinguished by a soda syphon, when exhibiting the pronation required to bow a cello properly. The lace cuff to her sleeve had burst into tiny flames.

'How terribly, terribly tiresome. Tell me, my dear,' Cissie continued blithely, quizzing her friend Bella Wallis with a solicitude that was far too tender to be genuine, 'do you ever hear anything of that frightful scrub Westland?'

Bella accepted a sugared almond from the plate proffered her by Lady Cornford's pride and joy, her Scottish servant Rankin, and held it expertly between her thumb and forefinger. She managed to stay calm by super-human effort.

'Is he such a scrub?' she asked.

'My poor child, they say he is in Baden Baden at this very moment, along with a French comtesse old enough to be his mother.'

'I had heard Mr Westland was in Rome.'

'Do you say so? He is a spy, is he not?'

'A spy!' Bella exclaimed. 'A moment ago you were telling me he was a philandering scrub.'

'Someone whispered something along those lines to me recently, I am sure. Who was it? I declare my mind is like a sieve these days. Ah, there is Sir William Skillane just come in with his wife and daughter. Do talk to them: nobody else will, I am sure.'

For the moment, Bella was left stranded in almost the centre of the carpet, contemplating the idea of Philip Westland moving like a shadow through the streets of Vienna, or wherever spies congregated. It was an absurd image but one with just enough itchy persistence to prevent her laughing aloud. Indeed, she frowned. She had hardly expected the name to come up at all and inside her bodice her heart was pounding.

Cissie Cornford's drawing room held forty people comfortably. The guest of honour for this particular soirée was the painter William Frith, recently returned from Italy. Though he was not yet sixty, Frith, an inveterate clubman, liked to play up the image of the genial old buffer. Many of his anecdotes had correspondingly hoary whiskers. People found him amusing because he took so much naive pleasure in the jokes he told.

Cissie had been right about the Skillanes. They stood just inside the drawing room's double doors, as awkward as railway passengers waiting for the down train. Frith was on song and they arrived just at the moment that a gale of laughter swept the room. Sir William Skillane regarded the painter with unsmiling suspicion.

'Has he anything about him?' he asked Bella. 'I have heard of him, but is he any good? That's the first question I ask of any man.'

He said this in such a loud voice and with such repellent unction that others nearby turned their heads and Bella herself flinched. Skillane wore evening dress with an easy air and sported a grey silk ribbon around his neck, at the end of which dangled some kind of foreign decoration. Most of the people in the room considered this a mark of the utmost vulgarity: Sir William liked to draw attention to his geegaw by constant touching. His hair and beard were snowy white and his eyes a watery blue. To look at someone, he had the habit of lifting his chin and sighting along a huge beak nose no wider than a knife blade.

'Now, there is a fellow I would not take to sea, no, not for a million in cash.'

'Mr Frith will be sorely disappointed to hear it,' Bella said. 'And you, Lady Skillane, would you sit to the artist?'

Agnes Skillane shook her head, wringing her hands. 'I don't believe we know too many people here,' she whispered, peering about her in agony.

'You are from Cornwall, I think.'

'And Cadogan Square,' her husband added with a smirk.

'Yes, indeed.'

It seemed the only sane Skillane was the daughter, Mary, who looked at Bella with such an air of pleading that the older woman took pity on her and led her off to meet Mr Eddinshaw, who was writing the parish history of Marylebone. Eddinshaw was earnest, youthful, and almost completely otherworldly. The two were made for each other. They fled to the furthermost corner of the room, behind the piano.

'Who is that uncouth giant with the white beard?' Billy Frith asked Bella a few minutes later. 'Is he an actor of some kind?'

'His name is Sir William Skillane. From Cornwall and Cadogan Square.'

'Good God,' Frith said reverently. 'What is that you are holding in your hand?'

'A sugared almond.'

The painter took it from her and dropped it into a floral decoration. 'They say that Bancroft might pitch up later. I very much hope so. I make of you an honourable exception but the rest of the crowd here are as alluring as scabbed sheep. I can't persuade you to jump on the table and dance a wild fandango?'

'You cannot.'

'It would make a pretty sight. The most handsome woman I ever knew was the Duchess of Manchester, as she was in her youth. One morning –'

'Forgive me,' Bella pleaded, 'but this is a story you have told me many times.'

'You are right,' Frith said, after a glum pause. 'I forget what a very intelligent woman you are. And what a ghastly old windbag I have become.'

'Do you not see merit in Sir William's face, I mean in compositional terms?'

'I do not. He looks like a parakeet that has swallowed poisoned thistles. Is that the daughter who blushes so prettily?'

Bella glanced. A deep flush was rising from Mary Skillane's bosom and burning on her cheeks. Eddinshaw seemed oblivious to the effect he was having. Bella smiled at Billy Frith and made her way over.

'We shall have an ice together, Miss Skillane,' she proposed. 'Mr Eddinshaw can cool his heels here for a moment.'

'We have been talking about bills of mortality,' he explained.

'I can't think of a more engaging topic,' Bella assured him. When she laid her hand on Mary's forearm, she was amazed to find the girl was trembling.

'He asked me how things stood along those lines in Cornwall,' she whispered. 'I answered that I was sure we had nothing of such an advanced nature.'

'Whereabouts do you live in Cornwall?' Bella asked.

'St Ives. Well, not St Ives itself, of course, which is nothing but pilchards and chapels –' Miss Skillane's voice trailed off and she smiled wanly. 'I am quoting my father now. I have no gift for conversation, Mrs Wallis. Pilchards and chapels and . . . there was something else, but I have forgot.'

Another fiery blush. Bella began to fear the girl would faint clean away from nerves. She cast about for something to say that would not prostrate her.

'Which do you prefer, tell me? Cornwall or Cadogan Square?'

'I would be happy to be away from either,' Miss Skillane answered with very unexpected vehemence. 'Indeed, away from everything altogether.'

'Well, that is straight enough. I have had those same feelings from time to time.'

'You have?'

'From time to time. Listen, I will give you my card, Miss Skillane, and you shall call on me whenever you are in need of idle conversation about hats, or shoes.'

'You are very kind,' the girl said. 'I know I should do better but I feel completely outfaced. So many intelligent people.'

'Most of whom would be delighted to meet you. Don't you go out in society at all?'

'Hardly at all,' Mary Skillane said.

'Do you read? Tell me what you are reading.'

'I know I should mention something improving but we are not much of a reading family. My mother has just finished a novel called *The Widow's Secret*.'

'Ah yes,' Bella said with guarded amusement. 'And how did she find it?'

'Perfectly shocking. It was written by a man called Margam – Henry Margam.' Mary looked about her nervously. 'I do hope he isn't here tonight.'

'Your mama would faint away?'

'I am sure she would.'

Bella thought of saying more but smiled and made her excuses. Across the room Cissie Cornford was engaged in explaining to Sir William who he really was, a disconcerting habit she had with everybody new to her acquaintance and one the Cornishman was suffering in spluttering silence.

'I have taken the liberty of inviting my good friend Mr Robert Judd here tonight,' he interrupted in a booming voice. 'I hope you have no objection.'

It took a great deal to stop Lady Cornford in her tracks, but the insolence of treating her home like a public house or wayside inn did for her. She stared at Skillane as though he were the wild man from Borneo. Bella was amused; but when she glanced back at Mary Skillane, she was astonished to see a quite unmistakable look of terror on the girl's face.

There were two or three hackneys waiting in Bayley Street. The first cab on the rank was in the care of a genially tipsy man who stirred up his horse with affectionate words and a light flick of a ribboned whip. Bella sank back against the leather cushions feeling vexed and out of sorts. The interior of the cab stank of men – of pomade, and boot polish and the general whiff of how men smell, even the most particular of them. She drew down the window and stared out at the crowded pavements as they swung very gently downhill towards Trafalgar Square, in convoy with dozens of other cabs.

As happened almost every time she parted from Lady Cornford, she vowed never to go there again. That consummate gossip-monger had mentioned the one name calculated to pierce Bella's heart. If Philip Westland was under one of the top hats bobbing down Charing Cross Road, she would make it her pleasure to jump out and dot his eye. Since the chances of meeting him in this way were slim, she hoped instead it was raining cats and dogs in Vienna or wherever else the secret shadows gathered over good-natured and utterly adorable spies.

THREE

Philip Westland was not of course in Vienna, nor in Constantinople, Kabul or anywhere else exotic, but could be found as large as life in Bella's drawing room, playing boisterous cards with his childhood friend William Kennett. Bella recognised the voices as she took off her velvet cape and examined herself in the entrance hall's gilt-framed mirror. Her hands trembled. Perhaps her eyes sparkled more than they had done for several hours and there was a small blue vein at her throat that she wished would go away. Mrs Venn, her housekeeper, appeared on tiptoe like a servant in a play.

'The gentlemen arrived an hour ago,' she whispered. 'And said they were sure you would be pleased to see them.'

'Thank you, Mrs Venn.'

'I told them you were round at Lady Cornford's,' the housekeeper added with a shy smile, 'and they said they would wait with impatience for your return, Mr Westland looking so bronzed and happy.'

Bella skewered the sentimental Mrs Venn with a glance and, heaving up a nervous sigh, entered her drawing room.

In many other locations across London when men sat

down to cards, there was money involved. The game these two played had been invented by Kennett when he was six and they were the only people in the world to understand or tolerate the lack of rules.

'Black Dog!' Kennett cried on the turn of a card – and not a black suit either.

'Stay, sir!' Westland cried, flourishing the three of hearts. 'I reply with Byron and again double Byron.'

'That is low of you, Westland.'

They looked up at Bella's entrance, grinning apishly.

'Mrs Wallis,' Kennett rose to greet her.

'How lovely to see you again, Mr Kennett,' Bella replied, extending her hand.

Philip Westland watched her with a half-smile. When she turned to greet him, he pre-empted whatever she might have to say by holding her lightly by her upper arms and planting a kiss on her cheek. The breath of a kiss. 'I have been abroad,' he murmured.

'So I imagined.'

William Kennett watched them with perhaps a little too much interest. He was tall and stick-thin, with a bright buzz of red hair and (Bella judged secretly) a beguiling mouth. As described by Westland, his friend was the cleverest man in England. At his house in Chiswick he had stables crammed to the doors with what he called his bright ideas: at the same time he had never made a single thing that worked.

'You are playing Black Dog, I perceive, Mr Kennett. How does the game end?'

'Oh, I should be mortified to think that it ever could.'

'But, say, if one player loses all his cards?'

'That would be quite terrible.'

'Bella wants to ask you what, then, is the point?' Westland smiled.

'The point?' Kennett frowned. 'A very deep question, one I have trained myself never to ponder. Perhaps it is to involve Westland and nothing more ambitious than that.'

'To divert him, you mean?'

'He has more than enough diversions. A very lazy man altogether. No, I like my verb better, I think.' His smile was humorous but Bella did wonder – and not for the first time – how much Kennett was in love with his friend.

'How did things go at Cissie Cornford's?' Westland asked gently.

Bella shrugged and raised her eyebrows. 'There was a man there tonight called Skillane. A very bumptious old man at that. With rather a lovely daughter.'

To both their amazement, Kennett sat down as if shot. 'I have met Mary Skillane,' he muttered. 'Did she look well?'

'She blushes very prettily.'

Whatever slight tension there had been in the room was dispersed as if by gunshot. Cognac was called for – an astonishing, because unexpected, story was revealed. Kennett was smitten with the girl Bella had dismissed only half an hour ago as a simpering nitwit. They had met at the mathematician Pybus's house in Draycott Gardens.

'You do not know Freddie and Cora Pybus but Philip does. A more rackety household cannot exist in London. Freddie is barely of this world at all and Mrs Pybus –'

'I know her to be a poet,' Bella warned.

'Then you know most of what there is to know. There are five children, all of them as wild as Dartmoor ponies. To make the story short, Adelaide, whose birthday party it was, stepped too close to the fire and her petticoats caught alight.'

Kennett studied Bella carefully. 'Miss Skillane doubtless struck you as idiotic in many respects. She has no conversation and is terrified of her father. But as the child screamed, she seized one end of the cloth covering the table and wrenched it free, scattering I don't know how many plates and cups into the bargain. She wrapped up little Adelaide and while I don't say she saved her life, she prevented serious burns to the child's legs. I have never seen anything finer. Quick, instinctive and completely the right thing.'

'My dear fellow,' Westland murmured.

'She is quite wonderful,' Kennett insisted, as much to himself as to anyone else. 'I am not sure how love strikes in the normal way of things but I must tell you I have not stopped thinking about her since this happened.'

'Have you spoken to her of your feelings?'

'Her father has her virtually under lock and key in Cadogan Square. I sent in my card and had it returned. A letter I wrote to Mary came back to me unopened, delivered by the hand of the butler.'

'There is a butler?'

'Sir William is as mad as a March hare. He has a house in Cornwall not much smaller than St Pancras station.'

'Let me ask you,' Bella said quietly. 'Who is Mr Robert Judd?'

There was a tight silence. 'Was he there tonight?' Kennett asked.

'I left before he arrived. The news of his coming seemed to upset Miss Skillane quite dreadfully.'

'She is promised to him. I shall do everything in my power to make sure he does not get her. Even if I have to kill him.' He stood, trapped by his feelings into a display of trembling Bella had never before seen in him and did not know he was liable to.

'You do not mean that,' she said.

'The man is an out-and-out scoundrel. To him, Mary is no more than an acquisition, like a new carriage or a pair of matched guns. She is a route to her father's wealth, which is enormous. Well, Judd simply shall not have her.' In an absent gesture, he turned over a card and laughed a bleak laugh. 'Look at that, if you will.'

'The seven of clubs,' Bella supplied.

'The Borodino,' Kennett corrected. 'It is a sign, Mrs Wallis. A sure and certain sign. Judd can go fish for her. She is – or perhaps it would be more honest to say – she will be mine.' He rose, tugging haplessly at the wings to his waistcoat. 'I have said too much.'

Westland touched him on the arm. 'If you intend to leave under such a cloud of anger, then please allow me to walk you home.'

'To Chiswick and back? I don't think so.'

'Must you walk at all?' Bella wondered. 'Wouldn't a cab be more convenient?'

'He walks everywhere,' Philip Westland explained.

In Bella's book, asking your occasional lover where he has been for the last three weeks would be very bad form. Asking him if he cared to unmask himself as an international spy was beyond her powers altogether. They lay in bed, holding hands like Hansel and Gretel. Unprompted, Westland gave a very funny account of a hotel in Cognac, without quite saying what he was doing there. Bella resolved not to ask. But love and silence are impossible bedfellows. She listened to Westland's breathing for a while and was relieved when he answered her unspoken question for her.

'I make these continental excursions because if I am not with you – I mean as we are now, tonight – London is intolerable,' he explained.

'It's not for me to ask where you have been.'

'Is it not?'

'Oh, Philip! I'm just happy to have you here now.'

They kissed. Westland smoothed out the neck to her nightgown. 'Did you know I have a sister?'

'I did not.'

'I have a sister eight years younger than me.'

'You have kept her very quiet.'

'She lives in Jarnac, on the banks of the Charente.'

'In a wonderfully elegant chateau?'

'No,' Westland said calmly. 'In an asylum.'

There was much more to say about Sarah Westland – her three attempts at suicide, her helpless indifference to the world outside, the frightening power of her silence – that always reminded Philip of the Alps under snow.

'Philip, I am so sorry to hear this.'

'No one can say whether she is happy. She is calm.'

'Calm is good,' Bella whispered.

'Perhaps. I suppose Cissie Cornford has a much more dramatic explanation for my absences.'

'Why do you say that?'

'The only time I met her she assured me that a man we both knew slightly was a spy in the pay of a foreign government.'

Bella sat up in the dark, alarmed. Philip laughed and dragged her down on to his chest. 'He was – he is – a perfectly respectable gentleman farmer from Sussex. His darkest deed, so far as I know, has been to take a party of sporting neighbours to play a fortnight's cricket in Corfu. Lady Cornford saw black iniquity in this. For her it was altogether too innocent an explanation.' Though, he reflected privately, that might be how a very different game was played. It was not much more absurd than buzzing about France like a postman.

Bella sat up again and pulled her gown over her head. She took his arm and drew it across her breast. 'Cissie Cornford is a foolish, interfering old woman.'

In the morning, Cognac hotels and Charentais asylums were not to be mentioned, any more than steamrollers or porpoises. They took breakfast in companionable silence, Westland reading his *Times* and munching thoughtfully on toast and marmalade. Bella watched him with the greatest affection. If he were a spy – and who would employ such a naturally open and honest man in such work – was it any business of hers, she thought? If she wanted to empty his life of all its secrets, honour demanded she must do the same herself. Meanwhile, the sun winked in the marmalade dish, Philip's newspaper crackled cheerfully, outside the windows Orange Street girded itself for another lazy and indulgent day.

'Would you say all's right with the world?' she asked, drenched from top to toe in happiness.

Philip lowered *The Times* for a moment. 'It says here that the steamer *Berwickshire* has run aground with a cargo of nitrates in Buenos Aires, but in every other respect I would judge we are managing to keep an equilibrium. So, yes, I might go so far as to say that.'

His smile was like a meadowful of birds.

Well, Bella thought, with the faintest touch of guilt, we have left out your friend William Kennett, poor fellow. He must be suffering a shadow or two in Chiswick. But then, that was love's pleasant agony for you. He must fight his own battles. On a day like this she was surely in the right of it: nothing much could go amiss. There were no dragons to slay and the waters of the lake that London sometimes seemed lay placid and undisturbed.

FOUR

Holborn Circus: bathed in sunshine though the day had started out frosty. On the south side lay St Andrew's, a very ancient foundation rebuilt by Sir Christopher Wren. At about ten in the morning, Constable Henry Darby was directed there by a pie-seller with a Christian conscience, a ratty little chap with a tray around his neck and a squared-off paper hat. He accompanied Darby as far as the graveyard and then nodded with his chin.

'Good man,' the policeman grunted. 'I'll have a tuppeny pie off you and then you can scarper.'

Fluttering beside a sixteenth-century vault was what seemed like a black shroud. Dust devils had blown paper and leaves against it. Darby laid down his pie on the tomb of one Cornelius Temminck, took off his helmet and wiped the band with a tobacco-brown handkerchief.

'Now then, Molly,' he said quietly. 'You're a bit out of your road up here. You haven't been sleeping out, I do hope.'

'Molly Clunn,' the fallen figure mumbled, as if answering roll-call.

'I know that, old girl. I know who you are. It's Harry

Darby come to see you. Sit up, if you can. I've brought your breakfast.'

Molly Clunn, the music hall darling. Darby had been taken across the river to Lambeth by his uncles to see her perform when he was ten. He'd seen her again the night before his wedding and yet again when Lily was still sucking on her mother's tit. Harry Darby was not the toughest copper in the division but still a hard man, as you had to be to do this job. Accordingly, he managed not to flinch as Molly struggled like a beetle to right herself. He breathed through the nose to minimise the stink of her.

'I'm a goner, Harry.'

'No, you ain't. But you can't lig about this old churchyard, good Lord you can't. And you with no boots on you.'

Molly plucked at her sodden skirts. 'I used to be so particular and that's no lie.'

'You've fallen on hard times. But it's not over for you yet, no, not by a long chalk.'

When Molly Clunn smiled her response, he saw that her four top teeth had disappeared. The woman he remembered as plumply seductive in fleshings and a skirt that opened at the front, a red bodice and fake diamonds in her hair was now a hideous scarecrow. Her half-exposed breasts were hardly more than flaps of skin, her shoulders bare to the bone. Old Molly was on her way out.

There was a footfall on the worn Yorkstone pavement and the sexton – if he was a sexton – (Darby was a bit hazy on church authorities but this one wore a cassock cinched with a leather belt with some silly bloody wallet hanging from it) – stood over them both. He was a stout and red-faced man with close-cut silver hair.

'Are you arresting this woman?' he demanded.

'No, sir, I am not.'

'Well, she can't stay here.'

Darby rose and put his helmet back on. That, and the set of his jaw, gave him what he thought of as the full majesty of the law.

'Now you don't want to go interfering with a police officer in the course of his duties.'

The sexton simply stared him down. 'I have taken your number and I want you both out of this yard at once.'

'Or?'

'Or he'll fetch a policeman,' Molly croaked with a cackle that turned into a paroxysm of coughs. In attempting to stand up, she collapsed like a tent whose poles had buckled.

'I will not have begging in the church precincts,' the sexton said. He picked up the pie. 'If this creature is a vagrant, you must apply the law.'

Experience had taught Darby that when it came to the poor, church people could be some of the most vindictive bastards on earth. The man in the cassock was in the way of being a gentleman; at any rate definitely not some shit-shoveller. With such as these, it was best to tread careful. Accordingly, he gave him his slow burn, an unblinking eye contact that did indeed unsettle the sexton.

'The lady is not a vagrant. She is out of her way this morning but her address is known to me.'

'A lady, you call her?'

'Is the vicar on the premises?' Darby decided, tugging down his tunic briskly. 'Because if he is, we shall just walk round there together, you and me.'

'The minister is preparing for matins.'

'Then off we go. Leaving the pie,' he added.

They saw the curate at the church door, a hand-wringing young man with a cruel centre-parting.

'Must there be all this fuss?'

'The lady – what this gentleman has called a creature – is Molly Clunn, once as well-known on the boards as any artiste who ever trod them.'

'But what is she doing in our churchyard, Constable?'

'It is not for me to teach you your duties, sir, but one explanation might be that she has a wish to be nearer to God.'

'What fiddlesticks,' the sexton snorted.

'Well, then,' Darby said. 'If you was to step around the corner with me, Reverend, you might tell her that's not possible. That you would like me to have her took up for trespassing.'

The curate bit his lip, considered, and then nodded. But when they came to the churchyard, Molly had gone.

'Is she a member of our parish?' the curate asked, uncertainly.

'Is Morton's Yard part of your parish?' Darby countered.

'I – perhaps. I cannot be sure.'

'You have never heard of it?'

'I think not.'

But the sexton knew what this exchange was about. His

face softened unexpectedly. Inside the church, the organ began to play and the first of the congregation were arriving. Disraeli had been christened in this church and Hazlitt married from it. That day's churchgoers were correspondingly well-heeled.

The curate's attention was beginning to wander. 'You say she is from Morton's Yard?'

'For a few days longer,' Darby said.

'And then what?'

'That's for you to say, sir. But no longer among us in this vale of tears. And that's no error.'

Darby touched the brim of his helmet and walked off. At the top of Shoe Lane he stopped to look for Molly over the heads of others. He searched to see whether the crowds were parting around some obstruction on the pavement or – as he told his wife that night – whether the Angel of the Lord was hovering. Nothing.

The way to keep your feet from playing merry hell on this job was to wiggle your toes and arch your instep. And, as Darby's sergeant was always reminding him with a good deal of sarcasm, to keep moving. He tucked his thumbs in his belt and began to walk up Holborn, steady as you like, one foot in front of the other, the law in motion.

Bella's office – or more accurately her place of work – lay in Fleur de Lys Court, off the Strand. It was here that she wrote the novels published under the name of Henry Ellis Margam. This nom de plume was very precious to her: not more than a dozen people in London knew Margam's real identity. It was as she wanted it. Though she did not like the fellow – no, not in the slightest – she very much liked being two people at once. There was mischief in it that not even the heady romance with Philip Westland could abate.

Margam was what was called a sensationalist – it was the heated pages of his latest book *The Widow's Secret* that had drawn a blush to Lady Skillane's cheeks, as reported by her daughter Mary. His more sophisticated readers found him alarmingly accurate about people and situations that they knew, or thought they knew. The moral of a Margam novel was not that love triumphs, nor that the meek will inherit the earth. It was that the world was a dangerous place and – once the thin veneer of manners had been stripped from it – unknowable.

There were by now eight such novels. This was not to say very much, for Mrs Toaze-Bonnett, with whom Bella shared a publisher, could write faster than she could knit and was on her thirty-fourth. She often protested to friends that she was sure she had no idea where these innocent tales came from. Bella could have told her: from a dusty and ramshackle barnful of clichés located in the otherwise empty pastures of Mrs Toaze-Bonnett's mind.

A Henry Ellis Margam novel was of a different order altogether. It came from Bella's uneasy sense of how the world really was – that was to say, how reason (and justice) was balanced precariously over an abyss. The trick was not to prate nor wring the hands but to find the story that might illustrate the metaphor. Every Margam novel, wherever it wandered, set out from London, both the view from such as Cissie Cornford's windows and the more brutal, less forgiving city land-scapes that lay beyond.

All the same, Bella was enough of a professional to know that happiness was the best pen wiper. It was this that Philip Westland gave her. Genial and good-natured man that he was, he had set off after breakfast for Chiswick. His friend Kennett was working on a steam launch (better to say a clinker-built rowing boat with a furnace and boiler amidships, topped by a seven-foot funnel). It was approaching the day of the vessel's second river trial. On its first outing, the boat had turned turtle.

'It sank under the weight of its own impudence,' Westland confessed. 'But since then he has cannibalised another boat and using the formers and risers from that has added all-important length to the keel. You could say a new seriousness has resulted. True, she is a little by the stern –'

'Westland, do you have the faintest idea what you are talking about?'

'No. But I like him. And admire him.'

'Has he ever been in love before?'

'Oh, love! What's that, dearest Bella? A momentary distraction. Good Lord, we inventors hardly have time for such nonsense. This is the elemental struggle, man against nature.'

But he kissed her lingeringly for all that.

Her pleasure at walking across the mossy paving of Fleur de Lys Court and pushing on the chocolate-brown door proved short-lived. Sitting at the once proud rosewood desk was Captain Quigley, eating a huge slice of veal and ham pie and spearing beetroot with his knife. His greeting was boisterous.

'And didn't I see you with your young man recently in St Martin's Lane?' he crowed.

'The boy you saw was my godson.'

'And every inch the warrior, the little chap! An officer any man would be proud to follow into the jaws of death and the Cape a safer place for his going there, I don't doubt.'

Bella stared in amazement at the entirely self-styled Captain Quigley. 'How did you know he was being sent to the Cape?'

'My dear lady! It is Quigley's business to know any detail touching your well-being. Why else would you employ me?'

'Do I employ you?'

'I think I have offered you some service in the past,' he smirked. 'Now, I have managed to get hold of some of that paper Mr Margam likes so much and also took the liberty of obtaining some of the German nibs he favours. The old office has been swept out, inkwells filled, everything ready for a bout of scribbling, if you are so minded.'

Quigley had a new trick – seething spittle through the gaps in his bottom teeth. He'd seen it done by a lawyer cove and admired it as a piece of punctuation. But he could not completely abandon waggling the eyebrows either. So he seethed and semaphored, his lips reddened by beetroot.

'And what are your plans now?'

'Me? I shall step round to the pub for a handy bit of business. Did you know,' he added formally, 'that down there in the Congo the currency of the country is brass stair-rods?'

'And you have some?'

'About four hundred,' Quigley confirmed, sliding out of the door with a final salute.

Bella settled at the rosewood desk with only the most sketchy idea of what she might write. The nibs that Quigley had procured lay nesting in a battered cardboard box. She tipped a few out and fitted one to her favourite holder, an ivory item the Captain had presented her with for the composition of *Deveril's Disgrace*. It was almost certainly stolen; if not, acquired from dubious sources. Bella liked its weary elegance. And at least the ink with which she wrote was honestly acquired, for she bought it herself from a stationer's in Fleet Street. But then this was only after Quigley had tried to persuade her to write in violet ink, of which he had several pint bottles in wicker sleeves, come by in the same way as his four hundred stair-rods.

She had been working no more than a quarter of an hour when Quigley returned. His expression was un-usually sombre. 'There is trouble,' he said, wiping his lips with the cuff to his jacket sleeve.

'And what trouble might that be?'

'I've just come across Billy Murch. Who sends his best regards, by the way. But otherwise much broken up.'

All the happiness Bella had felt at breakfast time dis-appeared in an instant. Murch was a name she recognised with a mixture of pleasure and dread. He had been the model for Meinherzen, the implacable hero of her latest book, *The Widow's Secret*. Even as disguised in the pages of a sensationalist novel, there was much to admire in Billy and not a little to fear. Quigley claimed him as a friend, but the gaunt and lonely figure was about as far removed from him as was a tiger from a tethered goat.

Bella laid down her pen carefully and looked Quigley in the eye. 'You say he is distressed?'

'Drunk, hardly fit to stand, the shakes on him like a wounded beast. He has found, or thinks he has found Molly Clunn,' the Captain nodded.

It took a moment or two for Bella to focus. 'She is in London?'

'You remember her, doubtless.'

Molly Clunn: bold and brash enough for two but reckless with the bottle. There had been loose talk that she and Murch might make a go of things – but all that had come from the Captain, who was of a generally sentimental cast of mind. Bella had met Molly once and once only and saw immediately that the very thing that Quigley admired so much in her and made her right for old Billy – her merriness – would in the end be her undoing. Murch had great qualities but a love of foolishness was not one of them.

Bella searched her memory. The two of them had set up somewhere along the Regent's Canal – a basement room, only to be got at through a thicket of alder. It was dry enough and clean enough but Murch (though he did not say so) detested it. Molly walked out on him a week or so later.

After that, reports of her were scant. She was in

Brighton, later on in Portsmouth. She was well, she was ill, she was in the gutter. Some said she was dead of the hard stuff. Murch himself shifted about in this same period, walking to Kent for the hop-picking, working the docks at Ipswich. When he came back to London, he stayed out on the wrong side of the river at Kennington and visited his friend the Captain only seldom. And now this.

'Is she in a bad way?'

'Hard to imagine worse.'

'Can we help?'

'I have sent word to Mr Urmiston, who values Billy highly. Doesn't know the lady but would cross an ocean for dear old Bill. Waiting on him now.'

Pat upon cue, Charles Urmiston arrived from his herbalist shop in Shelton Street, sidling into the office in his usual shy way.

'And if this isn't like old times,' the Captain exclaimed, after pumping his hand. 'Which I shall just run around to Tonio's for a jug of fresh coffee and a handful of biscuits.'

When he had gone, Urmiston smiled at Bella. 'You are looking wonderfully well,' he said softly.

She walked around her desk and kissed him, nuzzled her head in the crook of his neck and huddled him to her. There was a time in his life when Urmiston himself had been a sort of floating wreck. Bella had rescued him from the misery of losing his wife and then stood by astonished as he found what proved to be the true love of his life, the incomparable Mrs Bardsoe. In latter months she had seen him seldom and the role his commonsense had played in her judgement of what was right had passed to Philip Westland.

Comparison between the two men was inevitable. There never had been a romantic attachment with Urmiston, however, and while she admired him, she fancied she could never need him, not in the way she needed Philip. All that said, she was surprised how the snuff of his woolly collar, the familiar stoop to his back and gangling wrists made her eyes prick.

'How I have missed you,' she whispered.

Urmiston chuckled gently. 'We hardly live a mile apart, dearest Bella,' he chided. 'I should add that Hannah sends her love.'

They disengaged, each of them feeling a little foolish.

'This sounds a bad business,' Bella said to ease the moment.

'I fear the worst. We don't even know for sure where Molly is, exactly. But deep in some hellish slum.'

'Have you seen Mr Murch?'

'He took a bite with us at Shelton Street last night. He looked terrible, Bella. I have never seen a man so distraught. He blames himself for what has happened to Molly. He does not say so but I can see it in his eyes.'

'But he was under no formal obligation to her, surely?'

Urmiston shook his head gently. 'Once upon a time I would have agreed with you: he owes her nothing. But it doesn't work like that in Billy's world. She loved him and he let her down.'

Bella could not hold back a shudder. Urmiston, who had once been of her own class, had crossed a boundary and now lived far closer to that other, turbulent London she herself only visited. Molly's story was in its way the basis for a Margam plot: a woman loves a man who does not want her and as a consequence is flung into the pit. But Henry Ellis Margam's world was of dinner parties, white gloves and letters it might have been more sensible never to have sent. Bella's shudder came from having to acknowledge the basic emptiness of popular fiction.

'That poor woman,' she heard herself mutter.

'I have put myself at Murch's service for any rescue operation, which he has made clear is dangerous, very dangerous work.'

'I will come with you,' Bella said at once.

'No. That is gracious but it will not do.'

'I am not trying to be gracious. She will need a woman by her.'

Urmiston shook his head. 'That simply cannot happen. This is entirely man's work.'

'You do talk such piffle sometimes, Charles.'

He shrugged but did nothing to alter his expression, which was grave and – around the normally kindly blue eyes – a little bit fearful.

And shamefully, Bella herself was uneasy. Not because she was afraid, but rather that her alter ego, Henry Ellis Margam, whom she was hoping to encourage to enter the office and hang his hat, had turned at the threshold and disappeared. Evanesced. He was a man who preferred to stay on the sandy paths, among the parasols. He had told Bella many times that she was armed against life with nothing more than a pen and superb grey eyes. Mischief, to Henry Ellis Margam, was a monogrammed handkerchief found under the bed; or a cache of love letters hidden in the boathouse. Anything else was utter madness. There was enough folly in a misplaced lock of hair to furnish any novel with its plot.

FIVE

Quigley came back with his can of coffee and the three of them sat uncomfortably either side of Bella's desk, debating what to do. The Captain, like Urmiston, saw the search for Molly Clunn in expeditionary terms. It suited his nature to bluster and he tried to make clear that no African exploration could be more fraught than what he had in mind.

Quite suddenly, Philip Westland arrived, as if from a different story altogether. Even his clothes marked him apart: he wore a cream linen suit and a soft shirt, which were not in themselves so very extraordinary but had (in the perpetual gloom of Fleur de Lys Court) some of the effect of fancy dress. He shook hands with Urmiston and the Captain, stood about for a few uncomfortable minutes and then whisked Bella away to lunch at Fracatelli's.

He grasped at once that he had walked into some piece of business that was none of his own. That much he could see in Bella's uneasy smile and only half-effected introductions. But he knew she had an almost superstitious reverence for the Strand restaurant with its snowy white tablecloths and crystal chandeliers.

Fracatelli himself seated them and flourished the wine

list. 'We don't see you often enough, Mrs Wallis,' he protested, eyeing Philip surreptitiously at the same time.

'This is a very amiable place,' Westland said after he had gone. 'Are those gentlemen lawyers over there?'

Bella's glance towards the table he indicated with his chin was cursory. She found her hands were trembling. 'I was very surprised to see you, Philip. I thought you were over at Chiswick for the day.'

'As did I. But it seems there was a faint chance of Kennett meeting Miss Skillane at the Royal Academy and all other business was suspended. We came back into the West End together. Mrs Venn told me where I might find you.'

'And what did you make of Fleur de Lys Court?'

Philip examined his napkin before pulling it through its mahogany ring. 'Must I say?'

'Of course! Else why would I ask you?'

'This then: I was greatly startled.'

'I find it suits very well,' Bella said, brusquely.

'You mean, perhaps it suits Mr Henry Ellis Margam. About that, I can't comment.'

'That is true,' she snapped.

'But of course, in this instance, it is not he who is going to suffer if things go wrong.'

And that was it: even in such a brief and apparently casual visit to Fleur de Lys Court, he had learned enough to know what she was planning for that night. Not in any detail, she was sure of that, but either Urmiston or Quigley had said a word or two too many.

On a childlike impulse, she pushed away her plate. 'I cannot stay,' she decided.

Philip studied her without expression. 'Of course you

can,' he said in a steady and emotionally neutral tone. 'I have no right to insist, but –' and at last he smiled briefly '– I must.'

And when she looked suitably crestfallen, his smile became a soft and indulgent laugh. He covered her hand with his. 'Be easy, Bella. We are not quarrelling. We are merely two people taking lunch.'

She stayed; and for four courses and a very good bottle of Barolo he entertained her across a range of subjects, including a very scandalous account of how belly-dancing worked, or, perhaps more accurately, the amount of flesh it set in motion. That night's expedition to retrieve Molly Clunn was never mentioned once. They parted on the pavement outside, just as if things were as he had said they were – two close friends concluding a pleasant lunch. But then, at the last moment, Westland touched her sleeve. In fiction, squires' daughters came close to fainting when this happened, generally at the lynchgate when Captain Brooke looked into their eyes. Bella felt the same giddy sensations.

'The thing of it is,' Philip said gently, 'I had no right to spring myself upon you earlier. And certainly, dearest Bella, I had no idea what I might find. Without wishing to, I overstepped the mark.'

She stared after him as he sauntered away, holding his hat in his hand, arms swinging. Characteristically, he did not look back.

But then she knew him well enough to see that he had delivered, in his own inimitable fashion, a warning and a rebuke. Fleur de Lys Court was the door into a world he would far rather she did not enter.

* * *

Quigley insisted upon taking a gun, a French cavalry pistol with a dangerously weak breech. Urmiston was given a sawn-down pick handle – shortened so that it could be hidden in a sleeve and dropped out at a moment's notice, a trick he had tried repeatedly but could not master. He discarded Quigley's idea and went for a walk, coming back with a muddy stave from a building site.

The Captain did not want Bella Wallis to accompany the party, no, not for love nor money – but if she was going to be pigheaded about it, better she dressed accordingly. My word, yes.

Bella went to Shelton Street and consulted Urmiston's beloved, Hannah Bardsoe, as to what this might mean in a practical sense. That plump and good-natured woman ignored the question and begged her fervently not to go at all. 'The Captain is in the right of it for once. Leave it to him, as he is used to the perils of the underworld, tub of lard though he may be.'

'We're hardly going to the Congo, Mrs Bardsoe. And Charles will take care of me.'

'Charles? He cannot look after himself in even the smallest shower of rain,' Hannah cried. 'I know it has to be done but I will tell you straight: I'm afeared for the lot of you.'

'Tell me what I must do to disguise myself.'

'No perfume, not a hint of soap, no pins or brooches, combs or anything of the kind. No corsets nor stockings. Nothing in short that would make you a woman at all in the wider world. You go as an animal, Mrs Wallis, a brute thing.'

'You are not overegging the pudding somewhat?'

Hannah Bardsoe stood, distracted. 'My dear,' she said with great simplicity, 'you can have no idea.'

'Will you go with me to Coleman's, to help me choose some clothes?'

They walked to the end of Shelton Street and turned in at a stub of a passage where Ma Coleman kept her old clothes shop. At the bottom of this tiny cul-de-sac was a timbered Jacobean house bleached silver. Time had almost collapsed it: the structure leaned drunkenly against the blank brick walls of its neighbours. Ma had it for her warehouse, though it would have been risking death to move any higher than the ground floor. The door and windows had long gone and an acid stench came from the mountains of cast-off clothing that filled the property front to back. Death and destitution spoke to Bella from this hideous storehouse.

Ma had the knack of silence. Her face was filthy and her hands blackened, but she had intelligent eyes. She sorted her stock with a long pole, dragging this and that out on to the ruined pavement without comment. Bella found she could not so much as touch anything and so the choice was made by Hannah Bardsoe: a once white shawl, two torn chemises, a black tent of a dress in the cheapest cotton.

'Boots?' Ma asked, pointing with her pole to a cascade of them.

'No,' Bella said at once. Hannah laid a reassuring hand on her arm.

'Now for these old rags, Ma,' she said, 'if they are worth more than a few pence apiece, you can have 'em back without putting yourself to the trouble of searching out more.'

'This ain't no charity.'

'It ain't no emporium neither.'

The clothes were carried back to the little shop in Shelton Street and boiled up in the washer, then flogged in the tiny yard. Hannah examined every seam for lice, finding a few left alive and cracking them with her thumbnail.

'When do you go?'

'Quigley says tonight, as soon as it is dark.'

'Then you shall stop here and eat with us. These rags can go round to the bakehouse to be dried and then we shall see.'

London had grown heavy with the threat of summer storm. Cutting through its everyday smells – smoke, horse piss, dust, soot, pollen – many could identify the whiff of imminent electrical discharge. Ladies in Belgravia felt the sharp stab of unwonted headaches: across the river in Lambeth, round-shouldered men stood out of doors with their hands in their pockets, wondering at the lack of light. It was said that at Epping the storm had already arrived and that the great forests were on fire in several places. At their northern edge, the oak before the Woodbine Inn had been struck by lightning, killing two labourers sheltering under it. An oak is only an oak but this one was famous for having shaded the brow of the great Wesley.

But in central London it was eerily still. Many who had cause to cross the Thames during the late afternoon remarked on the river's unnatural colour.

Captain Quigley and Charles Urmiston stood outside the shop in Shelton Street, feeling the sky press down on them. What they could see of it was almost all black.

'You are very calm, Captain.'

'What it is, I am heartbroke. A man makes only a few pals of the true blue kind in his lifetime.'

'You knew her that well?'

'You should have seen her when she was young.'

'And Mr Murch – Billy? Did he know her when she was young?'

'Not so much.'

'Where is he now?'

'We meet at the bottom of Fetter Lane, as soon as it has come full dark.'

Bella joined them, her hair undone and artful smudges of soot on her cheeks and throat. The black dress hung open a little, revealing the slope to a far too white breast.

'No,' Quigley said gently. 'Will you go back inside and have Hannah decorate you with a little more dust?'

But in that instant the storm broke and in seconds they were drenched. They ran indoors and drank a full measure of rum each and shared the last cheroot from Urmiston's paper packet. Then, watched by a fearful Mrs Bardsoe, they hunched their shoulders and set off down the street. As Bella had seen done – but only ever at a distance – she linked arms with the two men and wore the white shawl over her head.

Murch was waiting for them, looming out of the dark, water streaming from a canvas jacket. When he saw Bella, he let out a stifled animal cry.

'The lady is to go back,' he commanded. 'I can't be responsible for her.'

'Listen to me, Billy –' Bella began.

He brushed her words away, white ridges high on his cheeks. 'I cannot have it.'

'She has come to help,' Urmiston said.

Murch stared at them all in turn, as if examining madmen. 'Maybe I should do this on my own,' he muttered.

'Well, you ain't going to, so lead on, Billy boy,' Captain Quigley said through chattering teeth. 'Let's get it done.'

Murch turned on his heel and marched up Fetter Lane. Water ran down the roadway like a black river. The others hurried to keep up. After only a hundred yards, Billy stopped. He pointed into the murk.

'Where we go now is as dangerous a place as any in London. You do exactly as I say. And mark me, Mr Urmiston: if you have to run, you retrace your steps and you run until your heart is fit to burst. Taking the lady with you. Understood?'

'Yes,' Urmiston said, his voice shaking.

'Then this way and God help us all.'

They felt their way into as evil a place as existed in all London. At the top of Morton's Yard a huge mound of dust and cinders had been reduced to a midden – mud and filth spread more than a foot deep across the cobbles. On the far side of this barrier the lights of a pub blinked wanly. A crowd of about thirty milled outside, roaring on the dance of two naked children, their scrawny limbs jerking, their feet splashing in the puddles. Dogs leaped at their heels. There was fiddle music from a hunchback man hardly taller than the dancers.

Murch held them back. 'Wait here,' he ordered in a low voice. 'And you, Mr Urmiston, put your arm around the woman we have with us. Hold that pacifier across your chest, ready for use. The Captain to come with me.'

Urmiston nodded and drew Bella under his arm. The stave he had found for himself was held tight in his hand. The two shrank back against a wall. Murch and Quigley pushed their way into the packed pub and were quickly lost to view.

'This is vile,' Bella whispered. 'I have never been so afraid.'

'Your hands are frozen.'

'From horror. We have done this badly. We must come back by day with half a dozen hired bullies.'

She screamed as an elderly man was pushed against her by the crowd.

He looked up into her face and gaped. 'Mrs Wallis,' he exclaimed, incredulous. 'Penwith, madam. I was in service to Lord Liddiment in better times. You don't remember me? I was under-butler to his lordship at the London house.'

'Mr Penwith!'

The old man put his fingers to his lips in agonised warning. 'Just Penwith. Old Pen, they call me here.'

'But –'

'You are going to ask what I'm doing in this horrible place. Starving, is the answer to that. Dying, the answer to that.'

Bella found that she was clutching both his hands in hers. 'But what has brought you so low?'

'Old age,' he whispered tearfully. 'And want of a house.'

'Lord Liddiment could do nothing for you?'

'I was turned off at a morning's notice. That was four years ago. His lordship was in Ireland. I doubt he ever knew or noticed.'

They were interrupted by a taller man who lunged at them, his expression wild with drink. 'Now, Pen, who's the judy with the lovely titties?'

'My daughter, Maggsy.'

'Your daughter, my eye.'

Urmiston seemed as if roused from sleep. He stepped between them, the stave in both hands. 'Enough of that.'

'Maggsy, he means no harm,' Penwith pleaded swiftly.

'Means no harm?' Urmiston laughed. 'I'd kill him as soon as look at him.'

But it was Bella who knocked the knife from Maggsy's hand and Bella who swung her forearm against his throat. The crowd that had been watching the naked urchins at once swung round to follow a more interesting story. The man called Maggsy was on his hands and knees and getting ready to spring. As he raised his head, Urmiston leaned into the stroke and drove through the covers as he had once been taught by the school professional, Henry Pye. Plenty of wrist, the bat angled downwards. There was a wet thud. Blood from Maggsy's nose wriggled away like worms in the downpour.

'Finish him!' a woman shrieked. 'Go on, bust him up!'

Her companion was already kneeling by the body, her hands plunging into his trouser pockets.

'We're looking for a friend of ours,' Bella shouted. 'And want no trouble.'

Murch was back by her side, his fingers closed like a

vice over her elbow. 'Don't speak,' he growled. 'Not a word more. Walk away slow. Perce, take her other side. Don't strut, for all love. Saunter.'

'You should have finished him, mister,' one of the naked children advised Urmiston. She hopped from foot to foot, shivering, her arms crossed over her chest. 'You let him off light. And now he'll have you, you see if he don't.'

'Is the white-haired old cove still with us?' Quigley whispered, groping for Penwith. 'Step ahead of us, dad, and lead the way. It's as black as a cow's insides down the lane here.'

'Where are we going?'

'Randall's,' Murch replied. 'You may know the house.'

There was no problem with rights of entry. The front door had long gone and by what tiny light there was Bella could see that so had the ground-floor windows. They were replaced by pennons of sacking blowing wildly in the tempest that had begun to rage. She held on to Urmiston's coat-tails and shuffled into a narrow hallway hardly less wet than the pavement outside. Her foot touched a sodden bundle. To her horror, it moved: inside the foul wrapping lay a child. Bella reached out with her hand anywhere and found Penwith's bony grasp.

'Breathe through your nose, madam,' he whispered, in the same tone he had once used when accepting her umbrella in Lord Liddiment's marble hallway.

There was a low curse from Billy Murch as his fifth match refused to flare; and then came a pale dish of light from the bulls-eye lantern he had carried hidden in his clothes. A gift from Constable Darby, not to be lost, not to be damaged; to be returned anonymous-like to the steps of the St Bride's nick by midnight sharp and no messing. Darby himself too bloody fly to put his nose anywhere near Morton's Yard, no, not for a sergeant's stripes.

From the back of the house a giant of a man reeled, if giants are measured by height. This one wore a whaler's cap with flaps and a ragged coachman's cape. 'Not here, you don't. You don't come in here, you sorry sacks of shit. Not 'less I see some coin in your hand, you don't.'

There was a sudden sharp coughing sound and he sank unexpectedly to his knees.

'What it is,' Billy Murch said in a low and seemingly reasonable voice, 'I will reach down your throat and rip your lungs out so soon as debate you. I will have your eyes out with these here thumbs, d'you follow me? Well, do you?'

'I am the lodging house keeper,' the giant whined. 'I have my orders.'

'See, but these are your new orders. You make one more peep and I'll finish you, so help me. I will break every fucking bone in your body.'

'She said you might come. She said one day you might come.'

Billy's piteous howl was like an animal's.

Molly Clunn had died that afternoon but already the rats had been at her. There were seven other people in the attic room where she lay. In the whole building there were forty more, all of them seemingly struck down by the same mystery illness, a sleeping sickness imported from some mangrove swamp or jungle floor. But it was much simpler than that: they were starving.

Old Pen held Bella back with trembling hands. 'She was ill when she came,' he whispered. 'I spoke to her a few times. A servant of yours maybe?'

'A friend. In her own way, a friend.'

'Now listen, old-timer,' Murch said in a thick voice. 'We cannot move her tonight. But if I was to give you a few coins, could you sit with her and see her took from this rathole in the morning so's we can bury her in the Christian way of things?'

Penwith stared. Murch reached in and dragged him forward by his lapels, his teeth bared. Urmiston, gentle Urmiston, brushed his hands away.

'Can you at least,' he amplified, 'have her taken from here to a place we will designate in the Farringdon Road where we might meet you with better arrangements – a hearse?'

The old man peered at them one by one. 'Tomorrow?'

'At eleven tomorrow.'

'And now,' Quigley added, 'we want a way out of this here attic such as will give us no trouble.'

But it was too late for that. Maggsy and his cronies were pounding up the stairs. Quigley took out the horse pistol and steadied it in both hands, before pointing it down into the dark. When he pulled the trigger, the breech blew off, whistling past his face and killing Penwith instantly. The firing pin had done its work, however, and though the bullet was travelling slow, it found the softest part of Maggsy's face, entering his enraged eye as sweetly as a masonry bee finds the one unmortared crack in a blank wall.

'Up on to the roof,' Murch shouted. 'Quigley to lead the way, the lady to follow. Mr Urmiston to stay with me. And make it quick.'

Bella held on to the tail of the Captain's jacket, shuddering to feel rats run across her feet. A child loomed for an instant and was knocked over. She supposed they would make their escape by skylight, but Quigley dragged her into an attic where the roof had collapsed. The same child they had knocked down took her hand.

'No mistakes now,' Quigley growled. 'One false move out on them tiles and you're a goner. Get up on the ridge. Straddle it and wait for the rest of us.'

'It ain't so hard,' the child boasted. 'Do it all the time. You can get to Creely's, what has a flat roof. T'aint no further than you can spit.'

'Come with me.'

'Not likely,' her guide cackled, disengaging her hand. In another second he had disappeared.

Bella and Captain Quigley clawed their way up the ruined section of roof and on to the ridge.

'To the right, to the right,' Quigley bellowed over the thunder.

'What about the other two?'

'Don't you worry about them.'

Illuminated by acid blue lightning, the dome of St Paul's seemed for a moment to be swimming towards Bella, as if to swallow all this misery like a whale in the ocean or better still (she thought hysterically) shaped like the shadow of God Himself.

Mrs Bardsoe had no tweezers but heated a needle over a candle, her left hand taking a firm grip of Bella's thigh. The men were downstairs, shaking the water out of their hair and clothes like rats.

'Now you can stop that sobbing,' Hannah Bardsoe said, 'for it is nothing but a jag of old wood that –'

Her breath fanned Bella's naked flesh and she grunted once or twice in concentration. 'You've had a night of it and no mistake. But now you're safe and – ah now! Out she comes, as sweet as a nut. A spell the size of my finger! Disinfectant for that and then a light bandage, I think. As for the bruises, why, arnica every time.'

She looked up past Bella's stomach and smiled. 'I'd be obliged for a pull-up, which my knees are creaking like some old gate.'

Bella obliged; and once she had Hannah upright, embraced her and kissed her hair. 'Is there a woman in the world more sensible than you?'

'None,' Hannah agreed. 'After a dab of lye and your bandage, on with your clothes and we'll step downstairs for a spot of refreshment. Unless I mistake, that is Mr Westland's manly voice mingling with the others.'

'How on earth did he get here?'

'Urmiston took the liberty of sending for him. And who give you these bruises on your lovely arm?'

'I'm afraid it was Billy Murch,' Bella replied.

'He's took it very bad, the poor devil. He'll stop with us tonight. And I do hope for long after that. Now listen to me, my dear. Let him and Percy Quigley arrange what is to be done. No more adventures.'

And reaching on tiptoe, she kissed Bella's trembling eyelids.

That night, in the dark of the Orange Street bedroom, she lay on her back like an exhausted swimmer, her arm trapped under Philip's head, his cheek against her shoulder. The rain hammered against the window panes and somewhere a gutter was overflowing, the cascade striking the pavement with a vaguely threatening force.

He knows so much, he has done this before, she thought. Some woman he has never mentioned and never will has taught him how patience unties the tricky knot. She wiped her damp skin with the flat of her hand and pulled her hair away from her face. She thought he was asleep, but his own hand came up and caught her by the wrist.

'It will not do, Bella,' he muttered. 'No more of this.'

For a terrible second she thought he meant the frenzy with which she had made love but of course his mind was on what had passed at Morton's Yard. In daylight, at the breakfast table, she would have been swift to contradict him, for squabbling like children was one of their most intimate activities.

'My arm has gone numb,' she whispered.

Westland raised his head and freed her, before flopping back on to the pillow, sending a puff of lavender-scented air into her mouth.

'Say you love me,' she begged.

'There is nothing of me, not one atom, that does not. But no more adventures. No more reckless journeys to the interior.'

SIX

Before the breakfast table had been laid in Orange Street, before even the curtains had been drawn back, Billy and Captain Quigley, along with another four men they had mustered from among their friends, returned to Morton's Yard and retrieved the bodies of Molly Clunn and Edgar Penwith. The third corpse, that of Maggsy, was nowhere to be seen, though a fourth and fifth – skeletal figures that had died in the night – had been thrown face-down in the mud, where they formed little sodden islands. There was not one dry foot of Morton's Yard from end to end – what was not mud was black water. The place was eerily quiet. Only one person was about, a child in a rag of a dress, cranking the handle to a cast-iron water pump.

Quigley had only once before seen anything to match this desolation: at a train wreck in Kent, where silence had screamed and even the morning air had, it seemed, been sucked out of the sky. Though too small a child to speak, he had had the feeling that something essential, some comforting ordinariness, had been stripped from the world and nothing put in its place. Bodies from the train lay scattered down an embankment – including those of his mother and father – and the engine's boiler was still venting steam. Three of the five carriages had over-turned, as if to draw urgent attention to the scene. Yet the overwhelming sense was of an ancient and aboriginal emptiness. And so it was now, at dawn in Morton's Yard.

Bella Wallis had a phrase she had once used against the Captain: for him, thinking was like trying to come it the toff in a duchess's house, tripping on the top step of her stairs and falling all the way to the cellars. This otherwise incurably facetious man sat down wearily on a worn stone, his head in his hands. It is true, he thought, I don't have the words. But if that child at the pump comes across to beg from me, I will kill her.

'Shift yourself, Perce,' said a quiet voice at his back.

It was Murch, bearing Molly's body in his arms. Both corpses were transferred quietly by closed van to a funeral parlour in Portugal Street run by a Mr Mustoe. There they were met by Urmiston, shaved, bathed and in his best suit. It was his job to persuade young Mr Mustoe what was to be done. To smooth over any questions, he carried a small doctor's bag, inside which was a cash box.

'Don't have nothing to do with the old man, he's a bit slow on the uptake these days,' Quigley warned, just before he lifted the door knocker. 'You deal with the boy. They call him Frank. And tell him that for Molly we want the glass hearse.'

For someone who had been roused from his bed at six in the morning by a stranger on the doorstep with two mutilated bodies wrapped in calico, Frank Mustoe displayed great sang-froid. As would follow from any acquaintanceship with the likes of Quigley, he was deft in asking only the question that mattered – that is to say, where the money was to come from. Urmiston passed him the leather bag. The first of the bodies he looked at was Mr Penwith's and, though he shook his head slightly at the ruined jaw and cheek, he made no comment. But when he looked into Molly's ravaged face, his response astonished Charles Urmiston.

'Poor old girl,' he muttered. Old Mustoe had appeared at the door of the office in his nightshirt. 'See who it is, dad.'

The old man peered, nodded, scratched his armpit and withdrew without a word.

The content of the cashier's box was examined and found agreeable. It was arranged that two professional mourners would walk in front of Molly's hearse, their top hats decorated with black crepe bands reaching halfway down their backs. The horses' bridles would be topped by plumes of black feathers.

'It will all be done according,' Frank Mustoe promised. 'I recognise the lady and I understand the interest that will be shown at her passing.'

'Do you say so?' Urmiston asked, faintly bewildered.

'Molly Clunn's a name that's not forgotten by many a Londoner. I don't want to teach you your grieving, Mr Urmiston, but so soon as you have a date for the funeral, you might wish to invite those as wish to pay their respects but cannot attend the church in person to send their carriages along. Even two or three empty carriages behind the hearse make a show, my word they do.'

'Do you happen to know someone called Captain Quigley?' Urmiston asked.

Mustoe's professional gravity cracked open in a smile. 'Percy Quigley? He sent you, did he? Hiding round the corner, is he? Him and the old dad had a falling out more than twenty years ago, but yes, I know the Captain. Tell him I will step down to Fleur de Lys Court later on this morning. And let him be ready with a list of the nobs that remember her fondly.'

Young Mustoe, who was forty if he was a day, laid his hand along Urmiston's sleeve. His voice was kindly. 'I've seen Molly out and about a few times recent and she deserved a better end. But it is our job to send her to meet her Maker with dignity and – if I may say so – a bit of joy. Yes, those are my words, Mr Urmiston: a bit of joy. Praise we the Lord, as the hymn has it. You have come to the right place.'

Bella had a small space permanently set aside in the morning room of the house in Orange Street. The plain oak desk with locking drawers that stood against one wall was used solely for the final draft of the Margam novels. Mrs Venn, who had a penchant for decorating the rest of the house with cut flowers or bowls of fruit, knew there was never to be anything on this desk but a brass inkstand and a Lyme Regis trilobite Bella used as a paperweight. The desk itself was to be dusted but never polished. Moreover, once seated behind it, her mistress was not to be interrupted by anybody. All visitors to the house were to be turned away and no letters brought in.

The morning after the disastrous Holborn expedition, Bella set herself up there and for a day and a half sat with a pen in her hand, perfectly ready to write, wanting to write, but paralysed by misery. Philip had left her a gently worded note to say that he would be away for a day or two, and this she interpreted (correctly) as an example of his tact.

Bella had once been told by someone she loved that she was at heart a moralist. The remark was meant to point to the essential seriousness of the Henry Ellis Margam books. The heroes and heroines of the stories stood aghast as they were drawn deeper and deeper into the maze created by the lust and greed of others. The trick of the thing was to make the idea of good seem natural and even commonplace. In Bella's world, choosing right over wrong was as necessary to life as breathing.

And yet Philip Westland's warning had touched a nerve: there was only so far one could go along the path into the horrors of the world. A fog hung permanently over that labyrinth and at some point even the most courageous adventurer faltered. There in the dark, like a canker, lay the multiplying evil of places like Morton's Yard. Bella had stumbled almost to the centre of it and it had left her struck dumb.

When at last her pen began to move, she found she was describing the sun bursting through elms into a broad and empty field. She could not explain to herself why this particular image surfaced rather than the terrors she had so recently experienced. The memory came from her child-hood: she was a six-year-old girl in a white smock and frilled pantaloons, sitting in a bank of buttercups, singing. Even the slight elevation the slope afforded gave her a view across the river to Chelsea, interrupted by the red sails of brick barges sailing upstream.

It is, her father seemed to say to her from beyond the grave, because you were alone in this landscape. That is why you remember it now. The house we lived in was not far away – it was along by the river – but this empty field was like another country, the first frontier you ever crossed. Can you remember what you were singing?

It was a characteristically wry touch. Henry Curtis had died when Bella was twelve and she remembered him most for his clumsy good nature and dry manners. From time to time, as now, he spoke to her as he was in life, a disappointed second son with a houseful of books and just enough invested wealth to live comfortably without the need to work.

'What should I have done?'

She spoke the question aloud. A startled Mrs Venn poked her head around the door.

'Did you ask for something?' she said in her most timid voice. Bella flung down her pen, greatly relieving her housekeeper, who had been going about the house on tiptoe all morning.

'I was calling for a pot of coffee, Mrs Venn. I have been away, I know, and now I am back.'

'Nothing could be more welcome,' Mrs Venn cried joyfully, as if welcoming her mistress home from a long voyage.

* * *

Three days later, Molly Clunn was interred in St Anne's, Wardour Street. Over two hundred mourners from the world of the music halls attended the service, many of them dressed in stage costume. Frank Mustoe had been right: eight carriages followed the hearse, their roofs banked with flowers.

Bella missed the service and the ensuing wake: she was seeing Mr Penwith buried in St Dunstan's in the West, a funeral attended by only two other mourners, one of them the former under-butler's distraught employer, Lord Liddiment. 'I might have helped, had I known. We have cottages, here and in Ireland: he would have been welcome to one. It shames me to say I never asked after him and now it has come to this. It is a black day, a bitter black day.'

Following Molly's funeral, Murch stayed the night with Urmiston and Hannah Bardsoe. He walked out without a word early the next morning. Quigley went down into Kent to look for him and was presently sleuthing, as he called it, in Gravesend. He sent a card to Orange Street, saying 'Wild Goose Chase'. There was no signature.

In the same post, a much fuller letter came from Bella's former companion, Marie Claude D'Anville. The Frenchwoman had fled, first to France and then back across the Channel to Worthing. Her new soulmate was a teacher called Iris Burton; they had taken to wearing identical clothes and had scandalised their Sussex neighbours by painting the interior walls of their little villa midnight blue. According to Marie Claude, this colour created an atmosphere of preternatural calm, though she was honest enough to add that the rooms could be gloomy during the hours of daylight. At night and in bed it was like being becalmed in the Pacific Ocean. Candles gave the appearance of watching Polynesian gods.

'She is very young,' Bella explained to Mary Skillane as they sat sipping sherry in Orange Street a few Sundays later. It was midday and the air was heavy with the sound of bells. Bella detested sherry but it seemed to be the only drink Miss Skillane had heard of. She held her glass pinched up in both hands, one at the stem, as though fearing the crystal might shatter. Or that her father might suddenly burst through the door like a rampaging bison.

'You don't worry about her?' she asked of Marie Claude.

'Never. I have not yet met Miss Burton and I worry for her sometimes,' Bella murmured. 'Her new companion can be excessively demanding.'

'Do they live together as man and wife?' Mary whispered, scandalised.

Bella remembered her former lover with the greatest fondness, even to the point of missing her touch once in a while, the scent of her body and her ridiculous neediness.

'Marie Claude would make a very unimpressive husband and an even worse wife. I would say the interests they share can be more poetically expressed.'

'Would I like her?'

Bella considered. 'If you like bedraggled birds of paradise,' she suggested.

But irony formed no part of Mary's experience. Nor was she amused by William Kennett's misadventures with the steam launch he was attempting to build. 'My father is a shipowner and knows the power of the sea. I wonder at Mr Kennett's foolhardiness.'

'Although of course this latest shipwreck took place not far from the Mortlake Brewery. But you must tell him what you feel to his face. He is expected shortly.'

The girl jumped up. 'He is coming here?' she wailed.

Bella laughed and drew her down again. 'You meet under perfectly respectable circumstances.'

'You will say nothing to suggest that I have been critical of his boat-building?'

And this, Bella thought, is love. Miss Skillane was thrilled and wretched all at the same moment, a vein in her throat throbbing, her hands shaking so badly that she actually tucked them under her thighs, like a schoolgirl.

'He comes to lunch. I hope you will join us.'

'Oh, I should like nothing better!'

'Later, you might ask him to escort you around a room or two of the National Gallery.'

'Is he artistic?' the girl cried in dismay.

'About as much as the average cab-horse. But he likes you very much, Mary. I am sure you have noticed. Talk to him about Cornwall. It's my impression that Mr Kennett will hang on your every word.'

'And now you are teasing me.'

For so it seemed when Kennett pitched up. He acted dumbstruck and sat down next to Mary, turning an apple over and over in his hand, one that he had plucked from a bowl of fruit in front of him. Bella indicated to Philip Westland that they should leave the two lovers alone for a few minutes. By way of an excuse, they sauntered up to Leicester Square together. Westland stopped before a familiar presence, the hurdy-gurdy man in his greasy soldier's Glengarry and paid him sixpence to give a turn or two outside the house in Orange Street.

'What does your chum Kennett make of us?' Bella asked.

'Us? There is an us?'

'In my mind there is an us.'

'He thinks me the luckiest man in the world.'

'As indeed you are.'

'And has offered me rather a pretty house he owns in Wiltshire. Village life, Bella. Big skies. A trout stream, I think. Cows and so forth. He describes it all as a writer's paradise.'

Bella seized his hand for a moment. Westland drew it to his lips. 'I told him you were perfectly happy where you were.'

'You understand, Philip?'

'Not for one moment, no. For example, shall you be Mr Henry Ellis Margam forever, do you think? I can quite see how that inkstained scoundrel will never be the man to be solaced by choral evensong in a Wiltshire village. But you and I might teach ourselves such an easy obedience, don't you think?'

'I am a Londoner,' she smiled ruefully. 'There must come an end to it one day – but not yet. Meanwhile, and in so far as I have a heart at all, it is yours.'

Walking back arm in arm, she thought about what she had said, or the part that had touched on London. To leave it would be the same as forsaking a library – a very mixed collection, to be sure, but alive in the way all books are. This sunlight they were bathed in, for example. In the city, sunshine was to be greeted with almost an apologetic grin, as if stolen from elsewhere. Who in Wiltshire gave it so much as a second thought? Bella laughed out loud and reached on tiptoe to kiss Philip Westland's cheek. When he glanced at her enquiringly for the reason, she pointed to a cat yawning in a doorway, its fur coated in dust. Next to the cat was old Abrams and his tray of ribbons and laces. He too was taking the sun while it lasted, his legs stretched out straight in front of him. The uppers to his boots had parted from the soles and by way of welcoming Philip's inspection, he wiggled his toes.

'A warm day, Mr Abrams,' Bella called.

'What of it?' he grumbled.

'A book, in its way,' Bella explained as they walked away.

It was Philip's turn to laugh. 'I had no idea inspiration was so easily come by.'

'What it is, I have asked Miss Skillane to lunch, and I have the most horrible feeling we shall learn more than we actually need to know from her.'

'Then,' Philip teased, 'would it not make more sense to send her packing and ask that old pedlar to lunch? He needs it more and you can winkle his story out of him. Did you not feel, Bella, he had the air of a ruined Russian diplomat with secrets too deep to divulge, with nothing between him and eternity but his wits and a tray of boot-laces?'

'How comical you can be!' she exclaimed. 'How

wonderful to sit listening to your chaff in Wiltshire and watching the parson clutch his sides with laughter. How I long for all that. I must be mad to turn it down.'

'Oh dear,' Philip Westland said.

SEVEN

When they returned to Orange Street, they were met with
smiles and blushes. Kennett had laid aside his apple and
was now holding Mary Skillane's hand. Mrs Venn's
eyebrows, as she busied herself laying the table, were
signalling a fleet message: Love is in the air! Catching the
mood, Philip uncorked and decanted the very best claret
to be found in the house.

'For the beef, to be sure,' Mrs Venn cried giddily. 'Which
though I say it myself –' But then remembered her place
and fled from the room.

'Mary has been telling me about Cornwall,' Kennett
murmured. 'It makes me long to go. Did you know the
origin of the phrase "hue and cry"? A man – he must be
a very gifted man – stands up on the headland and sees
the movement of the pilchards under the sea by certain
signs and indications. Then he calls out the boats. We could
do that, Westland.'

'I'm not sure I would recognise a pilchard if one were
on my plate. To know how to find them under the sea –'

'No, no. We shall be the fishermen, braving all weathers,
laughing in the teeth of adversity. Mary could wait for us
onshore, waving a white handkerchief.'

'Shall we eat?' Bella suggested.

They learned more of Sir William Skillane. Mary's father was from Gwithian, where he had been born in a farm labourer's hovel. At ten he had run away to Falmouth on the other coast. When he was twelve he was listed as captain's servant on board the 32-gunned frigate *Actaeus*. Dismasted by a typhoon in the South China Seas at seventeen, he left the service and took a position with the trading firm of Jameson and Wheatcroft, Penang. He bought his first vessel, a native junk, when he was not yet twenty-two.

'Thus,' Westland suggested, 'a driven man.'

'My father's kind are scattered all over the South China Seas. It is something he always emphasises to strangers. No, what made him was a handful of pearls. He came home, raised money on a Norwegian barque –' she blushed – 'this cannot be of the slightest interest –'

'The pearls are the story, Mary,' Kennett interrupted gently.

'Yes, the pearls,' she whispered. 'Of course.'

Kennett stood up from the table and began pacing, his fork still held in his hand. When he found he had it, he threw it absent-mindedly into the fire and there was an unseemly scramble as the whole company leaped to save it. Bella and Philip exchanged glances.

'There is a man,' Kennett said finally, dragging at his red hair, 'a Mr Robert Judd. The son of Beeston Judd, one-time partner to Jameson and Wheatcroft. The father is a notorious rogue and if anything Mr Robert Judd is a bigger scoundrel still. Mary spoke just now of a handful of pearls. There are twenty-seven of them, each as big as my thumbnail. The family legend is that Skillane himself gathered these pearls from a single lagoon and that they result from some especial freak of nature seen nowhere else in the Pacific. Their value is to be measured in the thousands. By now perhaps in five figures.'

'They still exist?' Bella asked. 'They were not used to buy the Norwegian barque that Mary just now mentioned?'

'They comprised the collateral for much of my father's early business affairs,' the girl explained. 'But were never sold. In recent years he has had no need of them.'

'No,' Kennett agreed with heavy emphasis. 'No, indeed. They rest in a Cornish bank vault, inside a red lacquer box. Mary has seen them once only in her life.'

'And Judd?' Westland asked. 'Where does he come into all this?'

Kennett looked towards Mary, who nodded, her fingers kneading the edge of the tablecloth so vigorously that her plate began to move dangerously in the direction of her lap.

'These monster pearls may well have come from some remote lagoon but they were not gathered there by William Skillane. I have Mary's permission to tell you this: her father stole them from a Chinaman in Semarang.'

'I'm not sure – swindled them, perhaps –' she whispered.

'Stole them, swindled them and fled with them back to England. Judd found all this out only two years ago and at once returned to blackmail him.'

'But isn't Sir William now rich enough to pay him off?' Bella asked.

At this point, Mary burst into tears and fled the room.

'The price he has demanded is Mary's hand in marriage,' Kennett said. 'And thus, in time, a small fortune.'

'And the pearls?'

'Stay right where they are. In the Trevoase Bank. I must go and look for Mary.'

'Philip shall go in your place. You'll oblige me by sitting still, William, and when the summer pudding comes in, eating your portion like a Christian.'

Westland ambled off. On an impulse, Bella reached across the table and kissed the distraught inventor lightly on his forehead.

'I love her!' he declared. 'But even if I didn't, I should count it my duty to set this thing right. I don't know whether Philip told you, but this Judd, this villain, has had the impudence to put up for our club. I saw him yesterday morning – a great beast of a man with the manners of the gutter. He had in tow another slavering idiot, a henchman of some sort. I mean, the very worst kind of thug –'

'Yes,' Bella said, heading him off, 'we can come to that. But tell me first about Sir William. His wealth, his interests.'

'He has eight grain ships in and about the Eastern Mediterranean. All registered to Penzance but considering their home port Tbilisi in the Black Sea, where Skillane has warehouses and godowns. Only four of the captains are British. Three are Russian and there is an American. It is a well-founded and highly profitable company.'

'And in his day Sir William was himself a blue-water sailor, as I think is the expression?'

'He built the whole enterprise up from nothing, using

only a complaisant Cornish bank and – I have to admit it – ferocious will-power. He has made a great many Cornishmen rich by their investments and down there he is considered a saint.'

'Poor William,' Bella smiled. 'You have set yourself quite a challenge.'

Just then, Philip Westland led in a red-eyed Mary Skillane. At once her champion jumped up, scattering further cutlery to the carpet, and embraced her. Against all the social proprieties usual for a Sunday lunch, they kissed. Nor was it such a kiss as is bestowed by a gallant uncle upon a swooning niece: Mary gave herself completely to Kennett and he to her. They clung to each other like honeysuckle and vine. Kennett's stance was particularly noteworthy: his eyes closed, an astonished half-smile on his lips, his hands joined in a clasp around her narrow waist.

Smiling herself (and perhaps just a little bit envious, for this was without a doubt first love for both of them), Bella experienced an additional tiny jolt. How it came about she could not say, but the beginning of another Henry Ellis Margam novel had, as it were, tiptoed into the room and laid its hand upon her shoulder. Sir William Skillane was the very figure of a Margam villain, right down to his surname. A coarse and ambitious man is laid low at the moment of his triumph, his nemesis a mysterious figure from the other side of the world. And, trapped in the middle, a girl quite unconscious of her delicate ivory beauty, the blushing champion of the world. The story practically wrote itself.

*   *   *

Bella's publisher, Elias Frean, was in London on a rare foray, staying at a suitably cheap hotel in Gower Street and taking his meals at a restaurant across the Tottenham Court Road.

'A good wine list,' he explained doubtfully. 'It was in this very place that the company was founded. Dear old Naismith, God rest his soul, thought the world of it. The menu has hardly changed in thirty years.'

Nor has the table linen, Bella reflected gloomily. She asked the usual polite questions about Mr Frean's life in France, or at any rate Boulogne. On the face of it the news was not good. His last young man had decamped to Sicily, taking with him a portmanteau of silver and whatever loose change he could find hidden about the place by the notoriously stingy Frean.

'But all that is so much water under the bridge. Indeed, I snap my fingers at it. I am here to engage a manservant of altogether a different cloth. Sergeant Griffiths. Of the 7th Hussars,' he added with a sly smirk.

'You astonish me,' Bella said gallantly.

'An unpolished diamond. Slow in the head, you understand, but a grand figure of a man.'

'And is he presently on duty with the Hussars?'

Frean laughed. 'Bless me, no. We met in Boulogne when he was somewhat on his uppers after twenty years' service to Queen and country. I gave him the fare home and he got work in Wilton, on the Earl of Pembroke's estate. His sister is in service there. She wrote to say that Arthur – that is his name, Arthur – had many fond memories of a certain English gentleman he had come across in la belle France and hoped to see him again one of these days.'

'That is a very romantic yarn,' Bella said admiringly.

The sixty-year-old Frean simpered coyly for a moment or two. 'High compliment indeed from such a weaver of dreams. But I suppose we must come to business. I hope to learn you have another book in prospect for me, Mrs Wallis.'

'It may be so. Have you ever heard of someone called Sir William Skillane?'

She was astonished to see Frean peer into his pudding with a face like thunder.

'I very much hope it was not you who recommended him to the firm. A poor joke if it was.'

Bella was perplexed. 'I am at a loss. You must explain yourself, Mr Frean.'

'His musings – that is the very word he used – his musings were sent to the office here with a request they be published. The world will find this hard to believe, but the manuscript was entitled 'From Cornish Hovel to Cadogan Square, A Sailor's Odyssey'. In a long life, I have grown well accustomed to the vanity of authors, but this fellow takes the biscuit.'

'It is a poor work?'

'Unreadable. Utterly unreadable. It is worse than Mr Motion's *Daphne, Queen of the Clouds*, a book I always hold up to fledgling talents as the worst book ever written.'

'You have corresponded with Sir William, I don't doubt?'

'I returned his manuscript and got back an invitation to Cadogan Square and a chance to meet a person called Judd, apparently as fine a villain as ever sailed the South China Seas.'

'Robert Judd?'

'Oh, don't say you have met these dreadful people!'

'Mr Judd and his companion, a Mr Lintott Edwards, have put up for a club of which friends of mine are members.'

'Lintott Edwards! Yes, that too is a name I recall from Skillane's importunate musings. They must be stopped! Your friends should act.'

Frean hesitated, his tongue flickering. Though they were the only people at table and the man who had served them was peaceably reading a paper by the door to the kitchens, he leaned as far forward as he was able and lowered his voice. 'I will tell you this in the greatest confidence. Skillane may have been all he says he was in the days of his pomp but I have heard rumours of some very ugly business dealings since.'

'To do with pearls, perhaps?'

'Pearls?' he asked confused. 'Are there pearls in the story? No, no, to do with property. I hear he is become one of the biggest slum landlords in London.'

Bella drank the last of her very indifferent wine, careful not to let Frean see the expression in her eyes. To stop the trembling in her hand, she laid it on the tablecloth. She was for a moment back in the cesspit that was Morton's Yard. 'Do you happen to know whereabouts he has invested in property?'

'No, and I shouldn't think he does either. That is all in the hands of this fellow Judd, whom he describes in his book as an inspirational companion. Sir William is far too grand a figure for petty detail. He is, by his own lights, a gentleman. A knight, after all. Though how he came by a title is surely a comment on this ghastly age and nothing at all to do with actual worth.'

'Can you say what was so particularly bad about the work he offered you?'

Frean shrugged. 'In many parts it was a list of ships he commanded, or caused to be built. The rest was shameless name-dropping. Brookes of Sarawak I can suffer but who in Christendom is William Featherstone of Surabaya? Or Chien Lu Tze and his half-dozen brothers? I lost the thread very early on. It is in the end a tale about money. Nobody prates about money, not even in the times we live in.'

'It is said he has built himself a castle in Cornwall.'

'Bah,' Frean retorted. 'I have seen the photograph. The house he has there resembles nothing so much as a county asylum.'

'I am interested in Sir William,' Bella confessed. 'He – or someone very like him – might make a story. But I don't think one can castigate a man merely for being vulgar. I am going to ask your indulgence, Mr Frean. Let me find out more before I commit myself.'

'All I ask, dear lady, is that you don't bring the sea and the Far East into things. Nothing written along those lines will ever succeed in English fiction, you may have my word on it.'

Bella liked walking and set off down Charlotte Street to recover her spirits. The better sort of passer-by raised his hat to a clear-complexioned and confident woman in her very early forties, elegantly dressed in a steel grey jacket with immense buttons and a matching skirt that she kicked out ahead of her with exceptionally beautiful kid boots.

Her destination was Urmiston and Hannah Bardsoe's house in Shelton Street. She arrived there with an armful of flowers, bought from a barrow in Cambridge Circus. Exercise had helped her digest Frean's ghastly lunch and she banged through the door of Hannah's little shop in fine style, making the bell jump on its bracket.

Sitting in the parlour with his boots off was Captain Quigley. He lay back in his chair with one arm thrown across his brow, tended to by a sardonic Mrs Bardsoe.

'Which he is back from his sleuthing and has had his eye blacked on the train from Gravesend, in an argument with a matelot about sail and steam,' Hannah said with great contentment.

'The argument was about face-whiskers. The naval cove was bearded like the pard, a comment I struck into a general discussion of the present-day navy. He had remarks of his own to make about fish-smelling former soldiers, et cetera, and fisticuffs followed.'

'He was caught a right wallop,' Hannah concluded. 'But enough of that. You shall sit down, Mrs Wallis, and take a pot of tea and a nice bit of ginger cake. Charles is out the back, whittling.'

Bella patted Quigley on the head and walked through the scullery into the tiny and sunless yard. Urmiston was sanding down a very lifelike representation of a hedgehog, fashioned from redwood and exact in every detail.

'For the shop window,' he explained shyly. 'My crouching hare has been much admired. I dare say you noticed it on your way in.'

'I believe I did,' Bella lied briskly. 'A fine piece of work. How long has Quigley been home?'

'He came straight from the station. I would say, restored to his former impossible self.'

'What it is, Charles, I need your help in a certain matter.'

Over tea and cake, she outlined to the others what little she knew of Sir William Skillane and his connections to slum properties.

'And he lives in Cornwall, the animal?' the Captain cried indignantly.

'And Cadogan Square.'

Quigley peered at her with what he hoped was affection but, what with the black eye, came across as something rather more sinister.

'I bow to your knowledge of the human heart but how on earth you can claim to be a Londoner gripes my guts something awful. Cadogan Square is nothing to write home about, nothing at all. It's not much more than a building site at present, dear lady. I doubt more than three houses have been built.'

'I imagined it somewhat different.'

'It might come nearer to your idea of a London square one of these days but, like I say, at present it's nothing much. You was perhaps thinking of Cadogan Place, though that's no better than it should be, neither. Pont Street's a reasonable address. But Cadogan Square is just so much earthworks.'

'I have been gulled,' Bella said, vexed. 'He made it sound like the best address in Chelsea.'

'Perhaps,' Urmiston suggested quietly, 'it gives a clue to his character. He might be one of those men who confuse the new with the valuable. Or he might be boosting the place for some perceived future advantage.'

'Or,' Mrs Bardsoe suggested, 'he might be just what he sounds like, some ignorant clodhopping peasant. All I know about Cornwall is dressed crabs and that horrible clotted cream they go on about.'

'What he is don't matter,' Quigley grunted, 'except in one respect. Does he have title to that place where Molly breathed her last?'

'That is the question,' Bella agreed.

'It is a point easily settled by half a morning's enquiry,' Urmiston observed uneasily. 'But I invite you to consider, Captain, that even if Sir William is found to own Morton's Yard, that doesn't make him a criminal. It might make him contemptible, but so are a great many men walking about London this evening.'

The swelling around Quigley's eye greatly altered his general expression of facetious good humour, but what he said next shocked them all, his face lending its ugliness to the retort. 'And I invite you to keep your long nose out of it,' he said in a thickened voice.

There was a shocked silence, ended by Mrs Bardsoe taking the Captain by his ear and dragging him out into the scullery. The door slammed behind them and immediately afterwards came the sound of a stinging slap.

'The moment he finds Billy Murch he will tell him of this,' Urmiston whispered. 'And then I wouldn't give a brass farthing for Skillane's life. We can't have it, Bella. You don't kill someone for being a grasping and heartless swine.'

If he was looking for a reply, he waited in vain. Bella refused his glance; and after a moment or two picked up her gloves and hat. She seemed about to say something – even walking down Shelton Street a few moments later she had the distracted air of a woman who regretted not speaking her piece. But finally she trudged on, her chin in her chest. Was Billy Murch – if ever the Captain found him – going to push his way into this story? If he was, then Urmiston was right: Sir William Skillane's life was not worth a brass farthing.

EIGHT

Sir William Skillane is in his carriage, on the way to a charity lunch in the City. Today is the first outing for an astounding morning dress of the palest pink cloth, a colour his tailor has described (not without anguish) as pearl blush. This tint, when seen next to men wearing a more conservative grey, or black, seems outrageous: but nothing in Sir William's wealth is to be understated. Money speaks. When it is asked in the clubs who made the largest donation at this lunch, it will be answered by some 'the man in the pink suit'.

By long habit, he rises at six. He makes his own coffee and enjoys what he thinks of as the continental breakfast. It was taught him long ago by a Dutch trader and accordingly Sir William is the only man in London to start the day with a slice of ham, a boiled egg and wafer-thin cheese. At eight he bathes and shaves.

Sir William goes direct from his bathroom to his desk. He has a balding blond – another Dutchman – he describes to others as a personal secretary. Wouters is discretion personified: he has the manners of an executioner and a completely fearless attitude towards money.

'Because it is not yours we play with, but mine,' Skillane has suggested more than once.

'Because it is only money,' Wouters invariably replies.

His wife would like him to steal from his employer, or at the very least search for advantage in his unusual position. But Wouters was in his day a professional gambler. He knows money is only a tide, a ceaseless ebb and flow of something essentially meaningless and unremarkable.

In 1871, at the height of the Paris Siege, Wouters was in Monte Carlo. He played the tables for eleven hours without missing a turn of the wheel and came away with as many francs as there are sparrows in London. In the hotel that night, three men broke into his room and beat him senseless. When he came round, the money had gone, save for a few hundred francs thrown carelessly on to the bed. Wouters shrugged and after a pause for breakfast, consulted the rail timetable.

Sir William never gambles and likes to know in detail where his money is working. However, he has a precept: only what is new need be discussed at these daily meetings. There is no map in his study, no works of reference. Wouters reads cables to him, some commercial, some of a political nature. No minutes are kept. Skillane prides himself on a prodigious memory and (if he were honest) a swindler's caution with the written word.

'You say Simeonovski is at anchor in Syracuse these last five days,' he interrupts Wouters suddenly. 'Why is that?'

'His wife is dying of cholera.'

Skillane inspects his secretary with pale blue eyes. 'You are sure of that?'

'The lady is not yet twenty years of age. They are devoted to each other.'

Skillane considers briefly, waves his hand for Wouters to continue. A bridge across the Mandru in the Bulgarian province of Burgas has collapsed, delaying a consignment of tobacco to the port. On the other side of the Black Sea, another of Sir William's vessels has clashed with brigands.

'Whereabouts?'

Wouters glances down at his notes. 'Ochyemchiri.'

'The dogs in the streets have more character than the Governor of that province. Pay him. Anything else?'

Wouters inclines his head to indicate that he has come to the end of his report. Sir William lumbers to his feet and leaves the room without a word.

And here he is at last in his newish carriage, rattling along Sloane Street, plucking his nostril, worrying a little about his health. There was a time when he could take a turn and turn about with the bow oar, rowing his ship through a dead calm, but those days are behind him. His gut hangs, his chest is white and plump. Even walking upstairs to bed is a burden.

His eye is suddenly caught by something untoward. Running alongside the carriage, sometimes in the roadway, sometimes on the pavement, is a gaunt, spare-looking man with an absolutely empty expression. In Knightsbridge the carriage stops for traffic: the man turns and faces directly into the window. To Sir William's amazement, he takes one step, two, until the men are as close as gentlemen in club armchairs, separated only by glass. When the coachman Joplin tickles up the paired horses, the man on the pavement steps back. Sir William relaxes. Though he has learned it is bad form to smoke inside a carriage, even one's own, he lights a cigar.

In Piccadilly, the man reappears, running without effort. Joplin has had enough and, leaning over from his seat, flicks his whip at the scoundrel. The man catches its tip, wraps it around his fist and there is a lurch as he mounts the box for a second or so. Something is said, Skillane cannot hear what.

'I wouldn't try that again if I were you, matey,' the man has commented in a horribly neutral way. He jumps off the box steps and resumes running.

All the way up the Charing Cross Road, all the way along Holborn, the runner keeps pace with the carriage. Skillane has tried to shrink back against the horsehair cushions. Even by the haphazard standards of sanity to be found on London streets among the poor, this is no ordinary fellow.

Sir William has with him a cane with an embossed silver top. Very well. As soon as his carriage reaches his destination he will jump out and roundhouse the madman, lash him across the face. If he goes down, he will kick him. Whether this is the action of a gentleman or not, Sir William does not care. He will not be outfaced by a beggarman. Sumatra rules will apply. The carriage slows, he braces himself for a leap down to the pavement. Within the space of ten seconds or so, however, the man has disappeared.

Skillane looks around him, annoyed at how foolish he must seem to the men and women greeting each other outside the restaurant before going into lunch. One of the most quizzical examinations he receives is from a blonde woman with grey eyes, dressed in what he judges to be a very fashionable costume of brown velveteen.

She shows every appearance of recognising him. But, red in the cheeks and mightily flustered, he cannot for the moment place her. After a moment, she turns away. He follows into the restaurant, the glamour of his pearl-pink morning dress somewhat diminished. He is still carrying his elegant cane halfway along the shaft, like a savage.

Bartholdy's was handsomely decorated with flowers presented by the Gardeners' Company, for the lunch was given by the philanthropist Walter Curtice, who was a liveried member. Bella could have done with fewer blooms: the long room in which they ate had a clerestory roof and the overall effect was that of a gathering held in a greenhouse. About sixty guests sat down to the plainest of plain fare, saved by some excellent wines. The purpose of the lunch was charitable, for the amiably earnest Mr Curtice wished to bring forward a scheme to create what he called sailors' lending libraries, depots of improving literature that would eventually encircle the world, bringing solace to lonely men in foreign ports. Sir William Skillane had put up a thousand pounds and was the guest of honour. Bella was seated next to a former Surgeon of the Fleet, an incredibly old and wrinkled man, who wanted to talk chiefly about petit point, a hobby he had taken up to please his wife, that had in time become an obsession. On her right hand was a sprawling and sardonic Robert Judd.

'I have found that sailors are perfectly capable of finding their own solace in foreign ports,' he said, with a curiously animal frankness. 'I will not name the means.

Are you a do-gooder, Mrs Wallis? Are you one who would Christianise the heathen, for example?'

'Why, Mr Judd,' she replied calmly, 'I have not the time to help you, I'm afraid. But if you are anxious about the matter, I can certainly point you in the direction of those who can. Across the table is Bishop Duddington, for example. He might take up your case.'

Judd hesitated quite a long time before laughing – or, perhaps a better description would be, barking like a seal. 'In my case salvation must wait.'

'I have always understood that to be the guiding principle of most business,' Bella agreed.

She was interested in him. Though Judd's clothes had clearly been tailored and were of the very latest cut, he wore them uneasily, as if having been forced into travesty. (Witness the cuff to his sleeve, bearing the marks of the butter dish.) No matter how hard he tried to disguise it, there was a kind of truculence about him that undid all his superficial polish. He was a boor.

'Where might one find you in London, Mrs Wallis?' he asked.

'What a very impertinent question, Mr Judd.'

'Is it? I am grown weary of London manners.'

'Things are ordered differently in the East, is that it?'

'Then you know who I am?'

'Your sentiments about good manners have preceded you. What is it like in Penang? What do you have there? Pearls? Coconuts?'

He studied her with pale green eyes, like a cat. 'What made you say pearls?'

Only then did she realise what she had said. 'Coconuts, then.'

'But you said pearls.'

'It's what one imagines,' Bella said. 'Rubies. Jade. Pirates.'

'Pirates,' Judd scoffed, still with his gaze on her.

'I have heard of pirates in that region, I fancy.'

'There are giants there. Or perhaps you need a giant's strength to make your way.'

'Say in the manner of your patron, Sir William?'

'Sir William,' he said in a neutral tone, 'is a great man. And as you have seen today, a very great philanthropist.'

'From Cornwall, I understand.'

'Yes, from Cornwall. Have you been there?'

'Not yet. Is it a man's world down there, too?' She had begun to resent his catlike attention. 'I will tell you what it is, Mr Judd: you are trying too hard. I know you to be very wealthy. It's true I know nothing of Penang or Cornwall. I know a little about men, however, and you are too full of your own conceit to be interesting.' She smiled.

Judd ducked his head as if in defeat but his neck was red with anger. 'You have a waspish tongue, madam.'

'I see the lunch is breaking up. Before she goes, I will introduce you to Lady Tenterden. I know for a fact she adores Cornwall. Her husband was a sea-officer for many years in Eastern waters.'

Sir John Tenterden was an Admiral of the Blue in his day. Buried in Trincomalee in '67, he was exhumed by his widow and reburied in the family vault at Staveley. As for a love of Cornwall, only a wit would ascribe that to Kitty, whose sole connnection to the duchy was falling into the sea at Falmouth, blown there by spring gales after an over-exuberant dinner aboard her husband's first command, the *Minerva*.

'Good God, Bella,' she exclaimed in the cab that took them back towards the West End. 'You do know the most incredible people. That fellow Judd has thighs on him like a carthorse. I worry for him. His trouser arrangements might burst at any moment.'

'Did you talk to him about Penang?'

'He asked me if I knew William Kennett.'

'How should you?' Bella asked, alarmed.

'Kennett is our neighbour in Chiswick. What this fellow wanted with the information I can't imagine. But about those thighs. Did you notice them?'

'I can't say that I did.'

Kitty Tenterden, like Bella a widow, was well into her seventies. She took Bella's hand, bouncing it on her bony knee. 'No gentleman has such legs. But let's ask the cab to drive us around a while. I want to know how things progress with that delightful man Westland. You can be quite frank with me, Bella dearest. Everybody knows I am the soul of discretion.'

They directed the cabman to drive to Park Lane and sat for a while looking out on to the Park. Lady Tenterden bored very quickly of Philip Westland's virtues and began a long account of the latest gossip from Marlborough House. A lady compromised by the Prince of Wales had been taken by her husband to Mentone to repent of her ways. There she had eloped with an

Austrian colonel of artillery, who spirited her away to his estate in Carinthia.

'Wherever that might be,' Kitty concluded sniffily. 'But altogether a very unfashionable address, I should imagine.'

Bella laughed gently but was taken aback by her friend's next remark, delivered in the same mannered and floaty way.

'Marry him, Bella,' Kitty Tenterden said. 'Westland, I mean. Someone told me the other day you won't marry him because you love him too much. What piffle you young girls do talk from time to time. It has to do with novels, I am sure.'

On his own initiative, Captain Quigley went undercover at Cadogan Square. But not quite undercover. He sat comfortably on a pile of sand, looking directly into the windows of the Skillane house, smoking a stub of pipe and scratching his thigh from time to time. It was a mild afternoon, with watery sunshine, and the trenches and scaffolds of the builders' site were empty. Quigley could hear a skylark.

'Every inch the British workman,' Jacko Watson cried, joining him with a bacon sandwich he obligingly halved.

'And I have my shovel to hand,' the Captain protested mildly. 'I don't see too many of your mates running amok with the hods and wheelbarrows.'

'Down the boozer,' Jacko explained. 'Waiting on the ganger to come back from looking for the clerk of works. Houses like these, you don't just run 'em up, Perce. Every detail has to be just so. All the plaster work's done by a set of jabbering Eyeties. At I don't know what cost a running foot. As for the bathrooms, the Queen could have her dinner off the floor in there.'

'If she was so minded,' Quigley said absently.

'Correct.'

'I was meaning to ask you, Jacko: have you heard tell of Billy Murch at all recently?'

'I get it,' Jacko Watson said. 'I was wondering what you was doing sniffing about down here. Lost your pal, have you?'

'You haven't seen him, then?'

'That middle house, the one you are eyeing so assiduous? Belongs to a cove called Sir Edward or Sir William Skillane. The usual bag of lard. Daughter a nice bit, though. Yes, Billy called by first thing this morning.'

'You don't say so?' Quigley yelped. 'This very morning?'

'Drunk as a skunk and the hour not gone seven by this here watch of mine. He had some business with his lordship, seemingly. But I told him, you don't want to mess with Skillane. Oh no.'

'So what did he say to that? Did he mention the nature of his business with the Cornish gent?'

'I think he'd like to blow him up. At the very least.'

'Could be,' the Captain mused uneasily.

'Blow him up while he's sat on the throne in one of his three bleeding bathrooms. Just raising one cheek to ease hisself, paper open at the racing tissue –'

'I have the picture, Jacko.'

'You haven't seen old Billy yourself, then?'

'Would I be asking all these questions if I had, like?'

'Well, don't get shirty. Where're you off now?'

'I have to report this to the Home Secretary. Who's waiting on my word.'

'Bollocks,' Jacko said comfortably.

'You expected to find Quigley here,' Bella suggested to the figure hunched in the Fleur de Lys office. He had the fighting man's caution with enclosed spaces and sat with his chair dragged around to the open door, his feet drawn up under his knees, boots flat to the floorboards. He was in silhouette and sat quite still. The only thing that moved was the smoke from his cheroot. It drifted for a brief moment and then was snatched by the tiny tornado that never left the deep well of brick they sat in.

'I came to see you,' he muttered. 'You sense that I'm in drink and you'd be right. I haven't been rightly sober since – since that night in Holborn.'

'Have you eaten today?' Bella asked in what she hoped was a neutral tone, as an another might enquire whether it was raining outside.

Billy Murch shook his head. 'Not important.'

'Billy, look at me. Turn your head and look at me.'

He did as she asked. Scabs of dried blood were caught in his growth of beard and his eyes were red-rimmed and tortured.

'I know you have been to lunch today with that villain Skillane – I ran alongside his carriage for a couple of miles or more, just so's he could get a proper gander at me. I was for dragging him out in front of his rich friends and killing him with my bare hands, you understand. And then I saw you.'

She waited. But he had exhausted what explanation he was going to make. He looked at his cheroot and threw it away. It bounced on the pavement of the courtyard, making a shower of tiny red sparks. Bella watched as he knuckled his eye-sockets with filthy hands.

'This man Skillane – not a man, this slug – owns the house that Molly died in. That rathole and a hundred others like it. He is a slum landlord to beat all.'

'How did you find this out?'

'By asking. By wading chest-high through his filth. D'you remember the lodging-house keeper at Randall's? He was my start. And don't he wish he'd never been born. You hear it said about people, they are maddened by grief. But not me, I thought, never me.'

'You say you saw me today and that altered things.'

Murch shrugged. 'She died in his house. Starved to death in Skillane's house and still paid him tuppence a day for the privilege. I want revenge, is what I want. Or justice. You and Mr Urmiston take the long view about this sort of thing, I know that. I've never met Mr Westland, nor his mate neither, though I would welcome the chance. I need help. That is the long and short of it. Thought I could handle myself. Find I can't.'

The chair he was sitting in was a recent acquisition of the Captain's, an applewood Windsor with handsome curved arms supported by pilasters. Murch's right hand tightened and the chair-arm on that side of his body snapped off with a crack like a rifle. Bella rose and took the debris from Billy before drawing him to her.

His head lolled against her chest and he sobbed like a child.

'You will come home with me. Mr Westland is the one to talk to, you are right. But first you will eat some soup and a plate of ham and pickles. Here's money. I put you upon your word to turn up at Orange Street within the hour. Do you understand me?'

'I'm in no state to be –'

She took a step back and held his chin in both hands. 'Within the hour,' she repeated.

Bella's instinct was right – Philip Westland was just the person to talk to Murch. After the merest of introductions, Philip waved Bella away out of the room. The two men sat with their feet in the grate in the downstairs sitting room, each with a brandy to hand and a cigar.

'I have been experimenting recently with a pipe,' Westland said. 'A friend invented something along the lines of a portable hookah – anyway, there's water involved. Draws well but makes a noise like pulling a boot from the mud. Did you ever –?'

'In the Crimea, yes.'

'Weren't you very young?'

'What it is, Mr Westland, sir, today I came as close to killing a man in broad daylight as can be imagined. A fat old man I did not know existed a fortnight ago. I ran alongside his carriage –'

'Yes, Bella told me about that.'

Murch studied him carefully. 'The actions of a madman, do you think?'

'Mr Murch, the one thing I do not think about you is that you're mad.'

They sat on for a few moments, listening to the heavy tick of a case clock. Westland had the great gift of patience. Though the two had met for the first time only twenty minutes or so ago, he had formed a view of the man opposite that he knew he would never change. He was responding to the honesty in Billy Murch, his elaborated seriousness.

'I have a friend,' he heard himself saying, '– the same friend who is the inventor of the portable water pipe – who also wants justice. And from the same family. Mrs Wallis has told me how resourceful you are. I propose we put you and Mr Kennett – that is my friend's name – together in some way. How, exactly, I don't know – but I think you should meet.'

'Does the gentleman live in London?'

'On the Surrey side of the river.'

'I am no man's servant,' Murch warned.

'You know about Mrs Wallis that she is also Henry Ellis Margam? You know she finds her plots in the immediate here and now? Your friend Skillane and another man called Robert Judd are in her mind – if you like, under her gaze. It is my job to care for Bella. And yours to look out for William Kennett – the man who invented the portable water pipe. Skillane and his partners look like black mischief to me, Billy.'

'She is writing about them?'

'I believe she is.'

'Then I am of your party,' Billy Murch said simply. The two men rose to shake hands.

'Nothing brutal now,' Westland could not help himself adding.

Billy Murch's smile was thin indeed. 'As to that, we must see,' he muttered. 'If you will give me a note, I will walk across to Chiswick now. And introduce myself.'

'Yes,' Westland said uncertainly. 'That would be the ticket.'

NINE

⁂

It was agreed by many a London hostess that there was nothing more bankable than an invitation to Mrs Bella Wallis at least once in the season. She was calm, pleasantly undemonstrative and adept at light and inconsequential conversation. Old men delighted in her company and women who had something to lose – like a gloomy husband or an over-romantic son – could find no danger in her. Quite the contrary – she was as chaste as Arctic snow. If she had a fault at all, it was that from time to time – as now – she simply disappeared.

'I know her very well,' Cissie Cornford explained. 'And I'm sure she would count me as her dearest confidante. This is nothing new. For three months of the year, she is not at home to anyone.'

'Some say she is very poor,' Mrs Titmarch suggested.

'Oh, as to that, who is poor these days? We are all comfortably placed. I know Titmarch is a mere rural dean but they look after such people quite well in Somerset, I believe. No, it is not money. I would never tell this to another living soul, you understand, but –' She touched a bony forefinger to her temple and tapped twice.

Mrs Titmarch was astounded. 'Can nothing be done?' she cried.

'Tragically, not,' Lady Cornford said with the greatest complacency, repositioning her false teeth with a gentle sucking sound. 'A little more of the almond cake, Mrs Titmarch?'

'But such an amiable figure of a woman! Is it the loss of her dear husband that causes the grief, do you think?'

'Oh dear,' Cissie sighed airily. 'I fear I have said too much.'

Like almost anything else she asserted for a fact, by nightfall she had forgotten she had said it.

The truth was much simpler. Bella was now in daily occupancy of Fleur de Lys Court; or better to say it was Henry Ellis Margam at the rosewood table, sending out for lunch, smoking a little too much, shouting for silence when the three clerks in the next-door office larked about or strangers came into the Court to settle differences that had arisen out on the main pavement. Each day, from mid-morning to four in the afternoon, the pages piled up slowly at Bella's elbow, a story that was hers yet not hers. Margam drank Niersteiner, Bella went home with the headache.

Captain Quigley was used to these early stages of composition – or fits of scribbling, as he put it. He moved a chair into the yard, where he sat with one leg cocked on the knee of the other, doing sentry duty. From time to time Bella heard him in low-voiced conversation with one or other of his circle of friends: it was an unbothering noise, like bees in a summer pasture. Sometimes he would pull out a turnip watch, glance at the time and slope off to the Coal Hole or the Cyder Cellars for a little refreshment. There he would harbour dark thoughts about Sir William Skillane.

'If a certain knight of the realm was to walk through

them doors,' he would observe to acquaintances like Welsh Phil, 'I would up and chin him, so help me. Not a word spoke, not so much as a how d'ye do, but boosh!'

'And how comes it like that, Perce?'

'There are dark deeds afoot, my old cocker.'

'There always is down your side of the street. This knight of the realm – a chancer, is he?'

'A right bastard.'

'Just asking for a visit from Uncle Slap, would you say?' asked Welsh Phil hopefully, who was the originator of that useful term.

'You put it very neat.'

But what grieved the Captain more than Skillane's skulduggery – though he sensed in some obscure way the two were connected – were the mysterious goings-on of his old pal Billy Murch. Quigley had walked over to Kennington, where he had been told Billy had a room in Stannary Place, next to the park: but his bird had flown. Or perhaps – most bitter thought of all – had never been there in the first place. The door was opened by a Russian beanpole with a beard down to his waistcoat, who signed in dumb-show that he spoke no English and (an eloquent shrug) had never heard of Billy Murch.

'How did you know he was Russian?' Bella asked.

'No snow on his boots but a very low sort of place for all that,' the Captain explained. 'Nothing but cabbage on the hob, children everywhere. A goat roaming about the front room.'

'Doesn't that strengthen the view that Billy did not lodge there?'

'Very like,' Quigley retorted, who had his suspicions that the lady knew more than she was letting on. 'But I know the regard you hold Miss Skillane in. I will just say this. Her esteemed dad could end up on the dining-room table with two pennies in his eyes. A great man for bearing a grudge, Billy.'

The plot that Bella devised for the tale of Sir William was all to do with a ridiculous old fraud and his beautiful daughter. It was a story of London society. Some parts were easier to create than others. The back room in Bartholdy's restaurant had become Skillane's conservatory. As to the famous address, Bella took Quigley at his word and moved the house from Cadogan Square to Holland Park, an area she associated with the more enigmatic rich. Her own dressmaker lived in the squalid end of Pottery Lane (where she was assembling a quiet fortune) and Skillane was now to be found in a fine stucco house at the top end.

Cornwall stubbornly resisted her attempts to describe it. She knew no one other than Urmiston who had been there or wished to visit: if there were to be rocks and wild men in the story, maybe Scotland would do, or further afield, Georgia. She considered she had a score to pay off with Cissie Cornford and that harmless gossip became a gypsy woman with a loose tongue, roaming the moors – if there were moors in Cornwall – in a donkey-cart, cadging tobacco from soldiers.

Mary Skillane was of course the damsel in distress. Bella liked writing about her, more than was strictly proper. Mary in bed, Mary dressing with extreme care in the morning, the better to conceal a gold chain no thicker than a hair given to her by her secret lover one delirious evening at the theatre. Mary at bathtime, Mary swimming illicitly in some rock-strewn cove, her pale limbs scissoring the green waves.

Skillane himself was straight out of Thackeray. Bella had once met a man who wrote to the master when *A Book of Snobs* was being serialised, asking if he, the poor innocent, could be considered a snob. Thackeray put him straight into the next episode, so thinly disguised that even his cook could recognise the original. Sir William was a similar gift to fiction: he passed from real life to caricature with no more fuss than a man changing trains at Reading. Mary's father spent a great deal of time in these early drafts eating mutton and bullying the servants. The piece of plot that pleased Bella most was when she sent him to a bookseller's in Museum Street, where he ordered fifty books on any old subject, providing the bindings were calf.

The Skillane pearls interested her but she was struggling to find a convincing portrait of her hero, using William Kennett as her model. She reinvented him as a soldier, the impecunious Lord Attlesford. Attlesford looked like his original – that beguiling mouth – but shared none of Kennett's reckless scientific enthusiasms. Lord Attlesford, on leave from the Blues, fought for the Turks against the Russians, spied for his country in Afghanistan and was a man possessed of daemonic fits of melancholy. At his house in Shropshire, he spent a great deal of time looking out on to the home paddock, reflecting bitterly on those who had the aristocratic virtues and those who had not.

And there he might have languished, dwindled and died (for Bella was growing bored with a man who spent so much time looking out of the window and was all for starting the novel again with less of Thackeray and a better hero) were it not for the stone thrown into these placid waters by Molucca Edwards, Robert Judd's colleague and myrmidon.

Molucca Edwards was finding London irksome. Skillane had Cadogan Square to amuse him, Bob Judd the simpering Skillane daughter. Molucca had a fat wallet and the company of Mrs Givens, a genial whore he met at Brighton races one dank afternoon. He brought her back to London and they set up together in Elm Park Gardens, off the Fulham Road. Four ground-floor rooms, never fewer than two dozen empty bottles ranged along the sitting room wall, a bed like a hayrick after it had been struck by lightning.

Liza Givens had wide experience of men but never had she taken up with quite such a rough diamond as dear old Molucca. He had money to burn, apparently, but about as much charm as an outside privy. He ate prodigiously, drank himself senseless most nights, and in between retold the course of his life in the China Seas. Most of his yarns involved biffing, as he called it. It seemed there was not a foreign devil he had not knocked senseless, gutted with Susan (the name he gave to his knife) or simply thrown overboard for the sharks.

'I squared up to him,' he was fond of saying, 'and looked him in the eye. I have my own way of doing that.'

'And don't I know it,' Liza Givens agreed feelingly.

'Looked him in the eye, never saying a word. He's holding a musket, remember, and I have nothing but Susan. Now then, I can feel the deck tremble beneath my feet, can sense what more's to come when we leave the lee of the island and the old tub falls off a point or two and I'm ready –'

'Was your pal Mr Judd with you this particular trip?' Liza interrupted.

Molucca stared at her. 'And ain't you always going on about Bob Judd?' he complained in a nasty sort of voice.

'He fascinates me.'

'He wouldn't if you knew him at all. I could tell you stories about Juddy –'

'Well, go on then, tell us one.'

But he was saved the trouble: the man in question arrived shortly after.

What fascinated Liza Givens about Judd was the way he treated Molucca, putting her in mind of a man with the ownership of a devoted but dim-witted dog. Disdaining the use of a chair (as if Molucca had invited him merely to a playful tussle on the carpet), he wiped the mantel with the palm of his hand before laying his elbow on it. And there he posed. His sneer was magnificent. Liza was entranced by his boots, of the finest kid. He was a thug, like Molucca; but a dandy into the bargain.

'I have found where Westland hangs his hat,' he said in his brutal languid way.

Liza immediately offered to excuse herself, for when business was being talked among such men as these, she had always found it wiser to be deaf and blind. Judd waved his hand with the greatest negligence. She was no more real to him than the fire tongs or the armchair in which Molucca sat. (And he, poor chump, looking as confused as a girl.)

'Westland? And who's he when he's at home?' Molucca asked.

Judd sighed, looking at his lieutenant as if at a black beetle, or an earwig. 'You may remember how we put up for membership of a toff's club in Ebury Street?'

'It was no skin off my nose that they wouldn't have us.'

'No, I'm sure it wasn't. This Westland and his chum had us black-balled, however. Which means he put the boot in with the committee. Perhaps we hadn't been to the right schools.'

Despite herself, Liza snorted out a laugh. She was rewarded by a boxed ear, delivered by Molucca with enough force to shake the pins out of her hair.

'There's more to it than that, though?' he asked.

There was: but what was the point of telling an oaf like Molucca? Judd had plans for the future that did not include his henchman and these plans were poised very delicately. The Wallis woman was a dangerous adversary, moreover one surrounded and apparently protected by a rum crew he was finding it hard to fathom.

'Let's say that this gentleman needs a warning-off,' he suggested, putting it in terms that Molucca could grasp. 'He is getting under my feet. So I asked myself, who could I depend upon to put the fear of God up him.'

At last Molucca's frown lifted. He understood. It was the kind of work he knew how to do. On jobs like this, it was an advantage not to delve too deep into Bobby Judd's motives. Dear old Bob had his way of going about things that often involved meetings down dark alleys: the outcome had always proved satisfactory in the past. Pointed in the right direction by the boss, Molucca had once taken a scrawny Australian chancer out to meet the sharks off Suyala Point, after relieving him of three hundred American silver dollars. Lifted him clean off the dock, decorated him with a few slashing wounds and later, after chucking in a few buckets of blood and fishguts, pitched him over the side.

When he reported back, Judd had told him to keep the money with as much nonchalance as another man might dust down his jacket. Good old Bob.

'What do you want done?' he asked Judd now.

'He must have something wicked happen to him.'

Molucca was struck by a bright idea. 'It isn't the other cove we should be talking about? The daddy longlegs from Chiswick, the one your girl is sweet on?'

Judd stared. 'What's that again?'

'No, no,' Molucca said hastily. 'I have it clear now. Do you want me to off him, this Westland?'

'Won't be necessary. Just give that knife of yours a bit of an outing. Give him something hideous to remember us by. Mark his card, if you want to put it that way. Mind, if you kill him, you're on your own.'

'And Sir William? How does he stand with all this?'

Liza flinched. She could have told Molucca: he was asking too many questions. Judd sighed. He swept his forearm along the mantelpiece, knocking everything that stood there to the grate. The landlady's lustre vases shattered, her clock lay on its back, shocked into silence. Judd took a fold of paper from his waistcoat pocket and laid it on the newly cleared black marble surface. He tapped it with his forefinger.

'A useful address. Remember, this is the fat-arse that had you pegged for an ignorant know-nothing son of a whore.'

'He said that? He used those very words?'

'Said you were neither use nor ornament to the human race. That he was surprised to find you could speak or walk upright. That your mother was nothing better than a mattress.'

'The blind impudence,' Molucca growled.

But in truth, he was not all that disappointed about being shown the door by the Waverdon Club; it was exactly the sort of place that made him feel uneasy. On his only visit he had tipped the waiter extravagantly and suffered the indignity of having his loose silver returned to him, less a sixpence. When interviewed by the committee, his remark that a man needed a place to drink from time to time without the company of thirsty women went down badly. His application for membership needed to be sponsored by an existing member. Molucca was on the back foot here, too. He could not remember the name of the man whom he had met at the Café Royal.

'An old gent,' he temporised. 'Mutton chop whiskers, some sort of Indian Army connections. Maybe a bit touched in the head.'

He was describing a past president of the Waverdon, Colonel Sir Ernle Hollis VC, hero of Shivavasrani.

'What it is,' he said to Liza Givens, after Judd had left, 'it don't sit with me too well, all this side of things.

Bob Judd loves it. But there's nothing much here in London for me, d'you see?'

'You was born here, wasn't you?'

'At Wapping, yes. I'm talking about all this mincing about with the how d'ye do and doncha know coves. All this "my good fellow, my dear old chum" malarkey. You know me. I'm a plain man.'

Yes, Liza thought gloomily, I'll say that about you. None plainer.

If it had been her job to mark Philip Westland for life, she would have gone about it with some urgency – that same evening would hardly have seemed too soon. She had a whore's realism in this: Molucca might be a violent man but his rages blew out quickly. His friend Judd was all the more frightening for being so icy cold. Molucca was the Catherine wheel, spinning haplessly on its pin. Robert Judd was the rocket. Aimed, she thought wincingly, right up the jacksie.

All these reflections she shared the next day with Daisy Lawrence, an old friend from Newport Street, when the world was younger. Daisy had done well for herself, finding and marrying a German butcher in a small way of business and working him to death. He dropped dead over the brisket one frosty January morning. She still had the shop, run these days by a gormless and adoring lad called Alf.

'This Molucca sounds a right turd,' she observed, her language not matching the elegance of her feathered hat and purple bombazine dress, nor her pale lemon gloves.

They were drinking in St Martin's Lane, at a pub favoured by theatricals. It was very much a venue to suit

Daisy, all etched glass and velvet benches, where champagne was served on tap.

'I have got myself in with a rum crowd,' Liza admitted. 'They're a no good lot and that's no lie. Molucca hasn't got the brains he was born with but his mate Judd is a dangerous bugger.'

She outlined the visit Judd had made and the plan to cut some unlucky gent called Westland. Daisy listened largely without comment as to the commission Molucca had been given: the kind of men both these women knew best were prone to sort things out with knives and clubs. But she had a duty of kindness to her friend.

'I should bunk off it if I were you, Liza. It don't sound right. Wasn't you after the cove that had the linen shop in Brighton?'

'That all fell through,' Liza said, tersely.

'Well, I never,' Daisy said in a scolding sort of voice. 'After all the hard work you put in.'

'It was going along fine and then he had his leg off.'

'No woman wants that.'

'There was a tearful parting. I go up the racecourse for something a bit more cheery and before I've finished me first glass, there's old Molucca in front of me. The big ape.'

'Staring at you like you was a choice bunch of bananas.'

'More or less.'

This thread might have been teased out much longer, had not Liza suddenly jumped up with a yelp. 'Blind me if that isn't old Percy Quigley passing outside.'

'The Captain? Ask the old sot to join us. I haven't seen

him for ten years or more. Go on, girl, run after him. Let's have his remarks pertinent to the problem.'

Quigley's report was rambling but unequivocal. Bella listened with a dark face. She was very unamused to learn that her address was known to Robert Judd. Nor was she made any happier to hear Philip Westland bluster that he was a match for Mr Edwards or any other thug who came at him with a knife. Quigley had gone on town patrol to Elm Park Gardens and reported that Molucca was quite as big as Liza described and, though he did not exactly trail his knuckles along the pavement, had shoulders on him that would not disgrace an orang-utanio.

'Which is?' she asked frostily.

'One of your bigger apes. A gorilla, if it's easier to picture.'

'The point is,' Westland said emphatically, 'I do not plan to hide under the bed here, waiting for him to turn up.'

Quigley's coughing harrumph was more eloquent than any speech he might have made.

'I shall get Kennett to teach me the rudiments of boxing,' Philip explained.

'And what on earth does he know about such a thing?'

'Very well then, a better idea. The Captain shall furnish me with a swordstick.'

'Can be arranged,' Quigley nodded quickly. 'From the estate of a Belgian gentleman, late of Tavistock Square. But, before you was to unsheath it, might I suggest a handful of ground pepper flung into the eyes first? Nothing assists the old cut and thrust more.'

Bella slapped the arm of her chair with impatience.

'I cannot see what they have to gain by mutilating you. Unless it is a thrust at Kennett, to warn him off canoodling with the Skillane girl. A high price for you to pay.'

'What is annoying you most,' Philip said quietly, 'is the fact that Judd knows where you live. I take it this has never happened before. It suggests to me that you are the real target of his viciousness. In some way we don't yet understand, art has collided with life. Taking them all together as a gang, they sense you know something they do not wish you to divulge.'

'Do you have a notion what that might be?'

'A man comes home from the East with stolen pearls of the highest value. They are the secret collateral in all his business dealings. Some years later he is made a knight of the realm. His whole standing in society is compromised if the story of the pearls comes out. He is prepared to pimp his own daughter to keep the secret safe.'

'My God,' Bella said faintly, suddenly remembering the conversation with Judd at the charity lunch in the City. 'What have I done?'

Westland and Quigley exchanged glances. 'What have you done?' Westland asked.

'When I met Mr Judd, I found him repellent enough to score points off him. I did not notice then that I had said too much.'

'You did not mention the Skillane pearls, for all love?' Westland asked.

'Of course not,' Bella said sharply. 'I am not quite so stupid. But I did say something careless about pearls in general.'

She held out her glass to be filled with a shaking hand. 'I have brought this down on us.'

'What you said gave him the idea that you knew more about the pearls than you revealed?'

'I think so,' Bella said in a very small voice.

'So, what are we going to do about it?' Quigley asked.

She moved to the window and peered out into Orange Street. There were few faces she did not recognise. Though it was not yet quite dark, Mr Gough the green-grocer had lit his naphtha lamps and stood among the boxes in his pavement display, eating an apple and talking to the musician Hubison. Mrs Allen was gossiping with Mrs Shipley. In fact, all the Orange Street neighbours were as carefully disposed as an operatic chorus: part of the pleasure in living in such a short street was that people did more or less the same things at the same time, from servants taking out the mats to be shaken in the early morning to their mistresses drawing down the blinds at night.

'How will he go about this work?' she asked Quigley absent-mindedly.

'Not by day. Stealth and sunlight don't go together. He won't try it in an empty street neither. Mr Westland is a novice at this kind of thing, but you don't need eyes in the back of your head to see the danger in that, not if he's the only other cove about, d'you see?'

Bella glanced at Westland, who nodded.

'I am generally cautious in such circumstances, yes,' he said.

'So, by night, in a crowded street? It doesn't sound too plausible.'

Quigley joined her at the window. 'I don't know about that. Those two fellows squaring up outside the pub, for instance. Are they going for the knives and dusters, or are they just a couple of drunks?'

'One of them is Mr Smallbones, the coalman. The other is his brother-in-law.'

Quigley raised his eyebrows and was about to say more but Westland laid a restraining hand on his sleeve. 'The Captain's point is that every pavement around here has such night-time scenes. It's not in the least unusual. It's the price we pay for living in London.'

'Well, I am very sorry it is not Wiltshire we are looking out on,' Bella snapped.

'Oh, Bella, is that really worthy of you?'

'It isn't,' she admitted, blushing.

Now Westland took his turn at the window. He stared out for a while, sipping his wine. Then he turned back to the room, with a faint smile on his face. 'Mr Edwards has just come into the street. If Henry Ellis Margam had control of what happens next, I should end the evening as a hero. Instead, I am going out to confront him with' – he searched the room briefly – 'this poker.'

'You'll do nothing of the kind,' Bella wailed.

Westland embraced her. 'Even a clumsy man with a poker is not entirely without menace, my dear.'

'Westland, if you love me, don't do anything so rash!'

'I haven't quite finished. The second part of my plan is that the Captain will run like the wind into Leicester Square and come back with a policeman.'

'Like the wind is good,' Quigley agreed. 'That part of it is very good.'

'Are you both mad? I will go out and face him,' Bella shouted, tugging at the poker end.

'You, for once, will do as I say. You will stay at the window and act as a witness to whatever ensues. Captain?'

'I'm your man,' Quigley grunted, hastily pouring himself a last brandy. 'Now then, sir. None of the old thrust and parry lark. Don't stand on no ceremony. Just lamp him with the poker before he gets his hands out of his pockets.'

The Battle of Orange Street was explained to Constable Swain by the musician Hedley Hubison, who had a God-given talent for getting hold of the wrong end of the stick. Hubison had been sacked from almost every pit orchestra in London for quarrelling with the conductor. The rows he created were of a very high-flown nature, to do with interpretation of the score. They often took place during the performance.

He peered into Swain's honest face, flecks of spit at the corners of his mouth. A tall man, he nevertheless stood on tiptoe in cracked patent-leather shoes. His beard wagged.

'If you could just speak a little more clearly, sir,' asked Swain.

'I was talking to Gough, the greengrocer, whose child I am teaching to play the fiddle. Fiddle-playing is nothing if not posture and the child is as round-shouldered as – an exact comparison escapes me for the moment –'

'Can we get on to what you saw, sir?'

'– because of course people think teaching the fiddle is hack work. Well, not in the way I conceive it, oh no.'

'You were talking to Mr Gough the greengrocer,' Swain prompted. 'Then what happened?'

Hubison pointed theatrically to Bella's door. 'Two men came out of that house, one a gentleman known to me by sight, the other an ill-found sort of fellow who ran away. He had a poker in his hand.'

'The one who ran away?'

'The other,' Hubison corrected. 'At which Gough said to me, in a half humorous way –'

'Where was the third party?'

'Who? Oh yes. He stepped from the shadows, I imagine with the intention of remonstrating –'

'The cove with the poker was saying what, exactly?'

'There was great confusion,' Hubison admitted after a few moments' hesitation. 'As to what his exact words were, I cannot say, but in a general sense it was "have at you" and that sort of thing.'

'While brandishing a poker?'

'Brandishing,' Hubison mused thoughtfully. 'I'm not sure that brandishing is quite the word –'

'Waving it about, then.'

'As I said before, he is a gentleman.'

'Well, was he waving it or not?' Swain demanded.

Hubison blinked. 'The man with the knife –'

'This is the one who stepped from the shadows?'

'Well, yes. Yes, of course.'

'He had a knife, did he?'

'A very large knife.'

'A carving knife, no doubt. To go with the poker.'

'You are being facetious.'

'Possibly,' Constable Swain admitted.

'I really wonder what it is you policemen do to earn your pay.'

'Oh, you do, do you? What I want to know from you, Mr Hubison, is why this cove with the knife come to be wearing this around his neck?' He held out his meaty hand. Hanging from a stubby forefinger was a length of cord with a weight at each end. Swain had recognised these easily enough – they were exactly equal stubs of pie-crust lawn edging. Terra cotta, but chunky enough for all that. He had something like it in his own back garden.

'Well,' Hubison muttered, 'they appeared as if from nowhere.'

Which was more or less what Molucca was explaining to the doctor across the river at St Thomas's. Attempting to explain. The livid bruise around his neck had played havoc with his voice box and he croaked like a raven. From time to time, his eyes crossed. Twice, to his great shame, he fainted.

Nobody in Orange Street had noticed the well-set-up toff who saw all this, walked into Charing Cross Road and hired a cab to take him to Chelsea and Cadogan Square. Nor did they hear – how could they? – how the man changed his mind and redirected the vehicle to Elm Park Gardens.

'You're the guv'nor,' the cabbie said.

TEN

'It is called a bolo,' William Kennett explained calmly, a glass of Bella's brandy at his lips. 'The gauchos of Argentina are very expert in its use. I have been practising on and off for several months. You whirl it over your head and let fly at the legs of straying cattle.'

'Do you have straying cattle in Chiswick?' asked Bella.

'Not in any great quantity. I have to admit it was a shot I couldn't repeat if you were to give me five years of practice.'

'But how did you know he was going to be in the street in the first place?' Philip Westland wanted to know.

Kennett waved his hand at Billy Murch.

'Sir William has gone away into Cornwall,' Murch explained. 'Judd stays in Cadogan Square, alone. I was giving the place the once-over in the manner of a standing patrol, as Percy Quigley would have it, when this Molucca came round to see him. Never got further than the front step. Instead, they walked to a pub called the Feathers. I followed and it was easy enough to get the gist of the conversation. Judd was telling his mate to get on with it. Orange Street was mentioned as the place where it had to be done and so forth.'

'Now why was that?' Bella wondered.

Kennett had an answer. 'Clearly, if Philip was to be attacked, he hoped you might witness it. Perhaps it was important you did witness it.'

'Billy?'

Murch shrugged. 'I don't know the gentleman. But if you ask me, he sees us as no better than heathen Chinamen. It's what you'd do to put the frighteners on the poor devils out there, so as to have your way of going on properly understood.'

Bella had to acknowledge the possible truth in this. Was Judd simply showing his strength in the way he knew best?

'You went home to alert Mr Kennett to the danger?' she asked.

'After following the other bloke home, yes.'

Billy Murch set down his glass and stood up, a tall and rangy figure with a natural grace. 'With your permission, I will hook myself out of all this and walk round to Fleur de Lys Court for a gab with the Captain.'

Philip Westland jumped up and pumped him by the hand. 'Mr Murch, you have done us proud. We will continue here a while and then I and my friend Kennett will join you for a drink or two later.'

Murch's smile was almost affectionate, the kind an older brother bestows on an over-eager sibling. Bella walked him to the door. There she astonished and embarrassed him by seizing his bony shoulders and planting a soft kiss upon his cheek. 'That is to thank you, Billy. I fear there may be much worse to come before this business is all over.'

'You can be sure of it,' Murch agreed, his face brick-red.

* * *

When Liza Givens opened the door to Robert Judd in Elm Park Gardens she immediately took a step back, her hand at her throat. Let him think it was coyness if he liked but she was extra-sensitive to the look of a man, the signals he was sending out, as she had to be in her profession. Danger came off Judd like a wreathing smoke.

'Molucca ain't here,' she said.

'I know that. You're looking particularly fetching tonight, Mrs Givens.'

For a moment it crossed her mind that he had come for sex. Taking all things together, that would be the least worst outcome to his visit. 'I was just about to take a wet, Mr Judd,' she lisped prettily. 'Perhaps you will join me?'

'I came to explain something to you, dear lady.'

'Well then, I am all ears.'

'I will put it very simply. I have a large business venture in hand. You could say it is a turning point in my life. I won't trouble you with the details but something of a make or break nature. Do you follow me at all, Mrs Givens?'

'At every point, Mr Judd.'

'I was raised in a hard school.'

'As weren't we all? Will you not sit down for a moment?'

'I came to say goodbye.'

'Goodbye?' Liza asked, very startled.

'Just that,' he agreed.

'Then I won't see you again?'

'You never will.'

*   *   *

That same night, towards ten o'clock, Judd rescued Molucca from St Thomas's and drove him by cab to a chophouse in Artillery Row. It was in its way a refined form of cruelty – the injured man was relearning how to swallow and left his plate untouched. The bandage around his neck gleamed in the candlelight. On the other side of the table, Judd chewed and swigged ferociously. The way he ate explained his discomfort at the charity lunch in the City. Food was not the accompaniment to something else: it was primal. Away from prying eyes, Judd ate like a savage in a cave.

'You don't say what happened,' he said through a last mouthful of meat.

'I wish I knew,' Molucca whispered painfully, his fingers at his throat.

'Let me tell you then. You were bushwhacked. And how do you think that came about?'

'Someone ratted on me.'

Judd pushed his plate away and lit a dark brown cheroot. 'Your whore ratted on you.'

Molucca nodded mournfully. 'She'll pay.'

'That's all taken care of,' Judd said. 'Where's your knife, Molucca? Your famous Susan? I'll tell you where, you sorry sack of guts! You dropped it in the street and the police have it now. Which is bad news for you. Very.'

'What have you done, Bob?'

And Judd laughed, actually laughed. 'Did you give them your address at the hospital?'

'They won't treat you otherwise.'

'Then don't go back there. If you know of a deep hole in which to hide, I'd go this very night. And if I ever clap

– 392 –

eyes on you again, even at a distance, even a glimpse of you on a passing train, you're a dead man. I hope all this is clear enough.'

'Is Liza dead?'

'Very much so,' Judd murmured, clicking his fingers to signal for the bill.

'You killed her?'

'Somebody did. Slashed her open with a very big knife. Like yours. Like Susan. I don't know who could have done such a terrible thing. I expect the police will have their own ideas about it, though.'

Molucca pushed back his chair. There were tears in his eyes, some of them from indignation, some – though he could not have phrased it this way himself – from un-requited love.

'All that time we had together in the East, Bobby, the scrapes we got into, the times I saved your arse? I've killed for you, I've taken the knocks for you. All that counts for nothing?'

Judd set down some coins beside his plate and rose. 'It's business,' he said.

Liza Givens lay face-down on the carpet, her body sprawled on what seemed like a red cloak, spread from her hips as far as her shoulders. Captain Quigley observed how small her hands were, and how white.

'Her old dad was a railway porter, did you know that?'

He and Billy Murch were drinking Molucca's gin and smoking curious little black cheroots with a bit of stick in the end. It was three o'clock in the morning and the streets were utterly silent. Only once, an hour earlier, had they stiffened at the sound of boots on the pavement outside. It was nothing but a young man passing with a canvas bag of tools, a carpenter's trestle slung over one shoulder.

'He ain't coming back,' Murch decided. 'Not that you'd expect he would, neither.'

'A railway porter,' the Captain repeated, following his own train of thought. 'Could be found any night of the week in the back bar of the Wellington. A bad house. As a maid, she would be sent to fetch him home.'

Murch gave a huge yawn. 'Molucca didn't do it. She came down to the street with him to see him off. Calling after him to be careful.'

'If he didn't kill her, who did, Billy?'

'Some other heartless bastard.'

The slip of paper on which Robert Judd had written Bella's address was still on the black marble mantelpiece. Murch picked it up and left his empty glass in its place.

'Offski,' he suggested.

They tiptoed outside in their socks and not until they were two streets away did they sit on the kerb and drag on their boots.

'For all her faults, she was a nice girl,' Captain Quigley muttered, probing with his tongue for a shred of tobacco.

Murch patted him on the shoulder and walked off into the gloom of what was promising to become a mid-morning pea-souper. Quigley blew his nose on his fingers and staggered to his feet. He was thinking of Liza Givens's father and the peculiar blue and mauve mottling on his face and neck. And the Wellington, where once the flash mob had gathered, now grown sadly ordinary. Ghosts, the Captain thought. This bloody city is full of them and that's no error.

William Kennett's house in Chiswick had been passed down through the family since 1772. Set back from the road and screened by trees, it retained (at any rate on the outside) an eighteenth-century suavity. Horace Walpole had dined there and in nearer times the artist William Hone and the statistician Chadwick.

Bella, whose mood was in any case nervy, was utterly dismayed by the interior. Books were piled in columns against the drawing-room wall and boxes of nondescript pottery shards jostled with rocks and fossils. On the exquisite little table where Kennett's grandmother was wont to preside over tea was a greasy iron clockwork engine and the tools to mend it. Kennett's hands hovered but he could not bring himself to move anything and instead began erecting a shaky card table.

The light was dismal. Outside, a gently swaying fog obliterated all but the nearest features of the gardens and seemed to cast a yellowy shadow over the room itself. Every corner was in gloom. The silence that comes with fog was very marked.

'What is that smell?' Bella asked.

'Embalming fluid,' Kennett explained. 'I have offered to preserve Mrs Rogerson's cat, of which she was very fond.'

Just at that moment, Mrs Rogerson came in with tea. Bella was expecting a long-suffering and doubled-over skivvy and saw instead a woman hardly past thirty with a broad face and merry eyes.

'Murch is in the kitchen,' she announced to her master. 'He asks me to tell you Captain Quigley patrols the lane outside.'

'Will you tell Mr Murch that the threat of invasion is very remote?'

'You can tell him that yourself. He has a loaded gun by him meanwhile.'

Kennett stared. Bella's stiff back and pursed lips made him ill at ease. 'Tell him that is a damned impertinence on his part,' he said.

Mrs Rogerson was entirely unperturbed. 'I'll pass the sense of that along, shall I? He'll cringe like a dog, I don't doubt.' She nodded to her employer's guests. 'You'll find the tea not much better than hot water but that is the way he likes it.'

'An outspoken widow,' Kennett mumbled after she had left.

'You have kept her very quiet,' Philip laughed, the way men do. But the moment was ill-chosen. Bella rose to pour the tea, which was indeed as pale as rosewater.

'Can we come to the point?' she asked, with far too much asperity. Because, she thought, we shall otherwise sink into a fog of our own. We shall give way to the fatuous and whimsical and end the morning playing with William Kennett's inventions, cribbed like small children in a world of make-believe.

These reflections disturbed her, all the more so for being apparently obvious to the two men. They added to an already foul mood. Mrs Rogerson's frank offhandedness annoyed her, the ridiculous tea annoyed her. Most of all, Philip Westland's passivity and good nature annoyed her. Last night, when they should perhaps have been closest, they had slept apart.

'We are here as a council of war,' he began, with a truly maddening deference, as if humouring a lunatic. It flashed through Bella's mind that what she would like to do most was to run up and kick him on the shins. When he saw the look in her eye, he examined the carpet between his boots, flushing slightly. My God, she thought, am I such a bully?

'Very well. Let us start with the poor woman Liza Givens. Judd killed her. Can we agree on that?'

'We cannot. There is no proof,' Philip pointed out. 'None.'

'But Murch thinks so,' Kennett replied in a low voice. 'It makes sense.'

'I also believe it to be true,' Bella snapped. 'But how can it make sense? What danger was she to Judd?'

Philip Westland answered, his good-natured face stricken almost to tears. 'She betrayed him. She thought she was doing no more than gossip with an old acquaintance – Quigley – without realising that whatever she said would come straight back to us. If you like, we helped to kill her.'

'What an utter fool you are sometimes, Philip,' Bella said with far too much vehemence, feeling a dam burst inside her.

Without a word, he rose and left the room. Perhaps it would have been better if he had slammed the door behind him but instead it closed with a polite click.

'That was harsh,' Kennett said.

He seemed to expect she would go after her lover. But instead Bella flung herself into an occasional chair, making the joints wince in complaint. To his embarrassment, she covered her eyes with her hands as if about to burst into tears.

'Philip was in the right of it last night,' she confessed. 'All this has come uncomfortably close to home. That is what is making me so awkward. I do not like what has happened and have no clear idea what to do.'

'Has it occurred to you that we are dealing with monsters?'

'I am a writer, William. I can't work without looking for the monstrous in people.'

'The monster you are searching for in Judd seems to me to be quite apparent. He stands to lose a great deal. Unless and until he marries Mary, Sir William's fortune must escape him. What won't he do to prevent that happening?'

'Is he truly so vile?'

'He is following Sumatra rules,' Kennett observed. 'That is, to do whatever is necessary.'

'Up to and including murder?'

'I don't think you have it yet,' William Kennett said. 'What happened in Orange Street last night was Judd's way of murdering you. By proxy, to be sure. Philip was completely in the right of it, though in a way he does not understand. The idea of attacking him was a way of warning you off. When that didn't work, something even more horrible happened.'

'This is very far-fetched.'

'Do you think so?'

'I could not write such a plot.'

Kennett looked at her with an expression on his face that hurt far more than outright contempt. 'If you will permit me to say this, Bella, whether you are a writer or not does not come into it. Judd doesn't know or care what you do for a living. You are simply in his way.'

'Doesn't he realise that this is London and not some woebegone shanty town or mangrove swamp?'

'He does not. There are millions at stake. Truly, millions. He would walk from here to Land's End on red-hot coals to get what he wants. This is not some social contretemps over the dinner table or a slight from a man you disdain. Nor is it an unwelcome review of a Henry Ellis Margam novel. This is war.'

She jumped up and began pacing, her heart in a turmoil. 'I have made a fool of myself,' she wailed, bursting into tears, something she had not done since she was a child. She was thinking of the little clockwork plot that animated the pages of the book she had so far completed. Whether Sir William Skillane, the slum landlord and shipping magnate, secretly ate peas off his knife or dropped his aitches was entirely beside the point. He was not the story. Sumatra rules were the story.

At which point, Philip Westland came back into the room and, ignoring Bella's tears, seized her by the arm and drew her to the window.

Out on the lawn, two smudged figures stood stockstill in the fog. One was unmistakably Quigley. The other – head hung low – was Molucca Edwards. Somewhere along the way he had lost a wig and a bald pate made his head seem huge. A figure approached from the house – Murch. The three men set off in file, heading towards the stables, paying not the slightest attention to the drawing-room windows, where Philip Westland was disengaging himself from Bella's sobbing embrace and Kennett was running to the door.

'We will bring him into the house when he is ready,' Murch said through a crack in the stable door. His voice was calm.

'I think this is my property,' William Kennett blustered.

'So it is and we will bring him to you in a while.'

'Tell me at least how Captain Quigley came to capture him.'

'The poor bugger gave himself up,' Murch smiled. 'He is here to throw himself on your mercy.'

'Then let me speak with him.'

'Soon enough.'

Molucca sat listening to all this on a broken-back chair, his chin in his chest. Quigley stood over him with a handy length of iron railing, as much in awe of his surroundings as the prisoner himself. The stables were filled top to bottom with things William Kennett thought one day might come in handy, of which the iron bar was one of the lesser examples. At a quick glance there were more than twenty cartwheels, the condensing boiler to a small locomotive, a small mountain of cogs, timber of all lengths, nautical blocks and pulleys.

'Is the cove you work for a chandler of some sort?' Molucca asked in his new (and permanent) throaty whisper.

'Never mind that, mate,' the Captain rejoined. 'It's your pal Judd we want to know about.'

Molucca raised his head at last. 'He turned me off.

As easy as kiss my arse. I have done him favours a prince would be grateful to accept. Go and lose yourself, he says. I'm telling you boys, that ain't easy.'

'Because of what's laid out on the floor round at your Chelsea gaff.'

'I never touched her,' Molucca said piteously. 'He did it, he told me as much.'

Murch pushed the Captain aside and put his face an inch from Molucca's. 'You haven't got the brains of a gnat, you poor bastard. That's why you're here with us and not up in the big house. Peaching on him isn't going to work. No court'll convict on what you say he said. So leave that out.'

'Leave it out,' Molucca agreed, forlorn.

'Take into account, Billy, he did give hisself up to us. Point in his favour.'

'As to that, Perce,' Murch growled, 'I'd as soon maim him as speak to him. Put his eyes out with some handy bradawl. Or a six-inch nail. Which there are enough examples right underfoot.'

'That's a way of looking at it,' Quigley admitted. 'I see where you're going with that.'

'Oh, and I'd stand for it, would I?' blustered what was left of the old Molucca. But long experience of tight corners told him that in any fight he would get no further than the door.

Billy smiled. 'Yes, that's right,' he said, as though reading these thoughts. 'I'm in the mood to smash you up, Molucca. Can't get my hands on Judd but I have got you sitting there. Pass me that length of iron, Perce.'

'No, no,' Molucca said hastily. 'I gave myself up

voluntary, didn't I? I have enough sea-time to get a berth and sod off out of it. Wasn't I at the docks this morning? But until this bloody fog lifts I'm a sitting duck. The police is after me. You know that. I'll tell you anything you want to know.'

'Captain,' Billy Murch suggested, 'step over to the kitchen and ask Millie Rogerson to brew us a cup of tea. Real tea, mind. He's going to tell us what we want to know.'

After Quigley left, Molucca seemed to perk up a little. Murch watched him with the same quiet smile.

'Fancy your chances a bit better now, do you?'

'Could give you a fight of it any day, mate.'

'Course you could. Big bastard like you. But you don't have the stomach for it. And for why? Because you're already beat. Coming home has done you no favours, Molucca.'

'And that's no lie,' the big man whispered, massaging his ruined neck.

'Now. If you was to tell me – which you have – that we shall see the back of you in a day or two –'

'Just watch my smoke,' Molucca promised.

'– then that might alter things. That might sit well, so to speak. But before you go, there's a lot you must cough about your mate Judd. Because I'd as lief kill you as wave you goodbye. Are you following this?'

'We're out of the same box, you and me.'

'No, no, no. I have spent my life scraping people like you off the sole of my boot. We're not brothers under the skin. So. I'll just tickle up your memory with this here iron bar, shall I?'

He swung the bar against Molucca's shins, getting in response a satisfying bull roar. The big man fell off the chair and rolled around the cobbled floor, cursing. He could be heard twenty yards away in the kitchen, where Mrs Rogerson had the kettle in her hand. She turned like a bristling dog.

'Be easy, girl,' Captain Quigley smiled. 'It's just Billy having one of his little chats. One of his little parley-voozes.'

The commotion was also heard in the drawing room. Philip Westland was at the window, watching the fog shift and slide.

'Is this how it's done?' he asked bitterly, as much to himself as anyone else.

ELEVEN

A man had once told Bella that if you were to climb a tree in Hyde Park you could look across what appeared to be uninterrupted forest all the way to the Surrey side of the river. It was a trick of the eye but there were certainly more trees in London than its bitterest critics supposed.

But not in the grimy canyon of Shelton Street, where the only green rose out of the gutters at rooftop level as defiant tufts of grass and the like. During the night the week-long fog had lifted, though not enough to allow the sun to shine through completely. Instead, a strange diffused light reduced the sooty houses and wet cobbles to something like the effects of black and white photography.

Bella arrived at the little herbalist shop in a very chastened mood. She kissed Hannah Bardsoe on the cheek and shook hands with a cautiously attentive Charles Urmiston. 'You once promised you would be there if ever I needed you,' she began without any niceties.

Urmiston studied her with a faint half-smile on his lips. The parlour was scented with laudanum, for Bella had interrupted him in measuring out throat linctus into little brown bottles. Their tiny corks were scattered like acorns across the table. Hannah Bardsoe sat watching with her chin in her hands.

'I believe I did say that.'

'I am in trouble, Charles. Or in a better phrase, trouble has found me out.'

'Ho,' Hannah cried in a boisterous attempt to rally her friend, 'any expression but that, my dear! That is the way foolish green girls announce themselves to me out there in the shop when they've taken a fall.'

'Nothing like that, Mrs Bardsoe,' Bella said.

'Don't mind me,' she said. 'That was just my little jest. I'll leave you to chew things over with Charles, while I walks down into the Market for a cauli. Which if I haven't got a pound or more of good red country cheese that'd go with it, enough to make your heart ache for the old days, the simpler times we used to live.'

Urmiston escorted her to the shop door, kissing her goodbye as if she were off to an expedition up the Niger, even going so far as to pat her black straw hat down on her head.

'How lucky you are,' Bella found herself exclaiming gloomily. 'Was there ever a happier couple in all London?'

Urmiston did not reply immediately. Finding a cork that had rolled to the carpet, he replaced it on the table as lovingly as a child with a toy soldier.

'The story you have to tell me concerns the Skillane family, I don't doubt. I propose we hear it with a glass of Mousseux to hand. It comes from Rheims, the wine, but more nearly from the docks, where one of our customers has a son who works as a clerk. His job is to write off warehouse breakage and spillage. As a consequence we are all wine drinkers in Shelton Street nowadays. Crime, I have discovered, is an elastic quantity,' he added shyly.

'I don't disturb you from your work?'

'Never in life, though I must jump up to serve in the shop as need arises. Unless you would like me to put up the closed sign for a while?'

'The story is simply told, Charles. What I am after is your advice.'

'Then let us see what we can do.'

She started with the easiest thread. But even then her tone was too dull, too maudlin. After only a moment or so Urmiston reached and took her hands in his, chafing them gently, his pale eyes very attentive. There was hardly another man in London who could have treated her so freely, a thought that made her feel, if anything, worse than she already did. She disengaged her hands and busied them with lighting a cigarette, smoothing down the chenille cloth, arranging the little corks in columns of three. Although her account was perfectly orderly, she was thinking of the coolness that had come between her and Philip Westland more than the story she was telling.

'I hope this is making sense,' she interrupted herself nervily.

Urmiston smiled. 'I am managing to follow your drift, I think.'

'I am very unhappy, Charles.'

'The bones of the matter first,' he suggested.

Bella nodded, licking her lips with the tip of her tongue. They were dry as dust. She thought for a second or two and then began to outline the outcome to the Molucca Edwards story.

As she spoke, Molucca himself was beating across the Bay of Biscay in a Dutch-owned barque bound for Surabaya, a tarpaulin jacket flattened against his chest and crotch, his seaboots filling with steel-grey water. There was a sun up there somewhere, not the one that warms the roofs of houses by land, but a colourless disc, skating in and out of long streamers of inky cloud.

Captain Van de Watering was on the afterdeck, his shrill voice scolding the officer of the watch. This was the kind of vessel where the petty officers carried rattan canes: the elderly Van de Watering, two days out from Rotterdam, would like to have seen them used more liberally on what Molucca also considered a surly and recalcitrant crew. As for himself, relief and a chance to put himself as far from Robert Judd as possible made him a model able seaman.

His parting words to Bella in Chiswick had been that she would never see hide nor hair of him again, no, not for a fortune in gold. At the time he meant to indicate a self-imposed and mournful exile; but now, staggering down the lee rail in a cloud of spindrift, he found himself actually happy for the first time in months.

'He got away scot-free,' Bella explained sourly.

'Good riddance to him,' Urmiston observed. 'But a lucky fellow, all the same. He put his head into the lion's mouth and Murch, you say, took pity on him. How did that come about?'

'It was all very strangely done,' Bella said slowly, remembering Molucca sitting in William Kennett's preposterous drawing room, his feet bare, his boots somewhere in the stables as a pledge on his promise not to run. Prepared by Billy and the Captain, the questions Bella put to him were frankly answered, but terse.

'Yes, I know about the pearls, as who could not? Sir William will be long remembered in the East as the man who stole them from the Chinaman. For many out there, it's who he is. And all he is.'

'Have you ever seen them, these pearls?' Bella wanted to know.

'Once,' Molucca said, unable to keep the awe out of his voice.

'Has Judd ever proposed stealing them back?'

'Getting the girl is the same thing as getting the pearls. Mind, he wants it all. Kit and caboodle. Little Miss Mary, the pearls, the whole business.'

'And how will that come about?'

Molucca shrugged.

'There is a plan?' Bella persisted. At the same time it was beginning to annoy her that, in the corner of her eye, she could see Philip Westland slouched in an armchair, arms folded, like a sulking child.

'With Bob Judd, there is always a plan. You've already seen that.' He nodded sheepishly in Philip Westland's direction.

But if Philip was content to stay stubbornly silent, William Kennett could no longer contain himself. 'You realise that

I will kill him long before he gets his hands on Skillane's daughter?'

'I wish you well of that,' Molucca said drily.

Because, after all, though he was slow and not from the same box as these grand people and their beautiful house, Molucca understood one thing very well. The lady was carrying the heavy end of the beam. And, naked feet or not, he could see freedom beckoning. He knew, as they did not, why his interrogation had begun in the stables with the two leery coves. They knew the score, spoke the same language, as the agonising throb in his shins could testify. Never mind that now. Give me another minute or two with this dozy lot, Molucca thought with some of his old cunning, and they'll be lending me money and a change of linen.

And there things might have stood, he might truly have disappeared back into the fog, had not Billy Murch suddenly burst into the room.

'Has he told you all?' he barked without the slightest deference.

'Have you?' Bella asked Molucca.

'I thought I was talking among gentlemen,' he blustered.

Before anyone else could move, Murch closed his fist and punched him in the face with colossal force. Molucca's head rocked back and blood flew from his nose in a fine spray.

Bella flinched as if struck herself. 'Is this necessary?' she cried.

Billy pushed her aside and seized Molucca by the jaw. The big man's eyes were still struggling to focus.

'I gave you your chance, you toe-rag, and now I come in here and find you've thrown it back in my face. I put you on your word to tell them everything.'

'I told them all I know,' Molucca insisted, but without much conviction. 'My nose is coming up like a marrow, you bastard.'

Murch turned back to Bella. 'What is best, is for me and the Captain to take him outside, tie him to that tree out there and remind him where he stands in this game. You might not want to watch.'

'Isn't he doing his best?' Philip Westland muttered. They were the first words he had spoken for ten minutes.

Murch's glance could have turned water into ice. 'This is a man who's never met you, who sets off with a knife to cut you up and leave you for Mrs Wallis to scrape off the pavement. No, Mr Westland, he is not doing his best. Has he told you about Linny? I see from your face he has not.'

In Mrs Bardsoe's tidy little parlour, the clock ticked a few dry seconds away. Charles Urmiston set down his glass. 'Linny?' he muttered, making the same mistake that Bella herself had made when she first heard the name, believing it to be a surname.

'That is Murch in a nutshell,' she said ruefully. 'Here were we three being fed unimportant titbits and he had already got out of Molucca – I don't know how – the key to the whole thing. The moment Murch mentioned the name, the poor fellow collapsed, just gave up the ghost. He had seen the chance of rooking us turn to dust in his hands.'

'But then, forgive me, who is Mr Linny?'

Bella nodded grimly. 'Just so,' she said.

In Cornwall, on a cliff path near St Just, with the Botallack mine chimneys half hidden by a high ridge of gorse and bracken, and nothing but the sea to the north and west, there was a miner's cottage built of boulder stone and scraps of wood. The roof was tarpaulin, painted nearly half an inch thick with ancient tar. The one piece of window glass in the place was cemented into the lee-side wall. The floor was unboarded, the walls black with peat. The tenant was a reckless girl called Linny Trethewey. She had been promised the earth. Fate and Robert Judd had given her a child and this miserable kennel.

Things had started very differently, with a gentleman riding by. Linny's father had raised his back from hoeing to see his daughter run to fetch Judd a cup of cider. Watching them, it was all too clear that to them he might as well have been a gatepost or a dung heap. Linny, sixteen, was laughing, her hand to her throat. Suddenly, Judd reached down and hauled her up behind him. Her bare leg flashed, as high as her thigh.

'Now, Trethewey,' he called with his trademark insolence, 'wouldn't you like to see your daughter here taken into service, such a fine figure of a girl as she is?'

'That would be something,' Trethewey agreed with enough irony to split staves.

'You know Sir William Skillane's place?'

'Who doesn't?' Trethewey, greatly daring, spat.

''Tis a chance, father, that don't come by often,' Linny said.

'Some would say it comes by often enough to trusting maids.'

'Are we going to spend all day gabbing?' Judd asked. 'If you don't like it, pull her down and I'll be on my way.'

Trethewey shrugged. 'Mind yourself,' he told his daughter, as if she were the kind to pay the slightest heed. 'See her straight now, sir. And bring her back to tell her old dad what's afoot.'

'Shall come back in a carriage,' Linny promised, making Judd laugh.

That night, Albert Moss came round, as he did three or four times a week, to see his girl, the light of his life.

Trethewey was drunk, not spewing drunk but dangerous. 'She'm sunk,' he laughed when Albert asked after her. 'Less'n you want to go and win her back with all your great wealth, my dove.'

'Could go and put his lights out,' Albert proposed, but none too eagerly.

'That's right,' Linny's father crowed. 'Put his lights out in your manly fashion. What could be easier?'

Albert, with his harelip and reddened lumps for hands, his spine already twisted from clawing in the potato fields. A shilling a day labourer, already half lunatic. He fidgeted. 'Your daughter's a whore,' he decided.

'That, and some,' Trewethey agreed.

Judd took Linny to Boskeriss House, easily the largest property she had ever seen and as alien to her as might be Windsor Castle. None of the Skillane family was in residence and the place was being looked after by the housekeeper and her husband. All the rooms on the ground floor were closed up. Judd left the barefoot girl shivering in the corridor while he went to find Mrs Rowe and order hot water to be sent to the bathroom. The green bathroom, mind. Hot water and a bottle – make that two – of champagne. Meanwhile, Rowe might shift his fat arse and stable the horse.

The Rowes exchanged glances and said nothing. They were country people (she from Land's End, he from the offices of a tin mine in Lostwithiel) but they were not stupid. They had seen Judd come up the drive and they knew before she did why Linny was there with him.

'Is it Miss Mary's bathroom you spoke of?' Mrs Rowe asked at last, very quiet.

'Just bring the water as fast as you can boil it and be damned with your questions.'

'If that poor whit has ever seen a bath afore it will be a miracle,' Rowe commented to his departing back, while planning how to catch a glimpse of her without her clothes.

And he was right: naked, Linny was brown with sixteen years of ingrained dirt. She sat in the bath with her arms crossed, watching Judd empty a jar of pale green crystals into the water and commanding her to kick. Alarming amounts of foam resulted.

'This ain't your bath I'm sitting in,' she accused him, playful but uncertain.

Judd smiled. 'No more than is that bed in the next room. When you finish here, you can stretch out in it like a young lady.'

'And where will you be?' she said with a child's attempt at archness.

'Use the little brush there. Scrub yourself pink. And wash the peat smoke out of your hair.'

An hour later, when he pulled away from her, he was surprised to see a flower of blood between her thighs. Linny was looking at him with darkened eyes, tears on her cheeks.

'I am not often the first,' Judd said, half to himself.

'Who is Mary?' Linny whispered. She pointed to a cross-stitch sampler framed and hanging on the gold and green wallpaper.

'What do you care?' Judd demanded, looking at her body without quite meeting her eyes.

'And he told you this? Molucca told you all this?'

Bella studied Charles Urmiston's anguished expression, in which disgust and compassion were mixed.

'He took a cottage for her in St Erth,' she continued. 'Bought her clothes, taught her manners after his fashion. Rode over to Trethewey's place and told him if he ever opened his mouth he was a dead man.'

'But the servants? Mr and Mrs Rowe?'

Bella smiled sadly. 'He is altogether very businesslike, Charles. Linny had never seen a three-storey house before and nor had the Rowes a five-pound note. After his own fashion, he got away with it. The Skillanes suspected nothing, least of all that poor innocent Mary. Then came the baby.'

She poured herself the last of the wine. 'She made the mistake of threatening to expose him as the father of the child. He turned her out of the cottage with the clothes she stood in and a sovereign. Her father would not take her back, this fellow Moss first belaboured her with a stick and then in a fit of remorse found her the place where she is now. Without Molucca Edwards – which is really to say without Billy Murch's way of dealing with him – we would not know any of this story, nor that she ever existed.'

'But now you have a chance to bring Judd's world down about his ears. And, I suppose, save Mary. That is your plan, I take it.'

'We have been discussing it in that light,' Bella said. 'Yes. But there is a problem.'

'Mr Kennett,' Urmiston guessed.

'How wise you are, Charles. William Kennett would stand to gain most from exposing Judd's infamy. Of course he would. But for him it is not enough. He truly wants to kill Judd. How it is to be done he cannot say. But he thinks it the only certain way to bring an end to the whole affair.'

Urmiston nodded. He stood, rubbing his thighs; and then walked into the scullery, where he filled a kettle with deliberate care. 'What you haven't said is the help you need from me.'

'Oh, nothing of a practical kind,' she called.

He was not a stupid man. He knew she had yet to reveal her true reasons for sitting there at his table, her head in her hands.

'Hannah will be back soon,' he said. 'I am making a pot of tea for all of us.'

'I don't know that Hannah –'

'Nonsense,' Urmiston said. 'You will tell her what's really troubling you and then she will tell me. That's the way it works best. Only then can I see what's in your heart, dearest Bella.'

*   *   *

The two women talked in Hannah's bedroom, the still air smelling very faintly of sweat and discarded shoes. It was the hour when the shop was busiest and downstairs they could hear Urmiston attending to customers with his trademark patience and courtesy.

'They come regular for their pills and potions – more than ever, now that Charles has tidied the business up, and me with it. But, like he says, it's not really their guts that are griping. Living is hard and tears come easy. My dear boy thinks we should change the name over the door and call the place the "Chat Shop".'

'Have you ever asked yourself what it's all about, Hannah?' Bella asked in her tiniest voice. 'Everything, I mean.'

'Lord love you! And you the famous writer!'

'You have probably guessed what's troubling me. It is that very thing. I could write a story about all these recent commotions without leaving the house, without so much as thinking twice. Instead, I have made Philip Westland witness some terrible things – and put his life at risk besides. Do you remember when Charles went down into Cornwall because he could not stand it any more?'

'I think I do recall that unhappy time,' Hannah said drily.

'That is how I feel now.'

'Run away, is it? Is there no other way?'

'Mr Westland and I are at sixes and sevens over our future together. Which is a pale way of describing it.'

'Now there is very unwelcome news.'

'We have a chance of a place down in Wiltshire. I know

he would make it perfect for us both. I love him, Hannah. I want him to be happy. But this, all this' – she waved her hand helplessly – 'is holding me back.'

'This bedroom, do you mean?' Mrs Bardsoe smiled. 'Or is it London, the dirty old place? I dare say there's much in Wiltshire that is pretty to look at and people there that are kindness itself. But I'd be buggered if I could live among them.'

In spite of herself, Bella laughed.

Hannah wrinkled her nose. 'I don't say as how a quiet life isn't worth having. And, oh, won't I jump at the chance of a little whitewash cottage next the church when the time comes. But as I see it, those days ain't come yet. And that's the long and the short of it with you and Mr Westland.'

'You are right, as always.'

'I don't doubt there is more to it than I can tell. But what keeps you here is wickedness and how to defeat it. He understands that.'

'I have begun to wonder.'

'Then you must unwonder. I have met the gentleman but the once, the night you put your life at risk out there in Holborn. But I know adoration when I see it.'

Bella blushed. Hannah Bardsoe patted her hand gently. 'He has chose you, and you him. It's that old Henry Ellis Margam that's queering his pitch, is that it? Well, similarwise, it does drive me to distraction sometimes to see my dear boy Charles acting like the Queen's physician to a bunch of old women without a pair of drawers to their name; but this here room is where we settle it, whenever it comes too much.'

So saying, she plumped up the pillows, helped Bella to her feet and smoothed down the counterpane. Her actions were brisk and businesslike but her cheeks were bright red.

'Running away won't help. That was my meaning. Shouldn't you give this Wiltshire place at least a lookover? Or speaking more frankly, Mrs Wallis my dear, closing the bedroom door on that old Henry Ellis for a few days?'

Bella resisted the impulse to hug her. 'Shall we share a touch of your best Martinique rum, Hannah?' she asked, pulling open the bedroom door.

'Oh yes, the rum! And if I hadn't forgotten that as a great peacemaker, too. Lead away downstairs. We'll see if we can't get Sir Charles Urmiston to finish his consult-ations and join us.'

He was waiting for them in the parlour, wearing his green baize apron and a strange felt hat that he put on when serving in the shop.

'Mrs Wallis has a mind to go down to Wiltshire for a few days, dearest,' Hannah lied briskly. 'For the holiday aspect of it. Same as we had them two days in Margate.'

'A capital idea,' Urmiston said gravely. 'I do hope Mr Westland will accompany her.'

'Well, would she go without him? I do declare, Charlie, sometimes you are as slow as some old snail. Wiltshire! Was ever such a romantic location? I am green with envy.'

Urmiston kissed her fondly. 'And do you know where Wiltshire is, my dear?'

'Why,' Hannah blustered, kissing Bella in turn. ''Tis where it always is, the month of September. Men, Mrs W! The questions they ask! And lost without women, if you follow my drift.'

TWELVE

Rain and more fog in London, but in Wiltshire a fine autumnal haze over the water-meadows. In the early morning the sound of marching feet as a full company of soldiers swung past, their red uniforms flowing like a ribbon against the green of the lane. Their helmets and belts were a dazzling white, the stocks of their rifles burnished like chestnut. As they marched, a grizzled old colour sergeant the size of a sentry box chivvied them along in a lulling, almost affectionate tone, like a man herding cattle. Yet-tchar! Chests out! Yet-tchar!

'A fine sight,' Bella exclaimed.

'They might say the same of you,' Westland replied. 'Not every cottage window they pass frames a beautiful woman; or at any rate, not a naked one.'

'This is the country,' she countered. 'Things are done differently here. We are closer to nature.'

She turned to face him and laid her arms around his neck. 'Does Kennett come today?'

'By mid-morning train.'

'I could wish him a thousand miles away. It really is a little corner of heaven here, Philip.'

'I concede nothing of my original idea, you understand – that we could be happy out of London. But I admit to being dismayed by the amount of walking about one has to do. You are nothing in this village if you haven't climbed that damn great hill out there at least once a week or strode along the river into Salisbury. Our neighbours are all perambulators.'

They kissed, skin to skin.

'You are intensely lovable. Have I told you that?' Bella whispered.

'You may have done. I live to make you happy, Bella.'

'But you don't like what I have made of myself.'

The pause before his reply was no more than a heart-beat or two; but for all that, it was too long.

'After breakfast,' he said, his lips against her neck.

As a consequence, this was a meal taken more or less in silence. After it, obedient to local custom, they walked; across the fields to a railway crossing, from thence down a narrow tunnel of blackthorn hedge more than a hundred yards long. Very disappointingly, it led into a stubbled field. To go on they would have to journey without paths to no obvious destination: it was more than Londoners could contemplate. They did what strangers to the country do and pretended to find beauty in a quite unexceptional view.

They were saved when Westland pointed out an ancient curiosity right in front of them – a quince, heavy with fruit, clinging to a fragment of brickwork.

'Were we to dig here roundabout, we should perhaps uncover a walled garden and in time the relics of a house. How cruel history can be.'

'This is maudlin of you, Westland.'

He picked her a green and ugly fruit. 'How I feel this morning, Bella,' he said slowly, 'is simple enough.

It falls out like this. We can stay in Orange Street, or I will buy you another house in London. But I would be lying if I said I was happy to see you risk your life – or mine, come to that – now or ever again for Henry Ellis Margam.'

'Is that really how it seems to you?'

'Shall we say this: poets who write about waterfalls don't always feel the need to live under one?'

'If you love me, you must not try to change me.'

'I hope I have shown that,' he protested mildly.

'I do not coax these stories into existence, Philip, they spring up like serpents. You wouldn't have me as soft-headed as Cissie Cornford, for example?'

'I don't know that Lady Cornford is a useful comparison.'

'Why not? Isn't she a fictionalist in her own way? Isn't the biggest fiction of all the idea that life is merely wallpaper and servants, coats of arms and French chefs? And the tittle-tattle that follows from them?'

She nodded 'good morning' to a hunched farmworker coming along the field edge, a sack across his back. He touched the neb of his ruined cap without so much as glancing as he passed.

'I could not live that life and be happy,' she said, meaning Cissie Cornford's comfortable banalities.

'You intend to hunt this fellow Judd down, I take it?'

'I intend to prevent your friend Kennett from doing something utterly reckless. I don't ask you to join me. And I beg you to believe I make a very reluctant warder.'

Westland walked into the empty field a few paces. 'At least

one thing can be settled,' he muttered distractedly. 'I could no more live here than fly in the air. Too much sky. And nowhere to hide.'

She laughed, in spite of herself. 'I didn't know you were in hiding from anything.'

'From things as they are.'

At their backs, a train thundered past, perhaps the one bearing Kennett. Philip had found a stick he pretended was of great interest. He swished experimentally. The stick broke in two.

'You will not marry me, I suppose?' he asked; and when she failed to answer, glanced over his shoulder with a wry smile. 'Never mind. We should walk to the pub and order something for Kennett to eat when he arrives. And if he attempts to walk from Salisbury by the river path, I shall wash my hands of you both.'

'How should he come then?'

'In a hansom, like Henry Ellis Margam on the way to the Garrick.'

'Philip, I am not completely cruel.'

'You mean that thing I said about marriage just now? Oh, that will come to pass one day. Like having to walk with a stick or taking the stairs one at a time. You will see.'

Though they held hands on the walk back, she found nothing to say that could break their mood. He left the quince he had picked balancing on a fence post, its glassy greenness winking in the watery sun. Some objects in the world are put there solely to provoke future dreams. This was one of them.

*   *   *

But it was not William Kennett who arrived in the village an hour later but Charles Urmiston. He had with him a brown paper parcel which turned out to be a cake from Hannah, a present he laid down on the sitting-room windowsill. 'Your surprise at my presence is understandable,' Urmiston began. 'I have taken William Kennett's place at extremely short notice – indeed, I had all to do to catch the train he designated.'

'Where is he?' Philip asked bluntly.

Urmiston looked about him, as if confirming to himself that this low-ceilinged room was indeed his destination. He had arrived wearing a ridiculous brown bowler that Bella knew without being told had been bought from a second-hand clothes stall. His jacket was of the kind that cattle auctioneers might wear. This was Urmiston dressed for the country by Hannah Bardsoe.

'Sit down, Charles,' she said.

'I am flustered,' Urmiston confessed. 'There is some kind of war scare in London and the train was stuffed with military men. All talking very loudly and being amazingly free with their opinions. Salisbury in uproar. Leave cancelled, provosts everywhere. The fellow who fetched me here from the station says he has it from unimpeachable sources that the Russians intend to occupy Constantinople. I took him to mean imminently.'

'Can we leave such eventualities to the care of the Foreign Office?' Philip Westland snapped, far too briskly.

Urmiston flinched. 'I beg your pardon.'

'Better to tell us why Kennett has failed to turn up.'

'The two things are connected – Russian intentions and William's reaction. Or not his, but Robert Judd's.'

Bella and Philip sat and waited, lips pursed, watching Urmiston scrub his temples with his knuckles.

'I can only tell this story one way,' he complained feebly. 'I asked William to furnish me with a note but he didn't have the time.'

Philip lumbered to his feet and began pacing the carpet, his hands pulling at his hair.

Bella caught him by the sleeve and begged him to look for wine and a corkscrew. 'And you, Charles, please continue.'

'Very well,' Urmiston said, rubbing the crease across his forehead where the bowler had been sitting. 'Skillane's Black Sea fleet is British registered. In the event of a Russian occupation of Constantinople there might follow at the very least a blockade of the Dardanelles. You may look at me like that all you wish, Bella, but I am only repeating the scaremongering that has attacked otherwise perfectly rational people in London.'

'And these rumours have caused Sir William to stir himself down in Cornwall?' she suggested.

'There you have it,' Urmiston exclaimed gratefully. 'Sir William wires his anxieties to Judd in London, Judd is galvanised. He receives a second intelligence from a man called Kashvili –'

'How do we know all this?'

'Murch,' Charles Urmiston said with the greatest simplicity.

'And how does he know?'

'The answer is, I'm afraid, burglary. And, I suppose, theft. We have the telegrams.'

Philip came back into the room with a bottle and glasses, still wincing.

'Who is Kashvili?'

'Wait. No sooner has Judd received this second cable than he cabs post haste to Cook's in Piccadilly and books himself on to the Harwich steamer to Holland. From there he goes direct to the boat train at Liverpool Street, taking with him nothing but the clothes he stands up in. Kashvili is a man who stays at the Metropole in Rotterdam.'

'And?'

Urmiston shrugged. Westland fixed him with a stare. 'You have no idea who he is?'

'None. Judd sailed for Rotterdam towards midnight of last night.'

'I have the most terrible feeling that you are about to tell us Kennett followed him.'

'Yes. By the morning service from Dover to Calais and thereafter by train. I can't say with what plan of action.'

'Taking Murch with him?' Bella asked sharply.

'Alone.'

The three of them sat trying to digest this. Then Urmiston remembered he had the telegrams in his wallet and fished them out, passing them to Bella, who skimmed the contents and passed them in turn to Philip.

'Kashvili is presumably an agent of the Skillane Company?' she asked.

Urmiston shrugged but Philip Westland nodded. 'It would seem so.'

'Then – and I may be missing the point somewhat – doesn't it make ordinary commercial sense for Skillane to instruct Judd to go to Rotterdam and find out what's happening?'

'You'll have noticed the Kashvili cable to Judd is in code,' Urmiston said.

Philip waved away the remark with a bitterly indulgent laugh. Bella looked at him. 'You think you could break it?'

'With patience, a child of ten could break it.'

'Then can we three try to match the ingenuity of a child of ten?'

Pencils produced, writing paper discovered in a desk drawer. The code comprised letters of the alphabet arranged in ten blocks of six. It read:

5KQJJY XFNQXX NHNQD2 9YMHMF SLJTKT
BSJWXM NUFLWJ JIHTSK NWRZWL JSYDP

'We can quickly discount the possibility that Kashvili's message contains ten nouns or verbs of equal length,' Urmiston proposed, with a nervous glance at the others.

'The groups might represent whole phrases or even sentences, if we knew the key,' Bella suggested.

Philip smiled. 'You are thinking of the commercial telegraphic code that the masters of merchant ships employ.'

'Kashvili is agent to a shipping company,' she pointed out.

'Maybe. He may be.'

'But it could be commercial code?'

'If so, there is enough here for a short story. No, I think this is what's called a substitution code. The letters represent other letters of the alphabet. Or at least, we might start with that possibility.'

Silent scribbling. Bella pointed out the presence of seven

Js, which could indicate a vowel. Urmiston drew atten-tion to the three numbers in the script and – after a few moments' reflection – the possibility that there were only two numbers, 5 and 29. More silence.

'Wait a minute,' Bella said. 'Suppose J to be a vowel. Then surely it can only be E or O.'

'If the first group is a single word.'

'But if not, what short English word ends in O?'

'Two,' Philip yawned. He lay back in his chair, hands folded across his chest. When Bella glanced at his work-sheet, she saw he had written nothing but instead had drawn a heart pierced by an arrow.

'If the 2 and the 9 because of their juxtaposition might indicate 29, what does that suggest?' he murmured, like a weary don conducting a tutorial.

'A date, perhaps!' Urmiston exclaimed.

'Very possibly. And the 5?'

'Maybe some other quantity. Five million in bonds. Five days. Five gentlemen in seaboots. I don't know.'

'If you know,' Bella snapped at Westland, 'perhaps you would stop pouting and tell us.'

He sat up, as if forcing himself to take the problem ser-iously for the sake of his friends.

'Schoolboys amuse themselves with stuff like this, Bella, in the long afternoons otherwise devoted to Latin gerunds or the cape and bay geography of Britain. Suppose the 5 indicates a shift of five letters forwards or backwards, what does that first group spell, if anything?'

Bella bent her head over her scrap of paper, Urmiston likewise.

'FLEET,' they cried together.

'And the whole text?'
More busy scribbling. The new groups now read:

5FLEET SAILSS ICILY2 9THCHAN NGEOFO
WNERSH
IPAGRE EDCONF IRMURG ENTLYK

'Sir William Skillane seems about to lose an empire, but
not to the Russians,' Philip Westland concluded. 'And it
might be worth pointing out that the 29th is exactly five
days distant. We now know what set Kennett off like a
terrier.'

Urmiston stirred uneasily. 'I was not charged to come
down here to tell you where your friend was. He asked
me to order you both – I'm afraid that was his word for
it – to return to London immediately and plan what to
do about the Cornwall connection.'

'And what does that mean?'

'He would not say.'

'We are on the back foot every step of the way,' Bella
said bitterly. 'A change of ownership might mean just that
– the business passes by some legal instrument or other
to Judd. It does not have to – in fact it would be stretching
the point to make it – bear a more sinister meaning. The
Skillane fleet is in danger of being bottled up in the Black
Sea and will repair to Sicily. Where new ownership will
be established.'

Westland took a turn to the windows and opened
them on what was turning out to be an idyllic autumn
day.

It was startling to Bella to realise she could read what

was in his mind from the set of his back and the way his hands splayed on the sill. What she saw was dispiriting.

'This is exactly the problem, Bella,' he said slowly. 'Leaving aside the murder of Liza Givens, which we cannot prove Judd committed, what we have here is the correspondence of a very unlikeable set of scoundrels who nevertheless sail well within the law.'

'And?'

'For you to make more of it is to tell a story that may or may not be true.'

'To tell a story?' she repeated, cheeks burning.

'To invent. To do Margam's work for him.'

Her salvation came from an unlikely source. Urmiston first asked for coffee, if there was any to be had, failing that the strongest tea.

'As to Bella's dilemma, I have never yet known her to tell a story that was not true. You discount Liza Givens and this other poor creature down in Cornwall because you have never met them. And you say, far too lightly, let the world roll on. Well, it's not good enough, Westland. It will not wash.'

'You are doing me the honour of calling my conscience into question, is that it?'

'Oh, for God's sake,' Bella shouted, storming from the room.

On the way back to London, the train stopped at Basingstoke for a scheduled four minutes, an opportunity some passengers seized as a chance to stretch their legs. Bella pushed past Urmiston's knees and opened the carriage door. He made no attempt to prevent her stepping down on to the platform. They had not spoken for more than an hour, and the atmosphere in the compartment was glacial.

Though a pale sun was doing its best, it could add nothing to Basingstoke station. The air was filled with steam and smuts; every surface was greasy to the touch. And – it struck Bella in her present mood – the landscape and the people in it were hideous beyond words. Enamelled plaques advertising cocoa, soap, proprietary medicines and washing products seemed to indicate to passengers that these things and their like were all they needed in life. In other places, prominent railway company notices told them what to do, where to go, how to avoid danger, how to walk down a simple flight of stairs, what was drinking water and what was not.

And all this while, sparrows flitted sardonically about under the platform canopy, feeding (or so it seemed) on what had leaked or been spilt from the human craving for order. The birds swooped and rose only a foot or so above the tallest beaver hats. Their tiny fallen breast feathers were swept up by miniature tornadoes, or blew like petals across the dusty floor.

Bella forced herself to acknowledge, as whistles blew and one by one the carriage doors slammed shut, that what she was experiencing was something close to hysteria. Honestly put, she could not give a damn about the arrangements of Basingstoke station, nor the people who used it. She was afraid of losing Philip Westland – which made it all the more absurd that the train was drawing out of the station without her, the guard hanging out of the last carriage, his green flag wagging. As he passed, he caught her eye, as if knowing full well what had happened and why she was being left stranded.

Henry Ellis Margam could have coped. A situation like this was meat and drink to him, though he would surely have transferred the scene to some more romantic location – a tiny halt in a Bavarian forest perhaps, or somewhere bleak and snowswept in Sweden. This man walking towards her now along the platform, breasting gouts of steam, his figure backlit by the sun, might be Robert Judd – vengeance in his heart, a silver pistol in his pocket, the blood of William Kennett on his hands.

In fact, standing in front of her was a hatless Philip Westland. Bella threw herself into his arms. 'Urmiston must think us both mad,' she sobbed.

'I was all for letting you stew. It was he who more or less bundled me out. May I propose tea? And perhaps an Eccles cake?'

He raised her head from his chest and kissed her full on the lips. 'Listen to me, Bella. Having once found you, would I ever let you go?'

THIRTEEN

The Hotel Metropole in Rotterdam lay halfway down a cobbled street of chandlers in the dock area of the city. Sentimental guests – and they were very few and infrequent – claimed they could smell the sea. What they actually smelt was tar and spice, mountains of Dutch potatoes – and a great deal of local sewage delivered into the river and sent back to its source by the stiff breeze that customarily blew across the estuary.

Right next door to the Metropole was a business selling uniforms, braided caps, solar topees, displays of gilt insignia and badges of rank. A printed card advertised that inside could also be purchased a patented double-lined tin trunk, suitable for the tropics and guaranteed termite-proof. Part of the window display was taken up by a sheaf of rattan canes and fly whisks, not at all arranged in a whimsical fashion but presented as the necessary and formal adjuncts of the East India trade.

It was not unusual for younger and more romantic customers to put on their new uniforms in the shop and then walk next door into the hotel bar as newly hatched third officers or assistant pursers. There they demanded the best in the house, clapped each other on the back, laughed uproariously, smoked luxuriously and offered complete strangers a drink. Many – especially those unwise enough to go upstairs with the Surinam whores who frequented the place – left in a sorry state, barely in a condition to find their ships, let alone their brand new caps.

Kashvili looked on them all with a father's fondness. His vantage point was a table in the shadows, where his piratical black beard put off all but the most delirious of these novitiates. The Georgian was one of those sprawlingly gross figures whose fat deceives the unwary, for when he stirred himself to stand up, he was revealed as a small but threatening mountain of a man. When Judd came into the bar, however, he hardly stirred, save for the flap of a hand in greeting.

'They have the innocence of children, these young gentlemen,' he explained. 'Papa puts up the money to send them to sea and the world beckons. I have yet to meet one who knows what he is in for.'

'Very touching,' Judd replied. But not so pointedly as to upset the Georgian, for Kashvili could be an awkward bastard when he set his mind to it. He had once been a ship's captain in the Skillane fleet, duties he discharged for the most part in a striped flannel kaftan and stocking cap, with felt slippers on his feet. Kashvili had been at sea since he was nine years old without ever serving under a captain in a navy blue serge uniform and brass buttons.

'My legs have gone,' he confided absently to Judd. 'What a terrible thing, to be old.'

'If all goes as planned, you can be carried about in a chair by Circassian slave girls.'

'That will be welcome,' the ruined captain said drily, running his fingers through his beard.

'Is it safe here?' Judd asked, looking around him into the gloom, alarmed momentarily by the clack-clack of billiard balls in an unseen annexe of the bar.

Kashvili laughed, reaching across the table and chucking Judd under the chin with a crooked forefinger. 'Can we be overheard? Of course! This fellow to your right is a poet. His subject is decadence. You see he drinks absinthe. Maybe he is listening. No, for sure he is listening! Is he safe in here? I don't think.'

The poet raised his shaven head from the table and, catching the glint in Kashvili's eyes, saluted sketchily and stumbled away.

'If he could only find the fare to Amsterdam, he would be among friends,' the Georgian explained. 'But he don't understand: everyone in here works at least as hard as the whores upstairs. Rotterdam! City without illusions! I like.'

Judd was barely listening, his face closed tight.

Kashvili folded his arms comfortably over his chest and peered. 'So, as to our present dealings, the captains are asking me how you intend to pull it off.'

'That is none of their business.'

'I have told them this.'

'You mean, *you* want to know how it will work.'

'Oh, please!' Kashvili protested, laughing. 'Am I looking so stupid? It will be done by trickery, blackmail. Poor Sir William, with his beloved knighthood and his dried-up wife. His ridiculous house in Cornwall, and his tame bank manager.'

Warning bells rang in Judd's head. He leaned in across the table. 'What do you know of all this?'

'He writes to me of course. "My dear old Kashvili, my trusted friend!" You think he don't remember me? I gave him his start when he got back from the East. A fat old man with a nose for business and Kashvili, master mariner. Two thieves, Mr Judd. Don't you got that expression in English, as thick as two thieves? I think so, yes.'

'What do you want?' Judd asked, his throat dry.

'I want the pearls.'

Useless to ask which pearls: the Georgian's smile was all-knowing.

'All that will come to pass.'

'You don't got them with you now?'

'Are you mad? They're still at the bank in Cornwall. I've told you this.'

'I want,' Kashvili said simply.

'All in good time,' Judd countered, feeling sweat run down his spine.

'We get proper valuation, maybe here in Holland and then Kashvili get his sweetener.'

'There is time enough for that,' Judd repeated.

'You think? Last week, Sir William writes me big letter. "Kashvili, what is going on? You understand the human heart. Do I got enemies in this crazy world? Nice old man like me? What should I do to sleep happy? Tell me please."'

'And what did you reply?'

The Georgian shrugged. 'When you get the girl, you get the business. This he understands. We all understand. You hang the old man by the heels, his money falls out of his pockets. Not all, but enough. Then, when he die, you got everything. Maybe you want it should go a little faster. What is this to Kashvili? It's business, he says to his pillow. Just business.'

'Then what is the problem?'

The Georgian examined his guest with unsettlingly feminine green eyes. 'The problem, my friend, is the lady with her throat slashed. The London lady you murder.'

'Molucca!' Judd divined at once.

'He came here. I find him ship. Nice ship. Before he goes, he wants to tell me story about' – he clicked his fingers impatiently – 'about Mrs Givens, yes. The poor lady.'

With surprising speed, he reached across the table and seized his companion by the shirt-front and lifted him halfway out of his seat. Though he spoke in a whisper, his breath roared in Judd's face. 'You get rid of Sir William just like you plan, everything nice. And then come the police and arrest you. Then they hang you! That's the problem, Mr Judd.'

He threw the Englishman back in his chair. 'Soon enough, everything goes back to what it was. Sir William has had a bad scare. He walks on the beach, thinks about business. Two, three days he walks, maybe a week. He don't shed no tears but he asks, "Who else was in on this? Who can I trust any longer? I thought I got friends and this new shit shows me I don't got none. Better I make other arrangements, marry my girl to a Scotchman with a castle, something like that. And for his part in all this other thing, Kashvili I kill. My eight captains I keep, maybe. But Kashvili, who call himself my friend, him I kill."'

'That won't happen,' Judd said, none too certain.

'You think? That old man is cunning like mountain bear. You think he sits in his house all day doing this?' He had not the word for it and mimed knitting with his thick fingers.

'If the police are after anyone, it's Molucca,' Judd said impatiently. 'They do not suspect me.'

Kashvili sank back into the shadows, his fingers at his beard again. 'You are big fool, Mr Judd,' he whispered softly. 'Tell me, please, what is doing the Englishman upstairs, a Mr Kennett? Has he come to Rotterdam to inspect new harbour?'

'Kill him,' Judd said instantly.

'But I like him,' the Georgian objected.

'Go upstairs and slit his throat. If you don't want to do it yourself, find someone who will.'

'I think you mean this,' Kashvili yawned.

'Of course I mean it. What's stopping you?'

'Yes, what can it be?'

'We are partners, aren't we?' Judd protested.

'Well, about this, I tell you something. I have nephew, my sister's boy, nice young man. He ask me once: "What is secret of long and happy life, uncle?" I tell him: Vassily, you have always to see around corners. Very important. You understand, Mr Judd?'

'We have a deal,' Judd said, his face white.

'We had a deal, maybe we still got a deal. But now, like I just tell you, we got a problem.'

'How did Kennett know he would find me here?' Judd asked, perplexed.

'That's not the problem,' Kashvili said. 'We tweak his

nose a little, he tells us his story. The problem is, how much Sir William knows. You want to get rid of him. He want to get rid of you. Maybe. Killing the whore was very stupid thing to do. Killing Mr Kennett could be worse. You don't think?'

Judd rose and pushed back his chair with enough force to topple it. For his part, Kashvili lit a cigarette, making enough blue smoke to wreathe his head, his beard and his unblinking eyes.

William Kennett really was upstairs. When the door to his room opened, he was sitting on the bed. In his hand was a toy of a revolver. He was expecting Judd and seemed utterly disconcerted by the figure blocking the threshold, roaring with laughter and facing him down with nothing more threatening than a chicken leg.

'Don't hide up here, English,' Kashvili bellowed. 'Come and drink. Your friend Mr Judd has gone.'

'Gone? Gone where?'

'He don't like the Metropole any more than you. Put your little gun away, Mr Kennett. Wrong to say you are among friends, but I don't got no bad intentions towards you. I swear.'

'I came here to kill Robert Judd,' Kennett said, greatly vexed.

Kashivili slapped his thigh with delight. 'And I come here to rob him of what he robs from Sir William. Maybe kill him, who knows? You play cards, Mr K? We go downstairs and play some cards.'

'Judd first.'

'Like you say in your country, the bird has flown.

And how he wish he could fly, that bastard. You bet. You want Mr Judd, you must look in Cornwall, I think.'

'He's gone back to England?' Kennett asked.

'For sure!'

When he saw the crestfallen look on Kennett's face, he burst out laughing all over again.

'Molucca tell me all about you. Nice house. Nice friends. Plenty money but very shy. You only got one problem in otherwise happy life – Miss Mary.'

'He will not get her,' Kennett warned.

'And that's why you bring your little pop gun to Rotterdam? Maybe you kill him when I have finished with him. But not today.'

'Today, if it's still possible.'

The smile vanished slowly from Kashvili's lips, as if the big man was at last noticing something about Kennett he had previously overlooked. He threw away his chicken leg into a corner of the room and pointed a greasy finger. 'That,' he said with great deliberation, 'would be big mistake.'

'It wouldn't help you, certainly.'

Kashvili blinked, as though it was the bed that Kennett sat on that had spoken with such impudence; or the wash basin and jug. 'You are long way from pretty house in London, Mr Kennett,' he said slowly. 'So don't talk stupid at me.'

'If I find him today, I will kill him. It's what I came to do. I'm not interested in anything else. Do what you like about all the rest of it. But now get out of my way.'

'Maybe you don't sleep so much last night. Maybe you're hungry. Maybe you're a little bit stupid, don't listen so good. This is not about pretty virgin girl with maybe secret moles somewhere nice, Mr Kennett. This is about money. Big money.'

'There is no money in it big enough to stop me.'

Kashvili sighed and wiped his hands on his shirt. 'Now you don't think straight. I got no time for dreamers.'

'I'm warning you. Get out of my way.'

It seemed that far from doing that, the Georgian was about to advance further into the room and tear him limb from limb. Kennett perked up the pistol.

Kashvili looked affronted. 'You don't got no manners,' he said. 'Now I got to be shitty with you.'

Kennett squeezed the trigger. He was aiming low but the Georgian fell back through the open door and into the corridor like a fallen tree.

'You killed him?' Westland cried incredulously.

'I hit his leg, I think. It was all very sudden.'

'And the pistol?' Billy Murch asked.

'I can't remember. I didn't have it at the train station. I threw it away, obviously, but as I say –' Kennett looked at each of them in turn. 'He is a very big man. I was expecting blood and so forth but there was very little of that. I jumped over him and legged it. Ran. Some people followed to begin with but in time they gave up. I hit upon the location of the station by the purest chance.'

'Well, sir,' Murch said with an encouraging smile, 'it seems to me you have come out of it very fair. For a beginner, so to speak.'

And really, what else was there to say? It was gone one

in the morning and Kennett had only been back in London four hours. He seemed, as well he might be, only half awake – and more than a little bit shame-faced.

Westland threw up his hands despairingly. 'You go to Rotterdam, you stay three hours and you shoot the wrong man. I wish I had your genius, William.'

'Fortunes of war, Mr Westland,' Murch said loyally. 'It happens. I've seen it before.'

'In the Crimea?'

'There it was more common than not.'

Kennett raised a weak smile and pumped Murch's hand. 'I do feel a bit of a fool, all the same, Billy.'

They waited until Murch had left and then Philip pointed a finger at his friend's face. 'No more, William,' he warned. 'You were not made for the role of assassin. No more guns. No more romantic gestures. We will bring these people down, but in a more orderly way.'

'By appealing to their better natures, I suppose.'

'Don't sulk. And don't scowl.'

'Why did I stay in that bedroom when I knew he would come? When I knew he was downstairs?' Kennett burst out.

'Because you placed love above hatred. Because you are no use to Mary in a Dutch jail. And because,' his friend added gently, 'she would never have understood. Chin up. Tomorrow you will find your mood much improved.'

'What has happened?'

'It is late. I shall sleep here tonight, with your permission, and in the morning we will go to Orange Street. We have been dealt the Borodino.'

'Tell me what has happened. Tell me now.'

'Tomorrow,' Philip murmured.

Kennett's housekeeper, Millie Rogerson, had the pleasant habit of eating biscuits in bed. Her wonderfully full and rounded breasts were scattered with crumbs and – as though these did not weigh them down enough – she dragged Murch's head to join them. 'Did he really shoot that man, Murchie?' she asked.

'The little gun he took with him could be put to better use starting foot races. But it was a bold stroke, all the same.'

No one before had ever called him Murchie; and there were other aspects to Millie that were even more startling. It had been a long time since Murch had shared a bed with someone so young, but that was not it either. None of that love talk about her, nothing that was coy – and absolutely no word about the future or what it all meant. Murch was (though he could not have phrased it this way) entranced.

'What happens now?' Millie asked.

'Cornwall. You could come too.'

'I never been on a train and have no wish to. And what says you have to go, either?'

'Come on, Millie,' he replied uncomfortably. 'I have to. Else, left to themselves, who knows what mischief they will all tumble into? I bet you have been on a train at that.'

'Never! Look at Rogerson. He'd never been on a bus, even. And then one ran him over. I've led a very sheltered life. Until I met you, of course.'

'Well, as to that, I had no idea what women were really like until you and me crossed paths.'

Her laughter was silent but had the effect of shuddering her breasts against his face. She tousled his hair. 'You don't want to leave them to it and stay here with me?'

He raised his head, kissed her lips and stared into her face. 'I want you to be here when I get back.'

'Got plans for us, have you?' She knew she was pushing him into areas he did not like to go and was very surprised when he answered.

'Yes,' he said.

'Well, if you get yourself killed, don't come back here looking for sympathy.'

She slid down the bed and wrestled him playfully on top of her. Murch, who knew all about the sabre and could drop a man at up to four hundred yards if the rifle was true, found his heart was banging fit to bust. Making love to Millie was like opening a door at the top of a five-storey building and falling out into the void. Falling out and not crashing, but flying. Answer me that, he asked himself.

FOURTEEN

In Cornwall, Sir William had exchanged the luxuries of his morning bath in London for a more austere regime. He still rose at the same hour but it was his Cornish habit to pull on broad linen trousers and a thick Guernsey sweater and walk down the hill to the beach. Men that he passed – men in the style of Kashvili, hardbitten sailors – rose from the mending of their nets and knuckled their foreheads or simply gave him the steady stare: he never acknowledged their presence.

Once at the lap of the tide, he waded out up to his hips and washed his face and scrubbed his hair, adding a particularly gross finale to these ablutions by taking in water through his mouth and blowing it out through his nasal passages. Then, dripping wet, he retraced his steps, entering the house through the front door, where his butler stood with a towel. In his hand was a second cloth with which he erased Sir William's footprints as the great man tramped upstairs. At a suitable point in the morning, his clumsy bathing costume was retrieved from the floor, washed and flogged free of salt and set to steam in the dungeon-like kitchens.

'And if he don't kill hisself of cold one of these days,' Connie Swift complained savagely, rinsing the sand from the Guernsey sweater with bright red fingers.

'My dad see'd him at high tide a day or two back. The rip tore the kecks clean off his limbs and left him naked in those parts. A spout on him like a donkey,' her friend Ada added.

'Ho! And much use that shabby old thing will be when he's got the double pneumonia. I wish.'

Skillane seldom left the house other than to bathe. Like a man with nothing on his mind but the pleasures of a retired country gentleman, he was supervising the creation of a library from one of the downstairs galleries, to which end he had bought several hundred books, sight unseen. They had come by cart from Penzance, along with various nautical memorabilia – the binnacle of the steamship *Orrin*, run aground at Whitesand Bay, an engraved telescope from the brigantine *Etoile*, lost with all hands at Nanjizal, and so forth. Skillane was buying history.

The truth was that he was happier in Cornwall than ever he could be in London. Boskeriss was a cold and miserable house as it stood now but there was something about its unforgiving bulk that pleased its owner. Choosing wallpaper in Cadogan Square could not compete with digging out an entire hill behind Boskeriss to lay the grounds to lawn; or, as now, fitting out an otherwise nondescript space as a panelled library, complete with false loft.

'With what purpose?' Mary Skillane asked of the loft. It was being built in sections under a canvas shelter erected on the terrace. Some of the completed frames were already indoors, lending the air a healthy sweetness.

'I am having a ship's model built of the vessel once named after you,' her father replied. 'The work is being done by the two brothers Morrison. When it is finished, we must take out that window to get the ship into the room at all. And then we shall boost it into the loft, all sails hung out to dry, so to speak, every detail truthful to the original. The masts are nine foot high, to give some indication of scale. And all this I do for you, Mary.'

'I barely remember the original.'

'And how could you? She ran against the rocks at Porthloe Cove when you were five. Smashed to pieces in under two hours. As fine a ship as ever swam and of the seventeen of us aboard, only three survived. I have never seen such hateful seas as that day.'

'A lesser man would have been broken completely,' Mary said in an entirely mechanical way, for this was how the story was usually concluded.

Skillane looked at his daughter with a surprisingly gentle reproach in his eyes. 'You find me foolish, I don't doubt.'

'I have not said so.'

He picked up a curl of planed wood from the floor and twiddled it in his fingers. 'Your mother says I am a cruel man.'

'No!' Mary cried in anguish, putting her hands over her ears. 'You must not talk to me about such things – about anything that touches how any of us thinks or feels! It solves nothing.'

'The *Mary Skillane* was my first and last attempt to set aside the past,' he continued, as much to himself as to his daughter. 'I have never been more proud of myself than the day she floated. We had a village band to play and there were fireworks – a great many, with rockets and such. You were a child, hardly more than a baby. We slept aboard that night. No masts, not a scrap of rigging, the very deck uncaulked. This was when we lived in a three-room cottage over to Falmouth.'

He walked to the window and looked out on to the men digging with pickaxes at the end of his lawns.

'You won't remember that either. But your mother does. They were happier days. Yes, indeed. Robert Judd comes down by train tomorrow,' he added, as though wiping the slate clean of such sentimental gush.

'And what is that to me?' Mary cried, as piteous as any seabird.

'I should think a very great deal.'

'I would rather kill myself than see his face again,' Mary said.

'Words I have heard often enough before. If you were a man – my son, I mean – I could explain the situation better.'

'Were I your son I would pistol Mr Judd before he destroys us all. I am not stupid, father. He intends your ruin.'

'Of course he does. Well, what should I do? Should I pistol him?'

'Yes,' Mary said with vehement simplicity.

There was a tap at the window and the master carpenter peered in, a short man with a purely white beard, set off by alarming black caterpillar eyebrows. Skillane glanced, nodded. He turned back to Mary. 'I have never been bested by another man, nor shall I ever be. I might have done more to make you and your mother happier but that is quite another story. One that we shall reflect on at our greater leisure, I don't doubt. That is Hargreaves at the window, Mary. I must give him his orders.'

'There is a gentleman in London,' Mary found herself confessing in a rushingly tremulous voice.

Her father held up his hand. 'One step at a time,' he muttered.

'But I have something to say! This gentleman –'

'I know what you wish to tell me, but it must be for another time. The loft goes in today, for tomorrow the Morrisons are bringing the *Mary Skillane* by cart from St Just. That matters more to me than the arrival of Robert Judd. By a long chalk.'

'You will not hear me out?'

'God's teeth!' Skillane roared. 'Cannot you see the rest of my days here hang by a thread? Is it too difficult for you to understand that this weekend and the party your mother intends for me is like a black waterspout on the horizon? If I am to outsail it, do I not need all my wits about me?'

'Then what is this nonsense with a loft and a toy boat?'

Sir William's expression hardened into loathing. 'What you call a toy is a reminder of the man I should like to have been and the son I never had,' he said, turning his back on his daughter and reducing her tears to a single cry of anguish.

It was the morning after William Kennett's return from Rotterdam. In Bella's drawing room, Captain Quigley was reporting on his standing patrol in Cadogan Square, where he shared the nightwatchman's sausages and made a bob or two on the side matching pebbles tossed into a bucket.

The nightwatchman was a ruined old sot called Thursgood, who had once been handy with his fists – enough to take on in his day the Dublin Mauler, who knew as much about Dublin as any Birmingham navvie, which is what in truth he was.

'Can we just get to the point?' Bella asked. Quigley nodded and flourished his cheroot. In his short and inglorious career as a soldier he had once been left as an unloved and unkempt recruit to stand guard over a haystack for two days and two nights without food or drink. Cadogan Square was by comparison packed with incident.

'Mr Judd comes back last night. Mid-morning, puts up a few necessaries, not many, enough for a small bag. Slings a canvas gun case over his shoulder, sets off for sunny Cornwall.'

'We know this for a fact?'

'Followed the gentleman to Paddington,' Quigley asserted. 'Saw him buy his ticket.'

'Did you see him get on the train?'

'He had a sharpener or two in the buffet and some sort of meat pie. Then, like I say, he sets off. If you want to be exact about it, the train left with him inside it. First-class carriage, a clerical cove as travelling companion. A bishop, maybe. Beard, eyebrows, hyena laugh and so forth. Improving book to hand. Penzance mentioned. My duties completed: returned to aitch-coo for further orders. No thanks required. The honour of the service is all.'

'Billy Murch is in the pub across the road,' Philip Westland added. 'Take a wet with him while we confer, Captain.'

Quigley nodded but, reaching the door, turned back.

'A word to the wise. You might want to keep up the watch on Cadogan Square. I can have an intelligent boy there inside the hour.'

'To what purpose?' Bella asked.

'I take it we're on a war footing,' the Captain replied with not a little asperity. 'He can't run a proper campaign down there in the land of the pasty, I shouldn't have thought.'

'Who is the "he" in that sentence?'

'Both. Neither Sir William nor his mate Judd can afford to give up Cadogan Square entirely, I shouldn't have thought. Gone today but here tomorrow, so to speak. After all, London is the capital of crooked dealings. Connections by sea and rail to all parts of the continong and beyond. Not to mention –'

'A shilling a day for the boy, then. Can he read and write?'

'What, on a shilling a day?' the Captain protested jovially. 'Can't do neither, but runs like a whippet. As good as a telegram for his promptitude.'

'Very well. He reports each night to Mr Urmiston in Shelton Street.'

'Mr Urmiston to command the rear party,' Captain Quigley nodded approvingly.

'Duties he will share with you,' Westland added, falling into the military way of describing things.

Quigley goggled. 'I'm not coming with you?'

'You are not,' Bella said, very bluntly.

'Well, there's a turn-up for the book and no mistake!'

But Westland had the knack of putting this demotion into a context Quigley could understand. 'You are forgetting, Captain, that it is upon you that the safety of this house and the one at Chiswick depends. We are not going to Cornwall for an entire campaign – say in the way Napoleon went to Egypt – but as a raiding party. What muffins we would look if our base of operations was meanwhile left unguarded.'

Quigley chewed his moustache for a moment or two, enormously upset. 'And Billy? How does he fit in?'

'That's to be decided,' Bella said. But the guilty look in her eye settled it.

The Captain wiped his mouth with the back of his wrist. 'Well then,' he barked, his eyes popping. Making an extravagant salute, he banged out. He did not cross the road to the pub but set off for Fleur de Lys Court, his normal slouch replaced by a straight back and swinging arms. His intention was to look martial but there was something faintly lunatic about him to those he passed. He realised this himself (and in any case the old hip was playing merry hell). Before disappearing from view, he turned and cocked a snook to whoever might be watching from behind Bella's curtains.

'Oh dear,' the kindly Philip Westland sighed.

William Kennett arrived ten minutes later. He had been promised a surprise and was given it the moment he stepped into the drawing room, in the form of an envelope handed to him by an attentive Bella. It was a letter posted in Penzance three days earlier and the envelope contained two sheets of stationery. One was a wildly written (and in places misspelt) invitation from Lady Skillane to join a weekend party to celebrate Sir William's sixty-fifth birthday. She was sure Mrs Wallis might not wish to come out of London for anything so 'triviall', though the weather was very 'clemment' and a display of fireworks promised. 'Nota benne', Mrs Wallis was on no account to judge the gardens as the finished article. Oh, and the majority of the guests were but simple Cornish folk. They had manners (some of them) but no breeding.

The second sheet was from Mary Skillane. Addressed to Bella, it was clearly intended for William Kennett's eyes.

'I add to my mother's invitation my own fervent wish that you will accept. I cannot tell you by how much I long to hear news of London and all who are dear to me there. You may ask why this birthday fete is taking place in Cornwall and not Chelsea. It is a question that has caused me similiar perplexity. But, come! I beg you. Yesterday they were fishing for pilchards in Carbis Bay and I recollect how much that once interested you. MLS.'

'You will go?' Kennett asked, hardly able to control his voice enough to ask the question.

'I have sent a telegram of acceptance.'

'We shall all go,' Philip Westland promised. 'To Cornwall, that is. I can't imagine you and I will be specially welcome at Sir William's table, William, though we can surely promise him fireworks.'

'Is Judd there?'

'We have Quigley's assurance that he set off by train for that destination, yes,' Bella confirmed. 'Carrying, I should add, a gun case.'

'Sir William has rabbits,' Westland murmured, by way of explanation.

His friend nodded absent-mindedly and re-read Mary's

note. And then fell to chewing his lip. 'This places you in very great danger, Bella.'

'I shall be slow to encourage any moonlight walks or trips around the bay,' she smiled. 'With these provisos, Philip was happy for me to accept the invitation. Not all Cornwall can be homicidally inclined. They live under the same law down there, I believe. According to Mr Urmiston, who knows the area a little, the people are too self-absorbed to be dangerous, except to each other.'

'You are not walking into a trap?'

'My dear William,' she protested. 'The alternative is that this thing descends to something far worse. Let us go and wreak havoc on all Judd's schemes and stratagems.'

'And how will we do that?'

Philip laid his hand on his friend's sleeve. 'We must get to the girl Linny and her child before Judd does. And then produce the evidence at the right moment. That is the key. More than the murder of Liza Givens, that is what will undo him. It hurts me to say so, but it's how the world wags.'

'And the effect of all this cheap theatre upon Mary?'

Philip was about to say something but Bella signalled for him to be quiet. She turned back to Kennett with glittering eyes. 'Will she be made to look a fool at the dinner table? It's possible. But perhaps I think more highly of her love for you than you appear to do. She needs to know the truth about Linny and the child. In a thunderstorm, it is better to be out in the open. Hiding under a tree is very poor counsel.'

'Do these revelations have to be made in public, though?'

'Where else, for God's sake?' Bella asked, very angry

indeed. 'Have you so little confidence in her? Such small regard for the truth? You talk about cheap theatre. Is Miss Skillane merely your china doll?'

Kennett blushed. He took a turn on the carpet, pacing up and down a few times, his face bright red. Bella jumped up and poured herself a brandy, her hands shaking on the decanter. There was an awful silence, broken only when Bella picked up the Bradshaw and flung it at the wall.

Kennett bit his lip. 'We take Murch with us?' he asked in a tiny voice.

'He is across the road, waiting on our orders.'

'And who commands us?'

'I do,' Philip said in a firm voice. 'Without that understanding, we do not go at all.'

Kennett combed his hair with his fingers. 'I do not say it must come to guns and bullets –'

'I am very pleased to hear it.'

'– but if it does?'

'If it does,' Bella interrupted, 'we shall have failed completely. We get rid of Judd, we save that poor girl he so casually ruined, and later, when we have united Mary Skillane with the man she loves most in the world, we turn our attention to the shortcomings of her father.'

'Nothing could be simpler,' Philip agreed, though with enough irony to stun an elephant.

'I should apologise,' Kennett said to Bella.

'You should thank your lucky stars you have a friend in Philip Westland, who would probably rather pick oakum than make this excursion, much less appoint himself the captain of it,' she snapped. Then she relented and opened her arms to Kennett, who came towards her gratefully.

Philip smiled. When he was invited by Bella's glance to join them, he did. The three of them stood in front of the fireplace, clasping each other like children, which was how Mrs Venn found them when she came in to ask what arrangements her mistress would like to make for lunch.

Kennett disengaged himself. 'I think you have met my dearest friend Miss Skillane, Mrs Venn?'

'Indeed I have, sir. A fine young lady of the very best stamp.'

'We are going to Cornwall to rescue her.'

'As I am sure will please her greatly. Oh my Lord, if it won't make her little heart sing! What a lovely thing to want to do, I am certain.'

FIFTEEN

West Cornwall; a nest of beaten-down ferns in a hollow a mile or so below Botallack, a little after ten in the morning. Looking towards the land, the clouds tumbling over the ridge are a strange cinnamon brown. But out to sea, the horizon is empty of anything but the palest light, stretched, it seems, like linen on the line. The wind is steady but spiteful. Though he has been in the Duchy less than a full day, Murch has learned to call the gust that did for his hat (sending it over the cliff edge like a falling chimney pot) a light breeze.

Murch has a very straightforward, phlegmatic approach to the task in hand. The gentlemen – Mr Kennett and Mr Westland – like to turn over all the possibilities that might arise from the Cornish expedition, many of which they rehearsed on the train going down. Though they travelled with first-class tickets, they sat with Murch for long periods in the lesser accommodation, something his fellow passengers regarded with the greatest suspicion.

'The law, are you?' a solicitor's clerk bound for Exeter asked.

'What makes you say that, chummie?'

'I know the Old Bill when I see it. Detectives, is it?'

'Do you know anything about brass-rubbings? No?

Well, that's what we're about. So smoke your pipe and read your book, you yellow-toothed old bugger.'

'Oh, very nice language, I must say,' the elderly clerk muttered. But resumed his study of *The Widow's Secret*, by that master of the genre, Henry Ellis Margam.

Murch yawned and closed his eyes, arms folded across his chest. It would be too much to say that he slept but neither was he in the least exercised by what lay ahead. There was an element of vanity in this: while talk was all very well, he knew he was there to finish this cove Judd and if possible keep the other two out of mischief. He could have done with a weapon of some sort but kept a polite silence when schemes and stratagems were being discussed – if you like, he indulged the gentlemen. In Murch's experience, the only sure way to finish someone was to get close, square up to the cove and punch his ticket for him.

With or without a weapon, he looked forward to doing just that. He admired William Kennett for his reckless passion (and choice of housekeeper). Mr Westland, however, was in his opinion not quite the finished article. Murch, though a shy man himself, did not understand shyness in others and Westland's gentle hesitancy occasionally dismayed him. When the party finally left the train at St Erth and a discussion began about where to stay – or as Westland put it – where to hide themselves away, Murch hoisted his knapsack and said, if it was all the same to the gentlemen, he would sooner walk over to St Just that night and make his number with this Linny girl as quick as may be.

'But how will you know where to find the place?' Philip Westland asked, bewildered.

'I have a tongue in my head,' Murch responded, with just enough of a smile for it not to be a complete reproof. He touched the brim of his battered beaver and strode away. Kennett attempted to call him back and got by way of reply a brief but emphatic wave goodbye.

'At ten tomorrow, then, at the girl's cottage,' Philip shouted. But this time there was not even a wave.

'What we were vain enough to call a plan in London looks very different down here,' Philip observed uneasily.

'Then how does it seem to you now?' asked Kennett.

'Like a recipe for disaster.'

A station porter ambled towards them with a note. It was from Bella, who was eight hours ahead of them and already installed at Boskeriss House. Philip read it with dismay.

'Where is Lelant?' he asked the porter.

'A fair step,' the man replied.

From his vantage in the ferns, Murch watched something he could not have bargained for in a month of Sundays: the replica of the *Mary Skillane* coming down the hill in a cart pulled by a fat-bellied grey horse. For a few magical stretches the horse and cart disappeared from view and then the ship seemed to buck and roll in a green Atlantic trough, stupendous mountain ranges to its lee. It sailed with bare poles (save for a whimsically hoisted jib), yet even so its detailed elegance sang like a seabird. The hull was painted a glossy black, decorated by a single line of darkest green. The deck was of varnished oak planking, the hatches in some darker wood. Every detail of the rigging and running lines was exact and to scale. The shrouds whistled and the halyards clattered just as they would if the *Mary Skillane* were really at sea. Murch was entranced.

Linny Trethewey lay on her back beside him, the baby asleep on her naked breast.

'You don't want to see any of this go by?' Murch asked.

'Wouldn't mind burning that old boat, tipping it out the cart and setting fire to it. And piss on the embers, I would.'

'Living up here has done you no favours. There's more than a ha'p'orth of patience has gone into that bit of carpentry.'

'You talk funny,' she said. 'The way you speak. And croaky like some old crow. And that silly hat! Baby likes you, though.'

Murch studied her much as if she were the baby's older and more slow-witted sister. 'Back to the cottage then,' he suggested.

'Cottage, you call it! That's what I mean. What do you live in, up there in London?'

'Button your blouse, Linny, and let's go make ourselves a pot of tea.'

Far from buttoning up, Linny ran a hand inside the dirty cotton and caressed herself luxuriously, with more than half an eye to the effect she was creating. This was a waste of her time: Murch's expression remained utterly neutral. She took him to be embarrassed.

'Would I like it in London?' she cooed from under lowered lashes.

'Not much,' he admitted with his usual honesty. 'But who's to say you must live there?'

'Well, you can keep bloody old Cornwall, I'll tell you that.'

'Don't tell me. Tell the two gentlemen who are coming to help you.'

'Yes, and where are they? I don't see 'un galloping to the rescue, same as you say they would. Don't see no purse of gold, same as you promised.'

Murch stood and pulled her up by her arms. 'Give me the child,' he said.

She was in the act of passing him across when a rifle shot rang out. The sound of it was like a dry crack, much amplified. Murch knew at once what it was, roughly where it came from, and from how far away. He threw himself on top of Linny and clawed the baby under his arm. The smell of fresh blood cut like a knife through the faintly sickly smell of crushed ferns.

'Be still,' he whispered. 'There won't be another so long as we don't stand up.'

'Am I dying?'

'Not for many a year yet. Lie still and bear the pain a moment longer. The baby's safe.'

Linny's eyelids fluttered and her eyes rolled back to the whites. Murch dragged back the fabric to her blouse. The blood was comfortingly bright red and ran down into her armpit in thin rivulets. He pulled his handkerchief from his neck and pressed it down on the puckered entry wound. The baby was bawling its head off. But that was what Murch supposed babies did, most of the time. He patted its stomach absent-mindedly.

'We have been sniped at,' he explained. 'But your ma's a big healthy girl and there's no need to take on. So give it a rest for five minutes, there's a good lad.'

'And then he spirited them both away,' Kennett concluded. 'The bullet passed clean through her. The child is uninjured.'

Bella's face as pale as paper. 'He did not take them both back to the cottage?'

'The pig sty,' Kennett corrected. 'Hellhole a better description still. Yes, they went back there and that is where we found his note. After we read it, we burned the place to the ground. Where they are now is anyone's guess.'

'You set fire to her only home?' Bella asked faintly.

'What Philip called forcing the pace. If you like, burning our boats behind us. If Judd was still there, still watching, that was the message it gave out, surely?'

They met by arrangement at an out-of-the-way inn along the road to Lelant Sands. It was a twenty-minute walk from Boskeriss House and to add plausibility to her absence Bella carried a stamped letter, addressed to Mrs Hannah Bardsoe of Shelton Street, but in reality a note to Kennett from Mary Skillane.

They had Mary's word for it that the inn was a safe rendezvous. Kennett and Westland had taken rooms there the previous night as London gentlemen with a taste for ornithology. Their mention of a hunt for the European fish eagle, which they hoped to accomplish on horseback, had caused convulsions of silent mirth when announced.

'Where is Philip now?' Bella demanded.

'Asking after the three of them along the road from St Just to Newlyn. But it will not be so easy as that. Listen, Bella. It is certain that Judd is the villain that tried to kill that poor child. I have seen the ground and it was not a close-to shot. He tried to pick her off at range. She is a very lucky girl.'

'He was not attempting simply to warn her, or frighten her?'

'Murch says not.'

Bella bit her lip. At the landlord's suggestion they were drinking hot rum punch, though it was hardly past four in the afternoon. The room they sat in was empty, though they could hear a low murmur of voices from the public side of the house. A buffeting wind rattled the windows and to Bella's dismay it had begun to rain.

Kennett laid his hand over hers. 'It is bad,' he said. 'How are things up at Boskeriss House?'

'Lady Skillane is doing her best.'

'And?'

'I imagine the news you really want to hear is contained in Mary's letter.'

'I was thinking rather of Judd's latest movements,' he replied sharply.

Bella ducked her head in contrition. 'The comings and goings in that place are almost impossible to track. Some people arrived today whom I took to be butchers, or greengrocers. They were the Mayor of Camborne and his lady. There is a very corpulent gentleman in a black velvet suit who describes himself as Sir William's agent in Falmouth. In point of manners, this place is hardly out of the eighteenth century.'

'And Judd?'

'Has not been seen since yesterday. It is said he went by horseback last night to oversee the transport of this cursed ship model from St Just. It forms the centrepiece of the celebrations being got up for the new library.'

'So off he set with a rifle around his neck,' he muttered.

Bella flushed with anger. 'Around his neck or across the saddle of his horse. I did not see him leave,' she said brusquely.

She and Robert Judd had paid each other only perfunctory greetings since meeting and her time had been largely taken up in trying to keep warm in the most uncomfortable house of its size she had ever visited. Lady Skillane seemed to think that tea was the only lubricant to conversation, so much so that Bella felt herself to be followed about by rattling trays, often moving from one room of cups and dainty little cakes, only to be ambushed an hour later in another. And, much as she liked Mary Skillane, she was being dogged by her wherever she went. The only place she could be alone to think was in her bathroom. It was also where she smoked, wrapped in a blanket with nothing to look at but the lavatory bowl.

The evening meal was suitably aldermanic – an immense leg of lamb, some sort of ragout that might or might not have been rabbit, heaped with wild mushrooms and spiced sausages, lobsters, and a mighty turbot. The service was chaotic and the wines seemed to appear randomly at the whim of the butler. It was clearly a mark of respect to eat and drink prodigiously. The sound of cutlery upon plates made a din that almost defeated what conversation there was.

'You have paid us the honour of travelling a very long way to share our Cornish home, Mrs Wallis,' Skillane boomed down the table.

'It is my first visit to the Duchy, Sir William,' Bella replied. 'I have much to learn.'

'Do you hear often of Cornwall in London?' the Mayor of Camborne's wife enquired.

'It is spoken of as the ancient nursery of seafaring,' Bella improvised. 'From Drake down, scratch a sailor, find a Cornishman.'

'That is well said,' Sir William laughed. 'Though I should tell you the most recent arrests for smuggling were made around the point in St Ives only a year or so since. Scratch a Cornishman, find a rogue.'

At which there was much cheerful banging of spoons and stamping of feet. Bella stole a glance at Judd. He was exploring his teeth with his tongue, as though too bored to be convivial. There were high spots of colour on his cheek. When the men joined the ladies for coffee after the meal, he was nowhere to be found.

Bella forced her mind back to Kennett and the here and now. The little wainscotted room they sat in stank of tobacco and woodsmoke and was decorated by a single framed print, a steel engraving of the 'Queen Visiting her Poorer Neighbours'. This great event had clearly taken place at Balmoral and Her Majesty, dressed in widow's weeds, was shown forcing an improving text on to a bewildered old couple at their cottage door. Two of her daughters watched unsmilingly.

For something to do, Bella rose and straightened this picture, her hands trembling on the frame. 'The weekend proper begins tomorrow with a semi-public dinner at which forty will sit down,' she said none too steadily. 'It is inconceivable that Judd should be absent from that. There will be toasts and speeches from Skillane's hangers-on and Lady Skillane has arranged for telegrams to be sent from what she calls more distant parts. We must have that girl safely under our hand long before then.' She turned back to Kennett with a downturned mouth. 'Something you planned to achieve this morning, of course.'

'We were late because we were lost,' he replied tetchily. 'We were lost because we had not a decent map between us. Westland on horseback is like watching Gladstone attempt to play polo. As for signposts, they are as rare in Cornwall as hens' teeth.'

'Well, we must find Murch and his party before the sun goes down today.'

'You are fractious, Bella,' Kennett said in a low voice.

'Oh, do you think so? I wonder how that can be.'

'And now you are waspish.'

'I am virtually a prisoner to circumstance, huddled up in Skillane's house with people I detest,' she exclaimed. 'I depend entirely upon you and Philip to effect our plan, such as it is, and yes, I am fractious. I will go further. I am very close to being distraught.'

'I hope Mary is some sort of comfort to you.'

She wanted to tell him that much as she loved Mary Skillane, her foot itched to kick her on the shins for the inexhaustible solicitudes she offered. But just at that point the door banged open and Philip Westland walked in, covered in mud from head to foot, the landlord hard on his heels with a kettle of rum punch.

'If God intended me to be a horseman, he should have given my parents an earlier indication of His wishes and desires,' Philip complained. 'I have been in company with – I cannot say I have ridden – an obstreperous mare called Sugar. The most misleading name in all ostlery. So soon as she sensed we were going home and not beating about the bush like fools, she came back at a gallop. Sometimes with me in the saddle and sometimes not.'

'Ah well,' the landlord commented, trying hard to keep a straight face. 'The old fish eagle is a flighty sort and hard to find in these parts. But see thee now, sir, do you have some of this here punch, that is hot and hot and will restore your good nature. As for Sugar, I shall speak to her, you have my word on it. Can be right moody when she's minded and only a master horseman could have brought her home so tidy.'

'You are not laughing up your sleeve at me at all, land-lord?'

'Never in life, sir.'

After he had left and Philip had dragged off his topcoat, he bent to kiss Bella on her brow. And then, briefly, her lips.

'They are safe,' he said in a low voice. 'Murch has them at an inn outside Newbridge and an arrangement has been made to bring them by covered cart to Penzance later today. She has been seen by a doctor and the baby is well. Our friend has performed wonders.'

'What is there in Penzance?'

'They will stay in Penalverne Drive, next door to the police station. According to Murch, the landlady of that place is a widow from Bermondsey, which he considers an advantage. More to the point, her late husband was a sergeant of the West Kents. In Murch's eyes there can be no higher commendation.'

'We seem to know a great deal about these lodgings.'

'Widow Harvey and the landlady of the inn at Newbridge are sisters.'

Bella considered, while watching Philip pull off his boots like any squire and extend his stockinged feet to the fire.

'We have the girl safe? You can be categorical about that?' she asked. Philip winced but managed not to shout out loud in exasperation. Bella rose and kissed him guiltily on the cheek. 'Poor Philip. I apologise. Kennett will tell you, I am fit to throw away,' she said.

'We have done as much we can, Bella. Better you tell us what you have planned for tomorrow.'

'At this dinner, or banquet as Lady Skillane is apt to describe it, there should be a telegram of congratulation from Linny Trethewey and her child,' she suggested. 'And, if it doesn't sound too ghoulish, one from Mrs Liza Givens and, if Murch will wear it, Molly Clunn. I will offer to explain them all for the benefit of otherwise mystified guests.'

Kennett looked up. 'You mean to unmask Judd there and then? In front of forty people?'

'I cannot think of a better moment.'

'Nor a safer one,' Philip added thoughtfully.

'I don't like it,' Kennett decided. 'It would lead to the

table being thrown into an uproar at any address in London to be sure, but may not hit the mark in this benighted wilderness.'

'I think we are doing all this to open Skillane's eyes and save Mary from Judd's clutches,' Philip said gently. 'I would have thought it will at least accomplish that.'

'And all the rest? Murder, attempted murder?' Kennett asked.

'Will fall out, choosing its own time.'

'As it might be the fox turning and trotting back towards the huntsmen, the better to oblige them. Is that your plan?'

'Do you have a better?'

'We need Linny to appear in person,' Kennett said.

'That is asking too much of her.' These words were spoken by a newcomer, a rain-soaked figure standing in the crooked doorway. His sudden entry had the effect of rendering them all speechless. It was of course Robert Judd. He nodded to Bella, pushed Kennett out of the way, sat down against the fire, and, like Westland, opened his coat.

'I very kindly volunteered to come and collect you, Mrs Wallis. The tide is on the turn and has brought in rain. I have the chaise outside and will take you home in it. Sir William is anxious you should not catch cold.'

'You have the cheek of the devil,' Bella said in a wondering tone. 'How did you know where to find me?'

Judd's smile turned into a laugh. 'Do you suppose it was so very difficult? Throw a handful of silver into the mud here and any of a dozen poor devils will scrabble to do your bidding.'

'You put it with your usual elegance, Mr Judd.'

'You don't like the picture I draw? What else is this but a story about money?' he continued in the most conversational tone possible. 'More money than you can begin to imagine. I don't think you have fully understood that yet, my dear Mrs Wallis. But that is how we must settle the question.'

'The question is about murder and attempted murder,' Bella rejoined. 'Blackmail and extortion. The ruination of a simple country girl who, for all you care, is bleeding to death out at Botallack this very minute.'

'These are relatively unimportant matters.'

'Are you quite mad?' Kennett shouted, his whole body trembling.

Judd merely waved the question away. His effrontery was breathtaking. When the landlord poked his head around the door, Judd ordered a brandy with the greatest nonchalance and then turned back to Bella. 'With a little ingenuity we can work things out to our mutual advantage,' he continued, his eyes fixed only on her. 'You and your friends have a shared mission in life – to interfere in matters which don't concern you. I'll pay you the courtesy of supposing you came here with a plan of action. It hasn't worked. How could it? I am the sort of man you cannot begin to understand or master.'

'We have the girl,' Bella said.

'And I have one of my own, Mrs Wallis. The sweet and virginal Miss Skillane.'

'You will leave her alone!' Kennett roared.

Judd pointed his finger at him. 'On the contrary. Unless you agree to see things my way, I will debauch that poor creature tonight in such fashion she will never entertain another man again. Mere rape won't come into it.'

'You unutterable swine!'

'Just so. Did you think to threaten me with Linny Trethewey? You poor fool, Kennett. I will send that girl of yours into an asylum for you.' The pistol that appeared as if by magic in his hand was very real. Even under the guise of a playful gesture, the weapon's muzzle was pointed directly at Bella's chest. 'Before you, Mr Westland, or you, Mr Kennett, contemplate anything foolish, I must warn you I will blow a hole in Mrs Wallis you can put your fist in. I will not hesitate.'

'And then you'll swing for it,' Bella said, surprising herself at the steadiness of her voice.

'Maybe. But this is a part of the country steeped in the idea of false witness. Put another way, money talks here. Some foolish horseplay with a loaded pistol, Mr Kennett maddened with desire, Mr Westland trying to remember exactly what day it was. All the parties dead drunk on rum punch. And the delightful Mrs Wallis there on the floor, dead as a door knocker.'

'You place a great deal of faith in the power of money,' Philip observed.

'Would you care to put it to the test?'

Kennett broke free from Philip's restraining grasp and with an inhuman howl threw himself at their tormentor. For a part of a second Bella felt her skin crawl, expecting Judd to keep his promise. Instead, the pistol came up and smashed Kennett in the mouth. He fell against a chair and sprawled face-up on the floor. Judd was on him like a flash, the muzzle pushed against one eye.

'You shall be the first to understand,' he whispered. 'You know who I am and what I am capable of.'

Later, months later, Bella would wonder why she and Philip Westland did not rush him then and there; or, less romantically, why she did not fling herself out of the door and run to the protection of the public bar. The answer was in Judd's next remark.

'I am teaching you all something valuable – that a really determined man will do anything if the stakes are high enough.'

'Let him up,' Westland said.

And Judd did scramble off Kennett's chest, brushing the sweat from his face with the hand that held the pistol. For the sheer crudity of doing it, he spat into the fire. His eyes were dark as coals. 'I see by the agitation of your breath you begin to understand, Mrs Wallis. So. This is how it will be. You will return with me to the great house and enjoy Sir William's generous hospitality. The gentlemen will settle their bill here and when they are safely on the morning train to London, things will return to how I wish them to be.'

'Put up your gun now, Mr Judd,' Bella said. 'That, or shoot me. But you are not going to do that, are you? That would hardly advance your immediate plans.'

Judd looked at her with something approaching respect. 'I think not. Or at any rate, not until we have agreed how things must be.'

'They can be however you want them. But the land-lord will be back in a moment. For your own sake, put up the gun.'

He hesitated a moment, and then laid the pistol in his

lap. 'You are worth two of any man of your acquaintance, Mrs Wallis. However. Kennett believes me. And now, I think, so do you.'

'That you are contemptible beyond words? I have always thought so.'

'You need not say any more, Bella,' Philip warned in his gentlest voice.

Judd laughed. 'The excellent Mr Westland! A little late in protecting the honour of his lady but then he has the outlook of a gentleman. The world as seen from clubhouse windows in Jermyn Street. Well, I spit on all that. I spit on you, all of you.'

He perked up his pistol in warning as Westland rose, but the big man simply shrugged, and with a half-smile, dug into his greatcoat pockets for his cheroots. 'You have us beat, Judd,' he said, amiably enough. 'And I suppose I must congratulate you for playing a weak hand with consummate skill.'

'Is it really such a weak hand?' Judd asked. 'Do as I say and by Monday next, you will have Mrs Wallis returned to you unharmed. Kennett will have his simpering ninny arranging the water-colours at the house in Chiswick – and not trying to wash herself clean of horrors and nightmares she cannot name. The clocks will still run forward, you will all have had a mild adventure, with the certainty that you will never see me again. As for the rest of it, none of which concerns you, you may read about it in the papers in due course.'

'You think that is who we are?' Bella asked.

Judd flicked the pistol at Bella one last time. 'I know

so. You are children when it comes to this game. Go back to your drawing-room tittle-tattle, Mrs Wallis. Buy a new dress. Read some diverting novel, maybe.'

'Your arrogance will win you prizes in any country in the world, Mr Judd.'

For a second or so, she saw something pass across his face she had not bargained for.

'You think that's what this is? You talk to me about arrogance? I am out of a box you should never have opened. What you are looking at, Mrs Wallis, is evil. You are not equipped to deal with it. Now, if you are ready, we shall leave.'

'Don't go back to the house with him, Bella,' Kennett mumbled through bloody teeth.

'I have to go,' she replied. She moved to Philip and kissed him on the lips. 'He has thought of everything. Or almost everything.'

It was a poorly coded remark that Judd destroyed with his most brutal laugh. 'You are referring to your man Murch, I don't doubt. He is dead – or if not yet, he will be before sunset.'

Though she felt as far from laughter as Cornwall was from Timbuktu, this promise from Judd brought out a broad smile. There were tears in her eyes to be sure; but with them came the sudden flash of something almost approaching a grin.

'You think as I have seen you eat, Mr Judd. I would back Billy Murch against you or any dozen of your hired cut-throats. As you will soon enough discover. My cape, if you please.'

'Fetch your own cape.'

'Do as I say, you ridiculous creature.'

Judd hesitated; and then threw the cape across the parlour. Bella caught it, smiling. 'And now fetch the chaise round to the door.'

SIXTEEN

That evening at Boskeriss House, the usual clatter of determined eating was drowned by the gunshot staccato of mallets, as elsewhere in the house the carpenters hired by Sir William assembled the pre-cut sections of the library loft. Sir William himself was supervising the work and the loudest of the imprecations coming from this distant uproar were his.

Accordingly, the duties of host fell to Judd, who sprawled silent, offhand and, to all outward appearances, drunk. Bella watched him carefully, nevertheless. Although she had won a small skirmish at the inn, the battle was still going his way. She was, as she had told William Kennett, completely a victim of circumstance while in the house. And Boskeriss House *en fête* was a little like a Hogarthian print or an opera by John Gay. The Skillane guests had a very simple view of dinner parties: they were a chance to rampage. Bella discovered the truth of an old cliché: she simply could not hear herself think.

For example, to paper over the cracks that were appearing, the Mayor of Camborne took it upon himself to entertain the company with a stream of anecdotes about the character of the God-bothered Cornish peasantry. The comic dialect he employed came not from an actor's repertoire but was his natural habit of speech, one that he had only smothered in recent years. His wife had the grace to look anguished. For her part, Lady Skillane looked as though she would like nothing more than to crawl across the table and hide in the trifle. Her daughter sat with silent tears coursing down her cheeks and collecting in little candlelit diamonds along her jawline.

Bella's dinner partner was a pleasant enough old man called Coombes, who hardly needed to mention that he had lost his wife some four years since, so gently abject was his address. The first part of the meal had been taken up with his monologue touching the mystery of the five red balls that decorated the Duchy's scutcheon: Bella had nothing to contribute to the subject. Coombes tried again with questions about the character of Mr Gladstone and (more impertinently) the Princess of Wales. There was no real harm in this – for Mr Coombes, London was as remote and unintelligible as St Petersburg. He had never been to either place. Some common ground could be had from a discussion about whether fish had feelings. The old Cornishman felt they must – trout and salmon certainly, but even (he dared assert) pilchards. And all this while came an infernal racket from the library.

'I know carpentry, Mrs Wallis,' he said, making one last effort, 'and that loft of Sir William's is a very clever piece of design. All the drawings are his, you understand, and there's a man –'

'There's a man could steal pennies from a beggar's cup,' Judd supplied, to the consternation of those who heard him.

'If there's a finer gentleman to come out of Cornwall I

should like to meet him,' Coombes quavered, at first defiant and then, when he caught Judd's ironic glance, blushing crimson.

'You know our host well, sir?' Bella suggested.

'I am his banker, madam,' he mumbled. 'Which honour I have had for twenty years or more.'

'And do you stay here tonight as his guest?'

'Tonight I sleep at home. Which is over to Cripplesease.'

Bella looked very meaningfully into his innocent blue eyes. 'And does your way lie by Lelant at all?' she murmured – but not low enough to escape Judd's rancorous attention.

'It does not,' he shouted from the top of the table. 'Beware, Coombes, you are in danger of being propositioned by a beautiful London widow.'

The old man flushed. Bella was astonished to feel his bony hand land suddenly high up upon her thigh, not lightly either, but with a firm pressure. She turned her head away from Judd so that he could not see her lips.

'I ask because I need your help,' she said.

'What are you telling him now, Mrs Wallis?' Judd demanded.

'That you appear to be drunk, sir,' Bella replied, careless of the reaction she got from an agonised Lady Skillane.

The old man's grip tightened on her for a moment, enough to stiffen her back. She began to wonder whether he had misunderstood the moment.

But then Coombes smiled and patted her leg gently before resuming his knife and fork. 'I go by back roads to Cripplesease,' he explained. Then he added something else cautious and for her ears only. 'In the normal course of things, Lelant is quite out of my way.'

But even this whisper reached the top of the table where Judd was watching them, his eyes glistening. 'Be sure you make it so tonight,' he bellowed, truculent.

After pudding and the usual confusion with cheese and fruit, it was considered a happy suggestion for the dinner guests to inspect the library. Bella excused herself for a moment and ran upstairs. Nor was there anything very suspicious in this – it seemed that in Cornwall people liked to get up from table and wander about helplessly, sometimes taking coffee, sometimes staggering out into the fresh air, like guests at a wedding.

The significance of the work taking place was well understood. The finale to the following night's banquet was to be the ceremonial hoisting of the *Mary Skillane* to its place of honour. There was already competition among Sir William's closer cronies to lend a hand to see it triumphantly home. The man appointed to oversee this work was the bosun of the St Ives lifeboat. When Bella came down from her room, Coombes was nowhere to be seen but Bosun Priddy stood with his hands on his hips, shaking his head in a very mannered way. Bella exchanged a few words with him.

'Ais, missus,' the man said, sucking his teeth gloomily, 'they heroes on the tally ropes tomorrow had better not be took by drink. For there's no more than an inch of clearance between the mainmast of the *Mary* and that there ceiling. And bugger all use will she be to anybody if she sits up there broached like some old Cardiff coal brig.'

'Have you sailed with Sir William ever, Mr Priddy?'

'I have not,' Priddy replied emphatically. 'I was – I am – an Edward Hain man. Not the boy, mind you: his father.'

'There is a boy?'

'A man in years. But a pen-pusher, a desk man. No, I speak of the father now. In the year '62 we took his old brigantine, the *Emily*, a fifteen-month voyage, as far as Brazil and up the seaboard all the way to Canada. Now there's a hero for you. Mr Hain would not take a morsel of food from this fellow's table, no, not if it was the last on God's earth. I speak frankly.'

'A different kind of gentleman?' Bella suggested.

'Why,' Priddy cried, 'there have been seagoing Hains here nigh on four centuries. This upstart bugger come out of a potato field. And don't it show?'

Bella realised tardily that though he wished sobriety on others, Bosun Priddy was himself catastrophically drunk.

'I am astonished you have agreed to help Sir William at all.'

'Ah, but when she struck that day at Porthloe, the *Mary*, fourteen souls were lost. One of them the wife's brother, a child, an unshaved boy. And where is he buried? Nowhere! How and for why? Because his body was never recovered. Him and two others. Never seen again.'

'And that's why you took the job?'

'Eh?' Priddy asked, momentarily confused. 'No, no. It was this. It is only ever this.'

He rubbed his thumb against his forefinger, managing to look sly and guilty all at the same time. Then knuckled his forehead and ambled away.

Bella turned and found Coombes at her elbow, already

in his old-fashioned topcoat, buttoned to the neck. On his head was a ridiculous sealskin cap, the flaps sticking out at right angles.

'Be quick,' he whispered.

'My mother is at her wits' end,' Mary confided dolefully an hour later in Bella's bedroom. 'She is not particularly worldly, as you have seen. But if I try to talk to her she buries her head in yet another list. Will there be enough proper serving spoons for tomorrow? Have we made sufficient arrangements for the coachmen and other servants? Above all, what if the accursed library is not finished?'

'Listen to me now, Mary,' Bella interrupted. 'I should like it if you stayed with me tonight. Go back to your bedroom, fetch your nightgown and then lock your door from the outside. Come straight back here.'

'What is happening?' the girl asked, bewildered.

'You are in mortal danger. And so am I.'

Not strictly true; not in mortal danger, she amended silently. Or at any rate, not yet.

Mr Coombes was an honourable man after his fashion, but he was, when all was said and done, a banker. He was (he reminded himself) obliged to Sir William above all others, a man who might have gone to Bolitho's with his business but had instead revived – plucked from disaster – a tiny bank that dealt with the petty people of that part of Cornwall. Sir William had made Coombes, snatched him from obscurity and brought him clients he might never have met otherwise. These reflections were made all the keener for the driving rain that filled up his eyes on the road up to Cripplesease. There was only one house worthy of any attention in that village and he was going home to it. Was that to be counted as nothing?

It was in his nature to act prudently, as does any man who is born to be afraid of the world and its doings. Balance sheets were Coombes's refuge, silent regiments of figures that he might command without fear of defeat. Yet now he had just been at a calamitous dinner, sitting next to a beautiful woman whose scent still filled his nostrils, charged by her to deliver a letter to persons unknown at an inn of which he had never heard. There was giddiness in that it was better not to contemplate. For this reason he turned off along the road to Lelant and headed home.

'You are fifty-eight years old,' he scolded himself, thinking of Bella's warm thigh and – by vague association – her comely bust and wonderful grey eyes. Because he was that kind of man, he felt the presence of his late wife in the chaise beside him and seemed to hear, above the hissing of the wheels, her habitual dry laugh.

When the horse stopped stone-dead, he was very nearly pitched out of his seat into the muddy lane. He peered into the dark and thought he saw a fallen bough. When it reared up on end, Mr Coombes screamed and Jupiter, the horse, shied as if it would much prefer to go back the way they had come.

'Who is there?' Coombes yelped.

Murch's effort to stand proved too much for him and he sat down again in a heaving splash. 'Are you going to help me or not, you bloody peasant?' he roared before falling once again on to his back.

*   *   *

Murch had been set upon by footpads or something of the sort. Not so much as a wet stick to defend himself, so took off across the moor, making a stand at a small quarry. Dished the young bloke with a handy rock to the head, fought a lengthy and seemingly inconclusive battle with the other cove; got him down at last with an abandoned shovel and near enough took his arm off at the elbow with it. For good measure, smacked him with the back of the blade, breaking his nose. Ran on. Felt a bit iffy. Found the road to Cripplesease, sat down for a rest. Keeled over.

The history of this adventure was written on his naked body. He lay on Mr Coombes's kitchen table with a bruise the size of a hen's egg at his temple, a flap of flesh where his right eyebrow should be, two broken ribs and a gash in his thigh as wide as a torn coat seam.

'And if you are not lucky to be alive,' Coombes's housekeeper said wonderingly.

'A few knocks and scratches,' Murch mumbled. 'The young one was neither use nor ornament but the other bloke knew what he was about.'

'Yes, and after you bested him, why did you bash him with that old shovel, break his nose and all?'

'To recognise him. We shall need to speak again tomorrow.'

The housekeeper nodded. She liked the way he submitted to her proddings and palpings, as though to be naked before a great fat woman like herself was nothing very special. She liked it too when he gasped and seized her hand as she set about stitching the gash in his leg. 'You are a rare plucked one,' she smiled, admiring the rise and fall of his surprisingly muscled stomach.

Coombes came into the room with a very large brandy. Murch indicated that his nurse should take the first sip. 'You understand,' he said to the master of the house, 'I have no idea where I am but I must set off again for Lelant quicker than jack spit.'

'Not while I finished this here embroidery,' the fat old housekeeper chuckled.

'To Lelant. Now why is that?' Coombes said with an awful foreboding.

'I have business with two gentlemen there.'

'Oh dear,' Mr Coombes muttered, fishing Bella's letter from his pocket. 'Oh dear, oh dear.'

Murch sat up with a racking groan, winced his way through a couple of breaths and held his hand out for the crumpled envelope. When Coombes hesitated, Murch shook his head to clear it, sending a little rain of grey sweat to the kitchen table.

'Be a gentleman now, sir,' he muttered. 'Unless I am mistook, this here note was given you tonight by what we might call the lady in the tower.'

'The lady –?'

'By Mrs Wallis,' Murch said, much more bluntly.

He fell back, exhausted. The housekeeper wiped the sweat from his brow.

Coombes passed across the envelope. 'Perhaps in a while a little of the chicken broth, Mrs Jeavons,' he suggested to his housekeeper, seeming to notice for the first time that they were standing over a stark naked man stretched out on the kitchen table, five candles at his head and feet, a bloody pudding cloth wedged against his thigh.

Murch was reading. When he had finished, he crumpled the note in his fist. 'Now we shall learn the full measure of your kindness,' he managed, before fainting.

'Which has been considerable,' Philip Westland told Coombes, pumping the old man's hand for the third time. He and Kennett paced about the old-fashioned sitting room, watched by two portraits that were of Coombes's ancestors and two more that might have been anybody. One wall was taken up entirely by a clumsy landscape tapestry, in which gentlemen on horseback leaped ditches and round-shouldered milkmaids huddled together in mob-caps. Dogs slunk around in the foreground, observed (perhaps commanded) by a parson in a tricorne hat, sporting a duck gun.

'To send your carriage to fetch us, that was handsomely done.'

'The thing is, I have no clear idea of what is happening,' Coombes said pitifully.

'There is mischief, great mischief,' Philip replied. 'Our friend Mrs Wallis is in the greatest danger from a man called Judd. I am sure you know the gentleman.'

'You do not make me any more easy in my mind,' the old man cried. 'I know Mr Judd to be a double-dyed villain.'

'Then you have some idea of our purpose,' Kennett said.

Coombes looked very uncomfortably from one to the other. 'And the half-dead fellow I found in the roadway?'

'Is of our party. We shall need to speak to him.'

Murch was in Mrs Jeavons's double bed, while that good woman sat with a candle at her side, hands folded on the bible in her lap.

'He has took a terrible beating, gentlemen,' she whispered.

'Now, ma,' Murch replied from under a huge mound of blankets, 'I am just taking a little rest here and regrouping my forces, so to speak.'

'Is anything broken?' Philip asked.

'Ribs,' came the reply. 'So, nothing serious. If you or Mr Kennett can find me my trousers, perhaps Mrs Jeavons could run us up a pot of coffee.'

'At this hour of the morning!' she shrilled. 'You'll never sleep, you great daft man.'

'Something to think about,' Murch agreed drily.

He insisted on dressing and coming downstairs, one tread at a time, his face running with sweat. He hobbled to a chair in the kitchen, fussed over by Philip Westland. Mr Coombes came in, took one look and excused himself to bed.

'Whatever need you have of me, I am at your disposition, gentlemen, but I shall be much improved for an hour or so of dark and silence. I am not used to such excitement.'

'There is nothing to be done until first light, sir,' Murch wheezed, grasping his hand briefly.

'You have been through the mill, Billy,' Kennett muttered when Coombes had gone.

'I see you have something of a fat lip and busted cheek yourself. If you gentlemen will tell me how we stand at present with that ugly bastard Judd, we can perhaps decide how to go on. Did you happen to notice whether the old gentleman who owns this place has any guns at all?'

'No,' Westland said, tightly. 'And we don't go down

that road. We must get Bella and Miss Skillane out of Boskeriss House and on the first train to London. Indeed, anywhere out of Cornwall. If you like, we retreat. Taking our wounded with us.'

'That don't sit well with me, not at all.'

'Whether it does or not, that is what I have decided.'

Murch's smile was vague enough to be a flat contradiction of Philip's remark and its tone. He took his mug of coffee from Mrs Jeavons and patted her amiably on the rump. 'You'd know if your master has a gun or two in the house, ma,' he murmured. 'Because I do not like to leave a thing unfinished. The gentlemen and their lady friends should by all means be got on to the London train. When they are out of harm's way, they should telegraph for the Trethewey girl to follow. But I stay.'

'You'll do as I say,' Philip snapped.

Murch looked him over with an unsettling calmness. 'Why, Mr Westland, I do believe you forget yourself,' he said in a very even tone indeed. 'I am not your dog.'

'Lor' lummocks,' Mrs Jeavons interposed hastily, 'I see the fever is beginning to talk in you, Murch. To speak that way to a gentleman! We don't have them manners down here, wouldn't last long if we had. As far as I can follow it, the job is to get the two ladies out of Boskeriss House and off to London. Does it have to be done surreptitious?'

'They will not be let go willingly,' Philip said.

'Why then, I do believe I am in the road to help you. For hasn't Mrs Ferris called on my help in the kitchens for this here banquet that has been spoke of for nigh on a fortnight?'

'Mrs Ferris?'

'Lady Skillane's cook, the ignorant old cow. I am called to be there at eight but I reckon I'll find her at six, running about with her pinny over her head. In I shall go with the fishermen and their lobsters – for they are to have lobsters cooked in champagne tonight if you please – and it will be my pleasure to find your ladies and lay out what is to be done.'

'Brilliant!' Kennett exclaimed. 'And if we then are in the drive –'

'There is still a great risk to you, Mrs Jeavons,' Philip warned in a slow doubtful way.

'From Mr Judd, do you mean? I ain't afeared of him, nonewise. I heard you speak of Linny Trethewey a moment back and I will tell you straight there isn't a Christian soul for miles around that doesn't know that sad story. Any man who is against Judd – which is to say most local men – will keep me safe. And more than that, I flatter myself my wits ain't completely deserted me, fat old whale as I may be.'

'Who says you're a fat old whale?' Murch laughed. 'Bring me that cove and I will lay him out like a rolled carpet.'

'Oh, you can leave this one behind!' Mrs Jeavons cried, delighted. 'I'll show him a bit of Cornwall he won't forget in a hurry.'

'What do you say, Billy? Can it be done?'

'Anything can be done, Mr Westland. If that's how you want to end it, then nothing could be simpler. Nor wiser. It is no place for a lady, that I grant.'

'And you'll come with us?'

'In a day or two, for sure. When the dust down here has settled.'

Westland looked at him with very uneasy feelings. To call what he had proposed a retreat was merely a more dignified way of describing running away – and not just from Cornwall either. What he wanted was an end to the whole story, like slamming shut the pages of a book. In this light, Billy Murch's battered countenance was a fairly obvious reproach.

'You have done what you could, Mr Westland, and come as far as any man in London would wish to go. Things will look very different by dinnertime tonight, when you are back safe in the smoke.'

'Have you ever been told you are a stubborn and awkward terrier of a man, Mr Murch?'

'Not in those exact words. But stubborn has come into it from time to time. Yes.'

Or remorseless, Philip thought. 'I don't want any more trouble,' he warned.

At which even Kennett laughed.

SEVENTEEN

Bella lay in bed half awake, Mary Skillane's arm flung across her neck. The two had talked and argued until past two in the morning. The older woman had discovered something about the elfin Mary that would one day tax William Kennett in ways he could not have foreseen. The light of his life snored. Gently, to be sure, but once in a while with a great shuddering sob that would wake a dead man. This would be followed by a lengthy brrrf! and what could only be described as random champing.

In every other respect, Mary Skillane was a perfect bedfellow, slim, chaste, and warm as toast. Having made up her mind about running away from her parents on probably the worst day possible for them, she fell asleep almost at once, her head in the crook of Bella's neck. And as for the physical contact that happens when two people share the same bed, she was joyfully unselfconscious of it. With only the very faintest tinge of envy, Bella judged that if Kennett could set aside the snoring, his future happiness lay before him like a field of poppies.

At six thirty exactly there was a gentle tapping on the door. Bella stiffened. She had only one weapon to hand, a silver candlestick, and with that she jumped out of bed and laid her ear to the door. 'Who is it?' she whispered.

'A friend,' a woman's voice whispered back. 'Open the door and let me in, for all love.'

It was Mrs Jeavons, in kitchen pinafore and mob-cap. She made a bob to Bella and grasped the lady's hands in hers, explaining who she was and where she came from, mentioning that the house was still asleep, save for the servants, and that two gentlemen were waiting outside in the rain, each with his own gig. 'And nothing will do now but that you dress as double-quick as can be and join them, for if there is danger in the plan it is that old Judd will throw up his windows and spy those same two sportsmen, what have come to spirit you away to London. And then who knows what?'

'Their names?' Bella demanded.

'Kennett and Westland. Oh, 'tis all quite as it should be. The password is Fleur de Lys.'

'We were otherwise planning on making a rope from sheets and shinnying down the outside wall,' Bella explained hazily.

'Stairs is more practical,' Mrs Jeavons said. 'Now wake up that young missy and let's be off. I have put up sangwidges for you to break your fast and they say there is something more substantial to be had on the train itself. And if this isn't today's most romantic thing to happen in all Cornwall, then I don't know what is.'

The fat old Cornishwoman busied herself with waking and dressing Mary Skillane. Perhaps without all the rush and whispered urgings the girl might have changed her mind about leaving. 'But I can't go to London dressed in an evening gown,' she protested feebly.

'And far better you be flustered about such small things,

rather than the earthquake you will leave behind,' Mrs Jeavons chided briskly. Mary at once burst into tears.

Bella cupped the girl's chin in her hands. 'This is a very big thing that you do, I realise. But you are doing it for a man who loves you. In time your parents will see it in the proper light. Your father has been most cruelly black-mailed into offering you to Judd and in the next two minutes both of you will be free of at least one disastrous consequence of that evil man's schemings.'

'Very well put, but enough said, my dear,' Mrs Jeavons interrupted. 'Now let us run down them old marble stairs like squirrels out of a tree.'

Though the house was as quiet as promised, the front door opened on to a very unwelcome scene. Standing on the gravel of the drive, dressed as for morning bathing, was Sir William Skillane. Unshaved, his white hair in wild disorder, the Guernsey sweater hanging from his shoulders in ruined swags, the master of Boskeriss swung his head this way and that from Philip Westland to William Kennett. He was trying to work out without being told what two carriages were doing drawn up in front of his house at that time of the morning.

Philip Westland raised his hat but could find nothing to say. Skillane narrowed his eyes. He glanced back to the house and saw Bella and his daughter on the threshold, as nervy as deer. He looked back and studied Kennett. 'You are the certain gentleman friend of my daughter's from London?'

'Yes,' Kennett croaked.

Skillane went over it all again, glancing from the carriages to the women in the doorway and back again.

Absent-mindedly, he fondled the muzzle of one of the horses.

'You must know that your house and family and your fortune are in the gravest danger from Mr Robert Judd and his schemes,' Philip stated defiantly by way of helping him make up his mind.

Skillane looked up sharply. Some of the steel with which he had made his fortune – and kept it – seemed to re-appear in his expression. 'You dare to presume what I should and should not know? And you tell me this on my own property?'

'I am explaining why we are here.'

'My daughter has invited you?'

'Sir William, you know very well you can command your daughter with a single word and she will stay. But I think you are wiser and perhaps nobler than that.'

When Kennett opened his mouth to add remarks of his own, Philip silenced him with a sharp gesture. There was a jingle of harness and the ugly screech of gulls over the roof of the house, but otherwise no human sound.

Skillane stood as still as a statue. 'Mary, come down from those steps, please,' he called at last.

In that instant, when the girl flew sobbing to her father, Bella thought they had lost the argument and William Kennett the love of his life. But Skillane surprised them all. Holding his daughter at arm's length, he looked into her eyes for a long second or two, embraced her – and then, without another word, tramped off down towards the beach.

'We may go,' Philip Westland said in his smallest voice, beckoning to Bella. Kennett reached down and helped

Mary into the chaise. The horses were woken up to their duty and the chaises began to roll. Once on the road a canter through the rain became a gallop, the carriage wheels scattering clumpy spews of sand. There was nobody about save a few men on the beach.

Out in the bay, a schooner-rigged vessel came up head to wind in a creamy curve and let all canvas go. It was, Bella considered, a fitting punctuation and the end to the Cornwall adventure. From the moment Skillane had let his daughter go, the curtain had begun to come down on the whole drama. She trusted to Henry Ellis Margam to transform this mad dash along the road to St Erth into something more poetical – the midnight flight from a Bohemian castle, or a frantic lunge to safety across the Mont St Michel causeway.

'How clever you are,' she shouted to Philip Westland meanwhile.

'It is the horse you should be talking to,' he shouted back. 'Because I am hanged if I know how to steer or stop.'

It was unromantic, but that in itself was deeply satisfying to Bella. Buffeted about by the action of the chaise's springs, her arms around the waist of the man she loved, who gave a damn about Margam and the world of sensationalist fiction. The pins to her hair were down, her arms and breast were blue with cold and she would have given a year's income for a cup of coffee.

Somewhere up ahead there was the sheer ordinariness of a two-platform railway station and the dusty comforts of a first-class carriage. After that, the mild terrors of the Tamar gorge, over which the trains seemed to tiptoe and the boats below looked no larger than toys. And after that, pleasantly empty hours leading at last to the calm and elegance of the house in Orange Street. It was not the perfect outcome to such an almighty confusion of hate and greed, but nevertheless that was how Bella thought it should end.

In the train, she snatched a glance at her companions. Mary Skillane was asleep on Kennett's shoulder, her one visible hand screwed into a tiny fist, like a baby's. As for Philip, he sat looking steadfastly out of the window, *The Times* across his knees. He sat with his back to the engine, so that he was studying the landscape as it passed and not as it came towards him. And this, she thought, is how we all must travel, with our backs to the future. How could it be worthwhile to try to read its dizzying, headlong rush? She moved her seat to join him and – after a moment or two – sought his hand.

In all his years of marriage Mr Coombes had never seen his wife naked and his knowledge of how his own sex looked was confined to the wardrobe mirror and one or two thrilling glimpses of a boy called Albert Triggs from the days of his childhood. Now, in the space of twelve hours, he had inspected at close range two grown men. One of them was Billy Murch and the other was the giant standing in his kitchen at that moment holding up his shirt.

'That was one bloody lucky miss, you bet,' Kashvili said, prodding the inside of his hairy thigh. 'I give Mr Kennett a thousand pounds, he can't make the same hole in me, not if he practise a year.'

'Of course,' Murch pointed out mildly enough, 'he was not aiming to kill you.'

'No, he shoot with his eyes shut!' Kashvili agreed uproariously. 'But brave boy all the same. What do you say, Mr Coombesy?'

'A lucky escape.'

Kashvili laid down his ham sandwich and, after retying a scabbed and bloody bandage, hitched up his trousers. Wiping his fingers on his beard, he swigged from the neck of a very good hock and burped like a sea-lion. 'Now we go to the bank,' he said.

Coombes's mew was like a terrified kitten. 'But surely you understand, I can't let you rob Sir William's deposit boxes in broad daylight. On a Saturday. At hardly past ten in the morning.'

'Coombesy, you don't got no choice. What is thing here, at end of table?'

'A mincing machine.'

'I put your hand in machine, turn handle. Which hand we start with? You choose.'

'But the pearls are not yours,' Coombes yelped.

'No, but for sure they are not his,' Kashvili countered. 'I don't got no wish to harm you, old man. Is just business. Every thing will work out good. You'll see.'

'I should do as he says,' Murch advised. 'On account of you don't have much of a choice. He knows you hold the keys somewhere in the house and there's no sense in getting knocked about for them.'

'You see?' Kashvili boomed. 'This fellow understands good. Better we go together, like old friends. You give me red box with pearls, I kiss you big goodbye, go back on to my ship, pfft.'

'Except that Judd will have seen the ship at anchor and made plans of his own,' Murch objected quietly.

'Possible,' Kashvili shrugged. 'But he don't know it's my ship.'

'He's a nosy bastard. The longshoremen saw you come in, I don't doubt. Word'll get back quick enough. No, this is the plan. You bring Mr Coombes and the pearls back here and we wait for him.'

'You try to tell me what I got to do, English?'

'Your pal killed a woman a week ago. Yesterday he tried to kill another. After you've gone and he's left to himself he will do some damage to Mr Coombes here. Then he'll come after you. That don't sit well with me, any of it. You get him back here and I will finish him.'

'You?' Kashvili laughed.

'Look into my eyes,' Murch said quietly. 'What do you see?'

The Georgian thought about it.

'Well, you have been in the wars!' Millie Rogerson said six days later. She and Murch lay in the attic bedroom of the house in Chiswick a little after dawn, a wonderful light in the sky and air as crisp as champagne. She was the same sardonic Millie but with some newly added catch of caution in her voice. For, seen against white sheets and more especially her own flawless nakedness, Murch did indeed look like a man who had been blown off a ladder at the Malakoff Redoubt (an event that had actually happened to him in the last days of the Crimean campaign).

'Like they told you, I was set upon by footpads,' he explained patiently. 'You expect a tussle or two with that sort of work.'

'My eye,' Millie said derisively. 'Mr Kennett has been wringing his hands the past week, crying woe on his mate Westland for leaving you in the lurch. Not that it hasn't all turned out for the best. That old Sir William is back in London, did you know that?'

'I did not.'

'Had the four of them to dinner Thursday night in Cadogan Square. All smiles there again, though if he knew the mischief his daughter was up to he might change his tune.'

'There's mischief, is there?'

'Well, not of the unheard-of kind. But it would be better the lovebirds married as soon as may be. You follow my drift, Murchie.'

'I think I've got the picture. Mr Kennett hasn't fallen out with his mate serious, has he?'

'Do I listen at doors?' she protested, laughing.

'I hope you do,' Murch said, swinging his leg over the side of the bed and standing up with only a few concealed winces. He walked to the open window and hung on the frame, gasping.

Millie watched him, her lower lip trapped by her teeth. 'You are a rare 'un and no mistake,' she said in a low voice. 'This cove Judd. Where is he now?'

Murch yawned. 'He has gone away,' he replied. It was difficult to be nonchalant with a black eye and a leg that throbbed like a second heart. But if his smile was crooked, it was out of shyness. He had yet to grow used to being naked in front of Millie and for sure he was never at his best in the early morning. She seemed to sense this and jumped out of bed to embrace him, her breasts warm against his narrow chest.

He kissed her. 'Mr Judd was an evil bastard, Millie – neither use nor ornament to the world. But now he's gone away. That's all them downstairs want to hear and the same should be true of you. He has gone.'

'Mrs Wallis knows how,' she warned.

'Thinks she does.'

Not even Bella could imagine the size of hole a duck gun could make in a bad man's heart. In Bella's fiction, there would have been a scene between Murch and the villain, in which the final strings of the plot were tied, followed by finger-wagging denunciations, a few words of civilised regret – and only then the meting out of justice. And although Judd was expecting something of the same kind when he walked through Mr Coombes's kitchen door, Murch had not read too many works of fiction. Coombes's gun was hidden on the table between Mrs Jeavons's cake tins and biscuit barrels, only the muzzle showing. As soon as he crossed the threshold, Murch pulled the trigger and despatched Judd to eternity. The spread of shot had also ruined several copper saucepans.

Kashvili took the corpse on a short cruise north and west to a point off The Carracks, returned on the after-noon tide to Carbis Bay and was rowed ashore in a captain's uniform from the outfitter's next to the Metropole in Rotterdam. He was, he explained to a tearstained Agnes Skillane, her husband's surprise guest and brought with him the compliments of all the other captains of the

Skillane fleet. Mary's absence and Judd's disappearance had thrown elements of doubt over that evening's banquet; but Kashvili knew how to enjoy a party. When a greatly shaken Coombes arrived in ancient evening dress, the Georgian embraced him like an old friend, lifting him off his feet and kissing him exuberantly on both cheeks.

'Anyoldhow,' Murch asked now, his face in Millie's hair. 'How have you been keeping?'

She was distracted from answering by squeals and screams from the garden. Racing around the lawn was an ecstatic Mary Skillane, pursued by William Kennett wafting an enormous butterfly net on a bamboo pole. Like the watchers in the attic, they had just risen from bed.

'Mrs Wallis –' Millie began.

'Ah yes, it's only fit that she should have the last word. What does she say?'

'She says I should take you down to Margate and marry you.'

Then, thought Billy Murch, she does know. Or can guess. 'A wise woman,' he said. 'And at the same time, what Percy Quigley calls a consummate weaver of dreams.'

'Is that a yes?' Millie Rogerson asked.

'Call it a yes,' Murch replied.

She seemed well pleased with the answer and disengaged herself to find her clothes. A thought occurred to her in the act of pulling on her second stocking.

'This foreign cove, this Kashvili you mentioned. He got the pearls then, did he?'

Billy smiled and jerked his thumb at the open window,

below which William Kennett and Mary were still scampering and squealing.

'He got the pearls,' he confirmed. 'But they got each other. Same as I got you. It all worked out reasonable, I would say.'

Millie studied him with the half-mocking smile he would come to know so well, the one that disguised her truest feelings about him for fear of spoiling the perfect man. Billy shrugged his shoulders humorously and walked across the bedroom carpet towards the perfect woman. Oh yes, the perfect woman. Said as much, dizzy with love.

In Orange Street on the same shiny morning, Bella sat up in bed with a small oblong package tied with lawyers' red tape. Philip watched her scrabbling at the gift paper with which it was wrapped.

'How have I earned this?' she asked. 'It is you who commanded us with such skill in Cornwall and you who deserve the reward.'

'I wish that were so on both counts,' Philip murmured. 'That we came out of it with our lives is something, I suppose. Saving the girl was also a good thing, and of course joining Kennett with Mary Skillane has been a spectacular success.'

'You might sound a little more pleased with yourself, therefore,' she scolded.

'Never to set foot in Cornwall again will be reward enough for me.'

The last of the paper came away from the package and Bella was left with a silver cardboard box. She opened it and peered inside.

'It is a stylograph,' Philip explained. 'Or, more accurately, an American stylograph. I'm told by the man who sold it to me that over there it is absolutely the *dernier cri*. Inkwells are a thing of the past, pen wipers, ancient history. In ordinary terms, it is a reservoir pen. This particular one is the invention of Mackinnon and Cross. Mackinnon should by rights be a sandy-haired Scottish inventor, but is, I'm told, a Canadian bigwig moonlighting in New York.'

'But it's wonderful!' Bella exclaimed. 'Why is there no ink?'

'There is ink but it is hidden in the barrel of the pen.'

'If it's there it's very shy!' She gave a few cheerful flicks and decorated the sheets, the pillow and the exposed part of Philip's chest.

'What a very romantic gift,' she said, kissing him and wondering how best to hide the stylograph in the weeks ahead. Such things could never replace the penholder and the inkpot. She wondered sometimes at how foolish the world was becoming. Without a blackened callus on the second joint of the middle finger, Henry Ellis Margam would cease to be. Perhaps, unconsciously or not, that was what Philip Westland had in mind.

THE
PLAYER'S CURSE

ONE

Jarnac, in south-west France, is a town made rich by brandy, as even the most casual visit can confirm. The always beautiful, always indolent Charente runs through it and though there is something a little asymmetric about the street plan – perhaps the want of a single grand boulevard or imposing hotel de ville – one glance at the cemetery tells the story of the place. What appears to be a small village of bourgeois houses are in fact the tombs of the great distillers and their families. Some travellers like to poke about a place to get at the essence of it: this cemetery tells them all they need to know about Jarnac. In death as in life, money counts.

The little nun was Belgian and as far as these things go, personable. Sister Mathilde was well known to the shopkeepers and hoteliers of Jarnac as a persuasive and gently insistent seeker of alms. Belgian or not, the French liked her. The handsome donations made to the convent at Easter – elegant envelopes of cash from the distillers and their families gathered up on the altar like plump fish – sprang from the affection everyone felt for the whole community of nuns; but especially the one they called Tilde la Belge.

Every Saturday for the past twenty years she had appeared over the bridge at ten on the dot and begun soliciting the townsfolk's charity, approaching rich and poor alike. An artist from Paris had taken her photograph standing under the catalpa tree in front of Demongeot's *tabac*. In the picture a serious child in pinafores was holding her hand while Tilde in turn held onto the little girl's hoop. This image exactly captured the nun, so much so that giant prints of it were to be found in Demongeot's and several of the other bars about town.

Her gap-toothed smile was much appreciated at the Café Turpin by the quayside, where the sailors met, their open boats moored up alongside. These men, who took the brandy barrels downriver and along the coast to Rochefort, were most likely to see Tilde for what she was: somebody's daughter, as it might be from their own family – a tubby little creature with a gimpy leg, driven into the church as a child by bad harvests and a too-innocent mind.

The weather turns in that part of Charente about the end of March. The mists lift off the river and the sandy eyots grow a pale green fuzz. Within a month, the palm of a hand laid flat against a wall or balustrade will find a faint warmth returned. The raked paths of the municipal walks and gardens lose their orange tint and are dry enough to coat a shoe or the hem of a skirt in dust. And then, sometimes in pairs, sometimes in larger groups, the nuns' tragic guests are led out from the gates of the convent – those who the world has driven mad. The women wear white embroidered surplices, the men tunics and trousers in the same colour, topped by floppy berets decorated with pompoms. It is particularly affecting to see grown men holding hands like children and shuffling along with lowered eyes.

'Why do we do this?' Jane Westland asked Sister Mathilde.

'You don't see how pleased everyone is to see you and how correct their address? Doesn't it make you happy to be out of doors in the good Lord's sunshine? I know it does.'

'You don't know anything. I want to sit down.'

Fitting the action to the words, the tall Englishwoman subsided to the path, her legs stuck straight out in front of her. Mathilde smiled and pulled her up by her wrists. For a small woman she had surprising strength.

'For me it is a pleasure,' she said. 'I enjoy your company and – when you wish to be nice to me – your conversation.'

'About the moles on my body.'

'That was harmless nonsense. I am sure you regret saying all those things.'

They sat side by side on a park bench, with a view of the men fishing.

'Can a curse ever be lifted, Tilde?'

'You must always use my full name.'

'If you have been cursed by a truly evil woman, can God take the harm away?'

'God can do all things.'

'Then can you ask Him to help me?'

Sister Mathilde took one of the Englishwoman's long pale hands and held it between her own.

'I do ask Him,' she said. 'I pray for you every day, you know that. I want you to be happy. When you hurt yourself with knives or pins, it pains me.'

'The Mother Superintendent thinks we are lovers.'

Sister Mathilde had inherited her laugh from her grandma, Edith. It was unbecomingly loud and derisive. She let go of Jane's hand and made a dusting motion (derived from her childhood in Edith's kitchen) as of a woman clapping her palms together to rid them of flour. Or foolishness.

'Oh, you wicked girl! Enough to make a crow blush.'

'If I tell you a name—'

'No, don't,' Sister Mathilde said, suddenly sharp. She had heard this name off and on for ten years, enough to blunt even her kindness. She looked up. A man – it was Jippy from the Café Turpin – stood in front of them with two overflowing ice creams in wax-paper cornets.

'This is M. Junot,' Mathilde explained.

'You are not in a zoo, m'sieu, and we are not animals to be fed,' Jane Westland shouted, knocking the ice cream he was proffering out of his hand. Jean-Pierre Junot glanced at the nun and shrugged. Mathilde noticed with a terrible pang of compassion that he had taken off his stocking cap to approach them.

'You do right to cry,' she said to her charge as he walked away. 'I hope these are tears of shame, Jane. You can be cruel.'

'Write to my brother.'

'That is for the Mother Superintendent to decide.'

'Tell *him* the name.'

He already knows it, Mathilde said to herself, the cornet held in front of her like a tiny torch.

'That bitch's curse has put me on this carousel for ever.'

'Nothing is for ever,' Sister Mathilde said.

Jean-Pierre Junot came from La Tremblade. One night he came ashore and found that in his absence at sea his wife and three children had died of typhus, along with forty others. Since that time, he had never uttered a single word. Yet God, whose mercy was infinite, saw to it that nothing was for ever. In time, everything was made straight.

That night, Jane was very bad, her howling loud enough to be heard in both wings of the convent. There were some nuns who hardly bothered to conceal their contempt for the Englishwoman and her arrogant ways. Every week without fail there came a letter from London, always in the same handwriting. Sister Loelie, the convent's post-mistress, made it her business to open these envelopes, for if she did not, they would remain just as they had been put into the postbox at the end of Orange Street.

'Your dear brother cares for you enough to send you letters. Why don't you ever read them?'

'Use them to wipe your fat bum,' Jane replied wildly. The violence and indecency of her speech horrified the nuns, more than the cuts she made on her wrists or the soft flesh of her thighs.

Once or twice a month – as tonight – her name was entered in the night ledger and against it the word: *Méchante*.

'What has the world done to her to merit all this?' Sister Loelie grumbled.

'It is a curse laid on her reason by a wicked woman,' Tilde la Belge explained, perhaps for the hundredth time.

'And you believe all that?'

'Does it really matter what I believe?' the little Belgian asked. 'In the men's wing, M. du Temple believes his wits were stolen by the Prussians and carried off back to Berlin for examination by the Kaiser. If I say I don't believe him, does it make it any better? It does not.'

'What a saint you are, Tilde.'

'And what a fool you.'

The howling had given way to a persistent drumming. Jane Westland was on her back, pounding the locked door of her cell with her naked feet. The violence of her attack made the air in the corridor outside tremble.

In London, it was a calm morning, at any rate as to the weather. Bella Wallis's doorstep in Orange Street was decorated by a tiny waif called Rosie Timmings who sat with her chin in her hands, waiting to be despatched to the shops by Mrs Venn, the housekeeper. These errands were urgent but haphazardly organised. The front door flew open and a floury Dora Venn coached little Rosie through another imaginary conversation before posting her off with a shove to her scrawny back. It was all very entertaining to the more raucous neighbours, who sped the child down the street with any amount of chaff and nonsense. Much did Rosie Timmings care. Old Mother Venn had a bark much worse than her bite and if she seemed a bit beside herself this particular day, she had reason.

'You give this bit of paper to *young* Mr Protheroe at the fishmonger's, not his dad, but the young boy with the squint, and you say that Dora Venn sent you. And you can tell him likewise that if it goes on like this, the poor woman will be carted off by the mad-doctors before nightfall.'

Inside the house, it was a day for treading carefully. Towards six, Bella came down in a favourite steel-grey gown and began setting the dining table. In a mild attempt to be sardonic, she brought out the best silver for the occasion, laid on starched linen from her mother's day.

The central decoration was a rose bowl stuffed – positively stuffed – with purple sweet peas. As was her habit, half an hour before the arrival of her solitary guest she paid a visit to the kitchen to express her thanks.

These were occasions to be finely judged and in a general way Mrs Venn shooed her and her compliments back upstairs with a few good-humoured grumbles. But on this particular evening she found Dora Venn red-faced and fractious, wondering in a thundering sort of voice what sort of a guest it was who must have Solway shrimps, followed by fish and two meats, followed by Russian salad, peaches in brandy and a summer pudding. No amount of joshing could amend her mood.

'You see me all of a fluster, Mrs Wallis, and that's no lie.'

'I know I can depend upon you, Dora. And you will make Mr Westland, whose menu it is, a very happy man.'

'Yes, and hasn't he been down here every ten minutes for the last two hours getting under a body's feet! I don't know who this great man is that's coming but according to the quantities laid down, he must be a powerful eater.'

'I believe he likes his food,' Bella admitted.

'A circus strong man, is he? I will just point out that we have only the one range to cook on and a kitchen table you wouldn't want to play whist at.'

'I shall get Mrs Poe's girl Elizabeth in to lend you a hand,' Bella suggested brightly, eight hours too late.

'You'll do no such thing,' Mrs Venn declared, bursting into tears.

In the dining room, Philip Westland was jumpy and defensive. Yes, his guest was something of a glutton at table but this was offset by his fame, as Bella surely must acknowledge.

'Is fame completely the right word?' she asked, who until last week had never heard of him.

'Dearest, dearest Bella,' Philip murmured in his most soothing voice, as if speaking to an aged aunt or the village idiot. She noticed that when fussing with the wineglasses, holding each up to the light to inspect their cleanliness, his hands were shaking.

'Are these flowers quite the right thing?' he suddenly asked.

'Touch them and I shall have to kill you,' Bella responded.

There was a commotion in the street outside. A giant of a man, not yet thirty, was alighting from a cab, reaching up to shake hands with the driver. Whatever he might have been saying was obscured by the sort of black beard ship-wrecked pirates might sport on desert islands. Half a dozen children, who had been running behind the cab, clustered about him, hopping up and down and yahooing. With the utmost nonchalance, he reached into his pocket and threw a shower of coins into the air. Then, jutting out his mighty beard and tugging straight his waistcoat, he searched for the house number. The rap he gave the front door knocker reverberated the glass in the picture frames decorating the hall.

'Ye gods!' Bella whispered.

When Philip fetched his guest into the drawing room, she noticed a strange thing. He was actually shorter than she had imagined and in truth no greater in height than his host. What made him gigantic was the aura of self-assurance that surrounded him, so insistent that it seemed to block the early evening light. You could say of Dr W. G. Grace, cricketer, that he was a burly man swaddled in his own importance. The piratical beard was the consolidation of this effect, as if all this psychic energy had materialised at one point on his body. All the same, his was an impressive physique. Handed a glass of sherry, the aperitif seemed to disappear into his paw as if already ingested. Invited to sit, the great Grace bottom challenged the joints and glue of the chair.

'My word, am I looking forward to a bite,' he boomed cheerfully.

'You are known as a good trencherman,' Philip responded, with a weak smile. Grace despatched the remark to the boundary without a moment's hesitation.

'You are what you eat,' he agreed.

Bella knew their guest to be a medical man, originally from Bristol; but any tentative pleasantries about the West Country were swiftly brushed aside. The good doctor had come on from Lords, where he had racked up yet another double century with trademark aplomb. It seemed he was perfectly happy to talk about himself with only the minimum of encouragement, while at the same time setting about his meal like a locomotive taking on coal. Even Westland, who had started out like a girl at her first dance, began to wilt under the furnace heat of W. G.'s self-advertisement.

'The secret of the game is in the front foot. There's your boldness, there's your decisiveness. I have played with men who have no more feeling for the front foot than a marble cat,' he rumbled, holding out his plate for a further helping of duck in orange sauce. 'Why, madam, I could teach *you* the off-drive faster than some of the gentlemen who are playing now.'

'And do you think there will one day be women's cricket?' Bella asked.

'I was speaking figuratively, of course,' Dr Grace laughed. 'No, cricket is all boiled beef and carrots or it is nothing. Brawn, in the first instance. It is a village game, played ideally by blacksmiths. I mind Tom Howard, for example, a bull of a man with all the stubbornness of that animal. Sadly gone away into exile.'

'And was his front foot an object of admiration?'

'It was passable,' Grace allowed, swigging from his claret. 'There were faults in it but it was passable.'

The good doctor was beginning to annoy Bella. Her smile was on the thin side.

'As you have discovered,' she said in her best little girl's voice, 'I know very little of the game but I conclude it is one that celebrates the healthy crudities of a male existence.'

'You are in the right of it!' Grace guffawed. This left him open to the unplayable ball, which Bella delivered with some zip.

'And as a consequence perhaps it is beyond a mere woman's understanding.'

The renowned cricketer looked at her under beetling eyebrows. He was, as Mrs Venn might have put it, not quite so green as he was cabbage-looking. Their eyes locked and after a moment he ducked his head with a wry expression.

'You do well to reprove me,' he muttered. 'To speak

truthfully, Mrs Wallis, I sometimes bore myself with these stories.'

'My dear Dr Grace, you must not act contrite. You are quite the most famous man I have ever met.'

'I believe not,' the doctor said, blushing. She softened. And the meal ended with Grace's most elegant stroke, which was to beg his hostess to bring the cook to the table that she might receive his thanks. To Bella's utter amazement, Dora Venn might as well have been complimented by the Prince of Wales, so deep were her curtsies.

'I count it an honour, Doctor,' she gushed. 'Why, if my dear departed husband could have been spared to see you here in this room, what a happy man he would be. He used to say to me that barring the talking horse of Shakespeare's day, never was such a prodigy, his exact words.'

'He followed the game?'

'Followed it? He could bore the hind legs off a donkey on the topic.'

Grace laughed and patted her hand with his own bear-like paw.

'Did he see me play?'

'He was the gateman across the river at the Surrey Club. You met him, sir, though you can't hardly be expected to remember. It was Charlie Venn who helped lift the madwoman's curse on you when you first played in London.'

'Now here's a famous story!' Grace exclaimed delightedly.

But if he expected Westland to laugh along with him, he was sorely mistaken. Philip threw down his napkin and turned his face away from Mrs Venn, scowling like a petulant child. The cook looked bewildered.

'I'm sure if I've said anything to upset –' she began hastily – but too late. Philip rounded on her, displaying a lack of manners akin to dragging in a dead cat from the street outside.

'This is mischievous, Dora. Mischievous! I will hear nothing of curses or madwomen, do you understand? Not in this house. Not ever.'

Grace looked perplexed.

'All the same, Westland, the thing did take place. It will cause me no offence at all to hear the story again. And of course it has made not the slightest difference to my batting averages. The contrary, if anything. So much for curses.'

Philip turned to Bella with glittering eyes.

'Are we to endure any more of this?' he barked.

'Let us leave it there, Mrs Venn,' Bella suggested, very alarmed.

'I will not be spoke of like that in front of honoured company,' Dora Venn insisted stubbornly. To everybody's amazement, Philip rose from the table with enough force to tumble his chair.

'And I will hear nothing more of any damn curse,' he shouted. 'Do you understand, all of you?'

There was an appalled silence. Very angry indeed, Bella reached and caught both Mrs Venn's hands in hers. It was a brief enough contact but constituted a complete reproach, though delivered to Philip's back.

After dinner, she did her best to turn the conversation into more general channels, as for example the total number of steamships now in service and whether their activities would have the effect of shrinking the world; the success of Mr Spencer Gore at the All-England tennis final; the course of Russian music, etc. Grace played up to her gallantly but nothing could save the evening. He left a little before half past eleven.

Bella was late to bed. Philip was waiting for her, a book in his hand.

'Bella, believe me, I had no idea what made me say those things,' he mumbled in a sombre voice.

'Mrs Venn is talking of handing in her notice.'

'But that is ridiculous! I shall make my apologies to Dora Venn in the morning. As for Grace, it's in the way of things that we shall never see him again.'

Bella took the book from his hand and threw it at the wall.

'Listen to me. Before this evening I had never heard of W. G. Grace and knew nothing of any curse. We have the great man's assurance that it has done his batting no harm, for which we must be for ever grateful. But you, Philip, are going to have to say more, much more.'

'I cannot.'

'I have never seen you so completely off the rails as you were tonight. We share everything, I believe. We hide nothing. Are you upset about your sister? About Jane? Is that it?'

'I have made it clear before,' he said stiffly, 'that I cannot – will not – speak that name any more, even to you.'

'This is ridiculous. Jane believed – believes—'

'I invited Grace tonight to hear what he has to say about cricket. And – this is the nature of male vanity – because he is famous. Because his fame made me feel important, God help me. Schoolboys think the same way.'

'Did you know about the woman at the Surrey ground before Dora mentioned her?'

Philip's face darkened. He beat with his hands on the counterpane, a muscle jumping in his cheek.

'I was infernally rude to you and Mrs Venn and that is where it must end. I will not be quizzed, Bella. Let it be.'

'You think I have nothing helpful to say on the incident?'

'I think it none of your business.'

Bella flushed. And Philip, seeing that he had wounded her horribly, put his head in his hands. She was amazed to see tears running down his cheeks. She managed to walk out of the room and along to the bathroom without collapsing in dismay. Washed her face, unpinned and brushed her hair for five long minutes, waiting for him to come and find her.

When he did, they kissed and made up. But long after, Bella lay by his side in bed listening to the sleepless city – pub-singing, cries and laughter, and the distant surf of traffic. The night air was sultry and the room smelled stale. She twiddled the edge of the sheet between her thumb and finger.

'Is he so very famous?' she asked, almost to herself. Philip took her hand.

'Grace? As far as cricket goes, he is incomparable. He is still young but already they say there will never be another like him. He is right. If there was a curse, it failed miserably in his case, to be sure.' There was a pause, a long one, and then he said, 'I love you, Bella. No one could love you more.'

In the dark, Bella frowned. An image came into her mind, of a feather falling through air, seemingly weightless but enough to upset the balance of (it was true) some exceptionally sensitive scales. And because she was a novelist, which was to say an intellectual fidget, it was not the quality of the curse that sent her into sleepless discomfort but the identity of the person who had made it.

As only a very few people in London knew, Mrs Bella Wallis was also the sensationalist author Henry Ellis Margam. In Margam's world, the curse was hardly likely to have been laid by a toothless old crone huddled in rags outside the Surrey grounds. A better candidate by far would be some ruined Hungarian noblewoman with connections to vampirism; or an octoroon with violet eyes. Quite what the motive was could only be teased out with further references to haunted houses, bleak moors shrouded in fog, even a ship burning to the waterline in some Arctic landscape.

And none of this helped explain tears at bedtime. Bella sighed. Philip was already asleep at her side, sprawled like a tiler who had fallen through the roof. One of his most enviable gifts was to treat each day as a new day, with the old erased, as surely as the tide destroys a sandcastle. And if it were not like that, to bury the pain so deep that it could never hurt again. In all but a very few things he had succeeded. His sister's madness was an exception.

There was little of imagination in his dreams. The most unintentionally telling was when he was handed a cucumber by the German Crown Princess, who happened to be dressed for skating with a perfectly adorable round fur hat and white kid gloves. The cucumber was, Victoria's favourite daughter explained, the key to eternal happiness. More phlegmatic than his beloved Bella – and twice as innocent – Philip Westland had put the whole thing down to indigestion and a bad pillow.

Bella planted a kiss on his cheek and fell back into a little shaft of moonlight, wanting to think deep thoughts about life and love but caring more for what to say to Dora Venn in the morning.

The following day was bright but blowy. In Fleur de Lys Court, off the Strand, dust devils scurried across the flagstones. Captain Quigley had chosen this unsuitable weather to paint the front door of what Bella thought of as Henry Ellis Margam's office and Quigley described as his occasional summer quarters. The paint came from a little bit of business he had conducted the previous evening at a pub in Bedford Street. A rustic-looking cove (it was the spotted red neckerchief that gave Quigley the idea) was selling the surplus from a job in Long Acre which had concluded that same afternoon.

'So was you on that job?' Quigley asked, sceptically.

'I was passing by as the ganger was loading his cart,' the rustic cove admitted. 'As a matter of fact, I was going to see my sister-in-law and the opportunity, as you might say, dropped in my lap.'

'You took the paint?'

'I took the cart, mate. Cart and contents. Brisk footwork needed.'

'You thieving rogue,' Quigley said admiringly. 'And this sister-in-law, is she also a countrywoman?'

'Watch it!' the rustic cove warned. 'I ain't no more from

the country than you are a peer of the realm, you fat-arse soak.'

'Well, what accent is that?'

Dutch, at one remove. The old father a steward on the Irish ferries, ma a wandering Dutchwoman from Dordrecht. The dodger himself born and brought up in the Smoke.

'This what you see me wearing now, including these here sideburns, is all the rage, matey. We can't all look like Chinese Gordon just before the fuzzie-wuzzies punched his ticket.'

'Point taken,' Quigley agreed, tugging straight his ruined tunic. To smooth over any feelings of ill will, he walked round the corner with the bloke, as the saying goes, and bought a couple of tins of the stolen paint and a good-looking brush or two.

Bella listened to all this while drinking a can of coffee from Tonio's and watching Quigley dab at the door, which he did from a sitting position on a chair that lacked its back.

'And this is why I am now having my front door painted in what appears to be lumpy cocoa,' she commented.

'How did things go with W. G. last night?' Quigley countered nimbly. She gaped.

'And how do you know anything at all about that?'

'It's my business to look after your interests in a general sort of a way. Also, I've had Dora Venn round here screaming blue murder.'

'You look after her general interests, too, do you?'

'Hardly know the woman but I did know Charlie Venn when he was alive. His mother and mine were in service together, over in Russell Square. Charlie a bit on the whimsical side to my taste, as can happen to chapel people. Forever chuckling and rubbing his hands together, if you follow me. Simple, another way of putting it.'

'Or devout,' Bella suggested in her most acid voice.

'Oh, nobody bothered God more regular. No doubt about that.'

'And his part in the lifting of the Oval curse?'

'Ah, the curse!'

'Yes, the curse! Mrs Venn didn't mention it?'

'She spoke of little else. Wondering what had got up Mr Westland's nose so dramatic, him as wasn't even there on the day. Him as calm as a horse pond in the general way of things and about as sporting as a length of stair-carpet.'

He laid down the paintbrush without too many regrets and adopted the pose suggesting commanding presence – one leg crossed over the other, a bunched fist tapping the knee from time to time and his free hand set to tugging his nose and stroking his chin. The poet Tennyson had many of the same gestures when in conversation, though in his case they did not lead to a face decorated by unsightly brown smudges.

'We go back ten years,' the Captain began.

TWO

In 1868, the very first party of Australian cricketers came to England to play forty or so matches. Gathered together by a bearded chancer in Sydney, these men had one startling thing in common. They were all of them Aborigines from the Lake Wallace area of Victoria, where they had been taught to play the game by white farmers. When they landed at Gravesend, they were described in a surly piece in *The Times* as 'the conquered natives of a convict colony'. As it happened, there were no convicts in Victoria and the cricketers, though they may have been conquered, were also accomplished stockmen and range riders. To *The Times* readers, as to the rest of England, it hardly mattered who they were, other than representatives of an inferior race, doomed to extinction. Looked at in this light, their presence was an insult to the hallowed game. It did not help their cause at all that they were rather good at playing it.

'Didn't suit,' Quigley explained. 'Perfectly all right as a circus act, say in the manner of footballing dwarves or something along those lines. I don't think you ever met Mad Jack Maloney, but he had rights in a mermaid who was very popular in her day. Tulalula from Tahiti. A homely little body from Battersea Rise. But then, one afternoon—'

'Can we stay with the cricketers?'

'Of course,' Quigley said, magnanimous. 'Ugly coves, most people found them. Black as a cow's insides, cousins to the monkey as regards the face. Big eyes. Sad eyes, as if they were always thinking of something else.'

'And what might that have been?'

'Ho! Perhaps they was musing on something along the philosophical line. Or maybe they was just wondering whether they had left a kangaroo stew on the stove back home.'

This witticism sent him into paroxysms of coughing, which Bella relieved by punching him hard in the back with her clenched fist.

'You met them?' she asked, when the fit was over. The Captain nodded weakly, tears running down his nose.

'The first big match they played was at the Oval. Twenty thousand turned up for the novelty of the thing. Having freely imbibed beforehand. Like I say, me and Charlie Venn were mates and him being the gateman and all, I was privileged to make their acquaintance on a face-to-face basis.'

'You shook their hand and so forth.'

'Better than that. We knocked back a few pints back with Bullocky, Jimmy Mosquito and some others. Yes, quite a few pints at that.'

'This was after the match?'

'Before, during and after. The hand of friendship extended and once extended, gratefully took. Sport knows no boundaries.'

'You mean your impudence knows none.'

'Let me tell you it was a warm day and refreshment much appreciated. By close of play most of the crowd was also in elevated mood, as the poet might put it. At the end of the cricket, the black boys came back out for an exhibition of boomerang throwing. The crowd was raucous, as I say, and for the cricketing purists among us—'

'Get on with it,' Bella snapped.

But the story needed dramatic punctuation and he lit a slightly battered cigar drawn from his tunic pocket.

'There's something about boomerangs,' he explained. 'Very un-English. It got up people's noses. You throw a stick away, you expect it to stay thrown. Anyway, the business over, out come the gentlemen of the Surrey Club and start hurling cricket balls at the black chaps, which they tried to fend off with their traditional shields. All part of the circus atmosphere but it suited the occasion. Old Jimmy Mosquito copped a couple that near enough laid him out. Twopenny caught one on the shins – I can tell you the toffs were not messing about, Mr Margam, sir.'

'These brave men were being deliberately humiliated?'

'That was the idea,' Quigley confirmed. 'The crowd baying and cheering, fat-arse schoolboys in their fifties scampering about, faces red as lobsters. Scenes to shock the faint-hearted.'

'How did it end?'

'The flash mob would have been happy to see the poor savages chased down the Kennington Road with only their boomerangs to cover their shame. I speak figuratively. But then someone came up with the idea of a last competition. Which was: who could chuck a cricket ball the farthest?'

'At which surely the aborigines excelled?'

'No one to touch 'em. Prodigious feats accomplished. So now the crowd's gone quiet and more than a bit surly. And for why, we hardly need ask? Tables turned, is for why! The black men is now putting it across the gentry.'

'Good for them!' Bella exclaimed. Quigley chortled.

'Spoken like a bishop. The black boys are chucking for fun when out onto the pitch strolls a portly-looking cove with thighs like a carthorse. Hands like buckets. Twenty years old but could pass for his grandfather. He picks up the pill, which is what we students of the game call it, and bungs it a very casual 118 yards, as measured by the umpires. Pandemonium in the crowd! Jeers of derision for the black coves! The mystery white man has taken 'em down a peg!'

Quigley drew on his cigar with a flourish of which any clubman in London might be proud. He was back in chortling mode.

'Now, dear lady, tell me: Who was this bearded young prodigy? A medical student to be sure. But what was his name?'

It took a moment to sink in.

'Dr Grace beat the aborigines?' Bella asked faintly.

'All ends up. I'll tell you this: they do a lot of magic, these coves, when they're running around the gum trees in Australia. And there, believe me, his name is mud.'

'The native Australians laid the curse?' Bella exclaimed. 'From twelve thousand miles away?'

'No,' the Captain allowed regretfully. 'That came from nearer to home, a witness to this whole sorry scene. To be exact about it, a lady. Much like yourself, Mr Margam. Out of the same box, so to speak. Only difference, she was hanging by the topmost spikes of Charlie Venn's gates and shouting her hat off.'

'A woman laid the curse?'

'A lady,' Quigley corrected. 'One of your lot, as you might say.'

A dreadful possibility occurred to Bella.

'Has any of this to do with Mr Westland or a member of his family?' she asked in a very small voice.

Quigley gawped. Normally, nothing would have pleased him more than to discover black conspiracy at the heart of things, but mention of Philip's name stumped him. He peered at Bella, genuinely perplexed.

'You have lost me, dear lady.'

'What I am asking is, do you know the woman's name?'

'Lady Gollinge.'

Relief flooded Bella. That, and shame at having asked the question.

She walked back to Orange Street in sombre mood. As Quigley pointed out, here was a story begging to be exploited by her writing persona, Henry Ellis Margam. What could be more sensational than a wildly uttered curse and its consequences? The triumphant conclusion Quigley had given to his story pointed like a fingerpost to something that would virtually write itself. And, she thought gloomily, that was it, that was the problem. All she had to do was strip out the aborigines, turn W. G. Grace into the Bishop of Matabeleland, identify the mystery lady as the Countess Paulette D'Ayraud and shift the action from the Oval to the Prix de L'Arc de Triomphe at Longchamps. That was all.

Why stop there? Why not turn Grace into Rupert von Gneisenau and have the lady become Eleanor Atkinson, a tall and willowy blonde who had come across an ancient book of curses in Paris, say in a *bouqiniste*'s bordering the Seine? Begged by her rather scatty mother not to read one aloud, she had done so just as von Gneisenau, a handsome brute of a man, had passed behind her back. Prior to this curse, the young Prussian had been stupidity incarnate. Even the royal house of Prussia, which had great forgivingness when it came to low intelligence, thought him insufferably slow on the uptake. But within months of Eleanor's curse landing on his innocent head, the lights burned at midnight in every Chancellory in Europe. It was war!

There were by now nine Margam books. What had started out as a widow's way of keeping herself busy (which was really to say fending off boredom and despair, not to mention any amount of attention from predatory men) was becoming profitably routine. There was a book going through the press right now, in which bosoms heaved and eyes narrowed, veins pulsed and hair flew in wild disorder. The *mise en scène* of this one was the coast of Pomerania, which was not entirely unlike the country around West Bay, in Dorset.

The public loved Henry Ellis Margam. Her publisher, Elias Frean, admired him, as well he might, for Margam novels comfortably headed the company's sales list. Frean was afraid of Bella, enough to have appointed a man of very different stamp to the London office. This languid fool thought of publishing as a disguised form of self-advertisement: his authors were doing their scribbling to smooth his path to the best salons and the most prestigious dinners. Barely energised enough to light his own cigarettes, certainly too weary of life to finish them, the new director wafted about London, trailing behind him carefully polished offhandedness, first rehearsed to his shaving mirror.

'A good bootmaker is an important fellow. The people who make embroidered waistcoats are quite important and I have heard interesting things said about lighthouse keepers. Authors are like grass, however. As lawns, they make a pleasing background to intelligent conversation.'

This to Bella at their only meeting. It was meant to intimidate her, the way a cruder man might raise a warning stick to an animal. It had a consequence that would have appalled the much more timorous Frean. His principal money-spinner came away from the meeting amused but thoughtful. There was only one response to this ambitious little jackanapes. If she had anything about her she should push Margam under a train and marry Philip Westland. She should do it today.

London was filled with sunshine, but the brisk wind, that in the country would hardly do more than make playful cat's paws in the barley, was here spiteful with grit and dust. The bottom of Charing Cross Road was black with cabs, their canvas roofs jostling each other as they tried to filter into Trafalgar Square. Bella wondered momentarily what all the fuss was about and then blushed for shame. The sculptor Musgrave, whom she knew slightly, was being buried in St Martin's in the Field. The vainglorious old fool Musgrave, with his chaotic private life and long history of sexual disasters. When she was much younger Bella herself had been cornered in his studio with only a broom to save her honour.

The memory did nothing to improve her mood. The air in the streets stank, window glass exploded with the sun's reflections, her feet hurt: it was a classic London summer's day. Like many people who passed her on the crowded pavements, Bella itched to hit someone. Turning into Orange Street, she calmed herself by stopping off at Liddell's and buying a walnut cake she did not need. Old Liddell, who knew a thing or two about human foible, boxed it slowly and carefully without saying a word.

'I will have the boy send it down to you,' he rumbled finally.

'It is hardly worth his trouble. The distance is so short.'

'It will taste better if it is delivered,' Liddell contradicted with a gentle smile.

Soothing encounters like these helped. But then, as Bella approached the house, she was startled to see a small but dapper man leave it, scooting down the steps and hurrying away towards Haymarket. She glimpsed Philip's face at the window for a second. When she came into the drawing room, he was standing in front of the hearth in theatrical pose, his arm along the mantelpiece.

'Where have you been off to this morning?' he asked, far too casually.

'Who was that man who just left the house? And Philip, if you answer, "What man?", which I see you half intend to do, I shall claw at the wallpaper with my fingernails.'

'Your new boots are pinching,' he guessed, entirely correctly.

'His name.'

He hesitated for only a second: Bella had long considered it one of his most lovable characteristics that when cornered he always told the truth.

'He is a naval officer called Alcock. However, it is very important that you forget what I have just said. I mean that, Bella.'

She sat down abruptly, as if all the air had been sucked from the room. Philip shrugged and began to pace about, hands in pocket.

'It had to come out sooner or later,' he muttered to himself, but only when he was behind her and could not see her face. The words were as good as a full confession.

Ever since she had known him, Philip Westland had disappeared three or four times a year on mysterious expeditions, seldom for more than a week yet never once properly explained. A friend had invited him to fish salmon in Perthshire, or an old school acquaintance was dying and destitute in Bath. He was going up to Anglesey to buy a marine picture he never brought home. Much more plausibly, his sister, in the charge of the Jarnac nuns, had taken a turn for the worse.

When she first noticed these absences, Bella supposed he had another woman somewhere, possibly even in London itself. If he did, it was no more than she deserved, for she had refused marriage with him three times and men were apt to misunderstand such matters. But it was not in Philip's nature to divide his affections between two women. Another possibility existed. He had not said and she could not ask but she had begun to believe that he was in the service of the government in some clandestine way.

'May I guess that you are going away for a while?'

'For a few days.'

The misery in his voice was painful to hear.

'Is it dangerous, what you do?'

'Bella,' he implored softly.

'I do not ask where you are going and for what reason; but is it dangerous?'

'No. Of course not.'

She reached into a tortoiseshell box, found a cheroot and lit it with trembling hands. Smoking was a vice he had begged her to give up. He stopped prowling and sat down opposite her, his hands between his knees.

'A week,' he said. 'Maybe ten days. You know all too well I am the least heroic man in London and until now the work has never followed me home here. We are just as we would be if I were a – I don't know, give me an example.'

'A jewel thief.'

'That is unfair.'

Close to an anger she could not explain, she threw her cheroot at the grate and plunged her head in her hands. No words of beseechment from him, no words of any kind. Nothing but the dry cough of the clock.

'Shall you go today?' she asked from between laced fingers.

'Yes,' he said with awful heaviness. 'I don't choose to but I must.'

She jumped up and walked upstairs to the second bedroom. Tore off her new boots and flung them at the wall, before crawling onto the bed fully dressed. She lay on her back, an arm across her face. To calm herself, she tried to remember the name of the sculptor Musgrave's last mistress, a girl he had picked up one night on Battersea Bridge. Flaxen hair, beautifully full lips fashioned into a permanent scowl. Bella had met her only once, walking in Green Park with the hobbling scarecrow that was Musgrave. She hardly spoke a word but the look she gave Bella was unmistakably direct, enough to make the older woman blush. They exchanged complicit glances while the sculptor prattled on about his most recent setback, which was falling off a scaffold in his studio. But her name? Her *name*?

When Westland tiptoed into the room only half an hour later, Bella was fast asleep. He put the note he had written her on the mantelpiece, next to a photograph of them both, she in a high-backed chair with barley-twist pillars, he behind her looking rumpled but content. Even a little smug, as a man might look who had won the great prize of life without really trying too hard.

'Well,' Cissie Comford remarked, helping herself to a third slice of the walnut cake, 'you can have no idea of the dreadful people who attended that funeral. Billy Frith I am sure was drunk; there was a man there who stank of tobacco and turned out to be Carlyle, quite *the* most disagreeable Scotchman in London but Musgrave's Chelsea neighbour; and two hundred others of dubious worth.'

So upset was she that Lady Cornford had gone straight from the service to Harrods (where she always bought her stationery); from there into the Park, where she met such a very nice old man who might well have been Dr Hornby, Provost of Eton; and now here she was on the homeward leg to Bedford Square. It was the arrival of her carriage that wakened Bella. Musgrave's funeral had furnished her with a week's gossip she was anxious to unload. Hornby (if it was Hornby) had endured some of it and now it was Bella's turn.

'Very poor hymns, all of the jocular variety; much prosing from the man who gave the eulogy and an overall lack of elegance. It was said that five of Musgrave's mistresses were represented, either in person or by what I suppose we should call his natural children. Or bastards.'

'And Alice Armstrong? What of her?'

'I can't imagine who you might mean.'

'His last companion.'

'Oh, the Battersea Bundle! She used to work on an asparagus farm, you know, and that's what gave her the soubriquet. Yes, she was there, wearing a veil as big as a tablecloth. We didn't speak, of course.'

'That wasn't very kind.'

'Percy Musgrave was a terrible lecher but his mother had connection to the Cathcart family. There are some unalterable truths, I think, and one of them is that the classes cannot mingle. As Frith said, rather wittily I thought, a few rows of asparagus can hardly compare with two thousand acres in Norfolk.'

'Frith's father was a pub landlord in Yorkshire,' Bella observed.

'I am sure he was nothing of the sort,' Cissie Cornford declared. She mumbled over her cake for a moment.

'Where is Westland, by the way?' she asked.

'He has gone into the country for a few days.'

'I see. Oh, yes, into the country, is it?'

'I don't suppose that just for once you could try to be a little less knowing,' Bella snapped. Lady Cornford smirked.

'I am sure it is none of my business where he is. How did you get on with Dr Grace? He came to Bedford Square a month or so ago and I declare I found him the most boring man in all Europe.'

'We learned of the curse laid on him in 1868.'

Cissie's cheeks at once coloured with two angry spots. Her thin little lips contracted to a slit.

'What rubbish you do speak sometimes. This is the Oval curse you speak of, is it?'

'I believe Lord Cornford was a Surrey member at the time.'

'He was President. You are so credulous sometimes, Bella. The whole thing was got up as a skit by an impudent young Guards officer. Who was later cashiered, incidentally, for throwing down his sword while on parade.'

'I have been told it was Lady Gollinge who laid the curse.'

'Then you were a fool to believe it,' Cissie snapped. 'Oh, I dare say Ursula Gollinge said as much at the time but she was quite mad. Her poor husband was in a straitjacket in Weybridge and she was if anything in worse condition. No house in London would receive them.'

'How was this?'

'Gollinge was something to do with government in Melbourne. Booted out, of course. Quite the wrong type, although one can never know at the outset. She, however, was lunatic from the cradle. It was in the family. Irish, of course.'

'Perhaps she was merely eccentric,' Bella suggested.

'When in Australia, she ran off with a German – a *German*, if you will – to explore the interior. I suppose that counts as mere eccentricity to you. Gone three months and found stark naked and babbling. Stark *naked*. Of the German, no sign. That did for Gollinge. He was invited to resign his post.'

Cissie Cornford had a generally good opinion of Bella but once in a while she closed her face against her. This was such a moment. She wiped her lips with her napkin and then threw it to the carpet.

'It is usual in such situations to draw a veil over events. We do not speak of such persons. I thought you might understand that.'

'Is she still alive?'

'I do not know and do not wish to know. I have explained: it was that scamp Harry Bagot who got up the idea of a curse. *His* family knew how to behave. A week after throwing down his sword in such an exhibition of petulance, the young man was sent to Canada. We shall not be hearing from him again.'

'The silence has closed over him,' Bella murmured.

'Yes, indeed! And what else, pray? I declare, you sometimes talk like one of those infernal novelists.'

Cissie indicated with a brusque gesture that she wished to be pulled up from her chair.

'Some things are regrettable and some contemptible. I hope I shall go to my grave knowing the difference. You don't have servants, I recall, so perhaps you will help me to my carriage. I am very disappointed in you, Bella.'

Are you, you foolish old woman? Bella thought, steering

her down the steps to her carriage. But Cissie, as so often happened as she grew older, overplayed her hand.

'I am sure Westland would understand. His mother was an Egerton.'

'He speaks of little else,' Bella assured her. 'We have a cannon on the roof that we let off in honour of that noble lady's birthday.'

And was rewarded by Cissie's peering upward glance to see whether this might just be true. It was only when walking back into the house that Bella remembered she could not tweak Philip's nose and ask whether he knew anyone called Gollinge. He was, she supposed, being sick on the Dover Ferry.

THREE

⁓

Bella sat with a pen in her hand, her face screwed up like a woman who had barked her shin against a chair, or found one favourite earring but not the other. It was half past four in the morning. Waking to find herself alone in the bed, she had dragged herself to a small writing table and a likewise empty sheet of paper, unless one counted the ink stars with which she peppered it. For something to do, she forged her lover's signature, feeling very baleful about it too.

What was a spy? A foreigner, was Henry Ellis Margam's predictable answer. A low fellow; failing that, a gentleman who was traitor to his class. Dr Johnson's scoundrel. The shadowy sort who is always on the outside looking in, never on the inside looking out. A cad. It was these and other such sniggerings that woke Bella from her sleep.

The ideal Margam spy hung about the champagne bar at British Embassy balls in Paris or Vienna. Masked by a black silk scarf, he rode like the wind down moonlit valleys towards some mountaintop schloss. Or then again (uncomfortable thought) he was illuminated by candlelight in a Hungarian spa hotel while his dupe, the foolish virgin with the palest and plumpest of white shoulders, cowered in the corner of the room, having tried to escape and found the door locked. The sheets on the bed were rumpled.

A spy must have at least one scar. He must be a crack shot with a grudge against all humanity. The cruelty of his lips would put a wolf to shame. There must be something additionally unspeakable about him, a secret lust that tickles the reader into guilty speculation as the chapter ends.

Philip Westland had none of a spy's attributes. He was as English as cheddar cheese, could not ride, shoot or defend himself with his fists. He was, she judged spitefully, at least two stone overweight, prone to bumping into furniture and laughing immoderately at his own clumsiness. He was certainly a wizard at looking up train timetables and retrieving interesting trivia from the pages of *The Times*, as for example the capital of Peru, or Abraham Lincoln's birthplace. But remembering to say he loved her, commending her choice of hats or shoes, finding pleasure in her skin or eyes, was beyond him. 'Everything about you is perfect,' he protested when she chided him for a want of compliments.

He could peel an apple with one continuous (though painstaking) passage of a knife. Seas – boisterous lakes, even – made him feel sick. Beautiful women tied his tongue; and as for dancing, there were bears all over southern Europe who could do as well, or better. At balls or soirées, he stood about grinning like an ape. He had only the one scar – a silvery crescent on his hip, got by tobogganing downstairs on a tea tray when he was eight.

He spoke excellent French and German and had tourist Italian. Without Bella in the world he would have gone to

India three years earlier and added Hindi to the list. He might even be married. Or, as Margam warned in her ear, he might be chained to the wall in some Afghani fortress, or dead in a ditch outside the Poona cantonments. But of one thing she was certain. Without her he would have remained loveless. Without *him*, she told her alter ego, Henry Ellis Margam, I might have died of crabbiness and boredom. Tears dropped onto her cheeks and ran towards her chin.

There was a rumble of iron rims in the street outside. The greengrocer was back from Covent Garden with a few boxes and crates of fresh vegetables. During his absence his boy had opened up the shop and swept the pavement. Together they began unloading the produce, talking to each other in low voices, like conspirators at the opera.

Bella shucked off her nightgown and lay down on the bed, letting the breeze from the open window cool her naked back. The curse laid on the ox-like Dr Grace caused him much less disquiet than the misery she felt now.

At breakfast there was a five-week-old letter with an American postmark. The wonderfully guileless Mary Kennett, so recently married to Philip's great friend, William, was writing from Denver at the end of a six-month honeymoon. By the greatest of good fortune, they had come across a gentleman from California who had sold them a map of some gold-bearing reefs in his part of the world that were hitherto unexplored. Now nothing must do but to make their way there as soon as possible – and under conditions of complete secrecy. The map was a little vague, for something that cost so much to purchase, but William had invented an improved separator that she felt well able to operate while he dug out the banks of the river along which the gold was located. Campfires and – a classic Mary touch – skylarks were indicated.

Yesterday Wm entered a shooting competition with the local gentry, if such they can be described. More accurately, he was given a pistol and invited to take aim at an empty whiskey bottle flung into a nearby creek. You well know his ignorance of firearms but at his first shot he removed the neck (at a range of forty paces) adding with the greatest offhandedness that he considered the body of the bottle too easy a target. A very large man with a red beard then accused him of a lucky chance, saying he had his eyes tight shut when he fired. Why, said Wm, he had no idea the rules were otherwise and gave back the pistol, saying he was d—d if he was going to be put upon for acting the way any English sportsman would, faced with such an easy task etc., etc. You are the dangfool dude who bought the gold map, Mr Redbeard countered, amid much laughter. That was a lucky chance, what you just did with the bottle. See and if you can shoot me, who is stood here right before you! So Wm took back the pistol and shot the man very satisfactorily, the bullet passing through his boot, to much ribaldry.

We take train to California tomorrow, in company with a dog sold to us earlier, one who it is claimed has an infallible nose for gold (tho I wd say he has been brought out from retirement for this present expedition, his nose likely to be his last fully functioning organ, for the poor fellow can hardly walk and barks only if you tread upon him).

Wd you please give Mr Murch an account of the shooting contest, for it is Wm's great regret that he was not here to witness it. Finally, dearest Bella, to you my deepest, deepest love, Mary. P.S. We have called the dog Quigley.

Mrs Venn observed the envelope and its frank with great contentment when she came in to clear the table, for the Kennetts were her favourites among Bella's friends, Mary especially. Her mood was sunny. Before he left so suddenly, Philip had gone down into the kitchen and made up with Dora, begging her forgiveness and going so far as to kiss her cheek. A few words now about his dearest pal in life would happily restore things to easy normality.

'How lucky that young man is to have found such a soulmate and that's no error. A prettier creature never was. And him such a Mr Head-in-the-Clouds for the most part.'

'He is prospecting for gold now, Mrs Venn,' Bella smiled.

'Hmmph,' Dora Venn snorted. 'Well, I hope he has bought his wife a sizeable hat and veil for it would be a crime to see her come home with that lovely complexion of hers ruined. Foreign parts indeed! Same as I said to Mr Westland—'

Her voice stopped in its tracks and she blushed guiltily. When she looked up she found Bella's gaze very level indeed – the notion of icy daggers occurred to her as a fancy.

'What did you say to Mr Westland?'

'Well, I shall not beat about the bush, though it costs me my position. I told him I thought it ripe that he should gad about all on his ownio over there, leaving you behind to wring your hands like a sailor's wife. Not that I say you do,' she added hastily, 'and not that the two of you are married.'

'You mentioned "over there".'

'France, is it? The way I see it, Mrs Wallis – and I've said too much to turn back now – we should leave these Frenchies and all the rest of them to stew in their own juice. Venn, when he was alive, was very hot on the subject. All the wailing and gnashing of teeth that goes on.'

'I have not heard that mentioned before in connection with Europe.'

'The Pope,' Mrs Venn explained. 'He encourages it. Just across from us in Coleman Street, when we lived on that side of the river, bless me if we didn't have half of Italy yelling and banging and cutting up on a Saturday night. Nice enough creatures but I couldn't help but think they'd be better off at home among their own. I used to say to Mrs Tubney —'

'Who sounds comfortingly English —'

'None more so. Well, indeed, her boy Arthur went across the river to be a constable with the police. I don't know as how you can get more respectable than that. Not from where we came from.'

'Do you ever see him, this Arthur?' Bella asked in a lazy sort of way, to indicate that she could hardly be bothered with the reply. She was imagining some chance encounter at a road crossing with a moustachioed giant. What Mrs Venn said next brought her bolt upright in her chair.

'He was the one that arrested Lady Gollinge for her wild words in that matter we was discussing two nights ago, to do with Dr Grace.'

'Mrs Tubney's son?'

'As I live and die. It was his first pinch.'

'Where can I find him? Do you know what division he is in?'

'I do not. I thought we was discussing the Pope.'

But Bella was reacting mostly to the previous day's acid conversation with Cissie Cornford. From being a story she could take or leave alone, a certain pride (and a good measure of exasperation) made it important to track down this curse and its author. She would not be put upon as nothing but a mere scribbler. Or woman, she added for Westland's discomfort, hoping to make his ears burn in whatever foreign bedroom he was taking off his trousers with trademark modesty.

Quigley vaguely remembered the bloke who laid his hand on Lady Gollinge's collar, though ten years had effaced the detail. And no, he did not propose to walk up to the nearest copper on the street and put the question about his present whereabouts. It was his experience of the Met that if you showed interest in them they were often of a mind to show a greater interest in you. This was a job demanding the calling in of favours from among those who were, as you might say, the best clients of the police – fellow professionals, so to speak. A good thief or burglar, if he had anything about him at all, could furnish a complete biography of the police force, down to what they had for breakfast. Why, hadn't he seen that very morning Topper Lawson sloping away down the Strand, a walking encyclopedia of rooftop London with broad experience of the Old Bill and its organisational structure?

'I do not wish to stir a hornet's nest,' Bella cautioned.

'Ho! As to that, no more do I. A few quiet words in the right ear, say towards lunchtime when the pubs have warmed up. Topper Lawson our man. Bald as an egg but a mighty brain beating there. Knows everybody. An ace up his sleeve for all occasions.'

'Can he be found easily?'

'He is the weather in the streets,' Captain Quigley explained. 'Meaning he is everywhere. As for the quality of his information, does a good bun have a cherry on the top?'

Under other circumstances, Bella might have taken advantage of Quigley's departure to do a little work on her next novel, for Margam worked strict office hours and liked to keep busy, as he put it. A chance conversation with a charismatic vicar from Norfolk a week or so ago had given him the germ of an idea. Big beaches clouded in spume, a girl's corpse rolling in the lap of the tide and the vicar, the great fool, sobbing like a baby on the altar rail of some forsaken village church. Up in the great house, General MacAlhone has dressed himself in his ancient blues, the better to blow his brains out in a final act of gallantry.

Quigley, with his unerring sense of what was in the air, had laid out her best German nibs and favourite ivory penholder. He had even gone so far as to tear a page from a child's atlas of Great Britain that indicated a broad sweep of the Norfolk coast. All to encourage a bout of word-smithery, his expression for it. It kept the lady cheerful. Or if not that, occupied. Mr Westland gadding about, as per. Naturally, the dear woman turns to her scribbling.

'Blind me if you ain't nothing but a wicked old gossip, Captain,' Hannah Bardsoe grumbled, half a mile from Fleur de Lys Court. 'Never you mind what she does or doesn't choose to do with her time. You as can barely write your own name.'

'Now who's being wicked?'

'She gave you a little commission this morning and you ain't going to get far with it sitting here in my parlour, drinking my rum and preening yourself.'

'Bear in mind I am carrying the heavy end of the wardrobe nowadays. I don't see the old gang gathering round, as used to be. You and Charlie tucked up here in Shelton Street like Hansel and Gretel. Mr Kennett wandering about America. And as for Billy Murch, I have seen neither hide nor hair of him these past three months.'

'And I wonder why?' Hannah asked cuttingly. 'You got to get this gang business out of your hair, Percy Quigley. The lady is an author. She don't want to be forever messing with the sort of rubbish that fills your head.'

'Oh, well, thanks very much for that,' he said, injured. 'Give old Perce a kicking, why don't you? I have done that woman a few favours in the past, my oath if I haven't.'

'Yes, you have. But suppose it is all over? Suppose she marries Mr Westland as by rights she should, the poor man? If he has a mind to marry her, that is.'

'Nothing more certain.'

'Well, there you are, then. Any old how, what is this thing she's asked you do for her this morning?'

When he told her, Hannah's face fell.

'That ain't right,' she said. 'Nothing but harm can come

from asking after the police. They take that sort of thing very bad, the jumped-up busybodies. Oh, this is very bad! Stop her, Perce. Don't let her go down that road. What's his name again, this cove?'

At that moment Bella was walking home to Orange Street, leaving the fictional General MacAlhone examining the handwriting on certain envelopes and wondering what the blazes was happening to him, a hero of Talavera. One minute he was being brought to life, cork leg, smallpox scars and all – and the next, pfft. Back in the goddamn desk drawer. My heart is not in it, Bella explained guiltily.

She passed two policemen along the way home, either of whom could have been Arthur Tubney. Her favoured candidate was a big-bellied constable carrying a lost child (or possibly an apple thief), his brawny forearm under her naked rump, her legs dangling like dirty paper streamers.

'Don't you listen to him, darling!' a wit yelled. 'He ain't got no 'ouseboat on the Thames, nor no doggie called Rufus neither.'

'You shut your mouth,' the child piped. 'He's giving me a lift up Long Acre is what he's doing.'

'That's how it starts, girl! Ask your ma, she'll tell you!'

Sergeant Tubney presented himself at Orange Street that afternoon. Bella was astonished on several counts. She had not expected him to come to her, nor was she prepared for how he looked. Tubney was only a little above medium height but what he lacked in inches he made up for in the basilisk calm of his expression. He wore plain clothes – a blue-black worsted suit and discreetly embroidered waistcoat. He wore his hair oiled and brushed straight back.

His stock was tied to perfection. All this Bella found faintly intimidating.

'You are a *detective* sergeant perhaps, Mr Tubney?' she guessed.

'I have been with the detective branch four years. In April we became what we call the Criminal Investigation Department.'

'An elite force!'

'A specialist department of the service,' Tubney corrected. The eyes were dark, almost black. The accent was unmistakably a London one; but, as to tone, neutral. In Bella's fictions, policemen were as awkward and clumsy as dogs when they were in the drawing room. This one had a stockbroker's poise.

'You wished to see me, I understand?' he prompted.

'I am first trying to recover from astonishment that you came to the house,' Bella countered. Tubney inclined his head.

'I have taken a small liberty in calling on you, that is true. I was on my way back to the office. To Scotland Yard, if you prefer.' The detective smoothed the fabric of his trousers over his knee. His self-possession was alarming, as was his next remark.

'I have read your books with some interest, Mrs Wallis,' he observed.

'Books? What books? I have written no books. You have been misinformed.'

Tubney said nothing but merely stared at her. The clock ticked. Bella chewed her lip.

'Very well. I wonder how you knew that?' she capitulated. 'It is a secret I have shared with very few people.'

'I understand. To reassure you, perhaps, the police are good at keeping secrets, when they have to.'

'What else do you know about me?' Bella asked.

'All that is for another time,' Tubney said offhandedly, as though there did indeed exist a bulging dossier somewhere on a windowsill in Scotland Yard. 'But on this occasion I think *you* wanted to ask *me* a question or two. If it would lighten the mood a little, I could say that it was a chance to meet Dora Venn again that brought me here. She was very good to me when I was a nipper.'

Maybe, Bella thought swiftly, but how did you know she was my housekeeper? A warning rocket went off in her head. Tubney, though he realised he had made a slip, watched her impassively, his hands on his knees, shoulders square to the back of the sofa. An unpleasant and faintly ridiculous idea occurred to her: Had her relationship with Philip Westland put the house under surveillance? Is this what happened to spies before they were recruited? That their personal dealings were investigated by the police at the behest of some shadowy government office, say in a memo scribbled by Commander Alcock, RN? She made a huge effort to put these thoughts to one side.

'Mrs Venn told me recently about your very first arrest and I was intrigued enough to hunt you down, as it were. That is all.'

Some of Tubney's aplomb deserted him. He looked genuinely puzzled.

'This is unexpected,' he said.

'In what way? You mean, you thought some other topic might be raised?'

The silence that followed suggested that was indeed what he thought he was there for. The two studied each other like cats on the same garden wall. Could it really be that this Tubney, with all his slightly sinister suavity, was gate-keeper to the world into which Philip Westland plunged from time to time?

'Do you happen to know a Commander Alcock, RN?' she asked, feeling heated and reckless (and silently asking forgiveness of Philip Westland). Just like a cat's, Tubney's blink was no more than a washing of the eyeballs.

'It hardly seems likely, does it?'

Mrs Venn came in with the tea. The detective smiled.

'Hullo, Dora,' he murmured.

'Well, here's a turn-up! Little Artie! And you looking so prosperous and all. So the police didn't suit you after all, eh? What line of work are you in now, you clever boy?'

'Mr Tubney is a detective sergeant, Mrs Venn,' Bella supplied. 'He has risen in the world somewhat.'

'Well, I'm blowed! Sergeant, you say? They don't hand those out every day of the week, I am sure.'

'Just leave the tray if you will, Dora,' Tubney said calmly. And even Dora Venn could see that it was not his place to order her about, sergeant or no bloody sergeant. She flushed.

'Yes,' she said. 'Now I remember you all right. They haven't learned you no new manners, I see. My mistress is Mrs Wallis here and not you, you bag of wind.'

And with that she clumped out, heartening Bella incredibly. She seized the moment, busying herself with the teacups.

'It's all very simple, Mr Tubney. At the outset of your career you arrested Lady Ursula Gollinge on a charge of – what was it? – a breach of the peace? To refresh your memory, the arrest took place at the Surrey Cricket Ground. The lady in question was hanging from the decorative gates.'

'She was only later identified as Lady Gollinge. I cautioned her and she struck me in the face with her fist. In such an instance, it was my duty to arrest her. For what it is worth, I was later commended by Assistant Commissioner Havelock for my conduct.'

'Wasn't that very unusual?'

'I had been mentioned favourably by name in a memorandum prepared by members of the Surrey Cricket Club. The situation was far from simple and straightforward, as I believe you already know.'

'Because of the curse?'

Tubney shrugged. It was a careless and even contemptuous gesture, meant to indicate she was asking the wrong question: What mattered was a youthful constable's sense of duty. He had arrested someone from a class that was not usually seized by the waist and dragged to the ground in a public place. The matter was hardly likely to be understood by what Tubney and his colleagues often referred to as civilians.

'It is the curse that interests me,' Bella pressed.

'Some wild words were uttered. Calling down woe on the Surrey Cricket Club, Mr Gladstone, and others.'

'Dr Grace, as he is now?'

'Dr Grace, the Archbishop of Canterbury and, unfortunately, Her Majesty.'

'These were wild words indeed. Did she have anything to say about you?'

Tubney hid his thumb inside his palm. His face darkened. He could remember in the most exact detail sitting on the lady's stomach and having her screech, 'This officer is touching my breasts! He is making a sexual assault! Is that what you came to see, you swine?' As he scrambled clear of her she kicked him in the groin, a pain that resembled being stabbed by an icicle. The crowd cheered.

'Most people assumed she was drunk,' he muttered.

'Was she charged as such?'

'For assaulting a police officer in the course of his duties. She was bailed to appear before magistrates a week hence.'

'And you never saw her again. Nobody saw her again. She never came to court for what she said and did.'

Tubney hesitated. She realised with sudden intuition that his value to the police was not an investigative mind at all, but merely a certain manner. And, just like any actor fed the wrong line, he could be knocked off his stride. She handed him his tea and then reached for the tortoiseshell box on the table between them and selected and lit a cheroot, without offering him one. Very satisfyingly, Tubney's sense of what was expected of a gentlewoman at four o'clock in the afternoon was offended. His cheeks reddened.

'May I pour you some tea, Mrs Wallis?'

'I shall do that for myself when I am ready. Do they smoke at Scotland Yard, I wonder? I should imagine it is like Euston station at certain times of the day. But you were saying, Detective?'

'Lady Gollinge had the protection of her class and sex,'

Tubney grumbled. 'She was also to be pitied. Her mind was deranged. I do not know what happened to her or where she went after she broke the conditions of her bail.'

'But of course you do! You were then a very junior police constable. But you are something rather grander now. You know exactly where she is, I am sure.'

'I cannot discuss police matters,' he said, much too stiffly.

'Isn't that rather lame? If this had ever been a proper police matter, she would have been found and brought to justice long ago. Instead, one can imagine a Treasury solicitor advising her ladyship to quit London if she had any sense left. And she took that advice and skipped, isn't that it? You got a punch on the nose for your troubles and a letter of commendation from Sir Edward Havelock. She got the liberty to rant and curse in some other part of the kingdom.'

'Why does any of this interest you?'

She thought about that. Nothing in what Tubney had revealed about the Oval incident could possibly have to do with Philip Westland. As Quigley said, he was not in the slightest bit sporty (apart from an accidental skill with archery) and – as far as Bella could remember – had never once expressed an interest in cricket, up to the time a club friend had taken him to Lords to see Grace face his first ball of the second innings, or some such nonsense. Nor had he ever mentioned Lady Ursula Gollinge. A further thought occurred to her. To curse a man like Westland would be like throwing the contents of a cup of tea at the face of Mont Blanc. He was not made for curses.

Which left her with the violence of his reaction when the subject had arisen at the dinner table two nights ago.

'I intend to visit Lady Gollinge,' Bella said in her most offhand tone. 'I will not trouble you for the address for I can get that from Sir Edward, I am sure.'

'You know Sir Edward?' he almost yelped.

'Isn't that something a good detective would already have discovered? Fie on you, Mr Tubney. I do believe you came here to intimidate me in some way. That was very reckless of you. You do not say for certain whether you do or you don't know Commander Alcock. That is, of course, also something I shall take up with him personally. What an interesting and entertaining hour of your time you have given me.'

She rose to indicate that he could put down his cup and leave, thinking guiltily at the same time that Philip Westland, wherever he was, must be wondering from whence the sudden griping pain in his guts had come.

The bit that alarmed Captain Quigley most was how the police had come to learn of Bella's other self, the scribbler Henry Ellis Margam.

'There's something naughty in that, dear lady, something very naughty. There are things in those books that come a bit close to home. They might be harmless tales to the innocent but raise a few questions to them as can put two and two together.'

'What do you have in mind?'

'What do I have in mind? One or two dead bodies is what I have in mind, one or two unexplained visits to meet the Maker. I don't like it. The Met can be a very nosy neighbour.'

She thought as much herself but had begun to wonder

whether it was the police who took the interest or merely the pushy and ambitious Sergeant Tubney.

'You need not trouble yourself. I am going away into the country for a few days.'

'Ho! *You're* going away, are you? Well, let me tell you, Captain Quigley is also pressed to leave London by urgent business in, say, Portsmouth. I don't say he's got our number entirely, this here Tubney, but it don't look good. So we shall lock up here tonight.'

'I shall need to warn Mr Murch.'

'That's it – warn all our mates – Mr Urmiston and Billy Murch – and bunk off out of it for a while. Muy pronto, as they say in France.'

'You think we are being watched?'

'I'm not stopping to find out. I don't know where you're going—'

'Yorkshire,' Bella supplied.

'Well,' Quigley exclaimed in admiration. 'Now that *is* a stroke and no error.'

Yorkshire, Finland, Greenland's icy mountains, they were all the same in the Captain's mental geography – places a long way off and peopled by self-absorbed coves who would not know the Metropolitan police from the Metropolitan Water Board. Vikings, many of them. Those that weren't, short arses with teeth like piano keys. He wished *he'd* thought of Yorkshire.

'I must go across to Chiswick and warn Mr Murch,' Bella said.

'Want me to do it?'

'No. I'll do it.'

She was making the tedious and expensive journey to

warn Billy, to be sure, but also to draw comfort from his imperturbable common sense. Quigley seemed to understand this in his habitually jealous way. He scrubbed his head with his knuckles. Was going to say something but his stock of facetiousness had deserted him. They both started up suddenly like criminals at the sound of a footfall outside. But it was only a gentleman who had ducked into the Court to relieve himself before moving on up the Strand.

FOUR

Billy Murch was as grave and attentive as anyone could wish. Living in William Kennett's Chiswick house as its caretaker had tidied him up, so that he no longer had the look of a man who would as soon sleep out on the lawn as anywhere else. Some of this new gravitas came from his marriage to Millie Rogerson, Kennett's housekeeper. Millie liked her man to walk her to church of a Sunday and while she was careful not to badger him too much about clothes and razors, some of her own haphazard sense of propriety had rubbed off. True, to anyone who had ever drunk a pint in a pub he was still a dangerous-looking cove, lean and lithe with the fighter's knack of watchful stillness. Yet something very good had come to him since marrying. He and his new wife were – or so it seemed to Bella – the poster advertisement of a contented couple. She was thunderingly jealous and said as much.

'I don't know that jealousy's just the right word,' Billy smiled. 'But Millie – and Mr Kennett's library – have helped me turn a corner and that's true enough.'

'This is certainly a house of books. What are you reading at present?'

'Did you know about the Ice Ages, both big and little?

There's a lot to chew on there. Though the greater education has come from Millie, of course.'

'Indeed. And I couldn't help noticing—'

'Yes,' he murmured shyly. 'She'll no doubt tell you about it when she comes back. She has gone to sit with her friend, who is in like condition.'

'My heartiest congratulations, Billy. I know Mr Westland will be delighted to hear the news when he returns from the Continent.'

She watched him closely. Murch merely nodded. Perhaps Philip abroad on the Continent was just that to him, an unimportant social note, a thing of no great consequence. Well, of course it was, she reasoned giddily. If Murch was party to this spying business, he would be shoulder to shoulder with Philip right now, primed pistols in his luggage. No better man in a tight corner, no more ruthless an opponent of wrong in the world. If she thought he would do it, Bella would gladly have paid Billy Murch to look after the wandering light that was her soulmate. Which uncomfortable thought brought her back to the reason for her visit.

They started out in the kitchen but at her suggestion moved into Kennett's sitting room, where most of the furniture was shrouded in dust-sheets. Without being asked, Murch lit a small fire in the grate, for while there was ample light left in the sky, the room smelled faintly of damp. So they sat, practically knee to knee, surrounded by icebergs.

Billy listened to her account of Sergeant Tubney's visit to Orange Street with his usual unblinking calm. When she mentioned Quigley's recruitment of Topper Lawson to locate the detective sergeant, he permitted himself a short and wintry smile. Otherwise he heard her out in silence. When she finished her report, he sat looking at his hands for a moment or two. Bella waited.

'We can start with Topper Lawson,' he said. 'There is no bigger cockroach in all London. I don't know what Perce Quigley thought he was doing messing with him. I have had my run-ins with that man before now, you understand. A sack of mischief from Shoreditch you wouldn't trust to point out Nelson's Column, not if you was stood in Trafalgar Square at the time.'

'Quigley described him otherwise.'

'Perce is very easily taken in,' was Billy's terse comment. 'It's my guess that Lawson gabbed to this Tubney cove, making up as much as he dared – and for why? Because he is a well-known copper's nark is for why.'

'He gabbed?'

'Told what he knew, or thought he knew. Which was nothing very much. See – forgive me, Mrs Wallis, if I speak frankly now – you might want to keep your book-writing a secret from the circle that you move in and all power to you for that. But I have to tell you, I knew Henry Ellis Margam was a woman long before I met you.'

'Quigley!' Bella snorted.

'No,' Billy corrected gently. 'It was a bargee's wife who told me, a Gravesend chum of mine with a taste for literature, as you might say.'

'And how did she know about it?'

Murch shrugged. 'How does anyone find out anything? Same as I am walking along Strand on the Green last week and an old bloke with a beard sticks his head out the pub window and shouts, "Looking forward to being a dad, then? Her brains and your beauty, what?" My hand to God, I had never seen this cove before in my life.'

'What did you do?'

'I had him out in the yard and we exchanged a few words, more for the form of the thing than anything else. An ex-Marine, he was. How he knew me was a mystery.'

'I think you're trying to be kind to me, Billy.'

'Not a bit of it. Think of it this way. Somebody says something to Topper Lawson. Could be anybody, could have been last week, last month, or years back. Well, now – begging your pardon once again – who cares? Among our sort of people, who gives so much as a monkey's if you are this Margam bloke? It don't alter the price of fish, as Millie would say. But then along comes Perce, the great chump, and Topper sees his chance to grass you up.'

'Me, or all of us. Quigley thinks that if the Margam books are read in the right way, they offer clues to – well, let's say certain real-life events. You're not afraid of what might be uncovered?'

Billy looked at her very levelly indeed.

'I don't believe I am,' he said.

'You don't think the police might put two and two together?'

'I've seen them try once or twice,' Billy said drily.

Impulsively, Bella jumped up and kissed him on the cheek. He blushed and fumbled for a cheroot.

'The Tubneys of this world are ten a penny,' he muttered. 'And it's my experience that the only use the law has for a long arm is to find its arse. Put it all behind you,

Mrs Wallis. I don't say how, but you can count on it going away. You say you have a mind to visit Yorkshire?'

'I need not go if I can be of help here.'

Billy smiled and smoothed back a glossy wing of hair.

'Nobly put, but I think I shall manage,' he declared, with just enough spin on the words to make Bella blush in turn.

'I feel guilty at having brought all this down on us,' she said.

'We have seen our way through worst scrapes. But on this one, you have been putting the terrier down the wrong rabbit hole, believe me. And now if I don't hear Millie and her bump banging about in the kitchen. I wonder at me saying these words but can I press you to a cup of cocoa, Mrs Wallis?'

Try as she might, Bella was a timid traveller. She arrived early at train stations, checked platform numbers and departure boards far too casually in an effort to appear nonchalant – and then worried she was on the wrong train, had mislaid her ticket, packed unsuitable clothes, was sitting with people who could not possibly be going where she wanted to go. The answer was to take some improving book and bury oneself in it at once. (Hers was on the hall table in Orange Street, where she had left it.) Someone once told her – it was the gloomily lubricious Musgrave, now departed this earth – that in the early days of train travel it was medical opinion that any speed exceeding forty miles an hour would displace women's internal organs. Their wombs would collapse. She was thinking about this ancient nonsense when the platform guard's whistle shrieked immediately outside the carriage window. It was very annoying to be seen to flinch.

As the train pulled out from King's Cross, it ran for a mile or so through sooty canyons but then the sun burst through the haze and smoke and revealed the tenderest landscapes of brick and tile, where people who would never pass Bella's windows in Orange Street sauntered about streets she too would never visit. Within another hour the view from the carriage was all green, green, green. What seemed to be untenanted countryside stretched and yawned all the way to the horizon. A church tower was an event; two naked boys up to their hips in a willow-lined stream were as startling as a visitation by angels.

She travelled dressed in a bulky tweed suit and yellow boots, topped by an unfortunate quasi-military cap, a sort of purple kepi. Though she was quite resigned to looking four parts out of five a complete idiot in this modest disguise, it served well, for she spent a genial hour exchanging pleasantries about perambulation with a parson from Sittingbourne who was on his way to walk from Lincoln Cathedral back to Canterbury, via Ely and Norwich. So detailed was his itinerary that when he left the train at Grantham, she was perfectly able to pass this off as one of her own former accomplishments to the man who took his seat.

'You are fond of walking,' Mr Buttersby of Sheffield observed.

'It stimulates the circulatory system and the historical imagination in about equal measure,' Bella explained, quoting her parson.

'Does it?' Buttersby muttered. 'Well, there's many as

walk the roads of this country in hope of a crust of bread and nothing more. Who keep moving for fear of the workhouse and to escape the cruel necessities of wage slavery.'

'You are a social philosopher,' Bella suggested.

'I am a cattle auctioneer, madam,' he corrected sourly.

After which, he folded his hands over an aldermanic belly and slept.

Bella played with her gloves and thought about Tubney and spies and madwomen, all without any useful conclusion. There *was* one obstinate and indigestible truth in her reflections, which was that she was making this journey, at any rate in part, to spite Philip Westland. Maybe there was a better way of phrasing it but if he could forgo the comforts of Orange Street (among which she counted a tangle of limbs in a crowded bed) then so could she.

Furthermore, this solitary expedition was a way of reasserting her professional independence. Let Philip go about the Continent, peering out of carriage windows and making notes on his cuff, hiding messages in loaves of bread (or whatever else spies did): she too had mysteries and enigmas. The previous evening, Captain Quigley had infuriated her by suggesting that he had better come with her to Yorkshire to keep an eye on things, as he put it. Her sudden flare of anger startled him.

'I was only thinking of your safety, dear lady,' he protested.

'And does every woman who travels alone require the services of a dishevelled drunk?'

'A military mind trained in the arts of reconnaissance is what you meant to say. At any rate, a man, d'you see? For when things get uppity. As you can rest assured they will.'

'And what makes you think that?'

'"Why, I should say you was the very lightning rod to evil,"' he quoted from a sentence she wished she had never written in *Captain Jeffrey's Downfall*. 'I should never forgive myself if you came to grief, never again hold my head up high to such as Mr Westland.'

'I am hardly going to the ends of the earth,' she countered weakly. 'And you can leave Mr Westland out of it.'

'Better you tell him that,' he grunted, always the man to have the last word.

Leeds was just such a town that might have been invented by Quigley for the general disparagement of those unlucky enough not to have been born in London. Bella arrived just when the day shifts were walking out of the Hunslet factory gates like an exhausted army, heads down, cloth capped, dogged. The tobacco-brown smoke of what looked like a great battle drifted eastwards over the rooftops. In Boar Lane it was difficult to see the road surface for a bickering concourse of horse-drawn buses, shays, carts and wagons. The pavements teemed. Bella thought how angry everybody looked.

'Aye,' the cabbie agreed. 'Bur tha's no call to go on abahr tit. From London, are ya? There y'are then.'

'Was I going on about it?'

'Y'ad that look, like.'

'You're proud of your town.'

'Am I that!' the cabbie said, with enough sarcasm to wilt lettuce.

The hotel he took her to *was* proud, if a little behind the times, say by fifty years or more. The main rooms were decorated by equestrian portraits of this, that or the other landowner in front of his house, interspersed among canvases depicting wild nature, noble ruins and allegorical nakedness. The clientele comprised businessmen, widows, governesses and militia officers. That day there had been – incredibly – an archery tournament on somewhere called Woodhouse Moor, which turned out to be hardly more than a mile away. Several of the competitors and the outright winner were dining that night but the undisputed centre of attention was a merry man not yet in his forties, with a nose that shone like a nightwatchman's lantern, Tom Emmett of Yorkshire County Cricket Club.

'Would the gentleman sign an autograph for my godson?' a timid woman asked, flourishing the menu.

'Tha can tell t'lad I am no gentleman, missus,' Emmett chortled, scribbling. 'But if he wants to come down to Sheffield for a county match, I shall be happy to shake his hand. And mebbe show him the old sostenutor at work.'

'He will be thrilled,' the godmother promised, with the tiniest flicker of alarm in her voice. Only when she returned to her table did her husband explain (and at some length) that the sostenutor was Emmett's ball that broke back from a length outside off stump, etc., etc. He took the autographed menu card and put it away in his wallet. Bella found the whole incident unintelligible.

'Is it true that there is a factory here that has sheep grazing on its roof?' she asked her dining companion, a frail gentleman on his way to the spa waters of Harrogate. He gave her what Quigley would have described as an old-fashioned look.

'It was once true, yes. Just as in my father's day you

could lift pike from the River Aire. I myself have shot for hares on the hill behind the cavalry barracks when a boy. But those times have gone.'

'In the name of progress?'

'So we are told. Is that why you came here, to see the sheep on the roof of Marshall's Mill?'

'I came to walk and sketch in the Dales.'

'There are sheep enough there,' the old man smiled. 'And a more ancient way of life. Do you have a particular destination in mind?'

'I was planning to visit Cruddas, I think it is called. Above Skipton.'

'Is there anything there worth your trouble?' the old man asked. But with just enough in the remark to alert Bella.

'You have heard of it?'

'My name is Foxton,' he murmured.

'Lord Foxton! Please forgive me. We have never met but I had a very particular friend in Yorkshire who spoke of you often and always in the kindest of terms. Yours is the great house a little before Wakefield – I saw it from the train this afternoon.'

'Was your friend Lord Broxtowe? Then you must be what he called his incomparable London rose. Well, well, Mrs Wallis, I see he did not exaggerate. Broxtowe and I were schoolboys together at Eton. To repay your generous compliment, I know that he liked and admired *you* a great deal. The happiest man I ever met. Happy is not quite the right word, either. Blithe would be better.'

Foxton smiled. He pushed back his plate and began to refold his napkin in an absent-minded gesture.

'I should add that he considered you a woman with more moral worth than the Archbishops of York and Canterbury combined. Rather a heavy burden of praise, I should have thought. You will not think me forward, I hope, if I propose a glass of champagne in the little snug they have here?'

'Champagne, my lord?'

'Bubbles,' Lord Foxton explained. 'I would not give the brandy they serve to a dying soldier. Bubbles will suit the occasion better. Come, and you shall tell me about your interest in Cruddas.'

It transpired that Foxton had lead mines in that part of Yorkshire and knew the area well, though the seams were exhausted and he had not visited his property for a dozen years or more.

'It is a very wild and unmanaged landscape you propose to visit. You would do better further east and north, say in Wharfedale, where things are more picturesque by far. Indeed, where Broxtowe had his place. But perhaps you are not going for the picturesque?'

He said this with such delicate insinuation that Bella was forced to face him down.

'There is a woman living there called Lady Ursula Gollinge.'

Foxton inclined his head.

'My tenant – or she would be if little matters like rent had any meaning for her. When the mine was still profitable, I installed the manager – a Swede, incidentally – in what I suppose we might call at a stretch a manor house. The Swede left and the Gollinge woman begged me to let her take it up in his place.'

'But how did she come to hear of it?'

'If you ever find out you must let me know,' Lord Foxton replied drily. 'Is Lady Gollinge a friend of yours?'

'We have never met. It is not very likely we could ever be friends.'

'I am pleased to hear it. The lady is said to be a terrible scandal to her sex, though in fairness I have to say what she gets up to in such a remote place is her own business. Do you read novels at all, Mrs Wallis?'

Bella watched him very carefully but the question appeared to be innocent. Foxton smiled again.

'From all I have heard, what goes on above Cruddas surpasses even the cheapest novel for sensation. Have a care, therefore. You will find Skipton an honest enough place and I can recommend the George Hotel. The vicar is a fund of useless information about birds and snakes and suchlike but a kindly man after his own fashion. The weather is of course execrable.'

'Even in summer, my lord?'

'At any time of the year.'

FIVE

Bella arrived in Skipton on market day with the town *en fête*, the cobbled streets strewn with dung and droppings, the pavements jostling with the families of local farmers, all of them got up in their best. The main street afforded a fine view of the castle which (this being Yorkshire) Bella was three times advised as being the finest example of this particular architecture to be found anywhere in the country.

'Do they have such a thing in Leeds or Bradford? They do not. Now, you say you have come from Leeds this day. And how did you find it? I'll tell thee – a dirtier hole does not exist. Up here, the air is pure. As my old dad says, we should bottle our air and send it down to those unhappy Loiners. You'll have noticed how fresh the streets are.'

This was true; but had much to do with a half gale blowing directly from Lancashire, carrying with it stinging sleet. This gave the faces round about their scrubbed and ruddy looks, as well as causing uproarious accidents, as when a youth's hat flew from his head like a rocketing pheasant and was walked over by a hundred or more sheep.

'And if that don't pay him out for coming it the gentleman, him as has not two ha'ppenies to scratch his arse with and only his poor old mother in work!' a woman shouted with great contentment. 'Yes, his mother washing floors and emptying grates while he laiks about every hour God sends with a bloody flower in his buttonhole and 'lasticated boots!'

'Is he not your Martha's young man?' her companion objected, mildly enough.

'Our Martha's a daft cat, but she aren't that stupid.'

The same two women came into the lounge of the George later, where Martha's mother unwrapped a bit of fish she had bought earlier and passed it to her friend for comment. To Bella's bemusement, they ordered a pint of porter each and fell to talking about haddock. At the next table, two gentlemen in shooting clothes were drinking schooners of sherry and discussing fatstock prices as they had been published in that day's *Yorkshire Post*.

Behind them was a wild-looking woman with blonde-grey corkscrew curls, talking animatedly to a sly-looking girl in a shabby green mantle. Quigley had always insisted to Bella that the eyes were the mirror to the soul. The wild woman had bulging and unblinking eyes that might have indicated unruffled stupidity but for the restless shadows that seemed to flit across their surfaces. A screeching monologue spewed from her box-shaped mouth, something to do with a slight or insult offered earlier in the day. Bella noted how studiously this ugly rant was being ignored, the way some of the same people were forced to ignore the parakeet in the Savile Arms, down by the canal, when they chanced to visit. But there was something more to it than this: the good-natured Skiptonians were acting as one in pretending that the couple were not in the room at all. It took some skill to ignore the physical presence of two other human beings in this way.

'Look at them all,' the woman crowed. 'Their blood three parts sugar, their piggy eyes glistening with lard! Afraid of the dark, afraid of dying. And so very anxious not to be different, not to stand out in the crowd. The herd, Amelia! Animals! Heads down, munching their way through their rotten little lives. With a bit of rutting once in a blue moon, yes, there in the dark with only the wardrobe for witness. And what's it all for?'

'The Empire!' her companion suggested unexpectedly.

'Yes, the Empire! Oh, how grateful we can be that all those lovely black men are shovelling coal for us and holding up umbrellas to keep us from the heat of the sun! While their children starve and their wives are beaten black and blue by soldiers for refusing their drunken and lecherous advances!'

Bella alone watched and listened. Though she still did not realise it, she was looking at Ursula Gollinge. Before she left to venture out into the streets once more, the manager of the hotel gave her a note written in bold slashing characters. It was from the Reverend Mr Sanderson, more or less inviting himself to dinner that night. Or, as he put it, to offer any help he could in deciphering the local character.

That evening, while dressing, it came to Bella: how many barking mad women were there in Skipton not to make the one she had overheard at lunch Ursula Gollinge? It was the image of the loyal black man shovelling coal while at the same time holding up an umbrella that gave the clue.

Bella sat down in her drawers and stays to write all that she could remember of how the woman looked and (more guiltily) the bearing of her young companion. A detail: Lady Ursula was entirely devoid of make-up or jewellery but the girl she called Amelia had so lined her eyes as to draw them out and give her the appearance of a cat. Every finger on both hands was decorated by rings – cheap market rings of Mexican silver, to be sure, set with miniature stones – but a bold enough touch.

As to what they were doing in the hotel that day, this was answered by the night manager when she finally went downstairs to meet Mr Sanderson.

'They come once a week to take a bath,' he explained gloomily.

'Then they have enough of the Empire's ill-gotten gains to book a room.'

'If only,' the manager said. 'Today they were discovered by a Mr Murray in the first-floor front, a gentleman who interests himself in parish churches. He, having been soaked to the skin in his explorations, was about to ease his rheumatism in the bath, when he found it occupied by the lady and her companion. *Together*,' he added in a low voice.

'They were in the bath together?'

'Mr Murray is sixty-four,' the manager said, with a weary shake of his head. 'He says he has never experienced depravity like it, not even he, a man born under a cannon at Waterloo. You will find Mr Sanderson in the residents' lounge, madam. And may I recommend the lamb shank tonight?'

*   *   *

'A curate with his own pony and trap!' Bella mocked gently. Mr Sanderson, lately of Trinity College, Cambridge, took it in good heart.

'The alternative would be a horse, you understand, but the animal that could carry me has yet to be born. It cheers people to see their curate carried about like a circus freak. I am brother to the Hottentot Venus, Mrs Wallis.'

Mr Sanderson was certainly a very large young man. Of only medium height, his fat was lumped onto him, so that for example his hands (which were girlishly delicate) peeped from under rolls of fat that threatened to overwhelm them. His thighs were each greater in girth than Bella's waist and when he laughed, his whole body shook like a blancmange. But Mr Sanderson had beautifully alert eyes. Lord Foxton had sent him a telegraph advising him of Bella's presence in the George and now here he was at dinner, as shrewd a mind as existed in the hotel that night. His manners were impeccable.

'Will you not tell me how you came into your curacy?' Bella asked.

'Oh, but don't you think the church needs jolly and uncomplicated men, Mrs Wallis? The parishioners call me Friar Tuck, which is very pleasing. What's needed in this vocation is a sort of holy innocence. People admire the vicar – Mr Mountain – for his learned ways and rather austere manners. They like me for a poor fat lad, as they style me, one who can never say boo to a goose. As a consequence I am told things enough to make a sailor blush.'

'Do you know why I am here, Mr Sanderson?'

'I am anxious to discover the reason,' the curate responded politely.

'Do you happen to know Lady Ursula Gollinge?'

'I see,' Sanderson said.

'You do know her?'

The curate left off eating long enough to spread his hands in the international gesture which the moderately sane use to indicate dismay in the face of what verges on the incomprehensible.

'Here, in the more remote parts of the tops, as they call them, people are known as much by their sins as their virtues. For example, Raybould, a name as famous as any in the Craven District. A farmer. When his wife died in 1855, he took leave of absence from the human race. Nobody has actually seen Walter Raybould since he was fifty-odd years old, not so much as a stolen glimpse.'

'But then what is his sin, to make him so notorious?'

'He killed his wife with a hatchet. Before two witnesses,' Sanderson explained calmly. 'The police have looked for him a hundred times since – in newspaper jargon, they have combed the moors. He has never been apprehended. Some say he lives underground. Children believe he can transform himself at will, say into a stoat, or a hawk.'

'We are in Transylvania!' Bella exclaimed wonderingly.

'Wouldn't it seem so?' the curate smiled.

'But what has this man to do with Lady Gollinge?'

Sanderson laid down his knife and fork with some regret and pushed away his empty plate.

'In practical terms, nothing. I use him as an illustration of the power the local folk have to reshape the world according to their lights. Raybould has decreed his own punishment. When he dies, there will be no burial and no fine words spoken over him. The people understand that. He has gone to live outside the tribe.'

'And so, it might be said, has Lady Gollinge,' Bella suggested.

'Maybe. But Raybould has touched something very ancient in the penance he has set himself. Put beside his example, Ursula Gollinge is merely a wilful and vexatious interloper. His is a human tragedy. She is a raree show.'

'Hasn't she too a right to live as she wishes?'

'Indeed,' Sanderson replied. 'But whether it earns her a scrap of respect is another matter. Decency is a virtue held very high among country people. She has none. I may pity her but those of the common people who have crossed her path despise her.'

'One last question, then: *do* you pity her?'

'Why,' the kindly and jolly Mr Sanderson said, forgetting his calling for a moment and speaking like the undergraduate he so recently was, 'I have never held another human being in such contempt.'

And so they sat; and so they ate pudding. Bella ended the evening better off by the loan of the curate's pony and trap – and the promise of a boy, Alfie Stannard, to drive it for her. She was grateful, too, for a hand-drawn map and some useful advice about the very few inns to be had in the district around Cruddas; but what stuck in her mind was this last remark of Mr Sanderson's and the unequivocal vehemence with which it was delivered.

'Unless you have personal dealings with Lady Gollinge, I would keep well away. There may be entertainment in the spectacle she makes of herself, the way that village simpletons are sometimes cruelly advertised. But truly,

Mrs Wallis, the lady is beneath your consideration. There is nothing worth your interest here.'

'Aren't all stories worth the telling?'

'I believe not.'

They said goodnight on the steps of the George, with the arrangement that the curate would drive himself back to his lodgings and in the morning the boy Alfie would return with the trap. The wind had dropped a little and the rain abated. Rags of white clouds moved across the roofs of Skipton, lit by an almost full moon. Though it was hardly past eleven, not a soul stirred. When Bella went to bed, the last sound she heard before sleep was that of a fox's dry coughing in the castle grounds.

She dreamed of Philip. Skipton had become a town on the Danube and its citizens Turks. Bella was looking for him in a crowded souk filled with sinister-looking characters, a place all the more frightful for birds, great swirls of them, swooping and diving. They were, she judged shakily, ravens. Guards on the castle roof were firing at them with impossibly long and old-fashioned muskets. Lord Foxton was in the dream, as was Mr Sanderson, who seemed to find the whole thing a cause for merriment. Easy for these two: they sat on cushions in a scented courtyard, drinking sherbet, while the world came to pieces outside.

It occurred to Bella that the place to look for Philip was down by the river and she ran there through rustling stalks of what she took to be maize, jumping sticks that terror taught her might also be snakes. She was not naked, but her feet were bare. When she looked down, she saw that she was wearing only a nightgown – the very nightgown in which she slept that night. The distant gunfire she heard could not possibly come from the shooting of ravens: the city was in a state of insurrection. She began to smell smoke.

When at last she found Philip, he was standing on the stern deck of a departing steamer, dressed in a cream suit. It seemed impossible that he did not see or hear her howling at him to turn back; but after a moment or two he sauntered away down the thrumming deck.

'He has gone,' an obliging old man in a turban explained.

Though the same moon that shone over the moors of the West Riding illuminated Westphalia, there was nothing romantic about Philip's landscape. Midnight in Essen disclosed a bleak network of railway lines, drifting in and out of definition as banks of yellow smoke moved about uneasily, generated from God knew where and seemingly with a mind of their own. A cruelly ugly iron bridge over the tracks was lit by a dozen darting naphtha lamps. Earlier in the night a man had hanged himself from its central span, some said a poor workman laid off by one of the foundries, some a farmer looking for his daughter – and finding her.

One of the figures on the bridge detached itself and sauntered towards Philip, who was half concealed in the shadows of a grimy warehouse.

'It is Wachter,' he murmured.

'You don't know that.'

'I know what the police told me. So now they ask what does an elderly clerk in the plans office of the mighty Krupps Works think he is about, trying on a hemp necktie?

It being our friend Wachter of course, he was wearing his best suit and newest boots. There was a briefly held theory that he had been attending a funeral, the poor fellow. But anyway, suicide.'

'Did he leave a note?' Philip asked. His companion's rich laugh was so loud and so out of place that several heads turned on the bridge.

'You are not quite as stupid as you look, Herr Westland.'

'We should search his lodgings. We should go now.'

'That is being done. But what if his note was in the nature of a detailed confession? And what if it is not propped against a greasy coffee pot in his lodgings but waiting in Herr Krupp's in-tray? Have you thought of that?'

'Let us meet again at breakfast.'

'Here? In Essen?' the man cried incredulously. 'By dawn I intend to be very far away indeed. You are not trying to rob a shopkeeper: this is Krupp you are dealing with. Steel is a ruthless business. Herr Krupp has a policy towards industrial spies. They are crushed like mice under one of his steam hammers. You have failed, Englishman. And now your life is forfeit.'

'You have a gift for melodrama, Herr Furst,' Philip said amiably enough. 'If you are planning to leave Essen tonight, I need hardly tell you that your silence will be taken for granted by my principals in London. You have already been paid well – not for your loyalty, of course, but discretion. Should that ever desert you, things would turn out very badly for both you and your family.'

Herr Furst studied the shadowed face in front of him, uncertain how to respond. This shambling Englishman, for all his easy command of German, was quite clearly an amateur at the game. Yet there was something about him Furst could not completely dismiss. The reason had to do with the one they called Alcock. Alcock, it was said, never left London but was known all over Europe for a feral ruthlessness. Furst had often tried to picture what he looked like and always came up with the uncomfortable image of one of those stolid unimaginative Englishmen to be found staring down the foreigners in Baden-Baden, like men inspecting cattle. A thought struck him: Maybe Westland *was* Alcock. Maybe he was being played for a fool.

'I have no wish to cause the slightest anxiety to your principals,' he muttered.

'They will be pleased to hear that,' Philip replied gravely.

'We could perhaps even travel back to London together?'

Or, Furst thought, I could put my mind at ease by breaking your neck here and now. He was in a panic. What he had said about the Krupp family's power to silence their opponents was a commonplace; if anything the son was more vindictive than the father. Nor was it simply a local matter. The dossier in question – the one poor Wachter had been suborned to steal or copy – was a commission given to Krupp by the Kriegsmarine. Which was to say, in the end, Bismarck.

Looking past Furst's shoulder Philip saw two policemen marching towards them across the bridge. Raising his voice, he thanked Furst profusely for such a handsome reunion dinner and begged to be remembered to Marthe and the little ones! Next year in Dusseldorf, that was for sure! Vogel would be there, and old Pappi Mundt. *Then* they would toast the regiment three times three!

Philip walked away, his hands shaking, but with enough sangfroid left to pause for a moment to light a cigar. There was a cab twenty yards ahead of him and the driver cracked his whip over the sleeping horse's head when he saw the match flare. A drunken whore scooted from the interior of the cab and stumbled into an unlit alley. Philip took her place. The leather bench she had vacated was warm.

'Where to?' the cabbie croaked. But before he could answer, Furst's face appeared at the open window, followed immediately by a blinding flash. Philip felt a bolt of pain in his shoulder and fell sideways onto the horsehair cushions. The bullet had passed clean through him, raising clouds of dust from the ancient upholstery. The cab rocked as the driver lashed his horse uphill over the cobbles, standing up on his box and shouting blue murder. Inside, Philip smelled gun smoke, burning cloth from the cigar that had lodged in the folds of his suit – and blood.

SIX

Alfie Stannard turned out to be a pleasant boy with excellent manners. Bella judged him to be seventeen or so, lean and sinewy with bright red hair and skin freckled like a thrush's egg. He wore chequered trousers and a patched linen jacket but it was his footwear that drew the eye. Bella was fairly convinced that his once-elegant boots, their soles as thin as paper, were cast-offs from his patron, Mr Sanderson. Fashioned for nothing more demanding than a walk across Trinity Great Court, perhaps to go as far as the post office or the Blue Boar, here in Skipton they were as out of place as a Chinaman's slippers. Alfie wore them with pride.

That he had also fallen in love with Bella at first sight was obvious to them both, yet he managed to get his feelings under control enough to drive her up the valley to Cruddas Bridge. There they rested the horse and sat down by the river on table-sized boulders, watching the water. Bella was intrigued. Alfie had suddenly grown jumpy, afflicted by nervous yawning and what Mrs Venn would have called a bad case of the fidgets. He pointed out the dark shadows of trout but his heart wasn't in it.

'Didn't think this was the place you wanted to come.'

'Yet it all seems very peaceful,' Bella said in an attempt

to calm him. And so it was if you liked silence and emptiness. They had passed the last drystone walls more than a mile back. The bridge was solid enough but it was the only indication that man had otherwise laid one stone upon another in these parts. Cruddas was nowhere to be seen. When asked where it was, Alfie pointed carelessly to the north.

'Can you not smell it?'

'I cannot. Is that how you find your way round up here – by sniffing places out? Is the nose your compass?'

As soon as she said this, Bella realised how fatuous she sounded. Philip would never have said anything so patronising, nor would he have noticed much if the boy's feet were stuffed into squelching marrows, or sandals made from string and cowpats. Alfie's mildly reproving glance was like a punch to the ribs.

'You can't smell a bone fire? Someone's burning summat.'

'Garden refuse, for example?'

'You mean like grass clippings and that? Nah.'

'Something more serious, then.'

'Just a fire, like. Thought you might smell it.'

He pulled a wet stalk of grass and chewed like a goat.

'Aren't many that come this high up,' he explained, 'except for the gentlemen from Leeds and maybe Halifax who fish. Right now it's too bright and the sky is too high.'

'You know about trout, Alfie?'

'Every boy does.'

'And do you come here to fish yourself?'

Amazingly, he blushed. Dropped his head and fell to examining his hands. Watched Bella from under his lashes.

'They'd be *your* friends,' he mumbled.

'Who? Who are you talking about?'

'The ladies that live over the ridge yonder.'

'What ladies can you mean?'

He pointed and resumed his blushing.

'Do you mean these waters are theirs? They've turned you off, have they?'

'No, no, oh, no. They're nobody to tell local people what they can and can't do. No, I was thinking on something else.'

'Can you tell me what that is?'

'Best not to mention,' he mumbled.

'You have the makings of a novelist, Alfie. You can see now that nothing will do but you tell me what this other thing is. I am on fire with curiosity.'

'I spoke out of turn,' he said.

'Don't be so gormless,' Bella snapped. 'I have not come all this way to admire the landscape. Those two ladies interest me quite as much as they do you.'

He flapped the remark away with bony hands and then burst into snotting tears, enough to startle even the horse. Bella was amazed – here was a solid enough country boy with his head in his hands and sobbing like a girl.

'You won't tell Vicar or Mr Sanderson?' he wept.

'Of course not. But you haven't said what it is I must keep secret.'

He wiped his tears away with the back of his wrist and stood.

'You had best see for yourself,' he muttered thickly and began walking downstream. Bella followed. There came a point in the river where they might cross, jumping from boulder to boulder, and this they did, at the expense of Bella's shoes and stockings. Once across, the boy pointed to a steep bank. A curlew cried piteously over their heads.

Only fifty yards from the road another country began, greeny-grey and largely featureless. What should have been a fine prospect of the Aire Valley running east to Leeds was obscured by a huge limestone bluff, maybe a mile off. The Pennines rose to the west in a green wall. There was plenty of sky to admire but not much else. The grass was as short as a lawn but scratchy and (as she discovered soon enough) filthy dirty. Dark banks of bilberries grew along the less exposed slopes and there were two or three forlorn stands of what looked like blackthorn trees.

They scrambled for half an hour before Alfie drew her down beside a little outcrop of rock. She was surprised how grateful she was for the respite. Sweat ran out of her hair and her eyes hurt from so much uninterrupted brightness. She found that for some minutes past she had been holding his hand and this she now disengaged, feeling alarmingly foolish and girlish about it, too. The tweed suit that had looked so well in the pony and trap clung to her hips and thighs as damp as any bath-towel. Alfie smiled at her.

''Tis easier for a man, perhaps.'

'Why is the grass so dirty?' she asked.

'Mills,' he answered. 'Over in Lancashire, like. Come winter, the snow is grey.'

'And why have we come here? To this particular spot?'

'You'll see,' he promised.

She lay back on the grass and closed her eyes, very conscious of him as an animal presence, child though he was. What had seemed like an oppressive silence was gradually resolving into a story – the curlew was still there but she could also hear the wind in the grass and even the very faint and syncopated sound of water tumbling through rocks. A very long way off, but carried to her by a trick of the wind, came the thrum of the looms at Slingsby's Mill, maddening to those who worked there but here no more than a whisper.

And then suddenly, unmistakably, a woman's voice cawing like a rook. Alfie laid his hand warningly on her forearm.

'Don't sit up,' he whispered. 'Don't show yourself. If you was to roll over onto your front – but slowly, like –'

At first she could see nothing. His hand was in the small of her back, pressing her down to the ground. They lay like lovers. Alfie took her finger and gently pointed it towards the low ground in the distance.

'Keep still,' he said. 'They are in that little beck. You see yon rock that looks like a cow?'

She did not, but then Ursula Gollinge obliged her by climbing up onto it, maybe a hundred yards away. After a moment, a younger woman joined her. There was something odd about the pair of them that Bella was slow to grasp. And then it dawned on her. Both women were stark naked and the sticks they seemed to be carrying were bows and arrows. They paused for a moment and appeared to look straight at Bella. Then plunged back down out of sight. The next time they appeared they were a hundred yards further off, showing their rumps like rabbits.

* * *

It did nothing for Alfie's peace of mind that Bella commanded him to take the trap further along the road to look for the women's house. She too was anxious she might be tipping her hand by doing so. On the other hand, what she had seen out on the fells begged for some sort of context. They crossed the bridge and struggled up a boulder-strewn ridge to Cruddas.

The entire village was crammed into a high-sided valley and comprised a single street of miners' cottages with stone roofs and tiny windows, more like pigpens than human dwellings. The few Cruddas folk who were about in the streets offered the traditional Yorkshire welcome given to incomers, which is to say they turned their backs on the pony and trap, some of them going so far as to face the wall until it passed. Bella took her cue from Alfie and stared straight ahead. Trickles of sweat ran down her ribs.

'There is the house,' the boy whispered, pointing with his chin down a steep dirt track. Even if they had wanted to visit they could not, for a hundred yards along the track a huge tree had been felled to block the way and left to rot, branches and all. Beyond, Bella saw the roof and yard of a fairly substantial building. Lashed to the chimney stack was a drunken pole, bearing – in place of a flag – a string of bones and feathers. Round about the yard there lay bits and pieces of what she assumed had once been mining machinery now glowing red with rust. The source of the smoke was explained. Lady Gollinge was not disposing of her grass clippings but burning a filthy mattress and – even more scandalously – a horsehair sofa. Bella shuddered.

'I have seen enough,' she mumbled faintly. 'This is a gate to hell.'

An hour later, they sat in the garden of a single-storey inn further down the valley, eating wonderfully nutty bread and thick slices of ham. Chickens scratched about under the table and several cats stalked. After Cruddas, the pure ordinariness of the scene acted on Bella like strong drink. This too was a poor and forsaken place but it was recognisably human. There were even little touches of ambition – a painted milk churn, pansies in a pot.

'How close have you been to them?' she asked, after a long silence. Alfie knew to whom she was referring.

'They have come closer to where we was earlier,' he admitted. 'Much closer once or twice. Say from here to that yew.'

'Did they discover you?'

He looked at her with something of pity in his eyes.

'I aren't that stupid, am I?'

'And you think they saw us today, however?'

'Saw *you*,' Alfie chuckled. 'She wor looking straight at you, the old bag. She won't like what she saw.'

'And what's she going to do about it?' Bella scoffed.

'Them Cruddas folk are tough, right tough. But they're all scared of her.'

'Look at me, Alfie. Do I look scared to you?'

'Not yet you don't.'

'And the nakedness and such. Do you have some idea of what that is all about?'

'They were hunting. With bows and arrows. The young

girl, she's Amelia from off the barges. Did you see the warpaint?'

'Is that what it was? And if you fall to blushing again I shall stick you with this knife.'

'That old thing? Couldn't cut water.' But he found some courage and touched his nipple briefly. 'Here? Round here? That is all painted black, huge black. Old Gollinge, she has a white face, like a skellington. 'Melia likewise. Feathers and that. But not a stitch of cloth anywhere. I dream about them,' he added unnecessarily.

'But what are they hunting?'

'Rabbits. I've seen them try to shoot at pheasants on the wing, the barmpots. Always stark bollock . . . always naked. Same as all the singing they do, the wailing. And dancing.'

'That must be worth seeing,' Bella said absently. When she saw that she made Alfie flinch, she patted his hand. 'You are a good boy to have taken me. Would you like the rest of my ham?'

He took it and stuffed it in his pocket.

'You would never do a thing like that?' he asked with a sudden arch smile, indicating they were in some sense co-conspirators. 'I mean, run about covered in paint?'

'You have my word on it,' Bella responded gravely, convulsing Alfie with silent laughter. 'But tomorrow we must get closer. I need to know what tribe they belong to. Would that suit you, too?'

'I think she knows who you are,' he whispered.

'And how could that be?'

'She has powers, no doubt about it.'

The hotel, Bella thought. Someone at the hotel has tipped her the wink, perhaps the lugubrious and put-upon manager.

'*I* have powers,' she declared grandly, patting Alfie on the head and then caressing his cheek. Earlier, she had asked the stunned landlady for coffee and now this buxom woman came out with what she imagined might be the next best thing, two earthenware mugs of nettle tea. The curlew that seemed to follow them round hung in the sky and for a moment life seemed to be good. Even the sweet treacly stink that floated from the inn's interior seemed apt and charming. Bella spoilt it for both the boy and the no-nonsense innkeeper by smoking, a scandalous way for a lady to be going on and something the two of them equated with distant manners in a part of England never to be imagined. In other words, London.

Well, Henry Ellis Margam asked, what did you expect? You are indeed far from London and – at least so far as discovering a suitable plot for a novel bearing my name – quite out of kilter with the modern taste. Madness has its own aesthetic. A beautiful woman maddened by grief, or a child struck dumb by a single fateful turn of fortune's wheel – both these are quite permissible when properly brought forward. But two women running about stark naked in the depths of Yorkshire is another matter. And the bows and arrows are a poor touch, one might even say a cheap effect. The castle at the bottom of this street is a far better location for a sensational tale. Let us imagine: Lady Mauleverer discovers a hidden passage in the picture gallery that leads . . . that leads somewhere or other . . . and is forced to keep this ghastly discovery secret from her husband, who, lamed in a recent riding accident . . .

Bella threw down her pen in disgust. Downstairs in

the hotel a wedding party was celebrating uproariously and she had elected to take her evening meal in her room. She had accordingly drunk two-thirds of a bottle of Niersteiner and smoked as much as any militia captain bored by his comrades but too lazy to make a sortie from quarters.

Both windows were wide open and the long dusk was finally giving way to night. What Lady Mauleverer needed to do was to brick up the secret passages in her castle to prevent her adorable husband from disappearing down them on his mysterious errands, buy herself a completely new outfit, give up the office in Fleur de Lys Court and go to live by the sea. Buy a telescope, take up painting, collect fossils, anything that had nothing to do with pen and paper. Take the inkwell and hurl it into the waves. Slam the door in Henry Ellis Margam's face and forget he ever existed.

She was startled by the dry crack of a pebble flung against her window. When she peered out she saw a moonstruck Alfie standing in the roadway in front of the hotel.

'What is it?' she called.

'At what time tomorrow?' he called back shyly.

'Alfie, it is near enough midnight.'

'I know. But they won't let me up to your room.'

'Go home and go to bed.'

'If you say so. But listen – I've had a right good idea.'

'Excellent!' Bella said. 'Tell me tomorrow. Be here at ten.'

There are things to do in a hotel bedroom that seem strange and difficult which in a home would pass completely unremarked. Cleaning one's teeth, hair-brushing, even reading in bed – all these became minor battles with mirrors and lamps, rucked carpets and inadequate curtains. When Bella finally flopped into bed, she felt exhausted but horribly wide awake. At home in Orange Street she would have padded round the house in her bare feet, even going as far as the kitchens to make tea. The mere act of thinking this made her homesick.

There came a point in every Bella adventure, before it became a Margam book, when it was sensible to ask no more questions of the raw material. She was not a detective, after all, any more than was Wilkie Collins or any of the other novelists in her field. She had set herself the task to find out more about Ursula Gollinge; discovering her as some sort of Red Indian out on the moors was revelation enough. Were she to go on and uncover some other madness, like plans for an attack on Leeds Town Hall by means of a hot air balloon, how much more would she actually learn? The one question she wanted to put to Lady Gollinge was foolishly querulous: What have you to do with my beloved Philip Westland?

The answer seemed obvious. It was against all probability the two had ever met. Bella sat up in bed and tried to punch the pillow soft, putting more bad temper into the effort than was ladylike.

There was a surreptitious scratching at the door. She got out of bed and for want of another weapon found her boot. Opened the door a crack, ready for battle.

Out in the corridor was an amiable-looking young man in his shirtsleeves, wearing a woman's hat and with his boots knotted round his neck. His socks had holes.

'I do beg your pardon,' he said with the elaborate courtesy of the roaring drunk. 'I was looking for Myrtle Longstaff. You are not her.'

As Bella closed the door on him, the woman's hat explained itself. The young man was a piece of flotsam from the wedding reception.

There was blood on the woman's apron and Philip supposed she had been slaughtering chickens. This was a farmhouse, he judged, or perhaps the summer kitchen to a larger building. The air was as thick as gravy and the flies that crawled across his face and neck seemed drunk on it. He could hear someone sawing wood nearby; further off, what might be the herding of cows. Daylight hurt his eyes. It slowly dawned on him that the blood on the woman's clothes was his own.

'Where am I?' he asked.

'My man will talk to you when he comes in.'

'Where is he now?'

'What does it matter where he is?' the woman shrilled. 'But if you don't lie still, you will start to bleed like a pig again. Be grateful you are not out in the ditch, where we found you.'

'Where is this place?'

'Naturally, this is heaven and we are angels.'

She held up his head and poured something disgusting down his throat, something he racked his brains to recognise. Finally it came to him. Milk.

'I have been shot,' he explained unnecessarily. 'I don't know how I came here but I have money—'

He stopped. They knew that. The woman's smile was

sardonic. She wiped his lips by rubbing her thumb across them.

'Everybody has a story they want to tell others,' she said. 'We will listen to yours later. Meanwhile, sleep.'

'Sleep!'

'Why not?' she said. 'It's not so difficult.'

SEVEN

Alfie's bubblingly bright idea was to take Bella to see Duxbury. At first she supposed this to be a nearby village; but Duxbury, who had shed his first name like a snake, was that inherently contradictory thing, a popular hermit. Not a local man, mind, for who could take seriously anyone daft enough to live in a limestone cave unless he came from exotic foreign parts – in his case, Woodhouse Street in Leeds. Five years ago, Duxbury had walked out on his hole-in-the-wall tobacconist kiosk opposite the Chemical Works and, after a year's adventures along the way, found his new station in life. In his wake, he left behind a wife, two daughters and five grandchildren. Bella was profoundly depressed by this story.

'It's a wonder he's still alive,' she commented sourly.

'Oh, it's a right roomy cave,' Alfie assured her. 'And Mr Sanderson says that folk used to live there in the Ice Age when the woolly mammals roamed.'

'I was trying to indicate how it's a great wonder his wife hasn't come up here and stabbed him to death with her umbrella.'

'It's no small thing being a hermit,' Alfie answered indignantly. 'He muses on things, is what he does. The older people go to see him when they've got a problem. My *mother* has been to see him.'

'And what was her problem?

'To do with her insides,' Alfie muttered.

And this is it, Bella thought: I am trapped in a very bad dream, such as comes at a noisy picnic after too much sun and a glass too many of wine. This child is the will-o'-the-wisp that is drawing me on. Madwomen running naked over the fells, and now a hermit. When he caught her scowling at him, Alfie managed to look pained and innocent, like a child being scolded for making up stories about bogeymen under the bed.

It was a mild morning with wan sunshine. Bella was entertaining the boy to a cup of coffee in the orchard garden of the hotel, where a convention of wasps was also meeting. It was her fixed London habit to swipe at things that buzzed and it did nothing for her temper that Alfie seemed not to notice the wasps, to the extent of letting one crawl across the orange hairs on the back of his wrist.

'You don't want to get them angry,' he advised.

'I want them to know that I am angry.'

In an effort to placate her, he picked up the wasp that was examining his shirt cuff and nipped its head off between his thumb and forefinger. Bella winced. The day had already got off to a bad start when he told her with artless candour that the coffee in front of him was the first he had ever tasted. Didn't like it much, neither. It stuck to your teeth, like. The hermit business came after.

'What do you think we can learn from this man?' she asked.

'Duxbury knows all,' Alfie promised. 'And he has a

right good view of that valley where the naked ladies do their hunting.'

'You've spoken to him about that?'

'I might have mentioned it,' Alfie confessed, blushing.

They were interrupted by the arrival of Mr Sanderson, wafting into the orchard like a great black balloon, carrying his Bible under one arm and encumbered by a string bag of sheet music and a pound or so of onions.

'I came to see how you are getting on,' he boomed in that jolly way that parsons have. 'Alfie, be a dear and fetch me some coffee. And perhaps a doughnut or two.'

Alfie was only too anxious to scoot off, though not before throwing Bella an imploring glance, easy enough to interpret: the less said about Ursula Gollinge, the better. But Mr Sanderson seemed to have other things on his mind. He was having his usual problem with chairs. He examined the one in front of him with suspicion, jiggled the back, and sat. There was a satisfying shriek as his mighty bottom tested the joints and then he leaned back with content. The legs sank into the turf like tent pegs.

'You are looking well, Mrs Wallis,' he smiled. 'I hope that boy is proving useful. He told me this morning he wished you to meet Duxbury.'

Sanderson by day was a slightly more formidable presence. She could account for this by supposing that he was in working mode (hence the Bible and possibly the onions, a gift to some housebound or indigent parishioner); or she could react to a faint steeliness in his voice that was not there before.

'We were discussing just that proposal when you arrived.'

'Yes,' Sanderson said. 'It is a pleasant enough drive and the weather is wonderfully clement. If you have the time, nothing could be more agreeable, I am sure.'

'I am not here on holiday, however. Alfie believes Mr Duxbury to be a valuable fund of local knowledge.'

'I doubt it,' Sanderson said shortly. 'What is agreeable about the expedition is the scenery. Particularly lovely chestnuts along the road.'

'You mean to warn me, however.'

'My dear Mrs Wallis, it is no part of my duty to warn you of anything. You are here for a purpose greater than sightseeing, I can see that, though I do not enquire what it is. I will simply say that sometimes it is better to let sleeping dogs lie.'

'Is that how parish duties are conceived here in Yorkshire?'

He flushed. Like a good curate, he was too astute to lose his temper completely. Instead, he steepled his fingers and touched them to his lips, all the while looking at her with a very level gaze indeed.

'Pay me the compliment of believing I have your best interests at heart,' he said finally. 'You saw Lady Gollinge and her companion yesterday, I understand.'

'In astonishing circumstances.'

'Alfie told me. I am sorry to have you witness that. It is a great scandal.'

'Everything has its explanation, however. Do you have views, Mr Sanderson?'

'Views? They have put themselves out of reach of normal society, this much we know. I don't think it is likely to turn out to be for any very sinister reason. They do not like the world as they find it. Nor do many others, albeit of different stripe. And so: let it be.'

'Their behaviour doesn't interest you?'

'It does not.'

'And Mr Duxbury?'

He flapped his hands, as though shooing away a fly.

'A harmless buffoon. I should add you have by no means exhausted Alfie's store of local eccentrics. According to him, Old Mother Marriot, a whiskery lady who smokes a pipe down by the canal, can spell warts and drive away the devil from a fractious child. Sergeant Lowden, late of the Green Jackets, speaks in tongues. It is said he can stop clocks just by looking at them. And so on. This is not society London, Mrs Wallis. We are neighbourly with our madmen, if you wish to see it that way.'

'I will put it to you bluntly, Mr Sanderson. What might I discover about Lady Gollinge in particular that is best left undisturbed?'

'To speak bluntly? Towering stupidity and self-regard. Most of all and much more serious, a vast emptiness. A desert.'

'I have never seen a desert,' Bella said.

'But then of course she has. In Australia, I understand.'

It suddenly fell into place: the nakedness, the tribal markings, bows and arrows, hunting and gathering. It was as though Sanderson had known about this all along but despaired of her making the connection for herself. Bella stared at him incredulously. The curate permitted himself something of an unchristian smirk.

'I have never seen these women out on the moor but any number of small boys have had their bottoms reddened for spying. The children think of them as grown-ups playing at Red Indians. Their parents take a more sanguine view.'

'You did not think to tell me about this at the very beginning?'

He dropped his eyes to poke about in his string bag.

'These onions are for old Mrs Jeffreys. She eats them raw to ward off the cold. Mrs Jeffreys was a babe in arms at the Peterloo Massacre. Her mother was sabred by a dragoon, you understand, and her father carried her as far from Manchester as was possible for a man with no work and sought by the police and their informers at every turn. I do not say this in any political sense, but Lady Gollinge is not fit to lick her boots. Ah, here is Alfie with my doughnuts.'

'You don't see a small mystery with these two women that is worth your solving, Mr Sanderson?'

'Whenever I want to be taxed by mysteries, Mrs Wallis, I open the piano lid and take a turn at Schumann.'

Prig! Bella almost shouted in his face.

The walk to Duxbury's cave was along the foot of an impressive limestone reef. Sheep and the locals had made quite a little path and the going was steep but easy. The hermit greeted them with great good humour, pulling Bella up by her wrists into a roomy opening in the rock. Presents were offered and accepted – a few links of sausages, a box of vegetables, a pound of tea and some twist tobacco.

Duxbury was a very unbiblical hermit. Despite his long hair and straggling beard he managed to persist with something of his former character, which was that of a chatty and whimsical tobacconist in good standing with his customers. There were certainly difficulties in his appearance to overcome, as for instance the woman's burgundy velvet frock he wore over some disgraceful trousers; and the bulkiness that came as a consequence of sporting two short jackets, one worn over the other. He smelled – the whole cave smelled – of wood smoke and this had also coloured his face yellow. On his hands were grey woollen mittens.

Duxbury smiled. 'You have come from London, I perceive. The Queen is sad. Today she lost a silver thimble and all the fine ladies are searching for it. No,' he chuckled, as if witnessing the scene, 'it is not *there*.'

'It has rolled under the piano,' Bella said firmly, astonishing Alfie and causing Duxbury to look at her in a different light.

'Take a pew,' he suggested, indicating a shelf of rock. 'The lad will mash us some tea. There is neither milk nor sugar in the house but you won't mind that.'

'You call this your house?'

'I speak as I have always spoke. It is my dwelling, if you prefer that way of looking at it. Yes, you can say that people of our class live in dwellings. You are looking at me out the corner of your eyes, widow-woman.'

Spencer Gore, all-England tennis champion, could not have put her on the back foot more successfully.

'How did you know I was widowed?'

Duxbury made little twittering gestures with his fingers. They were perhaps meant to indicate information that was carried on the ether.

'Is there no man in my life, then?'

'For sure! How could there not be, you as young and beautiful as you are? But there is trouble there, too.'

'What sort of trouble?'

Duxbury smiled and found a new job for his hands, palms up, as he once might have done when a customer commented on a week of rain.

'Isn't the heart nowt but a cabinet with hidden drawers? Who can say what troubles a man must keep therein?'

'Therein?' Bella scoffed.

'Therein,' the hermit repeated nonchalantly.

He was less flowery on the domestic economy of living alone in the cleft of a rock. Duxbury did not hunt rabbits with a bow and arrow like his neighbours: he trapped them with the help of a spool of silk line someone had bought him to catch trout by. Nettles grew a little way off and he enjoyed those for what he called their roughage. Docks would not kill you if boiled down to a green paste; and dandelions (though hard to find) had a fresh nip to them that was delicious. He had even feasted on wild strawberries in his time. And – as this morning – nobody who came to see him ever came empty-handed. He showed Bella his two tin saucepans and an iron kettle, his kitchen knife and coal hammer. There was a cabinet of curios arranged on rocks at the back of the cave – a mouse skull, ram's horns, a snakeskin, some blunt and orange teeth from the carcass of a sheep. Wrapped in a scrap of cloth were a belt buckle and a tin watch with a broken glass.

'These were Raybould the murderer's,' he said.

'He is dead?'

'Oh, I found *him* in a beck. Down there, where the

mine is. I buried him two years back. Leastways, covered him in rocks. So now he is a waterfall.'

'And you told no one? Not the police or anyone?'

'The police,' the hermit scolded gently. 'I think you are a free spirit, lass, same as me. What are the police to such as us? I have yet to meet a philosophical one.'

'Do you know how he died?'

'He was quite unable to help me on that.'

Duxbury's smile had the same power of insinuation as smoke or water. There is no smoke without fire, Bella thought wildly. For all his mask of amiability this is a dangerous hermit.

'How did you know I was a widow?' she repeated abruptly. 'And the truth this time.'

'It needed no special gift,' Duxbury replied. 'Alfie thinks I am a bit of a wizard, don't you, old lad? I am not. For thirty years I stood behind a counter selling folk stuff. I were very bad at it, for I cared less about the money than the look in their eye or the shape their mouths took when speaking. Each one was a walking history book. The money was just bits of copper or silver. Only a fool thinks about money. You're a lass that understands all that.'

'What else can you see in my face, then?'

'You're a wilful woman, that much anyone can see. You have no children and it says summat about you that you appear not to have paid much mind to that fact. You're not rich but then again you're not poor neither. You'd as soon live with women as with men.'

'You're very impudent, Mr Duxbury.'

'Aye, well,' the hermit smiled, taking his tea from Alfie and wafting it cool with a mittened hand. Living alone had given him the gift of switching off. He was waiting, Bella knew he was waiting, and try as she might, she could not bring herself to stay silent.

'And the man who is in my life now?'

'Is in some trouble,' Duxbury said calmly, fixing her with his pale blue eyes. 'He is that. Just at the moment, like, I would say he is arse over tip in calamity.'

Fog. No, not fog but clouds, the kind you look down on from mountain peaks. Philip knew he was nowhere near a mountain and that the lowering crag in front of him was a kneeling man. Better in the end to say fog. Mental fog. Better. It was the thing gnawing at his shoulder that was causing the problem. If he had the strength he would brush it away. But then all his strength was taken up in stopping his eyes from rolling.

'Listen to me,' the kneeling man said, slapping Philip's face gently to get his attention. 'My wife thinks we should rob you more and then kill you.'

'You already have everything,' Philip mumbled. His tongue seemed to have turned to wool in his mouth and he was finding it hard to hear himself speak for the singing in his ears. Stinging sweat ran into his eyes.

'Yes, that is true,' the man said. 'I have your watch, your wallet, your excellent boots. When people stay at hotels, they pay for their room, don't they? Ach so, this is not a proper hotel and we are poor. But not stupid. You have been talking in your sleep, Englishman. At first we thought you were from Berlin, such correct German, so fine an accent. But now we know.'

'Then you know my friends are coming for me.'

William Kennett, he thought deliriously. And Bella. Bella naked in the bedroom, turning a hip towards the door, a hairbrush in her hand. She is coming for me. She cannot abide fog. Or woolliness. He smacked his lips together a few times to bring his tongue to its proper duty.

'At least tell me where I am,' he said in a much clearer voice.

'You are four kilometres from Essen,' the man explained gently. 'They are looking for you everywhere.'

'Haven't I just said that?'

'No, not your friends! The police! And Krupp's men. Herr Furst has been arrested and taken by train to Berlin to answer certain questions. The cab driver who dumped you here has fled. He has relatives in Duisburg. One way and another, things are not good for you.'

'Then I must thank you for harbouring me.'

'Is that what you think? We are waiting to see whether there is a reward for your capture.'

'You say Furst has been arrested?'

'Your partner in crime.'

'I need a doctor and a telegraph office.'

'And us? For the risk we are taking? What is there in that for us?'

If I could sit up, Philip thought. If I could look out of the cobwebbed window and see the lie of the land. The road, for example: Is it a highway or some benighted farm track? This is not a house but it is not a cow byre either. This man is not a farmer: What farmers wear is not what he has on.

He racked his brains furiously before it came to him. He was talking to a postman.

'I am not worth anything to you dead. You're a sensible fellow. There is money in this for you. Are you going to kill me for a watch and a pair of boots?'

'Maybe you die anyway.'

'No,' Philip said with terrible lassitude, his eyelids quivering. 'If I was going to die of the gunshot wound I would already be dead. Listen to me. *Listen*.'

But whatever he was going to say floated away, like thistledown. He scrabbled feebly to find the man's hand, gave up and closed his eyes with an almost sensual abandon. For God's sake put some clothes on, Bella, he pleaded. You are acting as if it is Tuesday morning.

The postman's wife had joined her husband and stood watching Philip, arms folded. Unhappy marriage had turned her lips down at the edges and made her neck gaunt. She was insect-thin and breastless in a village of buxom and blustering neighbours but she had discovered a great truth in life. Once you are famous for never smiling, never deigning to look anyone in the eye, acting as though others did not exist, it is the easiest thing in the world to instil respect. Terror is a form of respect.

'What has he been talking about?' she asked. Her husband looked up at her.

'Gold,' he improvised. 'He wants a telegraph office.'

'Not here, for God's sake.'

'Of course not here.'

The woman thought about it, hugging her bony ribs. For something to do, she reached down and pulled the socks from Philip's feet, rolling them into a ball and stuffing them into the pocket of her pinafore.

'He can go to your brother,' she decided.

'The journey will kill him!'

'Hans-Georg can negotiate a price with London. He can do that for me.'

'For us,' her husband pointed out, without much hope of being listened to.

'Dig a trench,' she said. 'In case he does not recover in time to make the journey.'

'You want me to bury him?' the postman asked, amazed.

'What is *your* plan?' his wife retorted in her most cutting voice. 'Should we prop him up at the kitchen table?'

The postman's plan was to put him in a wheelbarrow and take Westland across the fields to the marshes and leave him to sink or swim. He had a horror of burying him in the garden. There was nothing religious about this. He was thinking of his neighbour's dogs.

'He isn't dead yet,' his wife said. 'Make him some soup.'

The postman seized his wife by her scrawny throat. It was not much of a marriage they had, but a man was a man.

'*You* make him some soup,' he commanded savagely and was rewarded by her mocking smile.

EIGHT

To her surprise – and a little to her irritation – Bella found herself increasingly taken with the hermit's conversation. What would have been tedious about Duxbury had she been trapped by him in a railway carriage or on some park bench was transformed by circumstance. Viewed from his cave, Yorkshire seemed huge, silent and invitingly empty. Reason told Bella that only two miles away there existed a town, a castle, a railway station, the canal and the River Aire itself – but they were all as if spirited away by some giant hand. It was a giddy feeling.

The sun helped, making Bella feel warm and relaxed for the first time in days. When Alfie pointed out a kestrel circling high overhead, the three of them watched it with the same patience it showed in hunting out its prey. It was a long time since Bella had given anything in nature more attention than she did habitually to the printed page. She was saddened to see the bird move away over their heads to begin quartering the limestone bluff.

'You were saying,' she resumed drily.

For how the former tobacconist liked to talk, even going so far as to rise in the middle of an anecdote and walk to the edge of the cave to empty his bladder without so much as a breath to interrupt his story, the next elements of which he threw over his shoulder. The noisy splashing he made meanwhile shocked Alfie but amused Bella. She liked Duxbury for his cheery nonchalance, which he salted from time to time with the sort of prophetic remarks hermits are supposed to make.

'Take young Alfie here. He has a small fortune in ha'pennies and pennies he keeps under a floorboard in his room. When he has enough, he will leave his old mother and make his way to London. For there he has a mind to open a little shop and marry a pretty girl.'

'How did you know that?' Alfie asked, amazed.

'A little bird told me.'

'No, I mean about where I keep my savings?'

Bella could guess easily enough: from his mother's several visits to see the hermit on other matters.

'And will he be happy when he is in London?' she asked.

'There will be setbacks,' the hermit said calmly. 'Selling sweeties is a difficult trade.'

'But how did you know it was going to be a sweetie shop?' Alfie yelped in anguish. Duxbury, who had sold a few hundredweight of sweeties in his day and had listened more than a few times to the boy's inventory of Minshall's stall on the market, gave Bella a sly glance.

What was to have been an hour's visit stretched into a day out. They made a round of Duxbury's rabbit traps (from one of which came his evening meal, despatched by Alfie) and listened to his unembarrassed prosing about Dame Nature, a lady who much resembled (one could say) a buxom apple-seller on Leeds Market. Alfie was a far more accurate guide to plants and insects, and his respect for the hermit was sorely tried on occasion; but the three dawdled the afternoon away in great content. Bella even found pleasure in watching Duxbury skin and quarter his rabbit.

Pressed by the hermit to stay and share the eating of it, she was torn between refusing and prolonging her visit to enjoy the late afternoon light washing the valley in water-colour tints. Moreover (she was forced to admit) for all his cheap theatrical effects and relentless jollity, there was something about the hermit she needed just as keenly as the credulous Alfie. After a few moments she accepted his invitation, on condition that Alfie returned to Skipton. She would follow in her own good time with the last hour of dusk to see her home.

'I am not happy with that,' the boy said.

'Then take the trap back and see to the mare, have a bite to eat yourself and then – if you must – come back on foot and I will meet you along the road. No harm shall come to me, Alfie, I promise.'

'What shall I tell the hotel?'

'You need tell them nothing. I am not a schoolgirl to be fussed over.'

Duxbury said goodbye to the disconsolate Alfie by ruffling his hair and patting him gently on the back.

'You can leave her safe with me, lad. I'll see to it she walks home before it comes full dark.'

'Y'ave talked all bloody day. What else is there to say to each other?'

'Well, I'll tell you next time I see you.'

'But Mr Sanderson has warned me to keep an eye on her.'

'Is that true?' Bella flashed. 'He used those exact words? Then be off with you right now, you impudent boy. And you may tell Mr Sanderson I shall not need your protection any longer, for I return to London tomorrow.'

Which was bluster of the worst kind, shaming enough to send her stomping out of the cave and heading towards the stream a hundred yards away, where Duxbury drew his water. Once there, she flung herself down onto a rock slab, her head in her hands. Her petulance was at full bore: had Alfie followed her down she would have brained him for certain – but when she looked round, he had gone. She calmed herself by taking off her boots and stockings and dabbling her feet in the water. It was cold enough to make her arteries jump.

Bella had an eye for nature, however uneducated it might be. By sitting still and letting her mind wander, she began to see more; and more deeply. Nor did Duxbury do anything, by a single word or gesture, to break this mood. When she looked back into the cave he was on his knees at the entrance, stewing the rabbit. Everything that was fanciful about him for the moment fell away. He was simply an elderly man who had to eat to live. It touched Bella that in a month, a year, five years hence, she might close her eyes at this time of day and imagine the hermit just as he was now.

She found herself thinking about the first time she and Philip had made love. That had taken place not in London but what had struck her at the time as the wilds of Shropshire. The same huge skies, the same unblinking indifference to human wishes. Set down in even the most commonplace of landscapes, how small she had seemed, how fatuous. She grimaced. For all his faults, the hermit had overcome something she did not like to admit in herself – a faint terror of nature. Trees could not love. Grass gave back nothing but stains. As if to punctuate these unhappy thoughts, a fly with brown mottled wings landed on the softer part of her bare calf and stung her painfully.

She walked into the stream with her skirts drawn up to her hips the better to dab water on the place, when something extraordinary caught her eye. Bobbing towards her was a paper boat, such as children make. It was broad enough in the beam not to have been capsized but with such plucky little ships things are usually undone so soon as they are waterlogged. This one showed no signs of foundering. It was only recently made.

Bella jumped out of the stream and scanned as far as she could see in every direction. Reason suggested she look for a child but her heart thumped out another possibility. She was being watched – and not by any adorable urchin. For a second or so her scalp crawled. Looked at in this new way, every shadowed fold or dip in the ground seemed malign. She sat down heavily and scrambled for her stockings.

And now is the time to get hold of yourself, she scolded, as clearly as if she had spoken these words aloud. If they have managed to get this close without being observed, you will not find them now – and even if you do, you are risking an arrow in your ribs. You are being toyed with: stay calm. For all they know, you are just another Skipton biddy come to see the hermit and this is their way of frightening you. But you are not frightened. You are their equal in brains and courage. You are Philip Westland's woman. He has not chosen a ninny to adore.

All the same, her defiance was not strong enough to make her call out or go and look for them. The idea of coming across two naked women and facing them down in a mutton-sleeved blouse and linen skirt was less than attractive. Quite right, a ghostly Philip agreed. Just this once, a lofty indifference is the better part. Perhaps a little insouciant whistling. I think moving back towards the cave could be seen as a mere tactical withdrawal, *reculer pour mieux sauter*. Scowling and scratching your insect bite is quite the wrong thing.

'I need to smoke,' she said aloud.

Duxbury was hymn-singing when she walked back to the cave. Mad as he was, the sight of him poking about in his saucepan of stew was very reassuring. Bella found her bag and lit a cheroot, scanning the ground in front of the cave for signs of movement. It was all as peaceful as a churchyard. For all that, she felt jumpy.

Ursula Gollinge could not have made the paper boat; no one who spoke in such a clacking humourless voice, who was so positive of her own worth, would waste time folding paper. But Bella could imagine Amelia doing it. It was the difference between the petulant child who cannot hear how she sounds to others, who never listens to others, never looks out of the schoolroom window; and the sly companion she has designated as her best friend. And if so – if Amelia had sailed the boat towards her – maybe it was merely a joke, a spur-of-the-moment tease. Maybe, she forced herself to think, it was harmless.

'We shan't be long,' Duxbury promised, forcing her to turn her attention back to the cave interior.

'Do you entertain often?' she asked in the most casual tone possible.

'Never,' he murmured, without turning his head.

'The ladies from Cruddas never come to see you?'

'They do not and nor would they be welcome. Any more than the Bishop of Ripon and his lady. Hermits are picky folk.'

'I am your generous exception, then.'

Duxbury glanced up at her with an unsettling absence of levity.

'I asked you to stay on because you have something to say to me you could not speak of in front of the boy,' he pointed out, as if to a child. Bella felt herself blush.

'I do want to talk. But the man I most want to talk to is not in the country at the moment I think you know that.'

'It is written in your face. You are worried for his safety. And of course, you have a great decision to make.'

'And what might that be?'

'Why, whether to marry him,' Duxbury smiled.

'So now you are setting up as a consultant in marriage? Are you really the right person, I wonder?'

'None better. I was married at twenty and lived with the same woman for thirty-two years. We gave it a fair go together, buried all four parents, had two children of our own, watched them go the same road as us. And it came to me one day that I had seen nothing and understood nothing.'

'And since then you have been up here?'

'No better off to be sure,' Duxbury admitted. 'Only lonelier. Of course, my sad story will never happen to you.'

'Can you say why, hermit?'

'You ask too many questions for a start! You're a well set-up woman, a fine woman, no doubt about that, but in a general way you're as jumpy as a cat on hot cinders. It will take a bold man to tame you. Mebbe a desert sheikh might do it. Or an Indian prince, summat of that ilk. I speak frankly.'

'You speak as you find, as I have heard them say up here.'

'You don't recognise the picture I'm drawing?'

'That I'm jumpy? That may be so.'

'To be bold about it: you have come up here on a wild goose chase. You're not going to tell me what, though I can guess. Today you had a good time of it and the frown went out of your face. Isn't that so?'

'I have enjoyed myself. You are a good host.'

'I am,' the hermit agreed calmly. 'And then all of a sudden you let yourself be trapped into saying you will go home on the morrow to spite a boy who has only half your brains.'

'I did not wish to spite him. The idea is ridiculous. I have things to do in London. Important things,' she blustered.

'I don't doubt. But what's in your mind right now is what brought you up here in the first place.'

'And do your powers extend to telling me what that is?'

'They do,' Duxbury said, pointing the stick he was using

to stir the pot. But the gesture was far from comical. 'You want me to say the madwoman and her chit of a lover, o' course.'

'What about them?' Bella asked.

'Aye, what about them? Circus animals, I call 'em. But I don't think it's them that brought you up here. Not really. They were just the excuse to get you on a train and hop off out of things for a while.'

'You can't know that.'

'Can I not? The top and bottom of this whole jaunt, my dear, has been that you don't like who you are.'

Bella flinched. What the hermit said might be true but it was hard to take. Who does like who they are? Duxbury's remark was of the kind that she would have demolished in any salon in London but was not so easy to deny here, with his lined and filthy face turned towards her, not even the ghost of a smile left on it.

'The reason is simple enough,' the hermit said.

Which is how she came to unburden her heart to a bundle of rags, while eating a rabbit stew she did not want and taking as her pudding a raw carrot he produced from a grimy paper sack. Duxbury was a good listener. Skipton was as far as he had ever travelled in his life but as she talked she sensed he could see and understand Orange Street and the intimacy it harboured. Alfie's idea of London was a fantasy and that was its appeal; but the hermit had the intuitive power the boy lacked. He did not see streets or buildings, but people. By her account of them, she saw that he recognised that Quigley would fail to understand him completely and that Billy Murch would find a way to use him, but the man he connected to most strongly was the mild-mannered and reclusive Charles Urmiston. Another shopkeeper, she thought hazily.

Like soldiers in their bivouac, they shared the last of Bella's cheroots. The hermit poked up the fire, for it was growing cold, and when she looked out of the cave's entrance, she saw that a vast mauve dusk had overtaken the valley.

'I must go,' she said.

'Aye and so you must.'

'I have said too much.'

Duxbury smiled and gently laid his blackened hand on her sleeve.

'You have told me nothing very much, widow-woman, and yet you have told me everything. The one gentleman you have not described in any detail is your friend Mr Westland. But were he to walk in here right now I should know him instantly, because of what you have told me about yourself.'

'Am I so very obvious?'

'I've told you about my marriage, haven't I? The kiddies and everything. *Their* kiddies. But the only time I ever understood another human being was with a man. His name was Franks. Nothing funny, if you take my meaning. We used to meet up once a week to play crib and sup ale. We did this for twenty or more years. I could get an idea of who he was just because he was another man, you understand. Married, like me. Ugly, like me. We got on famously.'

'What did you talk about?'

Duxbury laughed. 'We hardly said a word to each other in all that time. And certain-sure nothing deep. When he died, I saw that we had been made for each other. But he had to die first. People ask me what I miss about my old life. They mean armchairs and Sunday roast and the like. But the answer is Harry Franks. And you don't want to be going down that road.'

'Is there any hope for me, hermit?' she wailed.

'Tha'll do,' he murmured peaceably.

She bade him goodbye. It was by now dark enough to make the path back to the main road alarmingly hard to follow. What had seemed like a level walk in the morning was beset with rocks and unseen tussocks of grass that snatched at her feet. The safest way to navigate was to edge her way along the bluff, like someone feeling their way in a darkened room, their back to the wall. She was soon stranded on a narrow shelf that led nowhere and was forced to retrace her steps. To her dismay, she found herself walking downhill more than she remembered was necessary. Chilly though the night air was, she felt a trickle of sweat run down her ribs. She was lost.

The hand that closed over her mouth was warm and damp. The body that pressed against her back was unmistakably a woman's, soft and weighted in a way no man was fashioned. The low gurgling laugh in her ear belonged to the creature she had dreaded most to meet.

'Let me show you the way, my lovely,' Amelia whispered. And with that she threw her spare arm across Bella's stomach and ran her down a steep slope. Nothing could prevent them both from tumbling, which they did, rolling over and over. They fetched up in the beck, grunting like wrestlers, arms and legs flailing. Bella first had the breath knocked out of her and then her head hit a boulder. There was a flash as brief as lightning and the world disappeared.

'Mrs Bella Wallis, of 18 Orange Street,' Ursula Gollinge mocked. 'Such a very commonplace London address.'

'How do you know my name?'

'From your *carte de visite*. How thoughtful of you to carry it about. You need not feel your skull so tenderly. No skin has been broken.'

Bella looked about her. She was in what had once been a drawing room with plaster moulded ceilings and all the rest of what constituted eighteenth-century taste. A once-white marble fireplace, internal shutters to the long windows, an oak floor. This was a mine-owner's consolation prize to his wife for living so far from the Assembly Rooms in York, or the gathering of the gentry at Norton Ferrers or Castle Howard. Those who had once sat in this room were the remote echo of such taste and refinement but not without determination. In the Yorkshire way of things, they were as good as anybody else and a great deal better than some. And then, gradually, time had overtaken the property. From being a proud statement of intent, the room had dwindled to what it was now. Which was not much better than a cow byre.

What furniture there was had been stacked recklessly at one end of the room, higgledy-piggledy. Table stood upon table, rugs and carpets were rolled or draped in the gaps between and – in Bella's eyes most wantonly of all – two hundred or so calf-bound books were scattered about like autumn leaves. By the side of the hearth, piled any which way, were boughs, lengths of sawn wood and several hundredweights of loose coal.

'What an eye for good living you have,' Bella commented. 'Never let anyone tell you pigs could do better.'

Ursula was wearing what she took at first to be a penitential sack but the colour – olive green – and the decoration – crow feathers and scraps of cloth – proposed another possibility. Lady Gollinge had dressed for the evening.

'You are pondering how and when to make a dash for it, Mrs Wallis. I strongly advise against that. Amelia is a dead shot with a bow. You wouldn't get very far.'

'People will be wondering where I am,' Bella warned.

'You think they will come looking for you with torches? What a vivid imagination you have. The white man takes time to make up his mind.'

'You are yourself not white, of course.'

'I am white-skinned,' Lady Ursula allowed with magnificent hauteur. 'But there is an end to it.'

'And Amelia?'

'Is likewise gatekeeper to a better spiritual universe. Perhaps I should say a more real world.'

'You astonish me, Lady Gollinge,' Bella said with enough sarcasm to bring the ceiling down around their ears.

'I do not recognise myself in that title. The little fat woman in Windsor gave my husband a knighthood and then locked him in an asylum. All of that has nothing to do with me. People like you have nothing to do with me.'

'Then I wonder why I am here.'

'For my pleasure,' Ursula said. 'And to teach you something. Perhaps they will come here with torches. But only to ask whether I have come across any trace of you out on the moors. They don't like me but they have no reason to suspect me. The easiest explanation for your disappearance is that the earth has swallowed you up. Which is what I shall suggest.'

She leaned forward and stroked Bella's cheek with a grubby hand.

'How sad! You missed your way in the dark and fell into a disused mine. Which, when I have done with you, is just what will happen.'

'And what possible gain is there in that for you?'

'For me? None in particular. But the spirits who govern everything will be placated.'

'You are quite mad.'

'Do you know, I think I am,' Lady Gollinge said comfortably. 'There's great power in madness. The earth shall be cleansed by it. You are here to be sacrificed, Mrs Bella Wallis of Orange Street in London. Something wonderful will happen to you at last.'

NINE

What struck Alfie most was the noise, the raw ripping and shredding of sulphurous air by shrieks and hoots, booming crashes and frantic clatter. There was no calm, no shelter – the cacophony seemed to run up and down the yellow walls like a lunatic. Perhaps a thousand people were bustling and shouting and the half-glimpsed roads and pavements beyond were black with others. It was raining hard and the gutters overflowed with filth. Immediately at Alfie's feet the water ran red: a cab horse had been pierced in the belly by a badly loaded dray and was on its knees, dying. Two men with hammers were trying to kill it stone dead by a blow to its head. A woman bystander sank to the pavement in a faint.

And the stink! Of soot and tobacco, fish and cabbages, horse piss and cooking fat, sweat and bay rum, wet cotton and rotting teeth! In the middle of it all, as if dumped there by capricious gods, an honour party of Guards in long grey coats and huge busbies, slow-marched a coffin draped in a Union flag towards a gun carriage. The officer in charge of the party carried a drawn sword. General Powicke-Elsom, who had stood his ground and served his Queen all these many years, was on the last leg of his journey from Quatre Bras to the Guards Chapel. Welcome to King's Cross – welcome to the hub of Empire.

'Orange Street?' Alfie asked of a newspaper-seller sheltering under a canvas booth. The man jerked his chin by way of reply and the boy thought for a moment he was being given directions but all that was indicated was a policeman in a streaming tarpaulin cape.

'Now why would you want to go there?' this great man asked – Alfie's first taste of metropolitan condescension.

'Important message for a party.'

The policeman eyed him up and down in a leisurely way, wiping his moustaches by way of punctuation.

'Look like a drowned rat, you do.'

'Well, I aren't.'

'You're a lucky young sprout. And do you know for why? Wasn't I born in Bedford Street, which is not a thousand miles away from where you want?'

'Is it far?'

'Say an hour's brisk march,' the policeman said teasingly. Alfie merely nodded. Before this introduction to London he had formed no real idea of its size but the noise and confusion all around him indicated something huge, maybe a place as big as France, of which he had heard some details from Mr Sanderson. On the other hand, an hour's walk was nothing very much to a country boy and the policeman's jocularity fell flat. He was posted off down the Euston Road with a hearty shove in the back and instructions to bear left down Tottenham Court Road.

As Alfie squelched away, the constable straightened up and touched the brim of his helmet to a short and well-dressed man with a pale, unsmiling face.

'What is an hour's brisk march away?' Sergeant Tubney asked.

'Just a bit of fun with a country lad. A little gentle ragging to keep him up to snuff. The youth was asking after Orange Street.'

'Did he have luggage with him?'

'A cotton bag, slung over his shoulder, erm, on the right side if I recall.'

'Had he come out of the station?'

'Just popped up from nowhere. Swum up, if truth were known.'

'You called him a country boy.'

'Maybe a Yorkie. A Manc, maybe. Thick spoke, hard to understand. The way they rumble.'

'And a boy?'

'Wiry enough, but a boy, yes.'

'And why did he want to go to Orange Street?'

The policeman studied Tubney with just the tiniest flicker of fear in his eyes. Knew the bastard, a pushy cove if ever there was one and the scourge of the thieves and villains who worked the station. Attached to the Somers Town nick for the past month but never seen there. Had taken rooms for himself in Cartwright Gardens, if you please, as high and mighty as the Commissioner himself.

'Did you have an interest in the youth?' he temporised.

'Just answer the question.'

'Said he had a message to deliver.'

Tubney was already walking away.

'Well,' said Mrs Venn, pushing a strong cup of tea towards Alfie. Every stitch of clothing he had was hung on the backs of chairs in front of the open range. 'If this don't take the biscuit, coming in here like something fished out the Thames.'

'If I could have them clothes back—'

'Have them back! What, and have you die of cold right here in my kitchen? Hannah, my dear, give him another brisk-up with that towel.'

Hannah Bardsoe, who was visiting, beckoned Alfie to her.

'Come here, Carrot-top. And don't be shy about it. Me and Mrs Venn first seen what you've got to offer between your legs when we was blushing maidens ourselves.'

Unwillingly, Alfie gave up the towel round his waist and submitted to being buffed. Red as his skin was, his face was redder. Hannah kissed him absent-mindedly on his naked shoulder.

'Don't you worry. You're a good boy, I'm sure, and you're among friends. Cover your dignity and go sit near the range. And tell us your tale once again.'

It was five days since Bella's disappearance. The police had searched the house in Cruddas without result and though no one trusted Ursula Gollinge further than they could throw her, they were investigating her version of events: that this amiable London lady had called one night, having lost herself out on the moor. Had stayed for a meal and a bed and set off next morning with a view to inspecting the chapel at Ruthley before returning to Skipton. When the police investigated this location, they did in fact find a lady's bag. Empty, the way robbers leave bags.

'But you didn't believe this Gollinge creature, Alfie dear?'

'Not for a minute.'

'And for why?'

'Because there's nowt worth the seeing at the Ruthley chapel. It lacks a roof and is hardly bigger'n this here kitchen, just a pile of old stones. And more than that, I know Mrs Wallis. I have a fair idea of how she goes about things. They're lying.'

'They?'

'Gollinge and the lass 'Melia.'

'So then where is she, my mistress?' Dora Venn asked.

That was it, that was the reason why Alfie had prised up the floorboard in his bedroom and weighed out his hoard of coppers at the bank and taken the train to London. He did not believe she was dead or lost. He thought she was held captive somewhere by Ursula Gollinge, reasons unknown. There were details to his story that merely confused the two women: for example, Duxbury and Mr Sanderson. But the outline was clear. Something very nasty had happened to Bella.

'This Skipton place seems altogether a bit on the primitive side,' Dora Venn declared. 'I ain't ever been to Yorkshire but they don't seem to have their heads on the right way round. You have a few intelligent policemen up there, do you?'

'Out on the moors every day, additional sent for from Keighley. But the weather's turned, same as it has down here, and the search is going slow. Mr Sanderson thinks—'

'Yes, and is he the fat-arse one? He don't seem to have extended himself much – and him a man of the cloth.'

'What it is, Dora,' Hannah Bardsoe interrupted gently,

'this ain't going to be decided by the two of *us*. I'm wondering whether I shouldn't take this little ankle-biter back with me to meet my Charlie. Percy Quigley neither use nor ornament and in any case he ain't there, not at the present.'

'You think it needs a man's touch?'

'I do. *You* can't go nowhere, case she comes home. But Charlie might have an idea or two. He's very steady in this sort of situation.'

Mrs Venn passed Alfie his shirt and trousers and began pulling out the newspaper with which she had stuffed his very unsuitable boots. There was a point of etiquette here. She was Bella's servant and the meeting was taking place in her kitchen. It was for her to say what to do next, something Mrs Bardsoe understood only too well.

'We could run him round to that little chancer Tubney,' Dora suggested doubtfully. There was an eloquent silence, taken up in watching Alfie trying to get his strides on without making a peepshow of it. Then her common sense cut in.

'That's a very bad idea,' she admitted. 'I don't know what made me say it. Have your Charlie give the boy the once-over. But mind, Mrs B, I shall want to know what's decided.'

'Goes without saying,' Hannah agreed. 'He'll stop with us tonight and I'll be round in the morning with a full report.'

Which is how Alfie found himself walking up the Charing Cross Road, eating a toffee apple and being scolded to keep his feet out of the puddles by the good-natured Mrs Bardsoe. Neither of them noticed a sallow man with an impeccably tailored topcoat following after them, first on one side of the road, then the other.

'Well,' Charles Urmiston said in his usual quiet, kindly voice, 'I would say you have done exactly the right thing, Alfie. Mrs Wallis can be proud to count you as her friend. I don't suppose you saw into Lady Gollinge's house your-self? No, and how could you? But you think she might be hidden there?'

'They have her hid away somewhere for sure, the barm-pots.'

'Yes, I can see your thinking there. But here's a thing. Why would they want to do that?'

Alfie had no answer. Urmiston picked up Hannah's plump little fist and bounced it gently on the chenille cloth covering the table.

'Mrs Bardsoe here is unshockable, Alfie. Between us, we have met some very rum characters out there in the shop, not all of them twenty shillings to the pound. And there have been others,' he added. 'Now, put your manners aside and tell us in what way these two women are a danger, as I take you to mean.'

'Anyone can see it.'

'Yes. But suppose you tell us what *you* have seen?'

When the story came out of hunting naked with bows and arrows, Alfie was surprised to find it was the gentleman who blushed and not Hannah. She grabbed the boy delight-edly by the ears and wiggled his head from side to side, laughing at his description of sooty breasts and white-washed faces.

'If that don't merit the word "barmy", I don't know

what does. It's as good as anything in any book I've ever read and that's no error!'

Charles Urmiston winced and when she realised what she had just said, Hannah did the same. Alfie misunderstood this exchange.

'I only looked at them a few times,' he said, hot in the face. 'Just to get at the cut of their jib –' snorting laughter from Hannah '– and Mrs Wallis saw them, same as me, the day before she disappeared. I think she knowed 'em from down here. Duxbury the hermit says she had come to see them special.'

'Duxbury the hermit,' Urmiston repeated faintly. He did not wish to be disloyal to Bella but what dearest Hannah had blurted out rang true. Henry Ellis Margam had stumbled into one of his own plots – perhaps it would be kinder to say into a story by one of his racier competitors.

'We can do nothing more today, Alfie. You will sleep here tonight. Mrs Bardsoe and I will debate what to do and in the morning we shall have a clear plan.'

'There is a particular gentleman Mrs Wallis is attached to,' Alfie pointed out.

'There is indeed. But Mr Westland is out of the country at the moment and cannot be reached. You will have to put your trust in me,' he added half-humorously.

Before bed, Alfie was give cocoa with an eggcupful of rum in it, which he counted the best thing that had ever passed his lips. Urmiston showed him to the attic, the room where he himself had started out in the house. He was bidden to sleep well and warned about the bottom step of the stairs, should he wish to visit the outside privy.

It was easy to miss, as Urmiston could testify to by personal experience.

'You have seen little enough of London, you poor chap.'

'I shall come back one day.'

'One day soon, perhaps. We take breakfast at five. There is a good train to Leeds a little before seven. After that, I am in your hands.'

'And safe enough,' Alfie promised.

'Is it bad, Charlie?' Hannah whispered after they had all three gone to bed. Urmiston kissed her on her doughy cheek.

'Bella has survived worse. I would match her against most women in the given circumstances. But you know I shall have to take that boy back to Yorkshire tomorrow, dearest heart. I have no choice in the matter.'

'Could you not lay the whole thing before Billy Murch?'

'Would that I could! But time is of the essence here. We must travel by the first available train. And in any case—'

Hannah humped herself round in the bed and landed on him like the plumpest mermaid ever scrambling for a rock. Her kisses were hot and salty.

'Dear, dear boy! You think they care nothing of you! That you are not a man for a crisis. How foolish is that. You have their complete respect from top to bottom. For courage and wise counsel alike.'

'A petty shopkeeper,' Urmiston said bitterly.

'Ho! Well, as to that you can hang up your apron any time that pleases you and go off to be a hero in more dangerous climes and among younger women, if that's how you see yourself. I never said you was a flashing blade or the best horseman in England. All that is for books, you great daftie.'

'Hannah—' he protested.

'I wouldn't trust you with anything bigger than an egg spoon, if it comes to that. But then again I wouldn't Mr Westland, neither. Petty shopkeeper! Well, if that don't beat all! The kindest, noblest—'

He kissed her, his free hand stroking her back, prickly tears in his eyes. It had long ago come to him that all he knew of women was to be found in the short library of Hannah Bardsoe's desires and passions. He loved her with an ache that hardly ever went away. When she said, as she often did, that they rubbed along well enough, he knew she was teasing him. Or, as she would put it, blowing fate a raspberry. Their kisses lengthened and she rolled him onto his hip.

'Be quiet, woman,' he whispered. 'I am planning my campaign.'

'Not tonight, Josephine,' she retorted, her hand reaching for him with a boisterousness that made him gasp.

Midnight in the Ruhr Valley, measured by the tolling of a church bell – not distant but located practically outside the window. Philip had been taken a journey to get to this room, flat on his back and covered in straw. Two men, or possibly one man talking to his horse, a bumpy ride that made thought impossible. Only tiny slivers of his transfer from the postman's house remained intact as he slipped in and out of consciousness. Some sort of alter-cation with a cart passing in the opposite direction; later on, an attack by a determined dog. A woman's voice, the sound of geese being driven somewhere. A distant *train* passing.

Nevertheless, a good church bell and a bed to sleep in were decidedly steps in the right direction. Hock the wrong thing to order but possibly a glass of beer, were this a hotel. Which it resolutely refused to become. My name is Philip Westland and I am having the greatest trouble in getting the world to stand still for a moment or two.

'It is your liver,' Bella said in that absent-minded scolding tone she reserved for discussions about health. She was speaking from a balloon quite a way off, possibly with the help of a nautical speaking trumpet.

'The liver, eh?'

He spoke these words aloud and they caused a sudden stirring of shadows. There was a very large man in these new quarters called Hans Georg (not that he introduced himself) and his wife, or possibly his daughter, Anna. Hans Georg kept cows and understood enough of how to physic them to be able to dress a gunshot wound and reduce a fever. Philip was the better for a scalding poultice of what might have been horse radish and a pint of thin gruel. His naked body had been sponged by Anna with well-water so deliciously cold he could have wished her to continue with it all night long. Instead, she sat with her hair in a long plait reading the Bible, her finger following the lines of print. A single wavering candle lit the room.

'The thing to be remembered about Quigley—' he mumbled. Anna looked up again.

'Yes, what about him?'

'I have forgotten.'

'Is this man your superior?'

'Which man?'

'Herr Quigley.'

'We quarrelled on the train back from Wiltshire. Urmiston—'

'Yes, who is Urmiston?'

'Urmiston pushed me out of the carriage at Basingstoke.'

She was writing all this down on loose sheets of blue sugar paper. Philip reached out and touched the tip of her breast with his fingers. She stopped writing and sat very still. But unafraid.

'Where is the postman?' he asked.

'Franz? He is downstairs. You are still very feverish.'

'If I close my eyes, everything is purple.'

'That is normal,' Anna said, as though she spoke for consulting doctors Europe-wide. She took his hand from her nightgown and laid it across his belly. He felt lighter than a feather. And suddenly very tearful.

'I need to telegraph London.'

'In the morning you can do this thing. But be quiet now.'

'Who is that downstairs?'

'I have told you – Franz and my father. They are playing cards.'

'Shall we make love?'

The German girl's laugh was pleasantly low and intimate. She leaned over the bed and kissed him briefly on the forehead.

'An excellent idea. But first we must ask Bella.'

Philip peered, confused.

'You know about Bella?'

'She has been mentioned,' Anna said with great dryness.

'She says that if you carry a gun, you are more likely to be shot by a gun. Which is absolute nonsense.'

'I think so,' Anna agreed. 'But Bella is beautiful, no?'

Philip embarrassed them both by bursting into tears. Downstairs – but where downstairs? – there was the scrape of a chair being dragged back across stone flags. The noise gave an unmistakable indication of sudden exasperation. Then came heavy boots clumping on the stairs. Fee fie foe fum.

Hans Georg was certainly the height of the door but also half its width. At some point in the evening he had taken off his shirt, leaving a black forest of hair that ran from his gut, to gather under his chin and there form the undercroft of an impressive beard. In his hand he held a short-handled mallet with an iron head.

'Why don't I kill you, English? This fever you have, you hold onto like an old woman. Oh, look at me, oh, boo-hoo. Better I kill you.'

'Where is the profit in that?' Philip asked conversationally, as though discussing leading out trumps from a weak hand.

'Tonight comes a captain of police from Essen, yes, from Essen. Saying how much they would like to interview you. There is a man with him, a Berliner.'

'What did he have to say?'

'He don't say nothing. But before he sits down, he wipes the chair with his handkerchief. Eh?'

'You paint a very clear picture.'

'He doesn't know what he is saying,' Anna warned. 'He is burning up with fever.'

'He knows,' Hans Georg muttered. 'Why should we

– 633 –

fool with the police? Now, if it all comes out, I got problems with this captain, an ugly bastard with a silly fucking beard.'

'Some beards are beautiful,' Philip protested.

'You shut your face. Tomorrow we telegraph London.'

'Excellent.'

'I give your representative three days to get here. With a hundred gold sovereigns.'

'You flatter me.'

'Tonight Anna stays with you.'

'Not necessary. Very generous, but quite the wrong thing. Too kind.'

Hans Georg looked at him with fury.

'To stop you from running away.'

Fever or not, Philip thought this was the funniest thing he had ever heard. Snorting laughter, helpless beating of fists on the mattress, a threatening looseness in the gut, general mild delirium.

'Bring him more blankets.'

'Maybe a mattress?' Anna suggested.

'Good! And you, you fool: do you hear me? No more laughing! We sweat you like a horse, then you are better.'

Philip's whinny came near to extinguishing the candle.

TEN

Urmiston arrived at Skipton dressed in Hannah Bardsoe's idea of an outfit appropriate for the distant parts of the kingdom. His ginger wool shooting jacket was belted and had leather shoulder patches. No power on earth could have persuaded him to wear the breeks that went with this garment: Hannah knew that and had substituted a pair of corduroy trousers in duckpond green. Urmiston had big feet and these were encased in alpine climbing boots with metal clips to guide the laces. On his head he wore a soft tweed cap. All these things were second-hand and had been assembled by Hannah from clothes stalls over the last year or so against the day when her beloved Charlie would be recalled to the colours, so to speak. At King's Cross they had seemed woundingly eccentric but here in Skipton they passed without comment. A long nose and lantern jaw helped.

'Good day, maister,' the ticket collector at the station said, without the slightest suspicion of irony.

'He thinks you're somebody important,' Alfie whispered.

'Which of course I am. Now cut along and see your mother and we shall meet again at, say, two this afternoon.'

'Where?'

'At the George, I think.'

'Shall I walk you there now?'

'I doubt it is hard to find.'

They parted and Charles Urmiston walked into town, very conscious of being the representative of a loose-knit circle of London friends that had but one thing in common – their loyalty to a grey-eyed widow who had come to Skipton and somehow overreached herself. In all other respects, they were a most unlikely band of brothers. Among them, Urmiston counted himself the least.

As it happened (for all his weird and wonderful costume) he alone could be placed as a possible social acquaintance of Bella's, say a bookseller friend ruined by failure or a distant cousin driven mad by the study of Aramaic in some forsaken vicarage. He was, in the modest way of it, a gentleman. But how to explain – even under the elastic notion of six degrees of separation – Percy Quigley's quirky adhesion to Bella's cause? How to introduce the implacable Billy Murch as another of Bella's friends to this file of schoolchildren in pinafores being marched back into school?

It was Urmiston's habit to sell himself short. The truth was, he knew more of provincial England than any of the friends who gathered under Bella's banner. His work as a land agent to three successive railway companies had certainly taught him how to deal with bumptious local upstarts.

'I must warn you that gentlemen generally dress for dinner in this hotel,' the insolent day manager of the George murmured, having seen his clothes and cast a supercilious eye over his luggage, a single portmanteau. Urmiston stared him down.

'I do not like to be warned,' he said. 'The word you were searching for in this instance was "advise", I am sure.'

'One way or another, you won't be admitted to dinner in those clothes.'

'I see.'

Urmiston pulled a sheet of the hotel's writing paper from a wooden rack and studied it briefly. Something in the heading caught his eye and made him burst out laughing. 'Well, well,' he exclaimed. 'From this we understand the proprietor of the hotel to be Mr Herbert Lintott. Go and fetch him at once.'

'I cannot leave my post.'

Urmiston rounded on a cowering potboy in a red and silver striped livery waistcoat.

'Go to Mr Lintott's office and ask him to step along to the front desk. He will want to know why. Tell him you have been sent by Mr Charles Urmiston. Remind him the last time he met Mr Urmiston was in Swindon, when he had the Perceval Hotel. Go on, child. Skip away.'

The day manager could not be sure this ploy was genuine but prepared himself for the possibility that it was.

'I was merely pointing out to the gentleman—'

'Is that the residents' lounge? Ask Mr Lintott to join me there.'

Bravado was one of life's rich pleasures. He had almost forgotten how intoxicating it could be.

'My dear old Charles!' Bert Lintott chuckled, over and over. 'If this don't beat all. My word, I am so delighted to see you. And look, let's get the sad news out of the way first: my commiserations about the loss of your wife. Mary took it most feelingly. We wrote to the house in Campden Hill—'

'A lot had changed by then, Bert. We had fallen from grace somewhat—'

But he was sure Lintott already knew that. The hotelier would have followed the disgrace and dismissal Urmiston had suffered at the hands of the Great Western Railway as a matter of professional interest. That they were friends went without saying; but that all friendship was a matter of checks and balances was also understood. These two first knew each other in the days of Urmiston's pomp, when he was a highly respected servant of the railway company and Lintott as unctuous as any Yorkshireman ever wishes to be when among the condescending baboons that run the country to the south. Urmiston knew too that his old friend could price his travelling outfit to the last shilling – and in it, read his present fortune.

'You finally kept your promise to Mary,' he suggested, waving his arm to indicate not just the lounge but the whole hotel – and indeed the town.

'It was always what she wanted,' Lintott boomed. 'Be damned with all this, mind, but she said to me one day, "Bertie, I want you to take me back to Yorkshire and buy me that little white house on the road to Grassington, the one we used to gawp at when we were courting." Captain Shelley's house, as was. So we came up here for a poke about and blow me, Charles, if it wasn't on the market and just as we remembered it. As neat and comely as any house ever built. The hotel was an afterthought. A partner-ship,' he added primly. 'There's four of us own it.'

'Nobody could wish you more joy than me, dear old lad.'

'And I think you mean that,' the Yorkshireman said, wiping his eyes with a pass of his meaty wrist. Urmiston smiled his gentle smile.

'I do – and while we're at it, let's get something else out of the way. I haven't come up here to play the old soldier with you, as I think is the expression. You are looking at a solid citizen in good standing with his commu-nity. I live with a respectable widow and together we run a little herbalist's. I have never been happier.'

'In London, is it?'

'Oh, yes, but in such a London as you and I grew up knowing nothing of. Well, of course,' Urmiston added hastily, 'I must speak for myself there.'

Bert Lintott laughed and stroked his friend's sleeve with a very affectionate caress. 'By shots, but it is such a pleasure to see you again, old lad. Tell me, how did you know I was here?'

'Five minutes ago, I didn't. I came up here to look for a guest of yours.'

'Mrs Wallis,' the hotelier said at once in a changed voice. The smiles and laughs had disappeared. He and his entire staff had been interviewed by the police the previous day. Mrs Wallis might be a very nice woman but her dis-appearance was business.

'A very dear friend,' Urmiston explained artlessly.

'Is it a particular *kind* of very dear friend we're speaking of?' Lintott enquired cautiously. He was relieved by Urmiston's hearty laugh.

'She is just that, but not in the sense you mean. Good Lord, my Hannah would dot your eye for thinking so. No, she is a fine impetuous woman who may have got herself into bother.'

'You can say that again,' Lintott growled. 'I come straight to the point as always. Do you know about the cuckoos we have up at Cruddas?'

'A very bright boy called Alfie Stannard has given me the general background, yes.'

'Well, there you are. If those two women haven't a hand in it somewhere, I shall eat my hat.' But behind the bluster, Urmiston thought he heard a more sombre note. Lintott was repeating taproom gossip by way of preparing his friend for something worse.

'There has also been mention of the hermit Duxbury.'

The Yorkshireman slapped his thigh in irritation.

'This is a hard-working market town. In the ordinary course of things we would have as much use for the woman Gollinge and that fool of a hermit as a chocolate teapot. But they have suddenly become meat and drink to the local press, as if the place had become a nest of witches. None of it helps find Mrs Wallis.'

'Has Lady Gollinge spoken to the press, then, to put herself under such suspicion?'

'She has fired a dozen or more arrows at them and that's better than an interview.'

'And the police?'

'Searched the house and found nothing. Which proves nothing.'

'You are angry, Bert.'

'I am better than angry. Gollinge and her impudent chit

of a companion have made us a laughing stock. Which suits her, for she will never have a better stage to play on. She has found a printer – Rawson, the great fool – to publish her insane theories about hunting and gathering and all the rest of the tosh she talks.'

'A pamphlet of some kind?'

'Being set up in type right at this moment. And according to Rawson, the first edition already sold out by subscription.'

'Maybe I should start with this hermit fellow.'

'Ha! According to the locals, you'll find him struck dumb by the same mysterious power that abducted Mrs Wallis,' the hotelier said in disgust. 'A brisk kick up the arse is what these people need.'

'Will you tell me what you really think, Bert? As a friend?'

Lintott stirred uneasily. Always a touching sort of a man, he reached across and seized Urmiston's hands in his two meaty paws.

'The moors are a dangerous place for the foolhardy. I fear for your friend, old lad. There are pits out there that are no more than twenty feet deep but twenty feet is plenty when you fall down one. The bigger workings would swallow a regiment. The whole town would like it to be voodoo or devil worship that's taken her, but it could be something simpler.'

'That she fell down a mine shaft?'

'They have no proper headings, do you see? There's nothing much to give warning, even in full daylight. There are parts where I wouldn't walk or picnic – and I was born here.'

'Then we might never find her,' Urmiston guessed, his eyes prickling.

'Has she anything of the countrywoman about her?'

'She is as London as Westminster Bridge,' he answered brokenly.

'No, but let's see some more fight in you, Charlie,' Lintott said, alarmed by these tears. 'That bloody fool Duxbury was the last to speak to her before her disappearance, I believe. Since when nothing and no one can get him to utter. You must start there. He might just know something. And let it be a flying kick up the arse you give *him*, Charles. You have the boots for it.'

Alfie showed him the way. The boy was against using violence towards the hermit, though he knew in his heart it would never be offered. Urmiston had already impressed him by retrieving a magpie's feather and setting it upright in the turf. It was something local children were taught to do by their grandparents. That sat well with Alfie. The Londoner also stopped more than once to get the lay of the land, a thing practically unheard of among townies. Lastly, he seemed abstracted, as he had been for the whole train journey north. A puff of wind might blow him away, Alfie judged with the cruelty of the healthy young, but a deep thinker all the same. A bit of a brain-box, even. All the same he was completely taken aback when Urmiston asked him an unexpected question.

'You mentioned Mr Duxbury burying the bones of Raybould the murderer. Now where was that, exactly?'

'Turned him into a waterfall, he did.'

'Mmm. Would it be down there, at all?' Urmiston asked, pointing.

'I have never seen it.'

'Well, this is how it is, Alfie. We shall divide our forces. While I talk to the hermit, you shall scout for the place. But quietly and perhaps I should say secretly. So as not to tip our hand to prying eyes.'

'I can do that.'

'Good boy. When you have found it—'

'Mother has invited you to sup with us tonight, I forgot to say—'

'And I look forward to it. When you find the grave – or waterfall – come and fetch me. And now I think I see the hermit's smoke.'

'Is it important, about Raybould?'

'That is what we must find out.'

'You won't forget Mother's invitation?'

'No elephant has a better memory. Now be off with you.'

And watched with some envy as the boy ran straight down the side of the valley, as easily as if it had been Long Acre on a quiet Sunday. Like Bella before him, Urmiston was a little overwhelmed by the huge skies and empty spaces.

When he entered Duxbury's cave, he disconcerted the hermit by sitting down and saying nothing at all, not so much as a murmur of greeting. The two sat facing each other across a smoky fire. Urmiston had never met a hermit but – at the lowest point of his life – had known several deeply disturbed human beings. Only one or two were dangerous. For the most part, like Duxbury, they were losers with a gift for self-delusion. He was, accordingly, prepared to wait. A full five minutes passed.

'The Queen has lost her silver thimble,' the hermit said suddenly. 'All the ladies of the Court are looking for it.'

'Her Majesty enjoys these little games,' Urmiston responded gravely. 'The thimble is not lost but hidden. But I think you know that, for I have been told you are a very wise man.'

'Then where is the thing now?'

'That is what I am here to ask.'

Duxbury studied the fire of gorse twigs and rabbit dung for a while and then shrugged out a short smile.

'You are a friend of Mrs Wallis.'

'That is so.'

'Are you the one they call Urmiston?'

'Now that *is* very clever. She has told you about me, to be sure, but only a gifted man could have made the connection. Yes, I am Charles Urmiston. I have come to bring her home.'

'I cannot help. You are too late for that, I reckon.'

But Urmiston was ready for this answer; had anticipated it. Never a bold man, but not a complete ninny either. And he sensed that Duxbury was on the back foot. He played a weak card strongly.

'Hermit, I do not wish to threaten you but if I must I will go to the police and tell them how you poisoned Mrs Wallis with these pills that I recovered from your cave.'

He held out a tiny brown bottle of Bardsoe's Imperial Cough Lozenges, manufactured by him at the herbalist's in Shelton Street and slipped into his pocket by Hannah

Bardsoe to ward off any chestiness that might be about in Yorkshire.

'There could be anything in that bottle,' Duxbury scoffed.

'Mrs Wallis told you about my little shop? Four of these, mashed up with a few biscuits, will kill a dozen rats. You have heard of arsenic, I don't doubt?'

'The police will never believe you. They will want to have them examined.'

'You don't think it would work?'

'We may seem slow to Londoners but we are not daft.'

'Then I must try another tack. But be sure about something, Mr Duxbury. The police are very anxious to arrest someone and you are my candidate.'

'I never harmed a hair on her head.'

'But you were the last person to see her. You kept her back when Alfie Stannard went home and I think you know what happened after she left.'

'It was dark. She lost her way. Everybody thinks that. How should I know different?'

'Because you are a wise man. Would I come out here at all unless I believed in your powers?'

'Very well, then. She was taken by the girl Amelia,' Duxbury said without bothering to conceal a crooked smile at his visitor's reaction. 'You don't know whether to believe me, do you?'

'If you say it is so, it is so,' Urmiston said uneasily.

'I have never knowingly told an outright lie,' the hermit asserted far too grandly.

'Now this is better. Thank you for that. But you see, I still have a little problem that you can help me with. You liked Mrs Wallis?'

'As much as I knew of her.'

'Of course you did. I have never known anyone take against her on first acquaintance, as we might say. She paid you the respect due to you?'

'Enough,' Duxbury allowed.

'Yes. Quite so. A lady from London spends the day with you and accepts your kind offer of hospitality. After she has left, you see – or hear – her abduction and can identify the young companion of Lady Gollinge as her abductor.'

'Where's the problem with that?'

Urmiston rubbed the smoke out of his eyes. He examined his hands as though discovering them for the first time in his life. Sighed.

'I am not one of Mrs Wallis's bolder or braver friends. In many areas of life I am considered a bit slow on the uptake, even. But I do like an orderly story, Mr Duxbury. So here's my problem. Why did you not report these goings-on to the police? Oh, I know you have your dignity as a hermit to uphold and ideally the world should come to you. I see that very clearly. But then, next day, the police *did* come to you. And, bless me, you had nothing to say! In fact, you would not utter a single word.'

'It is none of my business. Let them work it out for themselves. The Gollinge woman is the chief suspect, if they have eyes to see.'

'Mmm.'

Alfie appeared all in a rush at the cave's entrance and Urmiston smiled and held his finger to his lips.

'I'm just getting it completely straight in my mind, hermit. On that strange night, Mrs Wallis leaves. A little later Alfie here arrives all of a fluster, just as he is now. She has not reached the road to Skipton. She might be lost on the moors. You say nothing. You know what has happened and you say nothing.'

'He put his finger to his lips, same as you just done,' Alfie piped.

'An important detail. You asked him to tell you what had happened and what did he do?'

'Pushed me out of the cave.'

'What did he say when he did that, Alfie?'

'Was struck dumb. They had laid a curse on him.'

'Bless me! A curse! Why hadn't I thought of that for myself?'

'Sarcasm now, is it?' Duxbury blustered.

'Alfie admires you, Mr Duxbury. He thinks you are a deep cove. And so perhaps you are. I think it very likely that Lady Gollinge *did* lay a curse on you. Not the night of Mrs Wallis's disappearance but somewhat earlier.'

'More riddles.'

'Maybe so. I am going from here to the waterfall you made of Raybould's bones. Raybould the farmer, who knew these moors as well as any man that lived, I dare say. And yet the poor fellow dies crossing a stream. A heart attack, possibly. So severe that he cannot as much as drag himself to the far bank. Tragic.'

'Who *are* you?' Duxbury whispered.

'A small shopkeeper like yourself. And like you, not a complete fool. So here's the thing. You find the man all Skipton has been looking for for twenty years or more and you say nothing. You tell no one in authority. Some hermits keep a vow of silence, I know. But you are not such a one. As Alfie said on the way here, in normal times you talk fit to turn a mill.'

'You can clear off out it now,' the hermit decided.

'In a moment. But first, shall I tell you what I think? That either you witnessed who killed poor Raybould, or you did it yourself. And now I shall leave, just as you ask. I shall go to where you buried him and keep a guard on the place. Alfie meanwhile will go back into Skipton and fetch the most senior policeman he can find. And then we shall all be a bit further down the road to the truth.'

'I did not kill him.'

'We shall need a senior policeman, Alfie, and a good doctor.'

'I had nothing to do with it,' Duxbury cried.

'Then I advise you not to bolt. One way or another, this is the second crime you have concealed, hermit, and it will go better with you if you don't dress up the facts with nonsense.'

Some of the smaller bones from Raybould's skeleton had washed into the pool below the waterfall. Urmiston found himself unable to touch them: they lay a few inches down on a bed of gravel. As to the stones piled on the rest of the farmer's mortal remains, he felt almost a religious inhibition from moving even one. Nor was there any need. Time and the brutal indifference of nature had laid bare all the evidence a man might want. Raybould's skull, which once had been the seat of such almighty remorse, was now a cistern. Luckily for Urmiston's stomach, only the back of the skull was visible, as an unmistakable round of bone. A ragged hole the size of a penny ruined its symmetry.

Through that hole dribbled a brown thread of peaty water. In summer dribbled. In winter spouted.

'However did you work it all out, sir?' Mrs Stannard asked.

'To say I worked it out is some exaggeration,' Urmiston smiled weakly. 'It was a nagging detail. Mr Duxbury is a mighty fantasist and I could not believe the waterfall story, except as an example of his rather feeble whimsy. But, as we passed through Wakefield in the train this morning, it occurred to me to ask: What if he was telling the truth? Wasn't there mischief in that? Mischief of some kind?'

'Another baked apple,' Alfie's mother proposed, filling his plate before he had time to answer. 'I will tell you straight, sir, you have done more in one afternoon than the police have managed over five days. The lady was a special friend of yours?'

'Is, Mrs Stannard. Is.'

'Just as you say, sir. I don't know what came over me to speak so careless. I put Alfie at your complete disposal, Mr Urmiston, for all that is left to do. A good boy and as for common sense, well, he has his moments. Not a great scholar—'

'He has already proved his worth in far more practical ways—'

'Which I thank you for saying. Yes, indeed, praise from you is worth the having. We shall soon see an arrest, I am sure; and if my Alfie can be of the slightest help to you in the meanwhile, you have but to ask.'

'With Mr Duxbury in police custody and shaken free of the curse laid on his tongue I think it likely that Lady Gollinge will join him at the station first light tomorrow.

And then perhaps Bella – Mrs Wallis – will be found safe and well.'

'May the Good Lord make it so.'

'Amen to that,' Urmiston answered dutifully.

ELEVEN

A dozen stubs of candles were spread across the floor, their flames bending and trembling to the only move- ment in the room. Amelia was dancing. Her naked body glistening, her hair tied in a towering topknot, she swooped and spun, her limbs making fantastic shadows. When she stamped her feet, ancient dust jumped out of the floorboards in percussive grey lines. This imitation of something ancient and primal in a ruined Yorkshire house had completely erased the girl she actually was, or had been before Ursula found her. She was not tranced but neither was she in the slightest way that other Amelia who once had loaded and unloaded barges along the Liverpool to Leeds canal. Whatever was ribald and feck- less about *that* creature had vanished. The dance had taken over.

Written down, Bella thought deliriously, all this would seem preposterous in the extreme. As it was, tied to a chair by her wrists and ankles, she watched the whirling body with something like terror in her heart. The room was insufferably hot. Behind her back, Ursula Gollinge drummed and chanted four notes over and over in a jagged corncrake voice. Bella felt her head falling into the same hypnotic rhythm. Against the wishes of her rational mind, she was as if nodding agreement to the thick air, the leaping shadows, the invocation of all that was dark and mysterious.

And then it was done. The candles were stamped out one by one, the drumming fell to a whisper, followed by a piteous shriek from the girl; and silence. One instance of how powerful the experience had been was that when Bella tried to gather her wits, she could not say for sure whether the others were any longer in the room or not. She slumped in the chair, her mind reeling, her clothes damp with sweat.

This is nothing, Philip said to her from a long way away. His tone was gently chiding, the way he sometimes spoke to her upon the pillow. You are not harmed, dearest Bella. It is more likely that the poor deluded Lady Gollinge will mend her ways and take up embroidery long, long before you bend the knee to an exhibition of such cheap magic. Wipe all this nonsense clean. Find your centre. For example, taking the drawing-room mantelpiece in Orange Street, identify the objects on it from left to right. Name three admirals of your acquaintance. What is the sum of fifty-two and seventeen?

'Are there spirits in the world?' Ursula Gollinge interrupted unexpectedly from the far end of the room. 'Is there a world of spirits, the least parts of which are more powerful than any temporal king or emperor?'

Bella blinked, the sweat from her hair running into her eyes. She found the salty sting reviving.

'Can we have some light?'

'Are you afraid of the dark?' the lulling whisper continued.

'Tonight it teems with spirits. Your father is here, for example.'

'I doubt it. He is rather fussy about the people he is seen dead with.'

'You should be much more afraid than that,' Ursula warned angrily.

'I am sorry not to oblige you. Standing on the roof of Westminster Abbey would fill me with terror. But not the gutters where your imagination lives.'

Well said, the ethereal Philip murmured, but with a more doubtful tone to his voice than she would have liked. Remember, we are not here to insult her but to escape. Bella chewed her lower lip, vexed. He made escaping sound like walking down a short flight of steps towards a waiting cab. But having pledged herself to stand and fight, there could be no turning back. Even when tied to a chair, she reflected groggily.

'Your inspiration for all this nonsense is the time you spent among the Australian aboriginals, I take it. What happened to your German, by the way? Perhaps he was of a more rationalistic turn of mind. Or less gullible, as we might put it.'

'What do *you* know of him? Who told you about him?'

'Try not to appear indignant, Lady Ursula. The poor man is an important part of your myth. He died nobly, I suppose. Is there some rock sacred to his name in the lonely outback? Is his memory kept alive in song and dance? Was he here tonight?'

Ursula Gollinge walked out of the shadows on stiff legs

and struck Bella's face with the flat of her hand, as hard as she knew how.

'You think you are better than me?'

'Saner,' Bella replied, feeling blood in her mouth. The taste was strangely invigorating.

'How could you understand what you have just seen, a complacent white woman such as you are?' Ursula demanded.

'Ah, yes. That again. *Was* your German noble, or did he plead with you to stop these foolish games and return to Melbourne where there were medicines and feather beds, white wine and all the other wicked contrivances of the imperialist master race? Was he a disappointing German in the end?'

'He was torn apart by wild dogs.'

'I am sorry to hear it.'

Something of the evening had wrought its magic, nevertheless. Bella had the clearest image of an emaciated young man being tossed to and fro by dogs in some stony gully under a pitiless sun. Imagination provided his leather satchel and silver repeater and all the other rags of his previous existence. In spite of herself, she shuddered.

'He came close to the mystery but it eluded him,' Ursula explained dreamily.

'The *mystery*? My God, what utter piffle you talk when you are excited, Lady Gollinge.'

'He was my husband.'

'You already had a husband.'

'My husband under the stars.'

'For as long as it lasted. Was it worth it?'

Having her face caressed was worse than being struck.

Ursula stroked her throat and jaw almost absent-mindedly, as another woman might smooth laundry.

'You don't have to understand a thing to know it is beautiful. You want me to say I understood nothing of what happened to me among the Aborigines and perhaps you are right. In your own mean-spirited way you are right. But I was given something you will never have.'

'And what might that be?'

'Why bother to explain? You could not begin to understand.'

'Are the Aboriginals a peaceable people?'

'They wish only to be left alone.'

'Your arrival must have been doubly vexing therefore. Two foolish Europeans, neither of whom could think straight for more than half a minute at a time.'

To say that Ursula laughed was to understate the noise that came from her – a wild howling bellow that fanned Bella's face. Bella felt her flesh creep. Then this, disgusting and unexpected: while her hands bore down on her captive's pinioned forearms, Ursula Gollinge spat full in her face.

'A curse on you and your kind!' she whispered. 'I call on powers that will shrivel you to dust!'

Amelia re-entered the room, dressed in a white shift, her face scrubbed clean of sweat, her hair undone. She went immediately to Bella's chair, pushed her mistress out of the way and began untying the ropes that held their captive there. It was an electrifying shift in authority.

'Go and fetch us to drink,' the barge girl commanded. 'You've said enough for one night.'

To Bella's amazement, the older woman filed obediently out of the room.

'Don't try nothing,' Amelia warned, as the last knot came undone. Bella chafed her wrists and plucked at her clothes, shaking like an aspen.

'How much longer can this go on, Amelia?'

'Until they catch us.'

'Are you not worth more?'

'You would know, of course,' the girl scoffed. 'I went on the barges when I was ten years old. I'm seventeen now. What would you have me do? Go back to shovelling spuds from out the hold or unloading forty tons of pig iron in some snowstorm? I'll take no lectures, thank you very much.'

'Your companion is heading straight for an asylum, you can see that, can't you? Does it have to end like that for you too?'

'I can look after myself.'

'And the police?'

'What of them? I can outrun any man set down on earth. And best of all, disappear when it comes to that, just vanish, pfft. Maybe she *wants* to be caught so's to kick up more dust. But not me. They can look as far as Timbuktu, they'll never find me. I'll run through mirrors first.'

All this with great good humour, as though explaining what was obvious. She pulled Bella up by her wrists and led her to the fire.

'She plans to kill you,' Amelia said. 'There are shafts round here that you can chuck a pebble in and never hear it strike. And you're right, she has bats in her belfry more than enough. But that's how it's worked out, like.'

'And that doesn't frighten you?'

'It's a laugh,' Amelia said, with the staggering cruelty of the half-formed.

'A *laugh*?'

'I don't say you would find it funny. But then you're not me, are ya? She's told me a lot about you, Mrs Bella Wallis.'

'Before all this, she had never met me. She has deceived you.'

'Happen so. But she goes on about you something cruel. So, do you want to be chucked down a lead mine?'

'It would take two of you and all your strength,' Bella blustered.

'Aye. Two of us,' the barge girl said with a derisive smile. 'So best keep in my good books, London woman. Can you hear what's outside?'

'I hear nothing.'

'You don't hear the dogs of Cruddas barking?'

Urmiston had been entirely correct in supposing the police would try to storm the Gollinge manor house but wrong as to timing. He had imagined a dawn raid but bargained without the confusion of having two police forces represented. After heated exchanges under the canopy of the Skipton railway station, twenty officers from two forces had been assembled and marched in column up the road to Cruddas, their boots cracking out a fine rhythm, while advertising their presence to every living thing. The dogs Amelia heard barking were responding to this heavy crunch-crunch up the hill to Cruddas: they had never known of such a thing and were more fearful than indignant. The fool of a farmer who added to the midnight confusion by letting off a twelve-bore from the gates to his midden saved Bella's life. The police fled into ditches, cursing and shouting. For an hour there were whistles and shotgun blasts, wild orders and the barking of chained dogs enough to beat the band. When the first constables arrived at Lady Gollinge's house, soaked to the skin and in a filthy temper, they found it deserted.

All of which Charles Urmiston witnessed, having been dragged from sleep by Alfie. The two of them followed the police up to the village in drenching rain and though told to turn back, managed to stumble their way by round-about route to the assault on the manor house itself. Much shouting and banging, the flitting of lanterns and exasperated cursing.

'They've bunked off out of it,' Alfie whispered.

'Perhaps only as far as one of the outhouses.'

'No. She's too canny for that, is Amelia. They've gone.'

The elm they sheltered under gave some relief from the weather but both Urmiston and the boy were drenched to the skin. Alfie watched as his new hero took out a moleskin purse (pressed on him by Hannah) and poked about inside. His fingers found one waterlogged banknote and a handful of coins. Urmiston dragged Alfie up by his wrist.

'Now we run – *run*, Alfie – to what used to be Captain Shelley's house along the Grassington Road. Do you think you can find it?'

''Tis two miles in the wrong direction!'

'It can't be helped. I have a friend there—'

'Mr Lintott—'

'Yes, Mr Lintott, who can fit us out with fresh duds and the loan of some money. For this could turn out to be a long search.'

'Mr Urmiston, sir, we have no time for that. The ladies have no more than half an hour's start. Running downhill to start with, for how else would you put distance between yourself and trouble? But by the time we've done with Mr Lintott and all such, who's to say where they'll be? We have to go *now*.'

They might have argued more but for a shout from the courtyard of the house and some excited pointing in their direction. This might have been the time to help the police with their inquiries, Urmiston reasoned. Instead, hand in hand with Alfie, he tobogganed down a muddy slope on his back and once upright, began running like a man trying to escape a dozen maddened bulls. A very small and inadequate moon lit the way.

Philip Westland woke to find the fever had left him. In its place was a draughty clarity, as though somebody somewhere had opened up all the windows in his mind and a cold breeze was blowing through. The sensation was not unpleasant. His first use of this return to sanity was to get his naked feet onto the floor and so escape the clamminess of a mattress saturated by sweat. This he managed to do, though with many premonitions of what life would be like when he was old. He sat with his hands on his knees, his lower lip pushed out, wondering about how to get to the little square window and open it. For the room stank. Open the window, lean out and let the sun warm him. Yes, that was the thing to do. He was still planning how to achieve this when the door opened and Hans Georg walked in, smelling of cows, his boots and gaiters flecked with mud and milk.

'Today you send the telegraph to England,' he announced.

'Get me some clothes. First, bring me some hot water and a towel. Some coffee and a slice of bread. And something to write with.'

'I see you are better,' the German guffawed. 'I send Anna.'

'No. We will do this my way.'

Hans Georg at least solved the problem of the window, opening it and then posting the sodden mattress through it like a particularly cumbersome parcel.

'Here it stinks. I am not your servant, English. I send Anna. How is your wound?'

'It hurts.'

'Show me, please.'

When Philip fainted, the German carried him downstairs and laid him on a wooden bench in the farm parlour, watched by a very old woman slicing beans.

'Is this the poor man you have robbed so cruelly?' she asked in a rhetorical sort of way. 'He doesn't look much to me.'

He walked outside, found the mattress and threw it on the roof of an outside privy. The first flies arrived, as juicy as blackberries. When he went back inside his grandmother was leaning over the figure on the bench, applying a smouldering chicken feather to Philip's nose.

'Take him outside and put him under the pump,' she suggested. 'The shock will start his heart.'

'I am not dying,' Philip protested. 'A little coffee will set me right.'

'I thought you were English,' the old lady cried.

'He *is* English,' Hans Georg said in great exasperation.

'Then where are his clothes? No Englishman wears only a shirt.'

'Listen, Grandma, you seem a very intelligent woman. I need clothes to be sure but first –' Philip managed a feeble smile – 'I need a cup of your coffee and a kind word.'

'Pfft,' she cried uncertainly. 'My last kind word was spoken many years ago. If you wanted coffee you should have come down at five this morning. I am having trouble understanding any of this.'

'I will make him another poultice,' Hans Georg decided.

'Good God,' Grandma exclaimed with great reverence, retreating to her beans. She mumbled to herself for a while and then looked up. 'Some clothes, or at least something to cover his manhood, would be a good idea. But then what do I know? I am just a poor old hunchback with nowhere to go and no one to love me.'

Urgent you bring one hundred sovereigns immediately this address. Of national importance. Sumatra Rules apply, as previously. Come alone. Westland.

Murch studied the telegram form for the fifth or sixth time, smoothing it out with his palm as if to release further meanings from the text. William Kennett's library had come up with some of the goods – the message had originated at a place called Feldhausen which resisted identification but had been passed through another place called Stoppenberg, which did exist as a dot on the map to the east of Essen. The wording was unambiguous and the clue was in the phrase 'Sumatra Rules', to be found in a Margam novel called *The Captain's Table*. The phrase spelt blood.

Billy Murch had no idea what Mr Westland was doing in Germany but that hardly came into it and he did not give it another thought. *Where* was not the question. The man was in trouble, maybe deep trouble. Half an hour's silent quizzing of the only evidence – this sorry-looking telegram form addressed to William Munch, MP – was never too long.

His wife Millie came in with a mug of tea strong enough to paint a fence. Murch took her free hand and kissed it.

'Seems he's got himself in a hole,' he said.

'Germany, is it?' Millie asked, peering at the book of maps. 'How far's that, then?'

'A good train ride.'

'And I suppose you'll go?'

'He don't give me much choice. See there? *Of national importance.*'

'What does it mean?'

'Buggered if I know. How much money do we have in the house?'

Millie sat down opposite him and laid a hand on her belly, where the baby pummelled with his tiny fists and danced a gentle hornpipe. Her smile was not without its element of derision.

'You should have been with Robin Hood and all his mates. I suppose you'd go to California if the Kennetts asked you.'

'Stretching it now, girl. No, California a bit out of the way. I don't say as Germany lifts the heart, neither. What would you do, Mill'?'

'Me?' Millie squealed. 'You're asking me?'

Murch waited. He could be as awkward as a sack of ferrets, he knew that, but being married to Millie had tempered his more saturnine aspects. Though he did not always ask her opinion out loud, he had come to depend upon it and could read the weather in her heart as surely as any country bumpkin standing at his garden gate. He loved her. These three words had yet to cross his lips but what else was love, if not this?

'Can you get there in time?' Millie asked.

'You think he's in that sort of danger?'

'Well, he didn't write to the Bishop of Southwark or What's-his-name—'

'The Duke of Cambridge—'

'No. What he wants is cross-eyed Billy Murch to go and hook him out of the mess he's got himself into. The distinguished MP,' she added teasingly.

'You make a good point,' Billy said thoughtfully. 'And all this about a hundred gold sovereigns?'

'Well, he knows you're rich but I'd say he was trying to mark your card along the lines of "nobody will do but you, Billy Boy. It's that urgent, God help me."'

'And what you're saying, we haven't actually got them sovs to hand?' he teased.

'What we've got is a cocoa tin in the kitchen with enough put by to buy the baby his first set of drawers, as well you know.'

'It's a facer,' Murch murmured.

'D'you hear that?' Millie asked her stomach. 'Your father's coming the old soldier with us again.'

'Again?'

Millie reached over and kissed him.

'You were probably born in a ditch with your arse as bare as a cow's bum. This child of yours knows that, already knows that, and he won't take it wrong if you steal the clothes off his back. You've made up your mind to go, you great lummox. I shall want to have words with Mr Westland when you fetch him back, mind.'

'If I can.'

'If you can! I wonder at you sometimes, Murchie, really I do. What, nip over to Germany and find some nothing place that nobody's never heard of? I'd do it myself if it wasn't laundry day.'

'Now you're talking!' Billy said, cracking one of his rare shy smiles.

TWELVE

By the light in the sky, however weak and diffused, Bella judged it to be an hour after daybreak. What before had seemed a grey blank slowly resolved itself into a prospect of distant trees, heavy with water, sleepy with it, so much so that she began to yearn for them with the same hunger she was already experiencing for a plate of egg and bacon, or best of all, a change of clothes. The idea of woodland was somehow comforting, filled with the promise of men with quiet jobs and children gathering mushrooms. Add in friendly dogs and a straggle of geese, why not?

The contours of the land that lay below her had softened, offering broad and largely empty meadows. Bella could make out the pale threads of roads – or at any rate lanes – and the blue smudge of what might be smoke. And all this was tantalisingly close, even as viewed through curtains of rain and the intimidating foreground of bare and scabby moor.

It had been Ursula's characteristically cruel idea to tie a halter round Bella's neck, made from a rotting length of rope found on the floor of the stone hut they sheltered in. The idea was that the free end of the rope would remain wound round her captor's wrist – but of the three women, Ursula was the oldest and, when it came to it, the most incompetent. She lay on her back, snoring noisily, unaware that Bella had slipped the halter without the slightest difficulty and was free to run away any time she liked. What held her back was hunger and – no matter that it was high summer in other parts of the kingdom – bone-chilling cold. When she held her hands out in front of her, she saw that they were lavender blue. Easy enough to explain: there was not a stitch of clothing on her that was not made sodden by rain and mud. Her flesh crawled.

Ursula stirred and gave a tug to the halter, only to find the business end hanging on a rusting nail driven into a roofbeam. She sat up in confusion, peering about her with gummed-up eyes.

'You're not at your best in the mornings, are you?' Bella observed coolly.

'Where is Amelia?'

'She has gone to find us something to eat.'

'Gone, gone where?'

'She didn't mention.'

'Was it she that untied you?'

'You have a very limited sense of story,' Bella snapped. 'You think she untied me and then put me on my honour to stay here and listen to you snoring? And that I said, "very well, Amelia my dear"?'

'Don't take that tone with me. Remember you are still my prisoner.'

'This is breathtaking. The only reason that I do not leave you here alone, you idiotic creature, is that I intend to bring you to justice. Look at me, Lady Ursula! Wake up and look at me! Without that girl, you are helpless. We will wait for Amelia, eat something and hopefully dry our clothes a little. Then we will continue downhill to the world of real things. Unless the police arrive first.'

'You don't understand,' Ursula said with a sudden arresting simplicity. 'I can't be taken.'

'It is too late for all that. Soon, what you are and everything you've done will be known to the world. Everything. Not as rumour and gossip but cold fact.'

'Why are you so filled with hate?'

'I will answer you with another question. What do you know of a woman called Jane Westland?'

Ursula peered at her for a moment. Her slow-breaking smile was horrible to witness. She shook her head in mocking wonderment.

'Well, well,' she muttered. 'That old story. Is that really why you came? There is a brother, I believe. Does he come into it? No doubt he does.'

'Jane Westland,' Bella demanded. Ursula laughed.

'Oh, such a stern voice! Such flashing eyes! You are a meddling fool, Mrs Wallis. You make a very poor avenging fury. Go home to your petty little existence and wring your hands there. Tell your diary what you have seen.'

One wall of the hut was blackened by smoke and in a corner were a few kindling sticks and what was left of a little wicket gate. Bella began searching. Jammed into a hole in the wall was a tin box, the lid depicting the pyramids of Giza. Inside, some provident shepherd had placed some stubs of candle and a handful of varnished matches.

'What are you doing?' Ursula Gollinge yelped.

'I am going to make a fire. To signal the police.'

'Put the box down. Put it down!'

Women do not hit other women. Bella put her hands

on Ursula's chest and pushed, enough to send her sprawling. Kicked her in the rump. Found she was shouting. Blood pounded in her ears.

Ursula rolled onto her hands and knees and clawed her way up the wall of the hut.

'Where is Amelia?' she screamed, wide-eyed and dishevelled. Pushing Bella aside she staggered out into the rain.

Running towards her, perhaps a hundred yards away, was an antic figure in a shooting jacket and muddy green corduroys, followed by a boy with red hair. Without a second's hesitation, Ursula turned and ran downhill, tumbling as she went but always bouncing back up. And as Bella watched, she saw a younger, lither figure running diagonally to join her. Then – but all at the same time, like the single shaking of a kaleidoscope – black dots appeared on the moor and the air was pierced by whistles and wild hallooing.

Urmiston crashed into the hut and seized Bella in a trembling embrace.

'Thank God you are safe,' he sobbed, before collapsing and pulling her down on top of him. Bella, laughing and crying, reached out an arm for Alfie and dragged him into the melee.

An orderly withdrawal to Herbert Lintott's lovely house on the road to Grassington was proposed and discounted, likewise the bridal suite at the George. No, nothing would do but Alfie's mother's cottage behind the cattle market and Mrs Stannard's own bed to crawl into. A hot toddy made from whisky and squeezed oranges, with just a dash of honey. Lizzie Stannard's goose-fat embrocation, applied by the lady of the house to Bella's blushing chest. A stone hot-water bottle to the feet. The cat for company.

Downstairs, Urmiston and Alfie sat in a mist of drying clothes, eating something new to the Londoner, fried egg sandwiches. Butter and dribbles of yolk ran down their chins. Tea the thing to drink with fried eggs – huge green mugs of it. Enough sugar to make the teeth ache.

'A couple of choice barmpots you two are,' Mrs Stannard said with great contentment. 'There's any amount of danger out there in the dark. It's a wonder you weren't both sent arse over tip – begging your pardon, Mr Urmiston – into some old mine shaft or such.'

'It was several times on my mind,' Urmiston confessed. 'But your boy is a wonder at the running. Rabbits could hardly do better. And since I was very careful never to let go of his hand, we survived.'

'Well, 'tis the talk of the town. I have had the neighbours coming round to pump my hand since ever you pitched up safe and sound. And how the police do love you for stealing their thunder, I don't think!'

'Have they found the two fugitives?'

'They have not. There's hue and cry all over, trains stopped and searched, all the canal boats with an armed constable on 'em. But not a sign. Not a sausage. My word but that old dressing gown sets you off a treat, Mr Urmiston. Quite the squire, you do look.'

'You spoke of armed constables?'

'Well, perhaps I was exaggerating a touch. But the warrant is out for those two wicked women on a charge of abduction, that I do know.'

'They will want to interview Mrs Wallis, no doubt,' Urmiston reflected uneasily.

'There's no policeman crossing that threshold before I says so,' Lizzie declared, pointing to the front door. 'Or to be more particular about it, before the lady herself says so.'

'Handsomely put, Mrs Stannard.'

'You are kind to say so. Now Alfie, do you take the gentleman upstairs – but quietly now – and go through the chest of your father's things and kit him out with some suitable duds. Paying attention,' she added meaningfully, 'to the fact that your dadda had but the one good suit and otherwise a taste for fabric that would shame a circus.'

'Is your father dead?' Urmiston whispered as they tiptoed upstairs.

'No. In Ireland, where he came from. Went out to buy some meat for our supper one night and never came back.'

'How long ago was this?'

'Ancient times. We don't miss him,' Alfie added.

'But, erm, was he a big man? Say about my size, would you say?'

'He was a giant,' the boy said, stifling a laugh and vaguely remembering just that – a red-headed giant with a taste for the stout and the knack of bending pokers in half.

The police called in the late afternoon. Inspector Bullard was a grave and methodical fellow in his fifties with something of the soldier about him. Bella wondered what that might be and found the answer in his unblinking calm. It was as though the inspector had spent an adult lifetime watching wickedness pass in parade, so much so that he had lost the capacity to be surprised.

The facts of the case were soon established. Bella had been lifted, as Bullard put it, by Amelia Jackson and carried to the house of Lady Ursula Gollinge. There she had been imprisoned for five days and nights in what she took to be a storage cellar, only being brought out to listen to what she called ranting monologues. Bullard was uncomfortable with the adjective – too wayward, too fanciful.

'Can you say a little more about the nature of this ranting?'

'That only simple people have any idea of the shape of the world and the only simple people left are what we in our ignorance call savages.'

'Savages?'

'I can't help you, Inspector,' Bella smiled. 'But Lady Gollinge has a very low view of civilisation. Things went to pot when the world gave up hunter-gathering, you understand. We grew fat and incredibly lazy. Our souls grew ugly. We turned to torture and exploitation as a way of life.'

'My word,' Bullard exclaimed, without losing a jot of his general imperturbability.

'Of course,' Bella continued, 'in those happier times any self-respecting hunter-gatherer would have knocked her on the head without a qualm of conscience. If indeed conscience ever came into it.'

'Weren't they morally superior to us?'

'Whether they were or not, Lady Gollinge would have been a strong candidate for being left behind or bashed on the head. I think for her, the idea of searching for nuts and berries is not work, but pleasure. Rather like picking daisies, or picnicking in the bluebell woods.'

'I am sorry to have missed it,' the inspector said sourly. 'Was anything else spoken of in these rants?'

'I'm afraid men came in for it hot and strong,' Bella smiled. 'White men, that is. The English in particular.'

'Yes,' Bullard nodded gloomily. 'A poor set of folk, white men. Now, Mrs Wallis, I will ask you this: Did either woman mention the name Raybould in the course of these rants? Or at any other time?'

'I know who Raybould is, of course,' she havered.

'From the hermit, yes. You had his character from Duxbury. But did his name come up when you were with the women? A white man, to be sure. And as English as Mr Gladstone. What you might call a neighbour of theirs out on the moors. A fellow who shared their happy hunting grounds, so to speak. Shared them – or ruined them. Do you follow my drift, Mrs Wallis?'

'I do indeed, Inspector Bullard.'

'And so how do you answer? I will put it plainly to you,' Bullard added. 'If enough evidence can be brought forward, then we shall be contemplating a charge of murder.'

'She killed Raybould?' Bella asked, alarmed.

'That is what I am trying to find out. Raybould was murdered, you can be sure of that.'

One part of Bella wanted to see Ursula become the victim of a sensational criminal trial and suffer all the consequences. Let the white men she despised so much take their revenge on her and make her name a subject of contempt all over Britain. The temptation for Bella to perjure herself was very strong. But honesty held her back – that and an unexpected pity for the confused and farcical woman. Bullard was all this time watching her carefully. It was as though, without either of them moving, he had manoeuvred her into the darkest corner of the room. Bella felt beads of perspiration on her upper lip.

'I do not remember them mentioning his name.'

The inspector sat back, his face still inscrutable, the movement alone betraying his dissatisfaction. Bella flushed.

'Certainly they claimed they knew how to deal with importunate men and there was a lot of giggling at that,' she suggested.

'Did they name anyone?'

'I have told you, no.'

'And what is importunate when it's at home?'

'Most women would understand me.'

'Do you say so?' Bullard growled.

'The only time I had seen Lady Gollinge before my capture was in conversation with the girl Amelia at the George Hotel. She spoke very freely and illiberally then and I took her to mean that sort of thing in general. Men, I mean.'

Bullard fell to plucking at his ear lobe, still with his eyes fixed on hers.

'Mr Urmiston has told me how you retrieved Raybould's remains,' she offered.

'Mmm.'

'And that the injury to the skull could hardly have been accidental.'

'Ah! Is Mr Urmiston a surgeon then? A bit of an expert, is he? We have him down as a shopkeeper.'

'Mr Bullard, I cannot tell you what I did not hear. You want me to say that I heard them confess to killing poor Mr Raybould. I did not.'

'Lady Gollinge threatened to kill you, though?'

'More than once.'

'And why was that?'

Bella did not have a ready answer. All at once, Bullard seemed to indicate that the interview was coming to an end, for he began fussing grumpily with a pipe and its pouch. She felt the most ridiculous guilt at not giving him the answer he wanted.

'Why should she want to kill you?' he repeated.

'Do you know, Inspector, I have no idea.'

'Unless, of course, it was in her nature.' He raised his pale blue eyes from the business of teasing out his tobacco. 'Or that she'd done it before. And was not sure how much the hermit had told you. Or was threatened by you coming up from London, for reasons we have yet to hear.'

'Is that how it looks?' Bella asked faintly.

'Any way you look at it, a lady from London turns up and is very far from being welcomed. Quite the contrary, in fact.'

'Inspector, I ask you to believe that until I came to Yorkshire I had never met Lady Gollinge in my life. She has a certain reputation in some circles as a deeply disturbed individual. That was all I knew of her.'

'And so, why did you come?'

Bella hesitated. Since her final confrontation with Ursula Gollinge she had found time to think. Dragging Jane Westland's name into the inquiry could do nothing but harm to Philip and might threaten her relationship to the man she loved most in the world. How to explain to this stolid Yorkshire policeman her arrogance – and wasn't that the word for it? – in believing she could shame a madwoman into repentance? Bullard watched these emotions flit across her face with a dreadful calm of his own.

'You were going to tell me why you came up north to meet her,' he said.

'I was curious,' Bella mumbled. The lameness of the remark was enough to make her blush.

The inspector pinched the bridge of his nose as if the pain of what she had just said had landed there, like the beginnings of a headache. In Mrs Stannard's sitting room the time was told by a German alarm clock that was carried down from the bedroom each morning. Its metallic clack was the only sound in the room for more than a minute.

'As far as I know there is no law against that,' Bella said.

Bullard thought about lighting his pipe and then regretfully put it away in his pocket. He smoothed crumbs of tobacco from his lap. She was being dismissed.

'You've had a bit of a do with the lady, and you've come out of it largely unharmed. Be thankful, as I'm sure you are. You'll no doubt be wanting to get back to London as soon as possible.'

'I hadn't begun to think of it.'

'Mr Urmiston has already booked your tickets, I believe.'

'Has he, indeed? He had no right to do that.'

'Perhaps it is the London way. There's importunate and importunate,' Inspector Bullard muttered.

* * *

London was the antidote to these adventures, there was no doubt about that.

'It is being home among your own things,' Mrs Venn explained Bella's mood, as if to a child. 'Sleeping in your own bed again. There is no better medicine. You have been among a very sorry lot and it's a miracle to me how you got by. Did you take a meal with this Mrs Stannard, by any chance?'

'You mustn't be jealous of her, Dora. You two would get along famously.'

'I doubt it,' Dora Venn declared. 'You have come home not much bigger than a skinned rabbit, Mrs Wallis, and your face as drawn as Mr Merriboy's, the chimney sweep, before they fixed his waterworks. And the clothes you set out in not fit to wear again. Now, I hope we shall have no argument about this but I have in mind a steak-and-kidney pie and a plate of the newest of new potatoes.'

'Dora, I would eat a raw herring if you put one before me.'

She took a bath and washed her hair, dressed herself in a high-necked linen blouse and wool skirt, meaning to go downstairs and glide about from room to room while waiting for her meal. But when Dora Venn came to look for her, she found her mistress curled up like a child and fast asleep. Leaning over Bella to wake her, she was astonished to have her start up with every appearance of terror. And then the tears began, blabbing tears. The two women sat side by side on the edge of the bed, their arms round each other, howling. Dora knew that small though the Orange Street house was, without Philip Westland in it

Bella had found it as echoing and empty as the Albert Hall.

'Hush, hush,' she murmured groggily, her throat full of her own sobs. 'They can hear us out in the street, I am sure, and will think the cat has died.'

'Dora, let us eat together tonight, not downstairs in the kitchen but in the dining room.'

'Good Lord above,' Mrs Venn exclaimed. 'That would never do! I shall sit by you and watch you tuck away my pie, in more of a nursie way, if you like. But sit down with you to eat? I never heard of such a wicked idea in all my years. I should never be able to look Mrs Bardsoe in the eye again. We'll sail this ship on an even keel.'

'Then where is he, Mrs Venn? Why wasn't he here to greet me?' Bella wailed. Dora kissed her cheek.

'Mr Philip? Looking for his socks, I don't wonder, and fussing over his blessed train timetables. There's only so much abroad a man can take, in my opinion. I believe he got as far as Cairo once and then doubled back for the love of you.'

'I have never told you that story.'

'No, but he did,' Dora Venn lied cheerfully. In fact, she had the bones of it from that wicked old scoundrel Percy Quigley, whose whole purpose in life was to mind other people's business. She pulled Bella up.

'I shall expect you downstairs in ten minutes,' she smiled shakily. 'As for that old Lady Gollinge, if she ain't taken up by the police already, she's hiding in a ditch some-where. So we can put her out of our mind. And good riddance!'

*   *   *

Ursula Gollinge was neither in custody nor cowering in a ditch. She was sitting in a gardener's hut in Roundhay Park, Leeds, having earlier robbed the Vicar of Roundhay of his parish funds, a change of clothes and some other knick-knacks that were too tempting to pass up. (The Reverend Mr Loveridge was at the Town Hall with his wife and daughters, listening to a concert of sacred music and finding it excessively boring. His true purpose in being there was to be in the same space, however huge, as one of his parishioners, a Mrs Neal. When he came home later that evening and found his house burgled, it seemed to him like divine punishment. His wife, who knew all about Mrs Neal, considered it the price one paid for leaving open a ground-floor window.)

The park-keeper's hut was Amelia's idea and smelled agreeably of mown grass and engine oil. When it was fully dark, the two women planned to walk down into Leeds and see how the trains ran. But for the time being they shared cold cuts from a sirloin of beef taken from the vicarage kitchen.

'I have never been to London,' Amelia said with a tinge of doubt in her voice.

'You will love it. And I will change, you'll see.'

'How will we live? For money, I mean.'

'I don't in the least mind robbing another house or two.'

Amelia watched her lover masticate. It was not a pleasant sight and the sound was disgusting. The plain fact was that the further Ursula Gollinge was from the moors around Cruddas the less lovable she was. The girl made allowance for the fact that the wild-haired hunter-gatherer was wearing Mrs Loveridge's garden-party best, the seams of which were already split under the arms to accommodate a far more generous bust than the vicar's wife could offer the world. But what had seemed blithe in Skipton seemed merely stupid now.

'And what if we come across Mrs Wallis?' she asked.

'Oh, I know how to destroy her,' Ursula replied cheerfully. 'She is the least of our worries. No, we shall have new names and, I fancy, a little cottage in somewhere like Chelsea.'

'And we'll set up as burglars, shall we?'

'To begin with.'

'You don't think we'd be safer a bit further from London?'

'As soon as we have the fares, we shall take ship for Australia. I have told you this, child, a thousand times. I cannot reward your loyalty more highly.'

It was agreed that while Ursula might take a cab to the station, if one could be found, it was folly for them to be seen together. Accordingly, Amelia must walk, or – if she thought it safe – take a tram.

She elected to walk. Ursula never saw her again.

THIRTEEN

Next day, it was Bella's whim to go to lunch at her favourite restaurant, Fracatelli's. As a way of cheering herself up, nothing could be better chosen, for this was a place she associated with all the good things in her life, a little haven of elegance set down in the otherwise brutally unromantic Strand. The restaurant, with its famous chandeliers, was neighboured on one side by a narrow house converted to half a dozen one-room offices. On the other was a theatrical costumier's that had seen better days. Sandwiched between, and with the same unimposing facade, Fracatelli had created a shrine to Mediterranean high seriousness without any of the self-advertisement that went with bigger premises in more favoured locations. His clientele were the very willing guardians of a well-kept secret.

Fracatelli never refused a customer but made sure that the worst of them never returned. American tourists who tried to talk down the bill and members of the House of Lords whose manners left something to be desired found on their next visit that, alas, all tables were reserved for the evening. The French got short shrift; especially, for some dark reason, those from Mentone. Children were tolerated for Sunday lunch only. Bella was the only un-accompanied woman ever to dine there. Her current bête noire, Cissie Cornford, considered Fracatelli the rudest man in London, an eminence he shared with the bleak old Duke of Cambridge, to whom she had once spoken eight unanswered words at an Aldershot Review.

'The fellow seems to forget he is Italian,' the painter Frith complained to Bella, after being refused a table for the simple faux pas of turning up in a peasant straw hat.

'It is because he *never* forgets he is Italian that the food is so good,' she retorted.

She dressed for this particular lunch in a favourite sprigged muslin gown that by its chic more or less commanded the rain to stop. And so it did, leaving the pavements smelling of wet pennies, lit by a sun smiling on London from somewhere over Green Park. This change in the weather did much to improve the capital's temper, so that perfect strangers exchanged nods and becks and even the cabbies were good-natured. The air was filled with the jingle of harness and hearty greetings from flower sellers and anyone else with wares to hawk. Balloon men were doing a brisk trade. Toy soldiers mustered and marched in Long Acre. Outside the Royal Opera House, a man was eating fire. Quigley had a cherished phrase for all this impromptu – the dear old city was showing her drawers.

Signor Fracatelli had caught the changing mood. He fussed over Bella, snapping his fingers to summon Alberto, one of the younger waiters. They discussed what La Signora might eat; meanwhile, a deliciously crisp spumante was proposed and accepted. Fracatelli himself uncorked the bottle, the better to complete the story of his niece's wedding to (imagine it!) a Danish boy from Esbjerg with already six ships in his fleet. Maybe not so big, these vessels; in fact, not much more than herring boats. But a young man with good manners and not a scrap of self-doubt in his make-up.

'And where did they take their honeymoon?' Bella asked. Fracatelli put his thumb to his cheek and flicked.

'St Petersburg! Can anyone explain this? She is surely the first Italian girl to go there, I mean from choice. My sister – her mother – cried for a week when she was told. But I do not need to tell you, signora. Love is blind, a most fortunate thing for Danes with blonde moustaches.'

'Is not your niece very beautiful?'

Fracatelli shrugged and gave the pristine tablecloth a last pass with his napkin. He dumped the wine bottle in its bucket of ice and span it with his fingers, producing a noise that always gave Bella a tiny frisson of her own.

'Like I'm telling you, love is blind,' he sighed. 'Which explains why all marriages are happy at the beginning. To answer your question, she is a little on the heavy side.'

Bella chose a dish of chicken livers and black grapes in a Madeira sauce, followed by a very welcome salad. The young Alberto hovered, his eyes as softly lashed as a girl's. She was on her second tiny cup of coffee when a shadow fell across the table.

'Mrs Wallis,' Sir Edward Havelock murmured. 'I was just on my way when I recognised you and thought to pay my respects.'

Havelock had more of the courtier about him than senior policeman. He was very tall and (though he was sixty) decidedly boyish in appearance. His white hair flopped forward over his brow and he had retained since youth that manner of tucking his chin into his chest, as if apologising for his existence to anyone not of his own class. A gentle smile peeked out from a lined and weary face.

'Will you not sit down, Sir Edward? I am poised between ordering a grappa and not. I should be very happy if you would help me make up my mind.'

The Assistant Commissioner had a much-remarked social knack. It was said of him by awed hostesses that he was either in the room or not, never to be seen entering, never taking his leave. This gift extended to sitting down. One moment he was towering over Bella and the next completely at his ease in the free chair at her table. He might as well have been there for the last hour.

'You have had some adventures in Yorkshire recently,' he said without preamble, as though changing the subject from the care of heated greenhouses, where to buy reliable oysters, or anything else they might have been talking about.

'Have they arrested her?' Bella asked eagerly.

'I fear not. There has been a great deal of breast-beating and the crying of woe about this in Yorkshire but I don't find it untoward.' He hesitated. 'The girl—'

'Amelia—'

'Yes, was found in Hull. Unfortunately, with her throat cut.'

Bella felt her eyes well. When she looked down at her hands, she saw they trembled.

'Poor creature!' she managed to say.

'It does seem a shame,' Havelock agreed politely.

'How did this happen? Do we know?'

'She was unlucky enough to fall foul of a Russian deck-hand without a word of English. This man was in turn murdered by those who witnessed the killing, which took place in a notorious dockside drinking den. It was all very sudden and very violent. Perhaps she deserved better.'

'Certainly she did. She was an intelligent girl. I liked her.'

Sir Edward tapped the table with his signet ring and bestowed on Bella his most affectionate smile.

'I believe only you among your sex could say such a thing, after having been so cruelly abducted, Mrs Wallis.'

'Believe me, I think much less well of her partner. Was Lady Gollinge with her when she died?'

'The people they have up there think not; nor does it seem very likely. If I had to guess I'd say she was making her way to London, if not already here.'

'And is this why you stopped by my table, Sir Edward?'

Havelock pursed his lips, before giving Bella his shrewdest glance.

'I thought you would want to know we are alert to the situation. A description has been issued to all divisions, yes. And you are of concern to me, rather more than I could wish.'

'As, for example?'

'Reflect a moment. Lady Gollinge has no idea what you might or might not have said to the police in Skipton that will make matters worse for her. It is just possible she may wish to renew acquaintance.'

'But here, of course, I am on my own ground.'

'Yes,' Havelock murmured.

'I don't claim to know London well but there are certain

parts of it known to me of which Lady Gollinge is, and will always remain, utterly ignorant. She fights on such ground at her peril.'

And never say more to a policeman than is absolutely necessary, she added instantly, greatly angered at herself. She searched for the phrase she wanted and grimaced when she found it: never prate.

'I know you to be a courageous and doughty fighter,' Sir Edward agreed.

Something in the way he spoke set off warning bells as loud as any fire engine. Bella studied the backs of her hands. Havelock seemed to find some detail at the far end of the room interesting.

'Are we talking about my ability to take care of myself?' she asked at length. 'Is it unfeminine for a woman to defend herself with all the means at her disposal?'

'My dear Mrs Wallis,' the Assistant Commissioner protested, laughing. He swept a crumb of bread away with the back of his hand and wiggled a forefinger in his ear with comical energy. Bella waited. The ear-wiggling was a punctuation mark. She guessed what was coming next.

'I believe you have been pestered recently by an officer of mine. You'll forgive me if I choose not to name him.'

'Was I being pestered?' Bella countered swiftly, as if watching a bomb roll towards her, its fuse spluttering. Havelock spent some more moments glancing round the restaurant in an abstracted way before returning his mild gaze to hers.

'He was perhaps being merely overzealous. It happens to some young detectives. However it was, four nights ago the uniformed police were called to help the unfortunate fellow down from a signal gantry at King's Cross. He was hanging by his ankles, covered head to foot in whitewash.'

Murch! thought Bella exultantly.

'How extraordinary,' she said, managing to keep her expression girlishly attentive. 'Had he fallen foul of some criminal gang?'

'He remembers being hit on the head from behind and so forth, but very little else. He is – or was – attached to the Snow Hill station. I'm afraid he made himself very unpopular with the natives in that part of the world. That might be one explanation of events.'

Or not, Sir Edward Havelock's steady gaze suggested.

'Might I ask what any of this has to do with me, Sir Edward?' Bella asked, determined to call him out. 'I think I was in Yorkshire at the time.'

'Indeed you were. But let us put it this way, Mrs Wallis. You are lucky to have the friendship and loyalty of some very admirable people. We might say they patrol your best interests. And long may they continue to do so. But –' he added, tapping out these last words with his fingers on Fracatelli's snowy tablecloth – 'there will be no more high jinks.'

'You choose a strange expression, Sir Edward.'

'Yes,' Havelock murmured. 'It is odd, to be sure. Let me speak even more plainly. At the first sight of Lady Gollinge in London – at the merest hint of her presence here – you will report yourself to the nearest police station. Dear me, dear me,' he added, with a mirthless chuckle. 'What a roundabout way of telling you to be careful. But I think you take my point. On all counts.'

He rose and extended his hand. Then, in that mysterious way of his, he was gone.

'And didn't I tell you not to go up to them heathen parts alone?' Captain Quigley scolded. He himself was back from Portsmouth with adventures of his own to relate – a close run-in with an over-amorous landlady and some complications with certain crates and cartons stamped 'VR'.

'I was out of my depth,' Quigley confessed. 'They do things differently down there. Not that every second cove you meet isn't bent as a butcher's hook. But the scale is different. At one stage I was stuck holding two hundred solar topees marked for Chandrapur. Don't ask me how.'

'I have no intention of doing anything of the kind,' Bella said. 'If you remember, the conversation we are supposed to be having is about Sergeant Tubney.'

'Yes, and how did *that* happen?' Quigley countered. 'He must have enemies we know nothing of. The whitewash a particularly bold stroke. And you may not have heard but Topper Lawson has been in the wars likewise. Found nailed to a hoarding by his overcoat, his boots on the wrong feet and a dunce's hat on his head. Well, it don't surprise me. He had it coming. Between them they had it coming.'

'Where is Billy Murch?' Bella demanded abruptly.

'Billy? Now what's he got to do with it?'

'Never mind that! Where is he?'

'Am I my brother's keeper? I did call over to Chiswick a couple of nights ago for a wet and a bit of a gab and Millie reports he's gone down to Chatham. Did you have something you wanted to ask him, dear lady?'

'An hour ago, I was warned off any further nonsense by Sir Edward Havelock. In the nicest possible way but – and understand me, Captain – definitively.'

'Good Lord!' Quigley exclaimed. 'Definitive, was it? That must have brought you up short in your tracks. Sir Edward known to be a flaming firebrand of an individual, the hammer and coking tongs of the fight against crime. My word, who would want to come up against *him* down a dark alley?'

'One day your facetiousness will get the better of you,' Bella fumed.

Quigley had an answer to that, too. He indicated the battered rosewood table, on which lay a neat stack of paper, her pen and a bottle of black ink. True, there was also a plate of empty whelk shells that he disposed of by chucking the contents through the open door; but the point stood.

'Looking after you, Mr Margam, sir, can be brisk work. For as long as you sit at that table, you will need the help and comfort of lesser mortals such as myself. We have seen very recent how you are when you're on your own. Next to useless, if you'll pardon the expression.'

'I am thinking of closing the office down.'

'Moving your base of operations temporarily. Agreed!'

'Shutting it down. Nailing up the front door. Quitting.'

Quigley goggled. What was Margam's office was also his quarters, his place of abode. It was, if a person wanted to put it this way, his support trench, firestep and sally port.

'Now we don't want to be doing nothing hasty,' he said. 'The dear old Court has been a friend to us both. And I fancy there have been some rare strokes of literature composed at that table there. I mind how before Captain

Deveril met his disgrace he hovered for more than a week poised between love and dishonour before being given a hearty shove by your good self when you was in a better mood and fortified by the Captain's Dutch gin in the stone bottle.'

'Which I never wish to taste again.'

'A delicacy greatly sought after by the more discerning palate.'

'Quigley, arguing with you is like trying to sculpt in frogspawn.'

'Yes,' he flashed back. 'And how did you first come by that useful phrase? From Welsh Phil is how, here in this very place. Abandon the Court? The Bard of Avon would have been pleased to get his feet under that table. Welsh Phil, College Pete, Billy Murch himself, not to mention Charlie Urmiston in all his pomp—'

'Suppose I say the game is up?'

'Then, dear lady, Mr Margam, sir, you would be making a sorry error of judgement. An egregious mistake,' he added, without the slightest idea of what the last adjective meant.

But Bella was wholly serious. She had come so close to saying too much to Ursula Gollinge and fighting Philip Westland's battles for him. It was as though loving him as much as she did gave her the licence to touch on the one secret torment he would never allow to be discussed. Shutting up the Fleur de Lys office was a guilty gesture, therefore, an act of contrition. The truth was that no amount of book-writing could ever replace love in the real world. With a sudden jump in her heart, she realised she might never take up a pen again.

Quigley watched her with one of his rare fits of perspicacity. It was as if he knew exactly what she was thinking and she could read in his eyes a certain shy but sincere kindliness, even. She jutted out her chin and faced him down.

'You don't understand,' she improvised. 'I have to defend myself against this Gollinge woman.'

'Ho! If she has come to London. And if she has, how would she ever know how to find you?'

'She has the Orange Street address.'

The Captain looked at Bella with a strange fondness, as sometimes happens when children say something so ineffably stupid that adult reality shivers like a dish of jelly that has been jogged. All this while, he had been wearing his park-keeper's kepi, headgear that he liked so much for its quasi-military associations. Sighing, he took it off and stood there like Livingstone staring numbly at Stanley.

'Never a dull moment in your employ,' he managed to croak.

Billy Murch was not in Chatham, of course, but marching up a muddy lane that led through the railway yards in Essen. Asking after this place Stoppenberg, as mentioned in Philip's telegram, he had fallen in with a far too obliging cove who claimed it was but a cock's stride away. No, no, my friend, really just over there, look, a few hundred metres only! But as the railway tracks ended and a few shabby-looking cottages came into sight, this Samaritan began to act up. He stopped his cheery grunting and babbling and became more thoughtful than was strictly necessary. A cudgel appeared in his hand. When he looked round, Billy had disappeared behind a linesman's hut. The guide walked back to investigate and was caught a blow across the side of his head with a muddy pick helm.

'*Kamerad!*' he yelped, staggering. Murch helped him upright by a hand round his throat.

'See, like you was telling me, you are fond of the old Englanders and I thank you for that. But I wasn't born yesterday. Do I look as if I was born yesterday?'

He pointed to the row of grimy cottages.

'Is that Stoppenberg?'

'No,' the man admitted, blood from his temple pouring into his eyes.

'Is there a pub there? Pub? Boozer?'

'*Stube, ja.*'

'Well then, let's have no more arsing about, no bad feelings, and we'll step across there and share a glass.'

But the man who had wanted to rob him turned on his heel and legged it, his overcoat streaming out behind him. Murch watched him hurdle a small stack of railway sleepers and disappear round the corner of a substantial brick building, one in which every single window had been broken. An engine shed, Billy guessed. Or maybe some kind of workshop. But never Stoppenberg, not for a single bloody minute. He threw down the pick helm and began walking. As it happened, he was going in the right direction, which was to say east.

To an outside observer, there was nothing nervous or guilty about Murch, nor was there the slightest concession to the novelty of his surroundings. When he came to the row of cottages, he found washing lines strung across the road, bearing sheets and nondescript items, fresh from the copper but already flecked with smuts. To make his way, he had to push these aside, so that he had the fancy of walking downstage, over and over. One or two pipe-smoking women watched him pass without comment – a foreigner to be sure, but not one to mess with lightly. A dog a very good indicator of what was what – several dogs sat up at his passing but not one came to challenge.

The truth was, Billy was carrying within him an entirely novel sensation. How this came about – a trick of the light, the soapy smell of the laundered sheets, the other-wise eerie emptiness of the streets, a touch of indigestion even – he could not say; but he wished Millie was with him. She was in any case right there in the forefront of his mind. It was a colossal surprise. Dear old Millie with her raucous laugh, her unapologetic way of breaking wind, the dab hand she gave to apple pie, her conversations with the unborn baby. What a time to think of her! It was enough to make a cove blush. Him, as had so accustomed himself to the solitary life that his entire reputation came to depend upon it!

'You never know what the beggar is thinking,' Quigley was fond of saying, not without awe in his voice. It was a habit that long preceded the Quigley years. Private Murch, as he then was, had distinguished himself as a soldier in the Crimea for just this capacity to keep himself to himself.

'I am done for,' the wounded Major Cathcart had wept. 'You may as well put me down, you dog, for your confounded jogging is shaking the lifeblood out of me.'

As Cathcart told the story later (and it was difficult to head him off from it, as his long-suffering wife knew only too well) this taciturn soldier had run the major two miles over broken ground to the head of the road into Balaclava.

'Slung over his back like a sack of potatoes. I make no bones about it, I was crying like a damned parlourmaid: but from him not a single word. He did not utter. Russian shells bursting all about, the ground littered with dead horses. Amazing fellow. The surgeons told me afterwards they wanted to examine him for wounds, so much blood was there on his tunic. It was all *my* blood, by God! And do you know –' the major always concluded, for he had very little sense of story – 'I never clapped eyes on him again! To the extent that the parson here once suggested I had dreamed him. Dreamed the whole bang-shoot. That he had never existed and it was the hand of God that saved me! Rum, what?'

Murch's version of the same events: had come across this tubby officer crawling about on his hands and knees, whimpering like a dog. Decided to save the cove's life. Spur of the moment thing. Ground a bit tricky but downhill all the way. He told the story while it was fresh in his mind, eating horsemeat steaks with a couple of chancers who had the word 'deserters' written all over them. Well, to say he told the story was an exaggeration: he had it dragged out of him by his incredulous audience. Paid for his steak with a pinch of tobacco and walked away, back to the lines.

But now! Billy, you have changed, he told himself wryly, feeling as light and blown as thistledown. Walking east to Stoppenberg with Millie for company – this is a turn-up for the book and no error. There is something in your heart that was never there before, that disqualifies you from biffing your way to eternity. Fetch Mr Westland out from whatever scrape he's got himself into and go home to your wife and child. And if there's a bit of an opportunity on the road back, give old Westland a nudge in the same direction. Show him the light, as Millie would put it. Lead him into the paths of righteousness. He'll thank you for it, blind me if he won't.

It was an incredibly liberating moment. Watery sunshine drenched the fields on either side, showing off hectares of slumbering cabbages – and in the distance, an embanked road along which plodded three carts and a file of peasanty-looking characters, every man jack of them singing. And here was an instant dividend from having Millie in your head – though Murch was about as musical as a wheelbarrow, he knew from churchgoing with his wife of a Sunday that what he was hearing was a hymn. One of the good old ones, in fact.

FOURTEEN

Philip Westland knew very little of the workings of his own body – in that respect he was one of the shyest men Bella had ever met, a reticence that shaded, when sickness came in one form or another, into downright cowardice. There never was a good time to discuss illness with him. Anything below the waist was completely beyond his powers to mention, as for example when he had poisoned himself with a bit of bad fish and spent three days flitting between the water closet and the spare room, doubled over in agony but too ashamed to ask for help. (On this particular occasion, his life was saved by Hannah Bardsoe, bustling into the house in Orange Street with a cure-all pill the size of a hen's egg: this and the hysterical laughter he could hear as Bella and Mrs Bardsoe discussed his case did the trick. It was a case of governing his wayward guts or dying of indignation.)

The wound to his shoulder was out of a different box. The fever dreams were gone, leaving in their place a clear mind savaged by a barking headache and – at the site of the wound itself – an ugly darkening of the flesh. Some of this was bruising but the suppuration that leaked from the blackened bullet hole itself was too frightening to contemplate. Philip began to believe the flesh was mortifying. When the heat in his shoulder began to spread across his chest, he was forced to confess as much to his captor, Hans Georg. After a bad-tempered examination – and an alarming amount of tooth-sucking – the farmer prepared a salve that resembled (and perhaps was) cooked spinach. When he applied it at near boiling point, straight from the stove, the patient fainted clean away.

'In the name of God!' Hans Georg's old mother exclaimed. 'He is not a beast. What you shove up a cow's arse might not work on an Englishman.'

When Philip came to, he was outside, flat on his back behind a low stone wall. His bloodied shirt lay over him. He was holding someone's hand – he guessed from its weight and softness, Anna's. He squeezed; and after a second or two, was squeezed back. Hans Georg passed him a hand-rolled cigarette.

'It wasn't me who shot you,' he grumbled.

'I am grateful to you for what you have done.'

'Yes, well, your friends from England had better arrive soon,' the German muttered. 'For if you don't get to a doctor, you will die.'

'Then get me to a doctor.'

To which there was no reply, for Philip knew that once lodged with a qualified doctor, his captors would lose control over him; and with that, any chance of the hundred sovereigns they supposed Murch was bringing.

'If I die,' he said, 'the retribution that will fall on you then will be terrible indeed.'

'You seem to forget you are a foreign spy.'

'So? Why not put on a clean shirt and go to see Herr Krupp and tell him the man he is looking for has been hidden from him for nearly a week by two bumpkins trying to extract a reward from the British Foreign Office? What's the matter, don't you have the stomach for that?'

'There had better be a reward,' Hans Georg threatened. 'Because I am getting sick of the sight of you, Englander.'

After he had gone, Philip dragged himself upright with Anna's help.

'If your friend doesn't come, my father will kill you,' she whispered. 'And if not him, then certainly his sister and her husband.'

'The postman and his wife.'

'Yes,' Anna said mournfully. 'We are not very intelligent people, I think.'

'Listen, Anna. The man who is coming is not a weakling like me. He has not come to negotiate. Do you understand?'

'There are no sovereigns?' she asked, a hand to her mouth.

'No. Instead there is a man who is utterly ruthless – believe me – whose sole purpose is to get me out of here, no matter what it takes.'

'My father has a shotgun,' the girl said, her lip trembling.

'A gun won't save him. If he is fool enough to discharge it, or even point it, he is a dead man. But you can help.'

'Me?' she squeaked.

'We shall need a pony and trap. If not that, a horse. A means of escape. If we get away, you have my word no harm will come to you.'

'A horse! There are only five horses in the whole village!'

'What about the pastor? How does he get about?'

'You want me to steal the pastor's horse?' she cried incredulously.

The old lady, who had been listening to all this with grim enjoyment, suddenly scrambled to her feet.

'Run and fetch the bed sheets,' she commanded. 'Two strangers are coming into the yard. Be quick, child.'

To make sure Philip did not show himself above the wall, she put a bare and blackened foot against his throat.

'My son will hold them off for a moment. But we are duty bound to offer them hospitality. Anna will cover you with the sheets. Lie still. And don't breathe.'

'Let me crawl somewhere now.'

'Do as I say. I'll tell you when to crawl.'

Anna reappeared with her arms filled with sheets. When they were dumped over him, Philip stifled a disgusted sob. But Grandma had found an actress within herself. He heard a stinging slap.

'Yes, and didn't I ask you to do this first thing? And now we've got visitors, to our great shame! Don't just stand there. Go and light the boiler.'

Murch had already come across the two strangers, bad-tempered men in town suits and starched collars. Murch in a ditch of watercress, the two men sitting with their legs dangling over the tailboard of a bullock cart as it passed in a cloud of mud. They were cursing, as well they might. Although Murch had not a word of German, he could piece their story together easily enough – tired of walking, they had hitched a ride they now regretted. Both a little bit drunk, one short and fat, the other a more formidable proposition, a lean-looking cove in

- 698 -

a soft black hat. A detail: the thin one sat with his fists on his knees – big hands, knobby knuckles. Drunk, but dangerous.

When it was safe to come out of the ditch, Murch sat with his back to a tree, letting the water drain from his clothes, and thinking. These two might be harmless chancers who had wandered in from some other story but he did not believe it. Billy had walked clean through Stoppenberg an hour earlier with a hunter's instinct that he had yet to come upon the freshest trail. There was just enough of what he considered civilisation in the main street for him to discount it as Mr Westland's hidey-hole. There happened to be half a dozen packmen selling ribbons and bonnets outside the village inn and the faces of the women gathered around were far too frank and open. Stoppenberg, as far as these things go, was an innocently happy place. He was even accompanied for a hundred yards or so by a child who held his hand and skipped along beside him, chattering merrily.

The lane he was on now had more promise, if only in the sense that the country round about was more woebe-gone. The cabbage fields had given way to thickets of blackthorn and the occasional ancient and untenanted cottage. Super sensitive to atmosphere, Billy considered the road to Feldhausen far more likely to lead to some-thing dark and sinister. Sighting the two strangers in the cart had done nothing to diminish this idea: What were obvious townies doing clattering through Mr No-man's-land in their Sunday best? Not police, he judged. But not Bible salesmen either.

* * *

The short fat man did the talking. Of the two of them, he was the more obviously drunk. His companion sat in Hans Georg's kitchen smoking and drumming his fingers. He looked bored and under-employed.

'My name is Wrangl,' the fat one blustered. 'It isn't my idea of a day out to come to this shit-heap. So let's get it over with. We are looking for an Englishman. When we find him, we will take him back to Essen. For the people among whom we find him, that's the end of the story. Nothing bad happens to them.'

'Is there an Englishman here? In Feldhausen? How can that be?' the old lady cried in a wondering sort of voice. 'Don't they have cabbages and potatoes in England? It seems a long way to come. But maybe he is mad. Old Sturmer went off his chump and they came for him.'

'Sturmer?'

'A neighbour,' Hans Georg supplied.

'When was this?'

'When she was still a girl.'

Wrangl ran his tongue over his teeth, thought about saying something, changed his mind.

'Naturally, I have never seen an Englishman but then I've never seen a Chinaman, either,' the old lady cackled. 'Nobody ever comes through here. Essen is the place to look for foreigners. They say there is a black man there. From Egypt, I think they said. Have you tried Essen?'

The lean and dangerous one stirred. He reached into his coat and took out a pistol.

'Where is the girl, Grandma?'

'Anna? Couldn't you see she was doing the washing?'

'Show me,' the lean one said.

'Show these gentlemen the wash-house,' Grandma said. 'Then you'll take something to eat with us, I don't doubt. Let me sweep the floor first.'

The three men walked across the yard to a small stone building. Inside, Anna was feeding chips of wood and dried cowpats to a fire burning under an iron tub. The sheets floated in milky water. Wrangl shook his head in disgust and took a swig from the bottle he had snatched up from the kitchen table. Anna offered his companion the dolly stick and he punched down some of the ballooning fabric. His free hand still held the pistol.

'If I thought you were playing the fool with me, any of you, your shitty little lives wouldn't be worth living.'

'Search the barns,' Hans Georg said. 'I don't know why you picked on us but we've done nothing wrong. If you have some quarrel with this Englishman, don't bring it here.'

'What quarrel can we have?' Wrangl asked mildly enough. 'What do you think is happening?'

'Perhaps you are robbers looking for an associate,' Anna suggested.

'Robbers?'

She shrugged. 'Perhaps he has made off with money that belongs to you. We know nothing about things like that.'

'Do we look like robbers to you?'

'I don't know. We are only trying to help you.'

The lean stranger pointed his pistol at the roof and fired. Anna screamed. Both she and her father flung themselves to the dirt floor of the laundry.

'You people ought to be in a zoo,' he said. 'This is not living, what you do here. Dogs lead a better life.'

Following the sound of the shot, a man ran to the court-yard's entrance, an old man with snow-white hair and blue-veined arms. It was Dietze, their neighbour, an interfering fool with one cow and half a hectare of potatoes.

'Help,' he cried. 'Murder!'

He had a peasant's sense of propriety, waving his skinny arms and bellowing but taking care not to cross an imaginary line that ran through the mud and rocks dividing Hans Georg's yard from the rest of the world. The two strangers watched him through a cobwebbed window, shouting and looking this way and that for the help he knew did not exist. The fat man laughed.

'Look at him jig! That is one stupid old bastard.'

The man with the pistol sauntered out of the washhouse, took aim in the most mannered and sardonic way possible and shot him dead. The fat man seized Anna by her hair and dragged her on her knees to Dietze's corpse.

'You have killed him!' she spluttered.

'That was the idea. By way of warning. Tonight we stay in Stoppenberg. If by noon tomorrow we have heard nothing from you, we shall come back and burn this rat's nest to the ground. We are not robbers. We are businessmen.'

'He is in the stable,' Hans Georg called, defeated.

'No!' Anna screamed.

The two Krupp's employees sprinted back across the yard. Hans Georg grabbed his daughter's wrist and ran into the house. Stumbled into the kitchen sobbing with terror. Bolted the door, jagging a flap of skin from his thumb. Turned – and came face to face with a complete stranger, holding his shotgun as if he knew how to use it.

'Cartridges,' Murch said. 'Go and get them. Stay away from the windows. You're a big man, so stop that bloody snivelling.'

'They don't speak English, Billy.'

'They don't need to, Mr Westland,' Murch said, very calm. 'But if you could just convey to this cove that we are up shit alley unless he wakes his ideas up—'

There were plenty of times in the coming months to piece together how, while the men were gassing inside, Anna dragged Philip to a tool shed attached to the house; how Murch, passing at just the right time, heard the shot fired through the laundry roof, jumped the farm wall and came into the house by way of a vegetable garden and narrow back door. How he found the kitchen empty, heard the second shot, saw Dietze's body fall, and then, miraculously, saw the old girl dragging Philip Westland inside by his heels.

'Tell Ma she's a good 'un,' Murch said now, throwing over the oak table and dragging it to the far wall, with just enough space for Philip and the womenfolk to crouch behind. He took off his jacket and hung it absent-mindedly on the back of the last upright chair.

'Now let's get this straight,' he said. 'Those evil bastards outside have already killed. I've arrived a bit tardy and don't have the full story but you can have my word on it that they won't pack up shop and go home. They'll want to come and join us in here. And that ain't going to happen.'

By way of demonstration, the two Krupp's men burst out of the stables in high old mood. When they saw the door to the house closed, they conferred briefly. Inside, Hans Georg passed Murch a battered cardboard box.

Lolling in the bottom were just three cartridges. To Billy's eye the brass bases looked suspiciously dull. He touched the breech of the gun and gave its owner an interrogative thumbs-up. Hans Georg nodded.

'Herr Westland,' the fat man called from the yard. 'We know you are in there. Already there has been such unpleasantness. We are not here to kill you but to take you back to Essen. Where everything can be decided in a proper fashion. Like gentlemen. No one will be harmed.'

'You have already killed an innocent man,' Philip shouted.

'No, he was not innocent! As our report shall show. He was assisting you in your attempt to escape. An accomplice, I think.'

'Oh, sod this,' Billy Murch said. He knocked a pane of glass from the window with the muzzle of the shotgun. Saw them flinch and dive behind a cattle trough. Considered a shot and then decided against it.

'Tell them you are not coming out and they are not coming in,' he commanded Philip. 'And best to add, sir, that if they so much as break wind behind that there trough arrangement, I will blow someone's head off. You might mention the notion of a crack shot and so forth.'

'If you come any closer I will kill you,' Philip yelled.

The answer was derisive laughter. Murch fired, just to wipe the smile off their faces. Hitting the trough was no good: he aimed at a lump of rock to one side and shattered it. The fragments sang as they flew.

'Now listen to me, Mr Westland. They are going to rush the house. They don't have any choice – even in this forsaken hole a crowd of witnesses is going to form.

They don't want that. When it happens – when they come through that door – this here German bloke will be with you behind the table. He should have one up the spout and the time to let fly is when they're framed in the doorway. Translate.'

Hans Georg listened to Philip with a green face, his head shaking vigorously. For all his size – and his was twice Billy's weight – he was in no mood at all to play the hero. When he was offered the gun, he pushed it back.

'Just what I thought. Tell him to get right out of it, then. He can hide upstairs. If they win down here, he's a dead man anyway. But get him out now. I don't want him in my squad.'

'Give Anna the gun. She'll do it.'

Murch thought about that and then shook his head.

'No. Tell Grandma I need her to do it.'

The old lady's head appeared above the table like a weasel's. Murch smiled encouragingly.

'When she was younger, did she ever fire a rabbit gun?'

'This isn't the Wild West, Billy.'

'Make sure she knows what to do. Frame 'em up in the doorway, then boom! Just point at the open doorway – boom!'

'This man has balls bigger than an ox,' the old lady decided. She wiped her nose with the back of her wrist and held out her hand for the gun.

'Not yet, not yet. Now I want Anna to tell them how no one's listening to you, they're all terrified and they are coming out. And make it convincing.'

As she spoke, Murch ran to the table and passed her

grandmother the gun. Then ran back and made a noisy business of drawing the bolts on the door. Pulled the door open slowly, slowly. Whatever the girl was saying, it was impressively passionate. A late addition to the plan: on the wall behind him, Murch found a glass-framed picture of the Lord Jesus Shining His Light unto the World. He took it off its hook and tested it for heft.

'They are standing up,' Philip called softly. 'They are arguing what to do.'

'Tell them that without help, you cannot fight them. You surrender. Beg them to save your life. Pour it on. Loads of gravy.'

And if this isn't the trickiest bit, Billy thought. If they decide to split up we are in trouble. If they don't take the bait at all, I don't have a better idea. Millie, old girl, I may have overreached myself at last.

'They're coming,' Philip called softly. Murch held up two fingers by way of a question. 'Yes,' Philip answered.

'Tell Ma to wait until they're right on the threshold—'

But the two killers had broken into a run. Murch ducked behind the door only a second before the shotgun went off. There was a gasp and an oath, followed by a pistol shot. The air was thick with white powder – the old woman had fired as instructed but missed the target and hit the ceiling, bringing down a shower of laths and perhaps a century of limewash and rat droppings. Billy held the religious print sideways on, stepped out from behind the door and swung the frame like an axe at the man nearest him. It was Wrangl. The blow caught him at eye level across the bridge of his nose and instinctively he turned away, his head in his hands.

In the smother of dust, the lean and dangerous one was cursing and firing his pistol across the kitchen. He turned his head to cope with this unexpected threat from his right – but just a second too late. Billy had changed grip and holding Jesus Shining His Light unto the World like a racquet, smashed it into the killer's face. The glass shattered.

As Billy had learned, having made his way down a long corridor of fights like this in the past, it was not the first blow that counted, but the second, third and fourth. And the trick of that was never to hesitate, never improvise. He was fighting a man with a pistol in his hand who was thrown back on his heels for only a split second. But in that tiny window of time he stepped across the killer's body, grabbed his gun arm high up near the armpit, seized his wrist and turned him against the wall. The German knew what was coming, dipped his shoulder and sank to the floor. It was a defence, he was strong, he held the gun. His elbow joint was intact.

But there exists a visceral understanding in fights, something that comes in well below the level of thought. The German's body was already accepting, on behalf of the brain, that it could not win. Though the two men fought on for another two minutes, the pistol became an irrelevance. To the outsider – to Anna watching in horror from behind the overturned table – the struggle seemed even-handed and the outcome doubtful. When Wrangl staggered back in and knelt beside the writhing figures to beat with his fists on Billy's back, it almost seemed that fortunes had changed. But, for his companion, it was the end. Cramped up by Wrangl's body, he exposed his neck for a fraction of a second too long. The shard of glass in Billy's hand plunged into his carotid artery, producing a fountain of blood. His boots began drumming on the stone-flagged floor.

'Not me, not me,' Wrangl cowered, his soft little hands held against his face.

'Look away,' Billy shouted to the girl.

Then slit the fat man's throat, the way that butchers slaughter pigs. When he stood up, the eye that he caught was Philip Westland's. And if he says anything, I will pick this bloody revolver up and kill the lot of them. Stone me if I ever pull a stroke like this again, Billy thought, wiping his face free of blood and spitting out a tooth. You and me are for some other world, Millie girl, some better place. In future we shall leave the gentlemen to settle their own quarrels. We'll hook ourselves right out of it – I don't say no to a lock-keeper's cottage and a corduroy suit, my oath if I don't. But anyway, far, far away from this.

Grandma floated towards him across the littered floor. She sat him down with his back against the wall, and stroked his face, his hair. Then laid her cheek against his shoulder for a moment. He patted her bony spine, wondering how to ask for coffee in her own lingo.

'Billy?' Westland said quietly. 'We must go home.'

'You won't get an argument from me,' Murch said drily. 'But what say we tidy up a bit first? Dig a deep hole and plant the bodies. Then a doctor for you. I dare say we could use a cart or something of the sort.'

Which is how Pastor Bisblinkoff came to find his yellow and black trap, his pride and joy and one remaining consolation in life, gone, along with Rudi the pony. Christian forgiveness could not answer the situation and when his wife suggested he calm down, he picked a massively heavy bust of Bismarck from the mantelpiece and threw it through the window.

FIFTEEN

Commander Alcock kept a desk at the Admiralty in a section to do with chart revisions, compiled and collated from reports by ships' masters across five oceans. For example, in 1876, the very dubious entrance to Puerto Deseado on the coast of Argentina was compromised by the collision of two merchant vessels just at the narrowest point of entry to the harbour. The wrecks remained unmarked until an apoplectic Captain Pottinger, RN, ran foul of them in the *Acheron*, toppling the smoke stack from his ship, shearing off the propellor and hazarding the lives of 247 men.

Alcock's civilian clerks were meticulous and patient men, none of whom had been to sea themselves. They enjoyed the celestial laughter that hung over some of the reports and signals: it was a pleasure to read as a footnote to Captain Pottinger's misfortunes how the Mayor of Puerto Deseado had shot dead his brother-in-law the harbour master for his dilatoriness in marking the wrecks, 'thus saving their Lordships the trouble of an official censure'. In another ocean altogether, volcanic activity had closed the small trading station at Bintochan on the Sumatra coast, isolating 700 tons of coal that had once stood dockside but was now three miles inland. Stranded along with the coal was a Baptist mission and its next-door neighbour, the notorious Lucky Boy brothel.

Alcock dealt with certain boxes whose contents were examined by his eyes only and filed in a green and gold floor safe to which he had the sole key. It was the Chief Clerk's understanding that what came across the Commander's desk contained information of a sensitive political or diplomatic nature that might not bear directly on revised instructions to mariners. He was content with that, as how could he be otherwise? Alcock, for all his fussy manners and demands to behold a tight ship when he walked into his dusty offices every morning on the stroke of ten, was otherwise the perfect boss. At half past twelve each day, he went to lunch and was not seen again until three and sometimes four in the afternoon.

'Your man had a miserable time of it among the Teutons,' Radley of the Foreign Office observed over lamb cutlets at the Travellers.

'The task was beyond him.'

'Bit harsh, what? Wasn't he shot by some chap supposed to be on our side?'

'It would seem so.'

'Herr Krupp set the dogs on him consequently?'

'You are remarkably well informed.'

'Well, he was trying to make off with what amount to state secrets. We tend to hear about that sort of thing. Do we know where he is now?'

'He managed to find his way to Duisberg and signalled from there that he was taking ship to Rotterdam.'

'When you say "taking ship"—?'

'Taking barge then,' Alcock said, greatly niggled. 'In any case, I do not intend to use him again. He lacks what I call the killer instinct.'

'Poor fellow,' Radley drawled.

'On that subject, did you receive my note on Pottinger?'

'Remind me.'

'Captain, RN.'

'The man who tried to start a war with Argentina.'

'You are very facetious,' Commander Alcock complained testily. 'The incident at Puerto Deseado was the only blemish on an otherwise impeccable record. Captain Pottinger has since resigned the service.'

'How did that go down with their Lordships?' Radley asked, who knew the answer.

'He is headstrong, I grant you. But I believe I can find him work.'

'Has he the killer instinct?'

'Great heavens, yes!' Alcock exclaimed, as though his companion had just asked the most redundant question possible. 'When he was a midshipman in the *Amphytriton*, he picked up a fractious mule in Valetta one afternoon and flung it bodily into the sea. A twenty-stone *mule*.'

'I did not know that,' Radley murmured. 'So Westland will give way to this fellow, is that it?'

'That is the plan.'

Lucky Westland, Radley thought, stirring the peas on his plate and wondering – not for the first time – whether there was a Mrs Alcock; and if so, what she found to console herself with in what was a very common sort of villa on Battersea Rise.

'Does your man speak a language?' he asked absent-mindedly.

'Welsh,' Alcock said, after a slight pause.

'If you ask me,' Charlie MacGill observed, 'your fellow was very lucky to have had you by him.'

'I didn't ask you,' Billy Murch replied. The little Scots engineer nodded. No offence taken. The two men sat on kitchen chairs on the afterdeck of the Dutch tug, watching the barge train strung out behind. It was night, and they were passing a small town on the German side of the Rhine, distinguished by a few strings of street lights. The only signs of life on the barges were washing lines and the sparks from galley chimneys. The very, very faint strains of an accordion – the sailor's piano – drifted down on them from the second boat in line.

'A hunting accident, you said,' MacGill prompted.

'Would you be a nosy bugger at all?'

'Not specially. I'm from Greenock, me. That's a Willis and Simms engine you hear down below. Not exactly the state of the art but I can claim to know it as well as the man who made the first drawings. Aye, I keep that pile of shite as fine-tuned as any concert violin. And to mark your card for you, Jimmy, what we are doing here is drinking my beer and making conversation.'

Properly rebuked, Billy rolled MacGill a cigarette and passed it across.

'He's had a bit of bad luck,' he said. 'I came to fetch him home. Reckoned a bed in this old tub better than a train ride any day of the week. Give his wound a chance to heal.'

'That would be right,' MacGill agreed. 'The pair of you master and servant, no doubt.'

'That sort of thing.'

'Aye, aye,' the engineer said musingly. 'Weel, as I say, he's lucky to have you by him. And what did you make of the German laddies you met with?'

'A bit on the slow side?' Billy suggested. MacGill struck his thigh in delight.

'Are they not! But terrible swift to take offence, wouldn't you say?'

'You've had dealings with them, have you?'

'Good God, man, am I not married to a Rhine maiden? Calm enough she is, the great lummox, as big in the beam as one of yon barges. A floating island, you might say. But her brother is a different proposition altogether. A frown on him enough to frighten horses.'

'There have had to be words with the cove from time to time,' Billy guessed. MacGill laughed and lobbed his beer bottle into the glassy river.

'You'd know all about that,' he said with Greenock shrewdness. 'We'll fetch to Rotterdam about three tomorrow. The Harwich ferry sails at seven. It's been a pleasure talking with you, sonny.'

He dropped through an open hatch to where the Willis and Simms chuntered in a fine mist of oil, every bit of brasswork, every copper tube polished up like Rob Roy's dinner service. Billy groped about in the thrumming dark and opened the door to Philip Westland's berth, finding an impossibly narrow bunk and a further four feet by nine of free space. Every inch of wall was taken up by hooks, or at any rate the clothes they supported. The triumphantly oily smell of MacGill's engines was mingled with more familiar stinks – sweat, sausage and onions, tar and canvas, tobacco.

Philip was awake. The bandage that the Duisberg doctor had applied glowed in the dark, possibly the whitest and cleanest thing ever seen in this cabin. He held out his hand to Billy with a wry smile.

'This is all very cosy,' he murmured weakly. 'Where do you sleep tonight?'

'On the floor here, I fancy.'

'You were a good man to come and find me, Billy.'

'It was nothing.'

'Well, no, it was quite a lot. I think you dug the graves of three people.'

'Shots were exchanged,' Murch allowed in his characteristically flat way. But Philip was thinking more of the sound a throat makes when it is slit from ear to ear; and the drumming of heels on a stone floor.

'I'll not put you to such trouble again,' he said – and hated himself for such an insipid and cowardly way of expressing thanks. 'This is my last excursion, I promise you.'

'What will you do?'

'Marry Bella. Mrs Wallis, that is.'

'I am very pleased to hear it.'

'You think I will make her happy?'

Murch was always a bit niggardly when it came to smiles but he bestowed one on Philip now that would have melted the polar ice cap.

'Never a dull moment between the pair of you,' he promised. 'Never a moment's regret, never a backward glance.'

'You sent her the telegraph?' Philip asked, suddenly anxious.

'All taken care of.'

'And you said nothing in it to alarm her?'

'Never in life.'

Bella had Billy's cable in her hand at breakfast that same morning. It read:

Everything tip-top considering. Weather rainy. On way home. Kind regards. Philp.

'And isn't that the news you've been waiting for?' Dora Venn exclaimed in delight.

'Philip didn't write this.'

'It's good enough for me,' Mrs Venn said. 'A leg of lamb, I think, for when he gets back; and a dish Mrs Bardsoe was mentioning, of summer fruits done up in a pudding. Unless you've got your own ideas, of course.'

'These are not words and expressions Mr Westland might use,' Bella repeated.

'The sense is clear enough, though. Now, I don't think he will want to find a moping woman when he steps through that door. I shall have Mrs Poe's daughter round to help me buff up this old place and it wouldn't harm to send the girl across to the Garden for an armful of flowers neither. But it will be *your* radiance that cheers his heart.'

Bella studied the cable form more closely. 'Where is Duisburg?' she asked.

'One place much the same as another over there,' Dora Venn declared. A joke occurred to her. 'I don't suppose they know where they are neither! The man to ask would be Charlie Urmiston. There's not a lot gets past him. A regular brainbox when it comes to where things are. Also the kings and queens of England, though that don't come into it in this particular case.'

She is trying to cheer me up, Bella thought when she was finally left alone. The conversation with Sir Edward in Fracatelli's had led to some very untoward behaviour and in consequence several instances of lips pursed and eyebrows raised from Mrs Venn. At first Bella kept to the house, not even venturing as far as Mr Liddell's for a cake, or a bag of his croissants. But yesterday she had spent a small fortune driving about the West End hoping to catch a glimpse of Ursula Gollinge. It was a deeply irrational impulse. She had the cab go up and down Regent Street twice (twice!) and into Piccadilly via Sackville Street. Thence all the way along the south side of the Park, up through Church Street and back down the Bayswater Road.

'Oxford Street or Park Lane?' the veteran cabbie called.

'Would you pull up and talk to me for a moment?' Bella asked.

'Talk to you?' the man said, greatly scandalised. 'I'd as soon drop you off and be done with it. Talk to you! This is a new one and no error. I took you for a lady, missus.'

Which was how she came to walk from Lancaster Gate all the way back to Piccadilly. Trees did not help; Speke's Monument (which she had not previously known to exist) did not help either. She sat on a bench with her back to the Serpentine and astonished herself by weeping.

Look at it this way, Margam said. You – let us call you

Lady Barbara Collins – spend a fruitless afternoon in searching for your bitter rival, Ursula Lapointe. Then, just as you are passing the monument to Speke, you see a white carnation laid on its topmost step. You investigate: there is a card. The handwriting is Lapointe's! But does it pay tribute to the great explorer? It does not. It reads, simply, *Ce soir à vingt heures*. (The ink is violet, I fancy.) Suddenly the whole mystery explains itself. This is a blackmail note addressed to your fiancé, Roderick Northland; for Lapointe has discovered that it was he, acting upon orders from the Admiralty, who shot dead John Hanning Speke—

'Oh, for God's sake,' Bella said aloud, disgusted.

If she could see Roderick Northland now, walking towards her across Kensington Gardens with his familiar clumsy gait and lopsided grin, these tears would turn to joy and Ursula Lapointe could go jump in the lake, taking Henry Ellis Margam with her. But the only person walking towards her was an elderly drunk with a sandwich board round his neck reading 'SEEK AND YE SHALL FIND'. He was saved from a kicking by falling over before he could reach her.

The same morning Bella's enigmatic telegram was delivered, Mrs Bardsoe made an excursion to Chiswick by bus and Shanks's pony. Her purpose was only partly charitable. From time to time it did a body good to get out into the fresh air and though she would never admit to being bored by Charles Urmiston, the earnest side of him could grate, occasionally. Across the river was about as far as she would like to go but she enjoyed stomping along, bad knee or not, in what she thought of as foreign parts.

She had a very pleasant conversation with a postman and a rather more guarded one with a clerical gentleman in a white straw hat.

And here she was, sitting with Millie Rogerson in the kitchen of the Kennetts' house, her boots off, reading Murch's second telegram from Duisburg, the message to his wife. It read, in its entirety, *Tiddly pom pom pom Murchie*, and Millie was so enchanted that Hannah Bardsoe forgot her aching feet and laughed along with the girl.

'Now my Charlie says there's many a message sent in code and I dare say this is such a one. And where's he been to send you a billy doo like this?'

'"*Tiddly pom pom pom*" says "You'll do for me", Mrs B. And he talks to the baby with those same words. You know,' Millie added shyly, touching her bump.

'Yes, but where's he been?'

'I don't see as how it harms to tell you. He's been to fetch Mr Westland out of a spot of bother in Germany.'

'Oh my lord,' Hannah exclaimed. She had a vague image of endless forests and the long snouts of wolves. 'Whatever was that good man doing poking about out there? He hasn't the brains he was born with, sometimes. And leaving Mrs Wallis to be snatched from the jaws of death in Yorkshire! I tell you, Millie, us women are going to have to put our foot down. I've had Charlie sneezing enough to blow a body's hat off, not to say waking up in a muck sweat babbling about naked women.'

'Go on!' Millie exclaimed in delight.

'As true as I'm sat here. So if your Billy comes home with some of the same ideas, you know where to come.'

'Murchie would run a mile from a naked woman, you

can have my word on that. He's as chaste as a pineapple in that respect.'

'And ain't I pleased to hear it. Now before I set off for the omnibus to come here, I walked down the market and bought us both a bit of fish. So do you sit quiet, you beautiful creature, and let old Bardsoe cook you a nice dinner.'

'You don't have to,' Millie protested.

'Well, I know I don't have to.' A thought occured to her. 'One more thing about these men of ours. The problem is, they're all in love with Mrs Wallis without knowing it. And she, poor creature, wandering about like Little Bo Peep. Not that I don't love her dearly myself.'

'It's London,' Millie said. 'It's that what's turned their heads. Rogerson, when he was alive, used to hang about the gates to the Palace, just on the off-chance that he'd be there when the old Queen came to her senses and pitched up back home.'

'Fat chance of that!'

'That's what I used to tell him. And that she aren't no more a Londoner than Garibaldi or one of that lot. But he would have none of it. He wanted to be there when Her Majesty leaned out of her coach and said, "Bobby, I've done this old city wrong, but I've seen the errors of my ways. Bring your pals round for a drink, why don't you?"'

'You say it's London: I say it's Bella Wallis.'

Millie laughed and jumped up to help Mrs Bardsoe light the range, which could be a bit tricky on a windless day. (The flue had been modified by her employer William Kennett, along rational lines, one lazy afternoon a year or so ago. Except in gale conditions, it had never worked properly since.)

'I will say this. Mrs Wallis is the biggest Londoner of them all. And that's why they love her.'

'Even Mr Kennett?'

'Oh,' Millie cried delightedly. 'Now there's a man who lives out among the fairies. We can't bring him into it. You want to hear Murchie on that subject.'

'And what does he say?'

'That he is Mary Kennett's humming bird.'

The Hooterville Assay Office was a clapboard building painted battleship grey. Next door to it a grandson of the original Hooter kept a dry goods store and general chandlery. There were another five businesses and then the smudged valleys of that part of California began, the home to snakes, wild dogs, rats and a handful of leathery men with spades and tents. Hooterville had no church, no doctor and only an intermittent supply of beer and whiskey. Old Henry Hooter had planted a few lemon trees at the back of his property and these provided the signature luxury of this little nightmare community – Ma Hooter's Lemon Barley. It was served in half-pint jugs at five cents a throw, ten with a jigger of corn whiskey added.

The assay office had of course no connections to the American Mint. Its existence was entirely cosmetic, a honey trap to lure dude prospectors such as William and Mary Kennett. Its manager was a man called John Joseph Beaminster, recruited by the Hooter family to add a little gloss to the idea that this was a gold town. Had anyone ever come off the hills with a strike worth more than a few flakes, the nearest official assay office was to be found in Idaho, where the premises were three storeys high and staffed by federal employees in wing collars.

The Hooters came originally from Illinois; Mr Beaminster was the last of five generations of Dorset folk who had blown like dandelion seed across America. In 1790, Jethro Smalls had changed his name to Beaminster in honour of the town where his grandfather was born. It was not a popular gesture, especially among barefoot neighbours who were called Scroggs, Shinner, Bluett or Raikes. But it had produced, after a succession of daydreamers, John Joseph, a reading man and halfway to being a gentleman. Just what he was doing swatting flies in Hooterville he left others to ponder. He liked the Kennetts for never asking.

'Ahah!' Beaminster exclaimed in kindly fashion to William. 'More rocks for me to look at! Not that I would rather cast my eye upon the only truly priceless nugget in these here miserable surroundings. I speak of Mrs Kennett.'

'She is in Hooter's, buying some bacon slab and drinking a lemon barley.'

'I knew that particular pig,' John Joseph quipped merrily. 'As good-natured an animal as ever walked. And hasn't the pig been as much a friend to this nation as the Constitution itself? If there is anything more toothsome than a gammon steak with a garnish of wild mushrooms, I should like to hear of it, sir.'

'I pine for a sirloin of beef, all the same,' Kennett admitted.

'It is the Englishman in you! No doubt you live in a castle back home. This must seem a far cry indeed from those native shores. A castle, and maybe as many as ten or fifteen gardeners. You have heard of Parnham House, I don't doubt?'

'I'm afraid not. In Dorset, that would be.'

When he first met Beaminster, William Kennett supposed him to be touched by the sun; or maybe congenitally damaged in some way or other. It took him a while to realise that his friend was simply bored and thus more often than not drunk. Later still, he learned that Beaminster was writing a history of his ancestral birthplace, derived from family legend. Central to the story was how the Smalls, as they were then, had lent money to the beardless youth Thomas Hine to find his way to France and so found (in a revolutionary year) Cognac Hine on the banks of the Charente at a place called Jarnac. The place name rang no bells with William Kennett and the point of Beaminster's book was to point out that a loan made in 1788 had by now accrued enough interest to change the scenery of his own life in a quite spectacular way.

'I admire you, Mr Kennett, I surely do. You are a man after my own heart, sir, a dreamer of dreams. Would it be impudent of me to describe you as a shameless romantic?'

He leaned forward with a leer and lowered his voice to a friendly whisper.

'I see you are packing iron, as they say out here. Now is that pistol and gunbelt a way of tipping your cap to the legendary West at all? Or does it, as we might say, lend a little local colour to your prospecting endeavours?'

'It is no more than a sensible precaution, Mr Beaminster, in the circumstances.'

'And what circumstances might those be?'

William hoisted his sack of finds onto the table between them. When Beaminster tipped out the contents, he rose, pushed back his chair and howled like a prairie dog. The dude, God blind his eyes, had struck it rich. Not just a little bit rich but filthily richer than the most leather-necked veteran could ever envisage.

'Do you know what you have here, sir?'

'Well, yes,' William Kennett murmured with his trade-mark shyness, indicating that Beaminster should return the nuggets to the sack and then the sack to its owner. The American fell to his knees and beat his head on the rough-hewn floor.

'If this don't beat all in the story of my miserable unhappy life,' he sobbed.

'Take heart,' William said. 'Come and have a lemon barley. But of course, if you blab one word to that swindling rascal Hooter, I shall have to shoot you. If you keep calm then we can surely find a way to make you rich – not unfeasibly rich but as we say in our English castle, comfy.'

'Comfy? That's a word?'

'My wife swears by it. And she is trying to persuade me to trust you.'

'Tell me what to do! Ask me for anything.'

'Well, it's like this. I never expected to find any gold. Now that I have, I don't know what to do with it.'

'You sell it,' Beaminster yelled, beside himself. 'Are you a goddamn idiot, sir? Are you *drunk*?'

'I am on my honeymoon,' William Kennett said rather stiffly. His own opinion of Mr Beaminster was far less flattering than his wife's. But then Mary had shown herself to be a shrewd judge of the American character – and so it proved to be in this instance. All Beaminster had ever wanted from life was for someone to love him and once he had that, he blossomed into the business manager from heaven.

SIXTEEN

Six months passed. How easy to say, as though clocks ticked, the sun rose and set, rain turned to sleet and then snow, coal was shovelled recklessly in parlours from Stepney to Shepherd's Bush, bringing in its wake the London fog, yellow and brown as dog fur – and all this as ordinary as teacups. But in these particular six months, Murch was presented with a daughter; William and Mary Kennett returned from America as proprietors of the Lucky Buckaroo gold mine; the boy Alfie Stannard was brought down from Yorkshire and set up in a tiny business selling not sweets but stamp packets for child collectors, a trade he adored. Percy Quigley came across (in his usual way of coming across things) enough tongue-and-groove boarding to refit the offices in Fleur de Lys Court as handsomely as any solicitor's – if the right person could be found to talk an innocent in to doing it for nothing. Equally amazing in its own quiet way, Charles Urmiston grew a beard to rival the Prince of Wales's – grey, close-trimmed and with the same elegant tip.

Two things did not happen. Ursula Gollinge, if she really was in London, did not show her face, not so much as a glimpse. And Bella Wallis did not marry Philip Westland.

'If I normally walked on my hands, these trips would

be the very thing to help recuperate a shoulder wound,' he complained as they paid their second winter visit to Brighton. 'But staggering about on the shingle here is doing very little for me.'

'Not very adventurous, I grant you.'

'Could we at least go somewhere where the sea is green? Better still, blue.'

'We are here for the air,' Bella chided. 'There are poor devils sticking pigs in Poona who would give their eye teeth for a bucket of this sleet.'

They kissed. No danger of compromising their dignity: the winter beaches were empty of everything but themselves and a raging squall. Driftwood and scraps of kelp flew past their heads. Out to sea, the sky was flecked by seagulls yet to make landfall on the town's roofs.

'We can go for a cup of tea now,' Bella decided.

Their failure to crown a dangerous and reckless summer by marrying was exercising everyone, though Hannah Bardsoe thought she had an explanation. As lovers (and what could be more romantic than the two of them tucked up in Orange Street, like sparrows squabbling under the eaves one day, cooing like vicarage doves the next?) they thought too much. Thinking was all very well in its way and folk had a right to carry on as they pleased, but in love too much brains could be as dangerous as too little. To see Bella in her edgiest moods was a sorry trial to the roly-poly Hannah and her own plain and straightforward way of going on. Being *clever* about love was utterly foreign to her nature. She would as soon believe in unicorns wandering out of the forests to lay their heads in a maiden's lap.

'I'm sure you've never looked at me in that light,' she challenged Charles Urmiston.

'In what light is that?' he asked cautiously.

'Like a bit of long division,' she explained, stunning him by the simile. 'Or anything else of that nature. Sums, I mean.'

'I think of you as my favourite prime number,' he protested. As a gallantry, it fell flat. Indeed, Hannah bristled.

'I was hoping for remarks pertinent and not some beardie nonsense.'

'Well, how about this? Certainly they love each other to distraction. Yet there is some small thing between those two admirable people that has yet to be resolved before they marry. Some final sticking point. If you like, a pea under their mattress.'

'Rubbish.'

'Just as you say.'

'Sticking point! They are made for each other, those two, as anyone can see. Why, 'tis plain as a pikestaff, Charlie. Unless—'

'Unless what?'

She was going to say that they – the two of them, along with Quigley and Billy Murch – might be just too much for Philip Westland to stomach any more. It was in her mind that both lovers had come up against the jaws of death in recent times, only to be saved (once again) by others. It did not seem like the recipe for a happy marriage. Hannah set great store in her own life by untroubled ordinariness. Confronted in the shop by some growth or swelling, perhaps some rash that ran red as raspberry jam across a shyly presented belly, she was worth any amount of pills to the worried patient.

'Ho! That's nothing very much! Didn't your neighbour Mrs Potts have the same? And isn't she still scrubbing out the Eagle Insurance at six every morning? Which I see her passing home when I takes down the shutters, as blithe as a cricket, always a kind word.'

Her beloved Charlie sometimes said she was a bit too free with her diagnoses but then he came out of the same box as Bella and could not be expected to understand that many of their customers could not afford a doctor and believed (rightly) that a turn in a charity hospital was as good as kissing the world goodbye. What they wanted from Hannah was the reassurance that nothing was so bad it could not be endured. Philip Westland, for all that he'd gone off to Germany on some unexplained jaunt and got himself shot, was Hannah's idea of a philosophical cove at heart, much in her own pattern. If you didn't like the way things were turning out, you had to learn to lump it. Bella was different.

'There is always someone riding to the rescue with her,' she muttered. Urmiston's sharp glance made her blush.

'Hark at me,' she exclaimed guiltily. 'What do I know about anything, a fat old body no taller than a Shetland pony?'

'Mmm,' Urmiston teased. 'You make a good point there, my precious.'

His beard was prickly but, at close range, comforting. Best of all, it did not smell of tobacco or stale soap but rather (though very faintly) of cough syrup, something they had begun to manufacture out in the kitchen and which flew off the shelves, people coming from as far as Southwark to buy it in the trademark red bottle. She sat on his lap, consenting to be kissed.

'You'd never leave me, Charlie?'

'The little Bienkowski girl came into the shop yesterday. I have always thought of her as very pretty. Well formed and so forth.'

'Oh, I dare say it will come to that one day. That's a story about men, not her and her kind, the impudent little cat. And good luck to you, for she'll leave you as skinned as a rabbit when she's had her fill of you. But you'd never leave me, all the same?'

'Never in life,' he promised. 'As if you don't know.'

There *was* a sticking point in Bella's relationship with Philip and it had to do with Ursula Gollinge. For it did not take much detective work from Bella to confirm that it was this vile woman who had undone Jane Westland twelve years earlier. Had she never gone to Yorkshire, Philip would have kept his silence, for just as Bella had nothing to say about her first marriage and subsequent affaire with the elphin Marie Claude, so he censored anything to do with the time before Bella. This reticence was simply a matter of form. Neither of them believed in love as an interrogation.

What came out of the past came unbidden; and as often as not, wearing an antic mask. So it was that Bella knew of the sixteen-year-old Philip being seduced by a much older woman in Florence; an ancient infatuation that had turned by now to moth-eaten farce. Likewise – because it was much in her mind after the sculptor's death – she told him the story of defending herself with a broom in Musgrave's studio, without mentioning that she was at the time stark naked save for a chaplet of laurel. (Nor that the broom came into the story as a late – a very late – rush of common sense after an afternoon's reckless flirting.)

Such episodes from the past flitted in and out of their pillow conversations without causing the slightest harm. They were shameless for the very reason that some dreams are shameless: they came from a place that has no real geography, where mirrors reflect back nothing but smoke. They were remembered only because they had been so long forgotten.

'What made you think of your Florentine adventure tonight?' Bella asked when she was first told of the voracious seductress of the Villa Danielli.

'I was just thinking vaguely about how hopeless I am at undressing in front of anyone,' Philip confessed, sending his beloved Bella into hoots of laughter.

Ursula Gollinge was a different matter. It was as if her burly, thuggish persona could never become anything whimsical and dreamlike. The reason was of course unfinished business, located in Jarnac, where Jane Westland languished.

'It is now or never, Philip,' she whispered one night. 'If we don't bring this into the open, it will poison everything between us for ever.'

'There are parts to the story I have never been able to tell you. Things that might hurt you.'

'Nothing you can say will harm me, Philip,' Bella said. And then for a long time there was silence, save for the rain in the gutters. She had a reasonable idea of the details he wished to keep from her but had the sense to keep quiet. He threw the covers off and got out of bed to watch the rain patter up and down the pavements, his cheek against the window glass.

'She was an incredibly gifted child,' he began. 'My mother died in having her and my father brought us up with the aid of governesses and the like. We were hardly affected by having only one parent, perhaps because my father was the most phlegmatic man in Christendom. As children we lived in Oxfordshire on a little island of wealth and security. I am far more of a country mouse than I've ever told you, Bella.'

'And Jane?'

'The same. We lived like savages, built treehouses, swam in the lake, slept outdoors.'

'But your father kept up a house in London?'

'In Dalmire Gardens. He gave dinners for his antiquarian colleagues and kept most of his books there. We went for walks, sailed on the river to Greenwich and suchlike, haunted museums and galleries. We were a very close-knit family. And horribly priggish into the bargain. But what we knew about life – or thought we knew – was all hidden away behind elms and attended by skylarks. London was –' he hesitated – 'less real.'

She thought about that. For her the city was everything, all the more alluring for being so difficult to master. London was the conversation that one never tired of having, the table that was constantly being relaid.

'I am cold,' Philip said suddenly. 'Could we go down and perhaps rekindle the fire? Take a little brandy together?'

It was half past one in the morning when they tiptoed downstairs, a dangerous time for letting truth slip the leash and run free. They sat in the dark at opposite sides of the hearth, watching the fresh coals fume.

'You have to think of Jane as bearing the burden of impossible expectations. My father wanted a consort, I suppose. At the back of his mind he saw Jane alongside him in the house at Radcot, enjoying a summer's day that would last until his death. She was not to change her character to accommodate him, nor suffer by the arrangement in any way. She would grow from a girl to a woman in his company and some magic or other would supply a happy outcome.'

'Instead, she ran away,' Bella divined.

'The first time when she was seventeen. We found her in Chelsea, living with a bachelor friend of my father's. Under his roof, that is, for the poor old man had as much need of a woman in the house as he might have for a pig, or a penfold of sheep. On the advice of an incredibly stupid doctor, my father took her to Bad Gastein for the waters. There she was seduced by an American woman. Is seduced the right word?'

'Please, Philip,' Bella whispered.

'I told you there were things you might not wish to hear. There was nothing physical about the relationship, I am sure. Jane simply ran about after this poor woman, much as a small child at a wedding pesters a glamorous guest. She ambushed her at breakfast, contrived to join her for walks and excursions – that sort of thing.'

He fell silent for a few moments, a picture of unhappiness.

'The hotel was a small one. There were letters and poems, all of which the American bore with good grace. I have tried to imagine it a hundred times, Bella – this glorious young woman in a white gown, searching and calling under the lanterns that lit the gardens—'

Bella jumped up and sloshed cognac into her glass, weeping tears that ran along the line of her chin. In the darkness, Philip sighed defeatedly.

'No,' she said sharply. 'I want to hear it all.'

'There are people who go to spas for nothing else but gossip. What greater topic than this wild swan of a girl making a fool of herself? Only after it was all over did I meet the American. She was an extremely intelligent woman and I think a good one. It was years later and we met completely by accident in Rome. She remembered Jane and asked after her with great tenderness. She was the first to suggest that my sister's troubles were deeper seated than we imagined. I am trying to be fair, Bella.'

'You are trying to avoid saying that you and your father believed she could change her nature if she wanted to. That she would learn to grow up. Isn't that the phrase for it?'

'I am trying to tell you that this girl, whom I adored, for whom I would willingly have given my own life, as being the better bargain, was already as unhappy as anyone I have ever met. To want happiness for another person and not to be able to provide it is a shattering thing.'

'Your father took her out of Germany?'

'He had no choice. He moved permanently to London in an attempt to bring her out into society. There were more scandals. He died in 1865 of a sudden stroke and the day of the funeral, Jane threw herself under a train at

Baker Street. The carriages passed completely over her. Standing on the platform was Ursula Gollinge.'

Philip threw his glass into the fire and the cognac in it ignited in a blossom of blue flame that made them both start.

'I am sorry,' he said in a broken voice, 'but I am going to dress and walk somewhere, to the river, perhaps. I can't stay here.'

'I will come with you.'

In the end they walked down Whitehall and up Victoria Street; thence, more or less aimlessly into Belgravia. The rain had stopped and they walked arm in arm, moving from pool to pool of lamplight, sometimes down tunnels of dark. The gutters ran black.

'Jane's American friend was very rich, very cultured. There was a calmness about her, a civility if you like. She was quite small, extremely fastidious in how she dressed, unsmiling, and I suppose the word is imperturbable. Maybe she was forty, maybe sixty. Who could say – and what did it matter?'

Bella suddenly tightened her grip on his arm. Thirty yards in front of them, a fox pattered up from a basement area and stood regarding them. Its coat was not sleek, but stirred up by the rain. It turned away and then looked over its shoulder one last time before trotting away towards Knightsbridge and the Park.

'A *fox*,' Bella whispered. 'How is that possible?'

'What is not possible in London?' Philip muttered.

The rest of the story came out in slow bursts, as though Westland had it all in his head as one continuous narrative but was editing it out of compassion for his lost sister.

Ursula Gollinge had organised Jane's release from underneath the train and whisked her away before the police arrived. They went to a hotel in York Terrace and hid there the rest of the afternoon. Later, a house in Marchmont Street.

'Gollinge was newly arrived from Australia and already notorious. The mad-doctors had taken her husband and she herself was without money or connections of any kind. No house in London would receive her. God knows what Jane thought about any of this. Hotels, rented cottages, even uninvited appearances at country-house weekends. There was family of some kind in Ireland and they made a half-hearted attempt to flee there. They got as far as Liverpool.'

'How do you know this?'

'There were letters to the house in Dalmire Gardens. Not from Jane, not a word from Jane, ever. But Gollinge had a taste for fire-and-brimstone denunciation. One of the packets we received was a missive thirty-seven pages long.'

'Did you employ a detective?'

'A man called Warrender, an Australian who claimed to know her. That might even have been true. But in the end she tired of us. I believe the Queen began to feel the heat of Gollinge's rants. The Queen, the Archbishop of Canterbury, Mr Gladstone. Dr Grace we know about,' he added bitterly.

'Did you know about the curse on Grace when you invited him to dinner?'

'Of course not! Do you think I am mad? I have spent the last ten years trying to obliterate the memory of Ursula Gollinge and all her stupidities.'

'And Jane, all this while the rants and curses were flying?'

'I cannot say,' Philip said. 'But somehow it ended. Her saviour and benefactress found someone else less difficult to command, perhaps. Or – and I would like to believe this – less honest.'

'But a curse was laid on her, all the same?'

Philip sighed. He took Bella in his arms and kissed her cheeks, her forehead.

'What does that really mean, though? She was cursed the very moment she was rescued by Gollinge at Baker Street. I found her in these same streets we have been walking, dressed in rags, begging for food. Would you come to Belgravia for such a thing? But she was like the fox, Bella. She lived in the Park. Ask your question.'

'Don't do this to yourself,' Bella begged, her voice as quiet as the empty streets.

'There is only one question – what did I do about it? I had her back, so what did I do? The answer is, I made just about every mistake a human nonentity could make. She needed a hero. She got me. And an asylum in Charente.'

They walked to Victoria and found a cab.

'Must a man always be a hero?' Bella sobbed.

'Hush,' Philip Westland said. 'Hush, hush.'

SEVENTEEN

Alfie Stannard had been offered lodgings with Charles and Hannah when he first came down from Yorkshire but had the good sense to refuse, finding a place of his own in a lodging house in Eagle Street. He had a single room in the fourth-floor attics and apart from the attentions of a lonely sous-chef, there he found the London he was looking for. It was a sparrow's-eye view of the city, for though his single sash window was small, it overlooked a forest of chimney pots and slate roofs stretching back across Holborn towards the river. This high up, even rain had its own beauty. He rose early every day and was rewarded on Christmas morning by a blood-red dawn, refracted through his iced-over window panes. He had not been slow in picking up the London gift for hyperbole and counted it the finest thing he had ever seen.

'You are very easy pleased,' his neighbour the sous-chef grumbled, patting him on the knee the while. They shared half a bucket of coal and the chef, who was called Arthur and came from Wolverhampton, showed him how to cook steak-and-kidney pie, using scraps of cardboard as examples of the ingredients.

As for the stamp trade, was there anything more romantic in the world? A rich collector might sit at his occasional table in smoking jacket and decorated slippers, poring over his treasures through a cloud of latakia from his meerschaum pipe; but Alfie was at the sharp end of the business, tramping the streets and begging banks and offices to give up their unwanted envelopes, wheedling clerks and junior partners, charming post rooms. It soon enough occurred to him that it was for this he had been set down on earth.

'It seems to me you have gone stamp-mad,' Arthur quipped, peering at him through the magnifying lens, his eye as huge and wet as an oyster.

Hatton Garden was a rich source of postal treasures. The diamond merchant Gorney took a shine to Alfie and passed on stamps from Holland, France and Germany. His more miserly colleague Steinitz struck a stiff price for a small suitcase of similar material that he had intended to study himself (or so he said). Alfie saw the whole trade as hunter-gathering. For him, stamp collecting was done on the hoof, almost as a form of postal delivery in reverse. There was no better way to get to know London at street level and he became a part of the tide that flowed and ebbed along the main thoroughfares and lapped secretly in half-forgotten alleyways.

When he was not searching for the raw materials of his business, he was hawking his made-up penny packets to toy shops, stationers and the bigger traders. The first Stanley Gibbons catalogue was now twelve years old and though stamps were printed in their millions, the chase for rarities had begun. So it was that already some water-holes had run dry, so to speak – the big dealers were there ahead of him in search of varieties. But Alfie worked on the principle that he would rather have three grubby stamps than one perfect example. Soon enough, one wall of the attic was stacked high with boxes and cartons.

He dressed very smartly for a youth of his age, was almost excessively polite to his superiors, did not smoke or drink, and lived for the most part on air. On Sundays he was summoned by Hannah Bardsoe to a roast dinner and plum pudding, an invitation he dared not refuse. After eating up as bidden, he and Charles Urmiston would sit either side of the parlour grate, talking men's talk, as Hannah liked to put it, while she went upstairs for a bit of a lie-down.

On a particular Sunday in March, when even in the sooty canyon that was Shelton Street, spring was announcing itself by some very mild weather indeed, Urmiston found the boy unusually reticent. Conversation about stamps languished and he could not be drawn out on whether he had found himself a young lady (a subject that fascinated Hannah and that Charles had been secretly instructed to enquire about).

'Your mind is elsewhere, Alfie,' Urmiston smiled. 'Last week you were all on fire in finding the four issues of the Danube Steam Ship Company – was it? – in Steinitz's suitcase.'

'Oh, and don't he wish he'd paid more attention to those items when he first came by them,' Alfie responded. But the tone was listless.

'You have had them valued?'

'I was going to ask you to act as my intromederary in that matter, so's not to tip my hand to Mr Gibbon direct.'

'I can see the sense in that,' Urmiston said, after a slight pause. 'But if they are worth what you think they are, shouldn't that be a cause for celebration? If this is your first big coup, why such a long face?'

'I was in Cock Lane on Thursday,' the boy said. 'And I saw someone. Someone you and me thought we would never meet again.'

Urmiston's note was to Philip Westland but in the event both he and Bella came. The five of them sat down to a council of war, Hannah Bardsoe tending the teapot and pressing toasted cheese on everyone, her idea of a Sunday afternoon snack. Alfie was taken through his story for the third time.

'And you can start by explaining why you left it until today to tell anyone about this here encounter,' Hannah chided. 'And only now because your pal Mr Urmiston winkled it out of you, you foolish boy.'

'Winkled is a bit strong,' Charles Urmiston protested. 'Our friend was quite properly in two minds what to do. Let him tell the story his own way, Hannah.'

'Let us be free and easy,' Bella agreed, hardly aware of the effect these words had on the still lovelorn Alfie.

'You had to have been there,' he explained.

'Yes, and isn't that always the way?' Bella agreed blithely, compounding the boy's embarrassment. He could not be aware that she too was secretly wracked: she was there to prevent Philip from doing something silly. By which she meant dangerous. Alfie sighed.

'Not much of a story. Either she had been in the pubs or she was took with some of her Yorkshire visions – any road up, she were making a bit of a spectacle of herself. And some.'

Cock Lane a short street, as agreed by all, and Alfie had recognised her the moment he stepped into it. She was wearing a long mauve cloak and a felt hat that was daffodil yellow. The corkscrew curls were uncombed and two savage lines had appeared either side of her nostrils, dragging down her lips. His first reaction on seeing her was one of pity. That took some explaining to Hannah Bardsoe.

'When I lived in Skipton, like, there was an old fighting dog, a bull mastiff that used to hang around the market. He was a famous enough dog in his day but all his real strength was gone. He just *looked* a dangerous beast. That was all that was left to him, you understand. The look of him.'

'And Lady Gollinge affected you in the same way?' Philip prompted gently.

'It was a shock. I think I felt a bit of shame, even.'

'Ho, shame! And whatever can that mean when it's at home?' Hannah wanted to know. 'Her as wanted to kill Mrs Wallis and by all accounts Mr Gladstone into the bargain! It's her who should be feeling a twinge of shame, I would say!'

'Hannah, my dear,' Bella protested. Alfie's glance was a grateful one.

'I am only saying what I felt, confused as it might be. Pity is better, perhaps.'

'Was she alone?' Philip continued.

'No, sir. The crowd that were round her had followed her from somewhere else, I would say.'

'These clothes,' the novelist in Bella murmured. 'They sound something of a mare's nest.'

'They were! And I forgot to say, she had bare feet.'

'Did she recognise you?' Philip asked.

'I kept well back,' Alfie promised. 'But if you ask me did I recognise *her*, the answer is yes. Ten times over, yes.'

'Did you follow her?'

'No,' Alfie muttered, blushing.

'You didn't think to follow her?' Bella cried.

'He is not our servant, Bella,' Philip objected, perhaps just a little too sharply. Alfie looked from one to the other in crimson confusion.

'I have a fair idea of where she was headed. And not far at that.'

'St Bart's,' Urmiston guessed at once. 'Isn't the hospital just across the road? Wasn't that where she was going?'

'You're in the right of it, Mr Urmiston. The kitchens end of it anyway. There's as many as fifty wait there all day long for the food bins to be put outside. The scraps, the vegetable peelings and such like. Sometimes scrag ends of meat, even.'

Hannah Bardsoe hauled herself up and fetched the Martinique rum from a side table. It was her indication that the story had taken a sombre turn.

'Then, like you, Alfie dear, I feel pity for the poor soul. It's a pound to a penny she sleeps rough and that will pull a body down faster than a fox in the chicken run. I don't say she should 'scape justice but she's headed for a terrible end nonetheless. I can say this without Billy Murch being present: leave us not forget poor old Molly Clunn and how she finished up.'

'Molly Clunn?' Alfie asked, bewildered. When Bella ruffled his hair, he was amazed to see her eyes filled with tears.

'Someone far more precious to us than the Gollinge woman.'

It was a very awkward moment, for all the way through the table had deferred to Philip Westland as being the arbiter of what should be done in the present instance. The fire crackled and the German case-clock ticked.

'You realise, Alfie,' Philip said in the same gentle voice he had used throughout, 'that the police have been looking for Lady Gollinge with a view to arresting her?'

'Mr Urmiston and me have discussed that from time to time.'

'Did you think to tell a policeman what you had seen in Cock Lane?'

'I wished I need tell no one, sir, and that's no lie. All that whole story has blowed away, to speak frank with you. I was only ever at the edge of it anyroad – and a boy into the bargain. I could see she were a monster all right but hoped never to hear tell of her again. Out of sight, out of mind.'

'But you did tell *me*,' Urmiston observed. 'And I honour you for it. For the rest of us round this table, putting her out of mind is not quite so easy.'

'And I wonder why that is,' Philip Westland said very unexpectedly. His tone was quiet and reflective. 'Do you think she has been punished enough – is that it, Alfie?'

'I think she has come to where she was headed all along, sir. If the police or anyone else wants her, she is not hard to find. Mrs Wallis might like to give her shins a good kicking and if she killed Raybould like they say she did, then I suppose she must pay. But I must tell you plainly, I wish I had not seen her, no, nor never again.'

'You have washed your hands of her,' Bella suggested.

'I have my own life to lead,' Alfie said with great simplicity.

Philip Westland rose from the table and excused himself from the company, saying he would welcome a short turn in the fresh air before it came full dark. To Bella he added that if she could make her way home, he would see her there shortly. Meanwhile, the toasted cheese snack a thing he would like to see introduced as Sunday ritual in Orange Street; hoped, however, they had not inconvenienced Hannah too much on this particular Sabbath. To Urmiston, he expressed the sentiment that they should meet more frequently, perhaps for a chophouse supper. For Alfie Stannard, nothing but a firm, dry and wordless handshake. And then he was gone.

'Have I said something wrong?' Alfie asked, bewildered. Bella walked round the table to him and hugged him, before stooping and kissing him on the cheek, dangerously close to his lips.

'You have said something that may turn out to be very important,' she said. And then, as if realising her first kiss might be construed as ambiguous, she kissed him again full on the lips, a thing he would remember for the rest of his life.

Philip was waiting at the corner of Eagle Street when Alfie walked home. The pair of them were like African explorers meeting in the middle of nowhere, Philip going so far as to shake hands and feeling very fatuous about it, too.

'I could not be sure which way you might come,'

he explained. 'But I wanted to talk to you for a few minutes, if you can spare the time.'

'Will you not step up to my room?' the boy asked. 'You can be my first visitor. Until I met Mrs Wallis, I had never tasted coffee and didn't make much of it. But Arthur has shown me how to make it in a jug and Sunday is my day for having some.'

'A cup of coffee would go down very well,' Philip promised.

The stairs to the lodging house were lit as far as the third floor by fluttering gas brackets; but to reach the attics, Philip tramped after his host in single file. He stood patient as a horse in total darkness while Alfie opened up the room and fussed about looking for matches and candles.

'I have a paraffin lamp but it ran dry last night. The smell you have is from something dead under the floor-boards.'

'A rat perhaps.'

'I should think so,' Alfie agreed. 'But anyway, welcome to my home.'

'Alfie, I had better say no to coffee,' Philip said after a glance at the tiny grate and its embers, the wall of card-board boxes and the single rush chair. 'For what I have to ask will take no more than a few minutes of your time and in any case Mrs Wallis will be waiting on me.'

'It is about Lady Gollinge, I suppose?'

'Indirectly.'

He went to the little square window and looked out, his hands blinkering his eyes. Nightfall had jostled the chimney pots into some semblance of a watching crowd, a fancy made all the stronger for the extreme quiet to be had only fifty feet above the pavements. Above the roofline was a clear night sky, with its own attendant watchers. Some of the constellations were vaguely familiar to Philip from the days of his childhood.

'Has Mr Urmiston been to see you here?' he asked.

'Not yet.'

'He would be very sorry to see what he had brought you to, after the open Yorkshire moors.'

'He is not a country man,' Alfie laughed. 'Besides, I like it here well enough for the time being. When I have enough money set by I shall rent a little premises and then you shall see me go.'

'I believe you,' Philip said.

He examined the rush chair as a place to sit and then rejected it in favour of the bed behind the door as a place to watch Alfie rekindle the fire. The fresh coals came from a paper sack and were measured out like sugar lumps.

'Mrs Wallis thinks you are a very gifted young man, Alfie.'

'Meeting her was the best thing that ever happened to me, sir. This is all a bit arse about face – this place, I mean, not London – but I do count myself a lucky lad.'

'You have found yourself,' Philip suggested.

'That is top and bottom of it.'

'I envy you.'

To his amazement, Alfie rounded on him, in so far as it was possible for a boy with a piece of coal in his hand, crouching over an unwilling fire.

'Mr Westland, if there is a luckier man than you from here to China I should like to meet him.'

Which was how it came about that Philip, speaking slowly and addressing the most part of his remarks to his boots, told Alfie the story of Jane Westland and her connections to Ursula Gollinge, the despair he felt at seeing her sink into madness, the guilt that came as a consequence. Alfie heard him out without comment, as though listening to a tragedian's soliloquy, or a prisoner's confession. When Philip faltered to a halt, the silence between them was very long indeed.

'And now,' Alfie suggested, 'you have the lady at your mercy. It would take us no more than an hour to find her, London being what it is, and then you could – well, then you could do whatever you wanted to her.'

'Or I could do what you did, and walk away.'

Philip stood and cracked his knuckles, wandering across to the window again and staring out into the dark. After a moment or two he closed his eyes.

'What did you come up here to ask me, Mr Westland?' Alfie murmured.

'I don't know,' Philip said truthfully enough. 'But it has been worth the journey. More than you realise for the moment, my dear friend. Yes, I will call you that, Alfie. A very dear and unexpected friend.'

Sister Tilde told Mother Superior and she slept on the problem for two nights. Then Tilde was summoned. The two *religieuses* sat in shade, watching the little fountain that burbled not very convincingly in the cloistered part of the asylum. Mother Superior was a tall rangy woman with not too much of the spiritual about her but a great deal of common sense. It was as though the madness of others had licked her into staggering matter-of-factness. It was this that distraught relatives seized upon in gratitude when they had their first interview with her. She had never been seen to smile and that somehow communicated itself to weeping mothers as a further reassurance. Men – fathers, uncles, sons – noticed her huge hands and determined jaw, from which sprang formidable yellowed teeth. Her speech was coarse and direct, unmistakably Parisian in accent. Though it was no part of Tilde's business to hold a personal opinion on her Mother Superior, she admired her enormously.

'Perhaps you will explain what the Englishman hopes to achieve from this particular visit? Has he not tried with his sister before? And were not the consequences – I mean in the short term – disastrous?'

'He believes he has something to say now that Jane has been waiting to hear.'

Mother Superior's glance was slashingly quizzical.

'Tilde, you are not getting sentimental in your old age? The knight in shining armour riding to the rescue at the eleventh hour? I do not think it our business to stage-manage an opera.'

'I have never seen one.'

'This business about a curse is more suited to the stage, nonetheless. You don't believe it, of course?'

'I believe that she believes it.'

A novitiate of the order came out with a glass of lemonade on a wooden tray. Mother Superior took it and drank it off like a workman from Belleville, banging the empty glass back down on the tray.

'Well,' she said. 'Tell him he may come. You may also

tell him with suitable asperity that all correspondence is normally addressed to me in the first instance.'

'He is very naive,' Tilde agreed tactfully. 'But his heart is in the right place and he loves his sister as a brother should.'

'Is there money involved? An inheritance, for example?'

But the Mother Superior regretted saying these flinty words as soon as they were spoken. She rose and pulled Tilde up by her wrist.

'You have got me at it now. Tell him to come, with my blessing. If he's as naive as you say he is, he'll turn up on the one day in July likely to cause us the most problems.'

In the men's wing, the twenty or so inmates were practising the Marseillaise, all of them doleful except for M. Dieumegard, a local man from Rouillac, and a former soldier. His stentorian tenor was champagne to the soul.

The Quatorze Juillet concert of inmates was held in the little cobbled courtyard that was in front of the main conventual building. A hundred chairs were set out with that French instinct for propriety that is worth more than rubies. They faced a small stage (later to be struck down and returned to the owners of a tivoli who intended it for dancing that night) decorated with chains of flowers. Philip Westland was noticeable in the audience for his great height and the shocking informality of his clothes – a linen suit and soft collar. That year, the average height set for compulsory service in the military was a little over five feet four: the giant Englishman loomed over his neighbours.

The concert was surprisingly good. A man and two women played accordion trios; half a dozen of the women inmates performed country dances in clogs; M. Tixier gave his annual sketch of a farmer trying to teach a dog to jump through hoops, all the patter delivered in a Charentais accent that had the audience in stitches. Mme Paridol sang; M. Lievremont juggled five oranges. The event concluded with the singing of the Marseillaise by all the inmates. Except one. Jane Westland, put in the front row for her pale beauty, did not open her mouth. Her head was cocked as if listening to another music altogether, as if carried on the air from another country.

At the end of the concert, the inmates filed away to their lunch and once they were safely locked inside, the courtyard gates were opened. Philip walked to the park bench Tilde the Belgian had picked out for him and waited patiently for two hours. Then and only then he came face to face with Jane. Tilde watched as without a word he passed his sister cuttings from three London newspapers.

'Is it true?' she asked.

'She was buried eight days ago. Yes, it is true. I went to the service. At Brookwood.'

'Where is that?'

'Near Woking. It is the largest cemetery in the world.'

Jane Westland crumpled the cuttings in her fist and let them fall to the ground.

'Who paid?'

'We do not know. It doesn't matter.'

'Did she suffer?'

'I think she did.'

'But we ought not to talk like that,' Tilde chided gently, taking Jane's hand.

'She did not suffer the way you have been made to

suffer,' Philip persisted. 'But she lost everything. I believe that, Jane. All her powers.'

'Can't she speak from the grave?'

'In Woking?' Philip asked and was rewarded with a short smile that skipped the years of madness and went all the way back to their shared childhood.

'This is my brother,' she told Tilde.

Philip took both Jane's hands and brought them to his lips.

'And this is my beloved sister.'

In 1933, Alfred Stannard died at his home in Thames Ditton, a sprawling mock-Tudor house with long lawns leading to the river. He left behind a philately business worth several hundred thousand pounds, and a personal stamp collection that took two days to dispose of at auction. Stannard was seventy-one when he died. He never married. Three of the many obituaries garnered at his death mentioned that he was among the last of the Victorians, occasioning a characteristically bombastic rejoinder from George Bernard Shaw, who was four years older and perhaps a hundred times more arrogant.

Among his papers was the original of a much reprinted photograph of the original Stannard shop, a tiny property in Fleur de Lys Court. The proprietor is seen as a very young man, standing with a woman far too carelessly described as his mother. The lady in question is Hannah Bardsoe, the only likeness that ever existed of her. Some historians believe this second figure to be his first customer; or more fancifully still, his financial backer. The truth is simpler. Urmiston, who took the photograph, had

Hannah's black canvas shopping bag at his feet. Inside, was a celebratory veal-and-ham pie and – for luck – a sprig of Yorkshire heather.

In his lifetime, Stannard published three books, all of them to do with philately. In between the pages of what is still a standard text on the plating of the Queen Victoria Penny Red, the auctioneers found the order of service of Mrs Arabella Wallis's wedding to Mr Philip Westland, which took place at St George's Hanover Square in 1878. Across the top of the folded sheet, in a woman's hand, were written the words '*To my dearest darling Alfie, with love from us both.*' As happens with ink, the superscription had grown faint and ghostly. But then ink is never the whole story. The whole story, like the whole world, is unknowable.

THE
WHOLE STORY

ONE

As almost always happens at weddings, the least attentive to their surroundings are the bride and groom. Quite properly, they only have eyes for each other. Time ties itself into a lover's knot: for them the service seems both nerve-rackingly protracted, while at the same time over in the twink of an eye. Afterwards, only a few unimportant details of this delirium stick in the mind – like a particular fold in the minister's surplice, or the scent of beeswax and lilies. Or perhaps it is the stubborn ordinariness of the world outside that registers, a dull hum as the traffic rolls by and the sun pours down with a complete disregard for whether it warms the church floor or, say, a furniture van on the way to Fulham.

So it was when Arabella Wallis married Philip Westland. At their backs was a congregation of strangely assorted characters, mostly drawn from Bella's acquaintance. Captain Quigley had gone to the trouble of acquiring – by his usual dubious means – the patrol uniform of a dragoon officer, complete with silver epaulettes. Mr and Mrs Murch sat beside him. Charles Urmiston gave away the bride, leaving his beloved Hannah to keep company with a certain naval commander called Alcock, squashed between herself and Dora Venn.

Alcock was greatly vexed, because he felt his place was at the groom's side of the church where the Westlands and Froggatts sat – all of them ancient, all of them dressed in country tweed. There was even a papery old man in a bath chair who listened intently to the service through a tin ear-trumpet. The youngest person present was Alfie Stannard. He too had been misdirected by the ushers, so that he sat next to the Assistant Commissioner of the Metropolitan Police, imposing in a handsome frogged uniform. Inexplicably, while waiting for the bride to enter, they had been discussing Russia, or so it seemed to their immediate neighbours.

'The 5 Krona black and blue, postmarked Moscow in red,' Alfie whispered conspiratorially.

'Indeed?' Sir Edward exclaimed, stroking his chin. 'I should like to see that.'

Hymns, to be sure: *Now Praise We All Our God* to set the company off at a steady and sober pace, without anything too elaborate to follow. It was the age when congregations took pleasure in singing, and perhaps for those present at Bella's wedding there was a special whole-heartedness, so that many would remember with fondness Billy Murch's astonishingly direct baritone and Dora Venn's ecstatic contralto, delivered from behind rivers of tears.

'My word, but you've got some pipes on you, Billy,' Hannah Bardsoe whispered when the parties to the wedding went to sign the register.

'No slouch yourself, Mrs B.,' he muttered. Hannah was amazed to hear a choke in his voice. Looking about her more carefully, she saw half a dozen in the same state.

Even that wicked old chancer Percy Quigley was dabbing his eyes.

'If you would kindly release me, madam,' Commander Alcock murmured at her side. She looked down – and found that in the transport of happiness that had overcome her she had been holding the spymaster's hand for ten minutes or more.

'It set me off,' she told her beloved Charles Urmiston that night. 'I was all right up to that point, but when the old naval gentleman tried to get his hand back, the floodgates opened. I couldn't contain meself no longer. Tears of joy, my beloved. Tears of unbounden happiness for those two dear, dear people.'

But then the final mystery of weddings; for in the very next week it seemed to Bella and Philip's friends that they had always been married. Love them though they might, the couple became in their eyes merely Mr and Mrs Westland – that is to say, fixed quantities, like the stars at night.

'And has he give up the spying?' Hannah Bardsoe asked her friend Mrs Venn over a pot of tea a month or so later.

'It never was in his blood, Hannah dear. It was always more of an absentminded sort of thing with him. They haven't asked and he hasn't volunteered. Oh no, we are all very quiet in Orange Street these days. Quite the dovecote, we are. All the billing and cooing, if you follow my drift.'

The two women nodded sagely at each other. It was a polite way of describing love's first fine careless rapture.

'Mind you,' Dora Venn added, 'she's put on more than a stone in weight since the weddding or my dad's a Dutchman.'

'She has the bones for it,' Hannah suggested.

'Oh, no doubt there. Still a fine set-up woman. None finer.'

So to a seasonally frantic London, three days before Christmas. Dawn is ushered in by light flurries of snow that melt the moment they touch the pavements. Shortly after 8 a.m. the Bank Piquet, which every night guards the nation's bullion, marches away down Cheapside to their barracks in Knightsbridge. Thirty men, two sergeants and a subaltern officer slamming their boots down on the glistening streets, with a drummer to warn of their coming. Though they would die to hear it said of them, the season offers an extra charm to their appearance. The busbies and long grey coats with the Coldstream double buttons are a child's dream of soldiery. Is there a boy alive who would not wish for a box of such as these at the foot of his bed on Christmas morning?

By tradition, on the night of the Piquet, the Bank of England lays the officer's table for two and the previous evening Lieutenant Garside invited his second cousin Philip Westland to dine with him. Though they had met hardly more than a dozen times, Philip left Orange Street with a keen anticipation. It was utterly improbable he should visit the Bank under any other circumstances and he took a cab there with his head buzzing with half-remembered nonsense about the Temple of Mithras on which the building stands. About his host, he remembered next to nothing, save for a gloomy boy at a picnic in Southwold.

'What marked him out then?' Bella wanted to know.

'He took a screaming fit when one of my other cousins put quite a small crab down his neck.'

'Poor little chap.'

'He was fourteen at the time.'

'He seems a bit wet to me.'

'He is from the damper side of the family,' Philip admitted. 'But we must support him, Bella. Tonight he is helping keep our money safe.'

'Well, do check,' she smiled, kissing him.

Marriage changes the nature of kisses. Though Westland was still in the delirium of having won Bella's hand, she – the minx – posted him out of the door that night like a small boy on his way to a party. Once upon a time they had kissed with a lingering ecstasy – or so he seemed to remember. The new Mrs Westland saw what he was thinking and wrinkled her nose humorously, tugged straight his shirt-front and handed him his top hat and gloves, kissed him again.

'You are the very picture of a happily married man,' she said teasingly.

Philip saluted her by touching his cane to the brim of his hat, but somewhat spoiled the effect by having trouble with the front door. He sighed. The wedding at St George's, Hanover Square, seemed like something that had happened a long time ago.

The evening was disastrous. The young Guards subaltern Sefton Garside was seriously high-minded and although seasonal pleasantries were exchanged, the conversation descended swiftly to the most unlikely of subjects – personal salvation. Philip's imperturbable good manners were tested by being asked to discuss his immortal soul with an unsmiling beanpole in military uniform who had a Bible to hand and proposed reading from it when they finished their meal.

In the ordinary way of things, any private feelings a Coldstream officer might have came second to the honour of the regiment, that is to say, they never compromised the carefully nurtured nullity of the professional soldier. Philip knew of a major in the Life Guards who had amassed a library of a thousand stolen books. It was a guilty secret only divulged at his death by his sister, on whom the parcels had descended over the years like a ceaseless shower of meteorites. Not one hint of this had he ever disclosed to his fellow officers, who took him to be an amiable barbarian, just like themselves.

As it happened, this man – Major Livesey of the Blues – was Sefton Garside's grandfather on his mother's side; but since he was dead, he was forgiven, both by the family and his regiment. Philip racked his brains to think of how Garside came by his own views and, more to the point, how he had concealed them from his fellow officers. Seen in a certain light, there was something raffish about stealing books; one might even say it was a gentleman's harmless foible. The grandson's holy-rolling was another thing altogether, more suited to, say, the Royal Engineers, a rum lot. All this made Philip feel a bit itchy.

'I wonder if you have chosen the right fellow to bring into your confidence,' he murmured uneasily. 'I have only the most conventional attachment to the Christian faith.'

'Well, part of the reason I have invited you tonight is to strengthen your commitment.'

'That might not be so easy,' Philip laughed.

'What is faith without struggle?' Garside asked with excruciating earnestness. His pale eyes searched his guest's. After a moment or two, he closed them and brought his hands together in an unmistakable gesture. 'Christ teaches us to love the sinner, not the sin.'

'I beg your pardon?'

'Cousin Philip, I have asked you here for a purpose.'

Philip was highly alarmed. The room in which they dined was small and windowless, a parlour of some kind to a larger chamber. The quiet was deafening. He had not liked the ambience when he was shown in and he liked it even less now. 'Perhaps you would explain yourself.'

'It has to do with your relationship with Mrs Wallis.'

'The conversation has taken a wrong turn. You are young, Sefton, and you'll permit me to say greatly impertinent. This is your Christmas present to me, is it?'

'Have I made you angry?'

Philip moved the candelabra an inch, his fingers trembling. 'Yes, I can say you have made me very angry.'

His cousin watched him carefully. 'You won't hear what I have to say?'

Philip pushed back his chair and threw his napkin down onto the table. 'I will not. In uniform or out of it, you have a very great deal to learn about life. Or sin, if it comes to that,' he added.

'It is my given duty to bring balm to troubled souls, at whatever cost.'

'Whoever gave you that duty has directed you to the wrong man, my dear fellow. Mrs Wallis and I were married four months ago.'

Garside did not quite reel back, the way that happens in books, but his jaw dropped and a blush rose from his neck to his hairline.

'My congratulations,' he said with a thick tongue.

'That is very kind of you. I do not say that Mrs Westland and I are beyond reproach and let's agree that your intentions were kindly. But since you hardly know me and have never met my wife, perhaps your aim was off.'

'It was my mother who first pointed out your situation.'

'Your mother – if it doesn't seem uncharitable to say it – is a damned fool. Your mother,' he added, warming to his theme with unchristian vehemence, 'invested most of her money in Paraguayan railway stock that fell to less than sixpence a share, which explains why you have ended up in the Army when you should be at Oxford bothering God in some more congenial setting.'

'I am resigning my commission,' Garside explained. 'I have found my true vocation. My whole intention now is to bring hope in this valley of despair.'

'I really wonder what that might mean.'

'Day to day, hour to hour, we are none of us far from Heaven's gate.'

'I did not expect to come to the Bank of England to hear of this.'

'Because your heart has yet to be opened to God.'

Which a furious Philip answered by blowing out the candles and, in pitch darkness, navigating the Chinese silk carpet to where he hoped the door might be. Looming on the threshold was the duty sergeant, who walked Philip down corridors of still and icy air.

'We do not smoke in the public parts of the building, sir,' this man said in a mild enough tone.

'I am under the stress of strong emotions,' Philip replied.

'Aye, I understand,' the sergeant murmured with unexpected dryness. 'Reflections on your immortal soul, I don't doubt. Mr Garside is very hot on the subject. Well, sir, may I wish you a merrier Christmas of it? I'd like to present you with a souvenir gold bar and all that but regulations is against it.'

Philip delved into his pocket and handed the soldier a sovereign. 'Will you be sure to share this among your fellows? From me and' – cursing himself for being such an owl – 'mine.'

'The missus,' the sergeant suggested.

'Just so. The missus.'

'A generous thought, Mr Westland, sir. As they like to say at this season of the year, peace on earth and goodwill to all men.'

'You don't seem too enthusiastic about it.'

'It's a fine sentiment, sir, but I have my job to think of.'

They shook hands on that and the sergeant opened a wicket in a vast bronze door. Outside, the snow was driving down the street in horizontal clouds. Philip set off into the polar night and did not find a cab until Upper Thames Street, by which time he was soaked through and restored to his normal cheerfulness.

'How was your cousin?' Bella enquired, holding out her arms to be embraced.

'In ripping form.'

'Should we invite him to dinner, do you think?'

'Not in this century,' Philip said.

'I heard from Elias Frean this evening after you left,' Bella said, changing the subject with far too studied negligence. 'He stays at a hotel in Charlotte Street and sent round a note.'

Philip's nod was a little grim. He had never met Bella's publisher and asked specially for him not to be included in the wedding list. Frean's name was too closely connected with that of Henry Ellis Margam, Bella's nom de plume in what Philip considered her bad old days. Very few people in London knew that Bella and the bestselling author Margam were the same person, but Frean was of course one of them. It helped that he lived for the most part in Boulogne these days. Philip wished him there now, preferably with both legs in plaster.

'What did the note say?'

'You are putting on your "Thunderclouds over Dogger Bank" kind of expression, my dearest.'

'I can guess what it said. He is dismayed to hear you intend to write no more.'

'He is mortified. He wants to come round and persuade me to go on.'

'And what do you say to that?'

'About him coming here? I think not. I might propose a farewell dinner at Fracatelli's.'

'You know what I mean, Bella.'

'Dear old hubbie! Didn't we push Henry Ellis Margam under a train two nights before the wedding? Didn't we go especially to Charing Cross to do so, and didn't you then buy me Irish stout and oysters at Finnegan's?'

Philip realised that was the only answer he was going to get. He bent and kissed his wife on the lips. There was a very faint whisper in his ears that he put down to the music of the spheres.

Although many firms and businesses intended to work up to Christmas Eve, there was nevertheless a feeling abroad in London that could only be described as reckless. Porters at the mainline stations wore paper roses in their caps and many omnibus horses were decorated with garlands of evergreen. This last flourish was popular. Later in the day in Fleet Street, an otherwise perfectly respectable junior in a solicitor's office scandalised the senior partners of the firm (who had just left an extended lunch at the Cheshire Cheese) by dragging a piebald rocking horse along the pavement, a collar of holly around its neck. He intended to walk it up to Museum Street, where his mother-in-law would stable it, she having offered a goose for the festive dinner, what with cousin Walter coming back from the Cape and the grandchildren – that is to say his own two ankle-biters – only too ready to blow out their kite, etc, etc. The rocking horse was second-hand, too old to enter the Derby Stakes and all that, but still a good 'un and would polish up a treat.

Kindly Mr Pardew gave his clerk half a crown for a cab: Mr Diamond made some facetious attempt to get the horse to share his cigar. Old Mr Shipley, wishing to reprehend such a vulgar display of fellowship and good feeling, no matter what the season of the year, stepped out into the roadway too abruptly and was knocked down by a passing cab. In the fullness of the Christmas spirit, this misfortune was greeted by ribald cheers, for it was assumed, not altogether incorrectly, that the old gentleman was up to his back teeth with the grog. And good luck to him!

Elsewhere, mothers roamed up and down an equally cheerful Oxford Street with parcels in one hand and adorable children in tiny fur hats and muffs in the other. The air stank of naphtha flares, fried onions, cinnamon, toffee apples and fir boughs. A fig for the real snow that caught in the eyelashes and when it wetted the lips tasted of soot: many stores had cotton-wool snow piled up in their window displays that would not have disgraced the North Pole. That year's street trader's toy was a monkey that climbed up a stick and then tumbled back down.

'Just like the old man trying to get his trousers off when he's had a few,' a jovial man encouraged a woman in furs who just happened to be the wife of the French Ambassador, at the same time giving her grand-daughter a lascivious wink. But the girl was looking down into Berwick Street, where Fancy Joyner, once of the 42nd Foot, was eating fire; or more accurately, cocking his head back and blowing it into a sky heavy with blue and gold clouds. It seemed to her the most beautiful thing she had ever seen.

In Mortimer Street, outside the Middlesex Hospital, a silver band played hymns and carols and for their pains were pelted by medical students with flour and soot bombs lobbed from the open windows of their hostel. Sergeant Copley led two constables into the premises, some words were exchanged and then, to a roar from the crowd that had gathered, the sergeant appeared at a second-floor window, dusted with flour but with enough seasonal cheer left in him to conduct 'Hark the Herald Angels Sing'.

These and scores more tiny stories played themselves

out like improvised scenes in the twopenny coloured toy theatres to be had from Mr Pollock's shop in Covent Garden. In Whitehall, the Home Secretary was having the principle of the toy explained to him by an enthusiastic colleague. Though not especially sentimental himself, he had nephews and nieces who enjoyed theatrical whimsy and he sent to Pollock for five packs. Later that night he would dine his sister's children at his favourite restaurant. He would then take his guns and himself to Norfolk for the holiday.

At 9.13 p.m. on Christmas Eve, a massive explosion in the Strand blew out the front windows of Fracatelli's, shooting a headless waiter into the street and injuring twenty-seven passers-by with the flying glass. The Home Secretary's party was dining in a mahogany booth at the back of the room and, apart from superficial injuries, survived. Nine people were killed outright and another twelve so badly injured that their lives were feared for. Among the dead was Elias Charles Arthur Frean, publisher, resident in France. Signor Fracatelli himself had been at his table when the bomb went off, supervising the serving of cannelloni al forno: his broad back took all the blast and Frean died from ingesting the restaurateur's life blood. Putting it bluntly, he drowned.

Among the injured rushed across the river to St Bartholomew's Hospital was Mrs Arabella Westland of Orange Street. Mrs Westland had been at the same table as Frean. The blast threw her towards the street, which is how she came to suffer fractures to her left arm and four ribs. Her hair and clothing caught fire but she was luckier than many. Mrs Westland was well known to the staff and a very quick-witted member of the kitchens smothered the flames with a bloody tablecloth. Better still, he tore away the smouldering bodice of her dress and so saved her from anything worse than second-degree burns to her side and chest.

Against police advice, the Home Secretary crossed the river to visit the victims of an outrage that was clearly directed at himself. He was a good man, perhaps a little too formal in his dealings with juniors and underlings; but those that saw him that night met someone barely able to conceal his anguish.

'Do we know who did it, sir?' an agonised parent asked.

'We do not, my dear fellow. Is this your daughter?'

'They are debating whether to take one or both legs off. If it was the Irish that did this thing, then God rot them. God send them to hell for all eternity.'

'It was not the Irish,' the Home Secretary said sharply. 'So much we do know. You yourself are from Devon, if I hear your accent right.'

But the man did not answer. He turned his back and held both his hands to his cheeks in an almost womanly gesture of grief. The Home Secretary found that he was concealing his thumb inside his fist, something he only did when he was extremely anxious, or afraid. The ward stank of coal gas and blood and antiseptic.

Pennington, his Scotland Yard protection officer, touched him lightly on the arm. 'This lady in the next bed is Mrs Westland, sir. I think you know her slightly.'

They peered down into Bella's face, which without Pennington's promptings he would never have recognised.

Her eyes were closed and her lips turned down. One side of her skull was completely without hair. The Home Secretary made a superhuman effort to control his feelings.

'We passed a few seasonal greetings earlier this evening. She was entertaining a friend as a Christmas gift. I can't remember his name.'

'A word now with the nurses and surgeons,' Pennington murmured, 'and then I think we might go.'

Over his master's shoulder he saw the hospital chaplain hovering, a notorious sermoniser. With a skill that went with the job, Pennington turned his man to avoid any encounter and the two of them walked away slowly under the hissing lamps.

Outside, it was very much colder and the snow had begun to settle. The hansom that had brought the two men there was more white than black. After all that had happened, it seemed quite extraordinarily quiet. Pennington relieved his overcoat pocket of the weight of his revolver and held it across his knee.

'Was it the Irish?' the Home Secretary asked unexpectedly.

'Not at all. You can be sure of it. Though it will be a brave Irishman that speaks out of turn in any pub in London tonight.'

TWO

Philip rose to the crisis with a mixture of tenderness in the sickroom and implacable authority outside it. As soon as it was possible, he fetched Bella back to Orange Street and installed her, not in her own bed, but in a smaller room next to the bath. He banned visitors altogether after they had made one brief visit and infuriated the housekeeper, Mrs Venn, with his notions on invalid diet.

'She ain't exactly dying on us, is she?' Captain Quigley asked cautiously. They were sharing his own sovereign remedy for the sick and faint of heart – bottled stout. This was a doubly guilty pleasure: Philip had banned all alcohol and Quigley, to evade his strictures on visitors, had entered the house via the coal-hole, as his face and hands testified.

'If bread and butter puddings can see a body off, she's not far removed from the end,' Dora Venn grumbled. 'We has porridge in the morning, bread and butter pudding for our lunch and a sliver or so of what he calls seethed chicken at nights, along with barley. I wouldn't make a poultice with what she eats.'

'He's took it very bad, I hear.'

'The poor man's in a worse case than she is. Never

leaves the house, a face on him like a sick bloodhound, tears in private. His pal, Mr Kennett, newly home from America, sloped round with his wife last week: gone by ten, the both of them.'

'It's a poor do,' Quigley agreed. 'Does she talk of that wicked night at all?'

'That's it! That's the clue to the whole thing. Has not mentioned it once, not once, which shows *me*, as has looked after her these nine years past, just how deep it's gone. It has struck her to the very soul, Captain. It has gone too deep for reason. I'm afeared for her.'

'What does she talk about, then?'

'Still as polite as any woman in London, still grateful for the little services as only a woman can offer to one of her own sex, but otherwise as quiet as a marble cat. And, o' course, him neither use nor ornament in a situation like this. Killing her with kindness.'

'Needs to be taken out of herself, that sort of thing?' Quigley suggested.

'Like you say, she ain't exactly dying on us. And changing the subject somewhat, Captain, I'd be obliged if you didn't come down the coal-hole no more. It ain't Christian and your boots have done my kitchen floor no favours. I wonder at your impudence.'

Bella herself was finding convalescence irksome. Philip had many sterling qualities but one overriding fault: he loved her too much. While Captain Quigley was tiptoeing out of the front door with exaggerated caution, Bella sat upstairs in a spoon back chair, a velvet turban on her head, smoking an illicit cheroot. It made her feel suitably sick and dizzy. The bedroom floor was covered in news-papers and periodicals, discarded bed-jackets and bottled spa water.

'What it is, Philip, I am bored with being cosseted. I am made dull by being read to, and if I don't have some-thing other than chicken to eat tonight, I think I shall go mad.'

'We might try taking a meal downstairs,' he conceded.

'We might go out. I don't know where – as far as Hyde Park perhaps.'

'For three days past there has been a nipping frost.'

'Good! Anything but this sickroom! I should like to be put in a cab to get thoroughly cold and red in the face and then come home and eat a very large chop. Better still, a steak and kidney pie. And a half bottle of claret.'

Philip sat back and threw his hands in the air. 'I congratulate myself on boring you back to such abrasive good health. I propose a balloon ascent, followed by twelve rounds of boxing with a young man of your choice.'

'It sounds heavenly,' Bella said, reaching out to be kissed. 'I shall dress, doctor. And then, after lunch, you shall take me to the park.'

'About *that*, though, seriously –'

They were interrupted by a thunderous knocking down-stairs, one which Philip indicated that he would answer. Their visitor was Superintendent Pennington.

'You have come to tell us how things go with the Fracatelli investigation?' Philip suggested, when they were seated in the drawing room. He found the superintendent faintly daunting, maybe because of the elegance of his tailoring and the exquisite suppleness of his boots. Pennington was a large – a very large – man in the peak of condition, with the assurance that went with total confidence in his own worth.

'I come about that matter, yes, but – as you might say – at an oblique angle, Mr Westland.'

'My wife will be down in a moment.'

Pennington smiled gently. 'Yes, but you see, there's the thing. It is you I wish to see.'

'Me?' Philip asked, surprised.

'I believe you know a Mr Sefton Garside?'

'Of the Coldstreams, yes.'

'Mr Garside resigned his commission at the end of January.'

'That I did not know.'

'He is your relation, of course. When did you last see him?'

'Just before Christmas.'

'And where was that?'

'In the vaults of the Bank of England, as it happens.'

Pennington smiled. The very gentleness of it suggested condescension, as though Philip had confirmed what the superintendent already knew, without him knowing what he might have given away. The visitor plucked imaginary fluff from the knee to his trousers.

'Mr Garside has taken himself from Knightsbridge and what we might term the bosom of his family to an address in Whitechapel. You didn't know this?'

'You amaze me, Mr Pennington,' Philip returned, now very much on his guard.

Pennington studied him at leisure. 'Faith has driven him there, apparently,' he murmured. 'He intends to go among the poor and bring them to their spiritual salvation. In short, he is become a missionary.'

'Is that a police matter?'

'Do you know a man called Piotr Komarev?' Pennington enquired lazily.

'I do not. He sounds Russian.'

'Garside is lodging with him.'

'Good for him. I don't want to seem more than normally obtuse, Mr Pennington, so if there is a point to these questions I shall be grateful to have you come to it much sooner than later.'

'Is your cousin Garside a political sort of fellow?'

'About as much as the average cauliflower, I should have thought. I can confirm from my conversation with him last Christmas that he is spectacularly devout. Who is Komarev?'

'In a moment. First, do you know a man called Percy Quigley?' the superintendent asked with the calm of a man who had just moved his bishop to threaten the king. Philip wetted his lips. Whatever he was going to say next was postponed by the arrival of Bella, wearing a favourite steel-grey dress and her green turban. Pennington rose as lithe as a boy and greeted her by taking and kissing her outstretched hand.

'Superintendent Pennington, Mrs Westland. I am pleased to see you looking so well. Part of my business here is the charge laid on me by the Home Secretary to ask after you. He will be delighted by my report of what seems a most happy recovery.'

'The superintendent wants to know if I have ever come across someone called Percy Quigley, Bella.'

She looked sharply at Philip before producing for Pennington her own warm and usually winning smile. 'This is my first day downstairs since leaving hospital,' she said. 'In celebration of which, I propose to sample a little of Mrs Venn's elderflower cordial, which I must warn you is powerful and ambiguous in about equal measure. The receipt of it comes from her grandfather, a Dorset man who fought with Nelson. A glass with you, Mr Pennington, before you leave.'

'Nothing could be more welcome,' the Superintendent said. 'I am something of a student of the ambiguous. Was Mrs Venn's grandfather at Trafalgar by any chance?'

'He was one of the four dozen men from the *Victory* chosen by lot to follow Nelson's body to Westminster Abbey,' Bella replied absently. 'But shall we come to the point? You were enquiring about Mr Quigley, I believe.'

'When did you last see him?'

'I gave him his Christmas box the afternoon of the explosion.'

'And you haven't seen him since?'

'This is all very dull, Pennington,' Philip interrupted, at his most lumbering. Two bright spots of colour deco-rated his cheeks, warning signs that Pennington ignored with sublime indifference.

'Perhaps you will allow Mrs Westland to answer a few questions however?'

Bella flushed. She was annoyed with the superintendent for spoiling her first moments downstairs for nearly two months, but doubly vexed to see Philip pushed onto the back foot by his presence.

'I lease a small property in Fleur de Lys Court and employ Mr Quigley there from time to time. I have not seen him since the afternoon of the bombing.'

'And this property is an office of some kind?'

'Yes, an office. He is presently renovating the interior. In tongue and groove boarding,' she added tartly.

'You have the intention to sublet, perhaps?'

'Isn't that my business?' Bella asked. 'Or putting it more directly, don't you have bigger things to worry about?'

Pennington smiled. He inspected his wonderful boots as though seeing them for the first time that day. When he spoke again, his voice was as calm as ever – but a good deal more official in tone.

'You mean to indicate the investigation into the Fracatelli bombing, perhaps?'

'If that is part of your duties, yes.'

'We have not been idle. Fifty officers have been drafted into the East End, quite apart from inquiries undertaken elsewhere. The case is generating a great many files, Mrs Westland.'

'Of which Percy Quigley's is one.'

'In a matter like this, our method has to be painstaking elimination. I am sure you will understand.'

'But why in the East End particularly?'

'In Whitechapel.'

'You mentioned someone called Komarev,' Philip reminded him.

'Yes, indeed.'

'Who is he?'

'Who indeed? Your cousin finds lodgings with him and two days later Mrs Westland's occasional employee turns up as bright as a button at the same address. What do you make of that?'

In all her years of writing novels about crimes and misdemeanours, under the pen name Henry Ellis Margam, Bella had steered clear of the police. There had been a few close encounters with the lee shore of illegality and things had happened to her and her friends about which she would rather keep silent. In spite of enough adventures to make the hair stand on end and the flesh crawl, she had managed to make herself believe that she was first and foremost a writer of fiction and not directly involved in the evil she described. Like most people of her class, she considered the police to be a flat-footed army of not very bright men, arriving only after the event and maddeningly slow to get hold of the right end of the stick. But now – and to be blunt about it – Pennington's languid charm was making her feel decidedly uneasy.

'Is there no such thing as a world of coincidence, Superintendent?'

'I believe even in the most high-minded fiction we see its operations,' Pennington suggested slyly.

'I am talking about coincidence pure and simple. If you were to tell me that Captain Quigley was in the Strand and outside Fracatelli's when the bomb went off, then *that* might make him a suspect,' she said. Even to her own ears, it sounded like bluster.

'It would certainly be something worth knowing,' the superintendent agreed. 'But of course, we know that his friend Komarev was.'

'And how do you know that?'

The silence that followed was as complete and startling as if the room, its furnishings and carpets had turned to ice.

'You are going to have to tell us much more, Pennington,' Philip said in a low voice.

'Have you ever broken, say, a crystal vase by letting it fall to the floor in a moment of clumsiness? It shatters and it is the devil's own job to find all the pieces. Tiny shards are dispersed everywhere, some to be found only by the most patient of searches. A glint in some distant part of the carpet, a sliver in the gaps between the boards, and so on.'

Pennington rose. His fingers went to his stock in what was obviously an habitual gesture, a reassurance that there was not the slightest thing out of place from his toes to the crown of his head. He smiled.

'Komarev is someone you would not wish to meet, Mrs Westland. He is very much from another part of the city. This is a police investigation and we must follow wherever it leads. We must, if you like, pick up every last piece of the shattered crystal.'

The cab ride to the park was cancelled and a new destination called for. Swathed in a plaid shawl, an immense Russian fur hat from Philip's wardrobe jammed on her head, Bella was half-carried into Fleur de Lys Court, to the place that had once belonged to Henry Ellis Margam. It was growing dark and the office was lit by half a dozen candles. The figure inside – casting such huge shadows – was not Margam, neither was it Captain Quigley, but a Kentish Town woman called Alice Cobb.

'A mate of his,' she explained. 'Well, not so much a mate as an old sparring partner.'

'And, apparently, a carpenter.'

'More'n what he is,' Alice agreed grimly. 'Not that there's much carpentry in tongue and groove. 'Tis mostly banging about with a hammer and a mouthful of French nails. But I hope you find it looks well when it's done.'

Miss Cobb was short and hugely fat, an appearance accentuated by two coats and a canvas apron of the kind worn by fishwives. 'Should you like some tea?' she asked with the greatest nonchalance, taking a blackened clay pipe out of her mouth to indicate a tin kettle.

'Where is my furniture?' Bella asked, bewildered.

'In store, such as it is. Oh, 'tis all safe. I see you are looking sideways at me, mister,' she said to Philip.

'There was rather a good rosewood table.'

'Like I say – in store.'

'And Quigley?'

'He seemed to have the idea I could work around him while he sat by and gabbed with his cronies. The brains of a newt, that one. Are you Mr Margam by any chance?'

'I am not.'

'I ask, because me and Perce filled a box with his books and papers, pens and blotters – all his *scribblings* – and hooked them out of here. Likewise in store.'

Bella sat down on a sawhorse and held her hands out to the meagre fire. 'I should very much like a can of coffee fetched from Tonio's,' she said faintly. 'And then you can tell me where Captain Quigley is tonight.'

'Well, he ain't rejoined the Colours,' Alice crowed, with

a laugh that resembled the siren of a Thames steamer running aground in fog.

Coffee sent for and delivered by Antonio himself, who took the liberty of kissing Bella on both cheeks to express his joy at her recovery. A flowery speech half rehearsed in English soon enough collapsed into Italian and was rounded off with a heartfelt snatch of traditional Neapolitan song. Handshakes all round but still Tonio was not done. He had not been gone more than a few minutes when a cheeky boy delivered a cake wrapped in a gingham cloth.

'Which we shall have to whistle for our brandy, seemingly,' Alice commented sourly.

In her sad story were bundled enough mysteries to occupy Superintendent Pennington for a fortnight. Her father had been transported for a term of fourteen years to Western Australia in 1851. More than half the ship's hold was taken up with Irish convicts and, some unfortunate words having been exchanged with one of these on the passage, Dick Cobb was stabbed to death only four days after arriving in Perth. Back in Dorset, things were no better. When the widow Cobb was taken up for housebreaking, the daughter went to live with someone she supposed was her grandmother and the two of them scratched a living gathering wild herbs and selling them on to shops. Then one night the police came and dug up the garden, unearthing Granny Ilstone's husband.

'You have been dogged by ill-luck,' Bella observed.

Alice looked at her uncomprehendingly. This was how life was, this was how the cards fell, her expression seemed to say.

'Might you say a word about how you came to meet Captain Quigley?' Philip asked.

'Him! I have knowed him off and on for all the time I been in London. Came up from Portsmouth, and the first person I met was that wicked old chancer. He was in need of a woman, as he expressed it, and it looked for a moment as if we was going to set up permanent, my brains and his beauty, I don't think.'

'When you say set up –'

Alice made a cheerfully obscene gesture with the fingers of both hands. 'But he ain't the homely kind, as was proved. No more 'n I was the bit of flash he thought he needed. He come down here into the Garden and I ended up with a gang of rogues in Kentish Town. Burgling,' she added.

'And the carpentry?'

'More recent. A la-di-dah cove by the name of Monbiot set me on. We was working for a landlord, putting up stud walls to rack the rent out in them big old houses up towards Hampstead.' She laughed. 'First I robs them. Then they're bought up one by one and I comes along to make rabbit hutches out of the bedrooms. Eh?'

Bella felt she had to ask. 'And it is with this Monbiot you live now?'

'Dear me,' Alice chortled. 'Oh dearie, dearie me. No, my heart is give to Peter, if he would only have it.'

'Peter?'

'Peter the Giant. The Russkie,' she added.

'Peter Komarev?' Bella asked in a flash of intuition.

'Wherever he is,' Alice agreed. 'For where he ain't is up in Kentish Town. So Perce, the old fool, says he'll go look for him, in lieu of paying me a wage to put this lot up, him strapped for cash what with this Margam bloke bunking off out of it. So I says, how are you going to find him? And he says, well, he's six foot six with a beard on him like a dead cat, he don't speak much English and he's walking about the streets with a bass fiddle for company. He ain't exactly incognito, is he?'

'A *bass fiddle*?'

'Which he is a musician,' Alice said, rather tart.

THREE

Why Sefton Garside had chosen Whitechapel for his missionary zeal was something of a mystery. He did not know the area any better than he knew Matabele Land or the remoter parts of Szechuan. Its one recommendation was that it was nothing like Norfolk, where he had been born. This was soon enough made abundantly clear.

In the space of only a few days going about God's work, he had the following items stolen from him: a pair of monogrammed hairbrushes, his best boots, an umbrella, an engraved silver turnip watch, two shirts and some underwear. Added to these was *The Imitation of Christ* in the India paper edition. Sefton took this particular theft to be a hopeful sign. Someone, no matter how stony the ground, was in search of enlightenment.

'Your book has gone to make some heathen his gaspers,' a street urchin called Walt explained with the patience one might show to another child.

'But how does that work?'

'Easy enough. Empty the old lady's teapot, dry the leaves out on the hob for a few minutes and then roll yourself one according. That particular kind of paper much prized. Anything else catches the back of the throat something chronic.'

'*Tea?*' Garside muttered, incredulous. 'You are smoking *tea?*'

'Well, it ain't *fresh* tea,' Walt chided. 'By the time we're talking about smoking it, a gnat would strain to produce anything stronger. As for the pleasure of smoking it, it's more of an indoor firework. By what I mean you wouldn't want to walk through the Woolwich Arsenal with one, but it offers a quantum of solace, yes.'

'You speak very well, Walter.'

'As to that, mate, I have been raised among princes.'

'Indeed?'

'Give us a couple of coppers and I'll go fetch us some coffee. Then I can tell you what's what in the old family tree.'

Sefton took out his purse and rummaged. 'Oh dear, the smallest I have is a shilling.'

'Then give us that and I'll bring you back the change.'

Of course he never saw the boy again. There was much else that Sefton was finding vexing about the East End. For some reason impossible for him to fathom, his very presence was a subject of mirth. This was before he opened his mouth, even. Taller than most, his spine more erect by far, what made him comical was his habit of standing about and peering like a caribou stork. In a homelier simile, he was like a turkey who knows an axe is being sharpened on a whetstone somewhere in the barnyard without being able to trace the source of the threat.

The only reason to stand still in the backstreets of Whitechapel was to assert a territorial dominance. You stayed put: the rest of the world passed by. Gang leaders had this habit. It pleased them to bend an ear to the petitions brought to them by the neighbours, about domestic quarrels, bad drains, bad debts, the chance of a little day labouring – all this while lounging against a wall, protected on both sides by young heavies. Thus the courts of Big Tony Neggs, Jimmy Slippers, the infamous Harry Coggins.

Coggins was barely five feet tall, as wizened as a winter apple and about as communicative. Over the years, seven unwise or unwary locals had gone to meet their Maker for saying the wrong thing, or even looking at this ancient dwarf the wrong way. They went with their throats cut from ear to ear. The gang-leader's weapon of choice for these executions was an antique German razor, inscribed '*Gott mitt Uns*'. It lived in Harry's waistcoat pocket.

It was all of a piece with Sefton Garside's innocence that he marked Coggins out on his very first day as a mild-looking chap who might know of a lodging house run by a clean and responsible Christian woman. This was doubly incautious. Coggins ran nearly thirty whores in nine houses and the question could have been construed as sarcasm. But more than that, he was not a man for idle conversation with strangers, under which head he placed Sefton's enquiry. He heard him out in silence, never meeting the missionary's gaze but staring down the street as if thinking of something else entirely. Sefton supposed he might be a little deaf and began to repeat his address. Harry Coggins simply held up his hand, palm outward.

'That was the sign to sod off out of it,' a bystander explained. 'You know, cease and desist. In other words, scarper.'

'Was I anything less than polite in my address?'

'You and him ain't got nothing to be polite about, you unhappy streak of piss. And *I* don't want to be seen talking to you, neither,' the man added, propelling Sefton backwards several paces with a warning cuff. There was always an audience for the untoward in Whitechapel and seeing the beanpole toff getting his ears boxed was rich entertainment. Funnier still was to see him retreat down an alley running in raw sewage.

'You don't walk on water, then!' a wit cried.

The missionary was unworldly down to the smallest details. Uncertain what to wear on his blond curls, but convinced he could not go about bareheaded, he settled at last on a ridiculous tweed deerstalker given to him by his mother as a Christmas present. Quite the thing in Norfolk, but in Whitechapel it had an almost sinister connotation. A beanpole in a foreign-looking hat, bearing a board reading 'COME TO JESUS' was somehow more than a mere novelty. Everywhere he went, he was followed about by a cloud of small boys, hooting and yelling.

Easily lost in the swarming warrens, he had the perfectly sensible idea of making sketch maps of his wanderings: these papers disappeared from his pocket as fast as he thrust them in. When he fell to chalking crosses on the walls, the marks he made caused alarm and consternation among the boys and spread quickly to their fathers. His mission, about which he had been so certain in Knightsbridge, descended now into episodes of the most humiliating kind. If he saw a troubled soul walking towards him with anything like the appearance of wanting to say something, he would cross to the other pavement, cheeks burning in shame. When he passed groups of idlers, their heads swinging around like cattle, he broke into a cold sweat.

He was right to think like this. This was territory where the merest signs of weakness or indecision invited disaster. Though his faith was strong, Sefton had never before defended it from attack by horse-droppings, rotting cabbages, dead rats and scoops of mud and filth. He was harangued wherever he went in German, Polish and Russian – and a particular sort of choked patois he realised after a day or so must be English. Sefton was used to conversation where a question was indicated by a gently rising inflection. In Whitechapel, questions of any kind took on the character of a hatchet, or club hammer. They had a downward force.

'Woss your game?'

'My name is Sefton Garside and –'

'Shut your face and answer the question!'

It took him three or four days to realise that many of the more unintelligible native speakers he met were not hapless lunatics discharged from some local asylum, but drunks. The most adhesive of these was a woman called Chunky Nora, who followed him about explaining how there was a fortune in stolen property waiting for them both in Ware. It was buried under a tree located in the graveyard of the parish church, a tree that had since been chopped down by the new vicar.

'And that's where you come in!' she would conclude, her yellowy-brown hands scrabbling at his sleeve, her jaws clacking. 'You're a man of the cloth, aincha? More or less, ennit? Then go give that bleeding vicar one up the throat! Give him gyp! We'll go dibs on the money and other items. What is called the loot.'

Thus it was a red-letter day when Sefton met Piotr Komarev, known locally as Peter the Giant. The gaunt Russian beckoned him from a doorway and when he hesitated, drew him inside with the gentleness of a mother. This one simple act of hospitality ended the worst of Sefton's torments. From being a man wandering about asking inane questions about hotels and boarding houses, Garside had – in the eyes of the many – stepped down to the level of the streets.

'Pete the Giant has took him in,' the bully boys commented, spitting vehemently into the gutter, as if franking his ticket to perdition.

Komarev occupied a single ground-floor room in a tiny street of properties run up by a speculative builder seventy years earlier. It was more than a single room at that, for in the much less distant past some desperado had knocked a ragged doorway through the back wall, affording a view of the shared scullery and a pocket handkerchief yard. In place of a door, the aperture was defended from the elements by a tarpaulin marked as the property of the North Eastern Railway.

Once, an honest artisan and his family had lived in this house, finding life good and praising God for it on Sundays, the tenant with a clean kerchief around his neck and his best boots on his feet. He and his kind had long gone from Berman Street; the floors his wife had scrubbed out twice a week had been sold for firewood, along with the beams that supported them. All that was left of the parlour was three and a half walls and a blackened fireplace. The floor was soil – and rocks.

'Eat,' Komarev commanded, pointing to a pan of cabbage soup. What appeared to the suspicious Garside to be mouse droppings turned out to be peppercorns. He ate and after a few spoonfuls, burst into tears. Komarev patted his shoulder absentmindedly, pulling out two sacks stuffed with ancient straw. 'After eat, sleep.'

Garside did exactly as he was told. At eight, the Russian put on an immense coat reaching to his ankles, took his double bass and sloped off to a penny theatre in the Whitechapel Road. He came back at midnight with a pinch of ground coffee in a paper cone, wiped out the soup can with his fingers, boiled some water, and made coffee. He woke his visitor and sat with him, fuming gently from half a dozen brandies tossed down his throat earlier. 'I am Komarev,' he said at last. 'Tomorrow we begin lessons in violin.'

Garside seized his hand and burst out crying all over again.

Captain Quigley's expedition to smoke out the Russian Giant was designed as a leisurely affair, for, as he had pointed out to Alice Cobb, the big man was not going to be very hard to find. The search was more in the nature of a holiday, even. The up and down of it was that Quigley was facing – though he hated to think about the details – a change of residence. The Fleur de Lys idyll was coming to an end. He was never short of bright ideas for the future but none of them now included Bella Westland, nor for that matter, his old sparring partner Billy Murch. Billy was the married man these days and, what's more, the dad of the world, a concept so foreign to the Captain that he could only guess at the rigours it implied. One way or another, the game was up with what he had already begun describing as the Henry Ellis Margam years. That shadowy figure had vanished like last night's smoke from a public house snug.

And eheu fugaces to the lot of you, Quigley concluded, taking a steadying draught at the Grapes, coming on, he hoped, like a man of affairs. Indeed, he was seen as just such, for a man with a ruined nose soon enough sidled up and offered him two dozen of claret, lifted from a warehouse in the Commercial Road quite recent, but not so recent as to be smoking hot.

'And would that be the Old Bill walking past right at this minute?' Quigley countered, indicating the pavement with his chin, where two policemen sauntered, thumbs in belts.

The man glanced. 'Them? Bigger fish to fry, old love. There's more coppers about here nowadays than at the opening of Parliament and that's no lie. The Fracatelli bombers is their quarry,' he added. 'They think the gang is hiding up somewhere in the East End, o' course.'

'What gang is that, then? There's a gang of them, is there?'

'*They* don't know. Could be Chinese laundry wallahs for all they know. Like losing a tanner down a dark alley and looking for it under a street light, that's what the poor old East End is for the coppers. Talk about pin the tail on the bleeding' donkey!'

'I heard King's Cross has been done over.'

'Done over? They have been through *there* like shit through a goose.'

'Turn up anything?'

'It's got so an honest dip can't earn his living no more on that particular terminus. All the working girls frightened out of their life. Some foreign gaffs turned over two or three times a week.'

'What about Frenchy Barnes?'

'You know Frenchy Barnes?' the man exclaimed admiringly. 'Sweet man, lovely geezer, God rest his soul.'

'Yeah?'

'You haven't heard? Goes down to Dover last Tuesday and he's only gone and got himself shot dead outside the dock gates that same evening. Persons unknown, which is to say, local villains. His old lady – Alice Noble that was –'

'– whose father was Bertie Noble –'

'– the same – she has rousted out the Barnes and the Nobles and gone down there mob-handed to sort it out. Anyoldhow, d'you want this 'ere dinner wine we're talking about or not?'

'I'll be in touch.'

'Take that for a no, then. But watch yourself, matey. Walls have eyes.'

'They have ears,' Quigley corrected amiably enough, as the cove sloped off, the soles of his boots slapping. Quigley could have done a little business with the wine at that but the thief was wearing a bottle-green topcoat and this was a colour the Captain disliked. Furthermore, when buying claret, it was better when the vendor wore boots where the uppers were still attached to the sole. And socks. Socks the thing for claret.

There was one other thing. The Grapes a pub well known to the fraternity, but not often the resting place for a geezer like the one watching him now, peering over the top of a paper like he was checking the time. My eye. This geezer had copper writ all over him, or Percy Quigley's a Dutchman.

If the truth were told, Quigley found Whitechapel daunting – and not just for the number of police hanging about. For one thing, there were far too many kiddies running about without shoes, the girls without drawers. Too many beggars trying to tap you up, too many leery coves with scars, with unknown business to conduct at street corners. It was a hard place to get a handle on, like trying to make a tobacco pouch out of frogspawn. He could be as light on the toes as the next bloke, but the sheer press of people was beginning to get him down.

He found Peter the Giant outside the theatre that same evening and introduced himself, naming a few connections but omitting for the time being any mention of Alice Cobb. They set off down the Whitechapel Road for a bit before plunging into the dark of a narrow street that was by day a vegetable market. Empty boxes were piled high on barrows and platoons of rats skittered about. The Captain very much on the qui vive. What might have been human brains under his boots proved nothing more than the heads of rotting cauliflowers, but all the same . . .

'You know Billy Murch?' Komarev asked doubtfully as they edged along.

'Me and Billy go way back. Married now, he is.'

'I love this man.'

'Does you credit, old lad. Now, Pete, I don't want to

put the wind up you but this cove as is following us is a copper down to his socks.'

'This I already notice.'

'Well, why don't we stroll along all casual and you can tell me how you and Billy came to be mates, mentioning no surnames, if you follow my drift.'

To the detective following them, they began a meandering conversation about people who played the halls. For Captain Quigley, what Komarev had to tell was iron to the soul. The connection between Billy and the huge Russian was poor old Molly Clunn, a name Quigley could not hear without being blinded by prickling tears.

'Molly is ill with the drink. She love Billy. He love her too, but there is pity also. Komarev is in the middle. She come to Komarev one night. Pete, she say, he is poisoning me with his pity. Now I move in with you.'

'I didn't know that.'

'I don't want no such thing and it don't last long. One night I come home from theatre, she is gone. I never see her no more again. Then comes Billy to say she is dead. He is very bad with drink. We fight. I make soup, we fight. Make soup, fight some more. One night he say, now I top myself. Chuck body in front of bloody train pretty soon. This Komarev don't allow. Tie him to chair.'

'Close arrest sort of thing?'

The Russian held up his fingers. 'Three days. No soup, no drink. Brandy, whisky, nothing. But tears, yes. Shouting, yes, plenty shouting. He love that woman. You know what is love?'

Quigley did not answer. It had begun to rain and the pavements were slick. The Captain bit the inside of his lip, wondering how many more streets like this he would walk down before death found him out. As for Komarev's question, he supposed Russians sat around in the cornfields asking this kind of thing all the time, gazing at the moon and so forth. No true blue Englishman would have a ready answer, balalaikas or no balalaikas.

'Well, he's married now,' he said shakily. 'Got himself a cushty billet down the river. Nice girl. Baby daughter. Your story a bloody gloomy one if you ask me, Pete.'

They were interrupted by a commotion taking place at the corner of Herschel Street. Four men, assisted by bellowed advice from a drunken crowd, were trying to boost a cow through the door to a terrace house. Half the animal was inside but the rump and back legs stayed stubbornly on the pavement. Sticks were flying.

'Now I've seen all,' Quigley said.

'It is Clausen. He have a dairy there.'

'What, in his front room?'

'Milk is milk,' Komarev said in his mild and neutral tone.

The crowds parted for the giant Russian. He crawled on his hands and knees between the legs of the cow and, lying on his back, began speaking to the beast in the pacifying voice taught to him by his grandmother, the one she used for children and animals alike. Quigley, left holding the double bass, watched in amazement as the cow's flanks quivered for a few moments and then disappeared into the dark. Komarev stumbled upright, wiping cowshit from his face and beard.

'This animal tell me she is new to Whitechapel,' he observed.

'Told you that, did she?'

But the biggest surprise of the night was when they got to Komarev's gaff. Quigley was badly thrown to find a tall and skinny gink in a deerstalker hat, playing scales on a ruined violin. It was one o'clock in the morning and upstairs they were hunting rats. He blinked. 'This is homely,' he said, producing a pint bottle of gin from his overcoat pocket. The evening ended with the three of them singing an old favourite of Molly Clunn's – 'I'm always the last out the door'.

Next day, after laying out a shilling for a handful of coal to try to coax a little warmth into these temporary quarters, Quigley, in his guileless way, considered it only right and proper to take Sefton off Pete's hands for an hour or two. It was also in his mind to give him a leg-up with the old God-bothering lark. With an unerring feel for local geography, the Captain took him to a falling-down property that had once been a stables. It was named Hackstraw's Yard, after the owner, who was still alive, though in a sorry state. He and his stableyard had gone downhill together. Chaff and wisps of straw blew about the cobbles, like the ghosts of horses. Mr Hackstraw sat on a kitchen chair at the gates to his property, reading the Good Book. He was the fattest man Sefton had ever met. Not that they had much to say to each other at first.

The Captain did the negotiating. 'Now we're walking down this here street and I pick you straight off as a soldierly looking cove,' he lied briskly. 'A cavalry type. I don't say the Royals and the Blues but an honest yeomanry regiment. Would I be right?'

'You would,' Hackstraw lied back, wiping his nose on his sleeve.

'Well, this is Mr Garside, late of the Coldstreams, who has had a call to come down here and do God's work. What he has give up the Queen's commission and a glittering career, abandoned all his mates up west, broken his old mother's heart and pledged himself to make the world a better place, starting here in dear old Whitechapel.'

'You don't say.'

Hackstraw had an unfortunate voice for one so obese – high-pitched and effeminate. Quigley, who had an eye for this sort of thing, however, judged him to be light on his feet over five yards or so. Run at you, fall on you and break every sodding bone in your body – like a piano falling from a first-floor window. The Captain licked his lips.

'Now, says I to Mr Garside, what makes you think Mr Hackstraw can help you in this difficult venture? Why, says he, is he not areading of the Good Book, as attentive to it as any Dorset parson?'

'Don't know Dorset, don't want to,' Hackstraw said, the unhelpful old basket.

Blushing, Sefton extended his hand in greeting. 'What it is, Mr Hackstraw, I am looking for somewhere to hold my meetings.'

'And what will happen at these meetings?'

'People will be asked to choose between heaven and hell,' he replied simply.

Hackstraw plucked at his nostril with a blunt and none-too-clean thumb. 'Bugger me,' he said.

'At present, Mr Garside stays with Pete the Giant,'

Quigley said. 'If there's a better character reference to be had, I haven't heard of it. Old Pete holds Ticket Number One in this great enterprise. He is all for it.'

'Pete the Giant draws no water here,' Hackstraw piped swiftly. 'He floats no boats. Harry Coggins decides what goes off round here.'

'Then I must meet Mr Coggins,' Sefton cried.

'You have done. Little chap. Bit of an artist with the razor. You arst him for help in finding lodgings.'

'Him!'

'What that has made you famous, molder. Aside from all which, I don't hear nothing about no rent being mentioned for these meetings of yourn.'

'Not a rich cove,' Quigley said hastily. 'The eye of the needle sort of thing. A oncer a week for two or three hours.'

'Two or three hours a day?' Hackstraw squeaked, incredulous. 'What's he going to do, walk on water?'

'And for that there stable as a place to lay his head. A sov for you when you square it with this Coggins cove.'

'Harry is not a man for the teachings of the Gospel. That don't figure much in his way of thinking.'

Quigley pointed to Sefton, who had wandered into the yard, his hands clasped in prayer. 'Look at him,' he said. 'Does he look dangerous to you? He's come here to have his heart broke and what skin is it off your nose if it does? As for Coggins, my old son, unless they catch these Fracatelli boys soon, his business here is down the Swanee. There's more coppers than brasses out at night and that's no error. But there's nothing the Old Bill like better than a justified sinner. Harry Coggins gives a missionary toff a leg-up? That'll sit well with the Commissioner, my life it will.'

'And you? Who are you?'

'You've heard of Charlie Spurgeon, I dare say?' Quigley improvised boldly, meaning to indicate the greatest revivalist preacher of the century and founder of the Metropolitan Tabernacle. It was satisfying to see Hackstraw's jaw drop. But then *he* was thinking of the Charlie Spurgeon who had talked his way into Windsor Castle and robbed the Queen of nigh on £4,000 in jewels. Now resident in France, at Cap Ferrat, as Charles Henri de Bougainville. A famous tickle, for those who followed these things.

'You was the sentry that let Charlie in,' Hackstraw yelped.

'The same,' Captain Quigley said gravely, wondering what the merry hell they were talking about.

Next day there was fog, such fog that made London famous. Quigley opened the door to Pete the Giant's gaff, expecting to see Sefton, whom he had sent for a small pail of milk to Jepherson's on the corner. Instead of the missionary beanpole, a garden roller of a man stood on the threshold.

'Harry wants to see you,' he said.

'And which Harry is that?'

'Just get your hat, if you got one.'

'I'm trying to be civil –'

'He didn't say nothing about not bashing your face in first.'

'Oh, that Harry,' the Captain said. He peered out into the street, intending to make some pleasantry about the weather. But the Coggins gang was as terse of speech as their boss. A second or so later, Quigley found himself stumbling along in a yellow universe, holding on to the thug's coat-tails, tripping over unseen hillocks of ash, dogs and small children.

Quigley expected the meeting to be held in a pub or something of that sort; but Harry Coggins was a creature of habit and they spoke out of doors, against the wall of a lodging house. The two men could barely see each other, so dense was the fog.

'Who is he?' the gang leader whispered, never one to waste words on preambles and introductions.

Quigley nodded. 'Name of Garside. About as harmless as stair-carpet,' he added. This facetious note was ill-judged.

'Did I ask you what he was like?' Coggins asked.

'You never did.'

There was a very awkward silence.

'He's straight up, is he?'

'Kosher,' the Captain promised.

'Not a police plant?'

'What, him?'

Coggins seethed some spit through his front teeth. A drunk stumbled past. 'And you? Are you on the take?

'Me? I dare say that tub of lard Hackstraw has marked your card about me.'

'The Windsor Castle blagging?'

'The same.'

Coggins seethed some more spit. 'When Spurgeon did a bunk to France, what did you do?'

'This and that. Ducking and diving. Nothing special,' Quigley replied.

'You got nothing? He never saw you right?'

'You know Charlie. Not a sharing kind of person.'

'I could have Arthur here practise his boxing on you,' Coggins warned.

'Won't be necessary. You are looking at one of the wretched of the earth, Mr Coggins, sir.'

'A comedian,' Arthur commented, cracking his knuckles in anticipation. But the boss held up his hand. He peered into the fog for a few moments, weighing up what had been discussed. The silence was unearthly.

'Put it like this,' Coggins said at last. 'I don't like you. I never liked Spurgeon and I don't like you.'

'Now whatever have I done to upset a goodhearted old gentleman like yourself?' Quigley asked in his most jocular voice. He woke an hour later with his pockets turned inside out and no boots. The fog seemed to have settled on his chest like a harmless but unshiftable cow. Then he realised he could not move a muscle, except for those that controlled his eyes.

FOUR

The breakfast hour in Orange Street was always formal to a fault. Philip could not imagine starting the day without *The Times* propped against the coffee pot, and Bella knew better than to speak at all while he was reading, even if it was to point out that the house was on fire or shoals of mackerel were swimming past the sitting-room windows. Each day a strained-looking Mrs Venn came in at exactly eight-thirty and laid the post down beside her mistress's elbow before tiptoeing out again. Though she had been encouraged several times to grasp the idea of companionable silence at this hour of the day, it was not her notion of what made a happy marriage. Better by far to hear a bit of shouting and banging about, to clear the decks, so to speak. But Bella liked the quiet clunk of the German case clock and the ambient noise of horse traffic and street cries. Today, for example, was the day that Mr Buckmaster, the knife grinder, made his rounds. And indeed, Dora Venn was taking out some of her exasperation by having the kitchen knives given a sabre's edge. Bella suppressed the desire to burst out laughing.

'Am I boring?' Philip asked out of the blue. It was as startling as if one of the chairs had suddenly spoken.

'Only intermittently, husband dear,' Bella replied. 'It is

your duty to bore me occasionally, otherwise I might get ideas above my station. And then who knows what frothy nonsense I might utter.'

'You might start to have opinions of your own,' Philip agreed, jumping up and embracing her. His mouth tasted of marmalade.

'What shall we do today?' Bella asked, perhaps holding him a little too tight. He pushed her away gently and held her at arm's length. The kindliness in his eyes was almost too much to bear.

'You miss the writing, don't you?'

'Not as much as you think.'

'Perhaps it is tedious being married to such a dull, prosaic fellow.'

'You are fishing, husband dear. It would be extremely tedious to have to simper every time the man of the house wishes to be reassured that he is the lord of all creation.'

'I beg your pardon,' Philip said. 'I thought I was getting you to see that without my emphasising it too boldly.'

'To answer your question, I miss the writing only in the way that people who no longer play bridge miss picking up the first hand of the evening. But you – don't you miss going out and doing all those manly things you used to do, like playing billiards at your club, or getting yourself shot for Queen and Country?'

'This is better.' He studied her face carefully. 'I will tell you what it is. I was not the one blown up, Bella, but I could heartily wish for all this late nonsense to carry on without us. I am sure Pennington is a very fine fellow but police work is something we have managed to avoid until now.'

'What do you propose?'

'That we become an old married couple, by which I mean staid and probably deaf and blind into the bargain. Devoted to each other, of course – but dull. Insufferably dull.'

'It sounds heavenly,' Bella said. 'How clever you are to think of it. With practice, we can communicate to each other in nothing but grunts and sighs. A fig for adventure.'

Philip knew when he was being mocked. He kissed her eyes, the tenderest expression he knew to show how much he loved her. When Dora Venn came in to clear away the breakfast things she was amazed to find her employers sitting in cocked hats made from the sacred pages of *The Times*.

'Roust out the crew, Mistress Venn,' Philip cried. 'Close haul the main braces and, um, jibber up the jib, for we're bound for the Rio Grande, be damned if we're not. A golden guinea for the first man to sight land.'

'Today is to be all about dance and skylark, bosun dear,' Bella added.

'What I was going to ask, if you you'd fancy a fillet of plaice for your lunch,' Dora countered, her lips still down-turned, but inwardly beaming, beaming.

At eleven, with Rio still obstinately over the horizon and Philip pottering about for second-hand books at the stalls in Cecil Court, there was a knock at the door. A uniformed constable stood on the step, young enough to blush, with an invitation to join Superintendent Pennington at the London Hospital, if Mrs Westland would be so kind.

'Is it serious?' Bella cried.

'Enough for me to fetch you by cab,' the constable mumbled, his face crimson. 'But nobody's dead, if that's what you mean.'

'Go down to the kitchen and ask Mrs Venn to give you a glass of lemonade, if she has any. I will be with you in five minutes.'

Lunch at the London was heralded each day by a clattering of trolleys and cutlery, carrying with it a stench of mince and cabbage that ran ahead down the corridors and woke all but the most heavily sedated. A flock of nurses arrived in the ward and darted from bed to bed, sitting the patients bolt upright, where necessary combing their hair and rubbing their mouths briskly with a damp cloth. All except at Quigley's bedside. Without being able to do anything more than blink and drool, he was already the least popular patient on the ward. Studying him, Bella's gloom was complete.

'He was found in the Liverpool Street goods yards, under a consignment of Wisbech potatoes,' Superintendent Pennington explained. Quigley lay before them, copping a deaf 'un, his eyes firmly closed. (So that was it, eh? Potatoes. What a bloody liberty.)

'How came he there?' Bella asked. It was a pleasure to hear her faintly acerbic tone.

'It was an exceptionally foggy day, of course. I imagine he was run round from Whitechapel by coster's barrow. The poor fellow had taken a fearful beating.'

'Of a political nature?'

Pennington laughed politely, as though she had said something light and amusing. Married woman or not, Bella

– 806 –

was very conscious of being flirted with by the detective. Pennington had a clubman's drawl – perhaps better to say the educated nonchalance of a university don. Nothing he said mattered, his voice and smile seemed to indicate. The human condition, about which the French made such a fuss, was a comedy, was it not?

For something to do, Bella reached for Quigley's hand on the counterpane and was startled to find her tiny pressure returned with vigour. She swallowed. 'How long will he remain unconscious?' she asked.

'The doctors cannot say. I fear you are going to tell me that this is just another scrape the Captain has got himself into, such as has decorated his conduct in the past.'

'He has had his moments,' Bella allowed.

'As may be. But I should tell you also, Mrs Westland, that his friend Piotr Komarev has disappeared.'

'This is very careless of you, Superintendent. The sad circumstance we find Quigley in now and the disappearance of the Russian are connected in some way?'

Pennington contrived to look world-weary and disappointed, as if a mere woman could hardly be expected to grasp the matter. 'In the Yard we pursue what we call lines of inquiry. I think I mentioned them at our first meeting. Komarev has disappeared and now we find his friend Mr Quigley landed in a hospital bed with a severe drubbing. I don't think we can say that lessens our interest in the two of them in any way. There may be mischief here.'

'There are probably a dozen men who would like to give Percy Quigley a good hiding.'

'Can you name any?' Pennington asked. 'I mean, in the Whitechapel area?'

'Of course not.'

'No, and how could you? Has he worked for you a long time?'

'He is not my employee.'

'I believe you told me he was.'

'The arrangements we made in the past have been more informal.'

'What a wealth of detail that tiny word conjures up.'

'What is this?' Bella demanded. 'Am I too to come under suspicion in your – what was it – line of inquiry? Is that why you have fetched me here? It seems to me you have been barking up the wrong tree.'

'My dear Mrs Westland,' Pennington protested gently. There was a pause, the detective looking away politely as Bella turned her back on him and gazed out of the window at another wing of the building and a patch of pale blue sky. Her cheeks were flushed with anger.

'Why does he call himself the Captain?' Pennington asked.

'For pleasure, I imagine.' Her back was still turned.

He shrugged and smiled his lazy smile. 'Well, I have arranged for a constable to be posted at the head of Captain Quigley's bed – in hope that he might soon be able to explain himself, but also to watch whether he regains the power of locomotion. In other words, to prevent him legging it. Finally, of course, to offer him protection.'

'I don't quite follow.'

'Hospital visits can take many forms. We wouldn't want anything else ugly to happen to this poor chap.'

'Is he really a serious suspect?'

'Mrs Westland, we believe the Fracatelli bombing to be

the work of men who might strike again. Anywhere, in any part of London – with utter disregard for human life.'

'And you genuinely believe this sad ruin of a man is part of that? Is being buried under potatoes a sure and certain indicator of criminal conspiracy? For shame, Mr Pennington.'

Bella stood, and gave a last squeeze of Quigley's dry and toasty hand. There was a crash as lunch arrived through the swing doors. Along with it came Constable Roberts, his helmet under his arm, his hair neatly parted. Roberts was elderly but, like the best horses, bomb-proof. He nodded by way of salute and sat down heavily in a chair level with Quigley's head.

'Look after him,' Bella said.

'Like a mother tends her baby, missus,' Roberts responded gravely.

'I know you can't hear me, Quigley,' Bella lied in parting. 'But I want you to know that when you are free of all this nonsense, you have only to visit Orange Street to have things set straight between us. We shall have a tidy-up of our affairs, you poor chap.'

'Let us hope it falls out that way,' Superintendent Pennington muttered.

And yes, my old matey, well may you blush, Quigley exulted. You are messing with the wrong woman here, you sack of horse feathers.

At that same time in Whitechapel, Sefton Garside was blissfully unaware that he was being followed by one of Pennington's men. The fog had dispersed, leaving behind it a smell of sulphur and a dull smear to glass and paintwork. Coughing and spitting were the order of the day. The tang of blood outside the horse slaughterers' was considered locally a great restorative for that sort of thing. Those that believed this stood about the yard like day visitors to Brighton, snuffing up the salty air, giving the pipes a chance to reinvigorate. Blood ran over their boots.

Meanwhile, Garside marched up and down with his placard, feeling lightheaded, a thing he put down to the intercession of the Holy Spirit but which more probably flowed from acute hunger. He took some comfort nevertheless from being left alone by the gangs of boys that normally dogged his steps, without realising that the presence of his police tail had warned them off. Sergeant Swift, who had this duty, sauntered half a street behind Sefton, thinking about women – more particularly of his sister-in-law, whose reckless carnality was a thing of wonder.

'Copper!' a ratty-looking man hissed. Swiftie steered him expertly into an alley, lifted him off the ground by his greasy lapels and kneed him in the cods, all in a calm and seemingly good-natured way. The man sank to the cobbles like a sack of coals.

'Yes,' Swift said. 'A copper. You ain't wrong there, my son.'

But when he walked back into the busy street, Sefton had disappeared.

So, too, had Captain Quigley. It had been a question of waiting for Constable Roberts to accept a whispered invitation to share a pot of tea with the kitchen orderly, whose job it was to gather up the lunchtime plates. This woman, who was Polish, liked a man in uniform and Quigley liked her for that. No sooner had the two of them disappeared through one set of swing doors than the Captain was out of bed and, though reeling a little, lightly away on his toes to the other end of the ward. Debouched into an empty corridor tiled out in dark green and as cold as an Arctic night, down the stairs to the ground floor, with the booming voice of the matron chastising some unlucky nurse.

Quigley was born with a rat's nippiness. It was the work of a moment to duck into a broom cupboard sort of space smelling of carbolic soap. Hung obligingly on the door peg were a couple of ankle-length white aprons. Nothing for the feet. He rummaged through some of the open boxes littering the place. Towels, dishcloths, women's nighties, and at last – yes!

So it was that the Captain left the hospital in a grey and white striped nightshirt, two crumpled aprons worn back to back and a pair of black felt slippers. In a final stroke of what he thought of as genius, he opened a tin of foot powder and tipped it over his head and chest, scooping up the last of the powder and flinging it into his face. There was no mirror in the cupboard but he felt suitably disguised as something other than a recent patient. A plasterer, maybe. On the way out he picked up a long pole used for opening the sash windows and this too was a stroke of genius, for although he looked as mad as a hatter, the pole suggested purpose, an errand of some sort. Far too weak for marching, none of the old how's-your-father left in him – not so much as a wry smile – he stepped out into the sunshine and sloped along by the sides of walls, just another ruined man in a cityscape of losers. Whenever he saw a top hat, he slewed to a halt and shrank back into a shop doorway, mumbling a few words about the Coming Rapture, when Christ would judge the just and the unjust alike. He sang a snatch or two of hymns, banging his pole on the pavement to keep time.

'Coming it a bit strong, aincha?' a match seller asked.

'I know whereof I speak, matey.'

'And *this*,' the old man said, 'is my pitch, so hop off out of it before I give you one up the throat, Second Coming or no Second Coming.'

'Bless this poor sinner,' Quigley cried, spotting a handy gap in the traffic and stumbling across the road. Right now, a pint of ale worth a gold sovereign, if nightshirts had pockets.

'So wait a minute,' Hannah Bardsoe said when he was safely on Tom Tiddler's Ground, 'you do a bunk out the hospital and, dressed in these here comical duds, you walk halfway across London to Shelton Street?'

'Where I knew I was sure of a warm welcome –'

'– dragging the police after you, hue and cry at every corner, I don't know how many crimes committed, but a general manhunt in progress. Very nice of you, I must say. Oh yes, very neighbourly.'

'Look at me, Hannah. Do you see a cove in the pink of good health? I was hoping for the healing balm of unbroken friendship, with perhaps a tincture of rum to ease the bodily pains. You are looking at a man who has been buried alive under a ton or two of Wisbech potatoes.'

'You don't say,' Mrs Bardsoe said sourly.

'See, this bloke I was lodging with – they call him Peter the Giant – has done a bunk. So, it was my job to hook him out of it and return him to the ample bosom of Alice Cobb. A Cupid sort of thing – are you following any of this?'

'I am not. You are making as much sense as McGinty's goat.'

'The thing to hang on to is that he's done a bunk. Now why's he done that?'

'To get out of your road, I shouldn't wonder.'

'No, but there's mischief in it somewhere.'

'I aren't listening, Perce.'

Quigley looked crestfallen. A bit slow on the uptake, old Hannah. 'Charlie not about today?'

'What his name is Charles and I'll thank you not to drag him into it, not this time, no, nor ever again. I'll make you up a bed in the attic where you can do your recuperations and all that. But I'm bound to warn you, Perce, if the coppers come looking for you, I shall give you up, my oath if I don't.'

'And how neighbourly is that? I'd have done better in Orange Street.'

'Don't you go near that poor woman's house!' Hannah Bardsoe cried. 'It's over, is all that!' She poured him a touch of rum – adding, before he could cry out in protest – a generous splash of warm milk. 'She's had enough of it, what with the wedding and being blowed to pieces. Them days are over.'

'Which I wish they was.' He tossed off his glass and held it out for more.

Hannah took pity on him. 'Take off your pinnies and

let's have a look at you,' she decided. 'What is all that white stuff in you hair and whiskers?'

'Penitential ash,' the Captain replied, who could rise to a useful phrase when the occasion demanded.

'Yes, but what is it?'

'Bragg's foot powder. From the original Cumberland recipe.'

Of the three disappearances that day, the one that would have been of greatest interest to David Pennington, had he knowledge of it, was that of Sefton Garside. As it fell out, the missionary was only lost for an hour and a half and Sergeant Swift thought it prudent not to make mention of it in his report. This was something he was to rue later, when returned to uniform duties and to be found pounding the beat along the Embankment, wreathed in dark thoughts about the unforgiving nature of criminal investigation as it was carried on in Scotland Yard, which, though he could see its lights as he passed, was a place as remote to him now as Ulan Bator.

Sefton was in Hackstraw's Yard during the missing hour and a half. He had cleared a small tack-room with the intention of making it a place of worship, against the day that the sinners would come to repent. It had a brick floor and any number of useful pegs on the wall. There was a lingering smell of rotted leather and horse sweat. Sefton had chosen this bit of the property because elsewhere rats as large as cats roamed, looking insolent and proprietorial, srolling about their straw castles. The advantage of the tack-room was that it had a stout door and unbroken windows. Furthermore, there was a rusty stove in one corner. True, it was missing its chimney, but Sefton put his faith in finding someone who might fix it.

And when he pushed open the door, it did for a moment seem that God had provided. A dark figure was wrestling with a length of stovepipe, trying to get it to rise through the roof and at the same time seat itself in the flange provided on the stove itself.

'Come in, Garside,' a familiar voice said in the most languid tone possible.

'Hough?' Sefton asked, incredulous.

'Steer this thing home while I take the weight.'

'*Hough?*'

'Watch your fingers,' this ghost from the past warned sharply. The stovepipe found its seating with a ringing clang.

'I thought you were dead.'

'Close the door, if you will.'

Every school has its complement of scallywags and chancers, boys who in Sefton's stratum of society went on with the same insouciance to be stockbrokers or hunting squires, clergymen or soldiers. Anton Hough was different. The last time Garside had seen him, he was sauntering away on foot, without a scrap of luggage, the Headmaster standing on the school steps bellowing for him to return to be properly expelled. The police were sent for to bring the boy back. After five days, they reported in their slow cumbersome way. As measured in that part of Sussex, Hough had disappeared without trace. Word was sent to Rye in Kent, where there was an aunt. She replied by postcard that she neither knew nor cared where her nephew was. Thrillingly, this card was written in German.

Pallings was a very modest school indeed, measured by educational attainment. Parents and potential parents understood this well – what the school had to offer was a polished mediocrity. It was safe. There were boys who went up to Oxford or Cambridge, to be sure, but none of them went on to be Fellows of their college. They broke their legs at point-to-point meetings, set fire to pub furniture and fought with glowering farm boys on race days. Gambled their inheritance and got young parlourmaids with child.

Pallings proposed a different pattern of Christian gentleman. Eubank, a frowning giant of a boy, had won a posthumous Victoria Cross in the Sudan and given his name to a school house. Mattingley, RN, was killed by Malay pirates when commanding the sloop *Dolphin*; Considine had a town named after him in Australia. There were Pallings boys like these scattered throughout India and Burma, in Hong Kong and Shanghai. The balance was tucked away in the shire towns of Britain, amiable and undemanding fellows, honest for the most part – but dull, dull, dull.

Anton Hough was quite different. To begin with, his self-possession was complete. He met praise or criticism alike with the same unblinking calm. The essays he turned in seldom exceeded fifty words. In class he slept for the most part. There were those who in later years swore they had never heard him utter a word in all his time at school. Foreign, of course. Wasn't Hough Huff, properly parsed?

Several of the staff thought it their duty to break him. After he refused to play sport of any kind, he was sent on a run comprising a two-and-a-half-mile circuit of irrigation ditches surrounding the school grounds (and the fording of the River Cheyney twice). This was a punishment invented by the Headmaster himself, one which he was proud of, enough to allow parents to witness it from time to time. It was underlining a point: there was no greater ignominy than submitting to a punishment that had no purpose. Humiliation was a dish a boy would seldom choose twice. On this particular occasion, Dr Peckett was astonished to see Hough plunging nonchalantly through the swollen ditches, wearing a cream summer suit and a straw boater. The month was November and the school lawns glistened with frost.

Peckett's eyes boggled in disbelief. 'Who is that idiot child running along beside him?' he demanded in fury.

'A new boy, Headmaster.'

It was of course Sefton Garside, as hopelessly in love with Hough as any girl.

'Is he mad?'

'He is not specially strong in the head, sir.'

'Bring him to me,' Peckett said with grim relish.

A beating came first, followed by close questioning. It was established that Garside 841 had never so much as spoken to Hough 736 and knew nothing of what the Headmaster liked to call Greek Love. The child had been moved to support Hough for what he thought of as aesthetic reasons.

'And what might those be?'

'It was something I had never seen before,' Sefton mumbled.

'There is a very great deal you have never seen before, you simpering ninny.'

That night, Hough came across Sefton blabbing in the latrines and threw his arm around the boy's bony shoulders. 'Chin up,' he murmured, before moving on.

Though this brief contact was the most wonderful thing that had ever happened to Sefton, the very thing he loved about his hero was also the source of his greatest torment. In any terms that made sense, Hough was unknowable. That night, hot with love, he tried to imagine the unknowable Hough as a gigantic waterfall in some undiscovered forest, thundering over the rocks and making rainbows whether there was anyone there to witness them or not. But as the days passed, a better and perhaps more accurate image asserted itself: Hough was an iceberg, alone in the ocean. Sefton was the abandoned child in the coracle.

'Where will you go for Christmas, Hough?' he dared to ask, the day before school broke up.

'I haven't decided,' the iceberg replied thrillingly.

'But won't your people be expecting you?'

'My people? I have no people.'

That night, the school pavilion blew up with a report that was heard in Mayfield, four miles away. Windows were broken in the school itself and the flash woke all the boys on that side of the building. Standing by the wreckage was Hough, hands in pockets. Some of his clothing smouldered, the way the devil appears in nightmares. The following day he was gone.

'And now, my dear Garside,' he said, wiping his hands clean of soot and rust in Hackstraw's tack-room, 'I have need of you.'

'You have come to Jesus!' Sefton cried ecstatically.

'I have come to Whitechapel,' Hough corrected with his customary eerie calm.

He left half an hour later, asking Sefton to stand guard over a carpet bag of things, some innocent and some not. But Sefton was not to know this, for it seemed wrong to poke about in a fellow's possessions.

That night, the last train from Fenchurch Street to Blackwall blew up at its destination. More accurately, the mail carriage of the train disintegrated, injuring two porters and showering the surrounding area with glowing cinders and hundreds of sheets of smouldering paper that swooped like a flock of gulls over the docks and installations of the Isle of Dogs. The captain of the Margate ferry was drunk, but thought it wise to get up steam and anchor out in the Thames. In the confusion, his vessel collided with an incoming Newcastle collier, the master of which was also drunk. One or other of these men fired a distress rocket which compounded the general panic by setting fire to the dock superintendent's house. Two hundred soldiers were rousted from their barracks and marched downriver.

'Who could have done such a thing?' Sefton Garside asked in the morning.

'Only a villain of the darkest hue,' Hough replied.

'Indeed,' Sefton cried.

'Or someone with a taste for explosions.'

At the time he was cooking bacon on the newly restored stove, stark naked, but with as much aplomb as the Bishop of Stepney.

FIVE

It was all very well Bella and Philip opting for a private life but events seemed to conspire against it. Quigley was on the run (though Bella had a fairly shrewd idea of where he might be); Komarev, likewise, was being hunted up hill and down dale; and now the explosion at Blackwall, news that came too late for the morning editions but was carried to Orange Street by bush telegraph – which was to say Mrs Geoghan's boy Bob, who was a porter at Fenchurch Street and, though a bit slow on the uptake, well able to put two and two together to make five. If blowing up Blackwall was not Pete the Giant's work, then Bob Geoghan would like to know what was.

'Do the police say it was Komarev?' Philip asked the boy, who had been summoned to Orange Street. Geoghan twirled his uniform cap, very aware of the state of his boots and the strong ammoniac smell of his trousers.

'"Had we noticed a giant cove with a beard?"' the porter agreed.

'And had you?'

'Not as such,' Geoghan havered, feeling very miserable. 'It was dark, mind.'

'Bob's not the complete shilling's worth of coppers,' Mrs Venn supplied, unexpectedly compassionate. The boy's mother was one of her lesser cronies, a martyr to her tubes and such. She ruffled Bob's hair. 'I believe he has told you all he knows,' she concluded.

'Was there any mention made of a Percy Quigley?'

'They asked,' Bob admitted.

Philip gave the boy a shilling, found some writing paper and dashed off a quick note. It was not answered until the evening, by which time the Blackwall bombing was the main topic of conversation in every pub. No newspaper editorials were needed to link Fracatelli's with the farcical events at on the Great Eastern line – they were obviously the work of the same man. The Blackwall explosion claimed no lives, but there was enough force in it to shudder windows and knock ornaments to the floor as far afield as – well, wherever the man who was telling the story happened to live. And hadn't the cab horses up and down the West End flinched and pricked their ears seconds before the explosion? Horses were like that, as it appeared were parrots, dogs and other house-hold pets.

'I am not quite sure what help I am being asked to give,' Commander Alcock said cautiously, like a chess player none too anxious to take his fingers off a piece. 'Is not the police your first port of call?'

Bella could tell that her guest, for all his spikiness and self-importance, could see past his own remark. He sat on the very edge of the seat cushion, his hands between his knees, looking glum. The police, as he knew only too well, were watching the house from the bottom end of Orange Street, which was why he had arrived bearing flowers

– hideously expensive early tulips – in an attempt to seem just another social caller.

'The thing of it is,' Philip explained, 'that while we do have an understanding with Superintendent Pennington, it doesn't extend to the fullest sharing of information. This nonsense with Quigley has upset us.'

Alcock grunted. The sound might have meant 'What did you expect?' but might also have indicated 'You don't know the half of it!' Philip regarded his former employer without pleasure. The whole of the spying game was in that grunt. He knew from bitter experience that for those like Alcock, the cards he held so close to his chest might contain five aces – in a word, his whole business was dissembling.

Bella could read what was going through her beloved's mind as easily as if he had actually spoken these thoughts. And she shared them. Alcock had never before been in her house by invitation and she knew very little of him. Philip had told her one of the departmental jokes about him, which was that he was forced to open his safe every night to confirm from a paper within where he lived. There was a dull kind of wife somewhere in Battersea, but no children. 'We are asking a favour of you,' she proposed quietly, 'as a friend.'

Alcock had the decency to blush. In his professional dealings with Philip, he had from time to time had reason to curse the famously inquisitive Bella. Friendship was an unusual way of describing their relationship. 'What do you want to know? Is it about this fellow Quigley? The man who absconded from hospital?'

'Not about him,' Bella said.

'Because, I must point out, I can do nothing for him.'

'It is not about him,' she repeated.

'Moreover,' Philip said, 'he has yet to be charged with any crime.'

'Ha! That's as may be,' Alcock said. 'Yet we can agree, can we, that a very great crime *was* committed no more than three months ago? And that last night an almighty explosion took place at Blackwall? In the circumstances, the police are free to pursue whatever line they like, wherever it takes them. I know nothing about Quigley.'

'I am quite sure I was not blown up by him at Fracatelli's,' Bella snapped. 'And to be frank about it, I don't much care who did. It was my idea to ask you here, meanwhile. What we need is background, the better to protect ourselves.'

'Yourselves, madam?'

They sat in the gloom of late afternoon, lit only by the white tulips on the table between them. Alcock was being asked to do something no spymaster should ever contemplate – that was, to tip his hand. Bella sat perfectly still, her beautiful eyes watchful. Alcock flickered his tongue across his lips.

'Very well,' he said at last. 'With this proviso. That whatever I tell you now can never be divulged as coming from me.'

'That goes without saying.'

'Forgive me, Mrs Westland,' Commander Alcock said feelingly, 'but long experience has taught me that *nothing* – nothing in this *world* – goes without saying.'

'What you tell us will be treated in the strictest confidence,' Philip amended. His tone was sour. 'You may recall that you have once or twice employed me on that exact same basis, to the distress of Mrs Westland, as she is now.'

Alcock blushed again, for this was true. Since the debacle in Westphalia, in which his former agent had very nearly died, he had gone out of his way to avoid Westland. He had been enormously flattered to have been invited to the wedding, but was careful to leave before the reception. His wedding present had been a copper engraving of the battle of Austerlitz, a gift that had woken him in writhing embarrassment more than once since.

'I will tell you enough to indicate why you are implicated in all this, that is, as much as you are. I think we can forget Quigley for the moment, who strikes me as a harmless buffoon. We all know who we're talking about. The Russian, Komarev.'

'Before Pennington mentioned his name we had no idea he existed,' Bella exclaimed.

'No, and how could you?'

'Yet he seems to hold the key to the story.'

Alcock could not help himself. A sneer flashed across his face. 'Oh yes,' he said. 'The *story*. I was forgetting.'

'Let me put you at your ease,' Bella said icily. 'You are not talking to Henry Ellis Margam. That gentleman has ceased to exist. He was pushed under a train at Charing Cross, a few nights before my wedding.'

'He was –?'

'My wife no longer writes fiction,' Philip explained.

Alcock looked from one to the other in confusion until gestured to go on. 'First, the fellow's name is not Komarev but Bestjuvev. He is not – or at any rate was not – trained as a musician. He started out as a chemistry student in Leningrad. In 1876 he fled to Geneva.'

'Was there a police warrant out against him?'

Alcock flapped his hand impatiently, as though the question was just too obvious to answer. 'There he found his way to the Café Kleist, where there was – and still is – a cabal of Russian émigrés. A few old graduates of the Peter and Paul fortress who are lucky to be alive; the others for the most part students. Poets,' he added with particular scorn. 'Bestjuvev found favour quickly. He was able to mend a printing press the group had cached in an old laundry. There is nothing more conspiratorial, Mrs Westland, than an underground press. Without it, the Café Kleist revolutionaries were barely worthy of the name. An intelligent child of ten could have mended the machine but Bestjuvev, who was already known as Peter the Giant, did the work and so gained a reputation for being expert in the practicalities of life.'

'This is leading somewhere, I hope,' Philip said grimly.

'Indeed. Five months after his arrival in Geneva, a villa belonging to a reactionary journalist called Verplanck was blown to smithereens. Inside was Verplanck himself, his wife and two children and his mother-in-law. They all perished.'

'And?'

'Two men and a young woman were arrested within the hour. Before dawn, another seventeen patrons of the Kleist were brought in for questioning. Bestjuvev was not among them. He had fled to Paris. He stayed there for eight months and came to England as Piotr Komarev, musician. This is the man your friend Quigley met recently in Whitechapel.'

Philip Westland rose and busied himself with lighting lamps. Bella had long ago learned to interpret his back, the set of his shoulders. He was angry.

'I do not like it,' he said at last. 'It is all very circumstantial. A man chooses the Café Kleist to frequent because there he can hear his native Russian spoken. He repairs a piece of machinery for the price of a few drinks or a meal. He has his doubts about all the wild words being uttered around him. We do not know that he built the bomb that destroyed Verplanck's house. We certainly do not know that he laid it, or was present at the explosion. You say he fled to Paris. I think that might have been a reasonable precaution in the circumstances. I would have done the same. From Paris he comes to England. He is walking down the Strand the night before Christmas when the Fracatelli restaurant blows up in his face.'

'And from all this you conclude?'

'That you know something you haven't told us,' Philip said calmly. 'For example, how did the police know he was present on that night?'

'Once he stepped on to the dock at Dover he became a Home Office concern. There are things about his movements since that neither you nor I will ever know. You think he is innocent. I believe he has questions to answer. And Pennington certainly thinks so.'

'We are getting nowhere.'

Alcock hesitated, a little man with a big idea of himself and the ingrained habit of wanting the last word. 'Very well, then,' he said slowly. 'I will tell you how it stands tonight. The area around Saffron Hill has been cordoned off since dawn and the police are conducting a siege there. They hope

– 826 –

to flush out Komarev and his associates on suspicion of having caused the bombing of Fracatelli's and the incident at Blackwall. In other words, they believe they have their man.'

Philip Westland bit his lower lip. *This* was the thing Alcock knew that they did not. He had told them in his own fashion, like an ace conjured from the magician's sleeve. It took a superhuman effort from Philip to stay civil. Out of the corner of his eye, he saw Bella reach for the tortoise-shell box wherein the forbidden cheroots were kept.

'Saffron Hill is near Hatton Garden, I think?' she said.

'That is one way of describing it,' Alcock said drily. 'It is also the address of a great many former communards who have found France too hot for them.'

'But, of course, our man is not French.'

'He spent eight months in Paris,' Alcock countered.

'And did you have him under surveillance all that time? I think not. Otherwise he would have been arrested the moment he set foot in England.'

'Do you say so?' the spymaster said with the greatest insolence. Bella rose, nodded to him and left the room without a word.

'I would be happy to have you call your wife back,' Alcock said, alarmed.

'My wife is not a dog, Commander Alcock. You were perhaps thinking of your own wife.'

The spymaster left soon after. Philip threw on a light coat and walked to Saffron Hill to see for himself what was going on. It was one those evenings when the air was still and the streets empty, as if the whole world was at dinner. The only people of any note that he passed were half a dozen young men in evening dress, students probably, looking for a renowned Hungarian restaurant and walking in quite the wrong direction. But as Philip came into Holborn he heard a distant commotion.

He arrived at the entrance to Saffron Hill just at the moment Peter the Giant was shot dead by a police marksman, if a shotgun blast can be said to be the same thing. An animal roar went up from several hundred onlookers. The sword the Giant had been waving above his head turned out to be the bow to his double bass.

Pennington was present at the scene and he had the grace to look ashen with guilt. A fierce hullabaloo was raging up and down and the police were being pelted with objects flung from upper-storey windows – shoes, candlesticks, chamberpots, the iron knobs from bedsteads. In a surreal finale to this bombardment, a chest of drawers crashed down and broke open on the cobbles. Shards of window glass reflected back the moon. For some reason, two engines of the fire brigade had been summoned and these now arrived in a clamour of bells. Men with axes leaped down and began attacking the doors and window frames on one side of the street.

Pennington had observed all the noise and confusion he needed to satisfy the Home Secretary that decisive action had been taken. All along Holborn, dozens more of the common people were running to witness the fall of Peter the Giant, bomb-maker and baby-eater, master criminal and godless revolutionary scum.

'Is he dead, is he dead?' a woman screamed in Philip's face. He pushed his way out of the crowd, mowing with his arms to make a space. People thought him drunk.

*   *   *

The Times could not quite bring itself to declare that the Fracatelli bombing had been avenged and the editorials in the provincial papers were even more sceptical. But the gutter press considered it had its man. Komarev was depicted as an anarchist revolutionary whose immense frame bore the scars of many another (unnamed) outrage. If he had not been arrested before, it was because he was a master of disguise, spoke seven European languages fluently and, in one particularly fanciful report, had covert connections to the very highest ranks of English society. He was abominably cruel to women, some of whom he had disfigured with acid and other mutilations too horrible to print. He was a loner. He was the leader of an international gang. He was a failed priest, a railway worker from the backlands of Siberia, a Rurik prince. He had come to this country from America, from France, or from Italy. Above all, in every habit and trait of character, he was foreign. Moreover, though the police had yet to make a statement, it was this same foreign devil who had masterminded the dastardly attack on the Blackwall Docks, a conflagration that had shocked all London.

'In short, just the man to invite a charge of buckshot,' Hough said negligently.

Sefton Garside shuddered. 'That is low of you.'

'Your friend Komarev was a walking dead man. He died a giant's death.'

They were eating in an eel and pie shop on the Whitechapel Road. A tank of live eels writhed in the window as an advertisement, and as a further touch of horror the restaurant was tiled out in white as brutally as any morgue. The restaurant stank of tobacco, vinegar and the ancient sweat that clung to the fibres of clothes and boots. It seemed certain to Garside that no woman had ever eaten there.

'You can't believe for a moment that he was guilty of anything!'

'Does it matter what I believe?'

'Are you really so heartless? He was a kind and gentle man.'

Hough pushed his plate away and belched. 'Had you stayed in the Army, you would doubtless have killed many dozens like him, often without even knowing. The fuzzie-wuzzies and that sort of thing, Garside. Afghans.'

'Are we going to be facetious? The thing was botched. The police have killed an innocent man.'

'How much do you know about the police?' Hough asked with icy contempt. 'I mean, apart from asking one of them the time, or directions to the Travellers' Club? I'll answer my own question. Nothing. If the police killed an innocent man, it was for a purpose, you little fool.'

'What purpose did they have in killing Peter the Giant?'

'To make a story. Stick to your glorious expectations of the life to come, my dear Garside. This world is far too wicked for you to understand.' He stood, pushing back his chair with a screech of wood on tile. At the door, he turned. 'Meet me back at Hackstraw's within the hour.'

And with this he was gone, leaving Sefton with the bill and a leaden feeling in his stomach. He knew very well why he was needed at Hackstraw's – to keep guard while Hough finished the coffer he was preparing in the brick floor of the tack-room. About the size of a suitcase – and certainly no deeper – the hole he had dug was lined with the panels from a ruined piano found at the back of one of the barns. Hough, it turned out, was a skilful and patient craftsman (or so it seemed to the cack-handed Garside). He had offered no explanation of why he needed such a hidey-hole, but when it was finished and its brick lid installed it would be indistinguishable from the rest of the floor. But to what end?

Hannah Bardsoe had had quite enough of Captain Quigley in his nightshirt and his incorrigible need to sit about her parlour smoking during what she thought of as shop hours. Asking him to stay upstairs was a waste of breath. He needed to talk – to gab – and she realised that he liked the company of women, the silly old fool. She was astute enough to grasp that the woman Percy Quigley was missing most was the lovely Mrs Westland. He was a storyteller without an audience. She had a vague image of some old Indian sitting cross-legged under a banyan tree, ready to begin but with no one to charm.

Her beloved husband Charles had explained that these old oriental tramps were much revered for their wisdom. This could not possibly apply to Perce and perhaps a more accurate picture was of a figure from her childhood, Uncle Chas. Like the Captain, he was merry without being wise. She could see him clearly, sitting against a whitewashed wall, his bowler hat on his knee, his cart whip leaning against his sausage thigh. Came to a bad end with a widow woman from Hornsey – both were found hanged in an apple orchard.

'Will you give it a rest?' she cried, making the Captain jump. He had been outlining one of his better capers, involving close work at Kensal Green and the honour of a lady called Lily Malone.

'I was just –'

'– you was just giving me gyp, is what you was just doing. Leave it out, for God's sake, Perce. I am trying to read my book.'

'Ah, yes. *The Prairie Schooner*. How are things going with Sheriff Jinks? Indians a bit uppity are they?'

Hannah was a devoted reader of Mrs Toaze-Bonnett's novels, at one time Bella's rival in fiction and now by default the bestseller on the Frean & Naismith list. The great thing about Mrs Toaze-Bonnett's work was that nobody ever died in her stories. Wrongs were righted and many a tale ended in church on a note of thanksgiving. Her lead character was Sheriff Jinks, a laconic character given to squirting tobacco juice, a thing Mrs Toaze-Bonnett had never seen but could easily imagine. She herself lived in Pinner, next to the vicarage, and the nearest she had been to the Wild West was High Wycombe.

'I don't say these here books are great literature,' Hannah harrumphed. 'But they do take a body out of herself. And yes, the Indians are uppity. Same as you, you wicked old chancer.'

An hour later, news of Peter the Giant's death reached Shelton Street, not from any official source but by the same bush telegraph that reported a collision of steamers on the Thames, a murder in Notting Hill or any of a dozen like calamities. When Old Mother Breen came knocking at the shutters with the story, it had already been passed by different routes all over that part of London. Quigley was eating a bit of cold pease pudding when he heard: he astonished Hannah by putting his head down on the table next to his plate and sobbing like a child.

'Get me some clothes,' he said brokenly.

'It ain't safe to be seen out, Perce,' she said, stroking his bony skull with real tenderness. Quigley snotting tears was a thing never before seen.

'They have murdered him. Just get me some duds and a pair of boots and I'll be out of your way.'

'Tomorrow,' she temporised. And in the morning she did walk over to Compton Street and scratted about among the stalls there. When she came home, she was astonished to find the Captain in conflab with someone she had never expected to see again – or at least, not more than once or twice a year.

Billy Murch had filled out a little since marriage and fatherhood had claimed him. His waist had thickened and his face was fuller. Most surprising of all, he had grown a black moustache worthy of the great Sheriff Jinks himself. Still the unnatural pallor to his skin, still the wary look about the eyes; but a citizen now, where before he was an unrepentantly awkward sod. Or so she remembered him.

'Blind old riley, Billy, you have give me a turn and that's no lie.'

'This is a bad day, Hannah,' he said gently, taking the bundle of clothes from her and passing them to a tear-stained Quigley.

'Is it about the Russkie?'

'It is, my dear. They have killed the wrong man.'

'But can we be sure of that?'

'There is nothing more certain.'

'For all love, Billy, don't do anything to bring the people at Orange Street into it.'

'This is just between me and Perce, Mrs B.,' he said in the same quiet voice. 'Pete the kindest, gentlest man in all London, and a friend. What's happened isn't right. Orange Street don't come into it. We owe the old boy something. That's how it works out with us and our kind. You know that.'

SIX

It was the age where social standing could be understood at a glance. Hats, shoes and boots, whiskers, walking sticks, wallpaper, dogs, pomade, corsets (or the lack of any of these) told a story, long before a word was uttered. It was a game of consequences, sometimes with painful outcomes. The man who turned up in your parlour to claim your daughter's hand might describe himself as a commercial manager at Liverpool Street Station, but Father, who worked for an insurance company in Holborn, knew a dreamer when he saw one. Frayed cuffs, soles of the boots a shade too thick because cobbled at home on the kitchen table. Red hands – and red hair. Dad (dear old Dad before he took against this poor devil in such a savage way) liked to think he had the shape of the world at his fingertips. He judged others as he knew they judged him. Same as at Margate last year when his bird-brained daughter had urged him to take off his boots and paddle. The senior clerk in the Annuities Department, showing his white and blue feet to the people, like any corner-shop tobacconist? Very likely, I don't think!

Anton Hough, on the other hand, had the ability to seem all things to all men. He had but one suit and that of a cut and colour that any tailor in London could see at once was foreign – but delicately stated, one might almost say unobtrusive, the way so many foreigners were not. He had never been received in any house of note in London and was unknown to the more distinguished of the immigrant population, who might be expected to claim him as one of their own. Yet in the lobbies of commercial hotels and restaurants of the second class, he always attracted a respectful glance. There was something enigmatic about him, something shadowed, that was – momentarily – beguiling. Perhaps the gentleman was an actor, or possibly an Austrian doctor of nervous diseases. He might be the better sort of fencing master (say, attached to a foreign court) or consul to a lesser European power with interests in the Levant. He was at any rate, in the English phrase, a man of affairs. So ran the verdict in the West End.

In Whitechapel, however, it was taken for granted that Hough was a chancer up to no good. Forget the floppy hair and sneering half-smile, this was a geezer yet to play his hand. The mistake Whitechapel made was to suppose his business was with money. If he spoke to no one and was never seen in pubs or with a woman, that was a pointer in the same direction. As to his friendship with the God-bothering Mr Garside, that could be explained as a bit of prior, dating from the missionary's previous existence. Nothing in the soldiering line, mind you, and little to do with the Gospel – more of a social connection, as far as anyone in Whitechapel could put pictures to this idea.

They were helped by an unexpected visit made to her son by Lady Garside, an immensely tall and bony woman with a nose as long as a horse. She arrived at Hackstraw's

Yard in a carriage rented in Kensington; and while the driver was in a cloud of anxiety about his surroundings, enough to make his groin crawl, Daisy Garside, whose father had been a colonial bishop, was of the no-nonsense school of womanhood.

'Are you the gateman?' she asked Hackstraw, who was in his usual lounging position at the entrance to his property.

'I am not,' he said in his squeaking voice.

'Do up the top buttons to your trousers and stand when you speak to me, my good man. Move that chair out of the way and allow my carriage to enter. What a miserably dirty place this is, to be sure. Have you no broom, or rake? Your employer shall hear of this.'

Hackstraw's jaw gaped. Daisy turned her attention to the coachman. 'You may as well go in search of refreshment, Mr –?

'Bannister, milady. I am perfectly happy to wait here.'

'Really? There cannot be an uglier place in all Christendom. I shall have my son send you out a mug of tea and a ham sandwich or something of the sort.'

'Obliged,' Bannister said gloomily.

Standing at the entrance to the tack-room was Anton Hough. He walked towards Daisy Garside with the nonchalance of an old friend, or even a family member. The two had never met before in their lives.

'Then the son comes back, looking as though his guts were griping him something cruel. And he goes into the chapel after them.'

'What chapel?' Harry Coggins wanted to know.

'The tack-room he is doing up. Chapel's maybe the wrong word. Meeting house or summat of that sort.'

'And what was said between 'em in this tack-room?'

'Blind me, Harry, I dunno what was said, do I? But the old girl comes out after an hour a lot happier than when she comes in. Hops up into the carriage and with a few more choice words directed at me, off she goes.'

'What words were them, then?'

'That if I got up off my arse a bit more oftener, I wouldn't be so lardy.'

'And what about the other geezer, the one with the suit?'

'Her and him were discussing aspects of the Gospel.'

'My eye, they was.'

'Blessed are the meek, he was saying by way of farewell,' Hackstraw explained.

'He's about as meek as a kipper nailed under the floorboards.'

'If you say so, Harry boy.'

'He's a wrong 'un,' the dwarf Coggins said, looking off into the middle distance. 'We shall have to do summink about him.'

Hackstraw wiped his face with both hands, unable to say what was the more shocking – the very great possibility that death and disaster were headed his way, or that little Harry had so far forgotten himself as to reveal what was in his mind, a thing as rare as having dogs speak. Though it was not specially warm, he felt the sweat run down his ribs; or, if you wanted to be particular about it, the rolls of fat that stood for where the ribs were buried.

'Where is he now?'

'Off out,' Charlie Hackstraw mumbled. 'Could be anywhere. There's one other thing. The religious toff – Garside – is thinking of holding a memorial service or something of the sort for Pete the Giant.'

'And who's going to come to that?'

'You got me there.'

They were interrupted by the arrival of a horse and cart delivering two dozen chairs, piled higgledy-piggledy. All of them were the sort of items to be found dumped on waste land. Some were missing backs, some legs. The driver of the cart reined in his emaciated horse.

'Is either of you gentlemen a party by the name of Garside?' Billy Murch enquired mildly.

'And who are you?' Hackstraw countered.

'I have some chairs on the back here donated by Christ in the City. Shoreditch branch.'

Hackstraw looked for his next cue from Harry Coggins, who merely shrugged. As was his wont, his eyes seemed to find consolation fifty yards away, where two dogs fought each other in the pale sunshine.

'You'd do better burning this lot,' Hackstraw said.

'I am just the carter, matey. Garside about?'

Hackstraw indicated the tack-room with his chin. He turned back to continue his conversation with Coggins, but the dwarfish little bastard was already twinking away down the street. His minders, who had been teasing a green girl called Maggie Allnut, pushed her aside and fell into step behind the boss.

Sefton Garside had learned very little of any value from his military career but he did have (knocked into him by circumstance) a respect for the common soldier. All his senses told him that this calm and unjudging carter had once served with the colours. His gratitude was pitiful to behold. Together they unloaded the chairs and carried them indoors.

'It is a sorry collection, I am afraid,' he muttered.

'Once made, a chair is always a chair,' Billy Murch corrected gently.

'That is true!'

'Glue and a pot of nails is the first item of business. Don't any of your parishioners have a way with wood-work?'

'Parishioners is not quite the word.'

'Your followers, then?'

When Sefton's face crumpled, Murch understood all.

'Look, Mr Garside, I will speak plain. Who knows but you'll make a great go of this place, given time? But just at present you are mixed up with a nasty bit of business. And we both know there's something not right about it. Pete the Giant couldn't have hurt a fly. Isn't that it?'

'You knew him?'

'He was a friend. A good friend. And I would go as far as to say a decent enough Christian into the bargain.'

Sefton had several times before embarrassed strangers by clasping their hands in his. 'It was for men like Piotr Komarev that I came into the East End,' the missionary declared. 'To meet such men! Who might join me in bringing salvation to the poor and unregarded!'

'Very noble. That's what I'm saying. And this other gentleman – this new friend – is he also a helpmate?'

'How do you know about him?' Sefton asked, amazed.

Because I have been following you about for two days.

Because I was sitting two tables away in the eel and pie shop this very morning, you daft bugger.

'Who is he?'

'A friend,' Sefton confirmed lamely.

'Yes indeed, but who is he?'

It happened that Murch was standing on the very spot where Anton Hough had built his underfloor cache. In the ordinary way of things, Sefton was as guileless as a stick of rhubarb, but common sense told him not to answer. There are ways and ways of doing this but Sefton's was to link his hands in front of his groin and writhe, go pink and pout.

'I see,' Murch said gently. 'And where is he now, this gentleman?'

'I cannot say.'

'Meaning you don't know? But going about God's work somewhere?'

'I hope so,' Sefton said, far too fervently.

Murch patted him on the shoulder. 'That's the ticket,' he said.

The firm of Beckmann's was a company that sold mostly to the Empire – indeed, its most famous product was Crown Imperial Ink, manufactured from premises in the Minories. Each bottle and flask bore a label depicting a fine town house in the eighteenth-century style. You were invited to imagine a few Johnsonian figures wandering about behind this elegant façade, urging on half a dozen journeymen in the search for the perfect blackness that was the hallmark of a bottle of Crown Imperial. The truth was a little more ordinary. The façade was more or less intact, but behind it three generations of Beckmanns had so altered the premises that what was on offer was a factory in all but name. The centrepiece of these arrangements were the newly installed vats. Young Mr Beckmann, as he was known, was a man in his fifties who understood that ink was a bulk business. He was not selling to sentimental old ladies with diaries to keep up: most of the overseas customers received their orders in gallon units, glass flasks with wicker corsets that were then sent on to police stations, rail depots, schools and government offices. It was an expensive but commercially astute detail that the cork to every flask was sealed by yellow wax, guaranteeing protection from evaporation. 'Are the seals intact?' the vexed resident magistrate would cry. 'The seals are in tip-top working order, sahib,' his clerk would respond gravely.

There were few secrets to the manufacture of ink. The trick was in the selling of it. Occasional glitches were all to do with shipping and dockside management in places with romantic names but idle agents. So it was that young Mr Beckmann was more than usually exasperated to be told that the exit valve to the Number Two vat was blocked by something much larger than a rat, or a workman's cap.

'There is something down there,' the foreman said. 'And buggered if I can say what.'

The vat was five feet wide and eight feet deep and filled with ink. Beckmann ordered it to be emptied by hand into tin troughs that resembled (and in fact were) pig feeding troughs. When the level in the vat was at about four feet, the women workers were sent away and a naked boy lowered to cast about with his feet.

And this was how the body was discovered. Even the slowest of Beckmann's employees could see that it was murder – the corpse was tied by the wrists to an iron bar. Not enough to pull him to the bottom immediately, but too heavy to endure for long.

But first he had to be identified. The boy that had fished for him with wriggling toes recognised him as a cove he had seen the previous afternoon coming out of a gunsmith's four doors down. As the police say, inquiries were made. The corpse was that of a Commander John Hubert Alcock, a gentleman wishing to shoot quail and lacking a gun fit for the purpose.

Kitteridge, the gunsmith, had been passed along from the usual plodding clowns (as he perceived the uniformed branch of the Met) to a far more senior, far more suave figure in an excellent suit.

'Were you able to accommodate him?' this fellow drawled.

'Oh, we had a most pleasant discussion about his particular needs, yes. Something at the Admiralty, I believe. He came recommended by Sir Arthur –'

'Did he come to the shop alone?'

'Quite alone. Save that another gentleman, catching sight of him, rapped on the window in a jocular sort of way before moving on.' The gunsmith lowered his voice apologetically. 'He was *hatless*,' he whispered.

'This was a chance encounter?'

'I cannot imagine it otherwise.'

'And your client? How did he take it?'

'He at once excused himself, saying he would come back a little later.'

'And did he?'

'He did not. It has all been most distressing.'

'Indeed,' Superintendent Pennington replied. 'But just to get this straight: Commander Alcock is engaged in conversation with you, there is a knock at the window pane, he looks up and there is some fellow without a hat.'

'As I have explained,' Kitteredge said.

'Very shortly after, the commander makes his excuses and leaves, which suggests he recognised the man. Was that your impression?'

'They were not friends,' Kitteredge said after a slight pause. 'I would not say they were social equals. But they had met, I would swear to that.'

'And you had never seen the man before?'

'Good heavens, Mr Pennington, this is a very highly regarded establishment. Many of our clients –'

'Yes, I understand. Could you furnish a description to my sergeant?'

'As to that . . .' the gunsmith havered.

'I am conducting a murder inquiry, Mr Kitteredge. So don't let's waste each other's time on the etiquette of selling guns only to the right sort of person. I will send a sergeant in to take a full statement from you, which must include a description of the man you saw. And now, for the moment, good day to you.'

He went back to the rear premises of Beckmann's, where Alcock's naked body was laid out on a trestle table in the open air, covered by a piece of drugget. The corpse was of course blackened by ink and revealed very little, except for a small tattoo on one of the buttocks.

'A bluebird,' the police surgeon murmured, with too

knowing a smile, as though they had in front of them a homosexual fiend and not an Admiralty legend for personal probity and the good of the service.

Alcock had been put into the vat with his wallet intact, his pocket full of coins and not a scratch on him. One of the papers found in the wallet was a waterlogged sheet of paper from someone signing himself 'PW'. Expressed in curt terms, it thanked the corpse for taking the trouble to visit Orange Street; and for help rendered.

'His senior clerk is being asked to formally identify the body. Mrs Alcock is staying with her sister in Bournemouth, apparently. A telegram has been sent.'

'Why didn't he scream blue murder when he was put in the vat?' Pennington wondered.

'Vanity,' Dr Rooney suggested. It seemed to the superintendent one of the most perceptive comments ever made by the police surgeon, who was generally known as a foolish and disappointed drunk. Alcock the spymaster, bested by a hatless man and dumped ignominiously in a vat of ink. Too proud – perhaps too vain – to raise an alarm. A thought occurred to him, but Rooney had beaten him to it.

'You are wondering why there was no earlier commotion, in the street. How it came that the two men walked here together.'

'I was wondering how the victim's vanity was so great that he scaled a ladder and fell into the ink without the slightest attempt to resist. Examine the corpse again and look for contusions to the head.'

'There are none.'

'Then for some other disabling event. Was he drugged?

Poisoned? Rendered unconscious by a thumb to a pressure point?'

'A thumb to a – aren't we snatching at straws a little?' Rooney sneered.

Just to relieve his ill-temper, Pennington reached for the surgeon's neck and applied his thumb to the carotid artery. After a second or two, Dr Rooney swayed and then fell. The Superintendent turned to the uniformed constable standing nearby. 'What did you see just now?'

'Nothing,' this man replied. 'Well, the doctor fainted. But nothing else.'

'Good man.'

Driving back to Scotland Yard, he reviewed the murder. Alcock leaves the gunsmith's to follow – perhaps to accost – the mystery man without a hat. There is no evidence whatsoever that this man was the killer. At the time Alcock was in the gunsmith's, Beckmann's was in full production at the back of their premises. The murder took place later, maybe as little as three hours later – that might be the sense of the police surgeon's remark about vanity. Maybe Alcock thought he could talk his way out of trouble, or maybe the two men were trying to work out a deal before it all went horribly wrong. But why there? Why not on waste land, or behind a city church? Why not in a railway carriage or on top of an omnibus? And why not by gun, or knife? Why all the elaboration of a death by drowning?

It came to him: it was the ink that was the story. A devoted servant of the status quo, whose pocket book was filled with secrets, whose office files were a history of what amounted to a covert war, had been drowned in his own ink. The more he thought about it, the more

Pennington grew convinced. He banged on the roof of the cab, which drew up outside a small parade of shops. There he sat for a while, staring out at a rainy pavement, criss-crossed with people going home, and tried to imagine a common murderer with such a perverse and elaborate sense of humour. Moreover, he reflected, someone with apparently supernatural calm.

'What's the game then, guv?' the cabbie called.

'Wait,' Pennington replied sharply.

He was not by nature an imaginative man and he knew this much about himself from some ill-fated relationships with women. Inside the Yard, he had the reputation of being a good policeman, but also something of a courtier, just too good at making himself agreeable. He was biddable and had never before gone counter to what his superiors thought. He had already delivered the result that the Home Office demanded: Piotr Komarev was the Fracatelli bomber. But now, standing in the shadow of that judgement was a man without a hat, who appeared as if by magic in just the right place and at the right time, perhaps to confer with Alcock, perhaps to kill him.

'Drive on,' he called. At the foot of Charing Cross Road he changed his mind about his destination and ordered the cab to go to Orange Street.

SEVEN

One part of Pennington's change of plan was the need to ask more questions of Philip Westland. There was something about this Westland that the policeman did not like. He was altogether too shapeless. Pennington's idea of a secret agent was a blunt man with maybe a touch of bitterness about the mouth – perhaps a background in an Indian regiment; a crack shot to be sure, but also someone who knew how to wring a neck at close quarters, or smash a kneecap. Philip was a sorry disappointment in these areas. Just as a matter of routine, Pennington had made some discreet enquiries at the fellow's club. There he was famous only for setting fire to a library armchair one somnolent afternoon. The general opinion of him was that he was a bit on the slow side.

'He reads novels,' the club secretary reported with the utmost contempt. 'That is to say, French novels, if you take my meaning.'

But then again, he was married to one of the most beguiling women in London. Another and guiltier consideration of Pennington's decision to visit Orange Street was to find Bella at home, not for any new light she might throw on the investigations, but for the sheer pleasure of her company. The superintendent was not the first man to fall under Bella's spell, nor to speculate whether – better to say in what way – he could have made her happy, had fortune delivered her into his lap. He was realist enough to be dismayed at his own impudence, but all the same what he needed now was an hour of her company. In this he was to be disappointed.

'She has gone to East India House,' Philip explained. Then, when he saw Pennington's confusion, smiled. 'Mr Liberty's new shop in Regent Street. It is her first expedition under her own steam since the bombing. The material for a new silk gown has been mentioned.'

'I know Arthur Liberty a little,' Pennington mumbled.

'You must tell Bella. She will have a hundred questions to ask of you. Meanwhile, this has been a good day. I think we can say she is returned to her former self.'

Pennington's heart sank. He realised from Westland's beaming face and characteristically chaotic hospitality that the news of Alcock's murder had yet to reach Orange Street.

'I'm afraid I'm the bearer of extremely bad news.'

When he was told about the murder, Philip's reaction was acute. For a full five minutes he paced about, asking disjointed questions, offering wine but failing to serve it, even plumping cushions in a hapless sort of way. 'It was good of you to tell me in person,' he said at last.

'You knew him well?'

'I think he saw it as part of his business not to form personal friendships. In that sense I hardly knew him at all.'

'You did not dine him?'

'Here, do you mean? That would have been quite the wrong thing. We had lunch once or twice at places of his choosing. He was exceptionally cautious. All these venues were hole-in-the-corner affairs – small hotels, dull restaurants. It suited his idea of himself – the faceless man, whom next day nobody would remember.'

'I think I catch you smiling, Mr Westland.'

'You do. Anyone who had met the Commander once, or even passed him in the street, would remember him for ever. He was a little marionette of a fellow. A sort of clockwork walk, you understand, much like a German tin-type toy.'

Pennington took out the ink-stained note found in Alcock's wallet and passed it across. Philip read it without curiosity and nodded, before passing it back. 'This is mine, yes.'

'You had some recent business to discuss.'

'We asked him here to learn more of Piotr Komarev.'

'And what could he tell you?'

'Nothing much,' Philip said, after a pause.

'But he came here at your invitation? Despite the caution you previously described him as having?'

'He had manners,' Philip replied. There was a further pause, during which Dora Venn's cackling laughter drifted up from the kitchen. She was entertaining Mrs Bardsoe to a pot of tea and a bit of cake.

'Let's get this clear,' Philip said uneasily. 'You are under no obligation to tell us anything at all about your investigations, but Bella and I feel exposed – and vulnerable.'

'Because of your association with Captain Quigley? He is of negligible interest to the police.'

'When you say negligible?'

'He has been eliminated from our inquiries.'

'I am pleased to hear it. Nevertheless, it would help to know more of what is in your mind.'

Which invitation Pennington treated with studied indifference. His next remark was seemingly addressed to the clock on the mantelpiece. 'I wonder if you could provide me with a list of the journeys abroad you made for Commander Alcock?'

'I have no problem with that personally. However, they were, I suppose, affairs of state and I should not like to do so without clearance from somebody or other in Government. I'm afraid I have no idea who that might be. You, perhaps,' he added after a moment's reflection.

'Who is Pankow?'

'I have no idea.'

'These are all names taken from his engagement diary. Metzger?'

'The same.'

'Oullebec? De la Riviere? Hough?'

'I'm afraid I can't help you. You already know more than I do, or ever did,' Philip murmured. 'I was called upon by Alcock from time to time, when more capable or more daring agents were engaged elsewhere. I suppose he had an office. I never visited.'

'You seem to have taken a great deal on trust.'

'As I do with you.'

An uncomfortable silence was broken by Bella's return, pink in the face and laughing with happiness. Philip took her hands in his and told her at once why Pennington was there. Perhaps lesser women would have sunk into a chair or clapped a hand to their cheek. Bella merely nodded and paced about, rearranging the cushions Philip had so recently knocked about. Her chin was up and she smiled politely at Pennington, as though he were a vicar come to solicit contributions to the village fete.

'I did not know Commander Alcock,' she said in the most conversational tone she could muster. 'My husband invited him to our wedding and he was kind enough to accept. He did not join us for the reception, however. In fact, I met him for the first time two days ago. But it is strange how all the threads of this story seem to lead back here – to us.'

'I hadn't thought of it like that,' Pennington lied quietly.

'We asked him here because we knew too little of Komarev. I mean, in his character of a man sought by the police. Yourself, indeed. As it happens, I have also yet to meet Philip's cousin Sefton; but it seemed to me quite incredible that two such ill-matched men could form a relationship that had any connection whatever to acts of terrorism. I think so still.'

'You are describing a feeling you have, a sentiment?'

'If someone told me you were married to a parlourmaid from Tunbridge Wells, I should have the same feeling, yes.'

'But then of course you have already told me that you knew neither man.'

'I know England, Mr Pennington.'

'Then you are very fortunate, Mrs Westland.'

'And you do not?' Bella said, far too sharply.

'Do you have suspects in this latest case?' Philip intervened.

'It is a complete mystery, save that it's very likely the Commander was murdered by someone he knew, or recognised. Other than that, there are no clues.'

'Do you have a motive?' Bella asked in her turn.

'Was he killed in his private capacity, do you mean, as an erring husband or a man with gambling debts and the like?'

'I hardly think a cuckold would drown a man in a vat of ink, however strongly he felt.'

'You think there is some more shadowy reason?'

'Is his death connected in any way to that of Piotr Komarev?'

Pennington searched her beautiful grey eyes. 'That is the question,' he confessed, feeling a fool now for having come there at all. Bella called for wine.

'No, really, I have not the time.'

'Nonsense.'

He thought for a moment of the sheer relief to be had from flinging himself into one of the Westlands' armchairs and letting go for an hour. But the traffic noise hammered on the window panes and the business of a great city, with its attendant wickedness, beckoned. All over London, his investigating officers were filing their daily reports. Somewhere, in the warrens of Scotland Yard, in some particular mountain of paper, there might be a clue that was waiting to be discovered.

Pennington's suavity did not come from a university education, nor yet a brilliant army career. He was that new thing, a public servant that had been formed and nurtured entirely by the service. He was suave because the rank demanded it. He insisted on leaving with just the right amount of regret in his voice and walked back down Whitehall, trying not to think too much of anything. Passing Downing Street, he saw several Cabinet Ministers leaving the Prime Minister's house, their top hats bobbing. That afternoon there had been a meeting to discuss their suspicions about the explosion on the Isle of Dogs.

Of the names in Alcock's appointment diary, only one was British, or so he supposed. It might be that of a work colleague or of another departmental head, or someone else – an informant or an active spy. When Pennington got back to the Yard, he had just enough time to stir up the Home Office lawyers before they went home to order a seal placed on the office in Admiralty Arch. As the Commander's staff arrived for work the following morning, they were to be detained for questioning. The chief clerk was on compassionate leave in Margate, where his mother was dying. He was to be brought to London by the earliest train.

'I don't like this any more than you do, Perce,' Billy Murch muttered. 'But it has to be done.'

'Recalled to the colours sort of thing.'

They were sitting in a pub in Sutton Row, off Soho Square, chosen for its gloom and quiet, with the additional protection of bad beer and a charmless landlord, Maltese Mick. Outside, it was dark and the street lamp across the way illuminated a windless drizzle that fell as softly as dust – or soot.

'What it is,' Murch continued, 'is how to settle scores with whoever saw off old Pete. But more than that, to get the two people at Orange Street out of it.'

'O' course, it don't matter about me and my problems with the Bill,' Quigley whined.

'No, mate, it don't. You was never arrested and this

Pennington cove had nothing on you in the first place. Say they do you for absconding from police custody at the hospital. What's that? Nothing.'

'Ta very much,' the Captain said bitterly.

He was still trying to get used to Billy's moustache. To which was added the indignation of being a captain in mufti. His beloved tunic was probably being cut up for floor mops over at the hospital and Hannah Bardsoe's replacement duds gave him the look of a railway ganger or, worse, a sewage worker. 'What about this geezer you saw at Hackstraw's place?' he asked.

'It was in an eel and pie shop adjacent.'

'Local, was he? Some local villain? Some Jack the Lad?'

'No,' Murch said, musing. 'Nothing of that.'

They sat in the kind of silence that sometimes invades pubs, two middle-aged men who might have been contemplating the death of a friend or planning armed robbery. Maltese Mick – who wasn't Maltese at all but a bruiser from Hoxton – sat reading yesterday's paper and eating boiled eggs from a dirty saucer. The only other customers were a brass whose pitch was at the top end of Greek Street, and a drunken kitchen porter with a bandage on his thumb.

'I ain't too happy about stirring up the Old Bill,' Quigley said.

'No,' Murch muttered absently.

'Mother Bardsoe thinks we should leave well alone. Says it's all over, what we had.'

'It has that feel to it,' Billy agreed.

'You don't buy it, though.'

'Pete the Giant was a mate, Perce. Don't that count

with you? Someone we both know had no more involvement in what went off at Fracatelli's than the Archbishop of Canterbury.'

'You're plain as a pikestaff there. I don't debate you there.'

'Well then. We set the record straight. Too late to help the old lad, God rest his soul, but necessary. And as for this other poor unhappy gink, Sefton, this missionary cove, he is in over his head out there in Whitechapel.'

'Got that right,' Captain Quigley said fervently.

'What I am saying, Perce, is that Orange Street *is* involved, whether they like it or not. Mr Westland a good bloke but a bit unworldly.'

'Wise words wisely spoken, Billy.'

'The key is this other geezer, the mystery man. He has bad 'un written all over him. What a bloody awful place that Whitechapel is and no error.' But then added in a much brisker voice, 'So now then, let's clear the decks. This Coggins bloke that had you done over, we'll deal with him first.'

'A well-connected villain,' the Captain warned. Murch smiled and ruffled Quigley's hair.

'A chiselling little ponce,' he corrected, with real affection.

The area around Cheshunt in Hertfordshire was a lake of glass, under which gnarly old men and very much younger girls in ragged white smocks cut flowers and – in season – tomatoes and cucumbers for the London market. The flowers were presented in metal bins filled with water and taken by cart to Waltham Cross, where they were loaded into goods vans to Liverpool Street. This work was done at first light. It was not unknown for the nursery workers to lock one of their number into a van – say a green girl about to be married, or an unpopular foreman – and post them down the line to the city. But it was very unusual to swing back the locking bars on one of the vans and discover someone who had come the other way. Who would want to arrive at a station out in the sticks at four in the morning?

When he was discovered, Harry Coggins was trussed hand and foot. Two further small details amused the crowd and baffled the goods agent (a grandiose title for a red-headed youth who had hardly commenced shaving). The victim was gagged and, when this was removed, found to have a very large potato jammed into his mouth. His genitals were exposed, generously coated with tar.

At that time of the day, with the mist driving in across the Lea, there was no one to decide the issue. The young goods agent was, as he said, faced with a bit of a poser. Trains run to timetables, signals must be obeyed, London was a long way away. This was a job for Liverpool Street. To the delight of the nursery workers, the potato was stuffed back down Harry Coggins's throat, the gag reapplied; and with the addition of a daffodil tucked behind his ear, the scourge of Whitechapel set off on the return journey.

'You'm maybe done a wrong thing there,' old Harold Campnett teased the red-headed boy. 'I thought I see'd a resemberlance in that old lad to one of they royal dukes. For all we knows there may be black reverloooshion afoot down there. The Queen herself involved. Bishops hanging by their guts from lamp-posts. No woman safe.'

'You shut your trap,' the goods agent shrilled.

'Do you say so, Carrot-Top?' Campnett asked wonderingly, who had started in the sheds when he was eight years old. 'I have got veins on the back of my hands biggerun your arms, m'older. I have a mind to pull down them railway trews of your'n and smack your little bottom for you, bebuggered if I don't.'

'You tell 'un, Harold,' the nursery workers chorused.

'Captain Quigley!' Sefton cried.

'Looking well, vicar,' Quigley returned uneasily. Murch, who stood a step or so behind him, cuffed the Captain affectionately behind the ear.

'I found this reprobate on his knees before God, Mr Garside, blow me if I didn't,' he said. 'Too shy to go on into any church but I smoked him out in the yard behind the Grapes in Bishopsgate. On his knees and seeking repentance. What he has given up the drink and written a pitiful letter to his old mother, begging her forgiveness. A lady of ninety-two as lives in Wandsworth in a little room no bigger 'n' a match box.'

Garside rushed across the cobbles of Hackstraw's Yard and hugely embarrassed the Captain by embracing him. 'You have come to Jesus!' he squeaked. 'You good fellow! Thy sins shall be washed away! Lay down your burden! Kneel with me and pray, my dear friend.'

But Murch was watching the doorway to the tack-room, where the mysterious Hough lounged. He sauntered across. 'How do, squire?' he murmured.

'What brings you back here?'

'I have come to Jesus.'

Hough had the knack of looking directly at people he did not trust. But then Billy Murch had met enough Houghs in his life not to be intimidated, no, not one little bit. True, these men were mostly youngish officers when he was nothing but a private soldier, but the principle remained the same. He smiled and shuffled his feet. For effect, he took off his battered beaver hat and stroked it glossier with his forearm. Spat. Your move, mystery man.

'And where do you stay?'

'Why, right here.'

'The barns are full of rats.'

'Good sport,' Billy chuckled. 'I like a rat-hunt as much as anything in life.'

Hough went back into the tack-room and shut the door behind him. He opened it again as if to add something threatening, looked at Billy Murch and changed his mind.

EIGHT

The memorial service for Piotr Komarev was held on a balmy Sunday in April. In the better parts of London the sun shone down with a kindliness that truly lifted the heart. Summery clothes that had been folded in tissue paper and laid in a chest or wardrobe were taken out, brushed and sponged; in some cases, leading to rueful matrons sending a note to their dressmakers to alter a bodice or let out a seam. Clocks and paintings were cleaned, pianos tuned, carpets taken up and beaten with rattan paddles in basement yards. Chimney sweeps were summoned, gardeners made their seasonal reappearance. Joyous children who had found toy yachts under the Christmas tree marched to the Serpentine for the first time with their boats under their arms.

The same sunshine lit Hackstraw's Yard and its environs but there it was a crueller light, for what was shown up was accumulated shabbiness. In Knightsbridge the spring air was declared to be champagne to the soul. But in Whitechapel there had been no clean air for a hundred years. The previous night a basement sugar factory not far from Hackstraw's had blown up, burning the building it was in to the ground. The streets stank of toffee and wet ash.

Sefton Garside had hoped for twenty at his service but found himself with four times as many. The chief reason for this was the free food on offer; damaged vegetables donated by stall-holders and cooked up in giant cauldrons, along with bits of the sheep and cow Mrs Beeton had never examined. The kitchens were supervised by Alice Cobb and a local girl who shortly succumbed to an epileptic fit. Some at least of the congregation attributed her distress to divine ecstasy.

There were far too few tin bowls for the watery stew on offer and this led to discord, not helped by a number of local drunks, some of them concluding quarrels that had broken out the previous evening, or even several days ago. Barefoot children ran about playing Tig and yahooing up and down the rotted straw bales. From time to time Sefton Garside made an attempt to preach and was listened to with passing interest, before the bickering and fisticuffs broke out again.

'Chin up,' Captain Quigley advised. 'They are enjoying themselves. And who's to say that heaven ain't like this on a quiet day?'

'I am trying to conduct a religious service,' Sefton mewed.

'And this is *it*. This is the whole point and purpose. You have given them something to remember. I should say your stock will have rose considerable in Whitechapel today, Mr Garside.'

'There was going to be music.'

'Which the musicians have done a bunk, the cowards. Though the cornet player did get a note or two off before he legged it. But look there in the crowd, sir.'

Sefton followed the direction of Quigley's pointing finger and found himself staring into the eyes of a burly giant of a fellow, bearded like the pard, with a leather belt cinching a huge blue shirt. A beautifully soulful girl hung on his arm. At her feet was a battered accordion. Sefton looked closer and saw that there was a small knot of similarly clad figures surrounding this man, all of them noticeable for their calm silence.

'Russkies,' the Captain explained. 'Of the Orthodox Church to be sure, but it's all one God.'

'Do you say so?' Garside muttered.

'Come to pay their respects to a fallen comrade. Camden Town, most of them, though there's a few here who drink at the Abbey, up the Kentish Town Road. The big lad, their geezer, a sportsman from Odessa, And, more recent, Wapping Steps.'

'But however did they come to know of this event?'

The answer was, of course, by means of Quigley and Alice Cobb, who had concluded a sentimental town patrol one night in Kentish Town by falling in with some of the Russians in the Abbey.

'At which, the old tom-toms started beating. Or maybe it was more the howling of wolves in the forest sort of thing. Leading to a decent enough turnout today, considering the number of police spies hanging about, Mr Garside, sir.'

'Police spies?'

'Narks. Don't ask me to point them out. Very bad form all round. A word to the wise is all.'

'Do the Russians intend to make speeches?' Garside yelped nervously. 'Are they political sort of chaps?'

'As much as the average cabhorse, I would say. No, they have come here to sing.'

'They're a choir!'

'They are Russkies,' Quigley explained patiently.

And a few moments later the Russians did indeed begin to sing, accompanied by the girl on the accordion. Huge booming baritones and basses, the sound dragged up from the swags of their bellies. Slow and stately hymns touched by that rarest of things in Whitechapel, male yearning. Such big men, caressing the note. Their unaffected tears were partly for the memory of Piotr Komarev, partly for the music itself and partly for Russia and the emptiness of its skies.

The spies – or narks – nevertheless identified three of these Russians, as well as a Frenchman and a hideously disfigured Belgian, all of interest to the police and present in Saffron Hill the night that Pete the Giant was shot. Captain Quigley's name also appeared on their list, but not that of the mysterious stranger who was Sefton Garside's sidekick and might have been expected to make a showing. Nor was there any sign of the moustachioed chancer who was Quigley's particular friend. These two coves had not been seen for three days. The bloke with the moustache was Billy somebody or other; the other bloke, the one with the pale suit seen knocking about the place, name unknown.

'His name is Anton Hough,' Billy murmured. 'Has lived in Geneva, has lived in Paris. Went to school here, where he met Mr Garside. But otherwise and since then a figure of mystery.'

He and Philip Westland sat under a row of plane trees

in Green Park, watching the better sort of people stroll about. Perambulators, hoops, matrons, grandfathers, the occasional man of affairs. Soldiers sauntered; a solitary policeman who was acting it up a bit, Murch considered – thumbs tucked into the belt and coming it all casual, like an extra in a play.

'You have not been idle, Billy.'

'At school, this Hough blew up a cricket pavilion or something of the kind. Perhaps that's important, I wouldn't know. But a dangerous cove.'

'You say you have been following him?'

'I lost him last night. No doubt that he knew he was being followed. Perce Quigley is keeping an eye on things over in Whitechapel but I could wish for someone a bit more solid. I arranged this meet because I think your cousin Mr Garside might be in trouble. And perhaps you, too. But you're going to tell me that Mrs Westland is ever your only concern.'

'Something like that, yes. But I don't quite see –'

'Perhaps this man has put your wife in mortal danger once already.'

Philip stared. Billy was peeling a green twig with his thumbnail and looking at the gravel between his boots. When he glanced up, his expression was sombre to a fault. The policeman he had noted earlier had turned about and was retracing his steps – still as unhurried as before, but what kind of a copper's beat was it that ended halfway across a park?

'I think the bloke we're talking about – Mr Garside's particular pal – may know something about the Fracatelli bombing,' he said quietly.

'That is a very huge assumption,' Philip said.

'For three days past I have been following him and I never saw him speak to another human being. But here's the thing: he knew I was on to him and that made him happy. Because, when he wanted to, he gave me the slip as easy as kiss my hand, as much as to say – well, you can guess the point he wanted to make.'

'That still doesn't mark him out as a bomber.'

Billy threw away his peeled stick and wiped his hands on his thighs. 'Your cousin,' he said heavily, 'is a very sincere sort of chap, but a few bob short of twenty shillings' worth of silver, if you don't mind me saying, Mr Westland. Under the floor of his little Whitechapel meeting house, or mission hall or however he styles it, is enough explosive to sink a battleship. Put there by this Hough.'

'You have seen this? And Garside knows it is there also?'

'Mr Garside would find it hard to believe ill of someone he might think of as an old schoolfriend. He knows there is something nasty under the floor but is too much the gentleman to ask what.'

'Now I will tell you something, Billy. Hough's name appears on a list found on Commander Alcock's body. The police told me this.'

Billy permitted himself a wry smile. He indicated with his chin that someone was crossing the grass towards them, a tall and heavy-set man in exquisite tailoring, wearing the most expensive kind of kid boots. Half a dozen paces behind him was the sauntering uniformed bobby who, on closer examination, looked comfortable about the gut but good for a respectable turn of speed over fifty yards or so.

'Gentlemen,' Pennington said, raising his hat. The constable, staring only at Billy, touched the brim of his helmet in a far more ironic salute.

'You are sharper than I give you credit for,' Murch muttered from under his moustache. Pennington smiled.

'I have no quarrel with you, Mr Murch. And to pay you a compliment, you have proved a very hard man to find.'

'And why were you seeking me at all?'

'It has to do with a mission in Whitechapel – and a fellow called Anton Hough. Shall we go?'

They took a cab to Hackstraw's Yard, where they found four policemen, two of them pipe-smoking old-timers enjoying the sunshine, but two more in the shadows with that flinty look in their eyes that goes with the issue of firearms. The fattest and most fatherly of the constables held the gate open for them and Pennington led the way to the former tack-room. Inside were Sefton Garside and Captain Quigley. The underfloor cavity was empty and beside it was piled its contents, shrouded by canvas. The Captain had some of his cockiness left intact and was resting both boots on the swag, drinking bottled stout from what appeared to be a jam jar.

Pennington kicked his feet away. 'Have a care, Captain Quigley. Perhaps you do not know for sure what is under that canvas,' he said. 'But I think your friend Mr Murch here does, and I believe Mr Garside has his suspicions.'

'I never gave you up, Billy,' Perce Quigley promised. 'On my oath.'

'Indeed not,' the superintendent agreed. 'Nor would we have found your friend today, were it not for the fact that

we have been tailing Mr Westland here for the past week.'
He turned to Philip. 'I'm afraid it was you who led us to
the meeting in the park.'

'That was clever of you,' Westland said quietly.

'It was averagely intelligent detective work. I read the
file on the Westphalen affair and the part Mr Murch played
in that. That was bravely done by both of you. And – how
shall I put it? – there have been other escapades you shared
in the past. It therefore seemed possible that you might
wish to reunite your forces, as it were.'

'We are not a criminal gang, Pennington. You are making
us more glamorous than we are,' Philip said, greatly
shaken. 'Murch is an old friend, nothing more.'

'An old and extremely useful friend. It is your nature
to protect your interests and solve your problems without
troubling the police. Murch here – and to some extent
Captain Quigley – have done you and the lady who is
now your wife some sterling service in the past. This
particular adventure – if that is how you see it – is, I am
afraid, of a different order altogether.'

'This is wild talk. I hardly know what you are talking
about.'

'But I think you do,' the superintendent said softly. 'In
another context, on another occasion, we might have much
to discuss.'

'Is that a threat?'

'I am simply telling you to keep out of it.'

'I took Mr Hough in merely as a seeker after Christ,'
Garside piped up.

Pennington turned to him much as if a child had spoken.
'Yes. You will forgive me for saying so but you are a

credulous fool, Mr Garside,' he replied. 'We are now looking for the most dangerous man in England. If it can be shown that you have colluded with him in any way whatever, then you are in dire trouble – the direst trouble. Meanwhile, be kind enough to make us some coffee.'

So began Pennington's report, delivered without notes, yet with a virtuosic attention to detail. The story began in the Café Kleist, Rue des Cordeliers, Geneva.

'How did Hough find them, these lost souls and parlour terrorists? The Kleist was a noisy, drunken den of dreamers, a smoky meeting place for the ranters and the dispossessed. Broken chairs and tables, crusts and newspapers littering the floor. The cheapest food and wine. When challenged, our enigmatic friend told them with the greatest offhandedness he was a civil engineer with experience in tunnelling. He had recently quit a job on the Gotthardbahn, the rail tunnel connecting Switzerland with Italy. He left, he said, because he was bored.'

'And this they accepted?' Philip asked, incredulous. 'Didn't boredom go against the grain of whatever it was that animated *them*? Wasn't that word offensive to everything they believed?'

'You'd think so, wouldn't you? Hough's trademark nonchalance was indeed disgusting to some patrons of the Kleist, because for them the Gotthardbahn was an instance of capitalist greed that was, so to speak, right on their doorstep. Two hundred workers had been killed in the construction work and where the tunnel enters Italy the army had been sent to the site to put down a strike, which it did by shooting directly into the crowd. But then the anarchists among the Kleist clientele began to reason that

Hough had actually said something rather profound. Capital *was* boring.'

'The upshot of which, they was flummoxed,' Quigley suggested in an effort to be helpful. He could see the Café Kleist in his mind's eye as clearly as if he was sitting there himself. The whiff of bad cigars and garlic. A slate behind the bar tallying up the credit extended. As to the clientele, a bunch of bloody foreigners with nothing but the old jabber-jabber to get them out of bed in the morning. Thus Quigley's fixed opinion of revolutionary politics.

'When you say they were flummoxed?' Pennington asked.

'He put the wind up them, must have done. If he wasn't a police spy, then what the merry hell was he? I'm sat there with a bomb in me pocket and otherwise not a ha'penny to scratch my arse with, when in walks this smartarse bastard –'

'I thought you were going to say something interesting about anarchy.'

'I could do,' Quigley allowed.

'It happened that he arrived in Geneva in the middle of a family quarrel among the Kleistians that concerned a Russian girl, Anna Lippatev, who had recently fallen pregnant and been abandoned by the poet Metzger. Mr Westland, do you have a comment?'

'I recognise the name,' Philip muttered.

'That's right, it was on Alcock's list. Lippatev committed suicide by taking rat poison. She died horribly. The question then became what to do about Metzger? These philosophers hit on the idea of arraigning the poet before a revolutionary court of honour, to be held in the Kleist.

Over seventy attended. With one exception. The accused failed to turn up to his own trial. Can we guess why?'

'He'd flitted,' Quigley decided. 'Done a bunk. Saw they didn't want to give him no medals and – bosh! – first express train out of Geneva.'

'That is a possibility,' Pennington conceded.

'Unless, of course, Hough had already seen to him,' Billy Murch said in a low voice.

Pennington nodded. 'Exactly so. Metzger, who was an athletic enough fellow in his twenties, fell out of the fourth-floor window of his lodgings. Could have been an accident, save for one detail. His mouth was stuffed with paper, which turned out to be his own poetry.'

'You say he fell?' Philip asked.

'Impossible to say whether he fell or was pushed.'

'Because?'

Pennington shrugged, as if to indicate the standard of criminal investigation in Geneva. 'The police liked it better that he was pushed. Indeed, five separate Kleistians confessed to having killed him over the next few days, including two women and an old man who walked with crutches. None of their statements could be corroborated.'

'They simply wanted him dead?'

'Just so. It remains an unsolved murder case. I don't say the Swiss authorities have exactly stretched every sinew to find out the truth.'

'You believe it to be Hough who killed him? Is that what you are saying?'

'Mr Murch?' the superintendent asked.

'The rest of the Kleist boys wanted *him* to take the

hero's part,' Billy suggested. 'But he just copped a deaf 'un. Said nothing, had no opinion.'

'Can you tell us what you think happened next?'

'At a guess, his stock went up. They took a shine to him.'

'Exactly. He stays the same quiet presence at a corner table, but what they thought of as his disdain begins to seem to them like ruthlessness. They *know* he murdered Metzger but only because none of them had the guts to do it themselves. Hough is invited to join some shadowy committee of would-be firebrands. He refuses. He talks to the giant Russian, Piotr Komarev occasionally. Lends him money. But otherwise walks alone.'

'Alcock mentioned the bombing of a villa,' Philip intervened.

'The Kleistians made much of the revolutionary precept that without violence, there can *be* no revolution. Before Hough arrived on the scene they interpreted this as defacing posters, flinging paint at the windows of banks and pushing the occasional cart into the lake. The villa that was blown up belonged to a reactionary journalist they did not like. The blast killed the entire family. It is out of character with the puerile nature of their usual activities.'

'It was Hough who blew up the house?'

'He was not asked to and had no personal animosity towards this poor devil and his family. Verplanck – the journalist – was investigating the deaths of Lippatev and Metzger, it is true, but in quite the most lazy and inept way. In his newspaper column, he was pointing the finger at a set of scruffy and work-shy foreigners. If you like, he was playing the indignant Swiss national. It made good copy.'

'Didn't these revolutionaries – or however they styled themselves – invite that kind of censure? Wasn't it publicity for their cause?'

'You mean was it good for business?' Pennington smiled. Philip frowned, but it was Murch who spoke next.

'Hough blew Verplanck up for the hell of it.'

'Go on,' Pennington prompted.

Murch shrugged. 'Mr Westland is probably in the right of it. The rest of them liked being in the paper – at least someone was paying them attention. But Hough just liked killing people. Did not need to explain himself, or justify what he did. Held no grudges. Killed for pleasure.'

'Have you met people like that before?' Pennington asked quietly.

'Some snipers are like that,' Billy Murch said, after a pause. He glanced at Captain Quigley, who alone among those listening knew that sniping had been Billy's special infantry skill in the Crimea, as any number of Russian widows could testify.

'A man without conscience?'

'I wouldn't like to say. A difficult and unpredictable bastard would be my summing up. Friendless.'

'What about Komarev?' Philip asked. 'Wasn't he a friend?'

'We shall come to him later,' Pennington replied. 'But back to the night of the villa bombing. When the police raided the Café Kleist, Hough and Komarev were not to be found, of course. Did they travel to Paris together? I think not. When they arrived, Komarev went to Belleville, where he found the kind of squalor he was long accustomed to.'

'And Hough?'

'We do not know. But one evening, a prostitute took her client down to the Seine and there in the water they found the body of a man the police identified as a respected member of the Bourse.'

'Now you have lost me, Pennington.'

'His name was Joachim Metzger. It was his son who had so tragically fallen out of the window in the Rue des Cordeliers, Geneva. Now, here was the father floating face down in the river. His throat had been cut. While he lived, Metzger the poet was fond of boasting how rich Papa Metzger was. He finally told the wrong person. Madame Metzger remembers a personable young visitor from Geneva who came to the house and expressed his sympathy for the loss of a dear but deluded son.'

'What was he after?'

Pennington shrugged. 'Money. A very great deal of it. Metzger *père* prided himself on knowing the ways of the world. He smelled a rat. He gave no money to this mysterious stranger but his unhappy wife did. She gave Hough some of her jewellery and several thousand francs. These transactions were discovered by Metzger, who forbade him to come to the house, on pain of being reported to the police. Two days later, he was dead.'

'The murder can be tied directly to Hough?'

'The evidence is circumstantial. But when the Sûreté looked for Hough, he had already crossed into England.'

Philip stood up and began pacing the little mission hall, a warning sign to those who knew him well. Picked up empty coffee mugs and set them down again, distracted. Looked out of the window and withdrew a handkerchief from his pocket and attempted to clean a pane. Found a dead moth that he held in his fingertips. When he saw what he had done, he threw it away as if were a cricket ball. It fluttered into a fold of his trousers.

'You are forgetting Alcock and our own interest in the man. What you are saying is that this monster was allowed into the country without a single let or hindrance to do whatever damage he liked. Since when he has indeed killed and maimed and has now disappeared – leaving not a single clue behind him. The police are powerless, and yet allowing the general public to think it was that poor devil Komarev who was the bomber.'

'Until we were able to study Alcock's files in detail, we did not know of the existence of Hough – or any other third party.'

'But you let, for example, my wife – my *wife*, Pennington – believe that she had been blown up by a harmless Russian exile. Hundreds of policemen combing London to discover a man who was a walking advertisement of simplicity and loving kindness. And then killing him as if he were a dog. Well, shame on you, Pennington. *Shame* on you.'

'You are getting over-excited.'

'Do you think so? Do you think we should all go away from here feeling there is nothing to be done about the real perpetrator? Or that it's none of our business to ask any more questions of the operations of the police?'

'I do think this is not the time or place to have such a conversation,' Pennington said with a glance at the others in the room.

'It's a matter for gentlemen, is it?' Philip asked cuttingly, enough to make the superintendent flush. 'Garside here's a gentleman and as much at risk as any other gentleman in London. We are not your dogs, Pennington.'

'I have gone out of my way to tell you what I know.'

'But not what you are going to do about it.'

'This is not a romantic adventure such as your wife used to write. You are out of your depth, Westland.'

'You have a name, you have a close description. You have background files that seem to indicate a history of murder and outrage. You have some very suggestive evidence. I would be obliged, meanwhile, if you kept your cheap remarks about my wife out of it.'

Quite unexpectedly, Murch lumbered to his feet and dragged Captain Quigley up by the wrist. 'Me and Perce are walking out that door now, Mr Pennington, taking Mr Westland with us. If I was Mr Garside here, I'd likewise pack up shop and leg it out of here. This cove Hough hasn't finished in England yet.'

'That is for me to decide,' an angry Pennington warned.

'I think not,' Murch said, handing Philip Westland his hat.

'You are a damned impertinent fellow,' the Superintendent spluttered.

'Pete the Giant was a pal of ours. Mr Garside here owes him more than a prayer or two. But like Mr Westland says, you shot the wrong bloke. And the one you should have nobbled, you let go, or knew nothing of. And now your best hope is that he's sloped off back to France, so's not to spoil a good story.'

'You are asking for trouble, Murch.'

'Now where've I heard that before?' Billy murmured in a calm and level tone, plucking Philip's sleeve sharply, to prevent him from speaking.

'I will have you all watched,' Pennington warned. 'At the slightest sign that you are hindering a police investigation, I will have you arrested.'

'I have been walking about after this bloke for three days past. In all that time I never saw a copper pay him the slightest interest,' Billy said. 'Of course,' he added scathingly, 'at the time, you was following Mr Westland. So *his* head can rest easy on the pillow tonight, I don't think.'

The three men left Hackstraw's Yard and went away down the deserted street, backlit by a feeble sun. Instinct told them to keep step, so that they resembled soldiers on the march. In Whitechapel there were always idlers and they shrank back a little as if at the passing of something important. Even the street urchins kept their distance, hands in pockets, their eyes watchful.

'My God,' Philip Westland muttered, 'what kind of fools have we made of ourselves?'

'Chin up,' Quigley chided gently. 'You are starting to shamble somewhat, if you don't mind me saying so, sir. Chin up, look to your front, bang the old boots down on the cobbles. Let's make a show, shall we?'

But Philip was facing a very uncomfortable truth. The police knew far more about Bella's recent history than they had ever before disclosed. Putting it another way, the Margam years were a matter of public record. As he stumbled along with blistering feet, Philip realised suddenly that some at least of the information they now possessed came from the files of the late Commander Alcock. The various scraps of information and conjecture the police might have garnered over time had been given shape from a source that could only have been him. Superintendent Pennington might not be an imaginative man but he knew how to add two and two.

'There is a file exclusively for us,' Philip said. 'I mean a pre-existing file, something that was in being before ever Hough set foot in this country.'

'I have never supposed it different,' Billy Murch grunted.

'Some of which comes from Commander Alcock's office.'

'Just so.'

'That while I was spying for the Commander, I was myself being spied on?'

'Let's say your background was being looked after for you, like a well-managed garden,' Murch suggested.

'I have no background.'

'Perce here has no background,' Billy corrected gently. 'But you have Mrs Westland. And, as it were, Mr Margam. And certain adventures, as the superintendent puts it.'

'In the very beginning, when you first met, you were all set to go off to India a day or so later, wasn't that right?' Quigley asked.

'What if I was?'

'You were just shoving off. Just an impulse kind of a thing.'

'Yes.'

'And that didn't bother Commander Alcock none?'

'I don't have to explain myself to anybody. If you want a motive, I did not like who I was. If you can possibly imagine that state of mind.'

'They don't like that,' Quigley said, brushing the sarcasm aside.

'Who doesn't like that?'

'People with pens, sitting in offices. Coves like the Commander, for example. Be that as it may, you get as far as Cairo and then you turn back. For love.'

'And what if I did?' Philip asked, blushing. 'What damned business is it of yours, you impertinent devil?'

'Well, I ain't the spymaster in the story, am I? But I bet it gave old Alcock a jolt. Assuming you was already on his books, if you see what I mean.'

Philip thought about that. It made sense. If it were true, then this might have been the first time Bella's name had become a matter of public interest. Maybe it was no more than a casual reference in the margins of Philip's personal file, as he was beginning to realise must exist among Alcock's papers. But turning back from India to tell Bella he loved her had started a train that had brought them to where they were now.

'Anyone who knows the both of you can believe no better reason to bring you home,' Murch reproached him. 'And look what great good came of it. You have the lady to your wife now. You have won the great prize in life, Mr Westland. Leave all this other stuff to that weasel Pennington. We're well out of it. Believe me.'

NINE

'So, what is to be done?' Philip asked, massaging his feet the while. He was ashamed to find his hands shaking. Those two accomplished pavement-pounders Quigley and Billy Murch had taken pity on his limping progress from Whitechapel and proposed calling in at a pub for what the Captain called a sharpener. It was a strangely aberrant thing to be without boots in public and Philip had already attracted the astonished glance of the land-lady. But the cool of the pine boards on his swollen soles was heavenly. As to the location of the pub, he had no clear idea where he was. He was, in all senses, lost.

'For you, there is nothing more to be done,' Murch said in answer to his question. 'Your duties begin and end now with looking after the missus.'

'Wise words,' Quigley agreed. This came with a scowl, for the Captain knew when he was not wanted and this was a pub with pretensions. What he thought of as knick-knacks were on every wall and the smell of beeswax stank the place out. Any minute now, the old bag who ran the place was going to come over and insist that Mr W. put his boots back on – at which time she would get a piece of Percy Quigley's mind, no error.

'I think we should convene a council of war,' Philip muttered.

'Hasn't he just said?' the Captain yelped.

'Look, Mr Westland,' Billy Murch said, 'we have had a fair run for our money over the years but what we face now is something very different.'

'I must all the same discuss it with Bella,' Philip said distractedly. 'With Mrs Westland.'

'No, sir. You and the lady should leave London tonight or tomorrow morning and not come back until it is over.'

'And how will it be over?'

'I mean when Hough is dead.'

'This is not exclusively about Hough.'

'With him out of the way, everything else will settle down.'

'Easy to say, not so easy to accomplish.'

'When all's said and done, the cove is a rank amateur,' Murch rejoined calmly. 'As to the time away, we are talking a few days, maybe a week.'

'You call Hough an amateur?' Philip asked, amazed. 'Isn't he the biggest villain we have ever faced? Enough for you to counsel me to run away?'

'He is a man who takes his pleasure in killing.'

'And?'

'He is a double-dyed villain to be sure, but his hours and days are numbered. I think he knows this himself. We shall do well to stay out of it.'

If Billy Murch had said he planned to open a wool-shop in Tiverton, or buy an ocean-going ketch and sail to Tahiti, he could not have amazed Philip more. The most ruthless and determined man in London, to whom the Westlands

– and Bella especially – owed so much – and now this? It seemed like the world turned upside down.

'You have no plan?' Philip whispered.

'Let Mr Pennington worry about what to do next. We are finished with all that.'

He said this with such finality that Philip could hardly take the words in. Instead, he stared at the man who had saved his life in Germany, trying to read this new thing in Billy's eyes. It was not unlike being told that he had suddenly been bankrupted. It did not help that Philip secretly agreed with the idea of cutting and running and an end to all the Margam connections. Swelling up in him with a vehemence was disgust at London itself. It came like bile in the mouth.

They were interrupted by the landlady approaching, looking down her nose.

'If the gentleman would put his boots on,' she began.

'Which you are talking to a foremost Arctic explorer, a hero just back from those snowy regions,' Quigley interrupted, 'a man who has risked his all for Queen and Country, a valued member of the Royal Geographical Society and Fellow of Balliol College, Oxford, who will be happy to put his boots back on as soon as the old frostbite eases.'

'And I suppose you two are also explorers?' the landlady enquired sardonically.

'Bosun and sailing-master,' the Captain said, saluting.

The landlady switched her glance to Billy Murch, who was looking at her with the horribly neutral expression that struck fear into men twice his size, let alone a woman with four combs holding up her hair. She thought about it for a moment and then licked her lips. 'Well, I don't want no trouble,' she conceded.

'Then there won't be none.'

'Be easy, Colonel,' Quigley remarked grandly, with a wave of his cheroot. 'She has understood. And, of course, your money's good in any pub in England.'

The landlady smiled weakly and retired. The knick-knacks that Quigley had identified were in fact Jacobean pewter plates, often inspected by visiting antiquarians, the whole display set off by a muster roll from Civil War days. In any other mood, Philip would have been delighted, for the one pleasure afforded by drinking with the Captain was his gift of finding interesting out-of-the-way pubs, like a pig hunting truffles. But now, it was a sign of his distress that he barely looked up. Murch watched him carefully. But even he was startled when Philip banged the table with his fist, causing every head in the pub to swing round.

'Very well!' he shouted. 'Let it go! Let it all go! If that is how it ends, so be it.'

He was talking about the future in the full knowledge that he was speaking only for his part in it, for Bella was about as immovable as one of the Landseer lions in Trafalgar Square. She was the kind of Londoner who flatly contradicts the gloomy Wordsworth. It was not nature that gave her a metaphor for universal health and wisdom. If it was to be found anywhere, it was in the hugger-mugger of tiles and slate, stone and glass. What nourished Bella's soul was the press of people streaming across Westminster Bridge in the early morning like a marching column; or shoppers swarming up and down Oxford Street. She loved crowds and the faces of strangers. Picnicking on Box Hill or the Brighton shingles might be fun for a day – but it was not life.

'It is London,' Philip muttered. 'That is what has done me down.'

'I am of that same mind about the shabby old town,' Billy Murch said very unexpectedly.

'But you think me a coward all the same!'

'I will tell you in full what I think of you some other day, Mr Westland. But you know you already have my respect.'

'I am a weakling.'

'You mean among men? Only averagely so.'

'You would really leave London, Billy?'

'It has been in my mind for some time,' Murch replied.

Philip stared at him, trying to read his face. In a broken sort of gesture, he reached out – not to grip his hand but to touch it with his finger-ends.

'I am afraid for her life,' he said in the tiniest of voices. Like a man in a dream, he rose from the table, his boots pinched up in the fingers of one hand, and wandered out into the street in his socks. He should be home now, guarding her life with his, he thought, instead of prosing away God knew where. It was just the sort of landscape Bella liked best – nondescript, rumpled by hard work and long-sufferingness and to all appearances unbudgable.

Philip sensed Murch and Quigley at his elbow. 'I am finished with all this, my friends,' he said. 'I must go home and tell Bella. Even if I meet this fellow Hough along the way and stop to tear his throat out, my mind is made up. There will be no more London.' Surprised to find he was holding his boots at such a critical moment in his life, he threw them across the road, where they skittered into the gutter like rabbits.

'Walk down there a bit and find us a cab, Perce,' Murch murmured.

Deciding to quit was one thing, persuading Bella that it was a good idea quite another. As she pointed out, she had said goodbye to the least impulsive man in Europe after breakfast, only to have him come home in the afternoon wild-eyed and babbling.

'I do not recognise the description,' Philip said stiffly.

'Without his boots.'

'Bella, we must find some other way to talk about this. I have told you, we are in the greatest danger from a random killer, a man without scruples of any kind.'

'Is there such a thing in nature as a random act? If there is, can it be forestalled, I wonder?'

'Very well, we are at risk of being killed like Alcock by a premeditating murderer. Does that make it easier to contemplate? I have a duty to protect you – and before you tell me you can look after yourself, if anything happened to you my life would end.'

'And you say that is not babbling? I married you because I perceived you as a generous man who knew where he left off and others began. Who would give me my space accordingly and not treat a wife like a chattel.'

'This is not a book, or a play.'

'Neither is it a conversation between two married people. You take it into your head that you can no longer live in London and I am to acquiesce like a canary in a cage. You simply take me with you? Is that it?'

'You left London once before, for the sake of your first husband.'

'Good God,' Bella said faintly. 'Has it really come to this?'

Seeing him blush crimson made her own eyes prickle. They found they could not stay in the same room together.

Sefton Garside was also leaving London, or at the least planning his tactical retreat. Pennington had left a solitary officer to guard the Hackstraw Yard premises, a man who had endured such sombre years in the police that he did not feel it any longer necessary to utter. Perhaps he might cry out Fire! in a crowded theatre if so ordered, but as a companion in a very tricky situation – as Sefton now regarded things – he was next to useless. When he made tea, it was only for himself. When he wasn't in the meeting room, arms folded over his stomach, he was clumping about in the yard gathering up bits and bobs. He had a hay rake and three buckets laid by to take home when he came off duty. That would happen when Sefton slung his hook.

Towards dusk, a boy turned up asking to speak to the vicar. Constable Daniels let this percolate for a bit. A ratty little chap, he concluded, but harmless enough. Stick arms, no boots, the cheeks of his arse hanging out of his kecks. Shaven head.

'What's it about?' he asked.

'Want to say goodbye.'

'And who says he's going anywhere?'

'Come off it! I weren't born yesterday.'

Once inside the meeting room, the boy opened his shirt and passed Sefton a scrap of paper as stiff as bone.

'Who gave you this?' Garside whispered.

'Party gave me a tanner to fetch it you, said you'd give me the same to receive it.'

Then it was from Hough, Sefton concluded.

'I have nothing smaller than a shilling.'

'Go on, then.'

'You must take me to him.'

'Not bloody likely,' the boy said, holding out his hand for the shilling.

The message, which was written on a corner torn from a poster said simply *19 Leyland St. Now.*

'Where is Leyland Street?' he asked.

'Well, it aint nowhere near Park Lane,' the boy scoffed. 'S'one of Harry Coggins's knocking shops, up by Carberry Street Market. You'll find it.'

Sefton told Constable Daniels he was going to buy a suitcase. Daniels digested this for a while and then gave a slow nod.

'Don't get one of them cardboard ones,' he advised. 'No matter how many steamer stickers it has on it. Leather the thing for suitcases.'

And while you're away, I'll just have a little riffle through your goods and chattels, he thought comfortably. Your little bits and bobs. Stuff you won't miss. Your little odds and sods.

'You'll look after things here, then?'

'I think I know my duty,' Daniels said.

Sefton was admitted to 19 Leyland Street by a lumbering woman wearing two shawls and a man's hat. Hanging down her back was a single plait of grey hair. He was irresistibly reminded of a Red Indian photographic portrait he had seen recently; but Ma Friedl was from Hamburg and spoke to him in German. This was a misunderstanding: Hough had spoken to *her* in German and she supposed Sefton to be of the same language group.

The brothel was noisy with the barking of dogs and the shouting of whores in four languages: it also stank to high heaven of sweat and stale beer. There was no allure about Ma Friedl's place: shoeing horses was done with more love and attention than had ever existed inside these walls. Sefton shuddered.

'You are too sensitive,' Hough laughed when they met. The crib he stayed in was eight feet by eight and had perhaps once been a scullery. Scraps of carpet and moth-eaten rugs covered the stone floor. The all-important bed leered. Like every other window in the building, felt had been nailed over the frame. They spoke by the light of a single candle.

'Why did you come back to Whitechapel?' Sefton whispered. 'You are risking your neck, even in a hellhole like this.'

The whisper came from anxiety about a third person he had discovered in the room, a broad-backed woman sleeping face down in the bed. She was the first naked woman Sefton had ever seen.

'This is Ekaterina,' Hough explained. 'You may say what you like in front of her, if she wakes. She has only a few words of English. And of course everyone in the establishment knows who I am and why I am here. This is brandy I am drinking. You might care to join me.'

'What stops them from giving you up to the police?'

'Money. I hope you have brought some with you. The daily rates for this room are comparable to the best hotels in London.'

'You have destroyed my life,' Sefton said in a broken voice.

'The road to excess leads to the palace of wisdom,' Hough rejoined comfortably. 'A text from the author of *Jerusalem* you might have studied with more attention when at school. I have not destroyed your life, as you so fancifully put it. You have no life. This Russian whore knows more about life than you will ever know.'

'You will be caught and hanged, Anton.'

'Oh, very certainly. There is not much news in that remark. But there are interesting things left to do meanwhile. I have a hankering to visit Norfolk, for example.'

'Are you mad?'

'I have a standing invitation from your mama.'

'You would drag her down with you?'

'My dear Sefton,' Hough said gently. 'Has it never occurred to you that we were put down here on earth not to praise God but amuse him? If there is another point to humanity I have yet to find it. You ask me if I am mad. The world is mad from end to end. Neither Norfolk nor your mother escapes this description. You came to save Whitechapel. I hope I have shown you how comically wide of the mark that is. What is there worth saving? Let us wake Ekaterina and ask her opinion.'

'I cannot help you, Hough. I will not help you.'

'But you must. You will pay my way here and then we shall hatch a plan to go back home to Norfolk. Your mother will provide me with the means to leave this country and we shall be quits. I will spare you the opportunity to save my soul.'

'You are an utterly evil man.'

'Now you insult me. I am a man, dearest Sefton. Your world will claim me long enough to put a rope around my neck, and sermons better than any you might write will be delivered in all the best places. The world, as you and your kind perceive it, will resume its course. And Ekaterina will stay right where she is.'

He stroked the girl's back and she rolled on to one hip, staring at them both with gummy eyes. She smiled a vague smile, exposing greenish teeth.

'Who is this?' she asked in Russian.

'The priest.'

'The one that helped Piotr?'

She reached out to take Sefton's hands in hers but the missionary misunderstood the gesture and recoiled. He jumped up, stumbling on the scattered rugs. Hough, who was prepared for this, levelled the rusty Colt he had bought from Harry Coggins, fired – and missed. Screaming, Garside fled the room.

'What happened?' Pennington demanded.

'He went to buy a suitcase,' Constable Daniels mumbled.

'Suspend this officer from duty and have him taken to the local nick. Put him in a cell,' the superintendent said. 'Find me the boy who came to deliver the message. Turn that damn brothel over and arrest Coggins and the madam who keeps the place for him.'

The driver of the cart that had run Sefton Garside down heard all this with terror in his heart. He had already told his story three times – How he's going along delivering five window frames and a door when this lanky cove comes running out of Ma Friedl's screaming and Bam! straight under old Walter's hooves. Rolls a couple of times, moves to get up, falls back and the cartwheel goes over his scrawny neck. An accident, the carter says, such as happens in a big place like London any day of the week, except he's been driving eighteen years and never so much as harmed a bleedin' fly. As God is his witness.

TEN

Sefton Garside was buried in a flintstone church in an almost forgotten village outside Dereham, in Norfolk. A wide and dusty street had in it the church, a too ancient pub, one shop and a straggle of miserable cottages. The only house of any quality lay a mile away, protected by elms and oaks, where the Garsides had their home, called locally the Hall. It seemed a matter of indifference to the family that so few attended the service, though it was shocking to Philip that nobody from the Coldstreams was there to see a former comrade laid to rest. The only man in uniform was a Commander RN recently returned from the China station, part of the Garside cousinage. He had discharged himself from a naval hospital to be present.

'And are we supposed to be impressed by that?' Garside's mother asked at the lych-gate. 'I understand the complaint he has is caused by some kind of intestinal worm, a quite grotesque thing to mention in general conversation. Of course, in my day, men were cut from an altogether different cloth. My brother came back from Hudson Bay in '53 missing four fingers and all his toes. That is my idea of a naval officer. Shall you walk back to the Hall, Westland?'

'I believe I shall, Lady Garside.'

He was accompanied by the Commander, who was called Benson. The two men ambled through fields of early corn, kicking up dust that a month or two earlier had been mud. Benson did the sun justice by sweating profusely.

'What is China like?' Philip asked.

'Like this somewhat, but without the skylarks. You live in London, I understand? That I should not like, no, nor any other great city.'

'Where would you choose to live?'

'Heligoland,' Benson said at once. 'Or maybe some quiet spot along the Baltic coast.'

'But nowhere in England? Here, for example?'

'I have lost the knack of being English.'

'You are very positive about it.'

'These people are my family, after a fashion. I find them unbearably stupid and the country round about as interesting as an empty dinner plate. Yet for Lady Garside, what it looks like is beside the point. It is hers and that's all that matters.'

'You have seen mountains, Commander.'

'I have seen the world,' he replied. 'And it is nothing like Norfolk.'

Philip thought about this. Although he had already crossed off East Anglia as a place to bring Bella, it was dispiriting to have to agree with Commander Benson. Norfolk was dull. He stood about on the lawns of Garside Hall, eating ham sandwiches and drinking what appeared to be Riesling, watching some very ordinary people making small talk. All of it had to do with family members, present or in other parts of the kingdom; their marriages and dogs, investments and ailments. There was barely mention of Sefton. The Garsides quite expected eccentricity to be present in any family – as instanced, for example, by Uncle Arthur, who had married the daughter of his local butcher – but missionary work in the East End was a little beyond their understanding.

The Hall, for all its local eminence, reminded Philip of nothing more grand than a property that would soon enough be past restoring. An impressive frontage was more or less maintained to some sort of standard but it was clear that the back of the house had not been seen to for many years. Philip could count seven broken panes of glass and the gutters were green with grass. Some of the garden statuary had toppled, so that, for example, Diana the Huntress had fallen flat on her face, exposing her mossy bottom. As for the lawns, they were scabby in the extreme. Only the most intimate of the family circle had been admitted to the house. The rest of the mourners stood about in mocking sunshine.

'Where is your wife?' a pleasantly stout and ugly woman enquired.

'In London. But I am astonished you should know I am married.'

'This is a family that believes in family. Better to say, insists on family. Mrs Westland is unknown to anyone here but she has her obligations.'

Philip studied her carefully before realising that the ugly woman was being sardonic. He bowed his head. 'And what branch of the family are you?'

'I am a Dorset Garside. A little out of the way down there but under direction to attend all weddings and funerals. If the world is to be made to stand still, as Lady Garside wishes, it requires the participation of the whole family, down to second cousins and great uncles, their wives and children.'

'And do you believe in any of that?'

The ugly woman laughed and threw her wine into a herbaceous border. 'No more than you. I am a widow, Mr Westland. I have other things to think about. An obscure and indolent Garside was my husband. If there was a stupider man in all England, I have yet to meet him. How do you find London?'

Just at present, like a ransacked library, Philip thought. He and Bella were living in icy civility far more painful than being apart altogether. The widow from Dorset quizzed him with fine blue eyes, a half smile on her lips. It was as though she already knew the answer to her question.

'I have lived there a long time. But I am presently looking to leave.'

'Aren't you a little young to retire from life?'

'This is more in the nature of a flight.'

'And where shall you live?'

'Is Dorset pleasant?'

'My dear man, it would bore you to death. It is the Garsides writ large. The world at a standstill. You should live by a more troubled sea, I think.'

'Commander Benson has a passion to live in Heligoland.'

'Poor fellow. But desire is appealing, whatever form it takes.'

'Well, and what is the problem between them, Dora dear?' Hannah Bardsoe asked, cutting her friend another slice of

Dundee cake. The two women sat in the parlour of the house in Shelton Street, the strongest tea at their elbows and a nice bit of Double Gloucester to give the cake a warning shot across the bows.

'I'm afeared for them both,' Dora Venn mumbled through her crumbs. 'She has an uncomfortable bold manner with men, there is no doubt of that. Always a woman to speak her mind. Only this time, she has maybe said a word too many, for I have never seen him so silent, which is to say, hangdog. A face on him like a sick cabhorse. Maps and railway timetables scattered all over. Most days off out of it before the streets have been aired, coming home more gloomy than what he set out.'

'Maps, you say?'

'Scattered all over,' Dora Venn confirmed. 'So I says to the missus, I says, would you like me to tidy up this little lot? And she says, no, Mrs Venn, you can leave them there until hell freezes over for all I care. Her very words. And how much grief is hidden in a vulgar expression like that, I wonder?'

'All is well in the bedroom, I trust?'

At which Dora Venn blushed, for she had not Hannah's earthy common sense. 'I do wonder how I would know anything about that,' she muttered.

'Has he took the death of his cousin bad?'

'That's where he is now, at the poor devil's funeral. In Norfolk or some such place. They say meanwhile the mission hall in Whitechapel has been burned to the ground. A party by the name of Coggins is said to be the culprit.'

'I sent Perce Quigley over for a looksie. Perce acting up a bit strange, too, now you mention it.'

The two women sat in silence, watched by the cat. Hannah was the more phlegmatic for the obvious reason that she had a man, whereas Dora Venn had not. Men were the despair of the world, on the whole, unable by nature to pick up a stick at the dry end, always asking how the story works out – impatient.

'I hope I am to go before Charlie,' Hannah said absently, 'for without me he could not find his way to the front door. And do finish that last knob of cheese, for I see that you like it so.'

But the silence had produced in Mrs Venn something of a revelation. At church on Sundays the vicar encouraged his flock to have a few moments of meditation before commencing the service. Dora usually spent the time staring at the flags between her feet, thinking about the roast she was to cook later; but once in a while she surprised herself by thinking of something she didn't know she could think. This was such a moment. 'What it is, my dear, being blowed up should have changed her more. I think he is more afeared for her in this wicked world than she is herself. And that has made him look weak. And that has got up her snout, more than somewhat.'

Hannah lumbered to her feet and found the Martinique rum and two glasses. 'I do declare, Dora, you are a clever old body when you put your mind to it.'

Fracatelli's closed their premises after the Christmas bomb that murdered its proprietor and destroyed half the property. But at a family meeting in Edmonton in the New Year, it was decided to continue with the business under the management of an energetic nephew, Franco, who came from Perugia with some handsome capital. At the reopening, the clientele was strongly Italian in composition as friends and relatives came to pay their congratulations and respects – and, inevitably, to pass judgement on the new owners. What they saw pleased them. There were no banners or advertisements, no speeches. It was business as usual. The waiters still flicked the chandeliers with their napkins as they passed, just as they had always done. There was more than ever reason to admire this tradition, for by one of the vagaries of the blast that had killed and maimed so many, the chandeliers had survived, all bar a few pendants. Each time the crystals chimed, there was a murmur of approval from the diners, who included the soprano Luciana, who had broken off rehearsals at Covent Garden to attend.

Bella and Superintendent Pennington were also at the reopening. She was greeted on the threshold by the waiter who had saved her life, who silently kissed her hand and led her to her usual table. Pennington was impressed, all the more so because this man could also clearly recognise a policeman when he saw one.

'You are remarkably calm,' he observed when they were seated.

'Do you think so? Inside, there is a tempest raging. But it would not do to reveal it. Have you never been here before, Superintendent?'

'It would give me great pleasure if you would call me David,' he replied. 'Who is the gentleman in the black corduroy suit sitting nearby?'

'Du Maurier,' Bella said without looking up.

Some of the turmoil inside her was to do with the

impudence of inviting him to lunch at all. That, and the alacrity with which he had accepted.

'I have never dined here,' Pennington said. 'But that night, if you recall, the Home Secretary was giving hospitality to members of his family in the booths at the back. I was on protection duty and Fracatelli laid me a place in the kitchens. Before I could sit down to eat, however – well you know what happened.'

'I have the dimmest of recollections. How good a detective are you, Mr Pennington?'

His laugh was rich and full, enough to turn a head or two. 'Well, of course, I am exceptionally gifted. You would hardly expect me to say less. I would never have appeared in any of Henry Ellis Margam's novels and we can put that down to the fine disdain of policemen shown in the books. He gave some bishops the nod, I believe, and certain elderly *cavalieri servanti* from the peerage. An interesting fellow, I should like to have met him.'

'You are being arch.'

'Mrs Westland, I have so very few opportunities to pay court to beautiful women, married or not.'

'Margam was a fool,' Bella said, only slightly shaken by his impertinence. 'He belonged to a profession stuffed with fools and charlatans, of course, but that is no excuse. More particularly, he was a flirt, of the kind that makes up the numbers at weekend house parties and elegant soirées. I am very glad to see the back of him.'

'You think flirting obnoxious?'

'Where is Hough?' Bella demanded, producing from nowhere the equivalent of an overhead smash at tennis.

The answer was that nobody knew. It was now sixteen

days since Sefton Garside's death and the burning of the Whitehall mission – or Hackstraw's Yard to be more exact about it. Some believed the two events to have been connected, but local police thought the fire might have been the work of a gang or gangs. Hackstraw, too, had disappeared, in the common way of talking about him, though he could be found most nights of the week across the river in Stockwell, where his cousin kept a pub. But of Hough – not a sign.

'Has he left the country?'

'I think not.'

'Has he left London, even?'

'I am beginning to answer no to that, too,' Pennington said slowly. 'We are trawling with a very wide net, you understand. But the mesh is also generous. It took us no more than a day to find Hackstraw, for example, but he is one of the more conspicuous fish in the sea. I mean, measured by weight and sloth. Hough is an eel by comparison.'

'Will he strike again?'

'What does your husband say?' Pennington asked, blushing when he saw how hard the question had hit home.

'My husband must speak for himself.'

'I did not mean to anger you.'

'We are of course one and the same person at law. Perhaps this is what you had in mind. What he thinks, I must think. That must have been in your mind.'

'Please,' Pennington muttered, greatly distressed.

'Are you a Londoner, Superintendent?'

'From Bishopsgate.'

'Mr Westland is a Londoner only by adoption. He spent his childhood idyll in Oxfordshire and is at heart a countryman.'

'You surprise me,' Pennington said faintly.

'I do not mean he rough-shoots or fishes for salmon. He has never, I think, ridden to hounds or lunged about in rivers otter-hunting. His general sense of direction and the value of knowing the points of the compass is woeful. I think I know more about wild flowers and suchlike than he ever will. I can read the weather more expertly. Nevertheless – or perhaps accordingly – I am altogether more overawed by nature than he.'

'And?'

And, what are you doing discussing your husband's character at all, Bella thought. What sort of trouble are you in that you can divulge your innermost thoughts to a stranger, no matter how suave his manners? A thought occurred to her. Perhaps Pennington was far cleverer than she gave him credit for. Red spots appeared on her cheeks.

'He thinks London an essentially violent city,' she said slowly. 'It is becoming more than he can contemplate to live here.'

'Sometimes a cruise or visit to a foreign land can wreak great changes,' Pennington murmured.

He has not understood, Bella thought, with a rush of relief. He is exactly that good-looking but stolid kind that I have avoided all my life. He will forget all this, or in some absurd manly way forgive me having uttered it. When she laughed, Pennington was careful to return his most non-committal smile. The conversation turned to more general subjects.

Only when she was walking home through a Covent Garden bathed in spring sunshine did she realise fully that she had been talking to a policeman, whose job it was to forget nothing. She had, as Captain Quigley would have put it (though never to Bella's face), shown the superintendent her drawers. And Philip, if he ever found out, would find that hard to forgive. Dora Venn was in the right of it: the longer it went on, the weaker she made her husband seem.

'Well, if this don't beat the band,' this very same Dora Venn exclaimed guiltily. When her mistress came in, she and Hannah Bardsoe were sitting over the remains of a plate of pork belly, garnished with pickled red cabbage. The two old Londoners stared at their visitor in such guilty amazement because it was she who had been the main topic of conversation for an hour or more. Bella took her troubles to Fracatelli's, Dora to the little house in Shelton Street. Indeed, she had only just finished outlining what a stubborn mare her mistress could be when she set her mind to it, when the poor woman walked in.

'I hope I don't intrude,' Bella said, in a tiny voice.

'You sit yourself down,' Hannah Bardsoe said. 'Mrs Venn here was just saying how brave you was to go back to that old Fracatelli's. Would a cup of tea suit at all? Pork belly is a champion dish but it does leave the tongue heavy in the mouth on occasion.'

Bella sat down. In the act of pulling off her gloves, she suddenly burst into wailing tears.

Dora was shocked, but Hannah had always been a freer spirit and not at all the person to stand on ceremony. She flung her arms around her visitor and hugged her close. 'You let it out, girl,' she crooned. 'You sit there and cry your eyes out, if you are so minded. There's nothing wrong with a good blab, when the occasion demands.'

And so it came out, in fits and starts. What the two older women did not know, or had not guessed, was little enough, but each put a different interpretation on the facts. For Dora, it was that Philip no longer wished to live in London and that had kicked up a stink something terrible between the mistress and her man. But Hannah Bardsoe, though she said nothing at first, knew that leaving London was for Bella like losing friends. It was saying goodbye to an era. Putting it bluntly, Bella was beset by the ghost of Henry Ellis Margam. Hannah imagined him as some sort of spectral dog, always under her feet or snapping at her heels.

'He suggests I should write poetry,' she wailed. 'Philip, I mean.'

'Not the thing at all,' Hannah exclaimed. She had never heard of Tennyson, but once bought a street market copy of verses by some silly old man called Martin Tupper. It was, she confided to her beloved husband, like having your breasts fondled when all you came in for was a tincture suitable for the bowels.

'You are a stern critic of contemporary poetry,' Charles Urmiston had said loyally, kissing those same breasts with timid ardour.

'He speaks of writing, when he speaks of it at all, as nothing more important than needlepoint. I do not want to spend the rest of my life describing the habits of a robin or the last rose of summer or some such. I do not wish to be admired by the local vicar as Philip Westland's clever little woman,' Bella sobbed.

'I should hope not,' Hannah agreed. 'Though it has to be said, you chosed him, my dear. There is that, at the end of the day.'

'And,' Dora Venn put in, 'though I risk my position by saying it, I shall say it nevertheless: he loves you as much as any man loved woman since time began.' And blushed for her impudence.

She was amazed when Bella jumped up and kissed her on her feathery cheeks. 'That is the truth of it! And I love him back. We could be as happy as cooing doves. But not out among the swedes and parsnips, talking to dull fellows and their wives about charity fetes and railway crossings.'

'Is that what they talk about in the countryside?' Dora Venn asked wonderingly.

'Hannah, you came originally from Uxbridge, I believe.'

'What the rich people talk about when they're at home will always remain a secret to me,' she laughed. 'It is true that when I was a girl it was all cornfields, my word it was, as far as the eye could see. But I wouldn't take Uxbridge to be a pointer to what you're on about.'

Bella left the house soon after, causing Hannah and Dora to reflect wonderingly on her ideas about life in the country. If it was as she described it, the greater part of England was no more inviting than Belgium on a rainy day, or Siberia without postmen.

'One thing's certain sure. She ain't going to leave London,' Dora said.

'Then it's all up between them,' Hannah replied. Which, she added privately, was about as likely as the Thames flowing backwards. She shrugged. 'O'course, if they catch that murdering devil he's so afeared of, that might make a difference.'

'Well, when it comes down to that, they've got everybody save the Archbishop of Canterbury out looking for him,' Dora Venn said doubtfully. 'What's the name of Percy Quigley's particular chum again?'

'Billy Murch.'

'He has a bit of a knack with this sort of thing.'

'Well, you can count him out,' Hannah Bardsoe said. 'He's hung his boots up. For the love of a good woman,' she added gloomily.

'Whatever next?' Dora wondered. 'And what woman is that?'

'His wife, Dora,' Hannah said, vexed, 'his wife.'

And don't I wish that spoiled child Mrs Westland could find a lesson in that, she thought, pulling herself up to fetch the rum to the table. There, I've said it.

Hough was blindfolded. Though the room he was in was dark as sin, the blindfold helped him think. And this he did, patiently and without too much fear, though there was a lump over his eye as big as a hen's egg. This was a time to ponder, weighing each fact. He knew that the two men who had lifted him from Magill's chophouse in Artillery Row, run him through the kitchens and bundled him into a waiting carriage, were now standing either side of the chair he sat in, easily recognisable by their smell. A third man had entered the room and was smoking a Russian cigarette of the cheapest kind. He guessed himself to be still in Pimlico and in what was probably a commercial warehouse of some kind. His hands were tied behind him and someone had removed his boots and socks. He yawned. 'Are we to sit here all day?' he asked in Russian.

'You will speak French,' a voice replied, after a pause. Hough smiled. His instinct was right: his captors were émigré Russians. Scribblers, dreamers, people of little account. Before the smile had faded he was knocked from his chair by a savage blow to the side of his head. Rough hands picked him up and dumped him back on to the chair. There was a trickle of blood gathering in the shell of his ear.

'We are not idle theorists, M. Hough,' the same gravelly voice explained, as if able to have read his thoughts. 'This is not the Café Kleist. You are here to receive a warning. We can make that as physical as you wish.'

'If you are not the parlour revolutionaries I take you to be, then let us talk like men. What have I done to upset you?'

'Better to ask what we want.'

'Very well,' Hough said after a slight pause. 'But I must warn you, I do not suffer fools gladly. For that reason I prefer to work alone.'

Gravel-voice chuckled. It was not an unpleasant sound but the sort of grandfatherly laughter that follows hearing a child say something unintentionally amusing.

'Let us understand each other . . . You work alone, as you put it, because you have a vanity as huge as Mont Blanc. In this room are men who are not so clever as you, I am sure. But neither are they complete idiots.'

'Who shall be the judge of that?' Hough mocked.

'We are at least realists. We took you out of Magill's chophouse ten minutes before the police arrived,' the voice said.

'Or so you say.'

'You can take it as true. Who sat at the table to the right, just inside the door?'

'A bald man and a woman, possibly his wife.'

'His name is Archer. A police informant.'

'He was there the whole time,' Hough said.

'And the woman you describe as his wife?'

Hough bit his lip. The couple had seemed as harmless as wallpaper. But now he remembered how she had risen from the table and sauntered out, carrying a bagful of shopping.

'Her name is Lizzie Barrass, a prostitute,' the Russian said.

'How did they know I would eat there?'

'They didn't. But every nark in London has been given an artist's sketch of you. Archer recognised you. It is the closest you have come to capture.'

'And you? How did you know where to find me?'

'We have been following you for three days.'

'Ekaterina,' Hough guessed.

'Yes. Coggins threw her out when your friend Garside was killed, in case she talked. We found her last Sunday at King's Cross.'

'I am grateful for your interest,' Hough said drily.

'I have told you, we want something from you. Or, better to say, we want something and you are it.'

'And what is it that you want, I wonder?'

'You will be our focusing glass,' the voice said.

There was a breath of air in the room as someone ran at Hough and punched him in the face with enormous force. The blow was intended to knock him out but failed. Half-conscious still, he was dragged out of the room by his heels and so down a short unlit corridor. Someone walking ahead unlocked a door. Hough's head bounced down two steps and he was flung into the dark.

ELEVEN

When Pennington arrived at Magill's, an hour and a half after the original incident, he found the confusion that is generated by policemen in uniform over-eager to look busy and on top of the situation. Helmets bobbed, officers darted in and out of the doorway, shouting orders and as quickly having them countermanded. Fifty or more bystanders had gathered. They were being pushed about and shouted at like cattle and in revenge had taken to throwing horse droppings and mud at the restaurant windows. Word had got out: some mass-murdering bloke had left Magill's customers in a sea of blood and guts and then bunked off out of it.

'What, he shot 'em?'

'Naval cutlass, matey.'

'He was a Jack Tar, then.'

'I could walk you around the corner and fit you up with a cutlass as easy as kiss my hand. He was Murdoch the newspaper seller, top of Vauxhall Bridge Road.'

'You don't say? But ain't he blind?'

'He only pretends to be blind, innit?'

Pennington was roundly booed as he alighted from his cab. To say he was in a foul mood was an understatement. His lunch with Bella sat in his stomach like a brick and he cursed himself for being a romantic fool. At the very moment he was finding her grey eyes so delightful, Hough had been a mile and a half away thinking of something else entirely. And God knew what.

He ordered the entire premises sealed off and the crowd in front of it dispersed. One by one, those who had been trapped inside by the police were taken upstairs for questioning. Some were sanguine, some bewildered. The calmest of all was the informer Archer.

'You would not be here if I had not acted prompt,' he said comfortably. 'If there is a reward going, I reckon I ought to have it.'

He was a small-time dealer in stolen property, over-weight, dishevelled and with nearly a pint of wine inside him. And that, he seemed to say in every gesture, every glance, was his business and nobody else's.

'Who were the two men who took Hough out of the restaurant?'

'Who indeed? A mystery. I thought they were your boys, until told otherwise.'

'Names.'

'I got no idea,' Archer smirked. 'I done my duty and that was that. What more can a man do?'

'Did he put up a fight?'

'Wouldn't have been no point.'

'Was he armed?'

'Not his style. You're wasting your time, Mr Pennington, sir. For the likes of Houghie, it was just another day at the office. You had him, almost. But he's too good for you. It was a surprise, seeing him lifted like that; but for him, not the end of the world. Never a more cleverer villain in all London.'

'He was abducted by some criminal gang?'

'It would seem so.'

'And you've no idea who?'

Archer twittered his fingers in front of his face, as if to indicate information flying through the air, all of it useful but much that resembled the fall of snowflakes. 'Am I my brother's keeper?' he asked, obscurely.

'Take him down to the station and book him,' Pennington said to the sergeant in the room.

'On what charge?' the man asked, bewildered.

'Go round to where he lives and turn it over, top to bottom. Find me enough charges to have him drawn and quartered by six tonight, understand?'

'Drawn and quartered, is it?' Archer scoffed. 'Dearie me.'

'And mind how he falls down those stairs on his way out.'

There was a satisfying series of bumps and yelps as Archer tumbled head over heels to the ground floor.

'Bloody Cossacks!' he yelled.

'Hard to say why, but he don't like you,' an elderly constable explained, standing on his hand with a size eleven boot.

Pennington had bigger things to think about. There was no evidence to support his theory, but he was working on the idea that Hough was lodging locally. Magill, who was a Liverpool Irishman, was one of those dependable witnesses the police dream about – an honest man with a clear mind. He explained how he had never seen Hough before in his life and supposed him to be a shopper at the Army and Navy Stores, looking for a cheap lunch. Which left the two men who had hustled him through the kitchens.

'Working men?' Magill suggested tentatively.

'You mean common labourers? We don't serve trench-diggers or those with cement dust on their boots. But we're not a grand sort of a place neither. If you like mutton stew or a bit of braised beef – the simple stuff to blow out your kite and all like that – d'you follow me now? – then this is the place for you.'

'You have your regulars, I suppose?'

'The publicans round about have always put business our way,' Magill explained. 'And then there's them that live local, so there is. Traders, a few clerks, a few old fellas and their biddies. All like that. But these two, the two that you're talking about, I never saw before in me life.'

'Foreigners perhaps?' Pennington suggested with a flash of intuition.

Magill smiled his congratulations. 'Jaws on them like Paddy's donkey,' he confirmed. 'Big lads. The big hands and feet, you know.'

'Is that what makes a foreigner?'

'Well, somebody loves them, I don't doubt. But not in this sceptred isle, I wouldn't have thought. About as English-looking as Jumbo the Elephant.'

'Russians? Frenchmen?'

'Aren't the French the world's waiters? I have never seen a tall one. These were sizable brutes.'

'Russians, then.'

'Only if you want to make 'em so. But big enough.'

'Let's go on. They come out through your kitchens and there's a carriage waiting. What sort of a carriage?'

'And did I get more than a glimpse of it, the arse end of it as it rattled off?' Magill thought for a moment, pulling at his nose. 'Four wheels. Box built.'

'A delivery van?'

'That sort of thing. But painted up with nobody's livery. Not a slogan on it. Had been black, once.'

'Windows?'

'Never a one. Doors at the back – and now here's the thing, though! – one door has the planking in a chevron style and the other up and down, like it's a replacement. Is that a help at all?'

'Are we talking about a milk cart?'

'That size? I should think not. Maybe a furniture van. But don't they have the writing down the side?'

'A four-wheel van with doors that don't match?'

'And isn't the luck coming your way at last?' Magill suggested.

As a child, Pennington had gone to sleep the night before a holiday, praying that nothing would happen to change the trip to the station, the dizzying wonder of the journey to Margate, the march behind his parents to Mrs Lack's boarding house. Something so dearly wished for might still, in some malign stroke of bad luck, be snatched from him. He felt the same dread now. He gave the order to release the other witnesses and send away the uniformed officers. On two paper napkins, he wrote down the names of fifteen men and a cover note to the Assistant Commissioner and sent his sergeant to Scotland Yard to convene a meeting at the restaurant in three hours' time.

Arms were to be issued. Then, his palms tingling, he walked down to the river and back as far as Victoria, trying to think through what he should do next. Caution was the thing – caution and planning. Other than that; Magill might be right. Maybe luck was coming his way at last.

At seven that night, Hough was brought out of his room. His wrists were untied and he was given back his boots. Bloody scrapes indicated how he had shucked off his blindfold by rubbing his head against a rough plastered wall. But no signs of panic, no fear in his eyes. No blinking at the light and not a word spoken, but a straight back, a condescending half-smile on his lips. He could afford to ignore the thug pushing him in the back. The real battle was yet to begin. And, being Hough, he looked forward to it.

He was led along a narrow corridor and shown into an old-fashioned office, piled with papers and cardboard boxes along the skirting. Above his head was a clerestory roof, the glass green with age, in places slashed diagonally with what seemed like brutal pen-strokes. These were the panes where the glass had cracked and moss had found a place to live and die. Once, bored clerks had gazed up into this roof and conjured fields and drystone walls from the ruined glass, perhaps seas and jetties.

'If he makes trouble, put him back to sleep,' his host commanded.

'There will be no trouble,' Hough said. 'I don't have any particular wish to stay a moment longer than necessary, but you clearly have something you want to discuss.

I suggest we speak in English and that you begin by telling me your name.'

'Nemerov,' the man said after a pause. Hough nodded. 'I know that name,' he allowed in his most languid voice.

'You are of course all-seeing, all-knowing.'

'You are too hard on yourself, comrade. At the Kleist in Geneva, you were always spoken of with respect. Of course, that may have had to do with the quality of your firebrand journalism, or it may have been jealous admiration for a man who has Manchester Square for an address. Scratch an intellectual, find a snob.'

'Does this look like Manchester Square to you?'

'It looks like what it smells like, a wholesale warehouse for rugs and carpets. Not very far from the restaurant in which you found me. We are still in Pimlico, I think.'

'You are a very clever man, Hough.'

'You say that only because most revolutionaries are ineradicably stupid. That's what brought me to your notice. I am not, of course, of a revolutionary disposition.'

'You think not?'

'The only way to make pigs fly is to blow up the pens in which they are kept.'

'Isn't that it, though? Isn't that the point?'

Hough yawned. And then smiled at Nemerov, with the sort of indulgence that some younger men extend to their elders. 'Is that why we are here? To talk about blowing up pigs? I mean, for a worthy cause? I have never yet found a cause that is worth crossing the road for. I am about something else.'

'And what is that?'

'Scratching an itch.'

'Then I pity you – with all my heart.'

Hough studied the Russian the way a chess player might consider his opponent. Nemerov smoked the foulest tobacco but his clothes – and his English – were impeccable. He wore a black suit, set off by a blue and black waistcoat, and his silver hair and beard were beautiful to look upon. His stock was held in place by a pearl pin.

'I grant you your noble heart,' Hough said, measuring the desk that separated the two men.

'Do I need your compliments?'

'I believe you do. Yet I would not wish to be Vassili Borisovich Nemerov tonight for all the gold in Russia.'

'Don't fool with me, Hough.'

They had resumed speaking in Russian, something that had happened almost accidentally but which Hough immediately exploited, for the sake of the thug who stood behind his chair.

'It is not easy, having a noble heart. You have probably fallen asleep many a night pondering the fate of that great anarchist, Oullebec.'

'His name is not to be spoken by such a man as you.'

'Why do you say that?'

'He was a hero.'

'I was in Paris the day the pitiable fool kissed his wife and children goodbye and set off on foot to the Elysée. His intention was to blow himself up along with the President of France.'

'How do you know this?'

'I lodged with him. He was a sincere admirer of your revolutionary pamphlets, by the way. And a bit of a scribbler himself.'

'Wasn't what he planned the act of a very brave man?'

'It was foolish. In fact, stupid.'

'I too knew Oullebec,' Nemerov warned.

'Then you know he gave his life for nothing.'

'Is it any less stupid to blow things up just for the pleasure of it? Just to scratch an itch?'

Hough shrugged. He folded his hands into his lap and lowered his eyes, perfectly equable.

Nemerov skidded a packet of cigarettes across the table they sat at. 'I hold your life in my hand,' he warned. 'You are the most wanted man in London. I can tie you up again right now and leave you outside any police station – come to that, anywhere public. Victoria Station, for example. Do you want that?'

'You are asking the wrong question. Is that what *you* want? They find me, charge me, I go to trial and they hang me. Do you really think I won't have a moment in all that time when I take the opportunity to say to the judge that I was betrayed by the great revolutionary socialist Nemerov? A bookish amateur from Manchester Square and a coward into the bargain? You think that mud won't stick, from here to Moscow? I should say it will finish you.'

'Then maybe you should never get arrested and never go to trial.'

'You mean, *you* will kill me?'

'Why not?'

'Just as you wish.'

'You are in earnest?'

'I am not pleading for my life now, but I know the character of those who are hunting me. There is a man

– 916 –

called Pennington, a detective with a little more intelligence than most. I would be surprised if he hasn't already found this place and had it surrounded. Killing me would have the same consequences as before. The heroic martyr Hough goes to Nemerov for sanctuary and is murdered instead.'

'The police will find nothing here but a legitimate carpet business.'

'How sure can you be of that?'

'The Nemerov Circle has eluded them before.'

'You believe that?' Hough laughed incredulously.

'You don't think we can protect ourselves from the powers of the state?'

'Only with their connivance. Oullebec was a dreamer like you, a harmless blond dolt of a man who came from a farm near Dinard. He put his wife out on the streets to get enough money for tobacco and absinthe. There are tens of thousands like him in Paris, lost in the fog, unable to think but desperate to be heard.'

'I have told you, he was a friend.'

'What a fool you are, Nemerov. How do I know you live in Manchester Square? Because that poor devil sent you an article and you published it. He spoke about it every day. Up until then he had contented himself with daubing slogans on walls in the dead of night. But now he had a friend in London, someone who commended his scribblings.'

'We sent him money.'

'He told me about that, too. What impressed him most was that the money you sent him did not come through the post but was passed to him clandestinely, across the crusts and wine stains of some hellhole café table. That was cruel but clever of you, Nemerov.'

'It was a necessary precaution.'

'Do you really think so? You bought Oullebec with that simple little deception. Nothing so exciting had ever happened to him. Such a conspiratorial gesture demanded an appropriate response. He was ashamed to have spent some of the money on a bit of sausage and the like. But then he took it into his head to blow someone up. He wasn't any longer a nobody but part of a vast international conspiracy. It came to him that he should blow up the President of France. After all, what could be simpler?'

'You speak very bitterly, my friend.'

'Do you know what was most remarkable about Oullebec's death? He was shot at a range of one hundred and fifty yards, by a single police sniper firing from the rooftops. No challenge was ever given. He was just a slow-witted man walking along with a carpet bag of explosive, still more than a mile from the Elysée Palace, who suddenly fell over with a hole in his forehead.'

'And yet, according to newspaper reports –'

'Yes, indeed,' Hough laughed. 'You got your money's worth. According to newspaper reports, he was shot at the very gates of the Elysée just as the President was leaving. A policeman was given a medal for wrestling him to the ground and extinguishing the fuse to his bomb, etc, etc. Wonderful! The French have always known how to stage comic opera!'

'There were twenty-seven witness statements.'

'For fifty francs I could find a platoon of witnesses to declare on oath that I was the Archangel Gabriel.'

'All this nonsense about a police sniper,' Nemerov blustered.

'You mean, how did he happen to be there? Because your friend Oullebec went back again and again to the Café Rostand hoping to meet the other revolutionaries he supposed that drank there.'

'It is a well-known meeting place.'

'I have the advantage of you. Unlike you, I have actually been there. It is a miserable thieves' kitchen – stuffed with informers. Oullebec talked too much. Only a little of your money had gone to his head. One night he said the wrong thing to the wrong person and, in that moment, he was already a dead man. I am going to make a guess, Nemerov. You too have a plan to blow up something of consequence. Windsor Castle or the Palace of Westminster or something of the sort. You don't know how to do it yourself but you think I can be persuaded to do it for you. You think you have found another Oullebec.'

'As I said, I have found the most dangerous man in London.'

'That may be so.'

'Whose vanity is almost superhuman.'

Hough laughed. 'Is that what you're counting on? And is that how I am to be paid? By the posthumous respect given to me by fools and idiots in prison cells all over Europe?'

'A hundred pounds in gold.'

'I am not a mercenary, Nemerov.'

'But you have a purpose.'

'Again I must disappoint you.'

'Then what is it that you want?'

'Suppose I helped you in some way. Boom! After which will come that glorious dawn when all men shall be equal. Is that it?'

'You will have reshaped human history.'

'Shortly after which, we shall discover that not all men wish to be equal – among them, most particularly, those with houses in Manchester Square, for example.'

'You are a hateful cynic! A leprous sore on society!'

'Yes,' Hough agreed. 'Better a simpleton like Oullebec to do your dirty work for you. But enough of this nonsense. I will show you how this ends.'

At which he leapt from his chair and vaulted the oak table at which Nemerov sat. The bodyguard drew a revolver and fired, but the bullet missed its mark. By that time, however, Hough had used the pencil he had been toying with to stab the Russian in the neck with a surgeon's precision. Blood flowed over them both like a fountain over its statues. The bodyguard's second shot ploughed Hough's forearm and ricocheted upwards. He fell back, seemingly in agony.

But, for all his bravado, he had expected to be killed and was astonished still to be alive. The bodyguard was clambering over the table to get at him. Hough rose from floorboards slippery with blood and using the edge of his hand first broke the man's nose and then his neck, the way that rabbits are killed. And this is why I do it, he thought exultantly, not because I must but because I can.

Outside the building, he could hear axes battering the gates to the delivery yard and the shrill of police whistles. He laughed, wiping Nemerov's life's blood from his face.

Of course, if there was an armed policeman posted on the roof, he was already a dead man.

But there was not. He sat against the stack of a chimney, his heart pounding, while the evening stars burst over him. There was even a crescent moon, as wet and yellow as a slice of mango. He tore the sleeve from his shirt and bound his forearm as tightly as he could. There was only one other man in London who possessed his preternatural calm – the one they called Murch, the man who had once followed him for three days. But Murch, he judged, was not all that interested. Only three people had ever seen Millie Murch naked: her first husband, Murch himself and Hough, from the vantage point of the gardens at Chiswick. Naked, and holding a naked child, looking out on the sunrise, completely unaware of how close she was to disaster. Hough had been completely unmoved by her nudity but had seen what he had come to see. Murch was a spent rocket.

He put on his jacket and flexed his hand experimentally. It worked, after a fashion. He walked to the edge of the building and studied the gap between it and the next property. It occurred to him how mild the night was, how welcoming. When he jumped, he was smiling.

In Orange Street next day, an event took place about as shocking to Mrs Venn as the Queen announcing her abdication: Bella failed to join her husband for breakfast. All the more shocking for it being such a lovely day, with sun pouring into the house like waterfalls, if you could imagine such a thing. But the missus was stubbornly insisting on a tray in her bedroom and only coming downstairs to go out – which was to say, sweep out – wearing her green velour cape and little fur pillbox hat, leaving Mr Westland to castle his fingers and look daggers at the carpet. And the two of them hardly married at all, Dora Venn thought wonderingly. Yes, barely wed. Then three hours later the front door goes bang and now he's off out too, leaving her with a lemon sole that she cooked and ate herself, for – as she said to the saucepans showing their copper bottoms – if they was going to play the goat then it was no skin off her nose, etc. (but feeling mightily guilty about it all the same).

Bella was not the first woman in history to sweep out of the house and then find she had nowhere particular to go. Shopping was one answer. She bought a wholly inappropriate tea gown, a dozen dinner plates and some Turkish slippers before common sense took over; or perhaps it was better to say she ran aground at Blumgarten's in Carnaby Street. Sitting at the very back of the restaurant, she ordered pork chops and Belgian beer, dropping hot tears on to the tablecloth.

There was a commotion in the street. First three, and then another two policeman ran past the restaurant windows. Like every other customer, Bella stood, willing the chase to be for Hough, the hated Hough who had caused her so much anguish. But the man the constables dragged back past the windows by his heels was not the most dangerous man in London but a sorry-looking nobody who had tried and failed to hold up a jeweller's in Regent Street.

Bella's Belgian beer winked sardonically in its glass. The one shortcoming she had never permitted herself in an adult life of small calamities was self-pity. But now she felt overwhelmed by the gloomiest kind of introspection, the one that leaves a sufferer not knowing whether to stay put or jump up, fight or submit. She could follow her morning's purchases home to Orange Street and there give way to tears. Perhaps better to make a defiant gesture by opening Westland's most expensive wine at quite the wrong time of the afternoon. She had never been drunk in her life, but wondered what it would feel like. She grimaced. It was as though the infernal Hough had broken into her life and burgled her self-possession.

An idea occurred to her, so absurd, so whimsical, that when she left the restaurant, she found herself almost running, pushing her way through astonished Londoners like a madwoman.

TWELVE

And, after all, what *was* London? An anthill? The overrun ruins of a walled city or the guts and lungs of the greatest empire the world had ever seen? Was it to be described by its restless excavations and improvements – new bridges, new sewers, new railway termini, taller buildings, a hundred new statues of the great and the good? Or by the faceless poverty that lay alongside these things? Was it a passport to the future or an indictment of the very idea of human progress?

Bella had plenty of time to ponder these questions as she made the awkward and exhausting journey that led from Carnaby Street to Battersea. Seldom can a sudden whim have caused more discomfort. Whatever else it was, London was dirty. Crossing the river, the Thames ran sluggish and brown. The skies had grown overcast since morning and while they could not be blamed for the gloom that seemed to have settled south of the river, they did not diminish it. There was very little of colour anywhere: it seemed that all the brown paint in London had been applied to shop fronts, factory gates, the doors of private homes. There was business enough – the streets churned with people – but such people as were seldom seen in Bella's neighbourhood.

She had gone there to visit her parents' graves. They lay together under the walls of the church, next to a standing headstone that marked the last resting place of Bella's grandparents. This ground had once seemed magical to her – she could remember laying meadow flowers on Granpa and Grammer's plot, moved by a childlike religious awe. When her parents followed, she was a young woman and a more doubtful believer. Her mother was the last to go, attended by only nine mourners.

Their resting place was characteristically modest but in the last twenty years had come to be overlooked by a small invasion of marble angels. The churchyard had once been protected by nothing grander than a low stone wall, separating it from the world outside. In those days the road had been mud and gravel. Beyond there had been empty fields and in the distance the fences and hedges of market gardens. She remembered – or thought she remembered – cowbarns and livery stables. It was here that Bella had heard her first skylark. All that had gone now. In place of the wall was a palisade of iron railings. In place of the rustic view, raw brick terraces and a public house called the Salute. In the churchyard, the nearest angel to Bella's parents had her plump arm snapped off above the elbow. It was the one that was formerly elevated, indicating by a pointing finger the way to salvation.

'You are paying your respects to the honoured dead,' a voice said at Bella's back. The speaker was a labouring type, wearing a torn tweed jacket and twill trousers. He was thin and dangerously pale, his skin almost parchment white. 'Is this your parents' grave?' he asked, leaning over her shoulder to read the inscription.

Bella had been kneeling. Now she stood. 'I would be grateful if you leave me be,' she said, as calmly as she could muster.

'There's a new church building up the hill. Roomier. A nicer class of people. Born here, were you?'

'Over there,' Bella said, pointing across the road.

'I don't think so. No, I certainly don't think so.'

'Are you here to rob me?'

'You have put the idea in my head,' the man admitted.

'Let me explain something. This is a very bad day for me. If you attack me, I shall fight back. You can have a shilling for something to drink but you must stand further off. Anything else and I will kick up such a hullaballoo that will end with you on the treadmills and good riddance to you.'

'Fighting words,' the man said.

'Yes,' Bella said. 'Exactly that.'

Something in her eyes made the man stand back. Bella opened her purse and flung a handful of coppers on to the gravel path before walking away on shaking legs to the road. When she looked back, the man was standing exactly as she had left him, his head sunk on to his chest, his hands hanging by his side. He was as much like a wraith as anything else, as insubstantial as smoke. It was, she thought, as though they had dreamed each other.

'And what does that mean, exactly?' Philip asked.

'Nothing, I dare say.'

They had fallen into a civil but distant way of talking to each other that was far more painful than argument. Dinner was at an end and they sat in lamplight on separate couches.

'I don't exactly know what it means. I was a fool to go there and it had a bad outcome.'

'You were there to find solace,' Philip suggested gently.

'To prove something to myself – that London is not always as black as it is painted. How wrong I was.'

'Bella,' Philip said, reaching for her hand, 'it never was my intention to turn you against London. But I think we have led a charmed life here. The man that wanted to rob you in the graveyard this afternoon might as easily have abused or killed you. You were right to offer him a feisty response but it might have gone very wrong.'

'And that wouldn't happen in the country?'

'In the graveyard of a parish church, in broad daylight? I think not. And if that makes the country a dull place to live, then there is nothing more to be said.'

'You think I went there for adventure?' she cried sharply.

'I have told you why I think you went there.'

The case clock sounded the hour: Bella looked up and was amazed that it was only eight o'clock. She had already forgotten what they had just eaten for dinner: when she looked down, she saw that her hands were clenched white. The world was falling down about her ears. Philip watched her with tears gathering on his eyelids.

'Where have you been today?' she asked in a trembling voice.

'To Rye, in Kent.'

'And is it good down there?'

'It has its virtues. A very good ironmongers, a church with a tower, cattle over the lea – that sort of thing.'

'What were you doing in an ironmonger's?'

'I have no idea,' he said miserably.

'You think I am an ungrateful woman,' she said.

'I think you the most wonderful thing that ever happened to me.'

'Please,' she sobbed.

He relinquished her hand and shortly after left the room. Mrs Venn, who had taken to listening at doors, tiptoed away. We are at a crossroads here, she thought. Things are blacker than they have ever been. And what kind of a dry old stick am I not to think of a way of making all better? This is where you need a man to talk things over with, she added, letting the unintended irony float away like a leaf on water.

In Norfolk the morning sky had the look of a vast and empty room, sunless but lit by a pearly light that had no obvious origin. It was the vault of heaven, if you wanted to look at it that way. Or perhaps the sky was simply reflecting back a terrible emptiness, of flat fields and deserted roads, mirror lakes and silver rivers. Hough was on foot, his boots kicking up dust and chaff, the only person on the road for miles around. His injured arm throbbed and his guts churned for want of something to eat. But even though there was no one to witness it, he made a point of striding out – marching, almost. His mind was comfortably empty. After more than an hour, he turned in at some ruined gates and walked down an avenue of rhododendrons, smiling briefly as the house came into view.

'I am astonished to see you again,' Lady Garside exclaimed, with the directness that had flattened many another uninvited guest.

'I have astonished myself,' he murmured. 'Faith has led me into many dangers, here and elsewhere in the world. It has beggared my purse and threatened my very life more than once. But I take Christian witness to be the essence of true humanity, as I know you do too, dear lady. It was one of the happier days of my life when we met.'

Lady Garside shrugged doubtfully. She had not asked Hough to sit, partly out of respect for the faded brocades of her couches, partly out of exasperation at having an eventless day given unexpected form, as when a flight of duck disturbs a lake or pond. She felt sulky, a thing she showed by pushing out her lower lip. What she wanted most was to blink her eyes and have her visitor disappear. This would have been the same if her peace had been disturbed by anyone at eleven o'clock in the morning, even the Bishop of Norwich. But Hough, looking as though he had been dragged through every hedge in the county, was especially unwelcome.

'Will you give some account of your present pitiable condition?'

'The immediate cause is a severe drubbing by the thugs and bully boys of Whitechapel.'

'What have you been up to, Mr Hough?' Lady Garside asked. The unfeeling tone would have terrified anyone else. In Hough it produced a soup smile.

'You probably know, the mission your son so nobly started has been destroyed by fire.'

'I did not know,' Daisy Garside said.

'I did my best to save it, but it will always be a brave man who speaks up for Jesus in Whitechapel. I am ashamed to come before you as I am.'

'There have been fisticuffs?' She had this image of men fighting outside a public house, something she had never witnessed but had heard spoken of.

'Bless you for putting it so simply,' he said, with a catch in his throat.

But he did indeed look utterly pulled down. His one suit was now a ruin and his face was drawn and pale. Silent tears began to run down his cheeks.

'You poor fellow,' Lady Garside said, tugging at a bellrope. 'I shall send you to the kitchens and you must tell Burling to look you out some clean clothes. The servants have their own bath, I imagine. Ask Burling about that.'

Hough wrong-footed her by falling to the carpet and praying, which was how Burling found him, with her ladyship at the window looking more than a bit aghast. And so she should, the butler reasoned grimly. Some dirty old tramp with wild hair and the stink of sleeping rough on him, bothering God with his blatherings on the morning room carpet. It was a great surprise to him that Lady Garside had agreed to receive the scoundrel. Burling was a Norfolk man who had joined the house as an under-footman and had risen to his present eminence by his own form of Christian forbearance, which was to take Lady Garside's wishes as inalterable. He glanced at his employer, who made a brisk gesture of dismissal in Hough's direction.

'Take Mr Hough to the kitchens and see that he is cared for. And have someone come in here and open the French windows.'

'Let me at least do that,' Hough cried piteously.

'Leave them be,' she said sharply. 'They can only be opened a certain way. See to him, Burling.'

'Very well, your ladyship. If the gentleman would accompany me?'

'Praise God this is a Christian household,' Hough declared, extending his hand to be pulled up from the carpet. Burling did not oblige. Like his mistress, he favoured austere manners. Hough scrambled on his hands and knees and dragged himself upright by the arm of a sofa. 'I have fallen among believers,' he cried.

'Indeed,' Lady Garside muttered, looking out across her lawns and thinking what a pestilential nuisance belief could be if it were not strictly limited to church-going on Sunday. As for her butler, he had already decided that what he had here was an awkward customer who needed close watching. This impression was reinforced as they made their way down a long corridor towards the kitchen. All of the stranger's wailing and gnashing of teeth had disappeared like snow in April.

'Bacon and egg the first item of business,' Hough declared briskly. 'And then a pot of strong tea.'

'Do you say so?'

'And then we'll talk.'

'I will consult with Cook,' Burling said stiffly.

'We must not get off on the wrong foot, Mr Burling. Does this corridor go on until it reaches the sea?'

'We call this the long gallery. May I ask what brings you to visit us in Norfolk, sir?'

'I was a particular friend and helpmeet of Lady Garside's son.'

And that explains all, Burling thought. Mr Sefton was about as much use as a chocolate teapot, in his opinion – a pipsqueak, as her ladyship was wont to call those of the young she did not like, among them her own child.

They clattered down the kitchen steps and the stranger astonished Burling by kissing Cookie's hand and then calling for his pot of tea straight away. He threw himself into the chair at the head of the table, which any real gentleman might realise was Burling's own place of honour, and confounded this impudence by lifting one cheek of his buttocks and breaking wind luxuriously. The cook, who came from Renfrewshire, did all but faint clean away.

'A stiff walk from the station,' Hough explained.

'You have *walked* from Dereham?' the butler asked, astonished.

'A very dreary countryside, Burling.' The more so if you arrived at Dereham by the last train and spent the night in a coppice, covered in beech leaves.

'And your luggage?'

'Will follow on,' Hough said calmly. 'You would not expect a fellow to carry his own suitcases? I noticed rabbits on her ladyship's lawns,' he said. 'Are there guns in the house?'

'The gardener looks after that sort of thing,' Burling answered.

'Well, the fellow is falling down on the job. It is a rabbit paradise out there.'

'Nevertheless.'

'Mr Gully has arthritis something terrible,' a scullery maid put in. 'And is knocking eighty. I doubt he has been out of bed this last week.'

'Did anyone ask you to speak, Dollie?' Burling asked.

Hough caught the girl's eye and smiled. She ducked her chin into her chest and smiled back. Dollie was fifteen, short, and a bit heavy in the beam. But what distinguished her more was a mass of red hair, a large mouth and an overly frank expression. She was punching Hough's ticket, as they were fond of saying in Whitechapel.

'Look me out a gun, Burling, and a dozen or so of cartridges. We'll put the devils to flight at dusk this evening.'

'For that I must have Lady Garside's permission. I should add, she has never once mentioned them to me as a particular problem.'

'Then she won't notice they have gone. Now, Dollie, ask Cook if you may boil up some water for my bath.'

'And what bath is that, sir?'

'Why, the one you use.'

Dollie, who had last had a bath on Christmas Eve, giggled.

The Home Secretary made Pennington wait a full half-hour, and when he summoned him he explained with great terseness that he was shortly to go to the Commons for a Division. He was agitated enough to smoke, a thing he had promised his wife he would never do in the office and certainly not in front of juniors. He thought longingly of the conservatory at his house in Dulwich, where he *was* permitted to smoke. To smoke, he thought and, if he wished, to run amok. Yes, to shuck off the cares of public office and behave disgracefully for the rest of his life – never wear a frockcoat again, never have to endure another Cabinet meeting. Instead he would grow orchids or, less ambitiously, peaches.

'The thing of it is, Pennington, you had the fellow and you let him go.'

Pennington winced. This was a grotesque misreading of his report, which described an armed assault on the carpet warehouse in Pimlico, the discovery of two dead bodies still warm to the touch, and then a painstaking search of the premises for Hough – and, more to the point, explosive charges. But the Home Secretary took his silence for guilt.

'Furthermore, the paper you sent me was what is called, I believe, typewriter-written. What damn nonsense is this? The Commissioner is good enough to submit reports in his own autograph and so it has been in this office for the whole of this century.'

'I apologise for any inconvenience caused,' Pennington muttered.

'Are you trying to show me impertinence, sir?' the Home Secretary demanded, flushed. 'It is not a matter of convenience. I am astonished at you, Pennington. I will have things done according to custom and precedence, do you understand me?'

'I shall, of course, resubmit the report in manuscript form.'

'And for the rest?'

'Sir?'

'Am I to tell the Prime Minister that we botched the job and this damn fellow is still at large?'

'He is still at large, though wounded and on the run.'

'You say he is wounded?'

'We found blood on the roof tiles that could only have come from him.'

'What in God's name was he doing up there?'

'We believe he made his escape by jumping on to the rooftops of adjacent premises.'

'Nothing wrong with his legs, then. Very helpful for a fellow on the run, what? The whole point is, where is he now?'

Pennington stared at the Home Secretary enough to make him flush again. He retreated to his desk, thought of sitting down, but changed his mind. Instead he took out his watch and studied it, biting his lip in exasperation. He laid down his cigar in the tray reserved for pens and paperclips. 'That was a very foolish thing to say,' he muttered with his trademark honesty. 'You must forgive me.'

'Home Secretary, everything that can possibly be done has been done. I think even Hough must realise that the days before he is caught are numbered. Of the two men he killed at the warehouse, one of them was a man called Nemerov. Today's *Times* describes this man simply as an expatriate Russian. In socialist and revolutionary circles he is considered rather more than that. As well as ourselves, the hunt is on from a great many outraged radicals of all persuasions – I would go so far as to say, a small army of them.'

'You exaggerate, surely?'

'As to their number? I think not.'

'These chaps are swarming all over London, you say?'

'There is great interest in the case. I think we might say Nemerov's murder has recruited some useful supernumeraries. I was trying to indicate the value to the police of their undoubted indignation.'

'Excitable sort of fellows, are they? Sabres and cavalry pistols?' The Home Secretary smiled at Pennington. Its melting quality was probably his most endearing foible, a smile that was grudgingly given but remembered by all on whom it was bestowed.

'Give me something I can tell the Prime Minister.'

'We are conducting the biggest police search ever mounted in London. Every constabulary in Britain has been alerted. The railway stations in a dozen cities are being watched, as are the ports. Every hotel, every boarding house in the metropolitan area, has been circulated with an artist's sketch of Hough. Perhaps the Prime Minister will understand that we cannot simply produce him like a rabbit out of a hat.'

'Though that would be quite excellent.'

Four brace of rabbits lay on the kitchen table. Burling, if he were honest, had enjoyed himself out on the lawns. It was not late – no more than ten at night – but the household had gone to bed. Hough was wearing new clothes, selected from Sefton Garside's wardrobe, which was one way of describing four tea chests stacked in a dank cellar room. He had a bed for the night – a room given to the more senior servants of guests in the days when the Hall had weekend house parties.

'While his lordship lived, we gave and received hospitality,' the butler explained. 'We have had the Duke of Cambridge here and many other notables. Thirty servants and enough candles burning to light up the lawn as far as the ornamental fountains. The full silver service once a week, visitors or not. A military band to play on the anniversary of Minden. And horses – my word, plenty of good horses.'

'Hard to imagine those times now,' Hough said.

'Indeed.'

'How did his lordship die?'

'Drowned at sea.'

Burling was drunk. Brandy had altered his impressions of the mysterious Mr Hough, who had been transformed into something the butler could recognise, a gentleman with severe money problems. In his fuddled way he was thinking of bookmakers and foreign casinos, young girls and diamond necklaces.

'How old was Sefton when his father died?'

'No more than two. Did you know of him in the Coldstreams, sir?'

'Is there a military tradition in the family?'

'His lordship was on Lord Raglan's staff in his day. You may have noticed a portrait –'

'In the long gallery, yes. Along with any number of bad paintings. Do you understand the notion of spying, Burling?'

'Do I ever!'

'Do you grasp the idea of state secrets?'

Burling nodded. But he was thinking of his own history of spying on his employer. He had been stealing from the household for the last fifteen years. His masterstroke had been the theft of the second key to the safe. Inside was hidden some of the more portable items he had lifted from her ladyship over the years – jewellery, silver boxes, not one but three gold watches. To which only he now had access. Yes.

'You are a spy of some sort?' he asked drunkenly.

'More than I am an evangelist. You wouldn't want me to say more, I know.'

'You are here on official business?' the butler whispered.

'Does it really seem so incredible? It is you and I that have the business, Burling,' Hough said gently. 'Though you have not said a word to implicate yourself, I know you to be a thieving rogue.'

'You are in the wrong of it, Mr Hough! How can you say such a wicked thing?'

'I know people,' Hough said. 'I know how they think.' And when that fails, I know how to wheedle the truth out of little trollops like Dollie, the kitchen maid. A girl in whom low cunning and stupidity lay like two spoons nestling in the same drawer.

'I resent and repudiate your remarks, sir.'

'Don't be an arse, Burling. I am not here on holiday.'

'I hope I have given nothing but good service to her ladyship,' Burling blustered. 'I have served here since I was fourteen years old.'

Hough pulled Burling's glass towards him and poured another two inches of brandy. 'But now, in the pomp of your years, I see all the makings of a tragic case. Tell me about the thefts you have committed.'

'I shall deny everything,' Burling spluttered.

'A guinea for every time I have heard that,' Hough said gravely.

'Are we talking about the safe? Her ladyship knows how certain items have been removed to there.'

'I doubt she even remembers she's got a safe. You are a fool, Burling. For as long as she had a key you might have talked your way out of it, had you been discovered. But she hasn't got a key any longer, has she? You took that too. That was bad thinking.'

Burling struggled to understand the turn the conversation had taken. He realised he was almost too drunk to focus his eyes. 'What do you want with me?' he asked, wiping his mouth with the back of his wrist.

'I'd like to keep you out of prison, if possible. Lady Garside has an unforgiving side to her, wouldn't you say?'

'She need never know. I'll put it all back, I swear.'

'That might work. But there's another problem. I think her ladyship is generally a bit slow on the uptake, but finding her butler has been having his way nightly with little Dollie, who as you know talks too much, would constitute another sacking offence. And then, of course, all the rest would come out as a consequence. Things of a more criminal nature.'

'What has this got to do with state secrets?' the butler asked with the last of his common sense.

'Work with me, Burling, and the day can still be saved.'

'What must I do?'

'Better I have the remaining key to the safe in my possession.'

'First thing tomorrow,' the butler promised.

'Go and get it now, there's a good chap.'

Earlier, before they started drinking, the two of them had cleaned the shotgun. While he waited for Burling's return, Hough broke the breech and looked at the lamp through the oily barrel. He was thinking of Pennington in his calm and unhurried way. Perhaps he was searching for the superintendent down a telescope, or perhaps waiting for him to appear at the end of a tunnel. He yawned and drank off what was left in the butler's glass.

And, he thought, this is the way the world ends. He had an absolute conviction that death was waiting for him, much sooner than later. This certainty he faced with stoic indifference. There would be no last-minute escape, no dash to the Continent or slow boat to West Africa or the Indies. The whole story of Anton Hough lay not in what might be but in what had been. One day soon, his name would pass from decorating the covers of a police file or newspaper headlines to a folk memory, in time to the great forgetting that covers any human life like soil, or turf. By sea, like rolling waves.

When Burling came back with the key to the safe, Hough stuffed it in his pocket without a glance. Holding on to the kitchen range so as not to fall down dead drunk, the butler tried to interpret this negligence as promising the way to his own future safety.

'Tomorrow, after the post has arrived, you will go to her ladyship and ask to borrow the pony and trap. You will tell her your mother is ill, and you urgently need to visit her before she dies.'

'She has been in her grave these twelve years,' Burling objected pitifully.

'She will ask you where I am, and you will tell her that I left after breakfast, you do not know where or why. And then we shall meet, Burling, along the way to Dereham.'

'I don't understand.'

'Everything will be made clear,' Hough said, snapping shut the breech to the shotgun.

THIRTEEN

Harry Coggins behind bars in Pentonville was a very different proposition to the same creature in his glory days. His Whitechapel empire had been dispersed among rivals. After a month of moonlit violence – and three murders – Big Tony Neggs now controlled Harry's old turf. In prison, he still kept up the image of an inscrutable generalissimo but all that charade was wasted on the prison inmates. If they considered him at all, he was just an elderly dwarf whose day was over.

He had not been in jail for thirty years and never before in Pentonville. Half the inmates were mad when they came in, the other half on the way to serious mental disorders. Reclusive by nature, Coggins found the noise and institutional briskness hard to bear. His cellmate was a violinmaker from Spitalfields who believed the Archangel Gabriel had fitted him up for the arson of three lodging houses. He and Gabriel had first met one rainy Sunday on Bethnal Green. The heavenly messenger was roosting comfortably in a tree, his wings and raiments spread about him. 'I trusted the geezer,' he explained. 'As you would.'

Superintendent Pennington's visit was therefore something of a holiday to Harry. It broke the routine. They met in an interview cell, the windows of which were ten feet above the floor. A steel plate table was bolted to the floor and the chairs were likewise anchored. By a trick of what light there was, Pennington seemed even larger than life, while Harry was made most acutely aware of how small he seemed in comparison. When he sat down as instructed, his feet barely touched the floor.

'You look in excellent health,' Pennington opened.

'Have you caught him?'

There was no need to identify who they were talking about.

'Would I be here now if I had?'

'No,' Harry said, 'you would not.'

Pennington smiled offhandedly. That day he was wearing a light grey summer suit and brocade waistcoat. To counter the stink of disinfectant, he was smoking a cheroot, which he took out of his mouth from time to time to yawn.

'Of course, I say you look in good health, but the prison doctor tells me otherwise.'

'Yeah?'

'Better you don't know what he has to say. But it boils down to this: don't buy any new shoes. The other bad news is that Ma Friedl has grassed you up for the murder of Rosie Dunnick.'

'Who?'

'One of your girls. The one who was given to answering back.'

'Never heard of her.'

'No?'

Pennington blew a little smoke and examined the tip of his cheroot. As if looking for something to fill the time, he took a letter from his pocket and read it idly before stuffing it back. And then smoothed down the line of his jacket. His chin fell to his collar, like a tired man about to snatch a little sleep.

'We are going to keep this up, are we?' Harry asked.

'Keep what up?'

'You know what. I had nothing to do with this Hough geezer.'

'Apart from putting him up in one of your brothels when you knew he was on the run.'

'It was business.'

'So it must have been a shock when you found out who he really was. What a real facer that must have been. Pull the other one, Coggins.'

Harry studied the wall above Pennington's head. But where previously this habit of his had seemed faintly awesome, now it seemed just fatuous. The cell was none too warm but he could feel sweat gathering in the small of his back. The superintendent threw his arms above his head and stretched, like a man who wished himself anywhere but where he was – perhaps someone on the beach who was finding that it was late afternoon and the breaking waves and the crash of shingle had lost their appeal.

'Did Hough have any visitors while he was your guest at Leyland Street?'

'Only Garside. Only that once.'

'And at Hackstraw's Yard, when he was there?'

'Quigley, maybe – and Quigley's mate. They was looking out for Garside, mostly. Hough just happened to be there too, sort of thing. So, yes.'

'They spoke together, these three?'

'No more than a few words, according to Hackstraw.'

'Nobody else came to the place?'

'Garside's old mum.'

'Lady Garside, we're talking about?'

'If that's who she was. I never met her.'

'What was she doing there?'

'Like I say, I never met the woman.'

'At her visit, was Hough also present?'

'May have been.'

'He was, according to that bag of lard, Charlie Hackstraw. Did Garside ask his mother inside the tack-room?'

'Well, he would do, wouldn't he?'

'And Hough was with them? Inside?'

'Maybe.'

'For how long?'

'I don't know, do I?'

'Didn't Hackstraw tell you?'

'Can't remember.'

'Talk to Hough in Leyland Street, did you?'

'What about?'

Pennington looked at him for a few moments, then, like the man on the seashore who had grown bored with the scenery, stood and left the room. On his way out, he made some pleasantly conventional remark about the weather to the warder at the door, leaving Coggins sitting in the chair wondering who had won this battle of wits. The Rosie Dunnick story was a bit of a jolt to the system, but then again that was four years ago and lippy little tarts like her were getting their throats cut every night of the week. Maybe. The point was, nobody called Harry Coggins a turd and got away with it. That was the point. He rubbed his knees and stood up.

'Who told you to move?' the warder barked.

Pennington travelled to Norfolk alone, more to get out of London for a few hours than with any fixed plan in his head. He would visit Lady Garside, so as to say that no stone had been left unturned; and later for the chance of a meal in what his imagination supplied as a bucolic inn, maybe with a village pond or something of the kind. Grizzled old men clasping their pints, buxom barmaids, dogs running about, that sort of thing. Haystacks, mill races, parsons in straw hats fishing under the shadow of the cathedral – Merry England in fact, he thought gloomily. But anyway far away from the slums of Pentonville and the utter squalor that surrounded the prison. The fourth or fifth child prostitute to proposition him had given him the urgent notion to waste a day in Norfolk.

Pennington had a superstitious dread of the country not entirely unlike Bella's. He had no idea of the England that existed outside London and could not guess at what its denizens were really like. The explanation was that he came from a country within a country. It went without saying that murders took place even in the smallest God-forsaken villages and hamlets, that people were as vile to each other there as they were in the city. But the superintendent knew nothing of the details of such things, save as anecdotes uttered by weeping soldiers in remand cells. They were news from elsewhere. Otherwise, he knew Margate and Brighton and had once visited Winchester

– he could not now remember for what reason. Rural England was a place hardly worth thinking of twice.

He travelled to Garside Hall from Dereham in a hired trap, still wanting to feel on holiday but overwhelmed by the huge skies and empty landscapes.

'From London?' the driver asked, and when he said yes, spat.

'You don't like it?'

'Don't know it. Don't want to.'

He might as well have been talking about Paris or Rome.

'It's easily reached by train, I think.'

'So is Wymondham. But I haven't been there neither.'

'What is growing in these fields?'

'Barley.'

'And the bird with the long tail that scuttled across us a little way back?'

'Cock pheasant.'

'I don't know too much about the countryside,' Pennington admitted.

'I can see that,' the driver replied cuttingly. He was letting the horse amble, not out of consideration for it, but because he was feeling truculent at having to come away from Dereham on market day, at a time when he should be raking in the coin.

The safe was empty, of course. Hough understood at once that while he had one key in his hand, Burling had been there before him with the second. Accordingly, the journey to say goodbye to a dying mother got no further than the village church, a safe enough place to bring the butler to his senses. They sat in the first row of pews, subscribed for by the Garside family and boxed off from the rest. It was from here that Daisy Garside communicated with her God each Sunday, more often than not asleep, and always alone. The vicar had long ago learned to ignore her, talking over her head to the dutifully attentive in the pews behind – though there were not many of those, either.

During the week the church was empty, save for the occasional visit from antiquarians who came for brass-rubbings and the transcription of memorial tablets. The Garside pew had almost the attraction of a private room to Hough. He sprawled comfortably, the shotgun across his knees, a thing that scandalised Burling but left him shaking with fear.

'I will give you until lunchtime to think things over,' Hough said. 'If you have the stuff with you, we can go on. But if not, you should go back to the Hall and fetch it. If you don't, I shall have to kill you, Burling. First you, then Dollie. I am not a man to be made mock of.'

'I swear I don't know what's become of the stuff,' Burling moaned.

'Well, we know Lady Garside doesn't have it and we can discount Cookie or any of the rest of the staff. Which leaves you and little Dollie. Never mind. Not all plans work out, not all clocks run to time, I understand that. I'm giving you your chance here. Go back to the Hall, talk things over with Dollie – or strangle her, I don't care which – and come back with what I want. If you don't, you can say goodbye to all your earthly pleasures, Dollie and everything else. By nightfall, you will be a dead man.' He brought up the shotgun and pressed the barrel hard against Burling's under-jaw. 'We should be very clear about one thing. You have never in your life met someone like me. It's important you grasp that one very simple point. Can you do that?'

'Be careful,' Burling begged, his head jammed back, his hands fluttering on the barrel of the gun. 'If that is loaded, you could blow my head off.'

'Did you understand what I just said?'

'Yes, for God's sake!'

'I want the contents of that safe. Be back here by midday, or I come looking for you.'

'Can I bring Dollie along with us?'

To his amazement, Hough burst out laughing. The church, which was fourteenth century, had never heard laughter before. A sparrow flew distractedly above their heads before darting through a broken pane of the west window. 'Now you are thinking like a real desperado,' Hough said mockingly.

'I can't leave her to blab.'

'She knows the whole story?'

'Enough.'

'Don't bring her here. Tell her to wait for us on the road to Dereham. She need not wear her best bonnet. It is now ten. I give you until midday.'

'Are we still on state business?' Burling asked, ashamed to sound so naive but hoping against hope that Hough would say yes.

'The highest,' Hough agreed. 'I will tell you everything when you return.'

'We aren't just robbing her blind?'

'That has already happened. No, we are playing a bigger game than that.'

'Can you tell me what it is?'

'You will know, soon enough.'

Only a mile or so from his destination, Pennington saw a girl in a white dress standing irresolute in the middle of the road, her hands lax at her sides and seemingly drunk.

'Pull up,' he ordered.

''Tis only some country girl who's lost her wits.'

'Do as I say.'

Fifty yards behind the girl was an empty trap, the horse placidly cropping grass from the verge. Pennington stood up to look into the ditch that ran alongside the road. He was searching for the driver, but instead the man he most wanted to meet in the world rose and levelled a shotgun at him from no more than a dozen yards. There was a blast and the superintendent flew backwards as if on elastic ropes. He was dead before he hit the roadway.

The girl screamed and ran away through the corn, scattering flocks of yellowhammers. Pennington's driver got down from the trap and after gazing at the hole in Pennington's chest for a moment or two, walked slowly down the road towards the other vehicle. Burling was on his back in the ditch. He was not drunk, or sleeping, but dead of a broken neck.

'It has been tiresome beyond belief,' Lady Garside complained the next day. 'I always thought Burling a stupid fellow but to end up in a ditch is just too vulgar for words. Whatever was he thinking of? He was on his way to see his dying mother. Quite enough for one day, I should have thought.'

'He was of course murdered.'

'So I have been told. They sent two men from Dereham, where they have a police station and so forth. Rather slow-witted, I found them.'

'I am here because of Superintendent Pennington, the man who was murdered in the same incident,' Bella said.

'Yes, the London policeman. We never met. Would you be kind enough to give a tug to the bell-rope? This food is quite disgusting.'

The lunch they had been given was indeed barely edible. Bella was startled to see real tears well in Daisy Garside's eyes.

'Nobody can know what it's like to live alone like this,' her hostess said.

No, indeed. Just as books that have been left in the sun lose their colour, so her ladyship's drawing room had a faded appearance. The wallpapers were grey with dust in places, elsewhere green with mould. Things that had been brought into the room years ago had yet to leave, so that, for example, three tall Chinese vases were ranged like milk churns against a far wall. A decorated screen lay flat on the floor with a heap of piano music piled on top of it. On top of that, a huge glazed bowl with the yellowed leaves of what might have been an acanthus hanging over its sides . . .

'The house is very old,' Bella suggested.

'Well, of course it's old. I know of no one who lives in a new house. You say your name is Westland. Is your husband that rather shambling man who came to Sefton's funeral? People have said he made a very poor fist at conversation.'

'I am happy to hear it,' Bella snapped, for a moment stopping her ladyship in her tracks. They were lunching off ancient card-tables in the drawing room and in an attempt to show petulance, Daisy kicked hers away, shooting her plate and the remains of a lamb chop to the carpet. A very old dog padded over, inspected the mess and then lay down beside it.

'You think me a foolish woman, no doubt,' she remarked.

'Lady Garside, I have no opinion of you. I am here about a murder.'

'Burling?' Daisy cried, incredulous. 'You are here about a servant of mine?'

'I meant to indicate David Pennington. He was well known to me and what happened has been very shocking.'

'Do people know policemen socially in London these days? I wouldn't have thought that possible. How did you come to meet him?'

'Through my friendship with the Home Secretary,' Bella replied icily.

'Your husband has political connections, therefore?'

'When I speak, the words that come out of my mouth are mine, and not my husband's.'

'You are very impudent,' Daisy Garside exclaimed. 'Yes, you are a very forward young woman. I think there are some manners that never change, Mrs Westland. You have overstepped the mark, I would say.'

'His murder took place more or less on your doorstep.'

'And whatever business is that of yours? These things happen. But nothing is to be gained by outpourings of sentimental gush. I'm sorry for your loss and so forth but I don't see how visiting me – at a very inconvenient time, mark you – can add anything to what you might already know.'

'The man who killed him was in all likelihood your last guest at Garside Hall. And this man – Hough – shot dead Pennington with a gun that belonged to this house.'

'Absolute stuff and nonsense.'

'Hough was not here two days ago?'

'He was Sefton's adjutant in the Whitechapel business. He had been most cruelly set upon by thugs there and came – well, I am not sure why he came, but perhaps to offer condolences at the loss of the mission.'

'You were not surprised to see him?'

'I am in a state of constant amazement at how the modern world wags, Mrs Westland. Like you, he came uninvited.'

'What did you make of him?'

'What did I *make* of him? Am I supposed to make something of everyone I meet?'

'Did Hough attend Sefton's funeral?'

'He did not. Attendance at funerals is by invitation,' Daisy Garside said tartly. 'Your husband is related to us on the Froggatt side. That explained his presence. I had met Mr Hough, but he was quite unknown to me.'

'Do you take a newspaper here, Lady Garside?'

'If there is war, I shall be told about it by my brother-in-law. Everything else in the newspapers is too dull to read. What is the point of your question?'

'I think you may be the last person in Britain not to know that Hough is a most notorious mass-murderer.'

One of the things Daisy Garside had retained from her schoolroom days was a trilling disbelieving laugh.

'Hough? He is an evangelist of a certain stripe and nothing more. He is pushy, the way some of the devout are, but otherwise quite unimportant. I'm quite sure you have hold of the wrong end of the stick.'

'How lucky you are to think like this.'

'What a very impertinent thing to say, Mrs Westland. I wonder at you.' She jumped up and tugged on the bell-rope, hard enough for it to disengage from its lever, bringing the whole lot down at her feet. 'You are an uninvited guest in a private house. I wonder if you can grasp the significance of that. I always thought Burling a fool and I suppose your policeman was here in pursuit of his duties. I'm sure it's all very sad and so forth but it hardly concerns me. Be good enough to see yourself out. Any further information you might need about the family can be found in *Burke's Peerage*. And now, good day to you.'

'Hough may have said to you where he is going next. That is the sole purpose of my visit.'

'Hough again! Would I much care if he *had* told me? And would I feel it necessary to tell you?'

'Lady Garside –'

'I believe I have bidden you good day.'

Murch was waiting for her in the hired trap. His expression was characteristically neutral. Bella felt very bad about bringing him with her from London. When the news of Pennington's murder reached the capital she had been so incensed with anger (and Philip so thunderstruck) that she could think of nothing but asking for Murch's help.

'I do not mean of a practical kind, but some judgement of how to go about finding him.'

'You mean Hough? Do we know for a fact it is him?'

'I go to Norfolk to have it confirmed.'

'And then what?'

'I shall find him and kill him.'

Murch studied her, his teeth nibbling at his lower lip. 'Killing a cove is not usually woman's work,' he said.

'I am not asking you to kill him for me, Billy. But I cannot have him walking about when David Pennington is lying in his coffin. Nor can I have him killing anyone else before he is finished.'

'Forgive me if I speak blunt, Mrs Westland. The state you are in now, you are very likely to be his next victim. That's if you ever catch up with him.'

'I have to do *something*.'

'And Mr Westland? What about him?' he asked gently.

'What about him?'

Billy gave her a searching stare. There was more compassion in it than she expected, much more. Her cheeks burning, she took both his hands in hers. 'He doesn't know I have come here tonight,' she confessed.

'I should hope not. Nothing I say can talk you out of this?'

'Nothing.'

'Then I had best come with you. To drive you about, you understand, and then to bring you home. That's as much as you can hope for. That bloody Hough could be anywhere by now. Anywhere.' He spoke as brusquely as he dared but knew she was hardly listening. For his part, he was trying to remember what he had been told about

Norfolk and the general lie of the land they had out there. As a boy he could remember drovers bringing geese into London from those parts, hundreds at a time.

Dollie's parents lived where her father had been born, one of five cottages at a crossroads deep among the corn. Mr Sands was a road-mender by trade, but much more importantly a cottage gardener of genius. Before Bella could go indoors and talk to Dollie, Sands explained in loving detail how the place would look in high summer when everything was in bloom. The two of them made a tour of the garden, he pushing Bella gently in the back, the better to steer her around. He had absolutely no social embarrassment.

'My wife says I have green fingers and that but I tell her 'tis all hard work. Yes, hard work and a good well of water. Green fingers my arse, begging your pardon, missus.'

'And do you also grow vegetables?'

'Why, yes,' Sands said, astonished. 'Who doesn't?'

'You must work very long hours, Mr Sands.'

'I have nothing much else on,' he responded drily. 'That driver of yours, gone for a walk, has he?'

Bella looked around. Murch had disappeared. Sands had begun watching her a little too closely.

'He is a very shy man.'

'He must be.'

'What plants are these?

'Delphiniums.'

'The whole place is a picture, Mr Sands!'

And so was the interior of the cottage. Bella was given tea and a bit of cake by Mrs Sands, a hugely stout woman with wild grey hair, whose manner was more reserved than her husband's. Neither of them asked a single question of Bella. Once she had told them she came from London, their curiosity switched off.

'You are here to see Dollie, I don't doubt. Not a bad girl, but a foolish one. There was a son; but he was done for by the drink. He had ideas to be a footman over at where you've just come from. Well, a clumsier footman never did exist and, like I say, the drink took him. Though where he found it in that bloody lunatic asylum I don't know.'

'Was this recently?'

'Recent enough,' Mrs Sands said grimly.

'So now nothing would do but Dollie going the same road,' Sands said. 'And look how that has turned out.'

'She was lucky to escape with her life.'

'I believe she knows that. Has done all but hide under the bed ever since. This Hough she mentions? Why, he'd be far, far away by now.'

'I need to find him.'

'Is that not a job for the police?' Sands asked.

'I need to have some idea where he might have gone.'

'Mr Pennington a London man?'

'And a friend,' Bella said.

The Sandses glanced at each other. The husband brushed his hands together thoughtfully. He looked down at his boots for a moment or two before fixing her with what she had learned from Captain Quigley to think of as a very old-fashioned look. 'We don't want to get mixed up in nothing awkward.'

'If I could just talk to your daughter for ten minutes.'

'To find out where this knave has gone, is it?'

'She doesn't know,' Mrs Sands put in.

'As it stands, she's just a silly young girl,' Sands agreed. 'And that's how we like it. So I'm saying no to you, mistress. Better she stays upstairs and keeps her mouth shut.'

'It is vital that I talk to her,' Bella said.

'Vital, is it?'

'He is a road-mender,' Mrs Sands said, pointing at her husband. 'And I am what you see. Your business is not our business. Jack has spoken and that's that.'

Then the door opened and in walked Murch.

FOURTEEN

'Now then, maister,' Jack Sands warned, laying his fists on the table with unmistakable meaning. Murch took some of the wind out of his sails by leaning across Bella and offering his hand.

'Murch,' he said. 'Another bloody Londoner. I am here to look out for Mrs Westland, as you have probably guessed.'

'We knock on doors out here,' Elsie Sands growled.

'Apologies, ma. No offence intended.' To show goodwill, he took off his cap, offering her that rare thing, a brief Murch smile. Only then did he turn back to the man of the house. The two men studied each other, like boxers just before they square up. 'We may have trouble,' Billy explained in a quiet, serious tone. The road-mender rose from the table, cottoning on at once to what that might mean.

'Go on,' he said.

'Should you and me walk out and take a turn in the garden for a bit?'

'Better you say your piece to all of us.'

Murch nodded, looked out of the window this way and that, and then turned back into the room. 'Here it is then. Do you have many coves sleeping rough in these parts?'

'Discharged soldiers from time to time, the occasional

tramp, but I know most of them by name. Decent enough men.'

'Mr Sands is a road-mender by trade,' Bella explained.

'Good,' Murch said. 'That's good.'

'Tell us what you've found.'

'About half a mile down the road, there's a little stand of trees. Hornbeam, mostly.'

'I cut my stakes from it. For the garden.'

Murch smiled briefly. 'I've seldom seen better. None of your tramps sleep out there in that wood?'

'We have a shed,' Mrs Sands put in. 'They know to look us up for a bait and a mug of tea. And there they can sleep if they wish. Like Jack says, we've knowed most of them a good few year. Tramping's not what the magistrates make out, I don't care what the law says.'

'Be quiet a minute, Elsie. Let the man tell his story.'

'Last night and maybe the night before you had what you might call a neighbour down in that coppice.'

Sands wiped his hand across his lips. He smiled at Bella, indicating Billy Murch with a jerk of his chin. 'I see I aren't talking to no common carter,' he observed. 'Give me a guess at it, I'd say he was a soldier in his time. First battalion sort of thing. No fires lit there? No ashes, scraps of food, feathers, nothing of that sort?'

'A few scrapes in the ground,' Billy murmured delicately, glancing at the women. 'A few footprints down by the dyke. Nothing else. In the ordinary way of things, an honest godfearing tramp would brew himself a can of tea, I take it.'

'A billy, yes. Soldiers are a wilder sort of people. Chickens, bread from the kitchen table – anything they can lay their hands on. Thieving bastards, most on 'em.'

'Very low people,' Mrs Sands agreed. 'I've had 'em walk in here as bold as brass, cadging money, as if we had any.'

'You've had one come in, Elsie. And that was five year gone.'

'We had no money then and we still have none now.'

'Soldiers travel in twos and threes,' Jack explained to Bella. 'It's a habit they pick up. That's how they drink and look for women. When they're in barracks, I mean.'

'The one I caught in here, I fetched him a clout he won't forget,' Elsie said sourly. 'Something to tell his mates, my word. Broke his nose for him.'

Bella turned back to Billy Murch. 'Is it Hough?' she asked quietly.

'It has crossed my mind that it might be him,' Murch said. 'A mild rainless night but it takes a determined man to sleep out with no grub and only ditchwater to drink, even with a shotgun for company.'

'You think that's how it is?' Jack Sands muttered. 'He's come for Dollie, is that it?'

'What stopped him come barging in here same as you did?' Elsie Sands wanted to know in her usual surly way.

'Short on cartridges, I'm guessing. He wasn't sure what he'd meet with. We don't know what Dollie told him exactly.'

'She's upstairs,' Bella said.

'I don't think we need to put the fear of God up the girl, or not just yet,' Murch said. 'I'm betting she told Elsie here more than she told her father.'

'She told him about Jack's garden, the daft cat,' Mrs Sands said. 'Which is how he found us, no doubt. Bring her down, Sandsie.'

'And you think she aren't listening to all this at the floorboards? I want to hear what Mr Murch has to say, if he has more to tell.'

'Do you have a gun in the house?' Billy asked.

'There's Ablett's.'

'And who's he?'

'Our neighbour. Shoots for pigeons and such.'

'Can you get to him across the fields you have at the back here?'

'You think our place is being watched?'

'If it is Hough, he's waiting for Dollie to come out.'

'Want me to fetch Ablett's gun?'

'I want you to take Mrs Sands and Dollie round by the back way, leave them there and come back with the gun.'

The stairs in the cottage were cased in, with a door at their foot. This opened a crack, revealing Dollie's frightened face. Murch smiled at her absently and beckoned her into the room. 'Your dad and me have all under control,' he said. 'But keep away from the window. You've an idea of what we're talking about.'

'He was going to Norwich next. That's what he told Charlie Burling. They were to drive the trap all the way to Norwich.'

'Taking you along with them?'

'That's what he promised.'

'Don't you start up with no tears, girl,' Elsie Sands said sharply. 'I have been to Norwich and it ain't all that much. You'm out of it by the skin of your teeth and this man here and your dad will put all right. They'll frighten him off and no mistake.'

'I want you to put your hair up, Dollie, and wear this

here cap of mine. Pull it down about your ears. And put on the biggest old coat you have in the house. Then you and your ma will creep round to Ablett's place.'

'I aren't wearing no dirty London cap,' the girl said indignantly.

After the Sands family had set off around the back of the cottage to walk to Ablett's, Bella made Billy Murch a fresh pot of tea. He sat at the table looking out on to the garden, drumming gently with his fingers while she pumped water to wash up the dirty cups.

'If they had let me talk to Dollie as I wished, you and I would be on the way to Norwich by now.'

He turned his head to look at Bella and nodded politely. 'Maybe.'

'I'm trying to say I never intended to drag you into this, Billy. It's true I wanted to find and kill him, but that was all comfortingly off in the future somehow.'

'Not many people have it in them to kill another human being. There's no shame in what you feel.'

'You haven't understood. I still want to kill him – *will* kill him. If it has to be here, then so be it. The shame comes in involving you. I am thinking of Millie and your child.'

'Millie understands.' But he said this with such an empty expression on his face that she knew what a gift he had made her of coming down to the country at all. She had never seen Billy at his most sombre and it frightened her.

'What are you thinking of?' she asked.

'That pony and trap outside. We should have hid it away, maybe.'

'We could do that now,' Bella suggested. 'But, really, you were thinking about what I just said – about Millie.'

'She'd go Napoleon for his garden and that's no error. This is just such a little cottage as she would want to live in. Not here, of course, but somewhere along the south coast. Hastings, maybe. Roses over the door and suchlike. Which we shall never see in London. No, this would do her very well.'

'And would you be happy?'

'I could be a road-mender in Sussex and not think twice about it.'

He stood and glanced into the roadway. Bella put her head into her hands.

When he heard her sobbing, Murch turned back. In all the time they had known each other, he had never once touched her. But now he took her hands away from her face and smiled his crooked smile. 'All is quiet. Nothing to report. Though I was just observing how much patience a horse has,' he murmured gently. 'Ours is out there now, cropping away as if nothing else was on his mind. I am going to put something to you now. We could walk out of here and be on our way back to Dereham with nothing to feel bad about. I would trust Sands with a gun sooner than many and once at Dereham we could send out the police.'

'Wouldn't that be running away?' Bella croaked, wiping wet cheeks with the back of her wrist.

'You asked me about Millie and now I ask you about Mr Westland. What would he prefer we did? You don't have to answer. It would be a foolish woman who settled a lover's tiff by getting her head blown off. Think a bit.

It is not us who are cornered, but Hough. He knows he is in the last few hours or days of his life. Whatever he promised Dollie, he knows he is done for. We can walk away from this, if you wish.'

'Leaving these people at the mercy of a desperate man? Is that what you want?'

'That would be the case whether we were here or not. Like you say, we could have been on our way to Norwich, purely ignorant of what's fallen out in this little place. But then again, we could as easily be stirring up that old horse outside and fetching the police from Dereham – which would shorten Hough's life quicker than playing hide and seek in that there garden.'

'We have a gun to fight him with.'

'A shotgun.'

'Isn't that enough?'

'What's needed is rifles.'

He was remembering dropping a man at four hundred yards. Not once but a dozen times, the target eating from a mess tin or studying a map, too far away for him to see the exact gesture or activity, but snuffed out all the same. Murch seldom mentioned the Crimea and had begun to forget his time there but what a rifle can do had never left him – which was to produce a bolt from heaven.

Bella shrugged, not at all clear about the distinction Billy was making. But something else he had said troubled her more. 'What is all this about a lover's tiff?' she asked.

'Before we came here, I went round to Shelton Street to make a few arrangements with Hannah Bardsoe.'

'What arrangements?'

'In the event of anything going wrong,' Billy said calmly.

'Stay away from the window,' he added, pulling her back by the sleeve.

'Hannah Bardsoe has a loose tongue,' she said, blushing bright red. 'There is an argument, yes, about whether to leave London. And, yes, I am a wilful and obstinate woman. I did not realise it was becoming a common topic of conversation.'

'So, what do you say to the idea we slope off back to Dereham?' Billy asked with just too much nonchalance, as though he had not heard what she said.

'Don't try to change the subject! And don't confuse two quite separate things. If it falls out that I kill that evil monster today, then that is the story. And you can keep your views on lovers' tiffs or anything else to yourself.'

'Yes, ma'am,' he said drily.

'Have I ever asked you about your relationship with Millie?' Bella plunged on, getting angrier by the second.

'You just have,' Billy pointed out. 'And to make all clear to you on that point, we are husband and wife. That is how we like to be seen and spoken of by others. Nothing fancier than that. Married, in other words.'

'My God,' Bella said. 'I never thought to hear impudence from you.'

It was Billy's turn to flush. He looked at her with the closest thing to anger ever to show on his face in all the time they had known each other. 'The first time I met your husband, I was obliged to tell him I was no man's servant. So it stands now. I said the man you came to kill is cornered but I didn't add that one of us or both of us could be stretched out on this floor as dead as doornails before nightfall. So no more of your talk of impudence.

If you're set on staying, what part you play depends on the number of cartridges that belong with Ablett's gun, and nothing else.'

'I have made you angry.'

'You have. These are the harshest words I've ever spoken to you but I'm saying what's in my heart now. You and your husband are the biggest couple of fools in Christendom.'

There was a rap and a tumbling chatter from the tiles above their head. Murch peered out of a small pantry window. Sands crouched by the side of his shed, a second pebble in his free hand. The other held the shotgun. Five cartridges. The gun itself was elderly but clean as a whistle, pulled through with a bit of bacon fat as like as not. Murch tested the trigger – hair fine – which was how poachers liked them, no doubt, but just a bit too sporty for the work that lay ahead. He was watched by an unsmiling Sands.

'Done this before?'

'Here and there. Off and on. Now listen, Jack. This is your house and he's after your daughter but if we sit here waiting for him to show his hand, we're giving up a good few moves of our own.'

'And?'

'Say I take the gun and go looking for him?'

'No,' Bella cried.

'Never mind Mrs Westland's opinions.'

'I will not let you risk your life!'

'I reckon I know the country round about as well as any man,' Sands objected slowly.

Billy laughed and cuffed him lightly on the cheek. 'I aren't that likely to get lost,' he chided. ''Tis but one bloody field after another. If he's up in the mountains, I'll come back for you.'

'Meanwhile, what do I do, you comical bastard?'

'There's not a breath of wind outside. If you could light not one but two big fires, with as black a smoke as you can make, that might give a signal.'

'And who are we signalling?'

'Buggered if I know,' Billy admitted. 'Once you've got them fires going, I want you to get in that shed out there and barricade the door. Block up the window, if there is one. A sickle would be good to have at hand, or anything that makes a weapon.'

'I don't like it,' Sands decided. 'I'm barricaded in and you're out there. No, I don't like that one bit. We stay here, in the cottage. I need to see what's going off. And if you come a cropper, God forbid, I need to get my hands on that there shotgun pretty quick.'

Billy considered and then smiled. It is your day for smiling all right, he thought ruefully. He took the cartridges and put two into his pocket, gave Jack two and passed the last one to Bella.

'As soon as he sees that smoke, he's going to come for us,' he said. 'He won't wait until night. Now listen to me, Jack. This cove's as dangerous as a sackful of ferrets. But I think the reason he didn't come for all three of you last night was because he hasn't got the cartridges. And he couldn't be certain what he'd find behind that door. Let's hope all goes well, but if it doesn't, we'll have done the best we can.'

'If it's cartridges we're talking about, I don't much like the idea of you going out with just the two.'

'If I get close enough, one will do it,' Billy said.

'And the one you have given the lady?'

'She has an idea she can take a man's part,' he said coolly. 'That is how it is among women, down there in London.'

'You are a very brave man,' Bella said. 'But you can also be too cocky for your own good. You think I am here just to make up the numbers? I want him dead – perhaps more than you do. If you doubt that, let me go first.'

'Well,' Jack Sands said. 'I vote we give the men a chance and then you can show us how to do it.'

'You agree? I go out and look for him?' Billy asked.

'I'd say that shows a mort of guts. Oh, yes, a mort of guts!'

Billy turned to go out the back. He stopped at the kitchen door a moment to glance at Bella – and then he was gone.

'I would like it dearly if they keep out of my flower beds when they set to,' Sands muttered. Bella obliged him by her own weak version of a smile, though in truth her heart was drenched in terror.

FIFTEEN

The shotgun's hair trigger was bothering Billy, and to be safe he crawled with the breech to the gun broken open an inch or so. A sensible precaution but – when push came to shove – a valuable second lost to time. It annoyed him to be distracted in this way and for a while he lay in the place he had chosen, trying to empty his mind of everything; or, rather, adding the vagaries of Ablett's gun to all the other information flowing through his mind, so that it had equal standing with the unnaturally calm air, the faint scent of wild garlic, and the kite that circled overhead. But he knew, after all he had seen of life and death, that he was in no way ready for the encounter with Hough.

It was a shocking realisation. There was a man that existed alongside Billy Murch, the same in features and habits but in essence a wholly different person he could call upon when the situation demanded. This was a man for tight corners and mortal danger, whose animal ferocity made the day-to-day Murch seem like a tabby cat. This other person, who walked and talked with an awesome simplicity, who could reduce the teeming world to a single empty landscape, save for the one present danger: where was he now when he was needed most? Sweat ran from Billy's scalp and a warning tremor fluttered his guts. Like an actor groping for his lines, he was as close as he had ever come to panic.

What he had said in the cottage was just so much window-dressing. There would be no roaming about the fields. He had no intention of hunting down Hough in such a flat and unforgiving landscape. His one strategy was to block his path when he made a run for the cottage. In other words, Hough would find *him*. Not much of a plan at all when it came down to it. No medals for gallantry promised: nothing but the squalor that comes with mutilation or sudden death.

The place he had chosen to hide out was in the ditch on the Sands' side of the road, at a point that covered both the cottage and the garden shed. It was not perfect, but then again in his present state he had been half prepared to find Hough already there. Billy frowned. He had seen Bella look fleetingly out of the cottage window two or three times, a sight that filled him with a wholly irrational anger – it had not taken her long to put Sands in his place as an amiable yokel. His protestations were useless as she glanced out of the window like someone waiting for the post to arrive. Soon enough, Billy thought gloomily. He supposed Hough to be no more than a hundred yards away at most, maybe even in the ditch opposite him. Bella – the imperious and impulsive Bella – was asking to be peppered.

The ditch was dry, with weeds growing out of the clods of earth. Murch crumbled some soil to powder his fingers, thinking fitfully of Millie. He had lied when he said she understood that he had a duty to help Bella; on the contrary, she had snorted out her indignation.

'Haven't you done enough for that woman? If she asked you round to paper the ceiling, you'd do that too, would you?'

'You don't know the whole story, Mill.'

'I do not, and am very happy not to. You have done with all that, Murchie.'

'This is the last time.'

'With such as her, there never is a last time.'

He was astonished to hear her say it, all the more because the conversation had not taken place in the dark of the bedroom but while making bread, with his daughter sitting on the kitchen floor, her little face –

He stiffened. There is never real quiet anywhere on earth, but some sense in him recognised a new hush. He looked down and saw the brass rim of the cartridge peering out from the shotgun breech. In a heartbeat, thoughts of Millie and his beloved daughter, Bella, the Sands family, vanished. Much of the material world likewise. Though he could hear nothing and see nothing, he sensed Hough very close, perhaps no more than the width of the roadway. Well, he thought, this is the ditch towards which my whole life has been leading me. He snapped shut the breech, making a dry click.

'Murch?' Hough called, like a voice from the underworld, but in a languid conversational tone, as if the devil had looked up idly from reading a newspaper.

'The same. Though how you knew that –'

'An intelligent guess. I am sorry to have to kill you first.'

All Murch's muscles were trembling with anticipation. This was it, this was the moment. When Hough showed himself, he would fire across the road from a kneeling position. It would be touch and go, but he thought he could get off the first shot. If it hit, he would run over and finish off his man without a second thought. But Hough did not oblige. The two men remained invisible to each other. Murch licked his lips. 'Police have been sent for from Dereham,' he lied.

'Then I shall require the loan of your pony and trap,' Hough answered mockingly.

'You will be captured or dead by nightfall.'

'Maybe. Probably.'

'Then what is the point?'

'Of this? Or anything else in the world?'

'This. The girl cannot help or harm you now.'

Hough laughed. 'The girl! You are not going to die because of some empty-headed girl. There must be terror, Murch. You know that. The world must take its full share of that medicine. Because without it –'

Billy saw the barrel of a shotgun flick into view for a millisecond and scrabbled to get his heels under his haunches. He has caught me off-balance with all this fancy talk, he thought wonderingly. I have let myself be gulled. But his mind cleared. When his enemy charged him from the other side of the road, as he must do in the next few seconds, Billy was ready for him. He was the pure form once again, the implacable –

The two shots were almost simultaneous, but not quite. Billy fell back into the ditch utterly astounded, blood spurting from his chest and shoulder.

'This is a botched job,' he said quite clearly and distinctly, seeing a black fog roll towards him as fast as a man could walk. 'I am done for, Millie girl. The bastard has killed me.'

He could hear distant shouting and the thunder of hooves. Saw Hough standing over him for a moment. Then, empty sky. Just before his eyes rolled back into his skull, he understood that what he took to be a beckoning eternity was furnished with a wheeling bird – the kite.

Hough was hit high up in both legs. He stumbled towards the approach of a pony and trap careering towards him with reckless speed. One man was driving and the other stood up in the bucketing trap, bellowing and waving what appeared to be a naval cutlass. It took him a moment or two to recognise Captain Quigley, beside himself with fury. Hough knelt and fired. The ridiculous and antic Quigley sat down suddenly, groped for a handhold and then flopped out of the trap, landing in the roadway like a child's rag doll. The driver roared like a madman and aimed straight for Hough, knocking him over and then dragging the pony to a standstill outside the cottage.

Hough staggered upright and reached for another cartridge, before realising that the last two had fallen from his pocket and lay in the dust at his feet. He straightened up, facing back down the road. He looked surprised at the person standing there and threw away his shotgun. 'I am unarmed,' he said, opening both hands, palms outward.

The charge of shot that hit him was spread from his chest to his groin. Bella lowered Ablett's gun and then let it fall, any way it wished.

Philip darted forward from behind the trap and caught her in his arms. The tweed of his jacket was soaked through with sweat. 'I thought we would be too late,' he sobbed.

'No,' Bella said in a dull, even voice. 'You were timely.'

'Are you all right?'

There was Hough's blood on her face and in her hair. She pushed Philip away and walked slowly into Sands' garden, sank to her knees and, after a moment more, fell forward on to the brick path.

Murch survived, but Percy Quigley – that greatest of all chancers – did not. He and Anton Hough were laid side by side in a police ambulance, covered by the same tarpaulin. For three days Billy knew nothing of how things had turned out and, when he was told, could not speak. It was as though he had been on a long journey, in which the cottage and everything in it had receded to a distant point. Millie sat by his bed, holding his too-dry hand in hers.

'Who brought you here?' her husband asked at last.

'It was Mrs Westland's doing. We stay at the George.'

'She is here?'

'No,' Millie said. 'It's me and the baby I am talking about. The Westlands have gone home to arrange for Percy's funeral.'

'I cannot be there,' Murch explained in a dreadfully tiny voice.

'Of course you cannot. Mrs Bardsoe will represent us. Alice Cobb stays with her in Shelton Street.'

'That is good,' Murch whispered absentmindedly.

'I am so sorry, Murchie.'

'Um? Oh yes. Percy was a good mate. Daft as a brush, but his heart was in the right place.'

'Don't talk.'

Billy turned his head to study her face, bringing the hand that held his to his lips. 'I never thought to see you again, Millie.'

'Well, here I am, as large as life and twice as ugly.'

'Tomorrow,' he promised, drifting into sleep. She sat holding his hand for another ten minutes, until budged by the matron. When she left the hospital, Sands was waiting for her.

'Elsie has taken the baby to the park,' he murmured. 'So shall us walk along to find them?' He peered into her face. 'How is he?'

'Indestructible.'

'You'm got that right, girl,' Sands laughed. 'A rare plucked 'un. A fellow to be proud of, that one.'

'You bloody men!' Millie cried, shocking Sands to silence. A rum lot, these Londoners, he thought, forgetting for the moment that Elsie Sands had said much the same thing but in even pithier language.

Bella and Philip stood in the Fleur de Lys office, now no more than an empty pine box boarded out in tongue and groove. There was a very agreeable scent of sawn wood and something Philip identified as stopper, a thing he had heard of but never before seen. Someone – but surely not Alice Cobb? – had rehung the door and painted over Captain Quigley's handiwork with the brush.

A man was watching them from the courtyard. 'Welsh Phil,' he announced himself. 'A friend of Perce's from the old days.'

'What part of Wales are you from, Mr—?'

'Name of Denny. I am about as Welsh as Robert the

Bruce, ma'am. But it pleased the Captain to call me such. We met at the Easter Hunt in Epping Forest when we were young 'uns. A very rowdy affair,' he added, with a glance at Philip.

'I dare say you've taken a drink or two since in this place?'

'Going on a famous London address, I would say,' Welsh Phil smiled. 'But my reason for being here today was to say what a very brave woman you are, Mrs Westland. Yes, indeed, a fearless brave woman.'

'You are very kind, Mr Denny. I would rather we shook hands to the memory of our mutual friend, Captain Quigley.'

And they did, with Welsh Phil solemnising the moment by taking off his beaver with a stage flourish. Genuine tears rolled down his cheeks.

'The end of an era,' Bella murmured.

'The very same. Shall you come back here to the old office at all?'

'I believe not,' she said, after the most delicate of pauses.

Welsh Phil's eyes flickered once again to Philip. He would not be Captain Quigley's mate if he did not already know the answer to his question. He seized Bella's hand once more. 'I wish you joy,' he said. 'Yes, with all my heart. You and your husband both.'

Bella burned the crates of paper that Quigley and Alice Cobb had gathered up and put in store while renovating the office in Fleur de Lys Court. As for the rather good rosewood table that had served her so well in the past, she gave it to Alice one balmy afternoon. By nightfall, properly waxed and buffed up by her, it had found a new home and so disappeared from the story as surely as Henry Ellis Margam's name and fortunes. The one thing she kept from her previous existence was the penholder with the ivory shaft that the Captain had found for her by his usual means.

She said goodbye to the Murches at a place of their choosing. On the city side of Hammersmith Bridge, just below the Dove, was an untidy scrap of green where they sat and picnicked, watching the river run by and amusing themselves by tickling the baby's ribs. Just as Quigley had foreseen, Billy Murch was now the dad of all the world. Millie talked to Bella with her usual naturalness; and when they parted, kissed the older woman with such unaffected fondness that for a moment Bella felt bewildered. Murch saved the day. He was a dozen or so yards off, holding his daughter in his arms, the two of them half obscured by the green branches of alder that overhung the path. He held Bella's gaze for a moment or two and then ducked his head with a shy smile before disappearing.

'He had a farewell speech all ready,' Millie laughed. 'The great awkward lump that he is. But you know what's in his heart, I am sure. Be happy, Mrs Westland, as I know you shall be.'

Hannah Bardsoe was by her own admission not much of a traveller but, as told by her, the journey to Winchelsea could not have been less eventful than a trip up the Limpopo or a search for Montezuma's gold. A year had passed since Bella and Philip had moved.

'Well, they do say, if a thing's worth seeing it's worth

a load of misery getting there,' she grumbled to her bosom pal Dora Venn.

'Do they say that? I never heard the expression before, though it borrows from the Scriptures somewhat, I fancy. Take off them boots, my dear, for I see they gyp you something awful. And now that you're here, tell me how you find the place.'

'They have bought the house at the end of the world. I came from Rye in a coach that belongs in a museum, along with most of the passengers. Grim old boys with gaiters, a woman with a live goose for luggage, and the vicar, who must be knocking a hundred.'

'But here you are. Let me press you to a little of this mincemeat pie, for I can tell you we have grown most adventurous in the kitchen department, my word, yes.'

'Are they happy, Dora?' Hannah asked when the pie was presented, eaten and commented upon.

'As much as two people can ever be. They say we are in the smallest town in England, which was a bit of a turn-up when he came home with the idea. But she has took to it like a duck to water. A quieter woman these days but a happier one.'

'And where are they now, for example?'

'Yes, well you are to keep a straight face when you meet them, Hannah. They are down the garden in what he calls his Temple of Venus, which is more like a cricket pavilion sort of structure.'

'He hasn't gone doolally, has he?' Hannah cried.

'He has took to roaming the fields looking for things of interest,' Dora admitted. 'Coins and the like, bits of old pottery. Oh, we are very enthusiastic about that. But as Mrs W. says, it's no more than a dog might do, once he's off the leash.'

'Has the doctor anything to say about it?'

'The doctor! Why, his house is full of Roman crockery! They go out together once a week, like schoolboys.'

'And the Temple of Venus?'

'How he scandalised the joiner that built it for him! They are somewhat lacking in our sense of humour, down here. We *are* thought to be a bit barmy, you're right, which is how she likes it. Wouldn't have it otherwise. But when you are rested, you must go down and see for yourself.'

The Temple of Venus was at the foot of the garden, approached through a tiny orchard of apple trees. On either side were massive beds of penstemons, delphiniums and phlox. Dora Venn had been right in describing the temple itself as a cricket pavilion in all but name. What scandalised the builder was the location and the colour the Westlands chose to paint the woodwork. No amount of pleading, no halting lectures on what was right and proper could change their minds. The Temple of Venus was the exact shade of blue to be found in the drawing room of their old house in Orange Street.

There was a railed verandah, with a faded red plush couch, on which Philip lay asleep, a straw hat over his face, the proceedings of the East Sussex Archaeological Society tented open on his chest. Bella swept past him to greet and embrace Hannah Bardsoe, hanging on perhaps a moment too long, but smiling and laughing. 'How wonderful,' she said.

She was changed. She was not quite who she had been.

But then again, the canny old Londoner reasoned, maybe it was because there was more of her.

She pulled Bella's face down and kissed her full on the lips. 'And so,' she asked, 'what news from paradise today?'

'Dance and skylark, dearest Hannah. Be an angel and kick my lord and master awake. And then tell me the longest and most complicated London gossip you have to tell. Omit no detail. And then, when you see me yawn delicately behind my hand, you will see how things stand with us, and who we have become.'